THE KINSMAN SAGA

BEN BOVA

THE KINSMAN SAGA

TOR

THE KINSMAN SAGA

First printing: October 1987

A TOR Book

Published by Tom Doherty Associates, Inc.
49 West 24 Street
New York, N.Y. 10010

Cover art by Pat Rawlins

ISBN: 0-312-93026-7

Library of Congress Catalog Card Number: 87-50484

Printed in the United States of America

0 9 8 7 6 5 4 3 2 1

Author's Foreword:
Reality and Symbols

I HAVE RETURNED to where I started, returned to Chet Kinsman, to the character who has haunted me since I first began writing seriously.

If you have read the Tor Books edition of *As on a Darkling Plain,* you know the genesis of this book: How I wrote a very early version of it in 1949–50, a version that predicted the Space Race of the 1960s, which culminated in the American landings on the Moon. How the novel was rejected everywhere, in part because publishers were afraid it would incur the wrath of anti-Communist witch-hunters such as Senator Joseph McCarthy. How Arthur C. Clarke encouraged me to keep writing, and how eventually I was able to hand him the first copy of the first edition of *Millennium.*

When *Millennium* was originally published, in 1976, the idea of putting laser-armed satellites in orbit to shoot down nuclear-armed ballistic missiles was widely regarded as fantasy. Except by a few of us who knew better. Today the concept is known as the Strategic Defense Initiative, or Star Wars. Billions of dollars are being spent on it. Passionate arguments have been waged over it among scientists, politicians, pundits, and even science fiction writers. But in the early 1970s the only place that such an idea could be explored seriously in print, outside of classified technical publications, was in the medium called science fiction.

To the large majority of the public, science fiction is regarded as a field that deals with the fantastic, as far removed from reality as fiction can be. In truth, science fiction examines reality, and explores it in ways that no other form of literature possibly can. I must admit, though, that I am speaking now of *my* kind of science fiction, the kind that I write and the kind that I published when I was an editor. There are many other types of stories being marketed under the name of "science fiction." They may deal with unicorns or video games, barbarian swordsmen or robot killing machines. It is these types of stories, and the films and TV shows made from them, that convince most of the public that science fiction has no connection with reality.

My kind of science fiction examines the future in order to understand the present. It is social commentary of a new kind, a variety of literature that has been developed and sharpened in this century mainly by a handful of writers in the United States and Europe who are familiar with the physical sciences, their resultant technologies, and the impact of these technologies on society. Those of us who practice this art are agreed that modern technology is the major force of change in society today—and will continue to be, for the foreseeable future.

It seems clear that technological developments, from nuclear bombs to birth control pills, are the driving force in our civilization. The engines of change begin with the scientists and engineers. *Then* come the industrialists, churchmen, politicians, and everybody else. In our fiction we attempt to examine how science and technology bring change. We do not try to predict the future so much as to describe possible futures. We are not prophets warning of doom or describing utopias. We are scouts bringing reports of the territory up ahead, so that the rest of the human race might travel into the future more safely and happily.

In *Millennium,* the concept of using lasers mounted aboard orbiting satellites to protect the nations of Earth from nuclear missile attack was both a symbol and a realistic extrapolation of technology. In science fiction, such a scientific concept can be used both as a symbol and as a part of the authentic technical background for a story.

I knew in 1965 that a space-based defense against ballistic missiles was inevitable. I was working then at Avco Everett Research Laboratory, in Massachusetts, where the first truly high-power laser was invented. We called it the Gasdynamic Laser, and the first working model was built and operated under the supervision of the physicist with whom I shared an office. In its first ten seconds of operation, that crude laboratory "kluge" produced more output power than all the lasers that had been built everywhere in the world since the first one had been turned on, five years earlier.

By January of 1966 I was helping to arrange a Top Secret meeting at the Pentagon to inform the Department of Defense that lasers were no longer merely laboratory curiosities. It was clear, even then, that a device which could produce a beam of concentrated light of many megawatts power could be the heart of a defense against the so-called "ultimate weapon," the hydrogen-bomb-carrying ballistic missile.

The meeting we set up in the Pentagon was snowed out by one of the worst blizzards ever to hit Washington. If you ever want to take over the government, wait for a two-foot snowfall. You can then take all of Washington with a handful of troops—if they have skis.

In February 1966 we finally met with the Department of Defense's top scientists and stunned them with the news of the Gasdynamic Laser. Seventeen years later an American President authorized the program that the media snidely calls Star Wars. I have told the story of the history, and future, of the Strategic Defense Initiative in a nonfiction book, *Star Peace: Assured Survival,* published by Tor Books in 1986.

But long before then, I used the very-real facts about laser-armed satellites as the background for my novel *Millennium.*

I had never given up on Chet Kinsman. He was too much a part of me, too deeply ingrained in my subconscious mind. I watched my first, unpublished novel become history as the Soviet Union did indeed put the first satellites and the first human space travelers into orbit and the United States roused itself to leapfrog the Russians and place the first men on the Moon. The way *I* had written it, that first step on the Moon was not made by Neil Armstrong; it was made by Chester Arthur Kinsman.

Kinsman would not let go of my imagination. I found myself writing short stories about him. He was a dashing young military astronaut who founded the Zero Gee Club, the first man to make love in weightlessness. He fought in orbit and killed a Russian cosmonaut, a shattering experience that altered his entire life. He got to the Moon, finally, and rescued a fellow astronaut who had gotten hurt while on an exploring mission. He battled the bureaucracy of Washington, as any modern pioneer must, in his efforts to get the United States to return to the Moon.

While these stories were shaping themselves in my mind, while I was writing them and seeing them published in science fiction magazines, the outline of *Millennium* crystallized and came to life.

Once *Millennium* was published, readers reacted powerfully, especially to the ending. I was encouraged to bring together the stories dealing with Kinsman's early life, and I wove them into a second novel, *Kinsman,* a "prequel" to *Millennium* even though it was written several years afterward.

In the meantime, of course, the scientists and engineers were making steady progress in the fields of space technology, lasers, and computers. So much so that in March 1983 President Reagan announced the start of the Strategic Defense Initiative. Once again I watched my fiction start to turn into history. Nothing in the original *Millennium* and *Kinsman* has been invalidated by the events of the past few years. But now many of the details that I had to sketch minimally can be shown in much clearer perspective.

Now, in this single volume, the whole story is played out from beginning to end. From a brand-new lieutenant on a joyride in a supersonic jet fighter plane to a man who literally carries the weight of two worlds on his shoulders. From a brash youngster who thinks of sex as nothing more than fun to a man who cares so much about the woman he loves that he is afraid of a relationship that will hurt her.

There are many differences between the original pair of novels and this new retelling of the Kinsman saga. For one thing, the human, emotional story of Kinsman and the woman he has loved all his life is told properly for the first time. Because the two novels were originally written the way they were, many details—and some larger aspects—of the story did not blend smoothly, one book to the other. Now they have been reexamined, rethought, and rewritten. All the characters and themes now mesh properly, and you can read the story of Kinsman's life from beginning to end as a single seamless garment.

The social and political implications of building a defense

against nuclear attack, however, remain almost exactly as I originally wrote them. That is because they have not changed. The ultimate result of space-based defenses against nuclear attack will be a unified world government. There is absolutely no doubt in my mind about that. Who runs that government, what kind of a government it will be, what role the United States will play in it and what role other nations will play—all those questions are unanswered. Their answers will be the political history of the twenty-first century.

There are many symbols in Kinsman's story. I mention this mainly because most critics have been blind to them. Or perhaps they think of symbolism only in its psychological sense, where rockets are considered phallic and a wheel-shaped space station is thought to be vaginal. That is not the sort of symbolism I am speaking of.

Kinsman himself is a symbol. A young American male, full of the adventure of flying, who brings both love and death to the pristine realm of outer space. In *Millennium,* he becomes a Christ figure, and his closest friend, Frank Colt, takes on the role of Judas. Colt himself symbolizes the dilemma of the black man in modern America.

The Christian symbolism is at its plainest in the section of *Kinsman* where he rescues the injured astronaut on the surface of the Moon. In that tale, titled "Fifteen Miles" when it appeared in a science fiction magazine in its original form, the surface of the Moon becomes a testing ground, a place of ordeal and punishment. The central question is redemption: Can Kinsman save his soul, or is he damned forever? This becomes the question for all the rest of his life, and forms his underlying motivation in *Millennium.*

The technological gadgets of the story also serve as symbols. Equating Moonbase's water factory with a human being's heart and blood is obvious enough. So, perhaps, is the symbolism of a lance of light that destroys the death machines of ballistic missiles. But the idea of humankind's reach into space *forcing* a change in human attitudes on Earth, which pervades the story of Kinsman's life, has escaped the attention of most critics.

There are two aspects to this, in the story. One is the laser-armed satellites, the Star Wars system, placed in orbit to defend against nuclear missile attack. The other is weather control, using technology to tame one of the most fundamental forces on Earth. Push and pull. Negative and positive. Yin and yang. The important point is that once the human race began to extend its ecological niche beyond the limits of planet Earth, all our old ways of thinking became doomed. Most people do not realize this yet. Most are oblivious to the fact that national borders are swiftly losing their meaning in a world of communications satellites, hydrogen bombs, continent-spanning missiles, and the expansion of human life into space.

The facts are there to see, but most people are not emotionally prepared to deal with them. It is through the symbolism of fiction that we prepare our minds for these new concepts. In the truest sense, Chet Kinsman does exist, and his message of hope and peace and love is the ultimate reality.

—Ben Bova
West Hartford, Connecticut
March 1987

BOOK I

KINSMAN

Fear death?—to feel the fog in my throat,
    The mist in my face,
When the snows begin, and the blasts denote
    I am nearing the place,
The power of the night, the press of the storm,
    The post of the foe,
Where he stands, the Arch Fear in a visible
    form.
Yet the strong man must go . . .

              —Robert Browning

To Mark Chartrand, despite his puns

Age 21

FROM THE REAR SEAT of the TF-15 jet the mountains of Utah looked like barren wrinkles of grayish brown, an old threadbare bedcover that had been tossed carelessly across the floor.

"How do you like it up here?"

Chet Kinsman heard the pilot's voice as a disembodied crackle in his helmet earphones. The shrill whine of the turbojet engines, the rush of unbreathably thin air just inches away on the other side of the transparent canopy, were nothing more than background music, muted, unimportant.

"Love it!" he answered to the bulbous white helmet in the seat in front of him.

The cockpit was narrow and cramped. The oxygen he breathed through the rubbery mask had a cold, metallic tang to it. Kinsman could barely move in his seat. The pilot had warned him, "Pull the harness good and snug; you don't want anything flapping loose if you have to eject." Now the safety straps cut into his shoulders.

Yet he felt free.

"How high can we go?" he asked into the mike built into the oxygen mask.

A pause. "Oh, we can leave controlled airspace if we want to. Better'n fifty thousand feet." The pilot had a trace of Southern accent. Alabama, maybe, thought Kinsman. Or Georgia. "Thirty thou's good enough for now, though."

Kinsman grinned to himself. "A lot better than hang gliding."

"Hey, I like hang gliding," said the pilot.

"But it doesn't compare to this. . . . This is *power*."

"Right enough."

Power. And freedom. Six miles above the tired, wrinkled old Earth. Six miles away from everything and everybody. It couldn't last long enough to suit him.

Ahead lay San Francisco and his mother's funeral. Ahead lay death and his father's implacable anger.

Life at the Air Force Academy was rigid, cold. A first-year cadet was expected to obey everybody's orders, not make friends. No matter that you're older than the other first-year men. A rich boy, huh? Spent two years in a fancy prep school, huh? Well, snap to, mister! Let me see four chins, moneybags! Four of 'em!

Yet that was better than going home.

His father had refused to stop off in Colorado when he had taken his ailing wife from their estate in Pennsylvania to her sister's home in San Francisco. And Kinsman had delayed taking leave to visit his mother there. Time enough for that later, after his father had gone back East to return to running his banks.

Then, suddenly, unalterably, she was dead. And his father was still there.

Instead of taking a commercial airliner, Kinsman had begged a ride with a westward-heading Air Force captain.

If t'were done, he told himself, t'were best done quickly.

Now he was flying. Free and happy.

Suddenly the plane's nose dipped and Kinsman felt his pressure suit begin to squeeze the air out of him. His arms became too heavy to lift. His head felt as if it would sink down inside his rib cage. He could hear the pilot's breath, over the open mike, rasping in long, regular panting grunts, like a man doing pushups, and Kinsman realized he was breathing hard too. They were diving toward the desert, which now looked as flat and hard and gray as steel. The pressure suit squeezed harder. Kinsman could not speak.

"Try a low-level run," the pilot gasped, between breaths. "Get a real . . . feeling of speed."

The helmet on Kinsman's head weighed two million pounds. He made a grunting noise that was supposed to be a cool "Okay."

And then they were skimming across the empty desert, engines howling, rocks and bushes nothing more than a speeding blur whizzing past. Kinsman took a deep exhilarating breath. The plane shook and bucked as if eager to return to the thinner, clearer air where it had been designed to fly.

He thought he saw some buildings in the blur of hills off to his left, but before he could speak into his radio mike the pilot blurted:

"Whoops! Highway!"

The control column between Kinsman's knees yanked back toward his crotch. The plane stood on its tail, afterburners screaming, and a microsecond's flicker of a huge tractor-trailer rig zipped past the corner of his eye. The suit squeezed at his middle again and he felt himself pressing into the contoured seat with the weight of an anvil on his chest.

They leveled off at last and Kinsman sucked in a great sighing gulp of oxygen.

"Damned sun glare does that sometimes," the pilot was saying, sounding half annoyed and half apologetic. "Damned desert looks clear but there's a truck doodling along the highway, hidden in the glare."

Kinsman found his voice. "That was a helluva ride."

The pilot chuckled. "I'll bet there's one damned rattled trucker down there. He's probably on his little ol' CB reporting a flying saucer attack."

They headed westward again, toward the setting sun. The pilot let Kinsman take the controls for a while as they climbed to cross the approaching Sierras. The rugged mountain crests were still capped with snow, bluish and cold. Like the wall of the Rockies that loomed over the Academy, Kinsman thought.

"You got a nice steady touch, kid. Make a good pilot."

"Thanks. I used to fly my father's Cessna. Even the Learjet, once."

"Got your license?"

"Not yet. I'll qualify at the Academy."

The pilot said nothing.

"I'm going in for astronaut training as soon as I graduate," Kinsman went on.

"Astronaut, huh? Well, I'd rather fly a real airplane. Damned astronauts are like robots. Everything's done by remote control for those rocket jocks."

"Not everything," Kinsman protested.

He could sense the pilot shaking his head inside his

helmet. "Hell, I'll bet they even have machines to do their screwing for them."

It was an old house atop Russian Hill. Victorian clapboard, unpretentious yet big enough to hold a hockey rink on its ground floor. The view of the Bay was spectacular. The people who lived in this part of San Francisco had the quiet power to see that none of the new office towers and high-rise hotels obscured their vistas.

Neal McGrath opened the door for Kinsman. His normal scowl warmed into a half-bitter smile.

"Hello, Chet."

"Neal. I didn't expect to see you here."

"He needed somebody to take charge of things for him. This has hit him pretty hard."

McGrath reminded Kinsman of a Varangian Guard: a tall, broad-shouldered, red-haired Viking who hovered by his Emperor's side to protect him from assassins. His ice-blue eyes looked much older than his years. He was barely twenty months older than Kinsman, but his suspicious scowl and low, growly voice gave him an air of inner experience, of wariness, that strangely made people trust and rely on him. Kinsman had known him since McGrath had been the ten-year-old son who helped their gardener mow their lawn. Now McGrath was his father's personal assistant, and was being groomed for one of the family's seats in the House of Representatives. He would be a senator one day, they all agreed.

Stepping from the late afternoon sunshine into the darkened stained-glass foyer of the old Victorian house, Kinsman asked, "Where is my mother?"

"In there." McGrath gestured toward a set of double doors that rose to the ceiling.

Kinsman let his single flight bag drop to the marble floor. "Is my father . . ."

"He's upstairs, taking a nap. The doctor's trying to keep him as quiet as possible." McGrath bent to pick up Kinsman's bag. "There's a room for you upstairs. How long will you be staying?"

"I'll leave right after the funeral, tomorrow."

"A lot of the family is flying in from the East. They'll expect to see you afterward."

Kinsman shook his head. "I can't stay."

"If it's a matter of fixing things with the Academy I can call . . ."

"No. Please, Neal."

McGrath shrugged and started toward the broad, stern dark-wood staircase, his footsteps echoing on the cool marble floor.

Kinsman went to the tall double doors. An ornately framed mirror hung on the hallway wall just before the doors, and he saw himself in it. His mother would not have recognized him. The blue uniform made him look slimmer than ever, and taller, despite the fact that he had never quite reached the six-foot height he had coveted so desperately as a teenager. His face was leaner, dark hair cropped closer than it had ever been before, blue eyes weary from lack of sleep. His long jaw was stubbly; his mother would have insisted that he go upstairs and shave.

He slid the doors slightly apart and slipped almost guiltily into the room. It had been a library at one time, or a parlor, the kind of a room where women of an earlier generation had once served tea to one another. Now it was too dark to see the walls clearly. The high windows were muffled in dark draperies. The only light in the large room was a ceiling spot illuminating the casket. Kinsman's mother lay there embedded in white satin, her eyes closed peacefully, her hands folded over a plain sky-blue dress.

He did not recognize her at first. The cancer had taken away so much of her flesh that only a taut covering of skin stretched across the bony understructure of her face. All the fullness of her mouth and brow were gone. She was a gaunt skeleton of the mother he had known.

Her skin looked waxy, unreal. Kinsman stared down at her for a long time, thinking, *She's so tiny. I never realized she was so tiny.*

He knelt at the mahogany prayer rail in front of the casket but found that he had nothing to say. He felt absolutely numb inside; no grief, no guilt, nothing. Empty. But in his mind he heard her voice from earlier years.

Chester, get down from that tree before you hurt yourself!

Yes, Mommy.

You could have a fine career as a concert pianist, Chester,

*if only you would practice instead of indulging in this ridicu-
lous mania for flying.*

Aw, Ma.

*I do wish you would be more respectful of your father,
Chester. He's proud of what he's accomplished and he wants
you to share in it.*

I'll try, Mother. But . . .

*If I give you my consent, Chester, if I let you join the Air
Force, it will break your poor father's heart.*

I've got to get away from him, Mother. It's the only way.
I'll put in for astronaut training. I won't kill anybody. It'll all
work out okay, you'll see. You'll be proud of me someday.

"So you finally got here."

Kinsman turned and saw the tall, austere figure of his
father framed in the doorway.

He got up from his knees quickly. "I came as soon as I
could."

"Not soon enough," his father said, sliding the doors
shut behind him.

Kinsman pulled in a deep breath. They had fought many
battles in front of his mother. He had been a fool to hope that
today could be any different.

"It . . . she went so fast," he said.

His father walked slowly toward him, a measured pace,
like a monster in a child's horror tale. "At the end, yes, it was
fast. The doctors said it was the Lord's mercy. But she
suffered for months. You could have eased her pain."

Kinsman realized suddenly that his father was *old.* And
probably in pain himself. The man's hair was dead white now,
not a trace of its former color. His eyes had lost their fire.

"I talked with her on the phone," he said, knowing it
sounded weak, defensive. "Almost every night . . ."

"You should have been *here,* where you belong!"

"The Air Force thought differently."

"The Air Force! That conglomeration of feeble-minded
professional killers."

"That's not true and you know it."

"I could have had any one of a dozen United States
Senators bail you out of your precious Academy. But no, you
were too busy to come and ease your mother's last days on
Earth."

"None of us knew she was that close to the end."

"She was in pain!" The old man's voice was rising, filling the nearly empty room with its hard, angry echoes.

"I couldn't come," Kinsman insisted.

"Why not?"

"Because I didn't want to see you!" he blurted.

If it surprised his father, the old man did not show it. He merely nodded. "You mean you couldn't *face* me."

"Call it what you want to."

"Sneaking around behind my back. Forcing your sick mother to consent to your joining the Air Force. The only son of the most prominent Quaker family in Pennsylvania —joining the Air Force! Learning how to become a killer!"

"I'm not going to kill anyone," Kinsman answered. "I'm going in for astronaut duty."

"You'll do what they order you to do. You surrendered your soul when you put on that uniform. If they order you to kill, you'll kill. You'll bomb cities and strafe helpless women and children. You'll drop napalm on babies when they order you to."

"I'm not going to be involved in anything like that!"

"My only child, a warrior. A killer. No wonder your mother died. You killed her."

Kinsman could feel waves of fire sweeping through him. Gritting his teeth against the pain, he said, "That's a rotten thing to tell me . . ."

"It's true. You killed her. She'd still be alive if it weren't for you."

The pain flaming through him was too much. Fists clenched against his sides, Kinsman brushed past his father and strode out of the room, out of the house, out into the bright hot sunshine and clear blue sky that he neither felt nor saw.

By the time he realized the sun had set, he found himself in Berkeley, walking aimlessly along a wide boulevard, carried along by the flow of students and other pedestrians streaming past shops and restaurants. Music blared from car radios passing by. Garish lights flickered from shop-front windows.

He stepped into a bar. The sign on its window said it was

a coffee shop, but the only coffee they served had Irish whiskey in it. Kinsman ordered a beer and hunched over the frosted glass, staring blankly into its foamy head. He heard a sweet woman's voice singing, looked up into the mirror behind the bar, and saw a girl sitting on a stool in front of a microphone, strumming a guitar as she sang.

> "Jack of diamonds, queen of spades,
>   Fingers tremble and the memory fades,
>   And it's a foolish man who tries to cheat the
>   dealer . . ."

The people sitting around the bar wore shabby denims or faded khaki fatigues. A couple of suits and casual sports coats. Kinsman felt out of place in his crisp sky-blue uniform.

As he watched the night deepen over the clapboard buildings and the lights on the Bay Bridge stretch a twinkling arch across the water, he realized he had spent most of his life alone. He had no home. The Academy was cold and friendless. There was no place on Earth that he could call his own. And deep inside he knew that his soul was as austere and rigid as his father's. I'll look like him one day, Kinsman thought. If I live long enough.

> "You can't win,
>   And you can't break even,
>   You can't get out of the game . . .

She has a really sweet voice, he thought. Like a silver bell. Like water in the desert.

It was a haunting voice. And her face, framed by long midnight-black hair, had a fine-boned, dark-eyed ascetic look to it. She perched on a high stool, under a lone spotlight, bluejeaned legs crossed and guitar resting on one thigh.

He sat at the bar silently urging himself to go over and introduce himself, offer her a drink, tell her how much he enjoyed her singing. But as he worked up his nerve a dozen kids his own age burst into the place. The singer, just finished her set, smiled and called to them. They clustered around her.

Kinsman turned his attention to his warming beer. By the time he finished it the students had pushed a few tables together and were noisily ordering everything from Sacred Cows to Seven-Up. The singer had disappeared. It was full night outside now.

"You alone?"

He looked up, startled. It was her.

"Uh . . . yeah." Clumsily he pushed the barstool back and got to his feet.

"Why don't you come over and join us?" She gestured toward the crowd of students.

"Sure. Great. Love to."

She was tall enough to be almost eye level with Kinsman, and as slim and supple as a young willow. She wore a black long-sleeved pullover atop her faded denims.

"Hey, everybody, this is . . ." She turned to him with an expectant little smile. All the others stopped their chatter and looked up at him.

"Kinsman," he said. "Chet Kinsman."

Two chairs appeared out of the crowd and Kinsman sat down between the singer and a chubby blonde girl who was intently, though unsteadily, rolling a joint for herself.

Kinsman felt out of place. They were all staring wordlessly at him, except for the rapt blonde. Wrong uniform, he told himself. He might as well have been wearing a badge that spelled out NARC.

"My name's Diane," the singer said to him as the bar's only waitress placed a fresh beer in front of him. "That's Shirl, John, Carl, Eddie, Dolores . . ." She made a circuit of the table and Kinsman forgot their names as soon as he heard them. Except for Diane's.

They were still eyeing him suspiciously.

"You with the National Guard?"

"No," Kinsman said. "Air Force Academy."

"Going to be a fly-boy?"

"Flying pig," mumbled the blonde on his left.

Kinsman looked at her. "I'm going in for astronaut training."

"An orbiting pig," she muttered.

"That's a stupid thing to say."

"She's wired tight," Diane told him. "We're all a little pissed off."

"Why?"

11

"The demonstration got called off," said one of the guys. "The fuckin' mayor reneged on us."

"What demonstration?" Kinsman asked.

"You don't know?" It was an accusation.

"Should I?"

"You mean you really don't know what day tomorrow is?" asked the bespectacled youth sitting across the table.

"Tomorrow?" Kinsman felt slightly bewildered.

"Kent State."

"It's the anniversary."

"They gunned down a dozen students."

"The National Fuckin' Guard."

"Killed them!"

"But that was years ago," Kinsman said. "In Ohio."

They all glared at him as if they were blaming him for it.

"We're gonna show those friggin' bastards," said an intense, waspish little guy sitting a few chairs down from Kinsman. He tried to remember his name. *Eddie?* The guy was frail-looking, but his face was set in a smoldering angry cast, tight-lipped. The big glasses he wore made his eyes look huge and fierce.

"Right on," said the group's one black member. "They can't cancel our parade."

"Not after they gave their word it was okay."

"We'll tear the fuckin' campus apart tomorrow!"

"How's that going to help things?" Kinsman heard his own voice asking.

"How's it gonna *help*?"

"I mean," Kinsman went on, wanting to bounce some of their hostility back at them, "what are you trying to accomplish? So you tear up the campus, big deal. What good does that do—except convince everybody that you're a bunch of loonies."

"You don't make any sense," Eddie snapped.

"Neither do you."

"But you don't understand," said Diane. "We've got to do *something*. We can't just let them withdraw permission to hold our parade without making some kind of response."

"I'd appeal to the Governor. Or one of my senators. Go where the clout is."

They all laughed at that. All but Eddie, who looked angrier still.

"You don't understand anything at all about how the political process works, do you?" Eddie sneered.

Kinsman smiled. Now I've got you! He responded with deliberate tempo, "Well . . . an uncle of mine is a U.S. Senator. My grandfather was Governor of the Commonwealth of Pennsylvania. Several other family members are in public service. I've been involved in political campaigning since I was old enough to hold a poster."

Silence. As if a leper had entered their midst.

"Jesus Christ," breathed one of the kids at last. "He's *really* Establishment."

Diane said, "Your kind of politics doesn't work for us. The Establishment won't listen to us."

"We've gotta fight for our rights!"

"Demonstrate!"

"Fight fire with fire!"

"Action!"

"Bullshit," Kinsman snapped. "All you're going to do is give the cops an excuse to bash your heads in—or worse. Violence is always counterproductive."

The night and the argument wore on. They swore at each other, drank, smoked, talked, yelled until they started to get hoarse. Kinsman found himself enjoying it immensely. Diane had to get up to sing for the customers every hour, and they would call a truce for the duration of her set. Each time she finished she came back and sat beside him.

And the battle would resume. The bar finally closed and Kinsman got up slowly on legs turned to rubber. But he went along with them down a dark and empty Berkeley street to someone's one-room pad, up four creaking flights of outdoor stairs, yammering all the way, arguing against them all, one against ten. And Diane stayed beside him.

Eventually they started drifting away, leaving the apartment. Kinsman found himself sitting on the bare wooden floor halfway between the stained kitchen sink and the new-looking water bed, telling them:

"Look, I don't like it any more than you do. But violence is *their* game. You can't win that way. Tear up the whole damned campus and they'll tear down the whole damned city just to get even with you."

"Yeah," admitted one of the girls. "Look what they did in Philadelphia. And with a black mayor, too."

"Then what's the answer?" Diane asked.

Kinsman made an elaborate shrug. "Well . . . you could do what the Quakers do. Shame them. Just go out tomorrow in a group and stand in the most prominent spot on campus. All of you . . . all the people who were going to march in the parade. Just stand silently for a few hours."

"That's dumb," Eddie said.

"It's smart," Kinsman retorted. "Nonviolent. Conscience-stirring. Like Gandhi. Always attracts the news photographers. An old Quaker trick."

"I could call the news stations," Diane said, smiling.

A burly-shouldered kid with a big beefy face and tiny squinting eyes crouched on the floor in front of Kinsman.

"That's a chickenshit thing to do."

"But it works."

"You know your trouble, fly-boy? You're chickenshit."

Kinsman grinned at him and looked around the floor for the can of beer he had been working on.

"You hear me? You're all talk. But you're scared to fight for your rights."

Looking up, Kinsman saw that Diane, the blonde smoker, and two of the guys were the only ones left in the apartment. Plus the muscleman confronting him.

"I'll fight for my rights," he said, very carefully because his tongue was not quite obeying his brain. "And I'll fight for yours, too. But not in any stupid-ass way."

"You callin' me stupid?" The guy got to his feet.

A weight lifter, Kinsman guessed. Pumps iron every day and now he wants to show off his muscles on me.

"I don't know you well enough to call you anything."

"Well, I'm callin' you a chicken. A gutless motherfuckin' coward."

Slowly Kinsman got to his feet. It helped to have the wall to lean against.

"I take that, sir, to be a challenge to my honor," he said, letting himself sound drunk. It took very little effort.

"Goddam right it's a challenge. You must be some

goddam pig—secret police or something."

"That's why I'm wearing this inconspicuous uniform."

"To throw us off guard."

"Don't be an oaf."

"I'm gonna break your head, wise-ass."

Kinsman raised an unsteady finger. "Now hold on. You challenged me, right? So I get the choice of weapons. That's the way it works in the good ol' *code duello.*"

"Choice of weapons?" The big guy looked confused.

"You challenged me to a duel, didn't you? You have impeached my honor. I have the right to choose the weapons."

The guy made a fist the size of a football. "This is all the weapon I need."

"Ah, but that's not the weapon I choose," Kinsman countered. "I believe that I shall choose sabers. Won a few medals back East with my saber fencing. Now where can we find a pair of sabers at this hour of the morning . . . ?"

The guy grabbed Kinsman's shirt. "I'm gonna knock that fuckin' grin off your face."

"You probably will. But not before I kick both your kneecaps off. You'll never see the inside of a gym again, muscleboy."

"That's enough, both of you," Diane snapped. She stepped between the two of them. The big guy let go of Kinsman.

"You'd better get back to your own place, Ray," she said, her voice flat and hard. "You're not going to break up my pad and get me thrown out on the street."

Ray pointed a thick, blunt finger at Kinsman. "He's an agent for the Feds. Or something. Don't trust him."

"Go home, Ray. It's late."

"I'll get you, blue-suit," said Ray. "I'll get you."

Kinsman replied, "When you find the sabers, let me know."

"Shut up!" Diane hissed at him. But she was grinning.

She half-pushed the lumbering Ray out the door. The others left right behind him. Suddenly Kinsman was alone in the shabby little room with Diane.

"I guess I ought to go, too," Kinsman said, his insides shaking now that the danger had passed. Or was it the thought of going back home?

"Where?" Diane asked.

"Back in the city . . . Russian Hill."

"God, you *are* Establishment!"

"Born with a silver spoon in my ear. To the manner born. Rich or poor, it pays to have money. Let 'em eat cake. Or was it coke?"

"You're very drunk."

"How can you tell?"

"For one thing, your feet are standing still but the rest of you is swaying like a tree in a typhoon."

"I am drunk with your beauty . . . and a ton and a half of beer."

Diane laughed. "I can believe the second one."

"The toilet's in there, isn't it?"

"You mean you haven't . . . ?"

Kinsman walked past her, carefully. "Nobody owns beer, you know. You merely rent it."

It was a narrow cubicle with an old-fashioned tub that stood on four rusted swans; the toilet was equally ancient. No roaches in sight. No sink. He bent over the tub and splashed cold water on his face, then patted it dry with a limp towel hanging on the back of the door.

He came out and saw Diane still standing in the middle of the room, eyeing him quizzically.

"How do you get a cab around here?" he asked.

"You don't. Not at this hour. No trains or buses, either."

"I'm stuck here?"

Diane nodded.

"A fate worse than death," he muttered.

The room's furnishings consisted of a bookcase crammed with sheet music and a few paperbacks, the water bed, a Formica-topped table with two battered wooden chairs that did not match, the water bed, a pile of books in the corner by the windows, a few colorful pillows strewn across the floor here and there, the water bed, two guitars, a sink and small stove with some cabinets above them, and the water bed.

"We can share the bed," Diane said.

He felt his face turn red. "Are your intentions honorable?"

She grinned at him. "The condition you're in, we'll both be safe enough."

"Don't be so sure."

But he fell asleep as soon as he sank into the soft warmth of the bed. His last thought was an inward chuckle that he did not have to spend the night under the same roof as his father.

It was during the misty, dreaming light of earliest dawn that he half awoke and felt her body cupped against his. Still half asleep, they moved together, slowly, gently, unhurried in the pearl-gray fog, touching without the necessity to think, murmuring without the need for words, caressing, making love.

Kinsman lay on his back, smiling peacefully at the cracked ceiling. Diane stroked the flat of his abdomen, saying drowsily, "Go back to sleep. Get some rest and then we can do it again."

It was hours later by the time Kinsman had showered in the cracked tub and climbed back into his wrinkled, sweaty uniform. He was peering into the still-steamed bathroom mirror, wondering what to do about his stubbly chin, when Diane called through the half-open door.

"Tea or coffee?"

"Coffee."

Kinsman came out of the tiny bathroom and saw that Diane had wrapped herself in a thin bathrobe. She had set up toast and a jar of Smuckers grape jelly on the table by the window. The teakettle was on the two-burner stove and a pair of chipped mugs and a jar of instant coffee stood alongside.

They sat facing each other, washing down the crunchy toast with the hot, bitter coffee. Diane watched the people moving along the street below them. Kinsman stared at the bright clean sky.

"How long can you stay?" she asked.

"I've got a funeral to attend . . . in about an hour. Then I leave tonight."

"Oh."

"Got to report back to the Academy tomorrow morning."

"You have to?"

He nodded.

"But you'll be free this afternoon?"

"After the burial. Yes."

"Come down to the campus with me," Diane said, brightening. "I'm going to try your idea . . . get them to stand just like the Quakers. You can help us."

"Me?" '

"Sure! It was your idea, wasn't it?"

"Yeah, but . . ."

She reached across the table and took his free hand in both of hers. "Chet . . . please. Not for me. Do it for yourself. I don't want to think of you being sent out to Central America or someplace like that to fight and kill people. Or to be killed yourself. Don't let them turn you into a killer."

"But I'm going into astronaut training."

"You don't think they'll really give you what you want, do you? They'll use you where *they* want you—Lebanon or Nicaragua or who knows where? They'll put you in a plane and tell you to bomb some helpless village."

He shook his head. "You don't understand . . ."

"No, *you* don't understand," she said earnestly. Kinsman saw the intensity in her eyes, the devotion. Is she really worried that much about me? he wondered. Does she really care so much? And then a truly staggering thought hit him. My father! Is he worried about me? Is he frightened for *my* sake?

"Come with us, Chet," Diane was pleading. "Stand with us against the Power Structure. Just for one hour."

"In my uniform? Your friends would trash me."

"No, they won't. The uniform will be great! It'd make a terrific impact for somebody in uniform to show up with us! We've been trying to get some of the Vietnam vets to show themselves in uniform."

"I can't," Kinsman said. "I've got to go to the funeral, and then catch a ride back to the Academy."

"That's more important than freedom? More important than justice?"

He had no answer.

"Chet . . . please. For me. If you don't want to do it for yourself, or for the people, then do it for me. Please."

He looked away from her and glanced around the

18

shabby, unkempt room. At the stained sink. The faded wallpaper. The water bed, with its roiled sheet trailing onto the floor.

He thought of the Academy. The cold gray mountains and ranks of uniforms marching mechanically across the frozen parade ground. The starkly functional classrooms, the remorselessly efficient architecture devoid of all individual expression.

And he thought of his father: cold, implacable—was it pride and anger that moved him, or fear?

Then he turned back, looked past the earnest young woman across the table from him, and saw the sky once again. A pale ghost of a Moon was grinning lopsidedly at him.

"I can't go with you," he said quietly, finally. "Somebody's got to make sure that the nation's defended while you're out there demonstrating for your rights."

For a moment Diane said nothing. Then, "You're trying to make a joke out of something that's deadly serious."

"I'm being serious," he said. "You'll have plenty of demonstrators out there. Somebody's got to pay attention to the business of protecting you while you're exercising your freedoms."

"It's our own government that we need protection from!"

"You've got it. You just have to exercise it a little more carefully. I'd rather be flying. There aren't so many of us up there."

Diane shook her head. "You're hopeless."

He shrugged.

"I was going to let you stay here . . . if you wanted to quit the Air Force."

"Quit?"

"If you needed a place to hide . . . or if you just wanted to stay here, with me."

He started to answer, but his mouth was suddenly dry. He swallowed, then in a voice that almost cracked, "Listen, Diane. I wasn't even a teenager when the first men set foot on the Moon. That's where I've wanted to be ever since that moment. There are new worlds to see, and I want to see them."

"But that's turning your back on this world!"

"So what?" He pushed his chair from the table and got to his feet. "There's not much in this world worth caring about. Not for me."

He strode to the door, then turned back toward her. She was still at the table. "Sorry I disappointed you, Diane. And, well, thanks . . . for everything."

Diane got up, walked swiftly across the tiny room to him, and kissed Kinsman lightly on the lips.

"It was my pleasure, General."

He laughed. "Hell, I'm not even a lieutenant yet."

"You'll be a general someday."

"I don't think so."

"You could have been a hero today."

"I'm not very heroic."

"Yes, you are." Diane smiled at him. "You just don't know it yet."

Unshaven, in his wrinkled uniform, Kinsman stood at his father's side through the funeral, rode silently in the cortege's limousine to the cemetery, and watched a crowd of strangers file past the casket, one by one, placing on it single red roses. His mother had detested red roses all her life.

As they rode back toward Russian Hill in the velvet-lined, casketlike limousine, Kinsman turned to his darkly silent father.

"I know I've disappointed you," he said in a low swift voice, afraid he would be cut off before he could finish, "and I also realize that you wouldn't be so angry with me if you didn't love me and weren't worried about me."

His father stared straight ahead, unmoving.

"Well . . . I love you, too, Dad."

The old man's eyes blinked. The corners of his mouth twitched. Without moving a millimeter toward his son, he whispered, "You are a disgrace. Staying out all night and then showing up looking like a Bowery derelict. The sooner you leave the better!"

Kinsman leaned back in the limousine's velvet uphol-stery. Thanks, Dad, he said to himself. You've always made it so easy for me.

* * *

Neal McGrath drove him down 101, toward the Navy's Moffet Field, weaving his new Chrysler convertible through knots of traffic and past hulking, hurtling diesel tractor-trailers.

"You're sure you can pick up a flight back to Boulder?" McGrath yelled over the rush of the wind.

"Sure!" Kinsman hollered back. "The guy I rode out with told me he was going back late this afternoon."

McGrath shook his head as he carefully flicked the turn signal and pulled around a station wagon filled with kids. The wind pulled wildly at his long red hair.

"The family's going to be very disappointed that you didn't stay for dinner."

"Not Dad. He threw me out."

McGrath snorted. "You know he didn't mean that."

"Sure."

"Where the hell were you all night, anyway? You look like you got rolled in an alley."

"Just about." Kinsman told him about Diane and her campus activists as the convertible zoomed down the highway.

"Sound like a bunch of Communists," McGrath growled.

Kinsman laughed. "We didn't discuss politics in bed."

"What an easy lay. She sure tried to recruit you, all right."

The Moffet Field turnoff was approaching. McGrath slid into the exit lane.

"Neal . . . I don't even know her last name!"

"So what?"

"So look her up for me, will you? Maybe the family could give her a little help . . . with her singing career."

"A Communist?"

"She's not a Communist, for Chrissakes."

"Worse, then. A liberal." But McGrath was grinning.

"See if you can help her."

"I'm a married man, kid," said McGrath.

Kinsman frowned at him. "I'm not asking you to get involved with her. But she's got a marvelous voice, Neal. Maybe somebody in the family can get her a break, some bookings . . ."

"Going to reform her, eh? Make her rich and turn her into a capitalist."

"Yeah. Why not?" Kinsman studied McGrath's face. He was smirking. You just don't understand, Neal.

Later that afternoon, thirty thousand feet above the Sacramento Valley with the sun at their backs, Kinsman felt the cares and fears of the Earth below easing out of his tense body.

"How'd you enjoy Frisco?" the pilot asked.

"I didn't see much of it," Kinsman said into his radio microphone.

"Didn't stay very long."

"Neither did you."

The pilot's voice in his earphones broke into a self-satisfied chuckle. "Long enough, pal. Overnight is plenty long enough if you know what you're doing."

Kinsman nodded inside his helmet.

They climbed higher. Kinsman watched the westering sun throw long shadows across the rugged Sierra peaks.

"Sir?" he asked, after a long thoughtful silence. "Do you honestly think that astronaut training would turn a man into a robot?"

He could see the featureless white curve of the pilot's helmet over the back of the seat. There was nothing human about it.

"Listen, son, *all* military training is aimed at turning you into a robot. That's what it's all about. You think a normal human being would rush toward guys who're shooting at him?"

"But . . ."

"Just don't let 'em get inside you," the pilot said, his languid drawl becoming more intense, almost passionate. "Hold on to yourself. The main thing is to get up here, away from 'em. Get flying. Up here they cain't really touch you. Up here you're free."

"They're pretty strict at the Academy," Kinsman said. "They like things done their own way."

"Tell me about it. I'm a West Point man, myself. But you can still hold on to your own soul, boy. You have t'do things their way on the outside, but you be your own man inside. Ain't easy, but it can be done."

Nodding to himself, Kinsman looked up and through the plane's clear canopy. He caught sight of the Moon, hanging just above the rugged horizon. It looked bright and close in the darkening sky.

I can do it, he told himself. I can do it.

Age 25

HE WAS FLYING west again, with the sun at his back. Two years of "peacekeeping" in the volatile Middle East had gone by. He had flown a fighter plane without firing a shot, happy that he was not assigned to the real fighting that flared intermittently in Central America. It had taken almost another two years before he had finally been assigned to astronaut training.

Two years of air patrols along the Gulf Coast, searching for smugglers' planes coming in from Latin America. Two years of watching the United States' economy slide disastrously as the price of foreign oil skyrocketed once again. Even Houston was hit by the new recession; the revitalized OPEC, backed now by Soviet arms, quickly squeezed all American companies out of the nationalized oil industries of the Middle East, Indonesia, and South America.

Diane Lawrence was on her way to stardom. Her haunting voice, singing of simpler, happier times, brought comfort to Americans who faced doubtful futures of unemployment and welfare. Kinsman dated her half a dozen times, flying to cities where she was appearing. He traveled on commercial airliners. New government austerity regulations prevented him from piloting an Air Force plane, except on official duty. He was shocked at the price of airline tickets; the cost of energy was more than money, it was freedom of movement.

But now Kinsman was relaxed and happy as he held the controls of the supersonic twin-engine jet. Months of training in the elaborate mockups of the space shuttle were behind him. Orientation flights on the "Vomit Comet," the lumbering cargo jet that flew endless parabolic arcs to give the astronaut-trainees their first taste of weightlessness, had gone smoothly. Now he was heading for the real thing: spaceflight duty. The cares and problems of the groundlings' world were far below him, for the moment.

Kinsman was sitting in the right-hand seat of the jet's compact cockpit. The plane's ostensible pilot, Major Joseph Tenny, seemed half asleep in the pilot's seat.

Far below them the empty brown desert of New Mexico sprawled. They had left NASA's Johnson Space Center, outside Houston, at sunrise. They would be at Vandenberg Air Force Base in southern California in time for breakfast.

The plane was as beautiful and responsive as a woman. More responsive than most, Kinsman thought. The slightest touch on the crescent-shaped control yoke made the plane move into a bank or a climb with such grace and smooth power that it sent a shudder of delight through Kinsman.

"Sweet little thing, ain't she?" Tenny murmured.

Kinsman shot a surprised glance at the Major. He was not asleep after all. Chunky, short-limbed, barrel-chested, Tenny looked completely out of place in a zippered flight suit and a visored gleaming plastic helmet. His dark-eyed swarthy face peeped out of the helmet like some ape who had gotten into the outfit by mistake.

But he grasped the controls in his thick-fingered hands and said, "Here . . . lemme show ya something, kid."

Kinsman reluctantly let go of the controls and watched Tenny push the yoke sharply forward. The plane's nose dropped and suddenly Kinsman was staring at the mottled gray-brown of the desert rushing up toward him.

"Shouldn't we get an okay from ground control before we . . ."

Tenny shot him a disgusted glance. "By the time those clowns make up their minds," he growled, breathing hard, "we could be having Mai Tais in Waikiki."

The altimeter needle wound down. The engines' whine was lost in the shrill of tortured air whistling past their canopy. The plane dived, screaming. The desert filled Kinsman's vision.

And then they zoomed upward. The yoke in front of Kinsman pulled smoothly back as his pressure suit hissed and clamped a pneumatic hold on his guts and legs to keep the blood from draining out of his head, to keep him alive and awake while the plane nosed up smoothly as an arrow, hurtling almost like a rocket, up, up, straight into the even emptier blue desert of the sky.

Kinsman wanted to let loose a wild cowboy's yell, but the weight on his chest made it hard even to breathe. Tenny said nothing, but the gleam in his devilishly dark eyes told Kinsman there was more to come. The afterburners were screeching now as the plane climbed higher, cleaving through the thinning air.

Kinsman grinned to himself as he realized what Tenny was going to do. Sure enough, the Major nosed the plane over again and suddenly Kinsman's arms floated up off his lap. His stomach seemed to be dropping away. He was falling, falling —yet strapped into his seat.

Weightlessness. Kinsman gulped once, twice. Despite everything his inner ear and stomach were telling him, he knew that he was not falling. He was floating. Free! Like a bird, like an angel. Free of gravity.

Tenny leveled the plane off and the feeling of normal weight returned. The Major eyed Kinsman craftily.

"Like the Vomit Comet," Kinsman said, grinning at him.

"You really *like* zero gee, dontcha?"

"It's great."

Tenny shook his head, a ponderous waddling with the bulky helmet. "You're the only guy in the whole group who didn't throw up once. Even Colt tossed his cookies a couple times. But not you. According to the reports."

"The reports weren't faked," Kinsman said.

Tenny grunted. "I didn't think so. But I hadda see for myself."

He gave control of the plane back to Kinsman and they resumed their flight toward Vandenberg.

"Sir?" Kinsman asked. "What's Colonel Murdock like?"

"I never served under him before. Desk jockey, from what I hear."

"I don't see why they didn't put you in command. You're due for promotion to lieutenant colonel, aren't you?"

Tenny made a face that might have been either a smile or a scowl. "Due for promotion and getting promoted are two different things. Besides, there's two other majors who've been running programs for two other squads of trainees, same as me. So we get a light colonel to sit on top of the whole group. That's the Air Force way: solid brass, all the way up the shaft."

Kinsman laughed.

But Tenny grew more serious. "There's something else I wanted to talk to you about. Colt. None of you guys have gotten close to him . . ."

"The black Napoleon? He's not easy to get close to."

"Maybe he needs a friend," said Tenny.

Kinsman thought of Frank Colt, the one night during training when the black man had joined the other guys in the squad for a game of pool. The intensity on Colt's face as he turned a friendly game into a gut-burning competition. How Colt had probed for the weakness in each of the other men; how he had finessed, angered, cajoled, or kidded each one of them into defeat.

"He's a loner," Kinsman said. "He's not looking for a friend."

"He's a black loner in an otherwise white outfit."

"That's got nothing to do with it."

"The hell it hasn't."

Kinsman started to reply, hesitated. There were a dozen arguments he could make, three dozen examples he could show of how Colt had deliberately rebuffed attempts at camaraderie. But one vision in Kinsman's mind kept his tongue silent: he recalled the squad's only black officer eating alone, day after day, night after night. He never tried to join the others at their tables in the mess hall, and no one ever sat down at his.

"If he wasn't the top man in the squad," Tenny said, "he'd have a lot of pals. But he's a better flier than any of you. He's scored higher in the training tests than any of you.

Higher than anybody in the other squads, too."

"And he's hell on wheels," Kinsman countered. "I don't think he wants any of us for friends."

Tenny scowled deeply. Then he said, "Yeah, maybe so. But he tossed his cookies. That shows that he's human, at least."

Kinsman said nothing.

Kinsman almost laughed out loud when he first saw Colonel Murdock.

Twenty-four astronaut trainees, all first lieutenants, twenty men, four women, all of them white except one, were sitting nervously in a bare little briefing room at Vandenberg Air Force Base. The air-conditioning was not working well and the room was dank with the smell of anxiety. It was like a classroom, with faded government-green walls and stained acoustical tile ceiling. The chairs in which the lieutenants sat had wooden writing arms on them. There was a podium up front with a microphone goosenecking up, and scrubbed-clean chalkboards and a rolled-up projection screen behind it.

"Ten-HUT!"

All two dozen trainees snapped to their feet as Lieutenant Colonel Robert Murdock came into the room, followed by his three majors.

He looks like Porky Pig, Kinsman said to himself.

Murdock was short, round, balding, with bland pink features and soft, pudgy little hands. He was actually a shade taller than Major Tenny, who stood against the chalkboard behind the Colonel. But where Tenny looked like a compact football linebacker or maybe even a petty Mafioso, Murdock reminded Kinsman of an algebra teacher he had suffered under for a year at William Penn Charter School, back in Philadelphia.

Colonel Murdock scanned his two dozen charges, trying to look strong and commanding. But his bald head was already glistening with nervous perspiration and his voice was an octave too high to be awe-inspiring as he said, "Be seated, gentlemen. And ladies."

Kinsman thought back to the algebra teacher. The man had terrified the entire class for the first few weeks of the semester, warning them of how tough he was and how difficult it would be for any of them to pass his course. Then the students discovered that behind the man's threats and demands there was nothing: he was an empty shell. He could be maneuvered easily. The real trouble was that if he discovered he had been maneuvered by a student, he was merciless.

Kinsman struggled to stay awake during the Colonel's welcoming speech. All the usual buzzwords. Teamwork, orientation, challenge, the honor of the Air Force, pride, duty, the nation's first line of defense . . . they droned sleepily in his ears.

"Two final points," said Colonel Murdock. The lieutenants stirred in their chairs at the promise of release.

"First—we are operating under severe budgetary and equipment restrictions. NASA gets plenty of bucks and plenty of publicity. We get very little. Almost everything we do is kept secret from the American public, and the Congress is constantly cutting back on funds for our operations. We are locked in a deadly battle to prove to Congress, to the people of this nation, and—yes—even to enemies within the Pentagon itself, that the Air Force has a valid and important role to play in manned space flight.

"It's up to you to prove that manned operations in space should not be left to the civilians of NASA. When the Congress one day approves the change of our service's name from just plain Air Force to Aero*space* Force—which it should be—it's going to be your work and your success that gets them to do it."

Kinsman suppressed a grin. He's never studied rhetoric, that's for sure. Or syntax, either.

"Second point," Murdock went on. "Everything you do from now on will be by the buddy system. You're going to fly in the shuttle as two-man teams. You're going to train as two-man teams. You're going to eat, sleep, and think as two-man teams."

Kinsman shot a glance at Jill Meyers, the only woman in his eight-person squad. The expression on her snub-nosed freckled face was marvelous: an Air Force officer's self-control struggling against a feminist's desire to throw a pie in the Colonel's face.

". . . and we're going to be ruthless with you," Murdock

was saying. "You will be judged as teams, not as individuals. If a team fu—eh . . . fouls up, then it's *out!* Period. You'll be reassigned out of the astronaut corps. Doesn't matter who fouled up, which individual is to blame. Both members of the team will be out on their asses. Is that clear?"

A general mumble of understanding rose from two dozen throats.

"Sir?" Jill Meyers was on her feet. "May I ask a question?"

"Go right ahead, Lieutenant." Murdock smiled toothily at her, as if realizing for the first time that there were women under his command.

"How will these training assignments be made, sir? Will we have any choice in the matter, or will it all be done by the Personnel Office?"

Murdock blinked, as if he had never considered the problem before. "Well . . . I don't think . . . that is . . ." He stopped and pursed his lips for a moment, then turned away from the podium to confer with the three majors standing behind him. Instinctively, he held a chubby hand over the microphone. Jill remained standing, a diminutive little sister in Air Force blues.

Finally the Colonel returned to the microphone. "I don't see why you can't express your personal preferences as to teammates, and then we'll have them checked through Personnel's computer to make sure the matchups are satisfactory."

"Thank you, sir." Lieutenant Meyers sat down.

"In fact," Colonel Murdock went on, "I don't see why we shouldn't get a preliminary expression of preferences right now. Each of you, write down the names of three officers you'd like to team with, in order of your preference."

Tenny and the two other majors looked surprised. The briefing room suddenly dissolved into a chattering, muttering, pocket-searching scramble for papers and pens or pencils.

Kinsman took his ballpoint pen from his tunic pocket and borrowed a sheet of tablet paper from the man sitting next to him. Then he found himself staring at the blank paper on the arm of his chair.

Who the hell do I want to team up with?

The magnitude of the decision seemed to hit everyone at

once. The room fell deathly quiet.

Kinsman glanced at the tall redhead sitting in the front row. He hadn't met her yet, but she had damned good legs and a pleasant smile. *But what if she can't hack it in zero gravity or she's a lousy pilot or something else goes wrong? Then I'm out in the cold.*

Jill Meyers was a smoothly competent pilot, Kinsman knew from their weeks of training in Texas. *But so is Smitty, and D'Angelo . . . and Colt.*

Frank Colt. He was the best man in their eight-officer squad. If what Tenny had told him was true, he was the best man of the whole two dozen trainees. The idea of teaming with the redhead had its charm, but . . .

He gazed across the room to where Frank Colt was sitting, bolt upright, staring straight ahead as if he were trying to burn a hole in the chalkboard at the front of the room with the laserlike intensity of his eyes.

Kinsman looked down at the blank sheet of paper and wrote three names on it:

Franklin Colt
Franklin Colt
Franklin Colt

That evening Major Tenny threw a party.

He had not actually intended to, but right after dinner at the mess hall most of his squad members congregated at Tenny's one-room apartment on the ground level of the new Bachelor Officers' Quarters. Kinsman had stopped off at the Officers' Club; he had heard there was a piano there, and it had been months since he had touched a keyboard. But it had been surrounded already by a dozen ham-fisted amateurs. So he trailed along with his fellow squad members to Tenny's quarters. It was well known that their major was seldom without a bottle of bourbon close to hand. And his quarters opened onto the poolside patio.

As the trainees from the other squads saw Tenny's people spilling out of the glass sliding doors and sitting around the pool, armed with plastic cups and a suspicious-looking bottle, they quickly joined the party. Some brought six-packs of beer from the PX. Others brought soft drinks. The leggy redhead that Kinsman had spotted that morning showed up in tight jeans and T-shirt, toting a half-gallon of Napa Valley rosé wine.

It was time to make new acquaintances.

By the time the sun had gone down and the few skinny palm trees ringing the pool were swaying in the night breeze, the trainees were all comrades in arms.

"So they turn off the damned flight profile computer, tilt the simulator forty degrees, and tell me I've gotta set it straight in twenty seconds—or else."

"Yeah? You know what they pulled on me? Total electrical failure. I told 'em they oughtta hang rosary beads on the dashboard."

"Y'know, these quarters are pretty good. I mean, I been in motels that're worse."

"This was a motel until a coupla months ago. They went outta business and the Air Force bought it up cheap."

Kinsman was sitting on the newly planted grass in a pair of brand-new fatigues. Beside him was the half-gallon of wine, and on the other side of it was the redhead. She had pinned her plastic nametag to her T-shirt. It said O'HARA.

"You do have a first name," Kinsman said to her.

"Yes, of course." Her voice was a cool, controlled contralto.

"I have to guess?"

"It's a game I play. You guess my name and I'll guess yours."

Why are women all crazy? Kinsman asked himself. Why can't they just be straightforward and honest?

"Well, let's see, now." He took a sip of wine. "With that last name and your red hair, I'll bet you get kidded a lot about Scarlett O'Hara. Is that why you're sensitive about your name?"

She smiled at him and nodded. It was a good smile that made her eyes sparkle. "And there was a movie star," she said, "years ago, named Maureen O'Hara. I get that a lot, too."

"But your name isn't that, either. It's something more down to earth."

"Plain as any name can be."

Kinsman laughed. "Well, then, it's either George M. Cohan or Mary."

"It's not George M."

Kinsman sang softly, "But it was Mary, Ma-ary . . ." He lifted his plastic cup to her. "Pleased to meet you, Mary O'Hara."

"Pleased to meet you, Chester A. Kinsman."

Now let's see how long it takes you to figure out that I was named after one of the great political disgraces of the Grand Old Party.

But an angry voice cut across everyone's conversation.

"I don't give a shit who they team with me! I left my paper blank."

Frank Colt. Kinsman saw him standing at the pool's edge, silhouetted against the Moon-bright sky. Like most of the others, Colt was wearing off-duty fatigues. But on him they looked like a dress uniform, perfectly fitted, creased to a knife edge.

All other talk stopped. Colt was glaring at one of the trainees from another squad, a stranger to Kinsman, a lanky rawboned kid with light hair, bony face, big fists.

"We already heard about you," the kid was saying in a flat Midwestern twang. "Top scores in the simulator. Best record in the group. Think you're pretty hot stuff, dontcha?"

"I do my job, man. I do the best I can. I'm not here to goof around, like some of you dudes. This isn't a game we're playing. It's life and death."

"Aw, don't be such a pain in the ass! You just think you're better'n anybody else."

"Maybe I do. Maybe I *am*."

Kinsman glanced over at Major Tenny, sitting on a folding chair a few yards away. Tenny was watching the argument, like everybody else. He was frowning, but he made no move to break it up.

"Yeah?" the other lieutenant answered. "Know what I think? I think they're givin' you all the high scores b'cause you're black and nobody wants a bunch of civil rights lawyers comin' down here pissin' and cryin' b'cause we flunked out our token . . ."

Colt's hand flicked out and grabbed the kid by the jaw, distorting his face into a ridiculous imitation of a fish: mouth pried open, eyes popping.

"Don't say it, man." Colt's voice was murderously controlled. "Call me black, call me dumb, call me anything you want. But if you say 'nigger' to me I'll break your ass."

Tenny was hauling himself out of the chair now. But too late. Colt released the kid's jaw. The lieutenant took a short step forward and swung at Colt, who simply ducked under the wild haymaker and gave a quick push. The lieutenant spun into the pool with a loud splash.

Kinsman found himself on his feet and heading for Colt. Everybody else went to the aid of the kid in the pool. Colt walked away, back toward his quarters. Kinsman followed him and caught up with him in a few seconds.

"Hey, Frank."

Colt turned his head slightly but he did not slow down.

Kinsman pulled up beside him. "Jeez, what a shithead! He got what he deserved."

"At least he said what was on his mind," Colt answered. "Plenty other guys around here feel the same way."

"That's not true."

"No? Suppose I started making time with that redhead the way you were? How many rednecks would come outta the woodwork then?"

"I thought you were married."

"I was. Ain't no more."

"Oh. I'm sorry."

"No big thing. Lots of chicks in the world. Why tie yourself down to just one?"

The grapes sound sour, Kinsman thought.

They had reached the doorway into the section of the BOQ where Colt and Kinsman were quartered. Colt pushed open the fiberboard door and they started up the steps to the second floor. As they headed down the corridor toward their rooms, Kinsman said:

"I hope you're not too tough to live with. I picked you for my partner this morning."

"You *what*?" Colt stopped dead.

Kinsman studied the black lieutenant's face. It was almost totally devoid of expression except for the suspicious, wary eyes. They were probing him, searching for the kicker, the payoff, the flick of the whip.

"This morning," Kinsman said. "Colonel Murdock's buddy system . . . I wrote down your name."

"Why the hell you wanna do that?" Colt started down the corridor again, not waiting for an answer.

Kinsman kept stride with him. "Because you're the best pilot in the group and I don't want to be washed out because my partner fucked up."

"That's it, huh?"

"Yeah."

"Wasn't your good deed for the day? Your contribution to the Air Force's affirmitive action program?"

Kinsman laughed. "Where I come from, we write checks for good causes. We don't *do* anything, especially if it means coming in contact with lower-income types."

Colt saw no humor. He reached his door, unlocked it, and swung it open. "I didn't write any names down. I left my paper blank."

Kinsman leaned against the doorjamb. "We all heard."

"Didn't think anybody'd want to be stuck with me."

"Because you're black."

"Because they're out to *get* me, man! They want to knock me off, pin my balls to their totem pole. And if they get me, they get my buddy, too."

"Nobody's out to get you, Frank. It isn't the Ku Klux Klan out there."

"Sure. Sure. Just wait. You want to be my buddy, man? Then they'll be out to get you, too."

"Listen," Kinsman insisted. "They're down on you because you've been behaving like a paranoid sonofabitch."

Colt smiled coldly. "Maybe you're right. Maybe I ought to act more humble . . . Yassuh, Massa Kinsman, suh. I's shore powerful grateful that y'all took notice of a po' li'l ol' darky lak me."

Grinning, Kinsman said, "Go to hell, Frank."

Immediately Colt replied, "Why this is hell, nor am I out of it."

With a shake of his head, "All I can say, buddy, is that you sure know how to break up a party. And I was just starting to get someplace with Mary O'Hara."

"That's her name, huh?" Colt made an enigmatic little

shrug, as if he were carrying on a debate within himself. Then he said, "Guess I owe you for breaking up the evening. Come on in, I've got a bottle of tequila in my flight bag."

"Say no more!"

By the time Major Tenny knocked on Colt's door he and Kinsman were sitting on the floor, passing the half-empty bottle back and forth with elaborate care. Colt climbed slowly to his feet and walked uncertainly to the door. The Major's squat bulk filled the doorway.

"Nice little show you put on down there. The poor bastard damn near drowned."

"Too bad," said Colt.

Tenny walked in and spotted Kinsman sitting on the floor, his back against the bunk. "What the hell are you guys up to?"

Kinsman waved the bottle of tequila at him. "Cultural relations, boss. We're studying the effect of tequila consumption on the gross national product of Mexico."

"Our good neighbor to the south," Colt added.

"Tequila?" Tenny strode swiftly to Kinsman, bent down, and yanked the bottle from his hand. He sniffed at it, then tasted it. "Dammitall, this *is* tequila!"

"What'd you expect?" Kinsman asked. "Hydrazine?"

Tenny shook his head, a frown on his swarthy features. "I can't let you men drink a whole bottle of tequila. You'll be in no shape for duty tomorrow morning."

"I have an idea!" Colt said brightly. "Why'n't you help us finish it up? Might save our lives."

"And our immortal souls," Kinsman muttered.

"To say nothing of our immoral careers," Colt added.

"That's immortal, not immoral."

"You have your career, I'll have my career."

Tenny scowled at them both. "If you think you can manage to shut the door, I'll do my best to help you out."

Within moments Tenny was sitting on the bare wooden floor between the two lieutenants, his back propped against the bunk.

"Did you know," Kinsman was asking him, "that ol' Frank and I were born and raised within a few miles of each other? Right in Philadelphia. Both of us."

"Only my neighborhood wasn't as classy as his," Colt said. "Not as many Quakers where I grew up. Kinsman's a Quaker, y'know . . ."

"Used to be. When I was a child. Not anymore. Now I'm an officer and a gentleman. No more Quaker. No more family ties."

Tenny let them ramble for a while, but he finally said, "Frank—you're gonna get your ass kicked outta here if you can't get along with the others."

"If *I* can't . . ."

"Murdock was puking into a wastebasket when he heard what happened at the pool tonight. He's got a very weak stomach and his first instinct was to transfer you to Greenland. Maybe farther."

"Sonofabitch."

Turning to Kinsman, Major Tenny asked, "You really want to be his partner?"

Kinsman nodded. Gently. His head was already hurting.

"Okay," said Tenny. "Frank, you've got a buddy. You're not alone. And you've got me. I think you're the best damned flier I've ever laid eyes on. Now keep your temper under control and your mouth zipped and you'll be okay. Got it?"

"Sure," Colt said, suddenly dead sober. "The Jackie Robinson bit. Anything else you want me to do, boss? Walk on water? Shine shoes?"

Tenny grabbed him by the shirt. "You stupid bastard! You wanna be an astronaut or not?"

"I want to."

"Then don't fuck yourself over. There's only one man can ruin things for you and that's *you*. Learn some self-control."

Colt said nothing as long as Tenny held his shirt. They merely glared at each other. But when the Major slowly released him, Colt said quietly, "I'll try."

"And stop going around with that goddamned chip on your shoulder."

"I'll try," Colt repeated.

Tenny turned to Kinsman. "And you . . . you help him all you can. He's too good a man to lose."

* * *

"How come you got the window seat?" Colt muttered.

He was lying beside Kinsman in the metal womb of the space shuttle's mid-deck compartment. Zipped into sky-blue coveralls, Kinsman lay on his back in the foam-padded contour seat next to the compartment's side hatch—and its only window.

"Lucky, I guess," he croaked back to Colt. His voice nearly cracked. His throat was dry and scratchy, his palms slippery with nervous perspiration.

Six astronaut-trainees were jammed into the mid-deck area, waiting in tense silence as the shuttle went through the final few minutes of countdown. They had no radio earphones and could hear only muffled, garbled voices from the flight crew on the deck above them.

Kinsman mentally counted the rungs on the ladder that disappeared through the open hatch to the flight deck. By the time I've counted the rungs ten times we'll lift off, he told himself. He counted slowly.

Up on the flight deck, at the other end of the ladder, the shuttle's four-man crew was going through the final stages of the countdown, Kinsman knew. They were watching instruments on their control panel springing into life, listening to the commands flickering across the electronics communications net that spread across the entire globe of the Earth. They could see the automatic sequencer's numbers clicking down toward zero.

Down in the mid-deck compartment, strapped into their seats, the trainees could only wait and sweat.

Kinsman gave up counting and turned his head to look out the small circular window set into the hatch. All he could see was the steel spiderwork of the launch tower, frighteningly close. Could the ship clear those steel beams when it took off? Kinsman knew that it had, hundreds of times. Yet the tower still looked close enough to touch.

He focused his vision on the distant shoreline, where the Pacific curled in to meet the brown California hills. But the nearness of the launch tower still pressed against his awareness.

Hell of a way to go, he said to himself. Lying on your back with your legs sticking up in the air like a woman in heat.

"Five seconds!" a voice rang out from the flight deck.

The time stretched to infinity. Then, a vibration, a gushing roar, a banging shock—Christ! Something's gone wrong! Abruptly the whole world seemed to shake as the roar of six million flaming demons burned into every bone of his body. Kinsman caught a brief glimpse of the tower sliding past the corner of his vision, then the brown hills slipped by as he was pressed down into the seat. The force pushing against him was not as bad as the g's he had pulled in fighter planes, but the vibration was worse, an eyeball-rattling shaking that felt as if all the teeth in his head would be wrenched loose.

With an effort he turned to look at Colt and saw that his partner's eyes were squeezed shut, his mouth gaping wide. Kinsman tried to see the other four trainees, but their seats were in front of his and he could not see their faces.

The pressure got worse and there was a jolt when the two strap-on solid rockets were jettisoned.

Going through fifty klicks, Kinsman knew. Maximum pressure ought to be behind us now.

The weight on his chest began to lessen. The bone-conducted rumble of the engines suddenly disappeared.

And he was falling.

Zero gravity, he told himself. We're in orbit. His arms had floated loosely off the seat rests. With a blink of his eyes, Kinsman rearranged his perspective. He was no longer lying on his back; he was sitting upright. They all were.

His stomach was fluttering. He made himself relax the tensed muscles. You're floating, he told himself. Just like at the seashore, when you were a kid. Beyond the breakers. Floating on the swells.

He turned and grinned at Colt. "How do you like it?"

Colt's answering grin was a bit queasy. "I'll get used to it in a couple minutes."

Major Pierce came floating down the ladder from the flight deck. He landed lightly on his booted feet, bobbed up off the metal deck plates. Back on Earth he had been a nondescript little man in his forties, patrician high-bridged nose, darting snake's eyes. Up here he could damned well be a ballet dancer, Kinsman thought.

"Very well, my little chickadees," the Major said, in a sneering nasal tenor. "Anybody feel like upchucking?"

The four other trainees had to turn in their seats to see Pierce, who was at the bottom of the ladder. Kinsman stared at the Major's boots, fascinated to see that they were not touching the deck.

"Very well," Major Pierce said when no one replied to his question. "Unstrap and try to stand up. By the numbers. And move *slowly*. Be particularly careful of sudden head movements. That way lies nausea." He pointed at Jill Meyers. "Meyers, you have the honor of being first."

Jill got up from her seat, her face going from brow-knitted concentration to wide-eyed surprise as she just kept rising, completely off her feet, until her mousy-brown hair bumped gently against the metal overhead. While the others laughed, Jill thrashed about and found an anchoring point by grabbing the handle of one of the electronics racks that covered the forward bulkhead.

"No matter how much training we give you Earthside, you still don't understand Newton's First Law of Motion," Pierce said, in a tone of bored disgust. "A body in motion tends to remain in motion unless acted upon by an outside force. In this case," he hiked a thumb upward, "the over-head."

Nobody laughed.

Jill's partner, the lanky, whipcord-lean Lieutenant Smith, got up from his seat next. Smitty was tall enough to raise a long slender arm to the overhead and prevent himself from soaring off his feet.

"That's cheating, Mr. Smith," said the Major.

"Yessir. But it works."

Kinsman smiled at the Mutt and Jeff look of the Meyers-Smith team. Jill was the shortest member of the trainee group; Smitty barely squeezed in under the Air Force's height limit for pilots.

Mary O'Hara and Art Douglas were next. Then Colt got cautiously to his feet, and finally Kinsman. It was like standing in the ocean up to your neck, with the waves trying to pull you this way and that.

"Well, at least you didn't toss any cookies," Pierce sniffed as the six trainees bobbed uneasily in their places.

"Very well then," the Major went on. "We're go for a three-day mission. By the time we touch down at Vandenberg again you will each know every square centimeter of this orbiter more intimately than your mother's"—he hesitated and smiled a fraction—"face. And each of you will get the opportunity to go EVA with Captain Howard, the payload specialist, and perform an actual mission task. In the meantime, stay out of the crew's way and don't get into mischief."

"Sir, will we get a chance to fly the bird?" asked Douglas. He was a shade smaller than Kinsman, prematurely balding, moonfaced, but sharp-eyed and very bright: the group's lawyer.

Pierce closed his eyes momentarily, as if seeking strength from some inner source. "No, Lieutenant, you will *not* touch the controls. You know the mission profile as well as I, or at least you should. We are not going to risk this very expensive piece of aerospace hardware on your very first flight into orbit."

"I know the plan, sir," Douglas replied agreeably, "but I thought maybe the commander would let us sneak in a little maneuver, maybe. Strictly within the mission profile."

"Majors Podolski and Jakes are the commander and pilot, respectively, on this mission. They will handle all the maneuvering. If you are a good little lieutenant, Mr. Douglas, perhaps Major Podolski might allow you to come up on the flight deck and watch him for a few moments."

"Oh, peachy keen!" retorted Lieutenant Douglas.

It was like living in a submarine. Outside, Kinsman knew, was the limitless expanse of emptiness: planets, moons, comets, stars, galaxies stretching out through space to infinity. But inside the Air Force shuttle orbiter, serial number AFASO-002, six young trainees and four middle-aged officers clambered over one another, stuck elbows in one another's food trays, and got in one another's way. Kinsman began to realize that a barrel of monkeys is not much fun for the monkeys.

"If it weren't for zero gee," Kinsman told Colt, "I'd be ready to murder somebody."

"I got my own little list," Colt said.

They were in the lower deck, wedged between canisters of lithium hydroxide and green tanks of oxygen. The metal bulkhead felt cold to the touch, and Kinsman realized that the vacuum of space was on the other side of the floor plates that he hovered a few centimeters above.

"Pierce really meant it when he said we were gonna lay our hands on every stringer and weld in this bucket," Colt grumbled. He was hovering above Kinsman in the hatch, head down, his feet floating above the floor of the mid-deck section.

The rest of the trainees were out in the cargo bay, with the officers, practicing EVAs in their space suits. Colt and Kinsman had been assigned to inspecting the air and water recycling equipment of the life support systems. They had already inspected the zero-gravity toilet, with its foot restraints and seat belt, and the washstand and shower stall. Now they were tracing the plumbing of the water pipes and the scrubbers that filtered impurities out of the air they breathed.

Kinsman consulted the checklist taped to his wrist in the light of the hand lamp that hung weightlessly by his ear. "Okay, that's the lithium hydroxide tank and it's all in one piece."

"Check," said Colt, making a mark on the clipsheet he carried.

"I still don't get it," Kinsman complained as they worked. "Why are we getting all the shit jobs? Jill and Smitty and the others are out there having fun and we're stuck inspecting the toilet."

He could not see Colt's face from where he was wedged in, but the expression came through loud and clear. "We're the special ones, man. You and I got the highest grades, so they're gonna take us down a peg. Keep our heads from getting big."

"You think that's it?"

Colt growled, "Sure. My being black's got nothing to do with it. Neither does your picking me for a partner. Nothing at all."

"It's good to see you're not being overly sensitive about it," Kinsman joked, pushing his way back from between the frigid green tanks.

"Or bitter."

"Well . . . they've got to let us go EVA tomorrow. There's no way they can keep us from going ouside."

For a long moment Colt did not respond. Then he said simply, "Wanna bet?"

The living quarters in the mid-deck were crowded enough when all six trainees were lumped together in the metal shoebox, but when a couple of officers came down from the flight deck the tensions became almost impossible.

The end of the second day, the trainees were bobbing around the galley, which looked to Kinsman like a glorified Coke machine. They were punching buttons, pulling trays of hot food from the storage racks, gliding weightlessly to find an unoccupied corner of the cramped compartment in which to eat their precooked dinners.

Kinsman leaned his back against somebody's sleeping cocoon, legs dangling in the air, and picked at the food. The tray was already showing signs of heavy use; it was slightly bent and it no longer gleamed, new-looking. The food, a combination of precut bite-sized chunks of imitation protein and various moldy-looking pastes, was as appetizing as sawdust.

Jill Meyers drifted past, empty-handed.

"Finished already?" Kinsman asked her.

"This junk was finished before it started," she said.

"It's chock-full of nutrition."

"So's a cockroach."

Major Jakes slid down the ladder and headed for the galley. Automatically the lieutenants made room for him. He had been an overweight, jowly, crew-cut, sullen-looking graying man when Kinsman had first seen him back at Vandenberg. His physical looks had changed in zero gravity: he seemed slimmer, taller, his cheekbones higher. And there was a happy grin on his face.

Jakes brought his tray to the corner where Kinsman was sitting, literally, on air. The Major was humming to himself cheerfully. After setting himself cross-legged beside Kinsman, anchoring his back against the other end of the nylon mesh cocoon, Jakes took a couple of bites of food, then asked, "How's it going, Lieutenant?"

"Okay, sir, I suppose," replied Kinsman. Never complain to officers, he knew from his Academy training. Especially when they're trying to buddy up to you.

"I don't see Colt around."

"Frank?" Kinsman realized that Colt was not in sight. "Must be in the pissoir."

Jakes made a small clucking sound. "Your redheaded friend is missing, too."

Kinsman took a sip of lukewarm coffee from the squeeze bulb on his tray while he thought furiously. "Maybe they're in the airlock. You go nuts down here trying to find some elbow room."

Jakes made an agreeable nod. "Yeah, I guess so. Like the fo'c'sle of an old sailing ship, huh?"

Why me? Kinsman wondered. Why is he buddying up to me?

"You're from Pennsylvania, aren't you?"

"Yessir. Philadelphia area . . ."

"Main Line, I know. My people have relatives down there. I'm from the North Shore—Boston. You know, the cradle of liberty."

"Where the Cabots talk only to the Lodges."

"Right." Jakes nibbled at a chunk of thinly disguised soybean meal. "And neither of 'em talk to my folks. We were sort of the black sheep of the clan. My old man could build the yachts for them, all right, but they never let us sail 'em."

"Black sheep," Kinsman muttered. Welcome to the club, buddy. Try to imagine what a black sheep you become when you leave a Quaker family to join the Air Force.

"Did you really pick Colt for a partner?"

"Yes," Kinsman said, warily.

"I hear he's a troublemaker."

"He's a damned fine man."

"Maybe. I hear you're just as good a pilot. Colt's got a reputation, well . . ."

Kinsman could feel his back stiffening. "Sir," he said, "if I were in a tight situation there's no one I'd rather have beside me than Frank Colt. Present company included."

Jakes grinned at him. "Snotty little shavetail, eh? Yeah, that's what I heard. Well, you and Colt are two of a kind, all right. Full of piss and vinegar. I guess that's good, in a way. This isn't a game for marshmallows."

They finished their dinners quickly and stowed the dirty trays in the galley's cleaning unit, which Kinsman knew from his inspection earlier that day was operating properly—after he had tightened a slightly leaky pipe fitting. Jakes swam back up to the flight deck, "officer country," and Kinsman was about to join Jill and Art Douglas in an argument about the Air Force's medical insurance plan for astronauts.

But Major Pierce and Captain Howard eased down the ladder and suddenly the mid-deck compartment was tense again.

"Mission control just sent us a change in schedule," Pierce said. "Meyers and Smith, you've got fifteen minutes before prelaunch inspection of Payload Number Two. Get rid of those trays and start suiting up for EVA. Captain Howard will brief you, starting now."

Howard was a dour, shriveled little man. Kinsman had never seen a crew cut manage to look messy before, but somehow Howard's did. He was gray-haired, old for a captain. Hell, he's old for a major or light colonel, Kinsman thought. But he must know his stuff.

Under Howard's direction, the O'Hara-Douglas team had operated the manipulator arm that had swung the mission's first payload—a small, laser-reflecting navigational satellite—out of the cargo bay and into orbit. And Captain Howard himself had gone EVA twice in the two days of the flight, once to check on a defunct observation satellite that had been orbited years earlier, and once to inspect a newly orbited Russian satellite.

Now Mutt and Jeff are going to go outside again while Frank and I sit around twiddling our thumbs, Kinsman grumbled to himself. They've already been EVA once!

Howard took them up to the flight deck for their briefing, space suits and all. Pierce followed right behind them. Suddenly the mid-deck compartment was empty except for Douglas and Kinsman.

"Where the hell did Colt and Mary get to?" Art asked.

Kinsman peered through the thick glass of the airlock window but they were not inside.

"Maybe they took a walk outside," he said.

Douglas looked annoyed. "I'll bet that sonofabitch has her out in the payload bay."

"If he does, about the only thing they can do out there is hold hands, with gloves on, at that."

"Yeah? And what happens when Pierce or Howard look out and see them out there? Unauthorized EVA? They go down the tubes, and we go down with them!"

Kinsman looked at the suit rack. Two space suits missing, all right. He pushed himself over to the airlock hatch.

"What're you doing?" Douglas demanded.

"Maybe they're just outside the airlock, down against the bulkhead where they can't be seen from the flight deck windows."

Douglas's round face was wrinkled with angered worry as Kinsman ducked inside the cold metal womb of the circular airlock. There was a window to the outside, just above the heavy hatch that opened onto the vacuum of space.

Kinsman tapped against the metal wall of the airlock with his Academy ring. Three quick taps, three slower ones, and then three fast ones again. SOS. He did it twice. No response. Feeling a little frantic, he went to the other side and tried again.

A thumping sound. Like a gloved fist knocking against the outer wall.

Kinsman pushed back into the mid-deck compartment and swung the inner airlock hatch shut. Douglas glided over and peered into the window. A pump whined.

"Christ," muttered Douglas, "I hope nobody's watching the indicators on the controls upstairs."

We'll know soon enough, Kinsman said to himself. After long minutes of breath-holding suspense, Colt and Mary O'Hara squeezed through the inner airlock hatch.

"Let's get you out of these suits, pronto," Kinsman urged.

"What's the rush?" Colt asked.

"Howard's going to be down here in another minute. Smitty and Jill are going out with him. Schedule change."

Mary was already unzipping her gloves, her face white with concern.

Colt complained, "Shit! Out there in the payload bay's the only place you can relax."

"You'll relax all four of us into ground assignments," Douglas snapped.

"In South Dakota," added Kinsman. "Come on, Frank. Move it!"

Grousing all the way, Colt allowed Kinsman to help him wriggle out of the space suit. Out of the corner of his eye Kinsman saw Douglas helping Mary. *Art's getting a lot more fun out of this than I am,* he thought.

They were almost finished when Captain Howard, Major Pierce, Jill Meyers, and Smitty came gliding down the ladder from the flight deck.

"Exactly what is going on here?" Pierce demanded, his voice thin and reedy.

Before Colt or anyone else could reply, Kinsman heard himself say, "I had to go out into the payload bay for a few moments, sir. I was getting a touch of claustrophobia in here."

Pierce glared at him.

"Lieutenant Colt came out with me—in accordance with the regulations that trainees should not attempt EVA without backup. Lieutenant O'Hara stationed herself in the airlock in case we needed further assistance."

Major Pierce looked from Kinsman to Colt to O'Hara and back to Kinsman. His eyes glittered with malice. "That is the dumbest story I've ever heard a shavetail try to pull, Lieutenant!"

"That's the way it happened, sir."

"Claustrophobia?"

"Only a temporary touch of it, sir. We were warned about it in training, if you recall. Since there's no qualified medical officer on board—"

"That's enough!" Pierce snapped. He closed his eyes for a moment. "All right, I'll let it stand. But I'm going to remember this, Kinsman. I'll be watching you—you and your claustrophobia. And the rest of you! Nobody budges out of this compartment without my direct approval. Is that understood?"

"Yessir!" from six relieved throats.

"You all know that you are not—repeat, *not*—authorized for EVA without my okay."

"Unless there's a medical or other type of emergency," said Kinsman.

Glaring, Pierce hissed, "I should put the whole squad of you on report for this."

No one said a word.

Pierce looked hard at Colt, who returned his stare evenly. Then he glared at O'Hara; she glanced toward Kinsman.

Shaking his head, the Major muttered, "You're on thin ice, Kinsman. Very thin ice."

"Yessir," Kinsman replied.

Pierce went back up to the flight deck and the tension cracked. Howard took Meyers and Smitty to the airlock. Kinsman puffed out a long, heartfelt breath. He felt as if he had been hanging by his fingernails from a very high cliff.

"Why'd you do that?" Colt asked him.

"Pure instinct, I guess. I figured you'd catch a lot more hell from Pierce than I would."

Frowning, Colt said, "What difference does it make? We're on the same team; he'll kick my ass out the same time he kicks yours."

Kinsman nodded. "Frank, you've memorized the book of regulations but you haven't figured out the people yet. He won't kick us out for something *I've* done. Not unless it's a lot more serious than this."

Colt's reply was a derisive snort.

"You could thank him," Mary suggested to Colt. "He was trying to save both our necks."

"And mine," Douglas chimed in.

"And his own, too," Colt said. "If I go, he goes."

Kinsman laughed. "You're welcome, buddy."

"Think nothing of it," Colt replied.

Kinsman looked at Mary O'Hara. He knew that she would have been in much more trouble, too, if Pierce thought she'd gone outside with Colt. But she doesn't say a word about that part of it. *La belle dame sans merci*. The beautiful lady who never says thank you.

It took an hour before Jill and Smitty came back in from their EVA. Howard, looking smaller and older than ever before, pointed a dirty-nailed finger at Kinsman.

"You and your buddy better get a good night's sleep. You're going to have a big day tomorrow."

But, wrapped in his nylon mesh cocoon after lights-out, floating weightlessly with his arms hanging in front of his eyes, Kinsman could not sleep. He could feel the warmth from Colt's body, bulging the sleeping bag a few centimeters above him, and smell the faint trace of perfume that Mary wore, in the next bunk down. Yet it was not her scent nor Colt's troubled groaning and tossing that kept Kinsman awake. Not even the anticipation of going EVA tomorrow, for the first time.

"To hell with Jakes," he mumbled to himself. "And Pierce. All of them . . . all of them . . ."

He saw in his mind's eye the crystal blue sky of the eastern Mediterranean as he flew his aging F-15 on a "peace-keeping" mission. When the Soviet Union finally admitted that its reserves of fossil fuels were no longer sufficient to meet its needs, and began bidding up the price of Middle Eastern oil, the political repercussions made the oil shocks of the Seventies seem trivial.

The Red Army gobbled up Iran in an eleven-day blitzkrieg while the rest of the world watched, stunned and vacillating. The Russians took over the Iranian oil fields, or what was left of them after the fanatical Iranians gave up their doomed defense and blew up everything they could. The Arab world split apart, some openly assisting the Iranian resistance, some trying to make an accommodation with the victorious Russian Bear. The industrialized world tottered as oil prices skyrocketed and stayed high.

It took a charismatic leader to bring the Arabs together again, and he focused his leadership on the obvious goal: the destruction of Israel. With relish, the Moslem world forgot its differences and invaded the Jewish homeland for the final time. No ally came to Israel's aid, not with the Soviets threatening nuclear war over the hotline to Washington. The American government, led by a born-again former schoolteacher, warned Israel against using its nuclear weapons against its invaders. To their credit, the victorious Arabs did not engage in a bloodbath. Israel simply ceased to exist, although its inhabitants continued to live in the newly constituted nation of Palestine. Only the leaders of the Israeli government and about a third of the Knesset were executed. In America the government that failed to help its ally won re-election on the strength of having avoided a nuclear holocaust.

Rationing and recriminations were the order of the day in every Western capital. Travel curtailments and restrictions on electricity became commonplace, and were used by governments to keep their people under control and make dissent, if not impossible, then at least more difficult than in the earlier days of easy travel and free speech.

The Greeks called for the total dissolution of NATO. The Turks made obvious moves to seize Cyprus. A new series of convulsions racked Lebanon, with Syrian-backed Shi'ites slaughtering Christians by the thousands and Syria itself —long a Soviet client—gaining new power from the Russian victory in Iran and the destruction of Israel but suffering such loss of prestige among its fellow Moslems that the assassination of Syria's president came as no surprise.

Flying out of Cyprus, the handful of Air Force fighter planes was a pitifully weak gesture, more of a public relations ploy than a military move. America was tacitly admitting that the Soviet conquest of Iran and the end of Israel were *faits accomplis*. Flying out of Damascus, a squadron of Soviet MiG-31's symbolized Russian determination to show America and the world that the Middle East was their sphere of influence now, rather than the West's.

In his half-sleep, Kinsman recalled all the feints and mock-dogfights he had gone through. It would have taken only the press of a button to destroy one of the Russian fighters. More than once somebody fired a burst of cannon fire into the empty air. More than once a missile "happened" to *whoosh* out of its underwing rack and trace a smoky arrow of death that came close to one of those beautiful swept-wing planes.

Each time Kinsman waxed the tail of a Russian and lined up the vainly maneuvering MiG in his gunsights he heard his father's stern voice: "Once you put on their uniform, you will do as they order you to do. If they say kill, you will kill."

No, Kinsman said to himself. There are limits. I can hold out against them.

They had not ordered him to kill. The squadron's orders were to defend themselves if attacked, and even then, only after receiving a confirming go-ahead order from ground command. Kinsman had never pressed the firing button on his controls, no matter how many times he centered a MiG in his gunsights.

He was overjoyed when his application for astronaut

training was finally approved. It was as if he had been holding his breath for four years.

Even grimy old Philadelphia looked good to him, after the months in Cyprus. He had dinner with Neal McGrath and his wife, Mary-Ellen, in an Indian restaurant on Chestnut Street, within sight of Independence Hall and the cracked old Liberty Bell. Neal, a Congressman now, informed him that Diane Lawrence had her first million-selling record to her credit and was fast becoming one of the nation's favorite folk-rock singers.

And Kinsman's father—sick, old, his home on the Main Line turned into a private hospital-cum-office—refused to see him as long as he wore an Air Force uniform.

When he finally peeled out of the nylon mesh sleeping bag he felt too keyed up to be tired, despite his wakeful night. Colt seemed also tensed as a coiled spring as they pulled on their space suits.

"So the Golddust Twins finally get their chance to go for a walk around the block," Smitty kidded them as he helped Kinsman with the zippers and seals of his suit.

"I thought they were gonna keep us after school," Colt said, "for being naughty yesterday."

"Pierce'll find a way to take you guys down a notch," Jill said. "He's got that kind of mind."

"Democracy in action," said Kinsman. "Reduce everybody to the same low level."

"Hey!" Art Douglas snapped from across the compartment where he was helping Colt into his suit. "Your scores weren't *that* much higher than ours, you know."

"Tell you what," Colt said. "A couple of you guys black your faces and see how you get treated."

They laughed, but there was a nervous undercurrent to it.

Kinsman raised the helmet over his head and slid it down into place. "Still fits okay," he said through the open visor. "Guess my head hasn't swollen too much."

Captain Howard glided down the ladder already suited up, but with his helmet visor open. The pouches under his eyes looked darker than usual; his face was a gray prison pallor. With six trainees aboard, the officers slept in their seats up on the flight deck, a factor that did not increase officers' love of trainees.

"You both checked out?" Howard asked in a flat, drained voice.

Mr. Personality, thought Kinsman.

Howard was not satisfied with the trainees' check of their suits. He went over them himself. Finally, with a sour nod, he waved Colt to the airlock and went in with him. The lock cycled.

Kinsman slid his visor down and sealed it, turned to wave a halfhearted "so long" to the others, then floated to the airlock and pushed himself through the hatch. The heavy door swung shut and he could hear, faintly through his helmet padding, the clatter of the pump sucking the air out of the phone booth–sized chamber. The red light went on, signaling vacuum. He opened the outer hatch and stepped out into the payload bay.

The orbiter was turned away from the Earth, so that all Kinsman saw as he left the airlock was the endless blackness of space. He blinked as his eyes adjusted to the darkness, and saw tiny points of light staring at him: hard, unwinking stars, not like jewels set in black velvet, as he had expected, not like anything he had ever seen before in his life.

"Glory to God in the highest . . ." Kinsman heard himself whisper the words as he rose, work forgotten, drifting up toward the infinitely beautiful stars.

When I consider thy heavens, the work of thy fingers, the moon and the stars, which thou hast ordained . . .

Howard's grip on his shoulder suddenly brought him back to the here-and-now. The Captain clicked a tether to the clip on Kinsman's waist, then pointed to his own wrist. Kinsman looked down at the keyboard on the wrist of his suit and turned the radio on.

Howard's voice immediately came through his earphones, a much higher fidelity sound quality than Kinsman had expected:

"We're using channel four for suit-to-suit chatter. Ship's frequency is three; don't use it unless you have to talk to the flight deck."

"Yessir," said Kinsman.

"Okay. Let's get to work."

Kinsman glanced out at the stars again, then followed Howard and Colt to the padded mound of insulation covering the final satellite in the payload bay. It was a large fat drum, taller than a man and so wide that Kinsman knew he and Colt could not girdle it with their outstretched arms.

"The checkout panels in the flight deck indicate a malfunction in the battery that powers the antenna foldout," Howard's voice grumbled in his earphones.

Under the Captain's direction they peeled the protective covering from the satellite. It was an aluminum cylinder with dead black panels of solar cells circling its middle and four dish-shaped antennas folded across its top.

"Kinsman, you come up here with me to manually unfold the antennas," Howard ordered. "Colt, check out the battery."

Floating up to the top of the satellite with the Captain beside him, Kinsman asked, "What kind of a satellite is this? Looks like communications, but it's going into a polar orbit, isn't it?"

"Seventy-degree inclination," Howard replied curtly. "You know that as well as I do. Or you should."

Kinsman did know. He also knew that the orbit was highly elliptical, so that the satellite hung over the Eurasian land mass for a much longer period of time than it sped past the other side of the globe.

"Start with that one." Howard pointed a gloved hand toward the largest antenna, in the center of the drumhead. "Unlatch the safety retainer first."

Hanging head down over the satellite, Kinsman read the instruction printed on its surface by the light of his helmet lamp, then unlatched and unfolded the antenna arm. His fingers felt clumsy inside the heavy gloves, but the task was simple enough. He remembered von Clausewitz's dictum from his Academy classes:

"Everything is very simple in war, but even the simplest thing is difficult."

That was as good a description of working in zero gravity as any, Kinsman thought as he slowly, deliberately unfolded the antenna arm and carefully opened its fragile, parasollike parabolic dish. No sound, except his own labored breathing and the faint, high-pitched whir of his suit's tiny air-circulating fan. This is hard work, he realized. They had told him it would be, back in the classrooms, but he had not truly believed it until now.

The first man to walk in space, Alexsei Leonov, told his fellow cosmonauts, "Think ten times before moving a finger, and twenty times before moving a hand."

We can do better than *that*, Kinsman told himself. Still, everything takes longer in zero gee than you'd expect.

"Now the waveguide." Howard's laconic voice startled Kinsman. He had floated slightly away from the satellite. The tether clipped to his waist was almost taut.

He returned to his work, voicing his curiosity into his helmet microphone. "No camera windows or sensor ports on this bird. At least, none that I can see."

"Keep your mind on your work," Howard said.

"But what's it for?" Kinsman blurted.

With an exasperated sigh that sounded like a windstorm in Kinsman's earphones, Howard answered, "Space Command didn't take the time to tell me, kid. So I don't know. Except that it's Top Secret and none of our damned business."

"Ohh . . . a ferret."

"What?"

"A ferret," said Kinsman. "We learned about them back at the Academy. Gathers electronic intelligence from Soviet satellites. This bird's going into a high-inclination orbit, right?"

He could sense Howard nodding sourly inside his helmet.

"She'll hang up there over the Soviet Union," Kinsman went on, "and tune in on a wide band of frequencies that the Russians use. Maybe some Chinese and European bands, too. Then when she passes over a command station in the States they send up the right signal and she spits out everything she's recorded on the previous orbit. All data-compressed so they can get the whole wad of poop in a couple of seconds."

"Really." Howard's voice was as flat and as cold as an ice floe.

"Yessir. The Russians have knocked a few of ours out, they told us at the Academy. With their ASAT—their antisatellite weapon."

Howard's response was unintelligible.

"Sir?" Kinsman asked.

"I *said*," the Captain snapped, "that I never went to the Academy, but I still know what an ASAT is. I came up the hard way, Kinsman. I'm not one of you bright boys."

Touchy! thought Kinsman.

"Colt, what the hell's the status of the battery?"

"Dead as an Edsel, sir," Colt's voice came through the earphones. "I just been listening to your conversation."

"All right. Get your backside up here and help unfold the antennas."

Colt glided up alongside Kinsman and together they opened up the satellite's antennas. It was like making a garden of metallic mushrooms bloom. As they worked Kinsman noticed a growing brightening, a flood of light that drowned out the feeble pool from his helmet lamp like the dawning sun overwhelms the stars of night.

He turned, finally, and saw that the payload bay was now facing the gigantic, overpowering splendor of Earth. Huge and bright, incredibly rich with vast sweeps of blue oceans and purest white clouds, the Earth was a spectacle that deluged the senses with beauty. Dumbfounded, speechless, Kinsman forgot what he was doing and drifted like a helpless baby, staring at the world of his birth.

"Fan*tas*tic!" Turning his head slightly, reluctantly, Kinsman saw that Colt was hovering beside him.

"Get your ass back here!" Howard's angry bleat was like ice picks jabbing at his eardrums. "Both of you!"

Kinsman realized his mouth was hanging open. But he did not care. Inside the helmet, with its tinted visor, inside the ultimate privacy of his impervious personal suit, he stared at the Earth, truly seeing it for the first time. He recognized Baja California and the brown wrinkled stretch of Mexico cutting between the blue of the Pacific and the greener blue of the Gulf.

"Kinsman! Colt!"

"I never realized . . ." he heard Colt's voice whispering, awed.

"All right. All right." Howard's voice was suddenly gentler, softer. "Sometimes I forget how it hits you the first time. You've got five minutes to enjoy the show, then we've got to get back to work or we'll miss the orbit injection time." And the Captain's space-suited form drifted up alongside them.

The Earth was *huge*, filling the sky, spreading as far as Kinsman could see: serene blue and sparkling white, warm, alive, glowing, a beckoning, beautiful world, the ancient mother of humankind. She looked untroubled from this distance. No divisions marred her face, not the slightest trace of the frantic works of her children scarred the eternal beauty of the planet. It took a wrenching effort of will for Kinsman to turn his face away from her.

"All right," Howard's voice broke through to him. "Time to get back to work. You'll get plenty chance to see more, soon enough."

Reluctantly, Kinsman turned away from the glowing Earth and back to the rigid metal enclosure of the payload bay. The satellite looked like a toy to him now. But something had softened Howard. He's just as wiped out about all this grandeur as we are, Kinsman realized. Even though he doesn't want to show it.

They finished checking out the satellite, and Howard led them back to the airlock hatch. But instead of going back inside, the Captain had them wait there while Major Jakes operated the manipulator arm from his control station in the flight deck. The arm smoothly, silently, picked up the weightless satellite, swung it out and away from the shuttle, and then released it. It hung in empty space.

Howard told them to switch their suit radios to the flight deck's frequency, and they heard Jakes and Major Podolski's clipped, professional crosstalk as they maneuvered the orbiter away from the free-flying satellite. Kinsman saw the orbital maneuvering jets at the bulging root of the big tail fin flare once, twice—each puff so brief that it was gone almost before it registered on his eyes. When he looked for the satellite again, it was gone from sight.

But Jakes was intoning, ". . . three, two, one, ignition." And Kinsman saw a tiny star wink out in the darkness: the thruster that would push the satellite into its predetermined orbit.

"All systems check. Payload trajectory nominal." Jakes's voice might have been a computer synthesis. But then he added, "Good job, you guys. The antennas are all working right on the money."

Kinsman expected that now they would finally go back inside, but Howard indicated he wanted to talk to them on their suit-to-suit frequency.

"We've got one more chore to do," the Captain said. "It's a big task, and we saved it for you boys."

Kinsman tried to glance at Colt, but his partner was slightly behind him and when he turned his head all he saw was the inside lining of his helmet.

"We haven't detached the booster fuel tank yet," Howard explained. "It's still strapped on to the orbiter's belly."

"Can't re-enter with that egg hanging on to us," said Colt.

"We have no intention to. We're now heading for a rendezvous point where the last six missions have separated their booster tanks and left them in orbit. One of these days, when the Air Force has enough astronauts and enough money, we're going to convert these empty shells into a permanent space station."

"I'll be damned." Kinsman grinned to himself.

"Like the station NASA's building," said Colt.

"Nothing so fancy," Howard countered. "Now, then, your task is to separate the tank from the orbiter manually, and then take it over to the assembly that's already there and attach it to the other tanks."

"Simple enough," Colt said. "We practiced that kind of assembly in the neutral buoyancy tank in Huntsville."

"It sounds easy," Howard said. "But I won't be there to help you. You're going to be on your own with this one."

"We can handle it," Kinsman said.

Howard said nothing for a long moment. Kinsman watched him floating before them, his tinted visor looking like the dead, empty eye of a midget cyclops.

"All right," the Captain said at last. "But listen to me. If something happens out there, don't panic. Do you hear me? Don't panic."

"We're not the panicky kind," said Colt.

What's he worried about? Kinsman wondered. But he pushed the thought aside as Howard helped them to take a pair of Manned Maneuvering Units out of stowage. The

MMUs were one-man jet backs, built like a seat back with arms that held the controls. No seat, no legs. It strapped to their backs over their life-support packs.

Colt and Kinsman spent the next half-hour convincing Howard that they could fly the MMUs. They jetted back and forth along the emptied payload bay, did pirouettes, flew upside down and sideways, even flew in formation, almost touching outstretched fingertips.

"There are no umbilicals or tethers," Howard warned. "You'll be operating independently. On your own. Do you understand?"

"Sure," said Kinsman. "We practiced with these in the simulator a hundred times."

"No funny stuff when you're out there. No sightseeing. You won't have time for stargazing."

"Right," replied Colt.

"Now fill your propellant tanks and oxygen supply."

"Yessir."

Howard busied himself with talking to the flight deck as Kinsman and Colt jetted themselves to the supply tanks down by the tail.

"He's pretty edgy," Kinsman said as he took the propellant supply hose and plugged it into the valve on Colt's MMU.

"Just putting us on, man."

"I don't know. He said this is the most difficult task of the whole mission."

"That's why they saved it for us, huh?"

"Maybe."

He could sense Colt shaking his head, frowning. "Don't take his bullshit seriously. They had other jobs—like inspecting that Russian satellite. That was a lot tougher than what we're gonna be doing."

"That was a one-man task," Kinsman said. "He didn't need a couple of rookies getting in his way. Besides, the Soviets probably have all sorts of alarm and detection systems on their birds."

"Yeah, maybe . . ."

"He's a strange little guy."

Colt said, "You'd think he would've made major by now."

"Or light colonel. He's as old as Murdock."

"Yeah, but he's got no wings. Flunked out of flight training when he was a kid."

"Really?"

"That's what Art told me. Howard's nothing more than a glorified Tech Specialist. No Academy, no wings. Lucky he got as far as captain."

"No wonder he looks pissed most of the time."

"*Most* of the time?"

Kinsman said, "I got the feeling he enjoyed watching the Earth just as much as we did."

"H'mp. Yeah. I forgot about that."

As Kinsman disconnected the hose from Colt's backpack he glanced out at the Earth again. "I wonder if you ever get accustomed to that."

"Sure is some sight," Colt agreed.

"Makes me want to just drift out of here and never come back," murmured Kinsman. "Just go on forever and ever."

"You'll need a damned big air tank."

"Not a bad way to die, if you've got to go. Drifting alone, silent, going to sleep among the stars . . ."

"That's okay for you, maybe. But I intend to be shot by a jealous husband when I'm ninety-nine years old," Colt said firmly. "That's how I wanna go: bareass and humpin'."

"White or black?"

"The husband or the wife? Both of them honkies, man. Screwin' white folks is the best part of life."

Kinsman could hear Colt's happy chuckling.

"Frank," he asked, "have you ever thought that by the time you're ninety-nine there might not be any race problems anymore?"

Colt's laughter deepened. "Sure. Just like we won't have any wars and all God's chillun got shoes."

"All right, there it is," Captain Howard told them.

The three space-suited men hovered just above the open clamshell doors of the payload bay, looking out at what seemed to Kinsman to be a stack of giant beer bottles. Except that they're plastic, not glass.

Six empty propellant tanks, each of them nearly twice the size of the orbiter itself, were hanging in the emptiness in two neat rows. From this angle they could not see the connecting rods holding them together.

"You've got three hours," Howard told them. "The booster tank linkages that hold it to the orbiter are built to come apart and re-attach to the other tanks . . ."

"We know, we know," Colt said impatiently.

Kinsman was thinking, This shouldn't take more than an hour. Two at the outside. Why give us three?

"Pardon me," Howard was saying, acid in his voice. "I should've remembered you guys know everything already." He grabbed at his tether and started pulling himself back inside the payload bay. "All right, you're on your own. Just don't panic if anything goes wrong. Panic kills. Remember that."

Almost an hour later, as they were attaching the empty propellant tank to the other six, Colt asked:

"How many times we practice this stunt in training?"

"This particular business?"

"Naw . . . just taking pieces apart and reassembling them."

Kinsman looked up from the bolt-tightening job he was doing. Colt was floating some forty meters away, up at the nose end of the fat propellant tank. He looked tiny next to the stack of huge eggs, each of them as big as a ten-room house. Sunlight glinted off them and the Earth slid by below, silent and serene.

The hardest part of the job was over: maneuvering the huge mass of the tank to the place where it was to be bolted to the others. Weightless though it may be, the tank still possessed mass, and in the frictionless vacuum of space, once a body starts in motion it keeps on going until something or somebody acts to stop it. The thrusters on their MMUs were pitifully inadequate to the task. The tank had its own thrusters installed at its nose and tail especially for this task.

"Well," Kinsman replied to Colt's question, "we did so much of this monkeywork in Huntsville and Houston that I thought they were training us to work in a garage."

"Yeah. That's what I was thinking. Then why's Howard so shaky about us doing this? You having any troubles?"

Kinsman shrugged inside his suit, and the motion made him drift slightly away from the strut he was working on. He reached out and grabbed it to steady himself.

"I've spun myself around a couple of times," he admitted. "But the tools work well, once you get used to them."

Colt's answer was a soft grunt.

"The suit heats up," Kinsman went on. "I've had to stop work and let it cool down a couple of times."

"Try to keep in the shadows," answered Colt. "Stay out of the direct sun. Makes a big difference."

"Maybe Howard's worried about us being so far from the orbiter without tethers."

"Maybe." But Colt did not sound convinced.

"How's your end going? I'm almost finished here."

"I got maybe another twenty minutes and I'll be through. Three hours! This damned job don't take no three . . . *Holy shit!*"

Kinsman's whole body jerked at the urgency in Colt's voice. "What? What is it?"

"Lookit the orbiter!"

Turning so rapidly that he bounced the upper corner of his MMU against the tank, Kinsman peered out at the ship, some two hundred meters away from them.

"They've closed the payload bay doors. Why the hell would they do that?"

Colt jetted down the length of the tank, stopping himself neatly as an ice skater within arm's reach of Kinsman.

"What on earth are they doing?" Kinsman wondered.

Colt said, "Whatever it is, I don't like it."

Suddenly a puff of white gas jetted from the orbiter's nose. The spacecraft dipped down and away from them. Another soundless gasp from the maneuvering thrusters back near the tail.

"What the fuck are they up to?" Colt shouted.

The orbiter was sliding away from them, scuttling crabwise farther and farther from the tank farm where they were stranded.

"They got trouble! Somethin's gone wrong . . ."

Kinsman punched the stud on his wrist for the flight deck's radio frequency.

"Kinsman to flight deck. What's wrong? Why are you maneuvering?"

No answer. The orbiter was dwindling away from them rapidly.

"Jesus Christ!" Colt yelled. "They're gonna leave us here!"

"Captain Howard!" Kinsman said into his helmet mike, trying to keep the tremble out of his voice. "Major Podolski! Major Pierce! Anybody! Come in. This is Kinsman. Colt and I are still EVA! Answer, please!"

Nothing but the crackling hum of the radio's carrier wave.

"Those sonsofbitches are stranding us!"

Kinsman watched the orbiter getting smaller and smaller. It seemed to be hurtling madly away from them, although the rational part of his mind told him that the spacecraft was only drifting now. It had only fired the vernier thrusters, not the rocket motors that would move it into an altogether different orbital plane. But the difference in relative velocities between the tank farm and the orbiter was enough to make the two fly apart from each other.

Colt was moving. Kinsman saw that he was lining himself up for a dash toward the dwindling orbiter. Grabbing Colt's arm to stop him, Kinsman snapped, "NO!" Then he realized his suit radio was still on the flight deck frequency. Banging the stud on his wrist, he said, "Don't panic. Remember? That's what Howard warned us about."

"We gotta get back to the orbiter! We can't hang here!"

"You'll never reach the orbiter with the MMU," Kinsman said. "They're separating from us too fast."

"But something's gone wrong . . ."

Kinsman looked out toward the dwindling speck that was the orbiter. It was hard to see it now, against the glaring white of the Earth. They were passing over the vast cloud-covered Antarctica. Shuddering, Kinsman felt the cold seeping into him.

"Listen to me," he commanded. "Maybe nothing's gone wrong. Maybe this is their idea of a joke."

"A joke?"

"That's what Howard was trying to tell us." Kinsman silently added, Maybe.

"That's crazy!"

"Is it? They've been sticking it to us all through the mission, haven't they? Pierce is a snotty bastard; this looks like something he might cook up. What would he like better than watching the two of us chasing the damned orbiter until the fuel in our MMUs gives out and they have to come back and rescue us?"

"You don't joke around with lives, man!"

"We're safe enough; got four hours worth of oxygen. As long as we don't panic we'll be okay. That's what Howard was trying to tell us." It was beginning to sound convincing, even to himself.

"But why the hell would they do something like this?" Colt's voice sounded calmer, as if he were trying to believe Kinsman.

Your paranoia's deserted you just when you needed it most, Kinsman thought. He replied, "How many times have they called us hotshots, the Golddust Twins? We're the two top men on the list. They just want to rub our noses in the dirt a little, make us feel foolish . . . just like the upperclassmen do at the Academy."

"You think so?"

It's either that or we're dead. Kinsman glanced at the digital watch set into his wrist keyboard. "They allowed us three hours for our task. They'll be back before that time is up. Less than two hours."

"And if they're not?"

"Then we can panic."

"Lotta good it'll do then."

"It won't do us much good now, either. We're stranded here until they come back for us."

"Bastards." Now Colt was convinced.

With a sudden grin, Kinsman said, "Yeah, but maybe we can turn the tables on them."

"How?"

"Follow me, my man."

Without using his MMU thrusters, Kinsman clambered up the side of "their" propellant tank and then drifted slowly into the nest created by the other huge tanks. Like a pair of skin divers floating in the midst of a pod of whales, Colt and Kinsman hung in emptiness, surrounded by the enormous, curving, hollow tanks.

"Now when they come back they won't be able to see us on radar," Kinsman explained. "And the tanks ought to block our suit-to-suit talk, so they won't hear us, either. We'll throw a scare into *them*."

"They'll think we panicked and jetted away."

"Right."

"Maybe that's what they want."

Kinsman laughed. Colt's paranoia had returned. "No," he said. "They want to scare us, not kill us. That would take too much explaining back at Vandenberg. Losing two cadets would ruin the whole afternoon for Pierce and the rest of them. Wouldn't look good on their files."

Colt laughed back. "Almost worth dying for."

"We'll let them know we're here," Kinsman said, "after they've worked up enough of a sweat. I'm not dying for anyone's joke—not even my own."

They waited while the immense panorama of the Earth flowed beneath them and the distant stern stars watched silently. They waited and they talked.

"I thought she split because we were down in Houston and Huntsville and she couldn't take it," Colt was saying. "White woman with a black husband—the pressure was on her a lot more than on me."

"I didn't think Houston was that prejudiced," said Kinsman. "And Huntsville's pretty cosmopolitan . . ."

"Yeah, sure. Try it with my color, man. You stuck around the base all the time, or you went into town with some of the other guys. Go try to buy some flesh-colored Band-Aids, you wanna see how cosmopolitan this country is."

"Guess I really don't know much about it," Kinsman admitted.

"But now that I think back on it, we were having our troubles in Ohio, too. I'm not an easy man to live with."

"Who the hell is?"

Colt chuckled. "You are, man. You're supercool. Never saw anybody so much in charge of himself. Like a bucket of ice water."

Ice water? Me? "You're mistaking slow reflexes for self-control."

"Yeah, I bet. Is it true you're a Quaker?"

"Used to be," he answered automatically, trying to shut

out the image of his father. "When I was a kid." Change the subject! "I was when that damned orbiter started moving away from us. A real Quaker."

With a laugh, Colt asked, "How come you ain't married? Good-looking, rich . . ."

"Too busy having fun. Flying, training for this . . . I've got no time for marriage. Besides, I like women too much to marry one of them."

"You wanna get laid but you don't wanna get screwed."

"Something like that. To quote the Bard, there's lots of chicks in the world."

"Yeah. Can't concentrate on a career and marriage at the same time. Leastwise, I can't."

"Not if you want to be really good at either one," Kinsman agreed. Oh, we are being so wise. And not looking at our watches. Cool, man. Supercool. But out beyond the curving bulk of the looming tanks the sky was empty except for the solemn stars.

"I don't just wanna be good," Colt was saying. "I got to be the best. I got to show these honkies that a black man is better than they are."

"You're not going to win many friends that way."

"Don't give a shit. I'm gonna be a general someday. Then we'll see how many friends I got."

Kinsman shook his head, laughing. "A general. Jeez, you've sure got some long-range plans in your head."

"Damn right! My brother, he's all hot and fired up to be a revolutionary. Goin' around the world looking for wars to fight against oppression and injustice. Regular Lone Ranger. Wanted me to join the underground here in the States and fight for justice against The Man."

"Underground? In the States?"

"Yeah. FBI damn near grabbed him a year or so back."

"What for?"

"Hit a bank to raise money for the People's Liberation Army."

"He's one of those?"

"Not anymore. There ain't no PLA anymore. Most of 'em are dead. The rest scattered. I watched my brother playin' cops and robbers . . . didn't look like much fun to me.

So I decided I ain't gonna fight The Man. I'm gonna *be* The Man."

"If you can't beat 'em . . ."

"Looks like I'm joinin' 'em, yeah," Colt said, with real passion in his voice. "But I'm just workin' my way up the ladder to get to the top. Then *I'll* start giving the orders. And there are others like me, too. We're gonna have a black President one of these days, you know."

"And you'll be his Chief of Staff."

"Could be."

"Where does that leave us . . ."

A small, sharp beeping sound shrilled in Kinsman's earphones. Emergency signal! Automatically, both he and Colt switched to the orbiter's flight deck frequency.

"Kinsman! Colt! Can you hear me? This is Major Jakes. Do you read me?"

The Major's voice sounded distant, distorted by ragged static, and very concerned.

Kinsman held up a hand to keep Colt silent. They were receiving the orbiter's signal scattered off the propellant tanks. No sense allowing Jakes and the others to hear them, even though their suit radios were not as powerful as the transmitter in the flight deck.

"Colt! Kinsman! Do you read me? This is Major Jakes!"

Colt leaned forward and touched his visor against Kinsman's. His muffled voice came through: "Let 'em eat shit for a coupla minutes, huh?"

Kinsman nodded, then realized that Colt could not see through the tinted visor. He made a thumbs-up gesture.

The orbiter pulled into view and seemed to hover about a hundred meters away from the tanks. The flight-deck radio switch was open, and the two lieutenants heard:

"Pierce, goddammit, if those two kids are lost I'll put you up for a murder charge."

"You were in on it, too, Harry!"

Howard's rasping voice cut in. "I'm suited up. Going out the airlock."

"Should we get one of the trainees to help search for them?" Pierce's reedy nasality.

"You've got two of them missing now," Jakes snarled.

"Isn't that enough? How about *you* getting your ass outside to help?"

"Me? But I'm . . ."

"That would be a good idea," said a new voice, with such authority that Kinsman knew it had to be the mission commander, Major Podolski. Among the three majors he was the longest in Air Force service, and therefore was as senior as God.

"Eh, yessir," Pierce answered quickly.

"And you, too, Jakes. You were all in on this, and it hasn't turned out to be very funny."

Colt and Kinsman, hanging on to one of the struts that connected the empty tanks, could barely suppress their laughter as they watched the orbiter's payload bay doors swing slowly open and three space-suited figures emerge like reluctant schoolboys from the airlock.

"Maybe we oughtta play dead," Colt said, touching his helmet against Kinsman's again so that he did not need to use the radio.

"No. Enough is too much. Let's go out and greet our rescue party."

They worked their way clear of the tanks and drifted out into the open.

"There they are!" The voice sounded so jubilant in Kinsman's earphones that he could not tell who said it.

"Are you all right?"

"Is everything . . ."

"We're fine, sir," Kinsman said calmly. "But we were beginning to wonder if war had been declared or there was some other emergency."

Dead silence for several moments.

"Uh, no . . ." said Jakes as he jetted closer to Colt and Kinsman. "We . . . uh, well, we sort of played a little prank on you two fellas."

"It's something we always do on first flights," Pierce added. "Nothing personal."

Sure, Kinsman thought. Nothing personal in getting bitten by a snake, either.

They were great buddies now as they jetted back to the orbiter. Kinsman played it straight, keeping himself very formal and correct. Colt fell into line and followed Kinsman's lead.

If we were a couple of hysterical, jibbering, terrified tenderfeet they'd be laughing their heads off at us. But now the shaft has turned.

Once through the airlock and into the mid-deck compartment, the two lieutenants were grabbed by the four other trainees. Chattering, laughing with a mixture of guilt and relief, they helped Colt and Kinsman out of their helmets and suits. Pierce, Jakes, and Howard unsuited without help.

When he was down to his blue coveralls, Kinsman turned to Major Pierce and said, tightly, "Sir, I must make a report to the commanding officer."

"Podolski knows all about . . ."

Looking Pierce straight in his glittering eyes, Kinsman said, "I don't mean Major Podolski, sir. I mean Colonel Murdock. Or, if necessary, the Judge Advocate General."

The blood drained out of Pierce's face. Everything in the crowded mid-deck compartment stopped. Jill Meyers, who had wound up with Kinsman's helmet, let it slip from her hands. It hung in midair as she watched, wide-eyed and open-mouthed. The only sound in the compartment was the hum of electrical equipment.

"The . . . Judge Advocate General?" Pierce looked as white as a bedsheet.

"Yessir. Or I could telephone my uncle, the senior senator from Pennsylvania, once we return to the base."

Now even the trainees looked scared.

"See here, Kinsman . . ." Jakes started.

Turning to face the Major, close enough to smell the fear on him, Kinsman said quietly, "This may have seemed like a joke to you, sir, but it has the look of racial discrimination about it. And it was a very dangerous stunt. *And* a waste of taxpayers' money."

"You can't . . ." Pierce somehow lost his voice as Kinsman turned back toward him. Past the Major's shoulder Kinsman saw Art Douglas grinning at him.

"The first thing I must do is see Major Podolski," Kinsman said firmly. "He's involved in this, too."

With a defeated shrug, Jakes gestured toward the ladder.

Kinsman glanced at Colt, and the two of them glided over to the ladder and swam up to the flight deck, leaving dead silence behind them.

Major Podolski was a big, florid-faced man with a golden old-style RAF Fighter Command mustache. His bulk barely fit into the commander's left-hand seat. He was half turned in it, one heavy arm draped across the seat's back, as Kinsman rose through the hatch.

"I've been listening to what you had to say down there, Lieutenant, and if you think . . ."

Kinsman put a finger to his lips. Podolski frowned.

Sitting lightly on the payload specialist's chair, behind the commander, Kinsman let himself grin.

"Sir," he said, nearly whispering so that Podolski had to lean closer to hear him, "I thought one good joke deserved another. My uncle lost his seat in the Senate years ago."

A struggle of emotions played across Podolski's face. Finally a curious smile won out. "I get it," he whispered back. "You want them to stew in their own juices for a few minutes, eh?"

Glancing at Colt, Kinsman answered, "Not exactly, sir. I want reparations."

"Repa—what're you talking about, Mister?"

"This is the first time Frank and I have been allowed up on the flight deck."

"So?"

"So we want to sit up here while you fly her back through re-entry and landing."

Podolski looked as if he had just swallowed a lemon, whole. "Oh, you do? And maybe you want to take over the controls, too?"

Colt bobbed his head vigorously. "Yes, *sir*!"

"Don't make me laugh."

"Sir . . . I meant it about the Judge Advocate General. And I have another uncle—"

"Never mind!" Podolski snapped. "You can sit up here during re-entry and landing. And that's all! You sit and watch and be quiet and forget this whole stupid incident."

"That's all we want, sir," Kinsman said. He turned toward Colt, who was beaming.

"You guys'll go far in the Air Force," Podolski grumbled.

"A pair of smartasses with the guts of burglars. Just what the fuck this outfit needs." But there was the trace of a grin flitting around his mustache.

"Glad you think so, sir," said Kinsman.

"Okay . . . we're due to begin re-entry checkout in two hours. You guys might as well sit up here through the whole routine and watch how it's done."

"Thank you, sir."

The Major's expression sobered. "Only . . . who's going to tell Pierce and Howard that they've got to sit downstairs with the trainees?"

"Oh, I will," said Colt, with the biggest smile of all. "I'll be glad to!"

Age 27

IN THE COOL shadows of the Astro Motel's bar, Major Joseph Tenny did indeed look like a slightly overage linebacker for the Pittsburgh Steelers. Swarthy, barrel-shaped, his scowling face clamped on a smoldering cigar, Tenny in his casual civilian sports shirt and slacks hardly gave the appearance of that rarest of all birds: a good engineer who is also a good military officer.

"Afternoon, Major."

Tenny turned on his stool to see old Cy Calder, the dean of the press service reporters covering Vandenberg and Edwards Air Force bases, where the fledgling Air Force astronaut corps trained and worked.

"Hi!" said Tenny. "Whatcha drinking?"

"I am working," Calder answered with dignity. But he settled his tall, spare frame on the next stool. He reminded Tenny of the ancient bristlecone pine trees out in the high desert: so old that nobody knew their true age, gnarled and weathered, yet still vital and clinging to life.

"Double scotch," Tenny called to the bartender. "No ice. And refill mine."

"An officer and a gentleman," murmured Calder. His voice was dry and creaking, like an iron gate on rusted hinges, his face seamed with age.

As the bartender slid the drinks down to them, Tenny said, "You wanna know who got the assignment."

"I told you I'm working."

Tenny grinned. "Keep your mouth shut till tomorrow? Murdock's gonna make the official announcement at his weekly press conference."

"If you can save me the tedium of listening to the chubby Colonel recite once more how the peace-loving Air Force is not militarizing space before he gives us the one piece of information we want to hear, I shall buy the next round, shine your shoes for a month, and arrange to lose an occasional poker pot to you."

"The hell you will!"

Calder shrugged. Tenny took a long pull on his beer.

"No leaks ahead of time? Promise?"

Calder sipped at his drink, then said, "On my word as an ex-officer, former gentleman, and fugitive from Social Security."

"Okay. But keep it quiet until Murdock's announcement. It's gonna be Kinsman."

Calder put his glass down on the bar carefully. "Chester A. Kinsman, the pride of the Air Force? That's hard to believe."

"Murdock okayed it."

"I know this mission is strictly for publicity," Calder said, "but Kinsman? In orbit for three days with *Celebrity* magazine's prettiest female? Does Murdock want publicity or a paternity suit?"

"Come on, Kinsman's okay."

"Really? From the stories I hear about him, he's cut a swath right across the Los Angeles basin and has been working his way up toward the Bay Area."

Tenny countered, "He's young and good-looking. The girls haven't had many unattached astronauts to play with. NASA's gang is a bunch of old farts compared to our kids. And Kinsman's one of the best of them, no fooling."

"Wasn't he going around with that folksinger . . . what's her name? Diane Lawrence, wasn't it?"

"Yeah, while she was out here. But lemme tell you about what he did over at Edwards. Him and Frank Colt have built a biplane, an honest-to-god replica of an old Spad fighter. From the wheels up. He's a solid citizen."

"And I hear he's been playing the Red Baron with it. Is it true he buzzed Colonel Murdock's helicopter?"

They were cut off by a burst of noise and laughter. Half a dozen lean, lithe young men in Air Force blues—shining new captain's double bars on their shoulders—trotted down the carpeted stairs that led into the bar.

"There they are," said Tenny. "You can ask Kinsman about it yourself."

Kinsman was grinning happily at the moment as he and five other astronauts grabbed chairs and circled them around one little table in the corner, while calling their orders to the bartender.

Calder took his drink and headed for the table, followed by Major Tenny.

"Hold it," Frank Colt warned the other astronauts. "Here comes the media."

"Tight security."

"Why, boys," Calder tried to make his gravelly voice sound hurt, "don't you trust me?"

Tenny pushed a chair toward the old reporter and took another one for himself. Turning it backward and straddling it, so that his chunky arms rested on the chair back, the Major told his young captains, "It's okay. I spilled it to him."

"How much he pay you, boss?"

"That's between him and me."

As the bartender brought a tray of drinks, Calder said, "Let the Fourth Estate pay for this round, gentlemen. I want to pump some information out of you."

"That might take a lot of rounds."

To Kinsman, Calder said, "Congratulations, my boy. Colonel Murdock must think very highly of you."

They all burst out laughing.

"Murdock?" said Kinsman. "You should've seen his face when he told me I was it!"

"Looked like he was sucking on lemons."

Tenny explained. "The selection for the mission was made by the personnel computer. Murdock wanted to be absolutely unprejudiced, so he went strictly by the performance ratings in the computer—and out came Kinsman's name."

"It was a fix," muttered Colt, mainly for effect.

"If Murdock hadn't made so much noise about being so damned impartial," Tenny went on, "he could've reshuffled the program and tried again. But I was right there when the personnel officer came in with the name, so he couldn't back out of it."

"We was robbed," said Smitty.

Calder's ancient, weathered face creased into a grin. "Well, at least the computer thinks highly of you, Captain Kinsman, even if Colonel Murdock doesn't. I suppose that's still some kind of honor."

"More like a privilege. I've been watching that *Celebrity* chick through her training. Ripe."

"She'll look even better up in orbit."

"Once she takes off her space suit . . . et cetera."

"Hey, y'know, nobody's ever done it in orbit."

"Yeah . . . weightlessness, zero gravity."

Kinsman looked thoughtful. "Adds a new dimension to the problem, doesn't it?"

"Three-dimensional." Tenny took the cigar butt from his mouth and laughed.

Calder rose slowly from his chair and spread his arms to silence the others. Looking fondly down on Kinsman, he said:

"My boy—more years ago than I care to think about, I became a charter member of the Mile High Club. It was in 1915, during the height of the Great War, when, at an altitude of precisely 5,280 feet—as near as my altimeter could tell me—while circling over St. Paul's Cathedral, I successfully penetrated an Army nurse. This was in an open cockpit, mind you. I achieved success despite fogged goggles, cramped working quarters, and a severe case of windburn."

"Nineteen-fifteen?"

"How the hell old are you, Cy?"

"You sure it wasn't your father you're talking about?"

"Or your grandfather?"

Ignoring them, Calder continued, "Since then, there has

been precious little to look forward to. The skin divers claimed a new frontier, of course, but in fact they were retrogressing. Any silly-ass dolphin can do it in the water."

He beamed at Kinsman. "But you have something new going for you: weightlessness. Floating around in zero gravity, chasing tail in three dimensions. It beggars the imagination!"

Even Tenny looked impressed.

"Captain Kinsman, I pass the torch to you. To the founder of the Zero Gee Club!"

As one man, they all rose and silently toasted Kinsman.

Once they sat down again, Tenny burst their balloon. "You guys don't give Murdock credit for any brains at all. You don't think he's gonna let Kinsman go up with that broad all alone, do you? The Manta isn't as big as a shuttle, but it still holds three people."

Kinsman's face fell, but the others' lit up.

"It's gonna be a three-man mission!"

"Two men and the blonde."

Tenny warned, "Don't start drooling. Murdock wants a chaperon, not a gang bang."

It was Kinsman who understood first. Slouching back in his chair, chin sinking to his chest, he muttered, "Goddammitall, he's sending Jill along."

A collective groan.

"Murdock made up his mind an hour ago," Tenny said. "He was stuck with you, Chet, so he hit on the chaperon idea. He's giving you some real chores to do, too. Keep you busy. Like mating the power pod."

"Jill Meyers," said Art Douglas, with real disappointment on his face. "At least he could've picked Mary O'Hara. She's fun."

"Jill's as qualified as you guys are, and she's been taking this *Celebrity* gal through her training. I'll bet she knows more about this mission than any of you guys do."

"She would."

"In fact," Tenny added, with a malicious grin, "she *is* the senior captain among you rocket jocks. So show some respect."

Kinsman had only one comment. "Shit."

* * *

The key to the Air Force astronaut's role in space was summed up in two words: *quick reaction.* The massive space shuttle that NASA had developed was fine for missions that could be planned months in advance, but the Air Force needed a spacecraft that could be sent off on a mission without such preparation. The smaller, delta-shaped Manta was the answer. Launched by throwaway solid rocket boosters, carrying no more than three astronauts, the Manta could put Air Force personnel into orbit within a few hours of the decision to go.

The bone-rattling roar and vibration of lift-off suddenly died away. Strapped into the contour seat, scanning the banks of controls and instruments a few centimeters before his eyes, Kinsman could feel the pressure and tension slacken to zero. He was no longer flattened against his seat, but touching it only lightly, almost floating, restrained only by his safety harness.

He had stopped counting how many times he had felt weightlessness after his tenth orbital mission. Yet he still smiled inside his helmet.

Without thinking about it he touched a control stud in his seat's armrest. A maneuvering thruster fired briefly and the ponderous, dazzling bulk of Earth slid into view through the narrow windshield before him. It curved huge and awesome, brilliantly blue, streaked with white clouds, beautiful, serene, shining.

Kinsman could have watched it forever, but he heard the sounds of motion through his helmet earphones. The two women were stirring behind him. The Manta's cabin made the shuttle orbiter seem like a spacious hotel: their three seats were shoehorned in among racks of instruments and equipment. And they rode into orbit wearing full space suits and helmets, thanks to some Air Force functionary who wrote the requirement into the flight regulations.

Jill was officially second pilot and biomedical officer for this mission. The photographer, Linda Symmes, was simply a passenger, a public relations project, occupying the third seat, beside Jill.

Kinsman's earphones crackled with a disembodied link from Earth. "AF-9, you are confirmed in orbit. Trajectory nominal. All systems green."

"Roger, ground," Kinsman said into his helmet mike.

The voice, already starting to fade, switched to ordinary conversational speech. "Looks like you're right on the money, Chet. We'll get the rendezvous parameters and feed 'em to you when you pass over Woomera. Rendezvous is set for your second orbit."

"Roger, big V. Everything here on the board is in the green."

"Rog. Vandenberg out." Faintly. "And hey . . . good luck, Founding Father."

Kinsman grinned at that. He slid his visor up, loosened his harness, and turned in his seat. "Okay, ladies, we're safely in orbit."

Jill snapped her visor open.

"Need any help?" Kinsman asked Linda Symmes.

"I'll take care of her," Jill said firmly. "You handle the controls."

So that's how it's going to be, Kinsman thought.

Jill's face was round and plain and bright as a new penny. Snub nose sprinkled with freckles, wide mouth, short hair of undistinguished brown. Kinsman knew that under her pressure suit was a figure that could most charitably be described as ordinary.

Linda Symmes was another matter entirely. She had lifted her visor and was staring out at him with wide blue eyes that combined feminine curiosity with a hint of helplessness. She was tall, nearly Kinsman's own five-eleven height, with thick honey-colored hair and a body that he had already memorized down to the last curve.

In her sweet, high voice she said, "I think I'm going to be sick."

"Oh, for . . ."

Jill reached into the compartment between their two seats. "I'll take care of this," she said to Kinsman as she whipped a white plastic bag open and stuck it over Linda's face.

Shuddering at the realization of what could happen in zero gravity, Kinsman turned back to the control panel. He snapped his visor shut and turned up the air blower in his suit, trying to cut off the obscene sounds of Linda's wretching.

"For Chrissake," he yelled to Jill, "turn off your mikes,

will you! You want me upchucking all over the place too?"

"AF-9, this is Woomera."

Trying to blank his mind to what was going on behind him, Kinsman thumbed the switch on his communications panel. "Go ahead, Woomera."

For the next hour Kinsman thanked the gods that he had plenty of work to do. He matched the orbit of the Manta with that of the Air Force orbiting station, which had been up for nearly a year, occupied intermittently by two- or three-astronaut teams.

Kinsman had thought that the Air Force would make use of the emptied propellant tanks from shuttle flights that were left in orbit to be clustered together in the "tank farm" where he and Colt had been initiated to orbital tomfoolery a couple of years earlier. But the tanks remained unused, and the Air Force sent aloft a completely separate little spacecraft that they were developing into a permanent station in orbit.

It was a fat cylinder, silhouetted against the brilliant white of the cloud-decked Earth. As he pulled the Manta close enough for a visual inspection, Kinsman could see the antennas and airlock and other odd pieces of gear that had accumulated on the station. Looks more like an orbital junk heap every trip, he thought. Riding behind it, unconnected in any way, was the squat cone of the new power pod.

Kinsman circled the unoccupied station once, using judicious squeezes of the maneuvering thrusters. He touched a command signal switch and the station's radar beacon came to life, announced by a blinking green light on his control panel.

"All systems green," he said to ground control. "Everything looks okay."

"Roger, Niner. You are cleared for docking."

This was more complicated. Be helpful if Jill could read off . . .

"Distance, eighty-eight meters," Jill's voice pronounced clearly in his earphones. "Rate of approach . . ."

Kinsman instinctively turned his head, but the helmet cut off any possible sight of her. "Hey, how's your patient?"

"Empty. I gave her a sedative. She's out."

"Okay," said Kinsman. "Let's get ourselves docked."

He inched the spacecraft into the docking collar on one

end of the station, locked on and saw the panel lights confirm that the docking was secure.

"Better get Sleeping Beauty zippered up," he told Jill.

Jill said, "I'm supposed to check the hatch."

"Stay put. I'll do it." Kinsman unbuckled and rose effortlessly out of his seat to bump his helmet lightly against the overhead hatch.

"You two both sealed tight?"

"Yes."

"Keep an eye on the air gauge." He cracked the hatch open a scant centimeter.

"Pressure's steady. No red lights."

Nodding, Kinsman pushed the hatch open all the way. He pulled himself up and through the shoulder-wide hatch.

Light and easy, he reminded himself. No big motions. No sudden moves.

Sliding through the station hatch he slowly rotated, like an underwater swimmer doing a lazy rollover, and inspected every millimeter of the docking collar in the light of his helmet lamp. Satisfied that it was locked in place, he pushed himself fully inside the station. Carefully he pressed his cleated boots into the gridwork flooring and stood upright. His arms tended to float out, but they bumped the equipment racks on either side of the narrow central passageway. Kinsman turned on the station's interior lights, checked the air supply, pressure and temperature gauges, then shuffled back to the hatch and pushed himself through again.

He re-entered the Manta upside-down and had to contort himself around the pilot's seat to regain a "normal" attitude.

"Station's okay," he said at last. "Now how in hell do we get her through the hatch?"

Jill had already unbuckled the harness over Linda's shoulders. "You pull, I'll push. She'll bend around the corners easily enough."

And she did.

The station interior was about the size and shape of a small transport plane's cabin. On one side nearly its entire length was taken up by instrument racks, control equipment, and electronics humming almost inaudibly behind lightweight plastic panels. Across the narrow separating aisle were the crew stations: control desk, two observation ports, lab benches. At the far end, behind a discreet curtain, were the head and the sleeping bags.

Kinsman stood at the control desk, in his blue fatigues now, his cleated shoes gripping the holes in the gridwork flooring to keep him from floating off. The desk was almost shoulder height, a convenient level in zero gee. His space suit had been stored in the locker beneath the floor panels. He was running a detailed checkout of the station's life-support systems: air, water, heat, electrical power. All operating within permissible limits, although the water supply would need replenishment at the rate it was being depleted. Recycling was never a hundred percent effective. He stepped leftward carefully to the communications console; everything operating normally. The radar screen showed a single large blip close by: the power pod.

He looked up as Jill came through the curtain from the bunkroom. She was still in her space suit, with only the helmet removed.

"How is she?"

Looking tired, Jill answered, "Okay. Still sleeping. I think she'll be all right when she wakes up."

"She'd better be. We can't have a wilting flower around here. I'll abort the mission."

"Give her a chance, Chet. She just lost her cookies when free-fall hit her. All the training in the world can't prepare you for those first few minutes."

Kinsman shook his head. But it's fun! he thought. Like skiing. Or skydiving. Only better.

Jill floated toward him, pushing along the handgrips set into the equipment racks and desk fronts. Kinsman pulled his feet free of the restraints and met her halfway.

"Here, let me help you out of that suit."

"I can do it myself."

"Sure. But it's easier with help."

After several minutes Jill was free of the bulky suit and standing in front of the miniaturized biomed lab. Ducking slightly because of the curving overhead, Kinsman glided to the galley. It was about half as wide as a phone booth, not as deep nor as tall.

"Coffee, tea, or milk?"

Jill grinned at him. "Orange juice."

He reached for a concentrate bag. "You're a tough woman to satisfy."

"No, I'm not. I'm easy to get along with. Just one of the guys."

That's a dig, Kinsman recognized. But who's it aimed at? And why?

For the next couple of hours they checked out the station's equipment in detail. Kinsman was re-assembling one of the high-resolution cameras after cleaning it, parts hanging in midair all around him as he worked intently. Jill was nursing a straggly-looking philodendron that had been smuggled aboard months earlier and was now inching from the biomed bench toward the ceiling light panels.

"How's the green monster?" Kinsman asked.

"It survived without us," said Jill, "but just barely. Maybe we could keep the temperature up a little higher in between missions once we get the power pack operating."

Linda pushed back the curtain from the sleeping area and stepped uncertainly into the main compartment.

Jill noticed her first. "Hi. How're you feeling?"

Kinsman looked up. She was in tight-fitting coveralls, coral red. He turned abruptly, scattering camera parts in every direction.

"Are you all right?" he asked.

Smiling sheepishly, "I think so. I'm kind of embarrassed . . ." Her voice was high and soft.

"Oh, that's all right," Kinsman said eagerly. "It happens to practically everybody. I got sick myself my first time in orbit."

"That," said Jill, dodging a slowly tumbling lens that had ricocheted gently off the ceiling, "is a little white lie, meant to make you feel at ease."

Kinsman forced himself not to frown.

Jill added, "Chet, you'd better pick up those camera parts before they get so scattered you won't be able to find them all."

He wanted to snap an answer, thought better of it, and replied merely, "Right."

As he finished the job on the camera he studied Linda carefully. The color was back in her face. She seemed steady, clear-eyed, not frightened or upset. Maybe she'll be okay, after all. Jill made her a cup of tea, which she sucked from the lid's plastic spout.

Kinsman went to the control desk and punched up the mission schedule on the computer screen.

"Jill, it's past your bedtime."

"I'm not sleepy," she said.

"Yeah, I know. But you've had a busy day, little girl, and tomorrow's going to be even busier. Now get your four hours and then I'll get mine. Got to be fresh for the mating."

"Mating?" Linda asked from the far end of the cabin, a good five strides from Kinsman. Then she remembered. "Oh . . . you mean linking the power module to the station."

Suppressing half a dozen possible retorts, Kinsman spelled out soberly, "Extravehicular activity."

Jill reluctantly drifted toward the bunkroom. "Okay, I'll sack in. I am tired, I guess, but I never seem to get really sleepy up here."

Wonder what kind of a briefing Murdock gave her? She's sure acting like a goddamned chaperon.

Jill glided into the shadows of the sleeping area and pulled the curtain firmly shut. After a few minutes of silence Kinsman turned to Linda.

"Alone at last."

She smiled back at him.

"Um . . . you just happen to be standing where I've got to install this camera." He nudged the assembled hardware so that it floated gently toward her.

She moved away slowly, carefully, holding the handgrip on the nearest equipment rack with both hands as if she were afraid of falling. Kinsman slid to the observation port and stopped the camera's slow-motion flight with one outstretched hand. He started mounting the camera into the fixture set into the observation port.

"You really feel okay?"

"Yes, honestly."

"Think you'll be up to EVA tomorrow?"

"I hope so," Linda said. "I want to go outside with you."

I'd rather go inside with you, Kinsman said to himself as he worked.

An hour later they were hovering side by side at the

observation port, looking out at the curving bulk of Earth, the blue and white splendor of the cloud-mottled Pacific. Kinsman was trying to remember the mission flight plan, comparing the times when Jill would be sleeping against the long stretches when the station would be orbiting between ground stations, with no possibility of interruptions.

"Is that land?" Linda asked, pointing to a thick band of clouds wrapping the horizon.

Glancing at the computer display of their orbital track, down by the control desk, Kinsman replied, "The coast of Chile, South America."

"There's another tracking station down there, isn't there?"

"NASA station, not part of our network. We only use Air Force stations."

"Why is that?"

"This is strictly a military operation. We have to be able to operate entirely separately from the civilian space agency."

"Doesn't that cost more money?"

Kinsman thought of Murdock, and the reason why the Pentagon had agreed to let *Celebrity* magazine send a photojournalist to the Air Force space station. "Maybe. But it lets the civilians do their thing without getting involved in military operations. And vice versa. Like the separation of church and state."

"So everything you do here," Linda said, "is strictly military."

He made himself grin at that. "Yep. But it's not very warlike. We don't have any weapons aboard. We couldn't hurt a flea."

"I thought you tested giant laser weapons up here. You know, for the Star Wars program."

"No," he replied, shaking his head. "No death rays. No killer satellites. We have reflectors mounted outside, to test laser beams fired at us from the ground. And someday we *will* test antimissile lasers and other SDI stuff, I guess. But for now, all we do is observe the Earth and check out hardware that's supposed to run in zero gravity. And people," he added. "We test people up here. Jill's specialty is biomedicine. She's studying how well people perform in zero gee."

Linda repeated, "But this station will become a testing

center for Star Wars weapons."

"When and if the Pentagon and the Congress can agree on the matter," Kinsman admitted. "Then we'll get a lot more secrecy, a lot more of the hup-two-three crap."

She smiled. "You don't like that?"

"There's only one thing the Air Force has done lately that I'm in complete agreement with."

"What's that?"

"Bringing you up here."

The smile stayed on her face but her eyes moved away from him. "Now you sound like a guy on the make."

"Not like an officer and a gentleman?"

She looked straight at him again. "Let's change the subject."

It's already been changed, he thought. We're off the weapons-in-space kick, and we're going to stay off it. "Sure. Okay," he said aloud. "You're here to get a story. Murdock wants as much publicity for us as NASA gets. And the Pentagon wants to show the world that we're not testing death rays in orbit. We may be military, but we're *nice* military."

"And you?" Linda asked, seriously. "What do you want? How does an Air Force captain get into the space cadets?"

"By dint of personal valor. I thought it would be fun—until my first orbital flight. Now it's a way of life."

"Really? You like it that much? Why?"

With an honest grin he answered, "Wait until we go outside. Then you'll see."

Jill came back into the cabin precisely on schedule, and it was Kinsman's turn to sleep. He seldom had difficulty sleeping on Earth, never in orbit. But he wondered about Linda's reaction to going EVA as he zippered himself into his mesh sleeping bag and adjusted the band across his forehead that kept his head from bobbing weightlessly under the pressure of the blood pumping through his carotid arteries.

Worming his arms inside the nylon mesh, snug and secure, he closed his eyes and sank into sleep. His last conscious thought was a nagging worry that Linda would be terrified of EVA.

When he awoke and Linda took her sleep shift, he talked it over with Jill.

"I think she'll be all right, Chet. Don't hold those first few minutes against her."

"I don't know. There's only two kinds of people up here: you either love it or you're scared shitless. And you can't fake it. If she goes ape out there . . ."

"She won't," Jill said. "Anyway, you'll be out there to help her. She won't be going outside until you're finished with the mating task. She wanted to get pictures of you actually at work, but I told her she'll have to settle for some posed shots."

Kinsman nodded. But the worry persisted. I wonder if Cy Calder's nurse was scared of flying?

He was pulling on his boots, wedging his free foot against an equipment rack to keep from floating off, when Linda returned from her sleep.

"Ready for a walk around the block?" he asked her.

She smiled and nodded without the slightest hesitation. "I'm looking forward to it. Can I get a few shots of you getting into your suit?"

Maybe she'll be okay, he hoped.

Finally he was sealed into the space suit. Linda and Jill stood back as Kinsman floated to the EVA airlock hatch. It was set into the floor, directly beneath the hatch that the Manta was linked to. Kinsman opened the massive hatch, slid himself down into the airlock, and closed the hatch securely. He always felt a little like a blimp in the bulky, pressurized space suit. The metal airlock chamber was roughly the size of a coffin; he had to worm his arm up to reach the control panel. He leaned against the stud and heard the whine and clatter of the pump sucking the air out of the cramped chamber.

The red light came on, indicating vacuum. He touched the stud that opened the outer hatch. It was beneath his feet, but as it slid open to reveal blackness flecked with stars, Kinsman's weightless orientation flip-flopped and he suddenly felt that he was standing on his head.

"Going out now," he said into his helmet mike.

"Roger," Jill's professional voice responded.

Carefully he eased himself through the open hatch, gripping its rim with one gloved hand as he slid fully outside, the way a swimmer holds the rail for a moment before kicking free into the deep water. Outside. Swinging his body around slowly he took in the immense beauty of Earth, overwhelmingly bright even through his tinted visor. Beyond its curving limb was the darkness of infinity, with the beckoning stars watching gravely.

Alone now. He worked his way along the handgrips to where the MMUs were stored and backed himself into the nearest one, then fastened the harness across his chest. He pushed away from the station, eyes still on the endless panorama of Earth. Inside his own tight, self-contained universe. Independent of everything and everybody. How easy it would be to jet away from the station and float away by himself forever. And be dead in six hours. Ay, there's the rub.

Instead, he used the thrusters to nudge him over to the power pod. It was riding silently behind the station, a squat truncated cone, one edge brilliantly lit by the sun, the rest bathed in the softer light reflected from the dayside of Earth.

Kinsman's job was to inspect the power pod, check the status of its systems, and then mate it to the electrical system of the station. It was a nuclear power generator, capable of providing the electricity to run a multimegawatt laser. Everything necessary for the task of mating it to the station —checkout instruments, connectors, tools—had been built into the pod, waiting for an astronaut to use them.

It would have been simple work on Earth. In zero gee it was complicated. The slightest motion of any part of your body started you drifting. You had to fight against all the built-in instincts of a lifetime; had to work hard constantly to remain in one place. It was easy to become exhausted in zero gee, especially when your suit began to overheat.

Kinsman accepted all this with hardly a conscious thought. He worked slowly, methodically, like a sleepwalker, using as little motion as possible, letting himself drift slightly until a more-or-less natural motion counteracted and pulled him back in the opposite direction. Ride the waves, he told himself, slow and easy. There was rhythm to his work, the natural dreamlike rhythm of weightlessness.

His earphones were silent. He said nothing. All he heard was the purring of the suit's air blowers and his own steady breathing. All he saw was his work.

Finally he inserted the last thick power cable to the receptacle waiting on the sidewall of the station. I pronounce you station and power source, he said silently. Inspecting the checkout lights alongside the connectors, he saw that they were all green. May you produce many kilowatts.

"Okay, it's finished," he announced, pushing slightly away from the station. "How's Linda doing?"

Jill answered at once, "She's all set."

"Send her out."

She came out of the hatch slowly, uncertainly, wavering feet sliding out first from the bulbous airlock. It reminded Kinsman of a film he had seen of a whale giving birth.

"Welcome to the real world," he said once her helmet cleared the airlock hatch.

She turned to answer him and he heard her gasp and he knew that now he liked her.

"It's . . . it's . . ."

"Staggering," Kinsman suggested. "And look at you—no hands!"

She was floating freely, space suit laden with camera gear, tether flexing easily behind her. Kinsman could not see her face through the tinted visor, but he could hear the awe in her voice, even in her breathing.

"I've never seen anything so absolutely overpowering . . ."

And then suddenly she was all business, reaching for a camera, snapping away at the Earth and the station and even the distant Moon, rapid-fire. She moved too fast and started to tumble. Kinsman jetted over and steadied her, holding her by the shoulders.

"Hey, take it easy. They're not going away. You've got lots of time."

"I want to get some shots of you, and the station. Can you go over by the power pod and go through some of the motions of your work on it?"

Kinsman posed for her, answered her questions, rescued a camera when she fumbled it out of her gloved hands and missed several grabs at it.

"Judging distances out here is a little wacky," he said as he handed the camera back to her.

Jill called them twice and ordered them back inside.

"Chet, you're already fifteen minutes over the schedule limit!"

"There's plenty slop in the schedule; we can stay out a while longer."

"You're going to get her exhausted."

"I really feel fine," Linda said, her voice lyrical.

"How much more film do you have?" Kinsman asked her.

Without needing to look at the camera she answered, "Six more shots."

"Okay. We'll come in when the film runs out, Jill."

"You're going to be in darkness in another five minutes."

Turning to Linda, floating upside-down with the cloud-decked Earth behind her, he said, "Save your film for the sunset, and then shoot like hell when it comes."

"The sunset? What'll I focus on?"

"You'll know when it happens. Just watch."

It came fast but she was equal to it. As the station swung in its orbit toward the Earth's night shadow, the Sun dropped to the horizon and shot off a spectacular few moments of the purest reds and oranges and finally a heart-catching blue. Kinsman watched in silence, hearing Linda's breath going faster and faster as she worked the camera.

Then they were in darkness. Kinsman flicked on his helmet lamp. Linda was just hanging there, camera in hand.

"It's . . . impossible to describe." Her voice sounded empty, drained. "If I hadn't seen it . . . if I didn't get it on film, I don't think I'd be able to convince myself that I wasn't dreaming."

Jill's voice rasped in his earphones. "Chet, get inside! This is against every safety reg, keeping her outside in the dark."

He looked toward the station. Lights were visible from the ports along its side. Otherwise he could barely make out its shape, even though it was only a few meters away.

"Okay, okay. Turn on the airlock lights so we can see the hatch."

Linda was still bubbling about the view outside long after they had pulled off their space suits and eaten sandwiches and cookies.

"Have you ever been out there?" she asked Jill.

Perched on the biomed lab's desk edge, near the mouse colony, Jill nodded curtly. "Eight times."

"Isn't it spectacular? I hope the pictures come out; some of my exposure settings . . ."

"They'll be fine," Jill said. "And if they're not we have a backlog of photos you can use."

"Oh, but they wouldn't have the shots of Chet working on the power pod."

Jill shrugged. "Aren't you going to take more pictures in here? If you want to get some photos of real space veterans, you ought to take the mice here. They've been up here for six months now, living and raising families. And they don't make a fuss about it, either."

"Well, some of us do exciting things," Kinsman said lightly, "and some of us tend mice."

Jill glowered at him.

Glancing at his wristwatch, Kinsman said, "Ladies, it's my sack time. I've had a very trying day: mechanic, tour guide, photographer's model. Work, work, work."

He glided past Linda with a smile, kept it for Jill as he went by her. She was still glaring.

When he woke up again and went back into the main cabin, Jill was talking pleasantly with Linda as the two of them hovered over the microscope and a specimen rack at the biomed lab.

Linda saw him first. "Oh, hi. Jill's been showing me the spores she's studying. And I photographed the mice. Maybe they'll go on the cover instead of you."

Kinsman grinned. "She's been poisoning your mind against me." But to himself he wondered, Just what in hell has Jill been telling her?

Jill drifted over to the control desk and examined the mission log on the computer display screen.

"Ground control says the power pod checks out all okay," she said. "You did a good job."

"Thanks." He hesitated a moment. Then, "Whose turn in the sack is it?"

"Mine," Jill answered.

"Okay. Anything special?"

"No. Everything's on schedule. Next data transmission comes up in twelve minutes. Kodiak station."

Kinsman nodded. "Sleep tight."

Once Jill shut the curtain to the bunkroom, Kinsman went to the control desk and reviewed the mission schedule. Linda stayed at the biology bench, three gliding paces away.

After a glance across the control board to check all the systems status indicators, Kinsman turned to Linda.

"Well, now do you know what I meant about this being a way of life?"

"I think so. It's so different . . ."

"It's the real thing. Complete freedom. Brave new world. After ten minutes of EVA everything else is just toothpaste."

"It certainly was exciting."

"More than that. It's *living*. Being on the ground is a drag. Even flying a plane is dull now. This is where the fun is . . . this is where you can feel alive. Better than booze. Better than drugs. It's the highest kick there is, as close to heaven as anyone can get."

"You're really serious?"

"Damned right I am. I've been thinking of asking Murdock for a transfer to NASA duty. Air Force missions don't include the Moon, and I'd like to walk around on the new world, see the sights."

She smiled at him. "I'm afraid I'm not that enthusiastic. And besides, not even NASA's been on the Moon for years."

"They will be," he replied. "Sooner or later."

"You really think so?"

"Sure. But what's really important is that up here you're free, really free. All the laws and rules and prejudices that they've been dumping on us all our lives—they're all *down there*. Up here it's a new start. You can be yourself and do your own thing, and nobody can tell you differently."

"As long as your air holds out."

"That's the physical end of it, sure. We live in a microcosm, courtesy of the aerospace industry and the scientists. But there're no strings on us. The brass can't make us follow their rules. We're writing the rulebooks ourselves. For the first time since 1776 we're writing new social rules."

Linda looked thoughtful. Kinsman could not tell if she was genuinely impressed by his line or if she knew what he was trying to lead up to. He turned back to the control desk and busied himself with the mission flight plan again.

He had carefully considered all the possible opportunities and narrowed them down to two. Both of them tomorrow, over the Indian Ocean. Forty-five minutes between ground stations and Jill asleep both times.

"AF-9, this is Kodiak."

He reached up for the radio switch. "AF-9, Kodiak. Go ahead."

"We are receiving your automatic data transmission loud and clear."

"Roger, Kodiak. Everything normal here. Mission profile unchanged."

"Okay, Niner. We have nothing new for you. Oh, wait . . . Chet, Lew Regneson is here and he says he's put twenty bucks on your butt to uphold the Air Force's honor. Keep 'em flying."

Keeping his face as straight as possible, Kinsman answered, "Roger, Kodiak. Mission profile unchanged."

"Good luck!"

Linda's thoughtful expression had deepened. "What was that all about?"

He looked straight into those cool blue eyes and lied, "Damned if I know. Regneson's one of the astronaut corps. Been assigned to Kodiak for the past six weeks. He must be going ice-happy. Thought it'd be best just to humor him."

"I see." But she looked unconvinced.

"Have you checked any of your pictures through the film processor yet?"

Shaking her head, Linda replied, "No. I don't want to risk them on Air Force equipment. I'll process them in New York when we get back."

"Damned good equipment," Kinsman said, "even if it was built by the lowest bidder."

"I'm fussy."

He shrugged and let it go. At least the subject of the conversation had been changed.

"Chet?"

"What?"

"The power pod . . . what's it for? Colonel Murdock got awfully coy when I asked him."

"It's classified," he said. "I don't know myself."

"It's a nuclear reactor, isn't it?"

"A little one."

"Isn't it dangerous?"

He laughed. "You're getting more cosmic rays through your pretty bod right now than any radiation that might come from the reactor."

"Cosmic rays?" She looked alarmed.

"Nothing to worry about."

"They're not dangerous?"

"Not as dangerous as living in Manhattan."

Linda spent a moment thinking that over. Then, "The reactor's going to power Star Wars stuff, isn't it?"

"We call it SDI: Strategic Defense Initiative."

"But that's what it's for, isn't it?"

His shrug would have lifted him off the floor if his cleated shoes hadn't been wedged into the grillwork. "Could be."

"So your brave new world is involved in war."

"Defensive systems like SDI won't kill anybody," he said. "Their purpose is to prevent nuclear war from happening."

"But this *is* a military station."

"Unarmed. Two things this brave new world doesn't have yet: death and love."

"People have died in space."

"Never in orbit. Three Russian cosmonauts died during re-entry. People have been killed in ground or flying accidents. But no one's ever died up here. And no one's made love, either."

Despite herself, it seemed to Kinsman, she smiled. "Have there been any chances for it?"

"Not among NASA's astronauts, not in the shuttle. And the Russians have had a couple of women cosmonauts, but you know how puritanical they are."

Linda thought it over for a swift moment. "This isn't exactly the bridal suite at the Waldorf. I've seen better motel rooms along the Jersey Turnpike."

"Pioneers have to rough it."

"I'm a photographer, Chet, not a pioneer."

Kinsman spread his hands helplessly. "Strike three; I'm out."

"Better luck next time."

"Thanks." He returned his attention to the mission flight plan. Next time will be in exactly sixteen hours, sweetface.

When Jill came out of the sack it was Linda's turn to sleep. Kinsman moved to the camera monitor screen, sucking on a container of lukewarm coffee. They were passing over Plesetsk, the Soviet military launching center. Clouds covered the area, so he switched the monitor to display the radar imagery. A space shuttle sat at one end of the ten-thousand-foot runway down there. And, as usual, at least six of the dozens of launch pads had boosters on them.

They launch their antisatellite stuff from there, he thought. Does one of those boosters have an ASAT on it, primed to take us out?

No, he told himself. That would mean war. Nuclear war. The rumors that unmanned reconnaissance satellites had been destroyed by ASATs were just the usual scuttlebutt that military people liked to scare each other with.

He pulled his eyes away from the screen and looked at Jill. She was taking a blood sample from one of the mice.

"How're they doing?"

Without looking up she answered, "Fine. They've adapted to weightlessness beautifully. Calcium levels have evened off, muscle tone is good. They're even living longer than they would on Earth."

"Then there's hope for us two-legged types?"

Jill returned the mouse to the colony entrance and snapped the plastic lid shut. It scampered to rejoin its clan in the transparent maze of tunnels.

"I can't see any physical reason why humans couldn't live in orbit indefinitely," she answered. "It might even be beneficial."

"You mean we'd live longer?"

Jill nodded. "Maybe. I'd certainly be better off up here. No allergies."

"That's right," he said. "No pollen or dust."

"I never sneeze up here. I never get headaches." Jill smiled, a trifle ruefully. "Living up here eliminates a lot of physical problems."

Kinsman caught a slight but definite stress on the word

physical. "You think there might be emotional problems, in the long run?"

"Chet, I can see emotional problems on a three-day mission." Jill forced the blood specimen into a stoppered test tube.

"What do you mean?"

"Come on," she said, her face showing disappointment and distaste. "It's obvious what you're trying to do. Your tail's been wagging like a puppy dog whenever she's in sight."

"You haven't been sleeping much, have you?"

"I haven't been eavesdropping, if that's what you mean. I've simply been watching you watching her. And some of those messages from groundside . . . is the whole Air Force in on this? How much money's being bet?"

"I'm not involved in any betting. I'm just . . ."

"You're just taking a risk on fouling up this mission and maybe killing the three of us just to prove that you're Tarzan and she's Jane."

"Goddammitall, Jill, now you sound like Murdock."

The sour look on her face deepened. "Do I? Okay, you're a big boy. If you want to play Tarzan while you're on duty, that's your business. I won't get in your way. I'll take a sleeping pill and stay in the bunk."

"You will?"

"That's right. You can have your blond Barbie Doll, and good luck to you. But I'll tell you this . . . she's a phony. I've talked to her long enough to dig that. You're trying to use her, but she's trying to use us, too. She was pumping me about the power pod while you were sleeping. She's here for her own reasons, Chet, and if she plays along with you it won't be for the romance and adventure of it all."

My God Almighty, thought Kinsman. Jill's jealous!

It was tense and quiet when Linda returned from the bunkroom. The three of them worked separately: Jill fussing over the algae colony on the shelf above the biomed desk; Kinsman methodically taking film from the surveillance cameras for return to Earth and reloading them; Linda clicking away efficiently at both of them.

Ground control called up to ask how things were going. Both Jill and Linda threw sharp glances at Kinsman.

He replied merely, "Following mission profile. All systems green."

They shared a meal of precooked boneless chicken and bland vegetables together, still mostly in silence, and then it was Kinsman's turn in the sack again. But not before he rechecked the flight plan. *Jill goes in next, and we'll have four hours alone, including a stretch over the Indian Ocean.*

He found himself whistling a romantic theme from *Scheherazade* as he zippered himself into his sleeping bag.

Once Jill retired, Kinsman immediately called Linda over to the radar display on the pretext of showing her the image of a Soviet satellite.

"We're coming close now." They hunched side by side in front of the orange-glowing radar screen, close enough for Kinsman to scent her delicate but very feminine perfume. "Only a couple hundred kilometers away."

"Should we blink our lights at them or something?"

"It's unmanned."

"Oh."

"It *is* a little like flying in World War I up here," Kinsman realized, straightening up. "Just being up here is more important than which nation you're from."

"Do the Russians feel that way, too?"

He nodded. "I think so."

Linda stood in front of him so close that they were almost touching.

"You know," Kinsman said, "when I first saw you on the base I thought you were the photographer's model, not the photographer."

Gliding slightly away from him, she answered, "I started out as a model . . ." Her voice trailed off.

"Don't stop. What were you going to say?"

Something about her had changed, Kinsman realized. She was still coolly friendly, but now she was alert, as wary as a deer in hunting season, and . . . sad?

She sighed. "Modeling is a dead end. I finally figured out that there's more of a future on the other side of the camera."

"You had too much brains for modeling."

"Don't flatter me."

"Why on Earth should I flatter you?"

"We're not on Earth."

"Touché."

She drifted, dreamlike, self-absorbed, toward the galley. Kinsman followed her.

"How long have you been on the other side of the camera?" he asked.

Turning back toward him, "I'm supposed to be getting the story of your life, not vice versa."

"Okay . . . ask me some questions."

"How many people know that you're supposed to lay me up here?"

Kinsman felt his face make a smile, an automatic delaying tactic. What the hell, he thought. Aloud he replied, "I don't know. It started out as a little joke among a few of the guys . . . apparently the word has spread."

"And how much money do you stand to win or lose?" She was not smiling.

"Money?" Kinsman was genuinely surprised. "Money doesn't enter into it."

"Oh, no?"

"No. Not with me."

The tenseness in her body seemed to relax a little. "Then why . . . I mean . . . what's it all about?"

Kinsman ran a hand across his jaw. It felt stubbly. "It's about making love. That's all. I mean, you're damned pretty, neither one of us has any strings, nobody's tried it in zero gee before . . . why the hell not?"

"But why should I?"

"That's the big question. That's what makes an adventure out of it."

She looked at him thoughtfully, leaning her tall frame against the galley paneling. "An adventure. There's nothing more to it in your mind than that?"

"Depends," Kinsman answered. "Hard to tell ahead of time."

"You live in a very simple world, Chet."

"I try to. Don't you?"

She shook her head. "No, my world's very complicated."

"But it includes sex."

Now she smiled, but there was no pleasure in it. "Does it?"

"You mean never?" Kinsman's voice sounded incredulous, even to himself.

She did not answer.

"Never at all? I can't believe that . . ."

"No," she said, nearly whispering. "Not never at all. But never for . . . for an adventure. For job security, yes. For getting the good assignments. For teaching me how to use a camera in the first place. But never for fun . . . at least, not for a long, long time has it been for fun."

Kinsman looked into those cold blue eyes and saw that they were completely dry and aimed straight back at him. His insides felt strange. He put out a hand toward her but she did not move a muscle.

"That's . . . that's a damned lonely way to live," he said.

"Yes, it is." Her voice was a steel ice pick, without a trace of self-pity in it.

"But how did it happen? Why . . . ?"

She leaned her head back against the galley paneling, her eyes looking away, into the past. "I had a baby. He didn't want it. I had to give her up for adoption—or have it aborted. The kid should be five years old now. I don't know where she is." She straightened up, looked back at Kinsman. "But I learned that sex is for making babies or making careers. Not for fun."

Kinsman hung there in midair, feeling as if he had just taken a low blow. The only sound in the cabin was the faint hum of electrical machinery, the whisper of air fans.

Linda broke into bitter laughter. "I wish you could see your own face: Tarzan the Ape Man, trying to figure out a nuclear reactor."

"The only trouble with zero gee," he grumbled, "is that you can't hang yourself."

Jill sensed something was wrong, it seemed to Kinsman. The moment she came out of the bunkroom she started sniffing around, giving quizzical looks. When Linda retired for her final rest period before re-entry, Jill asked him:

"How're you two getting along?"

"Okay."

"Really?"

"Really. We're going to open a disco in here. Wanna boogie?"

Her nose wrinkled. "You're hopeless."

For more than an hour they worked at their separate tasks. Kinsman was concentrating on recalibrating the radar mapper when Jill handed him a bulb of hot coffee.

He turned toward her. Even floating several inches off the floor, Jill was shorter than he.

"Thanks."

Her round face was very serious. "Something's bothering you, Chet. What did she do to you?"

"Nothing."

"Really?"

"For Chrissake, don't start that again! Nothing, absolutely nothing happened. Maybe that's what's bothering me."

Shaking her head, "No, you're worried about something and it's not yourself."

"Don't be so damned dramatic, Jill."

She put a hand on his shoulder. "Chet . . . I know this is all a game to you, but people can get hurt at this kind of game and . . . well . . . nothing in life is ever as good as you expect it will be."

Looking into her intent brown eyes, Kinsman felt his irritation vanish. "Okay, little sister. Thanks for the philosophy. I'm a big boy, though, and I know what it's all about."

"You just think you know."

Shrugging, "Okay, I think I know. Maybe nothing is as good as it ought to be, but a man's innocent until proven guilty, and everything new is as good as gold until you find some tarnish on it. That's my philosophy."

"All right, slugger." Jill smiled ruefully. "Be the ape man. Fight it out for yourself. I just don't want to see her hurt you."

"I won't get hurt."

"You hope. Okay, if there's anything I can do . . ."

"Yeah, there is something."

"What?"

"When you sack in again, make sure Linda sees you take a sleeping pill, will you?"

Jill's face went expressionless. "Sure," she answered flatly. "Anything for a fellow officer. And gentleman."

She made a great show, several hours later, of taking a sleeping pill so that she could rest well on her final nap before re-entry. It seemed to Kinsman that Jill deliberately laid it on with a trowel.

"Do you always take sleeping pills on the final time around?" Linda asked Kinsman after Jill had gone into the bunkroom and yanked the curtain shut.

"Got to be fully rested and alert for the re-entry," Kinsman said. "Trickiest part of the mission."

"I see."

"Nothing to worry about, though."

He went to the control desk and busied himself with the tasks that the mission plan called for. Linda hovered beside him, within arm's reach. Kinsman chatted briefly with Kodiak station, on schedule, and made an entry in the log.

Three more ground stations and we're over the Indian Ocean, with world enough and time.

But he did not look up from the control panel. He tested each system aboard the station, fingers flicking over the keyboard pads, eyes focused on the screen readouts that told him exactly how each system was performing.

"Chet?"

"Yes?" Without looking up.

"Are you sore at me?"

Still not looking at her, "No. Why should I be sore at you?"

"Well, maybe not angry, but . . ."

"Feeling put down?"

"Yes. Hurt. Something like that."

He punched in the final commands for the computer, then turned to face her. "Linda, I haven't had the time to figure out what I feel. You're a complicated woman, maybe too complicated for me. Life's got enough twists to it."

Her mouth drooped a little.

"On the other hand," he grinned, "we WASPs ought to stick together. Not many of us left."

That brought a faint smile. "But I'm not a WASP. My real name's Szymanski. I changed it when I started modeling."

"Another complication."

She was about to reply when the radio speaker crackled,

"AF-9, this is Cheyenne. Cheyenne to AF-9."

Kinsman leaned over and thumbed the transmitter switch. "AF-9 to Cheyenne. You're coming through faint but clear."

"Roger Nine. We're receiving your telemetry. All systems look good from here."

"On-board systems check also green," Kinsman said. "Mission profile nominal. No excursions. Tasks about ninety-five percent complete."

"Roger. Vandenberg suggests you begin checking out your spacecraft on the next orbit. You are scheduled for re-entry in ten hours."

"Right. Will do."

"Okay, Chet. Everything looks cool from here. Anything else to report, ol' Founding Father?"

"Mind your own business." He snapped the transmitter off.

Linda was grinning at him.

"What's so funny?"

"You are. You're getting very touchy about this whole thing."

"I'm going to stay touchy for a long time to come. Those guys'll hound me about this for years."

"You could always tell lies."

"About you? No, I don't think I could do that. If the girl were anonymous, that's one thing. But they all know you, where you work . . ."

"You're a gallant officer. I suppose that kind of story *would* get back to New York."

He grimaced. "You'd be on the cover of *Penthouse*, like that Miss America was."

She laughed at that. "They'd have a hard time finding nude pictures of me."

"Careful now." Kinsman put up a warning hand. "Don't stir up my imagination any more than it already is. It's tough enough being gallant, under these circumstances."

They remained apart, silent, Kinsman cleated firmly at the control desk, Linda drifting back toward the galley, nearly touching the curtain that screened off the sleeping area.

Patrick Air Force Base called in and Kinsman gave a terse report. When he looked at Linda again she was hovering by the observation window across the aisle from the galley. Looking back at him, her face was troubled, her eyes—he was not sure what he saw in her eyes. They looked different: no longer ice-cool, no longer calculating. They looked aware, concerned, almost frightened.

Still Kinsman stayed silent. He checked and double-checked the control board, making absolutely certain that every valve and transistor aboard the station was functioning perfectly. He glanced at the digital clock blinking below the main display screen. Five more minutes before Ascension calls. He started checking the board again.

Ascension called precisely on schedule. Feeling his innards tightening, Kinsman gave his standard report in a deliberately calm and detached way. Ascension signed off.

With a last long look at the controls, Kinsman pushed himself away from the desk and drifted, hands faintly touching the grips along the aisle, toward Linda.

"You've been awfully quiet," he said, standing next to her.

"I've been thinking about what you said a while ago." What was it in her eyes? Anticipation? Fear? "It . . . it *is* a damned lonely life, Chet."

He took her arm and gently pulled her toward him. He kissed her.

"But . . ."

"It's all right," he whispered. "No one will bother us. No one will know."

She shook her head. "It's not that easy, Chet. It's not that simple."

"Why not? We're here together . . . what's so complicated?"

"But life is complicated, Chet. And love—there's more to life than having fun."

"Sure there is. But it's meant to be enjoyed, too. What's wrong with taking a chance when it comes along? What's so damned complicated or important? We're above the cares and worries of the Earth. Maybe it's only for a few more hours, but it's here and it's now. It's us. Alone. They can't touch us, they can't force us to do anything or stop us from doing what we want to. We're on our own. Understand? Completely on our own."

She nodded, her eyes still wide with the look of a frightened doe. But her hands slid around him and together they drifted back toward the control desk. Wordlessly, Kinsman turned off all the lights so that all they saw was the glow from the control board and the flickering of the computer as it murmured to itself. They were in their own world now, their private universe, floating freely and softly in the darkness. Touching, drifting, caressing, searching the new seas and continents, they explored their world.

Jill stayed in her bedroll until Linda entered the sleeping area, quietly, to see if she had awakened yet. Kinsman went to the control desk feeling, not tired, yet strangely numb.

The rest of the flight was strictly routine. Jill and Kinsman did their jobs, speaking to each other only when they had to. Linda took a brief nap, then returned to snap a few last pictures. Finally they crawled back into the Manta, disengaged from the station, and started the long curving flight back to Earth.

Kinsman took a last look at the majestic beauty of the planet, serene and unique among the stars. Then they felt the surge of the rocket's retrofire and dipped into the atmosphere. Air heated beyond endurance blazed around them in a fiery grip as they buffeted through re-entry, their tiny craft a flaming falling star. Pressed down into his seat, his radio useless while the incandescent sheath of re-entry gases swathed them, Kinsman let the automatic controls bring them through the heat and pummeling turbulence, down to an altitude where the bat-winged craft smoothed out and began behaving like an airplane.

He took control and steered the Manta across the Pacific, checking the computer's programmed flight path against his actual position. Right on the money. The coast of California rose to meet him, brown and gray and white where the beaches met the ceaseless cadence of the surf. Gliding like a bird now, Kinsman brought the Manta back toward the dry lake at Edwards Air Force Base, back to the world of men, of weather, of cities and hierarchies and official regulations. He did this alone, silently, without the help of Jill or anyone else. He flew the craft with featherlight touches on the controls, from inside his buttoned-tight space suit, frowning at the instrument panel displays through his helmet visor. But even in the heavy gloves, man and machine acted together like a single creature.

The voices from ground control rasped in his earphones. He saw the long concrete scar of the all-weather runway laid across the Mojave's rocky waste. The voices crackled with information about wind conditions, altitude checks, speed estimates. He knew, without looking, that a pair of jet fighters were trailing behind him, armed with cameras in place of guns. In case I crash, he knew.

They dipped through a thin layer of stratus clouds. Kinsman's eyes flickered to the radar screen slightly to his right. The Manta shuddered briefly as he lined it up with the long gray slash of the runway. He eased back slightly on the controls, hands and feet and mind working instinctively, flashed over scrubby brush and bare cracked lake bed, flared the craft onto the runway. The wheels touched down once, bounced them up momentarily, then touched again with a shrill screech. They rolled for almost a mile before stopping.

He leaned back in the seat and let out a deep breath. No matter how many flights, he still ended oozing sweat after the landing.

"Nice landing," Jill said.

"Thanks."

He turned off all the spacecraft's systems, hands moving automatically in response to long training. Then he slid the visor up, reached overhead, and popped the hatch open.

"End of the line," he said, feeling suddenly exhausted. "Everybody out."

He clambered up through the hatch, his own weight a sullen resentment to him, then helped Linda and finally Jill out of the Manta's cramped cockpit. They hopped down onto the concrete runway. Two vans, an ambulance, and two fire trucks were rolling from their standby stations at the end of the runway, nearly half a mile ahead.

Kinsman watched their blocky dark forms wavering in the heat haze. He slowly pulled off his helmet as he sat on the lip of the hatch. A helicopter thundered overhead, cutting across the clear blue sky, but when Kinsman looked up at it the glaring desert sunlight annoyed him, made him squint, started a headache back behind his eyes.

Jill began trudging away from the Manta, toward the approaching trucks. Kinsman clambered down to the concrete and walked up to Linda. Her helmet was off, her sun-drenched hair shaking free. She carried a plastic bag of film rolls.

"I've been thinking," Kinsman said to her. "That business about having a lonely life. . . . You're not the only one. And it doesn't have to be that way. I can get to the East Coast, or . . ."

Her eyes widened with surprise. "Hey, who's taking things seriously now?" She looked calm again, cool, despite the baking heat.

"But I mean . . ."

"Chet, come on. We had our kicks. Now you can tell your pals about it and I can tell mine. We'll both get a lot of mileage out of it, won't we?"

"I never intended to tell anybody . . ."

But she was already moving away from him, striding toward the men who were running up from the vans. One of them, a civilian, had a camera. He dropped to one knee and snapped a half-dozen pictures of Linda as she walked toward him, holding the plastic bag of film up in one hand and smiling broadly, like a fisherman who had just bagged a big one.

Kinsman stood there with his mouth open.

Jill came back to him. "Well? Did you get what you were after?"

"No," he said slowly. "I guess I didn't."

She started to put her hand out to him. "We never do, do we?"

Age 30

Kinsman snapped awake when the phone went off. Before it could start a second ring he had the receiver off the cradle.

"Captain Kinsman?" The motel's night clerk.

"Yes," he whispered back, squinting at the luminous digits of his wristwatch. Two twenty-three.

"I'm awfully sorry to disturb you, Captain, but Colonel Murdock himself called . . ."

"How the hell did he know I was here?"

"He doesn't. He said he was phoning all the motels around the base. I didn't admit that you were here. He said when he found you he needed you to report to him in person at once. Those were his words, Captain: in person, at once. Something about a General Hatch."

Kinsman frowned in the darkness. "Okay. Thanks for playing dumb."

"Not at all, Captain. Hope it isn't trouble."

"Yeah." Kinsman hung up. For a half-minute he sat on the edge of the king-size bed. Murdock's making the rounds of the motels at two in the morning, Hatch is coming to the base, and the clerk hopes it isn't trouble. Funny.

He stood up, stretched his lanky frame, and glanced at the blonde wrapped obliviously in the bed's tangled sheets. With a wistful shake of his head Kinsman padded to the bathroom.

He shut the door softly and flipped the light switch, wincing. He turned on the coffee machine that hung on the wall above the light switch. It's lousy but it's coffee. Almost. As the machine started gurgling he rummaged in his travel kit for his electric razor. The face that met him in the mirror was lean and long-jawed and just the slightest bit bloodshot. He kept his hair at a length that made Murdock uncomfortable:

slightly longer than regulations allowed, not long enough to call for a reprimand.

Within a few minutes he was shaved, showered, and back in Air Force uniform. He left a scribbled note on motel stationery propped against the dresser mirror, took a final long look at the blonde, wishing he could remember her name, then went out to his car.

The new fuel regulations had put an end to fast driving. The synfuels were too expensive to waste, and when you tried to get some speed out of them they began to eat out the engine's guts. There were even those who insisted that the synfuels were specially doctored to tear up an engine's innards at anything over fifty: Washington's way of enforcing energy conservation.

His hand-built convertible was ready to burn hydrogen fuel, if and when the government made the stuff available. For now, he had to go with a captain's monthly allotment of synfuel. It was enough to keep him moving—cautiously —through the predawn darkness.

Some instinct made him turn on the car radio. Diane's haunting voice filled the starry night:

> ". . . and in her right hand
> There's a silver dagger,
> That says I can never be your bride."

Kinsman listened in dark solitude as the night wind whistled past. Diane Lawrence was a major entertainment star, with scant time for an Air Force captain who spent half his life in space. How long has it been since I've seen her? he asked himself. Could it be more than a year?

A limousine and an official Air Force car with a general's flag fluttering from its antenna zoomed past him, doing at least eighty, heading for the base. No fuel scarcity for them. Their engines whined and faded into the distance like wailing ghosts. There was no other traffic at this hour. Kinsman held to the legal limit all the way to the base's main gate, but he could feel the excitement building up inside him.

Half a dozen Air Policemen were manning the gate, looking brisk and polished, instead of the usual sleepy pair.

"What's the stew, Sergeant?" Kinsman asked as he

pulled his car up to the gate.

The guard flashed his hand light on the badge Kinsman held in his outstretched hand.

"Dunno, sir. We got the word to look sharp."

He flashed the light full in Kinsman's face, checking the picture on the badge. Painfully sharp, Kinsman groused to himself.

The guard waved him on.

There was that special crackle in the air as Kinsman drove to the administration building. The kind that only comes when a manned launch is imminent. As if in answer to his unspoken hunch, the floodlights of Complex 204 bloomed into life, etching the tall silver booster standing there embraced by the dark spiderwork of the gantry tower.

People were scurrying in and out of the administration building. Some were sleepy-eyed and disheveled, but their feet were doing double time. Colonel Murdock's secretary was coming down the hallway as Kinsman signed in at the security desk.

"What's up, Annie?"

"I just got here myself," she said. There were hairclips still in her sandy-colored curls. "The boss told me to flag you down the instant you arrived."

Even from completely across the Colonel's spacious office, Kinsman could see that Murdock was a round little kettle of nerves. He was standing by the window behind his desk, watching the activity on Pad 204, clenching and unclenching his fists behind his back. His bald head was glistening with perspiration despite the room's frigid air-conditioning. Kinsman stopped at the door with the secretary.

"Colonel?" she said softly.

Murdock whirled around. "Kinsman. So you're here."

"What's going on? I thought the next manned shot wasn't until . . ."

The Colonel waved a pudgy hand. "The next manned shot is as fast as we can damned well make it." He walked around the desk and eyed Kinsman. "Christ, you look a mess."

"It's three in the morning!"

"No excuses. Get over to the medical section for a

preflight checkout. They're waiting for you."

"I'd still like to know—"

"Tell them to check your blood for alcohol content," Murdock grumbled.

"I've been celebrating my liberation. I'm not supposed to be on duty, remember? My leave starts at 0900 hours."

"Your leave is canceled. General Hatch just flew in from Norton and he wants you."

"Hatch?"

"That's right. He wants the most experienced man available."

"Twenty astronauts on the base and you have to make me available."

Murdock fumed. "Listen, dammit. This is a military operation. I may not insist on much discipline from you glamour boys, but you're still in the Air Force and you will follow orders. Hatch says he wants the best man we've got. Personally, I'd rather have Colt, but he's back East attending a family funeral or something. That means you're *it*. Like it or not."

With a grin, Kinsman said, "If you saw what I had to leave behind me to report for duty here you'd put me up for the Medal of Honor."

Murdock frowned in exasperation. Anne tried unsuccessfully to suppress a smile.

"All right, lover-boy. Get your ass down to the medical section on the double. Annie, you stick with him and bring him to the briefing room the instant he's finished. General Hatch is already there."

Kinsman stood at the doorway, not moving. "Will you just tell me what this is all about?"

"Ask the General," Murdock growled, walking back toward his desk. "All I know is that Hatch wants the best man we have and wants him *fast*."

"Emergency shots are volunteer missions," Kinsman pointed out.

"So?"

"I'm on leave. There are eighteen other astronauts here who—"

"Dammit, Kinsman, if you—" Murdock's face began to turn red.

"Relax, Colonel, relax. I won't let you down. Not when there's a chance to put a few hundred miles between me and all the brass on Earth."

Murdock stood there fuming as Kinsman left with Anne. They paced hurriedly out to his car and sped off to the medical building.

"You shouldn't bait him like that," Anne said over the rush of the dark wind. "He feels the pressure a lot more than you do."

"He's insecure," Kinsman replied, grinning. "There are only twenty people on base qualified for orbital missions and he's not one of them."

"And you are."

"Damned right, sugar. It's the only thing in the world worth doing. You ought to try it."

She put a hand up to her wind-whipped hair. "Me? Fly in orbit? I don't even like airplanes!"

"It's a clean world up there, Annie. Brand-new every time. Your life is completely your own. Once you've done it there's nothing left on Earth except to wait for the next time."

"My God, you sound as if you really mean it."

"I'm serious," he insisted. "Why don't you wangle a ride on one of the shuttle missions? They usually have room for an extra person."

"And get locked inside a spacecraft with you?"

Kinsman shrugged. "There are worse things."

"Some other time, Captain. I've heard all about you guys and your Zero Gee Club. Right now we have to get you through preflight and then off to see the General."

General Lesmore D. ("Hatchet") Hatch sat in dour silence in the small briefing room. The oblong conference table was packed with colonels and a single civilian. They all look so damned serious, Kinsman thought as he took the only empty chair, at the foot of the table. The General, naturally, sat at the head.

"Captain Kinsman." It was a statement of fact.

"Good morning, sir."

Hatch turned to a moonfaced aide. "Borgeson, let's not waste time."

Kinsman only half-listened to the hurried introductions

around the table. He felt uncomfortable already, and it was only partly due to the stickiness of the crowded little room. Through the only window he could see the first faint glow of dawn.

"Now then," Borgeson said, introductions finished. "Very briefly, your mission will involve orbiting and making rendezvous with an unidentified satellite."

"Unidentified?"

Borgeson went on: "It was launched from Plesetsk in the Soviet Union. It's a new type, something we haven't seen before. We don't know what it contains or what its mission is. We don't even know if it's manned or not."

"And it is big," Hatch rumbled.

"Intelligence," Colonel Borgeson nodded at the colonel sitting on Kinsman's left, "had no prior word about the launch. We must assume that the satellite is potentially hostile in intent. Colonel McKeever will give you the tracking data."

They went around the table, each colonel adding his bit of information. Kinsman began to build up the picture in his mind.

The satellite had been launched nine hours earlier. It was in a low-altitude, high-inclination orbit that allowed it to cover every square mile of territory between the Arctic and Antarctic Circles. Since it had first gone up not a single radio transmission had been detected going to or from it. And it was big, twice the size of the *Soyuz* spacecraft the Soviets used for their manned flights.

"A satellite of that size," said the colonel from the Special Weapons Center, "could easily contain a beam weapon . . . the kind of laser or particle beam device that would be used to knock down missiles or destroy satellites."

"If it does," said Borgeson, "it could threaten every satellite we have in orbit; even the commsats up at geosynchronous orbit."

"Or it could be the first step in an effective antimissile defense," the Special Weapons man added. "You know, their version of Star Wars."

"Or it could be," said General Hatch, "a twenty-megaton nuclear weapon." His face was etched with deep lines of worry. Or is it hate? Kinsman asked himself. "A bomb that size, exploded at that altitude, could cause an electromagnetic pulse that would knock out every computer, every telephone, every auto ignition, every power station across the North American continent."

Borgeson nodded. "The chaos factor. It could be the precursor to a full-scale nuclear attack."

"And in a little more than two hours," Hatch went on, gloomy as death, "that satellite will be passing over the Middle West, the heartland of America."

"Why don't we just knock it down, sir?" Kinsman asked. "We can hit it with an ASAT, can't we?"

"We could try," the General answered. "But suppose the damned thing just zaps our missile? Then what? Can you imagine the panic in Washington? It'd make *Sputnik* look like a schoolyard scuffle. And suppose it *is* a nuke. Salvage fusing could set it off and the whole damned country will be blacked out. The Russians could even accuse us of starting hostilities by attacking their goddamned satellite."

Kinsman watched the General shake his head morosely. He puffed out a deep sigh. "Besides, we have been ordered by the Chief of Staff himself to inspect the satellite and determine whether or not its intent is hostile."

"In two hours?" Kinsman blurted.

"Perhaps I can explain," said the civilian. He had been introduced as a State Department man. Kinsman had already forgotten his name. He had a soft, sheltered look to him.

"We are officially in a position of cooperation, *vis-à-vis* the Soviets, in our outer space programs. Our NASA civilians and the Soviet civil space program people are working cooperatively on exploring the Moon and sending probes to the planet Mars. Officially, we are sharing information on our strategic defense programs, as called for in SALT III."

The State Department representative seemed unmindful of the hostility that Kinsman could feel rising from the others around the table. He went on in his low, Ivy League voice, "So if we simply try to destroy this new satellite it would violate our agreements with the Soviet government and set back our cooperative programs—perhaps ruin them altogether."

"On the other hand," Hatch cut in, his voice like a rusty

saw, "if we do nothing, the Russians will know that they can get away with bending those agreements whenever they feel like it."

"But . . ."

Hatch silenced the State Department with a baleful glance. Then he turned back to Kinsman. "This is a test, Captain. The Russians are testing our ability to react. They are testing our *will* to react. We have got to show them that we can detect, inspect, and verify that satellite's nature and mission."

"We ought to blow it out of the sky," snapped one of the colonels.

"And if it's a peaceful research station?" asked the civilian, with some steel in his voice. "If there are cosmonauts aboard? What if we kill Russian nationals?"

"Serve 'em right," somebody muttered.

"And then the Soviets will feel justified in launching a nuclear attack." The civilian shook his head. "No. I agree with General Hatch. This is a test of our abilities and our will. We must prove to the Soviets that we can inspect their satellites and see for ourselves whether or not they contain weaponry."

Colonel Borgeson said calmly, "If they've gone to the trouble of launching this massive vehicle, then military logic dictates that it's a weapon carrier. There's no point to placing a dummy in orbit, just to bother us."

"No matter whether it's a weapon or not, the satellite could be rigged with booby traps to prevent us from inspecting it."

Thanks a lot, Kinsman said to himself.

Hatch focused his gunmetal eyes on Kinsman. "Captain, I want to impress one thought on you. The Air Force has been working for more than ten years to achieve the capability of placing a military officer in space on an instant's notice, despite the opposition of NASA and other parts of the government."

He never so much as flicked a glance in the civilian's direction as he continued, "This incident proves the absolute necessity for such a capability. Your flight will be the first practical demonstration of all that we've battled to achieve over the past decade. You can see, then, the importance of your mission."

"Yessir."

"This is strictly a volunteer mission. Exactly because it is so important to the future of the Air Force, I don't want you to try it unless you are absolutely certain about it."

"I understand, sir. I'm your man."

Hatch's weathered face unfolded into a grim smile. "Well spoken, Captain. Good luck."

The General rose and everyone scrambled to their feet and snapped to attention, even the civilian. As the others filed out of the briefing room, Murdock drew Kinsman aside.

"You had your chance to beg off."

"And the General would've drawn a big red circle around my name. My days in the Air Force would be numbered."

"That's not the way he—"

"Relax, Colonel," Kinsman said. "I wouldn't miss this for the world. A chance to play cops and robbers in orbit."

"We're not in this for laughs! This is damned important. If it really is a weapon up there, a nuclear bomb . . ."

"I'll be the first to know, won't I?"

The countdown of the solid rocket booster went smoothly, swiftly, as Kinsman sat alone in the Manta spacecraft perched atop the rocket's nose. There was always the chance that a man or machine would fail at a crucial point and turn the intricate, delicately poised booster into a very large and powerful bomb.

Kinsman sat tautly in the contoured seat, listening to them tick off the seconds. He hated countdowns, hated being helpless, completely dependent on faceless voices that flickered through his earphones, waiting childlike in a mechanical womb, not truly alive, doubled up and crowded by the unfeeling impersonal machinery that automatically gave him warmth and breath and life.

Waiting.

He could feel the tiny vibrations along his spine that told him the ship was awakening. Green lights blossomed across the control panel, telling him that everything was functioning and ready. Still the voices droned through his earphones in carefully measured cadence:

". . . three . . . two . . . one . . ."

And she bellowed to life. Acceleration flattened Kinsman into the seat. Vibration rattled his eyes in their sockets. Time became a meaningless roar. The surging, engulfing, overpowering bellow of the rocket engines made his head ring even after they had burned out into silence.

Within minutes he was in orbit, the long slender rocket stages falling away behind, together with all sensation of weight. Kinsman sat alone in the squat, delta-shaped spacecraft: weightless, free of Earth.

Still he was the helpless unstirring one. Computers sent guidance corrections from the ground to the Manta's controls. Tiny vectoring thrusters squirted on and off, microscopic puffs that maneuvered the craft into the precise orbit needed for catching the Soviet satellite.

What if she zaps me as I approach her? Kinsman wondered.

Completely around the world he spun, southward over the Pacific and then up over the wrinkled cloud-shrouded mass of Eurasia. They must have picked me up on their radars, he thought. They must know that I'm chasing their bird. As he swung across Alaska the voices from the ground began talking to him again. He answered them as automatically as the machines did, reading numbers off the control panels, proving to them that he was alive and functioning properly.

Then Smitty's voice cut in. He was serving as communicator from Vandenberg. "There's been another launch, fifteen minutes ago. From the cosmonaut base at Tyuratam. High-energy boost. Looks like you're going to have company."

Kinsman acknowledged the information, but still sat unmoving.

Finally he saw it hurtling toward him. He came to life. To meet and board the satellite he had to match its orbit and velocity exactly. He was approaching too fast. Radar and computer data flashed in amber flickers across the screens on Kinsman's control panel. His eyes and fingers moved constantly, a well-trained pianist performing a new and tricky sonata. He worked the thruster controls and finally eased his Manta into a rendezvous orbit a few dozen meters from the massive Russian satellite.

The big satellite seemed to hang motionless in space just ahead of him, a huge inert chunk of metal, dazzlingly brilliant where the sun lit its curving flank, totally invisible where it was in shadow. It looked ridiculously like a crescent moon made of flush-welded aluminum. A smaller crescent puzzled Kinsman until he realized it was a rocket nozzle hanging from the satellite's tailcan.

"I'm parked off her stern about fifty meters," he reported into his helmet microphone. "She looks like the complete upper stage of a Proton-class booster. I'm going outside."

"Better make it fast." Smitty's voice was taut, high-pitched with nervousness. "That second spacecraft is closing in fast."

"E.T.A.?"

A pause while voices mumbled in the background. Then, "About twenty minutes . . . maybe less."

"Great."

"Colonel Murdock says you can abort the mission if you feel you have to."

Same to you, pal. Aloud, he replied, "I'm going to take a close look at her. Get inside if I can. Call you back in fifteen minutes, max."

No response. Kinsman smiled to himself at the realization that Colonel Murdock did not see fit to remind him that the Russian satellite might be booby-trapped. Old Mother Murdock hardly forgot about such items. He simply had decided not to make the choice of aborting the mission too attractive.

Gimmicked or not, the satellite was too near and too enticing to turn back now. Kinsman quickly checked out his space suit, pumped the air from his cockpit into the storage tanks, and then popped the hatch over his head.

Out of the womb and into the world.

He climbed out and teetered on the lip of the hatch, coiling the umbilical cord attached to his suit. Murdock and his staff had decided on using an umbilical instead of a bulky backpack and MMU because he was alone in orbit, without backup, and because they wanted Kinsman to be able to slide through the hatch of the Soviet satellite and inspect its interior. They had been confident that Kinsman could bring the Manta close enough to the Russian craft so that an umbilical could keep him supplied with air and electrical power, and provide a safety tether back to his own cockpit.

Kinsman pushed off from the hatch and floated like a coasting underwater swimmer toward the Russian satellite. He glanced down at the night side of Earth. City lights glittered through the clouds; he could make out the shape of the Great Lakes and a distant glow that had to be the Boston-to-Washington corridor.

They're right, he realized. A bomb set off here will black out the whole damned country.

As he approached the satellite the sun rose over the curve of its hull and nearly blinded him, despite the automatic darkening of his visor. He kicked downward and ducked behind the satellite's protective shadow. Still half-blinded by the glare, he bumped into its massive body and rebounded gently. With an effort he reached out and grabbed one of the handgrips studding its surface.

I claim this island for Isabella of Spain. Now where the hell's the hatch?

It was over on the sunlit side, he found after spending several precious minutes searching. It was not difficult to figure out how to open it, even though the instructions were in Cyrillic letters. Kinsman floated head-down and turned the locking mechanism. He felt it click.

For an instant he hesitated. It might be booby-trapped, he heard the Colonel warn.

The hell with it.

Kinsman pulled the hatch open. No explosion, no sound at all. A dim light came from within the satellite. Carefully he slid down inside, trailing the umbilical cord. A trio of faint emergency lights glowed weakly.

"Saving battery power," he muttered to himself.

It took a moment for his eyes to adjust to the dimness. Then he began to appreciate what he saw. The satellite was packed with equipment. He could not make out most of it, but it looked like high-powered scientific gear to him. He opened a few panels and saw capacitor banks, heavy-looking magnetic field coils, neatly stacked electronic replacement parts. A particle accelerator device? he wondered. It was not a laser, of that he was certain.

Up forward was living quarters, room enough for three cosmonauts, maybe four. Compact cabinets holding cans of food. Microwave oven. Freezer stocked with more food. Cameras and recording equipment.

"Very cozy."

He stepped back into the main compartment, where the enigmatic scientific gear was. Take home some souvenirs, he thought, opening cabinets, searching. No documents, no instruction books or paperwork of any kind. He found a small set of hand wrenches and unfastened them from their fixture.

Glancing at his watch, he saw that he had five or ten minutes before the estimated arrival of the second Soviet spacecraft. Holding the wrenches in one hand, Kinsman went forward again and looked through the living compartment for some paperwork he could take back to General Hatch and his intelligence aides. Nothing. A blank computer screen and a keyboard marked with Cyrillic letters and Arabic numerals.

Made in CCCP. He let the wrenches hang in midair and reached for the tiny camera in his leg pouch. Snapping away like a manic vacationer, he took pictures of the entire interior of the spacecraft.

As he tucked the camera back and reached for the wrenches once more, something flickered in the corner of his eye. He turned to the observation port and stared out. Nothing but stars: beautiful, cold.

Then another flash. This time his eye caught and held the slim crescent of another spacecraft gliding toward him. Most of the ship was in deep shadow. He would never have found it without the telltale burst from its thrusters.

She's damned close!

Kinsman gripped his tiny horde of stolen wrenches and headed for the hatch. In his haste he got his foot wrapped in the trailing umbilical cord and nearly went tumbling. He wasted a few seconds righting himself, then reached the satellite's hatch and pushed through it.

He saw the approaching Russian spacecraft make its final

rendezvous maneuver. A flare of its thrusters and it seemed to come to a stop alongside the satellite.

Kinsman ducked across the satellite's hull, swinging hand over hand along the grips until he was crouched in the shadow of its dark side. Waiting there, trying to figure out what to do next, he coiled his umbilical so that it would be less obvious to whoever was inside the new arrival.

The new spacecraft was considerably smaller than the satellite, built along the lines of Kinsman's own delta-winged Manta. Abruptly a hatch popped open. A space-suited figure emerged and hovered dreamlike for a long moment. Kinsman saw the cosmonaut had no umbilical. Instead, he wore bulging packs on his back: life support and maneuvering units.

How many of them are there? he wondered.

A wispy plume of gas jetted from the cosmonaut's backpack as he sailed purposefully over to the satellite's hatch.

Unconsciously Kinsman hunched deeper in the shadows as the Russian approached. Only one of them; no one else had appeared from the spacecraft. The newcomer reached the still-open hatch of the satellite. For several moments he did not move. Kinsman tried every frequency on his suit radio, to no avail. The Russians used different frequencies; they could not talk to one another, could not listen in on each other's chatter.

The cosmonaut edged away from the satellite and, hovering, turned toward Kinsman's Manta, still hanging a scant fifty meters away.

Kinsman felt himself start to sweat, even in the cold darkness. The cosmonaut jetted away from the satellite, toward the Manta.

Dammitall! Kinsman raged at himself. First rule of warfare, you stupid ass: keep your line of retreat open!

He pushed off the satellite and started floating back toward the Manta. It was nightmarish, drifting through space with agonizing slowness while the cosmonaut sped on ahead. The cosmonaut spotted Kinsman as he cleared the shadow of the satellite and emerged into the sunlight.

For a moment they simply stared at each other, separated

by some forty meters of nothingness.

"Get away from that spacecraft!" Kinsman shouted, knowing that their radios were not on the same frequency.

As if to disprove the point, the cosmonaut put a hand on the lip of the Manta's hatch and peered inside. Kinsman flailed his arms and legs trying to raise some speed. Still he moved with hellish slowness. Then he remembered the wrenches he was carrying.

Almost without thinking he tossed the entire handful of them at the cosmonaut. The effort swung him wildly off balance. The Earth slid across his field of vision, then the stars swam by dizzyingly and the Russian satellite. He caught a glimpse of the cosmonaut as the wrenches rained around him. Most of them missed and bounced noiselessly off the Manta's hull. But one banged into the intruder's helmet hard enough to jar him, then rebounded crazily out of sight.

Kinsman lost sight of the Manta as he spun around. Grimly he struggled to straighten himself, using his arms and legs as counterbalances. Finally the stars stopped whirling. He turned and faced the Manta again, but it was upside-down. It did not matter.

The intruder still had one hand on the spacecraft hatch. His free hand was rubbing the spot where the wrench had hit his helmet. He looked ludicrously like a little boy rubbing a bump on his head.

"That means back off, stranger," Kinsman muttered. "No trespassing. U.S. property. Beware of the eagle. Next time I'll crack your helmet in half."

The cosmonaut turned slightly and reached for one of the equipment packs attached to his belt. A weird-looking tool appeared in his hand. Kinsman drifted helplessly and watched the cosmonaut take up a section of his umbilical line. Then he applied the tool to it. Sparks flashed.

Electron torch! He's trying to cut my line! He'll kill me!

Frantically Kinsman began clawing along the long umbilical line hand over hand. All he could see, all he could think of, was that flashing torch eating into his lifeline.

Desperately he grabbed the line in both hands and snapped it hard. Again he tumbled wildly, but he saw the wave created by his snap race down the line. The piece of the cord that the cosmonaut held suddenly bucked out of his hand. The torch spun away and winked off.

Both of them moved at once.

The cosmonaut jetted away from the Manta, going after the torch. Kinsman hurled himself directly toward the hatch. He grasped its rim with both hands, chest heaving, visor fogging slightly from the heat of his exertion and fear.

Duck inside, slam shut, and get the hell out of here.

But he did not move. Instead he watched the cosmonaut, a strange, sun-etched figure now, drifting some twenty meters away, quietly sizing up the situation.

That sonofabitch tried to kill me.

Kinsman coiled catlike on the edge of the hatch and sprang at his enemy. The cosmonaut reached for the jet controls at his belt but Kinsman slammed into him and they both went hurtling through space, tumbling and clawing at each other. It was an unearthly struggle, human fury in the infinite calm of star-studded blackness. No sound except your own harsh breath and the bone-conducted shock of colliding bodies.

They wheeled out of the spacecraft's shadow and into the painful glare of the sun. The glorious beauty of Earth spread out below them. In a cold rage, Kinsman grabbed the airhose that connected the cosmonaut's oxygen tank with his helmet. He hesitated a moment and glanced into the bulbous plastic helmet. All he could see was the back of the cosmonaut's head, covered with a dark skintight flying hood. With a vicious yank Kinsman snapped the airhose out of its mounting. A white spray of gas burst from the backpack. The cosmonaut jerked twice, spasmodically, then went inert.

With a conscious effort Kinsman unclenched his teeth. His jaw ached. He was trembling and soaked in a cold sweat.

He saw his father's face. They'll make a killer out of you! The military exists to kill.

He released his death grip on his enemy. The two human forms drifted slightly apart. The dead cosmonaut turned gently as Kinsman floated alongside. The sun glinted brightly on the white space suit and shone full into the enemy's lifeless, terror-stricken face.

Kinsman looked into that face for an eternally long

moment and felt the life drain out of him. He dragged himself back to the Manta, sealed the hatch, and cracked open the air tanks with automatic, unthinking motions. He flicked on the radio and ignored the flood of interrogating voices that streamed up from the ground.

"Bring me in. Program the AGS to bring me in, full automatic. Just bring me in."

It was six weeks before Kinsman saw Colonel Murdock again. He sat tensely before the wide mahogany desk while Murdock beamed at him, almost as brightly as the sunshine outside the Colonel's office.

"You look thinner in civvies," the Colonel said.

"I've lost weight."

Murdock made a meaningless gesture. "I'm sorry I haven't had a chance to see you sooner. What with the intelligence and State Department people crawling around here the past few weeks, and all the paperwork on your citation and your medical disability leave . . . I haven't had a chance to, eh, congratulate you on your mission. It was a fine piece of work."

Kinsman said nothing.

"General Hatch was very pleased. He recommended you for the Silver Star himself."

"I know."

"You're a hero, Kinsman." There was wonder in the Colonel's girlish voice. "A real honest-to-God hero."

Again Kinsman remained silent.

Murdock suppressed a frown. "The Russians won't make a squawk about it, from what the State Department boys tell me. They're keeping the whole thing hushed up. We made a deal with them. We don't complain about them testing a beam weapon in orbit and they don't complain about losing a cosmonaut."

"We both lose," Kinsman said.

"But you've proved that the Air Force has an important mission to perform in space, by God! The only way we could tell they were cheating on the treaty was to look into their damned satellite. Bet the Congress will change our name to the Aerospace Force now!"

"I committed a murder."

For a long moment Murdock was silent. He drummed his fingers on his desktop. "It's one of those things," he said finally. "It had to be done."

"No, it didn't," Kinsman insisted quietly. "I could have gone back inside the Manta and de-orbited."

"You killed an enemy soldier. You protected your nation's frontier. Sure, you feel rotten now, but you'll get over it."

"You didn't see the face I saw inside that helmet."

Murdock shuffled papers on his desk. "Well . . . okay, it was rough. You're getting a medical furlough out of it when there's really nothing wrong with you. For Chrissakes, what more do you want?"

"I don't know. I've got to take some time to think it over."

"What?" Murdock stared hard at him. "What are you talking about?"

"Read the debriefing report," Kinsman said tiredly.

"It . . . eh, hasn't come down to my level. Too sensitive. But I don't understand what's got you so spooked. You killed an enemy soldier. You ought to be proud . . ."

"Enemy," Kinsman echoed bleakly. "She couldn't have been more than twenty years old."

Murdock's face went slack. "She?"

"That's right," said Kinsman. "She. Your honest-to-God hero murdered a terrified girl. That's something to be proud of, isn't it?"

Age 31

Lieutenant Colonel Marian Campbell drummed her fingers lightly on her desktop. The psychological record of Captain Kinsman lay open before her. Across the desk sat the Captain himself.

She appraised him with a professional eye. Kinsman was lean, dark, rather good-looking in a brooding way. His gray-blue eyes were steady. His hands rested calmly in his lap; long, slim pianist's fingers. No tics, no twitches. He looked almost indifferent to his surroundings. Withdrawn, Colonel Campbell concluded.

"Do you know why you're here?" she asked him.

"I think so," he replied with no hesitation.

Marian leaned back in her chair. She was a big-boned woman who had to remind herself constantly to keep her voice down. She had a natural tendency to talk at people in a parade-ground shout. Not a good attribute for a psychiatrist.

"Tell me," she said, "what you think you're here for."

When she tried to keep her voice soft it came out gravelly, rough. The voice had the power for an opera stage or an ancient amphitheater, despite the fact that its owner was tone-deaf.

Kinsman took a deep breath, like an athlete about to exert himself to the utmost. Or like a man who is bored.

"I've been under psychiatric observation for five months now. Suspended from active duty. Your people have been trying to figure out the effect on me of killing that Russian girl."

Colonel Campbell nodded. "Go on."

"You're the chief of the psychiatric section. I guess my case is in your hands for a final decision."

"That's quite true," she said. "It's up to me to decide

whether you return to active duty or not."

Kinsman regarded her steadily for a moment, then shifted his attention to the window. The blinds were half closed against the burning afternoon sun. For a moment he seemed like a little boy in a stuffy classroom, yearning for the bell that would free him to go outside and play.

"Colonel Murdock wants you permanently removed from duty. He'd like you honorably discharged from the Air Force, except that it might look bad in Washington."

"I'm not surprised," Kinsman said.

"Why not?"

He made a small motion of his shoulders that might have been a shrug. "Murdock would be happy to get rid of me. I'm not his type of marionette." He considered that for a moment, then added, "That's not paranoia. You can check it out with any of the other astronauts."

Marian chuckled. "We already have. You're not paranoid."

"I didn't think so."

"But you do seem to have some problems. I've got to determine if your problems are too big to allow you to fly again."

"That's what I thought."

She did not respond and he did not add anything. They sat looking at each other across the cluttered desk for several moments. Colonel Campbell's office bore the privilege of her rank and station. It was just another one of the starkly functional offices at the Air Force hospital, but a lieutenant colonel who is chief psychiatrist has more latitude in decorating her office than most others. The square little room was festooned with hanging plants. A young rubber tree sprouted in the corner near the window. Instead of a couch, there was a long metal stand bearing exotic tropical flowers.

He's outstaring me, thought Marian Campbell.

"Well," she said at last, "how do you feel about all this? What do you want to do?"

This time his answer was slow in coming. "I don't honestly know. Sometimes I think I ought to get out of the Air Force, accept a medical discharge. But that would take me out of the space program, and that's all I really want."

"To be out of the space program."

"No!" he snapped. "To be *in* it. NASA's sending astronauts to the Moon again. I want to be part of that."

"You want to go to the Moon?"

"Yes."

"To get away from here?"

"As far away as I can," he answered fervently.

She shook her head. "You can't run away from your problems."

Kinsman gave her a look of pitying superiority. "You've never been in orbit, have you?"

"No, of course not."

"Then you don't know. That business about not running away from your problems—it's a slogan. Pure crap. Like telling poor people that money can't buy happiness. You get your feet off the ground, get out of this office and up into a plane where you can be on your own—you'll get away from your problems easily enough."

"I've done my share of flying," she replied. "But you have to come down sometime. You have to return and face things."

"I suppose so." He looked toward the window and the hot Texas afternoon on the other side of the blinds. "You know, I sometimes wonder if some airplane crashes . . . some of the unexplained ones . . . aren't caused by the pilot's unconscious desire to get away from his problems for good."

"Suicide?" She suppressed an impulse to make a note in his file. Do it after he leaves; don't do anything now to break his train of thought.

"Not suicide exactly. Not the desire to die. But . . . well, every now and then a really good pilot wracks up his plane for no apparent reason. Maybe he just didn't want to put his feet back on the ground."

"How do you think you'd feel if you were allowed to fly again?"

His grin was immediate. "Terrific!"

"You wouldn't try to . . . avoid your problems?"

"No." The grin turned into a knowing smile. "I've got a better way to get rid of my problems. That's what the Moon is for."

Colonel Campbell thought, Never-never land.

"That's the one thing I want," Kinsman said. "The one

thing I need. To return to active astronaut status. To get in on the lunar program."

"But that's not an Air Force program," Colonel Campbell said. "The civilians are doing it—NASA and the Russians, isn't it? It's a cooperative program."

Nodding, he answered, "But they're looking for experienced astronauts. The Air Force is letting some of our people work for NASA on detached duty. Friends of mine have already been to the Moon."

He was set up for the tough questions now.

"What do you think your real problem is?" Colonel Campbell asked, letting her voice grow to its normal powerful volume.

Kinsman looked startled for a moment. "I killed that Russian girl . . ." His facial expression went from surprise to pain.

"She tried to kill you, didn't she?"

"Yes."

"You're a military officer. You were on a military mission. The satellite you were inspecting might have had weaponry on it that could have killed millions of people."

"I know that."

"Then why did you become . . ." She reached for the glasses on her desk and perched them on the tip of her nose. Reading from the file, ". . . despondent, withdrawn, hostile to your fellow officers." She looked up at him. "It also says you lost weight and complained of insomnia."

Kinsman hunched forward in his chair, clasped his long-fingered hands together. Looking up at her, he asked, "Have you ever killed someone?"

Marian Campbell moved her head the barest centimeter to indicate *no*.

"Lots of Air Force officers have," Kinsman said. "But at remote distances. You press a button and a machine falls out of the air or a building on the ground explodes. I killed her in hand-to-hand combat. I saw her face."

"You were doing your duty . . ."

"I could have done my duty without killing her!"

"In hindsight."

He ran a hand through his hair. "You ever hear of Richard Bong?"

"Who?"

"I've had the chance to read up on Air Force history quite a lot over the past few months," Kinsman said. "Dick Bong was a fighter pilot in World War Two. In the Pacific. Our top ace. Shot down forty Japanese planes in the first couple of years of the war. All in aerial combat, man-to-man victories, not strafing planes on the ground."

Colonel Campbell regretted that she had not turned on the tape recorder in the bottom drawer of her desk. Too late now, she chided herself.

"His commanding general came over to the island where he was stationed to pin a medal on him. The Japanese pulled an air raid on the base in the middle of the ceremonics. Bong and the general dived into the same slit trench. One of the Jap planes was hit by antiaircraft fire and started to burn. The Japanese pilot didn't have a parachute. Or maybe it just didn't open. Anyway, he jumped out of his burning plane and fell to the airstrip like a rock. He hit the ground just a few feet in front of Bong and the general."

"But what does—"

"Bong never shot down another plane for the rest of the war. He flew combat missions, but he couldn't hit anything with his guns."

"I see," Colonel Campbell said softly. "I understand."

"It makes a difference," said Kinsman. "It's one thing to kill by remote control. It's something else when you see who you've killed, face-to-face."

"And you think that's what's bothering you?"

Kinsman nodded.

"But you can handle it now?" she prompted him.

"As long as I'm not put into combat missions," he answered.

"And the fact that the person you killed was a woman has nothing to do with it?"

Kinsman's jaw dropped open and suddenly he was glaring at her. "How the hell should I know?" he shouted. "How high is up?"

"I don't know, Captain. You tell me."

He turned angrily away from her. There was perspiration beading his brow, Colonel Campbell noticed.

"That's enough for today, Captain. You may go."

She watched him stand up slowly, looking slightly puzzled. He went to the door, hesitated, then opened it and left the office without looking back.

Colonel Campbell opened the bottom drawer of her desk and pulled out the book-sized tape recorder. She turned it on and began speaking into the built-in microphone. After more than fifteen minutes she concluded:

"He's definitely looking for help. That's good. But we're nowhere near his problem yet. We've only scratched the surface. He's built a shell around himself and now not only can no one break through it to get to him, he can't crack it himself to get out. It could be something from his childhood; we'll have to check out the family."

She clicked the recorder's STOP button and turned to look out the window. The hot Texas sky was turning to molten copper as the sun went down. A helicopter droned overhead somewhere, like a lazy summertime dragonfly. The screeching whine of a jet fighter shrilled past.

She turned the tape recorder on again. "One thing is certain," she said. "Killing the cosmonaut was only the triggering trauma. There's more, buried underneath. If it's buried too far down, if we can't get to it quickly, he's finished as an Air Force officer. And as an astronaut."

The breeze whipping across the flight line did little to alleviate the heat. It felt like the breath from a hot oven. The sun beat down like a palpable force, broiling the life juices out of you.

Marian Campbell walked slowly around the plane, checking the control surfaces, the propeller, sweating in her zippered coveralls and waiting for Kinsman to show up. It was a single-engine plane with broad, stubby wings and a high bulbous canopy that made it look like a one-eyed insect. It was painted bright red and yellow except for the engine cowling, where permanent black streaks of oil stains marred the decor.

She saw a tall lithe figure approaching through the shimmering heat haze along the flight line. The sun baked the concrete ramp so that it felt like standing on a griddle. Come on, she groused to herself, before I melt into a puddle. Then she grinned sheepishly. It would be a damned big puddle, she knew.

Kinsman was in civilian clothes, an open-necked short-sleeved shirt and light blue slacks. He looked wary as he came up to the plane.

"No need to salute," Marian called to him. "We're off duty, okay?"

He nodded and put out a hand to touch the plane's wing. The metal must have been scorchingly hot but Kinsman ran his fingers along it lightly and almost smiled.

"Piper Cherokee. She's an old bird, but she still looks good," he said.

"Are you talking about the plane or about me?" Marian asked.

He looked startled more than amused. "The plane, of course, Colonel."

"My name's Marian . . . as in Robin Hood. And yes, I know the joke: 'Who's Maid Marian? Everybody!' "

Kinsman still did not smile.

With an inner sigh, Marian asked, "Do I call you Chet, Chester, or what?"

"Chet."

"Okay, Chet. Let's get upstairs where the air is cooler."

She climbed heavily up onto the wing and squeezed through the cabin hatch. Kinsman followed her and sat in the copilot's seat, on the right. He stuck his foot out to keep the hatch open as Marian gunned the engine to life.

He stayed silent, watching, as she taxied to the very end of the two-mile-long runway. It had been built to accommodate heavy bombers. This puddle-jumper could take off and land along the runway seven times and still have concrete to spare ahead of it.

They got the control tower's clearance, Kinsman dogged the hatch shut, and the little engine buzzed its hardest as they rolled down the runway and lifted into the air.

Marian banked the plane and made a right turn as ordered by the tower controller. They headed away from the Air Force base, across the Texas scrubland.

"Want to see the Alamo?" she asked.

"Sure," said Kinsman.

She asked the controllers for a route to San Antonio.

"Whose plane is this?" Kinsman asked as they climbed to cruising altitude.

"Mine," said Marian.

"Yours? You own it?"

"Sure. You think you jet jocks are the only guys who like to fly? Why do you think I joined the Air Force in the first place?"

He grinned at her. "You like to fly."

"Doesn't everybody?"

She could see him visibly relaxing. They were barely five thousand feet above the ground but already he felt safe and insulated from the pressures below.

"Want to take over for a while?" she asked.

"Sure."

She let go of the controls and Kinsman took the wheel in his hands.

"No aerobatics unless you warn me first," she offered.

"I'm not a stunt flier."

"It's a good thing you're slim," Marian said. "It's usually a pretty tight squeeze in here with most men. I take up more than my fair share of space."

He did not take his eyes off the horizon, but he asked, "Is this supposed to be some form of therapy? I mean, why'd you invite me for this?"

"Because I know you like to fly and I thought you could use some relaxation. We're not just brain-pickers, you know. We're doctors. We're concerned about your overall health."

Kinsman made a small sound that might have been a grunt. "One of your doctors liked to talk to me whenever I tried playing the piano down in the rec hall. Every time I'd sit down to play he'd pop up and start asking me questions. Then he said I was hostile and suspicious."

Marian laughed. "That was Jeffers. He's the idiot on my staff."

They flew for a while and chatted easily enough, but he never got close to anything about his emotional problems. Finally Marian had to dredge the subject up to the surface.

"We had to check back into your family history," she said.

"I know. I got a phone call from a friend."

"Senator McGrath?"

"Yes. He wanted to know if it was okay to talk to you. I told him it was."

"We had a good chat on the telephone."

"What did you find out about me?"

Marian pursed her lips for a moment and considered what she would do if he suddenly decided to dive the plane into the ground.

"He told me about your parents. The conflict with your father. He died while you were stationed in California, didn't he?"

Kinsman nodded. "While I was in orbit, as a matter of fact. I had gone to see him while he was in the hospital, like a dutiful son. He didn't recognize me. Or at least, he didn't admit to recognizing me."

"That's a pity," Marian said.

Very coolly, Kinsman replied, "We didn't see each other very clearly when he was alive and well, you know."

He talked easily enough, seemingly holding nothing back. But it was like a blank wall. All he wanted was to be reassigned to astronaut duty for the lunar missions. Nothing else seemed to matter to him. And yet there was something choking him. Something inside his brain that had put a wall around him, an invisible barrier that cut him off from any real human contact.

"I've been waiting for the zinger," he said, after nearly an hour of talk.

Marian's hands were resting in her lap. "The zinger? What's that?"

He glanced at her. "Aren't you going to ask me if I'm impotent? Jeffers and all your other shrinks did."

Is he asking for help? "I've read your file," Marian answered. "You told them you're not."

"I told them I don't think I am."

"Explain?"

"I've been more or less restricted to quarters for the past five months. Not much of a chance to find out."

"Go on . . ."

"I can get an erection easily enough," Kinsman went on, as clinically cool as if he were reading from a textbook. "I've awoken from my nightmares with a hard-on."

"Nocturnal emissions?" Marian asked.

"Wet dreams? Yeah, a few times."

"Then you're functional."

"The equipment works," he said, still as distant as the horizon. "What bothers me is I haven't felt much like trying. I mean, it's been five *months* and I haven't even felt horny. I haven't even made a pass at any of the nurses."

We know, Colonel Campbell said to herself.

"You're closer to me right now than any woman's been since . . . since . . ."

Suddenly his hands were shaking. The plane, built for amateur pilots, flew onward as steadily as a plow horse.

Marian took over the controls as Kinsman sagged back in his seat.

"Since when?" she prompted.

"You know."

"Tell me."

"Since I murdered that girl in orbit. Since I killed her. I ripped the air line out of her helmet and killed her. Deliberately. I could've backed off. I could've gotten back into my own craft and de-orbited. But I killed her. I murdered her."

"Good," said Marian.

"Good?" He glared at her with pain-filled eyes.

"It's good that you're showing some emotion. You've kept it frozen beneath the surface for too long. You've been acting more like a robot than a human being for the past five months."

Kinsman looked down at his hands. They were still trembling.

"It's all right, Chet. It's all over and done with. There's nothing you can do to bring her back. What you have to decide now is . . . where do you want to go from here?"

He pressed his hands palms-down on his thighs. "What did Richard the Third say? 'Let's to it, pell-mell. If not to heaven, then hand in hand to hell.'"

Marian gave an unladylike snort. "Neither one," she said, pointing off to her left. "It's only San Antonio."

The Alamo is the heart of San Antonio, but the four corners of the city are held by military bases. Colonel Campbell landed her plane at Kelly Air Force Base and they commandeered a synfueled gray sedan from the motor pool to go to town.

GENTLEMEN WILL TAKE OFF THEIR HATS, read the sign above the Alamo's front entrance. Marian saw that most of the visitors crowding the old shrine this muggy late afternoon were either Mexicans or Mexican-Americans. The signs on the displays spoke of the great American triumph that won Texas its independence. But it was only a temporary triumph, Marian saw. The erstwhile losers of the Mexican-American battle were winning the war over the long haul, simply outbreeding the gringos and reclaiming the territory they had temporarily lost.

Outside, in the shade cast by the graceful trees beyond the old mission's battered walls, Kinsman suddenly asked, "May I take you to dinner?"

Marian felt pleased. "It's been some time since a young man has invited me to dinner."

He grinned at her. "Maybe you can help me with my problem."

Her cheeks went hot and she cursed herself for an idiot. He's joking with you, she told herself sternly. You're old enough to be his . . . well, his big sister, anyway.

"You are qualified for I.F.R., aren't you?" Kinsman asked, suddenly serious again. "No problem if we stay out after dark."

Marian nodded. "I'd feel a lot safer, though, if you made the instrument landing. I don't like landing at night."

"Okay," he said. "So let's find some dinner. My treat."

They found a dinner theater in one of the hotels along the scenic riverway park. The ballroom floor was covered with small round tables jammed so close together that chairbacks touched each other whenever someone wanted to get up. Marian wrinkled her nose. This was too much like New York or Chicago. Where was the Old West, where cattle barons dined in the regal splendor of ornately paneled restaurants with high ceilings and crystal chandeliers?

The tiny stage set up at one end of the ballroom was for a revival of a show featuring songs written by a Parisian café entertainer named Jacques Brel. Only two men and two women, in street clothes. The management did not spend lavishly on the entertainment, Marian thought. But the singers were excellent and the songs highly charged, emotional, theatrical, pointed.

Marian began watching Kinsman in the darkened ballroom as the singers hit antiwar themes again and again. He sat calmly, laughed at the right places, applauded along with everyone else. Until a song titled "Next."

He sat straighter in his chair as the theme of the song became clear: a young European soldier being marched along with his comrades into a mobile army whorehouse, "gift of the army, free of course." Marian felt her eyes burning brighter than the stage lights as she watched Kinsman's face freeze in something very close to horror.

His hand slowly reached out toward her and she grasped it tightly. He hung on as the lead male sang:

> "All the naked and the dead
>   Should hold each other's hands
>   As they watch me scream at night
>   In a dream no one understands."

The song ended and Kinsman released her hand. When the show finally finished and the ceiling lights came on once more, he avoided looking directly at Marian. He seemed embarrassed, more than a little.

They drove back to Kelly through the muggy hot night in silence. Marian was content to wait until they were airborne again before trying to open him up. He talked better off the ground; he seemed more relaxed up there. They checked the car back into the motor pool and allowed a sleepy-eyed corporal to drive them in a jeep to the flight line.

Kinsman hopped up on the Cherokee's wing and pulled the hatch open, ducked inside, and took the pilot's seat. Then he helped Marian settle her bulk in the right-hand seat. He checked the control panel's gauges carefully, got his clearance from the tower controller, and taxied out to the runway. The edge lights stretched like glowing pearls, seemingly off to the horizon.

As he waited for final takeoff clearance he revved the engine. The whole plane shuddered and strained like an excited terrier being held in check by a leash. Somehow the engine roar seemed louder in the darkness to Marian. And then they were racing down the runway and up into the air. Kinsman handled the plane smoothly, his hands sure and steady. As they climbed to cruising altitude Marian saw a sky full of stars above them and the even more numerous lights of San Antonio below.

"One of the best Mexican restaurants this side of the Rio Grande is down there," she said, over the drone of the engine.

"Really?" Kinsman replied.

Marian nodded vigorously. "Too bad we missed it."

"Yeah. The food we had wasn't all that good, was it?"

"But I enjoyed the show."

Kinsman might have nodded in the darkness. She could not tell.

"How did you like it?" she asked.

"The show?"

"Yes."

Suddenly he started laughing, a soft, happy, satisfied chuckle.

Puzzled, Marian asked, "What's funny?"

"You are."

"I'm *funny*?" She did not know whether to be glad or angry.

"No, not you yourself," Kinsman corrected. "It's the situation that's funny. The relationship between us."

He turned to their homeward course, changed the frequency on the radio for the mid-route controller, then turned in his seat toward her.

"Look," he said, "you know damned well that something clicked in my head during the show, when I grabbed for your hand. And I know you know. But you're trying to lead up to the subject subtly, to see if you can get me to talk about it."

"What clicked?" Marian felt eager, as if she were a hunter close to her quarry.

"During that song I finally realized what the hell has been bothering me."

"Yes?"

"They got to me," he said flatly.

Marian felt her eyebrows rise. "They got to you? Who . . . ?"

Kinsman said, "All these years I've been telling myself

133

that I'm my own man. I joined the Air Force to get into space, to get away from all the ugliness of Earth. But I didn't escape it. I couldn't."

"You brought the ugliness along with you."

"Yeah." He was silent for a long moment. "I murdered that cosmonaut. Maybe if she had been a man I wouldn't feel so badly about it. But the thing is—they got to me."

"Who?" Marian demanded.

"The Air Force," he said. "The training. The military mind-set."

"I don't understand."

Gesturing with one hand in the cramped cabin, Kinsman said, "Look, when I joined the Air Force it was strictly to be an astronaut. Sure, they put me through the same training everybody gets and even made me fly combat in Cyprus. But I never fired a gun or a missile. Never."

"So?"

"So once I got into the astronaut program I thought I had it made. I had what I wanted. The Air Force hadn't gotten to me. Their training hadn't turned me into a military machine. I was my own man."

Marian began to feel the inner tingle she always got when a puzzle became clear to her.

"But I was wrong," Kinsman went on. His voice was serious now, but not somber. Not morose or wooden. "When I got into a combat situation—hand-to-hand fight, yet—all that military training took over. I wasn't an astronaut anymore. I was a fighting machine. A trained killer. A military automaton. I killed her just the way an infantryman becomes conditioned to sticking a bayonet into another human being's belly."

"And you think that's what's been bothering you?" Marian asked, as softly as she knew how.

"For the past five months I've been trying to figure it out. How could I have done it? How in the hell could I have deliberately ripped out a human being's air line? How could I willingly kill somebody?"

"And now you have the answer."

"Yes." It was an unshakably firm response. "I'm not as smart as I thought I was. The military training got to me. God knows, put me in the same situation and I might even do the same thing all over again."

"Chet, listen to me very carefully," Marian said slowly. "You *think* you have the answer and you're feeling pretty good about it . . ."

"Damned right!"

"But what you have is only the beginning of the answer. There's still a lot more, buried down inside you. A lot that you haven't brought up into the light yet."

He shook his head. "I don't think so."

"Listen to me!" Marian urged. "You've kept a shell around yourself all your life. Your Quaker upbringing. Your conflict with your father. Your Air Force duties. The one time you let go, the one time you let your emotions override your self-control, you kill a person. A woman. A girl. Now you've clamped that self-control down again and made your shell thicker than ever. You've isolated yourself from any real human contact . . ."

As if none of her words had penetrated his awareness, Kinsman said, "If you keep me off-duty, under observation, for much longer, Murdock's going to drum me out. You know that."

"I can protect you."

"You can't keep me proficient. He can drop me from the astronaut corps—for good."

"Yes," she admitted. "That's true."

"What I need now is to get back to active duty. But not with the Air Force. I want to get into NASA's lunar exploration program."

"You want to run off to the Moon?"

"It's not running away. I know better now. I know myself better."

"Well enough to risk your life, and the lives of others?"

He grinned at her. She could see his teeth in the faint light from the instrument panel. "You're trusting me with your life right now, aren't you?"

Almost ruefully she admitted, "I suppose I am."

"Just tell it to Murdock."

The next morning Lieutenant Colonel Marian Campbell was back in uniform, back in her office, sitting behind her desk. Colonel Murdock's round, bald face looked distinctly unhappy, even in the small screen of the telephone display.

"Just what are you trying to tell me, Colonel Campbell?" he asked testily.

She took a deep breath, then replied, "In my opinion, Colonel, Captain Kinsman is now fit to resume his duties."

"Resume . . . ? But I thought he was psychologically, er, well . . . unbalanced."

"He was troubled by what happened to him on his last mission, of course. Anyone would be. But in my opinion, he's worked through those troubles and he's ready to go back to active duty."

Murdock's face wrinkled with suspicion. "I don't get it. For five months you shrinks have been working him over without a word of progress. Now all of a sudden you say he's okay?"

Feeling almost as if she should cross her fingers, Marian Campbell answered, "It happens that way sometimes. He's gained the insight he needed to understand what happened to him. He's adjusted to it. He's fit for duty."

"Not under me," Murdock said fervently. "I'm going to transfer him out of here just as soon as he comes marching through my door."

"You can't do that!"

Murdock looked startled. Her voice had boomed.

"I mean," Marian said, trying to tone it down, "that I would recommend he be allowed to continue in the astronaut program. It's what he's trained for and what he enjoys doing."

"That doesn't mean—"

She overrode him. "I understand there's a shortage of trained personnel with his qualifications. It would be against Air Force policy to waste a man of his training and experience in a different slot."

"If he's psychologically fit for such duty," Murdock retorted.

"He is," Marian said.

The Colonel gave her a shrewd stare. It seemed almost ludicrous, his face was so tiny on the phone screen. But still it sent a shiver of apprehension along Marian's spine.

"You are guaranteeing that he's mentally sound?" Murdock asked.

Marian Campbell stiffened her back. "There are no guarantees in the medical profession, Colonel. But I will personally draft the report on Captain Kinsman, recommending that he be returned to the duties for which he has been trained."

"That ties my hands if I want to transfer him."

"Unless you transfer him to the NASA program," Marian blurted.

Murdock's face took on a knowing leer. "So that's how he worked out his emotional problem. Twisted you around his little finger, didn't he?"

Just to wipe the smirk off his face, Marian made herself smile and say, "It wasn't his *little* finger, Colonel."

Murdock's face flamed red. He snapped, "Well, then write your report and make your recommendation! I'll handle my own problems my own way." He cut the connection and the phone screen went blank.

Marian leaned back in her chair. Well, old gal, now you've got a reputation for screwing around with your patients. She almost wished it were true.

She hauled the tape recorder out of its drawer and started to dictate her final report on Kinsman. But in the back of her mind she was thinking, What else can you do? Keep him here? That will kill him just as surely as cutting off his oxygen. You've got to let him go.

Over the faint hum of the air-conditioning she thought she heard distant piano music. From the recreation hall. A light, happy piece of Mozart. She listened for several minutes. No one interrupted the pianist.

So now he can go to the Moon. Maybe he'll find what he needs there. But he won't. He's locked up inside himself. If you let him go, he'll never break free. He'll carry that shell around him forever. You know that. You know it and you're letting him go. He's going to kill himself, one way or the other. Himself, and maybe others besides. And you're letting him go out and do it because you're too weak to keep him here and watch him die one day at a time.

She turned on the tape recorder and watched the cassette slowly turning as she fought back an urge to cry.

Age 32

"ANY WORD FROM him yet?"

"Huh? No, nothing."

Kinsman swore to himself as he stood on the open platform of the little lunar rocket jumper. It was his second trip to the Moon and it was not going well.

"Say, where are you now?" Bok's voice sounded gritty with static in Kinsman's helmet earphones.

"Up on the rim. He must've gone inside the damned crater."

"The rim? How'd you get . . ."

"Found a flat spot for the jumper. Don't think I walked this far, do you? I'm not as nutty as the priest."

"But you're supposed to stay down here on the plain! The crater's off-limits."

"Tell that to our holy friar. He's the one who marched up here. I'm just following the seismic rigs he's been planting every three, four klicks."

He could sense Bok shaking his head. "Kinsman, if there are twenty officially approved ways to do a job, I swear you'll pick the twenty-second."

"If the first twenty-one are lousy."

"Mission control is going to be damned upset with you. You won't get off with just a reprimand this time."

"I suppose mission control would prefer that we just let the priest stay lost."

"You're not going inside the crater, are you?" Bok's voice edged up half an octave. "It's too risky."

Kinsman almost laughed. "You think sitting inside that aluminum casket you're in is *safe*?"

The earphones went silent. With a sigh, Kinsman wished for the tenth time that hour that he could scratch his

138

twelve-day-old beard. Get zipped into the suit and the itches start. He did not need a mirror to know that his face was haggard, sleepless, his black beard mean-looking.

He stepped down from the jumper—a rocket motor with a railed platform and some equipment on it, nothing more —and planted his boots on the solid rock of the ringwall's crest. With a twist of his shoulders to settle the weight of his bulky backpack he shambled over to the packet of seismic instruments and the fluorescent marker that the priest had left there.

"He came right up to the top and now he's off on the yellow brick road, playing Moon explorer. Stupid bastard."

Did you really think you'd leave human stupidity behind you? a voice in his head asked. Or human guilt?

Reluctantly he looked into the crater. The brutally short horizon cut across the middle of its floor, but the central peak stuck its worn head up among the solemn stars. Beyond it there was nothing but dizzying blackness, an abrupt end to the solid world and the beginning of infinity.

Damn the priest! God's gift to geology. And I've got to play guardian angel for him.

Kinsman turned back and looked outward from the crater rim. He could see the lighted radio mast and squat return rocket, far below on the plain. He even convinced himself that he saw the mound of rubble marking their buried base shelter, where Bok lay curled safely in his bunk. The Russian base was far over the horizon, almost on the other side of the Mare Nubium. He could talk to the Russians by bouncing a signal off one of the commsats orbiting the Moon. But what good would that do? They were much farther away from the wandering priest than he was.

"Any sign of him?" Bok's voice asked.

"Sure," Kinsman retorted. "He left me a big map with an X to mark the treasure."

"Don't get sore at me!"

"Why not? You're sitting inside. I've got to find our fearless geologist."

"Regulations say one man's got to remain in the base at all times."

But not the *same* one man, Kinsman replied silently.

"Anyway," Bok went on, "he's still got a few hours'

oxygen left. Let him putter around inside the crater for a while. He'll come back under his own power."

"Not before his air runs out. Besides, he's officially missing. Missed his last two check-in calls. Houston knows it, by now. My assignment is to scout his last known position. Another of those sweet regs."

Silence again. Bok did not like being alone in the Base, Kinsman knew.

"Why don't you come on back in," the astronomer's voice said at last, "until he calls in. Then you can go out again and get him with the jumper. You'll be running out of air yourself before you can find him in the crater."

"I've got to try."

"You can't make up the rules as you go along, Kinsman! This isn't the Air Force; you're not a hotshot jet jockey anymore. NASA has rules, regulations. They'll ground you if you don't follow their game plan."

"Maybe."

"You don't even like the priest!" Bok was almost shouting now, the fear-induced anger making his voice shrill, ugly. "You've been tripping all over yourself to stay clear of him whenever you're both inside the base."

Kinsman felt his jaw clench. So it shows. If you're not careful you'll tip them both off.

Aloud, he replied, "I'm going to look around. Give me an hour. Call Houston and give them a complete report; all they've got so far is a gap in the automatic record where the priest's last two check-ins ought to be. And stay inside the shelter until I come back." Or until a relief crew arrives, he added silently.

"You're wasting your time. And taking unnecessary risks. They'll ground you for sure."

"Wish me luck," Kinsman said.

A delay. Then, "Luck. I'll sit tight here."

Despite himself, Kinsman grinned. I know damned well you'll sit tight there. Some survey team. One goes over the hill and the other stays in his bunk for two weeks straight.

He gazed out at the bleak landscape surrounded by starry emptiness. Something caught in his memory.

"They can't scare me with their empty spaces," he

muttered to himself. There was more to the verse but he could not recall it.

"Can't scare me," he repeated softly, shuffling to the inner rim of the crater's ringwall. He walked very deliberately, like a tired old man, and tried to see from inside his bulbous helmet exactly where he was placing his feet.

The barren slopes fell away in gently terraced steps until, many kilometers below, they melted into the cracked and pockmarked crater floor. Looks easy . . . too easy. Like the steps to hell. With a shrug that was weighted down by the lunar suit's backpack, Kinsman started to descend into the crater.

He picked his way across the gravelly terraces and crawled feet-first down the breaks between them. The bare rocks were slippery and sometimes sharp. Kinsman went slowly, step by careful step, trying to make certain that he did not tear the metallic fabric of his suit. His world was cut off now and circled by the dark rocks. Inside the vast crater he was cut off from the direct radio link with Bok; in the shadow of these terraced rock walls, he could not even make contact with the communications satellites orbiting over the Moon's equator. The only sounds were the creaking of the suit's joints, the electrical hum of the pump that circulated water through its inner lining, the faint wheeze of the helmet air blower. And his own heavy breathing. Alone, all alone. A solitary microcosm. One living creature in the universe.

They cannot scare me with their empty spaces.

Between stars—on stars where no human race is. There was still more to it: the tag line that he could not remember.

Finally he had to stop. The suit was heating up too much from his exertion. He took a marker beacon from the backpack and planted it on the broken ground. The Moon's gray rocks, churned by eons of infalling micrometeors and whipped into a frozen froth, had an unfinished look about them, as if somebody had been blacktopping the place but stopped before he could apply the final smoothing touches.

From a pouch on his belt Kinsman took a small spool of wire. Plugging one end into the radio outlet on his helmet, he held the spool at arm's length and released its catch. He could not see it in this dim light, but he felt the spool's spring fire the antenna wire high and out into the crater.

"Father Lemoyne," he called as the antenna drifted slowly in the Moon's gentle gravity. "Father Lemoyne, can you hear me?"

No answer.

Down another flight, Kinsman told himself.

After two more stops and nearly an hour of sweaty descent, Kinsman got his answer.

"Here . . ." a weak voice responded. "I'm here . . ."

"Where?" Kinsman snapped, every sense alert, all fatigue forgotten. "Do something. Make a light."

". . . can't . . ." The voice faded out.

Kinsman reeled in the antenna and fired it out again. "Where in hell are you?"

A cough, with pain behind it. "Shouldn't have done it. Disobeyed. And no water, nothing . . ."

Great! Kinsman raged. He's either hysterical or delirious. Or both.

After firing the spool antenna a third time, Kinsman flicked on the lamp atop his helmet and looked at the radio direction-finder dial on his forearm. The priest had his suit radio open and the carrier beam was coming through even though he was no longer talking. The gauges alongside the radio-finder reminded Kinsman that he was about halfway down on his oxygen. More than an hour had elapsed since he had last spoken to Bok.

"I'm trying to zero in on you," Kinsman called. "Are you hurt? Can you—"

"Don't, don't, don't. I disobeyed and now I've got to pay for it. Don't trap yourself, too . . ." The heavy reproachful voice lapsed into a mumble that Kinsman could not understand.

Trapped. Kinsman could picture it. The priest was using a canister suit, a one-man walking cabin, a big, plexidomed, rigid metal can with flexible arms and legs sticking out of it. A man could live for days inside it, but it was too clumsy for climbing. Which is why the crater was off-limits.

He must've fallen and now he's stuck, like a goddamned turtle on its back.

"The sin of pride," he heard the priest babbling. "God forgive us our pride. I wanted to find water; the greatest discovery a man can make on the Moon. . . . Pride, nothing but pride . . ."

Kinsman walked slowly, shifting his eyes from the direction-finder to the roiled, pockmarked ground underfoot. He jumped across a two-meter drop between terraces. The finder's needle snapped to zero.

"Your radio still on?"

"No use . . . go back . . ."

The needle stayed fixed. *Either I broke it or I'm right on top of him.*

He turned a full circle, slowly scanning the rough ground as far as his light could reach. No sign of the canister. Kinsman stepped to the terrace edge. Kneeling with deliberate care, so that his backpack would not unbalance him and send him sprawling down the tumbled rocks, he peered over.

In a zigzag fissure a few meters below him was the priest, a giant armored insect gleaming white in the glare of the lamp, feebly waving with one free arm.

"Can you get up?" Kinsman saw that all the weight of the cumbersome suit was on the pinned arm. *Banged up his backpack, too.*

"Trying to find the secrets of God's creation . . . storming heaven with rockets. . . . We say we're seeking knowledge but we're really after our own glory . . ."

Kinsman frowned. He could not see the older man's face behind the canister's heavily tinted visor. Just as he could not see the face of the cosmonaut, years ago.

"I'll have to bring the jumper down here."

The priest rambled on, coughing spasmodically. Kinsman got to his feet.

"Pride leads to death," he heard in his earphones. "You know that, Kinsman. It's pride that makes us murderers."

The shock boggled Kinsman's knees. He turned, shaking. "What . . . did you say?"

"I know you, Kinsman. Anger and pride. Destroy not my soul with men of blood . . . whose right hands are . . . are . . ."

Kinsman ran. He fought back toward the crater rim, storming the terraces blindly, scrabbling up the inclines with four-meter-high jumps. Twice he had to turn up the air blower in his helmet to clear the sweaty fog from his faceplate. He did not dare to stop. He raced on, breath racking his lungs, heart pounding until he could hear nothing else.

Finally he reached the crest. Collapsing on the deck of the jumper, he forced himself to breathe normally again, forced himself to sound normal as he called Bok.

The astronomer listened and then said guardedly, "It sounds like he's dying."

"I think his regenerator's shot. His air must be pretty foul by now."

"No sense going back for him."

Kinsman hesitated. "Maybe I can get the jumper close enough to him." But his mind was screaming at him, The priest found out about me!

"You'll never get him back here in time," Bok was saying. "And you're not supposed to take the jumper near the crater, let alone inside it. It's too risky."

"You want to just let him die?" He's hysterical. If he babbles about me where Bok can hear it . . . Christ, it'll be piped straight back to Houston, automatically!

"Listen," the astronomer said, his voice rising again. "You can't leave me stuck here with both of you gone! I know the regulations, Kinsman. You're not allowed to risk yourself or the third man in the team in an effort to help a man in trouble. Those are the rules!"

"I know. I know." You've already killed one human being. Are you going to let another one die because of it? Where does it end, Kinsman? Where does it end?

"You don't have enough oxygen in your suit to get down there and back again," Bok insisted. "I've been calculating—"

"I can tap the jumper's propellant tank."

"But that's crazy! You'll get yourself stranded!"

"Maybe." If NASA finds out about it they'll bounce me straight back to the Air Force. Back to Murdock.

"You're going to kill yourself over that priest! And you'll be killing me, too!"

"He's probably dead by now," Kinsman said, as much to himself as to Bok. "I'll just place a marker down there so another crew can get him out when the time comes. I won't be long."

"I'm calling Houston," said the astronomer. "You can't make a move until mission control okays it."

"By then he'll be dead for sure."

"But the regulations . . ."

"Were written Earthside," Kinsman snapped. "The brass never planned on anything like this. I've got to go back, just to make sure."

"Kinsman, if you go . . ."

"I'm gone," he said. Then he turned off his suit radio.

He flew the jumper back down the crater's inner slope, leaning over the platform railing to see his marker beacons while listening to their radio peeps. In a few minutes he eased the spraddle-legged platform down on the last terrace before the helpless priest, kicking up a small spray of dust with the rockets.

"Father Lemoyne."

Kinsman stepped off the jumper and made it to the edge of the fissure in two lunar strides. The white shell was inert, the lone arm unmoving.

"Father Lemoyne!"

Kinsman held his breath, listening. Nothing . . . wait . . . the faintest, faintest breathing. More like gasping. Quick, shallow, desperate.

"You're dead," Kinsman heard himself mutter. "Give it up. You're finished. Even if I got you out of here you'd be dead before I could get you back to the base."

The priest's faceplate was opaque to him. He saw only the reflected spot of his own helmet lamp. But his mind filled with the shocked face he had seen in that other visor, the horrified expression when she realized that she was dead.

Kinsman looked away, out at the too-close horizon and the uncompromising stars beyond. Then he remembered the rest of it.

They cannot scare me with their empty spaces
Between stars—on stars where no human race is.
I have it in me so much nearer home
To scare myself with my own desert places.

Like an automaton he turned back to the jumper. His mind was a blank now. Without thought, without even feeling, he rigged a line from the jumper's tiny winch to the metal lugs in the canister suit's chest. Then he took apart the platform railing and wedged three rejoined sections into the fissure above the fallen man, to form a hoisting lever arm. Looping the line over the spindly metal arm, he started the winch.

He climbed down into the fissure as the winch silently took up the slack in the line, and set himself as solidly as he could on the bare, scoured-smooth rock. Grabbing the priest's armored shoulders, he guided the oversized canister up from the crevice while the winch strained steadily.

The railing arm gave way when the priest was only partway up and Kinsman felt the full weight of the monstrous suit crush down on him. He sank to his knees, gritting his teeth to keep from crying out.

Then the winch took up the slack. Grunting, fumbling, pushing, Kinsman scrabbled up the rocky slope with his arms wrapped halfway around the big canister's middle. He let the winch drag them both to the jumper's edge, then reached out and shut off the motor.

With only a hard breath's pause Kinsman snapped down the suit's supporting legs so the priest could stand upright even though unconscious. Then he clambered onto the jumper's platform and took the oxygen line from the rocket tankage. Kneeling at the bulbous suit's shoulders, he plugged the line into its emergency air tank.

The older man coughed once. That was all.

Kinsman leaned back on his heels. His faceplate was fogging over again, or was it fatigue blurring his vision? The regenerator was hopelessly smashed, he saw. The old bird must've been breathing his own juices. Once the emergency tank registered full, he disconnected the oxygen line and plugged it into a special fitting below the regenerator.

"If you're already dead, this is probably going to kill me, too," Kinsman said. He purged the entire suit, forcing the contaminated fumes out and replacing them with oxygen that the jumper's rocket motor needed to get them back to the base.

He was close enough now to see through the canister's tinted visor. The priest's face was grizzled, eyes closed. His usual maddening little smile was gone; his mouth hung open slackly.

Kinsman hauled him up onto the railless platform and strapped him down to the deck. He saw himself, for an absurd moment, as Frankenstein's assistant, strapping the giant monster to the operating table. Then he turned to the control podium and inched the throttle forward just enough to give them the barest minimum of lift. Steady, Igor, he said to himself. We can't use full power now.

The jumper almost made it to the crest before its rocket motor died and bumped them gently onto one of the terraces. There was a small emergency tank of oxygen that could have carried them a little farther, but Kinsman knew that he and the priest would need it for breathing.

"Wonder how many Jesuits have been carried home on their shields?" he asked himself as he unbolted the section of decking that the priest was lying on. By threading the winch line through the bolt holes he made an improvised sled, which he carefully lowered to the ground. Then he took the emergency oxygen tank and strapped it to the deck section also.

Kinsman wrapped the line around his fists, put his shoulder under it, and leaned against the burden. Even in the Moon's light gravity it was like trying to haul a truck.

"Down to less than one horsepower," he grunted, straining forward.

For once he was glad that the scoured rocks had been smoothed by micrometeors. He would climb a few steps, wedge himself as firmly as he could, then drag the sled to him. It took a painful half-hour to reach the ringwall crest.

He could see the base again, tiny and remote as a dream. "All downhill from here," he mumbled.

He thought he heard a groan.

"That's it," he said, pushing the sled over the crest, down the gentle outward slope. "That's it. Stay with it. Don't you die on me. Don't you put me through all of this for nothing!"

"Kinsman!" Bok's voice. "Are you all right?"

The sled skidded against a meter-high rock. Scrambling after it, Kinsman answered, "I'm bringing him in. Just shut up and leave us alone. I think he's alive."

"Houston says no," Bok answered, his voice strangely calm. "They've calculated that his air went bad on him. He can't possibly be alive. You are ordered to leave him and return to base shelter. Ordered, Kinsman."

"Tell Houston they're wrong. He's still alive. Now stop wasting my breath."

Pull the sled free. Push it to get it started downhill again. Strain to hold it back. Don't let it get away from you. Haul it out of the damned craterlets. Watch your step, don't fall.

"Too damned much uphill . . . in this downhill."

Once he sprawled flat and knocked his helmet against the edge of the sled. He must have blacked out for a moment. Weakly, he dragged himself to the oxygen tank and refilled his suit's supply. Then he checked the priest's suit and topped off its tank.

"Can't do that again," he said to the silent priest. "Don't know if we'll make it. Maybe we can. If neither one of us has sprung a leak. Maybe . . ."

Time slid away from him. The past and future disappeared into an endless now, a forever of pain and struggle, with the heat of his toil welling up to drench him in his suit.

"Why don't you say something?" Kinsman panted at the priest. "You can't die. Understand me? You can't die! I've got to explain it to you. I didn't mean to kill her. I didn't even know she was a girl. You can't tell, can't see a face until you're too close. She must've been just as scared as I was. She tried to kill me. How'd I know their cosmonaut was just a scared kid? When I saw her face it was too late. But I didn't know. I didn't know . . ."

They reached the foot of the ringwall and Kinsman dropped to his knees. "Couple more klicks now. Straightaway. Only a couple more . . . kilometers."

His vision blurred and something in his head was buzzing angrily. Staggering to his feet, he lifted the line over his shoulder and slogged ahead. He could just make out the lighted top of the base's radio mast.

"Leave him, Kinsman!" Bok's voice pleaded from somewhere. "You can't make it unless you leave him!"

"Shut . . . up."

One step after another. Don't think, don't count. Blank your mind. Be a mindless plow horse. Plod along. One step at a time. Steer for the radio mast. Just a few . . . more . . . klicks.

"Don't die on me, priest! Don't you . . . die on me! You're my penance, priest. My ticket back. Don't die on me . . . don't die . . ."

It all went dark. First in spots, then totally. Kinsman caught a glimpse of the barren landscape tilting weirdly, then the grave stars slid across his view, then darkness.

"I tried," he heard himself say in a far, far distant voice. "I tried."

For a moment or two he felt himself falling, dropping effortlessly into blackness. Then even that sensation died and he felt nothing at all.

A faint vibration buzzed at him.

The darkness started to shift, turn gray at the edges. Kinsman opened his eyes and saw the low curved ceiling of the underground base. The hum was the electrical generator that lit and warmed and brought good air into their tight little shelter.

"You okay?" Bok leaned over him. His chubby face was frowning worriedly.

Kinsman nodded weakly.

"Father Lemoyne's going to pull through," Bok said, stepping out of the cramped space between the two bunks. The priest was awake but unmoving, his eyes staring blankly upward. His canister suit had been removed and one arm was covered with a plastic cast.

Bok explained, "I've been getting instructions from the medics in Houston. They contacted the Russians. A paramedic's coming over from their base. Should be here in an hour. Lemoyne's in shock and his right arm's broken, but otherwise he seems pretty good. Exhausted, but no permanent damage."

Kinsman pulled himself up to a sitting position on the bunk and leaned his back against the curving wall. His helmets and boots were off, but he was still wearing the rest of his lunar suit.

"You went out and got us," he realized.

Bok nodded. "You were less than a kilometer away. I could hear you on the radio, babbling away. Then you stopped talking. I had to go out."

"You saved my life."

"And you saved the priest's."

Kinsman stopped for a moment, remembering. "I did a lot of raving out there, didn't I?"

Bok wormed his shoulders uncomfortably. "Sort of. It's, uh . . . well, at least the Russians didn't pick up any of it."

"But Houston did."

"It was relayed automatically. Emergency procedure. You know . . . it's the rules."

That's it, Kinsman said to himself. Now they know.

"They, uh . . ." Bok looked away. "They're sending a relief crew to fly us back."

"They don't trust me to pilot the return rocket."

"After what you've been through?"

That's the end of it. NASA won't want any neurotic Air Force killers on their payroll. It would ruin their cooperative programs with the Russians.

"You haven't heard the best of it, though," Bok said, eager to change the subject. He went over to the shelf at the end of the priest's bunk and took a small plastic bottle. "Look at this."

Kinsman took the stoppered bottle in his hands. Inside it, a small sliver of ice floated on water.

"It was stuck in the cleats of his boots."

"Father Lemoyne's?"

"Right. It's really water! Tests out okay and I even snuck a taste of it. It's real water, all right."

"It must have been down in that fissure, after all," Kinsman said. "He found it without knowing it. He'll get into all the history books now." And he'll have to watch his pride even more.

Bok sat on the shelter's only chair. "Chet . . . about what you were saying out there . . ."

Kinsman expected tension, but instead he felt only numb. "I know. They heard it in Houston."

"I'm sure they'll try to keep it quiet."

Kinsman heard himself replying calmly, "They can't keep the lid on something that big. Somebody will leak it. At the very least it means I'm finished with NASA."

"We'd all heard rumors about an Air Force astronaut

killing a Russian during a military mission. But I never thought . . . I mean . . ."

"The priest figured it out. Or he guessed it."

"It must've been rough on you," Bok said.

Kinsman shrugged. "Not as rough as what happened to her."

"I'm . . . sorry." Bok's voice trailed off helplessly.

"It doesn't matter."

Surprised, Kinsman realized that he meant it. He sat upright. "It doesn't matter anymore. They can do whatever they want to. I can handle it. Even if they ground me and throw me to the media wolves, I think I can take it. I did it and it's over with and I can take whatever I have to take."

Father Lemoyne's free arm moved slightly. "It's all right," he whispered hoarsely. "It's all right."

The priest turned his face toward Kinsman. His gaze moved from the astronaut's eyes to the plastic bottle in Kinsman's hands. "It's all right," he repeated, smiling weakly. "It's not hell we're in. It's purgatory. We'll get through. We'll make it all right."

Then he closed his eyes and relaxed into sleep. But his smile remained, strangely gentle in that bearded, haggard face; ready to meet the world or eternity.

Age 33

IT LOOKED LIKE a perfectly reasonable bar to Kinsman. No, he corrected himself. A perfectly reasonable pub.

The booths along the back wall were empty. A couple of middle-aged men were conversing quietly as they stood at the bar itself with pints of light Australian lager in their hands. The bartender was a beefy, red-faced Aussie. Only the ceiling of raw rock broke the illusion that they were up on the surface in an ordinary Australian city.

Kinsman ordered a scotch and walked slowly with it to the last booth, where his back would be to the rock wall and he could see the entire pub. Tiredly he wondered when the British Commonwealth was going to discover the joys of ice cubes. Half a tumbler of good whisky and just two thumbnail-sized dollops of ice that immediately melted away and left the scotch lukewarm.

Like the Wicked Witch of the West, he thought. Melting, melting. Like me.

Kinsman glanced at his wristwatch. The dedication ceremonies should soon be over. The pub would start to fill up then. Better finish your drink and find someplace to hide before they start pouring in here.

He gulped at the whisky, but as he put the glass down on the bare wood of the booth's table, Fred Durban walked into the pub. Durban looked damned good for a man pushing seventy. Tall and spare as one of the old rocket boosters he had engineered, back in the days when you pressed the firing button and ducked behind sandbags because you had no idea of what the rocket might decide to do.

Kinsman felt trapped. He could not get up and leave because he would have to walk past Durban and the old man would recognize him. If he stayed, Durban would spot him. Even in a civilian's slacks and sports jacket, Kinsman could not hide his identity.

The old man walked slowly toward the bar, looking almost British in his tweed jacket and the pipe that he almost always had clamped in his teeth. He looked down the bar, then toward the booths. His face lit up as he spotted Kinsman. Briskly he strode to the booth and slid into the bench on the other side of the narrow table.

"You couldn't take all the speechifying either, eh?"

Wishing he were somewhere else, Kinsman nodded.

"Can't blame you. I've been in this game for a thousand years now and the *only* part of it I don't like is when those stuffed shirts start congratulating themselves over the things you and I did."

"Uh, sir, I was just leaving . . ."

"Hey, come on! You wouldn't leave me here to drink all alone, would you?"

Before Kinsman could answer or maneuver himself out

of the booth, Durban turned toward the barkeep and called, "Can I have a mug of lager, please, and another of whatever my friend here is drinking?"

The bartender nodded. "Ryte awhy, mate."

"Now then, the logistics are taken care of." Durban put his unlit pipe in the battered ashtray, then fished in his jacket pockets to produce a pouch of aromatic tobacco, lighter, and all the surgical instruments that pipe smokers carry.

"I really should be going," Kinsman said, starting to feel desperate.

"Where to?"

"Well . . ."

"There's nothing going on except that damned dedication ceremony. Everybody else is there, except for thee and me. And except the miners." He started reaming out the pipe and dumping the black soot into the ashtray. The barkeep brought their drinks and put them down on the table.

"How much?" Durban asked.

"I'll keep a tab runnin'. Got a bloody computer t' keep track of you blokes. Prints up your bill neat an' clean when you're ready t' go. Even keeps track o' the ice!" He laughed his way back to the bar.

"I haven't seen much of the mines yet," Kinsman said, still trying to get away.

"Nothing much to see," Durban muttered, putting his pipe back together. "Take the tour tomorrow morning. Just some tunnels with automated machinery chipping away at the rock. The real work's done by a half-dozen engineers in the control center. Looks just like mission control at Kennedy or Vandenberg."

"I haven't even seen the surface. We landed last night . . ."

"Desert. They won't let you up there by yourself. Fifty degrees Celsius. That's why the miners live down here."

"I know." The sun will broil you in minutes. And it's empty up there. Clean and empty. No one to see you. No one to watch you. They wouldn't find your body for days.

Durban took a long swallow of beer. "Fifty degrees," he murmured. "Sounds hotter if you say 120 Fahrenheit."

"Like the Moon."

Durban nodded. "That's why we're opening this training

center here. People will have to live underground on the Moon, so we'll train them here at Coober Pedy."

"It was your idea, wasn't it?"

Another nod. "Not mine exclusively. Several other people thought of it, too. Years ago. But when you live long enough to be an old fart like me in this game, they give you credit for enormous wisdom." He laughed and reached for his beer again.

Kinsman sat quietly, wondering how he could break away, while Durban alternately sipped his beer and packed his pipe. The old man still had a tinge of red in his silvery hair. His face was thin, with a light, almost delicate bone structure showing through skin like ancient parchment. But the cobalt-blue eyes were alive, alert, inquisitive, framed by bushy reddish brows. Durban had seen it all, from the struggling beginnings of rocketry when people scoffed at the idea of exploring space to the multinational industry that was now on the verge of colonizing the Moon.

"You look damned uncomfortable, son. What's wrong?"

Kinsman felt himself wince. "Nothing," he lied.

Those bushy eyebrows went up. "Am I bothering you? Did I say something I shouldn't? Am I keeping you from a date or something?"

"Nosir. None of the above. I'm just . . . well, I guess I feel out of place here."

Durban studied him. "You were on the plane with me, the L.A. to Sydney flight last night, weren't you?"

"Yessir."

"I thought I recognized you. Saw your picture in the papers or something a few years back. But you were in uniform then."

He can't know, Kinsman told himself. There's no way he could possibly know.

"I'm still in the Air Force," he said to Durban. "I'm on . . . inactive duty."

"Astronaut?"

"I was."

Durban said, "Do I have to buy you another drink to get you to tell me your name?"

"Kinsman," he blurted. "Chet Kinsman." He grabbed the whisky in front of him and took a long pull from it.

"Chester A. Kinsman," Durban murmured. "Now where did I . . . of, of course!" He grinned broadly. "The Zero Gee Club! Now I remember. Old Cy Calder told me about you."

Kinsman put his drink down with a trembling hand. "The Zero Gee Club. I had forgotten about that."

"Forgotten about it?" Durban looked impressed. "You mean you've gone on to even greater things?"

"No." Kinsman shook his head. "Different. But not greater."

"Calder died a couple of years ago," Durban said. "Ninety-three."

"I didn't know."

His voice lower, "Just about all my old friends are dead. That's the curse of a long life. You get to feel that you're the last of the Mohicans."

"You think dying young is better?"

Instead of answering, Durban picked up his lighter and started puffing his pipe to life. Clouds of bluish smoke rose slowly, swirled around his head, then were pulled ceilingward toward the vents in the solid rock.

"You said," he asked between puffs, "you're on . . . inactive duty. . . . What brought that about?"

"Accident," Kinsman said automatically, feeling his insides congealing.

"Where? In orbit?"

"Yes."

"You got hurt? Funny, I didn't hear anything—"

"It happened a long time ago," Kinsman said, seeing the face of the cosmonaut screaming as she died. "It's just . . . one thing led to another. You know how it is."

Durban blew out another cloud of smoke. "Still, I've got a pretty good network of spies in all parts of this business. Odd I never heard about it."

Stop pumping me, Kinsman snarled silently. "Maybe it wasn't important enough to make the scuttlebutt rounds," he lied. "Except to me."

Durban looked skeptical. "An able-bodied astronaut sitting on his backside? For how long now?"

"A while."

"H'm. And what are you doing here?"

Kinsman shrugged. "Looking for a job, I guess."

"A job?"

"I can get an honorable discharge from the Air Force. I thought I might get a civilian job."

Durban's bushy brows knit together. "The Air Force is willing to let an experienced astronaut go? Who's your boss out there at Vandenberg?"

"Colonel Murdock."

"Bob Murdock?" Durban broke into a grin. "I've known Bobby since we used to fill out requisition forms over his forged signature. Don't tell me he's still a light colonel!"

"No, he's got his eagles."

"And he's willing to let you quit the Air Force? Why?"

Kinsman shook his head. Because I make him uncomfortable. Because I don't follow the rules. Because I'm a nervous wreck and a murderer. Or is it the other way around?

"Personal, eh?"

"Very."

"I can introduce you to some NASA people who . . ."

"I've done a tour of duty with NASA. They shipped me back to the Air Force. The big aerospace corporations are where the jobs are now. Or so they tell me."

"And that's why you're here. To talk to the corporation people. Any luck?"

"All negative. They won't touch me without seeing my Air Force record, and my record shows a big blank space where it counts most."

Durban stared at him. "What the hell happened?"

Kinsman did not reply.

"Okay, okay . . . it's very personal. I'm just plain curious, though. Not much happens in this game without me hearing about it, you know."

Kinsman picked up his drink again, thinking, You've heard about this one. You've heard the rumors. You just haven't connected me with the story. He drained the thick-walled glass and put it back on the table again.

"I hope you won't go probing into this, Mr. Durban. It's very sensitive . . . to me personally, as well as to the Air Force."

"I can see that," Durban said.

"I wouldn't have mentioned anything at all about it,"

Kinsman went on, "except that you . . . well, you seem like someone I can trust."

"But only so far."

"Believe me, I've told you more than anyone else. But please don't push it any father . . . I mean, farther."

"All right."

"I'd like your word on that."

The eyebrows shot up again. "My word? You mean there's a gentleman left in this world who'll take a man's word and a handshake on something bigger than a five-dollar bet?"

Smiling despite himself, Kinsman answered, "I don't even need the handshake. Your word is good enough for me."

"Well, I'll be . . ." Durban turned slightly on the bench and looked toward the front of the pub. "Looks like a couple more fugitives from the ceremonies just slinked in."

Kinsman glanced toward the pub's front entrance and saw Frank Colt, in his sharply creased Air Force blues, looking slightly uncomfortable next to a lanky, sandy-haired Russian in the tan and red uniform of the Soviet Cosmonaut Corps.

Durban stuck his head out from the booth and called, "Piotr . . . over here."

"Ahah! An underground meeting," the Russian boomed out in a voice three times his size.

The two men came over and slid into the booth: the Russian next to Durban and Colt beside Kinsman.

Durban said, "Chet, may I introduce Major Piotr Leonov, Cosmonaut First Class. And a fine basso, if you ever want to get up an operatic quartet."

"We have already met," the Russian said, taking Kinsman's extended hand in a friendly but not overly strong grip.

"We have?"

"At your base near Aristarchus. I piloted the craft that brought medical aid for your renegade Jesuit."

Comprehension began to light in Kinsman's mind.

"You were quite asleep at the time," Leonov went on, in English that had a slight British accent. "Apparently, you had gone through a strenuous time, rescuing the priest."

Kinsman nodded. "Well, it's good to meet you when my eyes are open."

Leonov laughed.

"This is Captain Frank Colt," Kinsman said to Durban. "Top flier in the Vandenberg crew. I don't know how well he sings but he's a damned good man to work with in orbit."

"I've got a natural sense of rhythm," Colt said, straight-faced, testing Durban.

"I've heard about you," Durban said. "Aren't you the one who saved that cee-cubed satellite when its final stage misfired and it looked like the whole damned thing was going to splash in the Pacific?"

With a nod, "I got a replacement thruster mated to the bird, yeah."

"And damned near fried his ass off," Kinsman added.

"You should have asked us for assistance," Leonov said, grinning. "We would have been happy to help you save your command-and-control satellite."

"You sure would," Colt snapped. "You'd tote it back to Moscow with you."

Leonov shrugged elaborately. "Wouldn't you, with one of ours?"

A waitress appeared at their table: very young, miniskirt showing smooth strong thighs, low-cut blouse showing plenty of bosom, long blond hair, and a pretty face with placid cow eyes.

"Service is improving," said Durban.

"The ceremonies are breaking up," Colt told him. "This place'll be jammed in a few minutes."

The waitress took their order and flounced off to the bar.

"Nothing like that in Cosmograd, eh, Piotr?" Durban nudged the Russian.

"My dear Frederick," Leonov countered, an enigmatic smile on his bony face, "just because you did not see any of the beautiful women of our city does not mean that they do not exist. Being good Soviet women, naturally they hid themselves from the prying eyes of capitalist spies."

"Hid themselves? Or were hidden by others?"

Leonov shrugged. "What difference? The important fact is that I know where they are and you do not."

As the girl came back with their drinks, Colt asked Kinsman quietly, "How's it going?"

Kinsman jabbed his thumb toward the floor. "Lousy."

"I still wish you'd let me help. We can go over Murdock's head. The other astronauts will—"

"You don't want to get involved in this, Frank. It won't do you any good."

Colt made a disgusted face.

"A toast!" Leonov called, raising his glass. It looked like a tumbler of water. Kinsman guessed that it was at least four ounces of straight vodka. "To international cooperation in space. An end to all military secrets. Peace and total disarmament. Brotherhood throughout the cosmos. Friendship among all . . ."

"Is this a toast or a speech?" Colt grumbled.

"*Nazdrovia!*" Leonov snapped back and tossed down half his drink in one gulp.

"I've got a toast," Durban said. "May the work that is done here, underground, result in the four of us meeting underground again . . . on the Moon."

They drank again. And again. The waitress brought fresh drinks. Through it all Kinsman kept wishing he could get away, escape. The whisky was not making him drunk. It couldn't. He would not let it.

"Frank, my friend," Leonov said over their glasses, "why are you scowling? It is no crime to be drinking with a Russian."

Colt hunched his shoulders and leaned forward over the table. "Pete, I'm just drunk enough to tell you to go to hell. You know I don't believe a word of this peace and friendship bullshit."

"And I am drunk enough to know capitalist brainwashing when I hear it."

"Come on now," Durban said, relighting his pipe for the nth time. "Let's not get into a political squabble."

"Easy enough for you," Colt growled. "Mr. International Astronautical Federation. You can go around the world being friendly and setting up programs where we gotta cooperate with the Reds. But we"—Colt's gesture included Kinsman—"we gotta figure out how to cooperate with 'em without letting 'em steal the whole fucking store! We gotta defend the nation against 'em and cooperate with 'em at the same time. How d'you do that?"

"By giving up all weapons in space," Leonov answered. "Put an end to this Star Wars program of yours and dismantle your antisatellite weapons and we will do the same."

"Uh-huh. And you'll let me come over and inspect your boosters and satellites to make sure you're not cheating?"

"Allow you to spy on our space bases? Never!"

Kinsman leaned back in the booth, utterly sober, staring at his emptied glass and wishing he could disappear from the face of the Earth. Colt's superpatriotism always surprised and embarrassed him. Childhood prejudice, he knew. Blacks were anti-Establishment when you were a kid and you expected them all to be anti-Establishment forever.

But America was truly multiracial now. There were black generals, Hispanic bank presidents, Oriental board chairmen. The talk was that there would be a black President before much longer.

What will they call the White House then? Kinsman wondered. Will they repaint it? More likely they'll repaint the new President.

Leonov was chuckling. "Frank, my hotheaded friend, I refuse to get angry with you. We are both alike! You want to fly in space; so do I. Your government has ordered you to be an intelligence-gatherer for the duration of this international conference and ferret out as many of our secrets as you can. My government has ordered me to be an intelligence officer for the duration of this meeting and ferret out as many of your secrets as I can. How do you think I can roam around this underground rabbits' nest without a KGB 'guide' at my elbow?"

Intelligence officer? Kinsman snapped his attention to Leonov's eyes. The Russian met his gaze, smiling pleasantly, a bit drunkenly. There was no hatred there, not even suspicion. He doesn't know about me. Still, Kinsman's knees felt suddenly weak.

"You already know all our goddamned secrets," Colt groused.

"Just as you know ours," countered Leonov.

"Then let's get off the subject," Durban suggested, his voice a bit edgy, "and talk about something more congenial."

"Such as what?"

Durban sucked on his pipe for a moment. It was out

again. He took it from his mouth and jabbed the stem in Kinsman's direction.

"Chet here is looking for a job. What can we do for him?"

Jesus Christ, he's going to spill it all over the place! Kinsman heard himself stammering, "No, really . . . there's no need . . . I'd rather . . ."

"Defect!" Leonov suggested jovially. "We will treat you handsomely in the Soviet Union."

Colt glowered. "Yeah. In the basement of some psychiatric prison."

The Russian pretended not to hear.

"I'm serious," Durban insisted. "There are too few experienced astronauts—and cosmonauts—to let one walk away from the game."

For God's sake leave me alone! Kinsman screamed silently. But he could say nothing to them. He was frozen there, pinned into the booth. Trapped.

"They don't want experience anymore," Colt said. "They want youth. Murdock's even got *me* slated to train the little bastards instead of doing the flying myself."

"The private corporations . . ." Durban began.

"Are all talk and not much else," Colt said. "Chet and I are executive timber, as far as they're concerned. But they're not hiring fliers. They'd rather let Uncle Sam take the risks while they sit back and wait till everything's set up for them at the taxpayers' expense. *Then* they'll move in and make their profits."

"In all honesty," Durban said, "the military space program has gotten so big that it's swamping the civilian program. The corporations can make assured profits working for the Air Force. That makes it damned hard for them to justify the risks of private operations in orbit."

Suddenly serious, Leonov said, "I know how you must feel. If I thought that I would have to spend the rest of my life at a desk, or training others to do what I most want for myself, I would go mad."

"We need a new program," Durban said. "A priority program that's got to get going *now*, before they have time to train the next generation of kids."

"Such as what?" Colt asked.

"Not a military program," Leonov said. "Both our nations are putting enough military hardware into space. Too much."

"I agree," said Durban. "It ought to be an international program . . . something we can all participate in."

"Something that needs a corps of experienced astronauts," Kinsman heard himself chime in. "Something that will get us out there to stay. Away from here permanently."

"I've been mulling over an idea for a while now," Durban said. "Maybe the time is ripe for it."

"What is it?"

"A hospital."

"Huh?"

"On the Moon. A lunar hospital, for old gaffers like me, with bad hearts. For people with muscular diseases who are cripples here in this one-gravity field but could lead normal lives again on the Moon, in one-sixth gee."

Leonov smiled approvingly.

"Nobody's gonna put up the funding for an old soldiers' home on the Moon," Colt said.

"Want to bet?" Kinsman was suddenly surging with hope. "What's the average age of the U.S. Senate? Or the Presidium of the USSR?"

"My father . . ." Leonov realized. "He is confined to bed because of his heart's weakness. But in zero gravity, or even on the Moon . . ."

"And Jill Meyers," Kinsman added, "with all those damned allergies of hers." I can stay in the Air Force! If they go into a medical base on the Moon I can stay and work on that. I can stay on the Moon, away from it all!

They drank and made plans. Kinsman's head started to spin. The pub filled up with dignitaries from the conference that had officially inaugurated the underground training facility. The four men stayed in their booth, drinking and talking, ignoring everyone else. The international businessmen and government officials drifted away after a while and the pub began to fill up with its regular customers—the hard-drinking, hard-handed miners who dug for opal and copper, who lived underground to escape the searing heat of the desert above, the miners who were being crowded out of half their living area to make room for the space training facility.

The noise level went up in quantum leaps. Laughing, rowdy men. Blaring music from the stereo. Higher-pitched laughter from the extra barmaids and waitresses who came on duty when the regulars came off shift.

Durban was yelling over the noise of the crowd, "Why don't we adjourn to my room? It's quieter there and I've got a couple of bottles of liquor in my luggage."

"Gotta make a pit stop first," Colt said, nodding toward the door marked GENTS near their booth.

"Me too," said Kinsman.

Inside the washroom the noise level was much lower. Colt and Kinsman stood side by side at the only two urinals.

"Y'know, I think the old guy's really got a workable idea," Colt said happily. "We can lay this hospital project on top of everything else that the Air Force is doing . . . and with Durban pushing it, with his connections . . ."

"I still won't get off the ground," Kinsman suddenly realized.

"Huh? Sure you will. Murdock can't . . ."

Kinsman shook his head. "It doesn't matter, Frank. My psychological profile will shoot me down. They won't let me back into space again."

Zipping up and heading for the only sink, Colt said, "You can't let it beat you, man. You can't let it take the life outta you."

Wonderful play on words.

Gesturing Kinsman to the sink ahead of himself, Colt said, "What happened is over and done with. You gotta stop acting . . . well, you know."

Kinsman looked into the mirror above the sink, into the haunted eyes that always stared back at him. "I act sick? Mentally unwell? Disturbed?"

"You act like a goddamned dope," Colt grumbled.

Wiping his hands on the cloth toweling that hung from a wall-mounted fixture, Kinsman said, "Frank, for a minute back there I got excited. I thought maybe Durban was right and this hospital project would make enough new slots for astronauts that I'd get another chance. But we both know better. They won't let me fly again. You, sure. But not me. I'm grounded."

Colt went to the sink as a couple of miners banged

through the door and headed for the urinals. A gust of noise and raucous laughter bounced off the tile walls as the door swung shut.

"Listen, man, one thing I've learned about the Air Force—and everything else," Colt said over the splashing water of the sink. "If you take just what they want to give you, you'll get shit every time. You gotta fight for what you want."

Kinsman shook his head. "My family were Quakers, remember?"

Colt was moving to the towel machine when one of the miners jostled him.

"D'ya mind, mate?"

Wordlessly Colt stepped away from him, turned, and started wiping his hands on the toweling.

"Bloody foreigners all over th' plyce, ain't they?" said the miner's companion.

Kinsman looked at them for the first time. They were no taller than he or Colt, but they were heavy-boned, big-knuckled, and half drunk.

Colt was wiping his hands very deliberately now, looking at Kinsman with his back to the two miners.

"Bad enough they're tykin' up half th' bloody pits to put their bloody spyce cadets in," said the one at the sink, "but now they're goin' t' stink up th' bloody pub."

"An' myke goo-goo eyes at th' girls."

"We oughtta bring in a few bloody chimpanzees t' serve 'em their drinks."

"Foreigners," said the second miner, loudly, even though the washroom was small enough to hear a whisper. "You remember what we did t' those Eye-Tyes back in Melbourne, Bert?"

"They weren't Eye-Tyes; they were bloody Hungarians."

"Wops, Hunkies, whatever. Treated 'em ryte, din't we?"

"Gave 'em what they deserved."

Kinsman was between Colt and the door. He wanted to tell his friend to leave, to ignore the drunken Aussies and walk out. But he couldn't.

Colt was slowly, methodically, wiping his black hands on the white toweling. The first miner stepped from the sink to stand a few inches away from him.

"Least we never had t' deal with bloody Fiji Islanders before."

Colt said nothing. He surrendered the towel. The miner grinned at him with crooked teeth.

"Or Yank niggers," he added.

Colt grinned back. His right fist traveled six inches and buried itself in the man's solar plexus. The miner gave a silent gasp and collapsed, legs folding as he sank to the tiled floor. The other miner stared but said nothing.

Kinsman opened the door and Colt followed him out into the noisy, crowded pub. They saw Durban and Leonov already standing at the end of the bar, near the door that led to the corridor.

"See what I mean?" Colt said as they elbowed their way through the press of bodies. "Gotta fight for respect, every inch of the way."

Out in the corridor Leonov said, "I was about to call your embassy to send a searching party for you."

"We got into a small discussion with a couple of the friendly natives," Colt replied.

"Say, if you youngsters will slow down a little," Durban pleaded, "I'll show you where my room is."

"And the liquor!" Leonov beamed, immediately slowing his pace to walk beside the elderly Durban.

They labored up the rising slope of the corridor. It had originally been a tunnel hewn out of solid rock. Only the floor had been smoothed and covered with spongy plastic tiles. The walls and ceiling were still bare grayish-brown unfinished rock. Fluorescent lights hung every ten meters, connected by drooping wires.

The others were busily chatting among themselves about the new hospital project. Kinsman stayed silent, thinking, Could I talk Murdock into it? Would they let me fly again? I'd have to work it out so that I was assigned to the hospital project permanently. They'd never let me get away with that. They could reassign me whenever . . .

"HEY, YOU THERE! THE YANKS!"

Turning, Kinsman saw a dozen or so miners advancing up the tunnel corridor toward them. In the lead were the two from the washroom. They all looked drunk. And violently angry.

"That's the black barstard that beat me up!" the miner yelled. "Him an' his friend there."

Colt moved to stand beside Kinsman. And suddenly Leonov was on his other side.

The miners halted a few feet in front of them. They wanted to fight. They were spoiling for blood. Kinsman stood rooted there, his mind blazing with the memory of the moment when he had felt bloodlust. He was sweating again, panting with exertion, reaching for the cosmonaut's fragile airhose . . .

Not again, he told himself, trying to control his trembling so that the others could not see it. Not again!

"What is this?" Leonov demanded. "Why are we accosted by a mob?"

"Back off, Russkie," said one of the miners. "This is none of your fight."

"These are my friends," Leonov said. "What concerns them concerns me."

"He beat me up," said the miner Colt had hit.

"An' him." His companion pointed at Kinsman. "He helped th' black bugger."

"Beat you up?" Leonov asked mildly. "Where are your scars? Where is the blood? I see no bruises. Are you certain you did not merely faint?"

The miner turned red as the men around him grinned.

"I was there with 'im," the other miner said. "They jumped Bert and pummeled 'im till he dropped. In the midsection."

"While you watched?" Leonov asked.

"We ain't tykin' that from no foreigners!"

The mob surged forward.

"Now that's enough!"

Frederick Durban stepped between Kinsman and Leonov to face the angry miners. "We are the guests of the Australian government," he said firmly, "and if any harm comes to us you'll all go to jail."

"What about 'im?" one of the miners yelled. "They can't go beatin' up our blokes and get awhy with it!"

"Nobody beat anybody up," Colt shouted back. "The guy called me a nigger and I punched him in the gut. He folded like a pretzel. One punch."

166

"That's a bloody lie! The other one held me and the black barstard kicked me, too!"

Very calmly, Durban took the pipe from his mouth and said, "All right, let's settle this here and now. But not with a riot."

"How then?"

"There's an old custom where I come from . . . mining country, back in Colorado." He turned slightly back toward Kinsman and winked. "When two men have a difference of opinion, they settle it fairly between themselves. Do you two want to fight it out right here . . . Marquess of Queensberry rules?"

Colt shrugged, then nodded.

"Oh, no, you don't!" screeched the miner. "He's a bloody tryned killer. A soldier. Probably a karate expert . . . chops bricks with 'is bare hands an' all that."

Durban scowled from under his shaggy brows. "Very well then. Suppose *I* represent the American side of this argument. Would you be afraid to fight me?"

"You? You're an old man!"

"I may be almost seventy," Durban said, stuffing his pipe into a jacket pocket, "but I can still take on the likes of you."

The miner looked bewildered. "I . . . you can't . . ."

"Come on," Durban said, very seriously. He raised his fragile-looking fists.

One of the other miners put a hand on the first one's shoulder. "Forget it, Bert. He's crazy."

Bert wavered, uncertain. Durban was ramrod straight, looking like a slim rod of knobby bamboo next to a snorting red-eyed bull. Kinsman watched, unable to move. That guy'll kill Durban with one punch. Then what can we do? What can I do?

The miner finally stepped back, muttering and shaking his head. They all turned and began walking slowly back down the tunnel corridor, toward the pub.

Durban let his hands drop to his sides.

Colt puffed out a breath of relief. "Thanks, man."

"Very courageous of you," Leonov said thoughtfully.

But Kinsman said nothing. What would I have done if it had come to a brawl? What would I have done?

The four men walked slowly back to Durban's room, two

levels up closer to the surface.

"The whisky's in the brown carryall," Durban said as they entered the windowless room. "Help yourselves." He went straight to the bed and stretched out on it.

Colt and Leonov went to the whisky. Kinsman took a close look at the old man. His face was ashen, his thin chest heaving.

"Are you all right?"

"I've got some pills here . . ." He fished in his jacket pocket. The pipe fell out and dropped to the floor, spilling black ashes across the cheap carpeting.

"I'll get you a glass of water."

Kinsman went to the sink across from the bed and took a plastic cup from the dispenser on the wall above it. Durban propped himself on one elbow to drink down the pill, then dropped back onto the mattress and stared at the ceiling.

Leonov had taken the small room's only chair. Colt was sitting on the dresser top next to the open whisky bottle. They both had plastic cups in their hands.

"Hey, you need a doctor?" Colt asked.

"No . . ." Durban closed his eyes and took a deep breath. "Just a little too much excitement for my heart. That, and the climb upstairs."

Leonov said, "We have a cardiac specialist with the Soviet delegation."

Pushing himself up to a sitting position, Durban waved a hand at the Russian. "No, it's all right. I'll be okay in a minute."

Kinsman sat on the edge of the bed and helped the old man out of his jacket, then pulled off his shoes.

"You see," Durban said, sinking back against the pillows, "I really do need a low-gravity home. Damned heart's not fit to live on Earth anymore. It wants to be on the Moon."

"We'll get you there," Colt said.

"Yes," Leonov agreed, raising his cup to the proposition.

Kinsman shook his head. "If that miner had punched you, it probably would have killed you. You were taking your life in your hands."

Durban smiled at him. "Oh, I knew he wouldn't hit me. He couldn't."

"He came damned close."

"Not a bit of it. I'm obviously a frail old man. It would ruin his self-image if he hit me. He knew that I'd go down with one punch. I could see it in his eyes. Where's the *machismo* in beating up an old man?"

"Then why . . ."

"I got in front of you fellows so that he would be forced to hit me before anybody else started fighting. That was the best way to prevent a fight from starting."

"You still could've gotten hurt. Killed."

Durban's shaggy eyebrows rose a bit. "Well, sometimes you have to put yourself on the line. You guys know that, you've all done it yourselves, one time or another."

"More than once," Leonov murmured.

"We could've taken on the bunch of them," Colt said. "They were brawlers, not trained fighters."

Leonov took a swallow of whisky and said, "I, for one, am glad that the fight did not come about. My training is not in hand-to-hand combat."

You have to put yourself on the line, Kinsman was repeating to himself.

"Maybe you could have taken them all single-handedly, Frank," Durban said. "But I doubt it. Besides, there are better ways of winning what you want than punching people. Much better ways."

"The tongue is mightier than the fist?" Colt jabbed.

"The brain is mightier than the biceps," Durban replied.

Kinsman got to his feet. "I've got to phone Colonel Murdock."

"Bobby? Why?"

"To tell him that I'm not quitting the Air Force. I'm not going to take an honorable discharge or any kind of discharge. I'm not quitting."

Colt broke into a wide grin. "Great! And tell him for me what I think of being assigned to training."

Leonov said, "You realize, of course, that if you start a high-priority program to build a hospital complex on the Moon, my superiors will become very suspicious of you."

"That's fine, Piotr," Durban said. "I'll put the idea before the International Astronautical Federation and get them to make this an international cooperative project. Then you can come in on it, too."

"We shall all meet on the Moon," said Leonov.

"The sooner the better," Durban agreed.

"To the Moon." Colt raised his cup.

"I'll be there," said Kinsman.

Age 35

As soon as he stepped through the acoustical screen inside the house's front doorway the noise hit Kinsman like a physical blow. He stood there a moment and watched the tribal rites of a Washington cocktail party.

My battlefield, he thought.

The room was jammed with guests and they all seemed to be talking at once. It was an old Georgetown parlor, big, with a high ceiling that sagged slightly and showed one hairline crack along its length. The streets outside had been quiet and deserted except for the police monitors in their armored suits standing at each intersection. They looked like a bitter parody of astronauts in space suits.

But here there was life, chatter, laughter. The people who made Washington go, the people who ran the nation, were here drinking and talking and ignoring the enforced peace of the streets outside. America was on a wartime footing, almost. The oil shock of ten years ago had inexorably pushed the United States toward military measures. The Star Wars strategic defense satellites that could protect the nation against Soviet missiles were being deployed in orbit, despite treaties, despite opposition at home, despite—or because of—the Soviet deployment of a nearly identical system. Unemployment at home was countered by a new public-service draft that placed millions of eighteen-year-olds in police forces, hospitals, public works projects, and the armed services. Dissidence was smothered by fear: fear of dangers real and imagined, fear of government retaliation, fear of ruinous unemployment and economic collapse, and the ultimate fear of the nuclear war that hovered remorselessly on the horizon waiting for the moment of Armageddon.

In the midst of these tightening tensions Kinsman was devoting every ounce of his energies to creating a permanent medical facility on the Moon.

As he stood at the doorway looking over the crowd, he recognized fewer than one in ten of the partygoers. Then he saw his host, Neal McGrath, now the junior Senator from Pennsylvania. Neal was standing over at the far end of the room by the empty fireplace, tall drink in hand, head bent slightly to catch what some wrinkled matron was saying to him. The target for tonight. McGrath was the swing vote on the Senate's Appropriations Committee.

"Chet, you did come after all!"

He turned to see Mary-Ellen McGrath approaching him, hands outstretched in greeting.

"I hardly recognized you without your uniform," she said.

He smiled back at her. "I thought Aerospace Force blues might be a little conspicuous around here."

"Nonsense. And I wanted to see your new oak leaves. A major now."

Promoted for accepting hazardous duty: lobbying on Capitol Hill.

"Come on, Chet. I'll show you where the bar is." She took his arm and led him through the jabbering crowd. Mary-Ellen was small, slender, almost frail-looking. But she had the strength of a tigress and the open, honest face of a woman who could stand beside her husband in the face of anything from Washington cocktail parties to the tight infighting of rural Pennsylvania politics.

The bar dispenser hummed impersonally to itself as it produced a heavy scotch and water. Kinsman took a stinging sip of it.

"I was worried you wouldn't come," Mary-Ellen said over the noise of the crowd. "You've been a hermit ever since you arrived in Washington."

"Pentagon keeps me pretty busy."

"And no date? No woman on your arm? That isn't the Chet Kinsman I used to know back when."

"I'm preparing for the priesthood."

"I'd almost believe it," she said, straight-faced. "There's something different about you since the old days. You're quieter . . . more subdued."

I've been grounded. Aloud, he said, "Creeping maturity. I'm a late achiever."

But she was serious, and as stubborn as her husband. "Don't try to kid around it. You've changed. You're not playing the dashing young astronaut anymore."

"Who the hell is?"

A burly, balding man jarred into Kinsman from behind, sloshing half the drink out of his glass.

"Whoops, didn't get it on ya, did . . . oh, hi, Mrs. McGrath. Looks like I'm waterin' your rug."

"That won't hurt it," Mary-Ellen said. "Do you two know each other? Tug Wynne . . ."

"I've seen the Major on the Hill."

Kinsman said, "You're with Satellite News, aren't you?"

Nodding, Wynne replied, "Surprised to see you here, Major, after this morning's committee session."

Kinsman forced a grin. "I'm an old family friend. I've known the Senator since we were kids."

"You think he's gonna vote against the Moonbase program?"

"I hope not," Kinsman said.

Mary-Ellen kept silent.

"He sure gave your Colonel Murdock a going-over this morning." Wynne chuckled wheezily. "Mrs. McGrath, you shoulda seen your husband in action."

Kinsman changed the subject. "Say, did you know old Cy Calder? Used to work for Allied News Syndicate out on the West Coast."

"Only by legend," Wynne answered. "He died four, five years ago, I heard."

"Yes, I know."

"Musta been past eighty. Friend of yours?"

"Sort of. And he was past ninety."

"Ninety!"

"I knew him . . . lord, it was almost ten years ago. Back when we were just starting the first Air Force manned space missions. Helluva guy."

Mary-Ellen said, "I'd better pay some attention to the other guests. There are several old friends of yours here tonight, Chet. Mix around, you'll find them."

With another rasping chuckle, Wynne said, "Guess we *could* give somebody else a chance to get to the bar."

Kinsman started to drift away but Wynne followed behind him.

"Murdock send you over here to soften up McGrath?"

Pushing past a pair of arguing, arm-waving cigar smokers, Kinsman frowned. "I was invited to this party weeks ago. I told you, the Senator and I are old friends."

"And how friendly are you with Mrs. McGrath?"

"What's that supposed to mean?"

Wynne let his teeth show. "Handsome astronaut, good-looking wife, busy Senator . . ."

"That's pretty foul-minded, even for a newsman."

"Just doin' my job," Wynne said, still smiling. "Nothing personal. Besides, you got nothing to complain about, as far as news people are concerned. The rumor is that you're the astronaut who killed that Russian cosmonaut several years ago."

It was the hundredth time since Kinsman had arrived in Washington that a reporter had faced him with the accusation. The Aerospace Force public relations people had worked assiduously to keep the story "unofficial," citing the slender thread of cooperation that still remained between the Soviet and American civilian space programs. The media had backed off, spurred more than a little by the government's tough new regulations on licenses for broadcasting stations and mail permits for newspapers and magazines. But individual newsmen still braced Kinsman with the story, trying to get an admission from him.

Freezing his emotions within himself, Kinsman answered merely, "I've heard that rumor myself."

"You deny that it's true?"

"I'm not a public relations officer. I don't go around denying rumors. Or confirming them."

"Look," Wynne insisted, "the Air Force can't cover up this story forever."

"Aerospace Force," Kinsman said. "The name's been changed to Aerospace Force."

Wynne shrugged and raised his glass in a mock salute. "I stand corrected, Major."

Kinsman turned and started working his way toward the other end of the room. A grandfather clock chimed in a corner, barely audible over the human noises and clacking of ice in glassware. Eighteen hundred. Royce and Smitty ought to be halfway to Copernicus by now.

And then he heard her. He did not have to see her, he knew it was Diane. The same pure, haunting soprano; a voice straight out of a fairy tale:

"Once I had a sweetheart, and now I have none.
Once I had a sweetheart, and now I have none.
He's gone and leave me, he's gone and leave me,
He's gone and leave me to sorrow and mourn."

Her voice stroked his memory and he felt all the old joy, all the old pain, as he pushed his way through the crowd.

Finally he saw her, sitting cross-legged on a sofa, guitar propped on one knee. The same ancient guitar; no amplifiers, no boosters. Her hair was still straight and long and black as space. Her eyes were even darker and deeper. The people were ringed around her, standing, sitting on the floor. They gave her the entire sofa to herself, an altar that only she could use. They watched her and listened, entranced by her voice. But she was somewhere else, living the song, seeing what it told of, until she strummed the final chord.

Then she looked up and looked straight at Kinsman. Not surprised. Not even smiling. Just a look that linked them as if all the years since their brief time together had dissolved into a single yesterday. Before either of them could say or do anything the others broke into applause. Diane smiled and mouthed, "Thank you."

"More, more!"

"Come on, another one."

"'Greensleeves.'"

Diane put the guitar down carefully beside her, uncoiled her slim legs, and stood up. "Later, okay?"

Kinsman grinned to himself. He knew it would be later or nothing.

The crowd muttered reluctant acquiescence and broke

the circle around her. Kinsman stepped the final few paces and stood before Diane.

"Good to see you again." He felt suddenly awkward, not knowing what to do. He held his drink with both hands.

"Hello, Chet." She was not quite smiling.

"I'm surprised you remember. It's been so long . . ."

Now she did smile. "How could I ever forget you? And I've seen your name in the news every once in a while."

"I've listened to your records everywhere I've gone," he said.

"Even on the Moon?" Her look was almost shy, almost mocking.

"Sure," he lied. "Even on the Moon."

"Here, Diane, I brought you some punch." Kinsman turned to see a fleshy-faced young man with a droopy mustache and tousled brown hair, carrying two plastic cups of punch. He wore a sharply tailored white suit with a vest and a wide floral scarf.

"Thank you, Larry. This is Chet Kinsman. Chet, meet Larry Davis."

"Kinsman?"

Diane explained, "I met Chet in San Francisco a thousand years ago, when I was just getting started. Chet's an astronaut."

"Oh, really?"

Somehow the man antagonized Kinsman. "Affirmative," he snapped in his best military manner.

"He's been on the Moon," Diane went on.

"That's where I heard the name," Davis said. "You're one of those Air Force people who want to build a permanent base up there. Weren't you involved in some sort of rescue a couple of years back? One of your people got stranded or something . . ."

"Yes," Kinsman cut him short. "It was all blown up out of proportion by the news media."

They stood there for a moment, none of them able to think of a thing to say, as the party pulsated around them.

Finally Diane said, "Mary-Ellen told me you might be here tonight. You and Neal are both working on something about the space program?"

"Something like that," Kinsman said. "Organized any

more protest demonstrations?"

She forced a laugh. "There's nothing left to protest about. Everything's so well organized in the Land of the Free that nobody can raise a crowd anymore. Public safety laws and all that."

"It does seem quieter. Nobody's complaining."

"They can't," Diane said. "You ought to see what we have to go through before every concert. They want to check the lyrics of every song I do. Even the encores. Nothing's allowed to be spontaneous."

"You manage to get in some damned tough lyrics," Kinsman said. "I've listened to you."

"The censors aren't always very bright."

"Or incorruptible," Davis added, smirking.

"So everybody's happy," Kinsman said. "You get to sing your songs about freedom and love. The crowd gets its little thrill of excitement. And the government people get paid off. Everybody gets what they want."

Diane looked at him quizzically. "Do you have what you want, Chet?"

"Me?" Surprised. "Hell no."

"Then not everybody's satisfied."

"Are you?"

"Hell no," she mimicked.

"But everything *looks* so rosy," Davis said, with acid in his voice. "The government keeps telling us that unemployment is down and the stock market is up. And our President promises he won't send troops into Brazil. Not until after the elections, I bet."

Diane nodded. Then, brightening, "Larry, did I ever tell you about the time we tried to get Chet to come out and join one of our demonstrations? In uniform?"

"I'm agog."

She turned to Kinsman. "Do you remember what you told me, Chet?"

"No . . ." It was a perfect day for flying, for getting away from funerals and families and all the ties of Earth. Flying so high above the clouds that even the rugged Sierras looked like nothing more than wrinkles. Then out over the desert at Mach 2, the only sounds in your earphones from your own breathing and the faint distant crackle of earthbound men giving orders to other earthbound men.

"You told me"—Diane was laughing with the memory of it—"that you'd rather be flying and defending us so that nobody bombed us while we were demonstrating for peace!"

It was funny now; it had not been then.

"Yeah, that sounds like something I might have said."

"How amusing," Davis smirked. "And what are you protecting us from now? The Brazilians? Or the Martians?"

You overstuffed fruit, you wouldn't even fit into a cockpit. But Kinsman replied merely, "From the politicians. My job is Congressional liaison."

"Twisting Senators' arms is what he means," came Neal McGrath's husky voice from behind him.

Kinsman turned.

"Hello, Chet, Diane . . . em, Larry Davis, isn't it?"

"You have a good memory for names!"

"Goes with the job."

Kinsman studied McGrath. It was the first time they had been physically close in many years. Neal's hair was still reddish; the rugged outdoors look had not been completely erased from his features. He looked like a down-home farmer; Kinsman knew he had been a Rhodes scholar. McGrath's voice was even softer, throatier than it had been years ago. The natural expression of his face, in repose, was still an introspective scowl. But he was smiling now.

His cocktail party smile, thought Kinsman. Then he realized, Neal's starting to get gray. Like me.

"Tug Wynne tells me I was pretty rough on your boss this morning, Chet." The smile on McGrath's face turned just a shade self-satisfied.

"Colonel Murdock lost a few pounds, and it wasn't all from the TV lights," Kinsman replied.

"I was only trying to get him to give me a good reason for funneling money into a permanent lunar base."

Kinsman said, "The House Appropriations Committee approved the funding. They're satisfied with the reasons we gave them."

"Not good enough," McGrath said firmly. "Not when we've got to find money to reclaim every major city in the nation, plus new energy exploration, *and* crime control, *and*—"

177

"And holding down the Pentagon before they go jumping into Brazil," Diane added.

"Thanks, pal," Kinsman said to her. Turning back to McGrath, "Look, Neal, I'm not going to argue with you. The facts are damned clear. There's energy in space, lots of it. And raw materials. To utilize them we need a permanent base on the Moon."

"Then let the corporations build it. They're the ones who want to put up solar power satellites. They want to mine the Moon. Why should the taxpayers foot the bill for a big, expensive base on the Moon?"

"Because the heart of that base will be a low-gravity hospital that will—"

"Come on, Chet! You know it'll be easier and cheaper to build your hospital in orbit. Why go all the way to the Moon when you can build it a hundred miles overhead? And why should the Air Force do it? It's NASA's job."

Kinsman could see that McGrath looked faintly amused. He enjoys arguing. He's not fighting for his life.

Glancing at Diane, then back at McGrath, Kinsman answered, "NASA's fully committed to building the space stations and helping the corporations to start industrial operations in orbit. Besides, we've got an Air Force team of trained astronauts with practically nothing to do."

"So build your hospital in orbit. Or cooperate with NASA, for a change, and put your hospital into one of their space stations."

"And running the hospital will cost twenty times more than a lunar base will," Kinsman said. "Every time you want a Band-Aid you'll have to boost it up from Earth. That takes energy, Neal. And money. A permanent base on the Moon can be entirely self-sufficient."

"In a hundred years," McGrath said.

"Ten. Maybe five."

"Come on, Chet. You guys are already spending billions on the strategic defense system. You can't have the Moon, too. Let it go and stop pushing this pipe dream of Fred Durban's."

"A lunar base makes sense, dammitall, on a straight cost-effectiveness basis. You've seen the numbers, Neal. The base will pay for itself in ten years. It'll *save* the taxpayers billions of dollars in the long run."

A crowd was gathering around them. McGrath automatically raised his voice a notch. "That's just like Mary-Ellen saves me money at department store sales. I can't afford to save that kind of money. Not this year. Or next. The capital outlay is too high. To say nothing of the overruns."

"Now wait . . ."

"There's never been a military program that's lived within its budget. No, Chet. Moonbase is going to have to wait."

"We've already waited twenty years."

The rest of the party had stopped. Everyone was watching the debate.

"Our first priority," McGrath said, more to the crowd than to Kinsman, "has got to be for the cities. They've become jungles, unfit for human life. We've got to reclaim them and save the people who're trapped in them before they all turn into savages."

"But what about energy?" Kinsman demanded. "What about jobs? What about natural resources? You can't save the cities without them, and space operations can give us all those things."

"Let the corporations develop those programs. Let them take the risks and make the profits. We're putting enough money into space and too much into the Pentagon—including plans for a manned antisatellite spaceplane that your brass won't even tell us lowly Senators about."

The spaceplane, Kinsman realized. Neal's pissed because nobody's briefed him on the new spaceplane interceptor concept.

Aloud he was still arguing, "The corporations aren't going to develop anything, Neal, unless the government backs them. You know how they work: let Uncle Sam take the risks and when it's safe they'll come in and take the profits."

McGrath nodded. "Sure. Fine. But NASA's the agency that's running with that particular ball. The Aerospace Force has no business extending its gold-plated tentacles all the way to the Moon."

It's like he's running for re-election, Kinsman said to himself. Then he realized, Of course he is! They always are.

"Sure, Neal, play kick the Pentagon," he said. "That's an

awfully convenient excuse for ducking the issue."

With the confident grin of a hunter who had finally cornered his quarry, McGrath asked, "So you want to build a permanent base on the Moon, despite the fact that we've signed treaties with the Russians to keep the Moon demilitarized . . ."

"This base isn't going to be a fortress, for god's sake. You know that. It's a hospital. We're just using military astronauts to get the job done because we have a trained corps of people who aren't being utilized. The Russians *want* to work with us on this."

"All right, all right." McGrath waved his hand, still grinning. "Even so. You put up this hospital of Durban's, this super geriatrics ward on the Moon, at a cost of billions. How's that going to help the welfare class in the cities? How's that going to rebuild New York or Detroit?"

"Or Washington," someone murmured.

Kinsman said, "It will create jobs . . ."

"For white engineers who live in the suburbs."

"It will save lives, for Chrissake!"

"For rich people who can afford to go to the Moon to live."

"It'll give people hope for the future."

"Ghetto people? Don't be silly."

"Neal," Kinsman said, exasperation in his voice, "maybe space operations won't solve any of those problems. But neither will anything else you do. Without a strong space effort you won't have the energy, the raw materials, the new wealth you need to rebuild the cities. Space gives us a chance, a hope—space factories and space power satellites will create new jobs here on Earth, increase the Gross National Product, bring new wealth into the economy. Nothing that you're promising to do can accomplish that, and nothing short of that can solve the problems you're so damned worked up about."

His smile a bit tighter, McGrath said, "Perhaps so. But your Moonbase won't do that. Industrial operations in orbit might do it. The corporations could do it, if they wanted to take the risks."

"But the corporations aren't moving fast enough. They're waiting for us to pave the way for them."

"That's why NASA's building the space stations," Mc-Grath said. "To encourage the corporations to push harder on industrial operations in orbit."

"But that's not enough! The most economical way to supply those space stations and orbital factories is with raw materials from the Moon."

Diane touched his arm, a curious gleam in her dark eyes. "Chet, why do you want a Moonbase so much?"

"Why? Because . . . I was just telling you . . ."

She shook her head. "No, I don't mean the official reasons. Why do *you* dig the idea? Why does it turn you on?"

"We need it. The whole human race needs it."

"No," she repeated patiently. "*You*. Why are you for it? What's in it for you?"

"What do you mean?"

"What makes you tick, man? What turns you on? Is it a Moonbase? Power? Glory? What moves you, Chet?"

They were all watching him, the whole crowd, their faces eager or smirking or inquisitive. Kinsman looked past them, through them, remembering. Floating weightless, standing on nothing, alone, free, away from them all. Staring back at the overwhelming beauty of Earth, rich, brilliant, full and shining against the black emptiness. Knowing that people down there are killing themselves, killing each other, killing their world and teaching their children how to kill. Knowing that you are part of it, too. Your eyes filling with tears at the beauty and the horror. To get away from it, far away, where they can't reach you, where you can start over, fresh, clean, new. How could they see it? How could any of them understand?

"What moves you, Chet?" Diane asked again.

He made himself grin. "Well, for one thing, since they started using synthetic coffee in the Pentagon . . ."

A few people laughed, a nervous titter. But Diane would not let him off the hook. "Get serious, Chet. This is important. What turns you on?"

They don't really want to know, he told himself. They would never understand. How could they?

"You mean, aside from the obvious things, like women?"

Diane nodded gravely.

"I never really thought about it. Hard to say. Flying, I guess. Getting out on your own responsibility, away from all the committees and chains of command."

"There's got to be more to it than that," Diane insisted.

"Well . . . have you ever been out on the desert, at an Israeli outpost, dancing all night by firelight because you know that at dawn there's going to be an attack and you don't want to waste a minute of living?"

There was a heartbeat's span of dead silence. Then one of the women asked in a near-whisper, "When were you . . . ?"

Kinsman said, "Oh, I've never been there. But isn't it a romantic picture?"

They all broke into laughter. That burst the bubble, Kinsman knew. The crowd began to dissolve, fragmenting into smaller groups. Dozens of conversations began to fill the silence that had briefly held them.

"You cheated," Diane said, frowning.

"Maybe I did."

"Don't you have anything but ice water in your veins?"

He shrugged. "If you prick us, do we not bleed?"

"Don't talk dirty."

He took her by the arm and headed for the big glass doors at the far end of the room. "Come on, we've got a lot of catching up to do."

He pushed the door open and they stepped out onto the balcony. Shatterproof plastic enclosed it and shielded them from the humid, hazy Washington evening—and from the occasional sniper who might be on the roofs across the street.

"Being a senator hath its privileges," Kinsman said. "My apartment over in Alexandria is about the size of this balcony. And no air-conditioning allowed."

Diane was not listening. She stretched catlike and pressed against the plastic shielding. To Kinsman she looked like a sleek black leopard: supple, fascinating, dangerous.

"Sunset," she said, looking toward the slice of red sky visible down the street. "Loveliest time of the day."

"Loneliest time, too."

She turned to him, her eyes showing genuine surprise. "Lonely? You? I never thought of you as being lonely. I always pictured you surrounded by friends."

"Or enemies," Kinsman heard himself say.

"You never did marry, did you?"

"You did."

"That was a long time ago. It's even been over for a long time."

"I orbited right over your wedding," he said. "I waved, but you didn't wave back."

Her eyebrows went up. "You walked out on me, remember? More than once. It wasn't my idea for you to go. You chose a goddamned airplane over me."

"I was young and foolish."

"You'd still make the same choice today, and we both know it. Only now you want to go to the Moon."

Kinsman looked into her deep, dark eyes. She was not angry with him. Curious, perhaps. Puzzled. Hurt?

He said, "That doesn't mean I *like* making the choices that way, Diane. We all have our problems, you know."

"You? You have problems? Weaknesses?"

"I've got a few, tucked away here and there."

"Why do you hide them?"

"Because nobody else gives a damn about them." Before Diane could reply, he said, "I sound sorry for myself, don't I?"

"Well . . ."

"Who's this Larry character?"

"He's a very nice guy," she said firmly. "A good agent and a good business manager. He doesn't go whizzing off into the wild blue yonder . . . or, space is black, isn't it?"

"As black as the devil's heart," Kinsman answered. "I don't go whizzing off anymore, either. I've been grounded."

She blinked at him. "Grounded? What does that mean?"

"Clipped my wings," he said. "Deballed me. No longer qualified for flight duty. No orbital missions. No lunar missions. They won't even let me fly a plane anymore. Got some shavetail to jockey me around. I work at a desk."

"But . . . why?"

"It's a long, dirty story. Officially, I'm too valuable to risk. Some shit like that."

"Chet, I'm so sorry. Flying means so much to you, I know." She took a step toward him.

"Let's get out of here, Diane. Let's go someplace safe and watch the Moon come up and I'll tell you all the legends about your namesake."

He could hear her breath catch. "That's . . . that's some line."

He wanted to reach out and hold her. Instead he said lamely, "Yeah, I suppose it is."

She came no closer. "I can't leave the party, Chet. They're expecting me to sing."

"Screw them."

"All of them?"

"Don't talk dirty."

She laughed, but shook her head. "Really, Chet, I can't leave."

"Then let me take you home afterward."

"I'm staying here tonight."

There were things he wanted to tell her, but he checked himself.

"Chet, please . . . it's been a long time."

"Yeah. Hasn't it, though."

The party ended at midnight when the sirens sounded the curfew warning. Within fifteen minutes Kinsman and everyone else had left the stately red-brick Georgetown house and taken taxis or buses or limousines homeward. Precisely at twelve-thirty electrical power along every street in the District of Columbia was cut off.

Kinsman fumbled his way in darkness up the narrow stairs to his one-room apartment. It was still unfamiliar enough for him to bark his shins on the leg of the table alongside the sofabed. The long, elaborately detailed string of profanity he muttered started and ended with his own stupidity.

In less than an hour of staring into the darkness he drifted to sleep. If he had any dreams he did not recall them the next morning. For which he was grateful.

The Pentagon looked gray and shabby in the rain. It bulked like an ancient fortress over the greenery of Virginia. The old parking lots, converted into athletic fields for the Defense Department personnel, were bare and empty except for the growing puddles pockmarked by the raindrops. Off in the mists, like enchanted castles in the clouds, the glass-walled office buildings of Crystal City lent a touch of contrast to the brooding old concrete face of the Pentagon.

Feeling as cold and gray within himself as the weather outside, Kinsman watched the Pentagon approach through the rain-streaked windows of the morning bus. As always, the bus was jammed with office workers, many of them in uniform. They were silent, morose, wrapped in their own private miseries at 7:48 in the morning.

The Pentagon corridors had once been painted in cheerful pastels, but now they were faded and grim. Kinsman checked into his own bilious green cubbyhole, noted the single appointment glowing on his desktop computer screen, and immediately headed for Colonel Murdock's office.

Frank Colt was already there, slouched in a fake leather chair in the Colonel's outer office. Otherwise the area was unpopulated. Even the secretaries' desks were empty. Frank always arrives on the scene ahead of everybody else, creases sharp and buttons polished, Kinsman thought. Wonder how he does it?

"Morning," said Colt, barely glancing up at Kinsman.

"I'm glad you didn't say *good* morning," Kinsman replied.

"Sure as shit ain't that."

Kinsman nodded. "Murdock's not in yet?"

Colt gave him a surly look. "Hey, man, it's only eight o'clock. He told us to be here at eight sharp, right? That means he won't waltz in here for another half-hour. You know that."

The Colonel's got his own car, he doesn't have to hit the bus on schedule.

"How'd the party go last night?" Colt asked.

"Lousy. Neal's getting more stubborn every year."

"We're gonna hafta lower the boom on him."

"That might not be so easy."

"I know, but what else is there?"

"Maybe if we got somebody to brief him on the space-plane interceptor . . . he's pissed about not being in on that."

"Murdock don't have the guts to suggest that upstairs."

"I know."

The secretaries began drifting in, chatting over their plastic cups of synthetic coffee. True luxury now consisted of obtaining real coffee, smuggled in through the embargo that extended from Mexico's borders southward.

Sniffing at the aroma, Colt said, "How can they make it smell so good and taste so lousy?"

Kinsman shook his head.

"Damned Commies won't stop at nothing," Colt complained to the world in general. "First they cut off our oil, and now our coffee."

The Colonel's private secretary, an iron-gray woman with a hawklike unsmiling face, arrived last—as befitted her rank.

"Colonel Murdock is upstairs," she informed Kinsman and Colt. How she knew this was a mystery they did not question. "He's briefing the General on yesterday's testimony."

Yesterday's fiasco, thought Kinsman.

The two majors sat in front of the chief secretary's desk. Kinsman felt like a traveling salesman kept waiting before being allowed to make his pitch to the prospective customer.

"You catch the late news last night?" Colt asked.

Kinsman shook his head.

"Shoulda seen our beloved leader," Colt said solemnly.

The secretary glared at him, but quickly returned her attention to the morning mail on her desk.

"Murdock was on the news last night?"

"Sure was. Big floppy handkerchief and all."

"Terrific."

"They showed the part where he got mixed up between miles and kilometers and wound up saying the Moon's bigger'n the Earth."

They both laughed. The secretary glowered at them.

Colonel Murdock burst into the anteroom, his usual worried frown etched into near panic, his uniform jacket unbuttoned, his tie pulled loose.

The secretary rose with a handful of papers.

"Not now!" Murdock's voice was high and shrill.

Christ, Kinsman thought, he's already four o'clock nervous and it isn't even eight-thirty yet!

"Get in here, both of you!" the Colonel snapped as he opened the door to his private office.

By Pentagon standards, Murdock's room was almost sumptuous: a real wood desk, several cushioned chairs, even a synthetic leather couch along the far wall, beneath the National Space Society map of the Moon. The Colonel had a standard-issue desktop computer, but no less than four television sets bunched side by side against the wall opposite the desk. Most impressive of all, it was an outside office with a real window that looked out on the gray river and the fog-shrouded National Airport.

That's the only thing he's really good at, Kinsman said to himself: feathering his own nest. He doesn't believe in Moonbase any more than McGrath does, but he'll use it to worm his way farther up the ladder.

"We've got troubles," the Colonel said. He sat at his desk hard enough to make his jowls quiver.

Colt and Kinsman took the chairs closest to the desk.

"What kind of troubles, sir?" Colt always addressed the Colonel in the formally correct manner. But he always looked to Kinsman as if he were on the edge of laughing at the man. Something about Murdock amused Colt; probably the same flustered incompetence that infuriated Kinsman.

"The General is apeshit over the way the Appropriations Committee hearings are going. He's getting pressure from the Deputy Secretary and the Deputy Secretary's getting it from the Secretary himself. Which means that the White House is putting on the squeeze. The White House!"

Kinsman smiled inwardly. Newton was right. For every force there is a reaction. If the Senate weren't putting up resistance to Moonbase, the White House wouldn't even know it was in the budget request.

Colt was saying, "Sir, if the White House is interested why don't they put the squeeze on the Committee directly? If they leaned on Senator McGrath, for example . . ."

"Can't, can't, can't!" Murdock panted. "McGrath is aiming at Minority Leader next time around. He'd use the pressure from the White House to show his people how good he is—fighting against the Pentagon and even against the President to save the taxpayers' precious dollars."

"Politics," Colt said, making it sound disgusting.

"We've got to come up with something, and *fast*," Murdock said, his pudgy little hands fluttering around the desktop. "The General wants us to go with him to the Deputy

Secretary's office at three this afternoon."

No wonder he's terrified, Kinsman realized. It's guillotine time.

Colt seemed completely unawed. "It seems to me, sir, that there's only one thing we can do."

Murdock's hands clenched into childlike little fists. "What? What is it?"

"Well, sir, of course I'm not in on all the details of the upper echelon's big picture . . ."

He's deliberately drawing it out. Kinsman suppressed a grin as he watched Murdock's wide-eyed, open-mouthed anticipation.

". . . but it seems to me, sir, that Senator McGrath would be much more sympathetic to the entire Aerospace Force program if he were fully briefed on the spaceplane interceptor program."

Sonofabitch! Kinsman almost laughed aloud. You stole that right out of my pocket, Frank.

"No!" Murdock shrieked. "Can't do that! He'd run right to the media with it! We can't let them know we're designing a manned interceptor to knock out the Russians' satellites! McGrath would *love* to leak that one!"

"But the Senate Appropriations Committee already knows about the program," Colt said. "Sir."

"Only the chairman," Murdock snapped. "Nobody else has been briefed. Nobody!"

"But they all know that the program exists," Kinsman pointed out. "McGrath knows about it, and he's steamed because he hasn't been formally briefed. He *is* the ranking minority member of the committee."

Murdock shook his head. "There's no connection between our Moonbase program and SDI's interceptor."

"There could be," Colt answered. "There *will* be, sooner or later."

"The Moon is not a militarized area," Kinsman said.

"Then why the fuck are we tryin' to set up a base there?" Colt's profanity, like his cool, was carefully planned and judiciously used, Kinsman knew. But Murdock's reaction was a startled gasp.

"We're *military* men," Colt went on. "We can talk about hospitals and peaceful applications of space technology and even cooperate with the Russians here and there, but we're in this for military reasons. Anything else is just bullshit."

"We are bound by the Space Treaty of 1967," Kinsman said, keeping his voice low, calm. "Military weaponry cannot be put on the Moon."

"You think the Soviets won't put weapons there?"

"No, they won't, because we'll be right alongside them on the Moon. We'll watch each other."

Colt edged forward in his chair. "Listen, man. Both sides are starting to deploy their Star Wars stuff, right? We're developing the spaceplane so we can knock out their ABM satellites as fast as they put 'em in orbit, right? They're gonna be doing the same to us, you can bet on it. There's gonna be a war in orbit, man. Maybe it'll be only the machines that get hurt, but it's gonna be a war, all the same."

"We can't tell people like McGrath that we'll be fighting in space!" Murdock's voice was quaking. "He'd have it all over the media in a hot second. We'd go down in flames."

Kinsman glanced at his wristwatch. "Sir . . . I've got to get over to the Capitol. The committee hearings resume at ten."

He left the Colonel's office like a suburban businessman fleeing a downtown pornography shop, hoping that nobody had seen him there. Once in his own office he squeezed behind his battered metal desk and punched out a phone number.

Mary-Ellen's face filled the tiny display screen on his desk. "Hello, Chet! How are you feeling this morning?"

"Okay, I guess. It was a good party. Aspirin helps."

She smiled ruefully. "I've got to get this place into some semblance of order for a dinner party tonight."

"Uh, Mary—I've got to bug out of here and get to the hearings. Is Diane there?"

Her face clouded briefly. "I don't think she's awake yet."

Dammitall! "Look . . . when she gets up, would you ask her to meet me at the hearings at noon? I've got to talk with her. It's important."

Mary-Ellen nodded as if she understood. "Certainly, Chet. I don't know if she'll be free, but I'll tell her."

"Thanks."

The District Metro connected the Pentagon with the

Capitol, so Kinsman did not have to go out into the bleak morning again. The subway train was bleak enough: crowded, noisy, dirty with graffiti and shreds of refuse. It was hot and rancid in the jam-packed train. Smells of human sweat, a hundred different breakfasts, cigarettes, and the special steamy reek of rain-soaked clothing.

The morning's hearing was given over to an antimilitary lobby consisting of, it seemed to Kinsman, housewives, clergymen, and public relations flaks. The old rococo hearing chamber was buzzing with witnesses and their friends, photographers, reporters, senators and their scurrying aides. TV cameras were jammed into one side of the chamber, their glaring hot lights bathing the long green-topped table where the committee members sat facing the smaller table for witnesses.

Who signs the TV stations' energy permits? Kinsman wondered idly as a middle-aged woman with too much makeup on her face read from a prepared statement in a penetrating voice that jangled with New York nasality:

"We are not against the development of useful programs that will benefit the American taxpayer. We support and endorse the efforts of American industry to develop Solar Power Satellites and thereby provide new energy for our nation. But we cannot support, nor do we endorse, spending additional billions of tax dollars on military programs in space. Outer space should be a peaceful domain, not a place in which to escalate the arms race."

Kinsman slouched on a bench in the rear of the crowded hearing chamber, watching the TV monitors because they gave him a better view of the witness. He wished that he did not agree with her.

The woman looked up from her prepared text and said, "Let us never forget the words that we left on the Moon, engraved on the *Apollo 11* landing craft: 'We came in peace for all humankind.'"

The crowd she had brought with her applauded, as did several of the senators. Kinsman snorted at the misquotation. Feminist revisionism. He saw that McGrath was smiling at the woman as she got up from the witness's chair, but not applauding her.

An aide came to McGrath's side, appearing magically

from behind the Senator's high-backed chair and whispering into McGrath's ear. He looked up, shading his eyes against the TV lights, and scanned the room. Then he spoke briefly to the aide, who disappeared as magically as he had arrived.

The next witness was a minister and former Army chaplain who now headed his own church in Louisiana. As he was being introduced McGrath's aide suddenly popped up beside Kinsman.

"Major Kinsman?"

Kinsman jumped as if a cop had suddenly clapped him on the shoulder.

"Yes," he whispered.

Wordlessly the young man handed him a note which read: *See you in the corridor when the session ends. Diane.*

It was neatly typed, even the signature. She must have phoned Neal's office, Kinsman realized. By the time he looked up from the yellow paper the aide was gone.

Kinsman sat through two more witnesses, both university professors. The first one, when he was not toying with his mustache, was an economist who showed charts which he claimed proved that *private* investment in space industries would help the national economy greatly, but *government* investment in space would only increase the inflation rate. The other, an aging, grossly overweight biophysicist, insisted that space development of any kind was unsound ecologically.

"It will cost more in energy and environmental degradation," he intoned in a deep, shaking, doomsday voice, "to place large numbers of workers into space than those workers will ever be able to return to the people of this Earth in the form of energy or usable goods. Space is only good for the very rich, and it will be the poor peoples of the Earth who will pay the price for the privileged few."

As soon as Kinsman saw that the committee chairman was going to gavel the session into adjournment he ducked out the big gleaming oak double doors and into the quiet, marble-walled corridor. Diane was walking up the hall toward him.

"Perfect timing," Kinsman said, taking her by the arm.

Her smile was good to see. "I can't make it a long lunch, Chet," she warned. "I've got to meet Larry and fly up to New York for a contract negotiation."

"Oh."

"I'll only be gone overnight. I've got a concert up there Friday night, then the whole weekend's taken up with briefings and medical checkups . . ."

"With what?"

The click of their footsteps on the marble floor was lost as the rest of the crowd poured out of the hearing chamber and into the corridor.

Raising her voice, Diane said, "I've been invited to fly up to the opening of Space Station Alpha. Didn't Neal tell you?"

"No, he didn't."

"I thought he had. We're going up on the special VIP shuttle Monday. Just for the day."

Kinsman felt stunned.

Diane was grinning at him. "I thought it'd be fun to see what it's like up there. Maybe I'll find out what fascinates you about it so much."

Nodding absently, he led Diane to the elevators that went down to the basement cafeteria. "You've been invited to Alpha," he muttered. "That's more than anybody's done for me."

Diane said nothing.

An elevator opened and he ushered her into it, then slapped the DOOR CLOSE button before any of the crowd coming down the corridor could reach them.

"You'll be tied up all weekend?" Kinsman asked.

"That's what they told me."

"I thought maybe we could get together for dinner or something."

Diane gave a little shake of her head. "I don't think so, Chet. I'm sorry."

The elevator door slid open and they were faced with another crowd, the clerks and secretaries who were lined up for their cafeteria lunch. Silently, numbly, Kinsman got into the line behind Diane. They picked up their trays and selected their food: Diane a fruit salad, Kinsman a bowl of bean soup. Both passed the steam tables with their pathetic-looking "specials." Both took iced fruit drinks.

Kinsman led Diane through the crowd to the farthest corner of the busy, clattering cafeteria and found a table that was big enough only for the two of them.

"It's not the fanciest restaurant in town," he said as they sat down. "But it's the toughest to bug."

"What did you say?" Diane's eyes went wide.

He gestured at the crowded cafeteria. "Nobody knows who's going to sit where. And the background noise is high enough to defeat mikes hidden in the ceiling."

"You're serious?"

Kinsman nodded. "You remember last night, you were asking me why I want Moonbase so much?"

She nodded.

"It's not just a lunar base, Diane." He hesitated, wondering how much he could tell her, how far he could trust her. "It's a new world. I want to build a new world."

"On the Moon."

"That's the best place for it."

"You *are* serious, aren't you?"

"I sure as hell am."

She tried to laugh; it came out as an unsure giggle. "But the Moon . . . it's so desolate, so foresaken . . ."

"Have you been there?" he countered. "Have you watched the Earth rise? Or planted footprints where no human being has ever walked before? Have you been anywhere in your whole life where you really were on your own? Where you had the time and the room and the peace to think?"

"That's what you want?"

"Being here is like being in jail. It's a madhouse. I'm locked into Pentagon level three, ring D, corridor F, room number—"

"But we're all in that same jail, Chet. One way or another, we're all locked up in the same madhouse."

"It doesn't have to be that way." He reached out to grasp her hand. "We can build a new world, a new society, all those things you sing about in your songs—love, freedom, hope. We can have them."

"You can have them," Diane said. "What about all the billions of others who can't get to your new world, no matter what?"

"We've got to start someplace. And we've got to start now, right *now*, before we sink so far back into the mud that we won't have the energy or the materials or the people to do

193

the job. Civilization's cracking apart, Diane."

"And you want to run away from the catastrophe."

"No! I want to prevent it." Realizing the truth of it as he spoke the words, Kinsman listened to himself, as surprised as Diane at his revelation. "We can build a new society on the Moon. We can set an example, just the way the new colonies of America set an example for the old world of Europe. We can send energy back to the Earth, raw materials—but most of all, we can send hope."

"That's not your real reason," she said. "Nobody ever did anything for the sake of philosophy. That's not what's really driving you."

"It's a part of it. A big part."

Diane studied his face. "But only part. What's the rest of it, Chet? Why is this so important to you?"

"It's the freedom, Diane. There are no rulebooks up there. No chains of command. You can work with people on the basis of their abilities, not their rank or their connections. It's—it's so completely different that I don't know if I can describe it to you. There's nothing like it on Earth."

"Freedom," Diane echoed.

"In space. On the Moon. A new society. A new world. A world that you could be part of, Diane."

She shook her head. "Not me. I can see how important it is to you, Chet, but it's not for me." Her hand slid away from his. "If I'm going to help build a new world, it'll be right here on *terra firma*. That's where we need it."

He leaned back in his chair. "By singing folk songs."

"They give people hope, too, you know."

Kinsman clenched his empty hand. "You'll never make a new society on Earth, kid. Too many self-interests. Too much history to undo. Society's locked in place here. The only way to unlock it is to build a showplace . . ."

"A Utopia?" She grinned at the thought.

"It won't be Utopia. But it'll be better than anything here on Earth."

She started to shake her head again, but Kinsman leaned forward intently. "Listen to me," he said urgently. "Whether you agree with me or not doesn't matter. But you've got to tell Neal that the longer he fights against the Moonbase appropriation the closer he's pushing us into a major confrontation in space, a full-scale conflict with the Russians that can only end in nuclear war."

Diane stared at him. "I should tell Neal . . . why do you think that I—"

"You've got to!" Kinsman insisted. "I can't talk to him directly. Not even through Mary-Ellen. They'll know what I'm doing: the brass, the people who are pushing us toward war. But you can warn him. He'd listen to you."

Her face was a frantic mixture of fear and disbelief. "But I won't see him until—"

"See him! Tell him! It's important. Vital."

"But why can't you—"

"He'd want specifics from me that I can't give him. And any conversations I have with him are probably monitored."

"How did you—"

"You can talk to him," Kinsman went on, ignoring her objections. "Tell him it's either a peaceful Moonbase or the spaceplane interceptor. He'll understand."

Kinsman walked Diane to the front entrance of the Capitol and down the long granite steps that gave the building its impressive facade. Larry Davis was waiting for her in a real limousine, long and luxurious, pearl gray, with a liveried black driver.

"Come on!" he yelled out the car window. "We'll miss the flight and there's not another one till six!"

Kinsman deliberately held Diane for a moment and kissed her. She seemed surprised.

"Call me when you get back to town," he said.

"Okay," she answered shakily.

"And talk to Neal."

"Yes . . . yes." She ran down the last few steps and into the waiting limousine.

The car pulled away with a screech of tires on the wet paving, a rare sound in conservation-conscious Washington. Kinsman watched the limousine thread its way through the sparse traffic. Not a bad way to travel, he mused, for somebody who sings about the hungry poor.

The weather had cleared enough for Kinsman to take the bus back to the Pentagon. The sky was still gray as he waited for the bus in the L-shaped enclosure at the curb, but the rain had ended. The enclosure was filthy with litter, its plastic walls scribbled with graffiti. It stank of urine. Finally the steamer came chugging into sight. Just as its doors opened for Kinsman, another man came running down the sidewalk hollering for the driver to wait for him.

Kinsman saw that it was Tug Wynne puffing toward the bus, and silently wished the driver would close the doors and hurry on. But the sallow-faced Hispanic was in no hurry. He waited patiently for the burly newsman.

Kinsman took a back seat in the nearly empty bus. Sure enough, Wynne came over to him.

"Mind if I sit with ya?"

"Not at all," Kinsman lied. "Go right ahead."

Wynne slid into the seat, wedging Kinsman solidly between the window and his own bulk. From the smell of it, Wynne's lunch had been mostly bourbon.

"Not much fireworks in this morning's hearings, eh?"

"Not much," Kinsman agreed. The bus lurched around a corner and headed down Delaware Avenue, chuffing.

"You see the look on the chairman's face when that perfessor started talkin' about the dangers of beaming microwaves through the atmosphere?"

"That's when he closed the session, wasn't it?"

"Sure was. He's not gonna give any eco-nut a chance to scare people about power satellites. Not with GE back in his home state!" Wynne chuckled to himself.

"It was time to break for lunch anyway," said Kinsman.

"Yeah. Say, wasn't that Diane Lawrence in the cafeteria with you?"

"Yes. She was singing at the party last night. Didn't you hear her?"

Wynne looked impressed. "And now she's breaking bread with you. Fast work. Or is she an old family friend, too?"

"I've known Diane for years," Kinsman said, staring out of the bus window at the passing buildings. This part of Washington was drab and rundown. Not much money between the Capitol and the Navy Yard. Just people's homes. Kids playing on the sidewalks. They'll grow up to stand in unemployment lines.

Wynne jarred him out of it. "Haven't seen you with any women since you arrived in Washington."

"My private life," Kinsman said, still staring out the window, "is my private life."

"Sure. I know. And I guess it must make some kinda mental block . . . killing that girl like that."

Kinsman whirled on him. "Stop fishing, dammit! I've got nothing to say to you on that subject."

"Sure. I understand. But you know, reporters hear things . . . rumors float around. Like, I heard you got hurt pretty bad yourself up there." He waggled a forefinger skyward.

"Bullshit," Kinsman snapped.

"I know you gotta deny it, and all. But what I heard was that you got hurt . . . radiation damage, they say. And now you're impotent. Or sterile."

Thinking of the thousands of nights he had spent alone since returning from that mission and the agonies of the few times he had tried to make love to a woman, Kinsman laughed bitterly.

"That's what they say, do they?" he asked Wynne.

The older man nodded, his expression blank.

"Well, you can tell them for me that they're all crazy."

Wynne nodded gravely. "Glad to hear it. But how come nobody's ever seen you go out with a woman? In all the time since you've been in the District . . ."

The sonofabitch thinks I'm gay! "Listen. I am heterosexual and I'm not sterile. I've never been involved in any accidents in space or anywhere else that would impair my ability to make a woman pregnant. Is that clear?"

"Major, you have a way of making your points."

"Good." And it's not a lie, either. Not completely. I'm not impotent—except when I'm with a woman.

The office of the Deputy Secretary made Colonel Murdock's painfully acquired luxuries seem petty and vain. The office was huge, and in a corner of the Pentagon so that it had *two* windows. Rich dark wood paneling covered the walls. Deep carpeting. Plush chairs. Flags flanking the broad, polished mahogany desk.

General Sherwood was a picturebook Aerospace Force officer: handsome chiseled profile, silver-gray hair, the piercing eyes of an eagle. He sat before the Deputy Secretary's desk looking perfectly at ease in his blue, beribboned uniform, yet so alert and intelligent that one got the impression he could instantly take command of an airplane, a spacecraft, or an entire war.

He carries those two stars on his shoulders, thought Kinsman, with plenty of room to add more.

The Deputy Secretary, Ellery Marcot, was a sloppy civilian. Tall, high-domed, flabby in the middle, and narrow in the chest, he peered at the world suspiciously through thick old-fashioned bifocals. His suit was gray, his thinning hair and mustache grayer, his skin as faded as an old manila file folder. Kinsman had never seen the man without a cigarette. His desk was a chaotic sea of papers marked by islands of ashtrays brimming with cigarette butts.

"Gentlemen," he said after the polite handshakes were finished and the four uniformed officers seated according to rank before his desk, "we have reached a critical decision point."

General Sherwood nodded crisply but said nothing. It would have been easy to assume that his Academy-perfect exterior was nothing but an empty shell. His eyes were *too* sky-blue, his hair just the right shade of experienced yet virile silver. But Kinsman knew better. He'll get those other two stars. And soon.

Marcot blinked myopically at them. "For the past four years the Aerospace Force has struggled to maintain some semblance of an effective program for manned spaceflight. We have had to battle against NASA, the Congress, and the White House."

"And our own SDI Office," Colt added.

Murdock turned sharply toward Colt. But then he saw General Sherwood smiling and nodding.

"Yes, the Strategic Defense group," Marcot agreed, "and their ideas of doing everything with automation."

"But we have made significant progress," the General said.

"Along the wrong road," Marcot snapped.

"It was the only road available at the time," General Sherwood replied, his voice just a trifle harder than it had been a moment earlier. "We had no way of knowing that the SDI Office would try to outflank us with this manned interceptor program."

Kinsman spoke up. "Sir, if it hadn't been for our Moonbase program, and the cooperative Soviet program that's linked to it, the Aerospace Force would have had to surrender its entire manned spaceflight capability to NASA several years ago."

"I understand that, Major," said Marcot. "But the Appropriations Committee is not impressed."

"Their attitude is disastrous," General Sherwood agreed. "If they have their way, they'll shoot down Moonbase *and* the spaceplane. They'll leave us entirely defenseless in space. What good are the ABM satellites if we can't protect them against Soviet interceptors?"

Marcot lit another cigarette, then rummaged through his messy papers. "State Department doesn't agree. Sent a memo . . . it's here someplace . . ."

"The State Department," Sherwood muttered, real loathing in his voice.

Colt said, "It's like our military presence in Antarctica. We've got to show the Soviets that we're able and willing to defend our interests, wherever they are."

"The Russians are going ahead with their share of the lunar base," Colonel Murdock said, his voice sounding almost hopeful.

"All the more reason for us to be up there alongside them," Sherwood said. "We must not allow them to have the Moon for themselves."

Feeling like a tightrope walker, Kinsman said, "With all due respect, sir, the Appropriations Committee won't be impressed by that argument. Senators like McGrath are dead-set against anything that looks like the old Space Race of the Sixties."

Marcot peered at him through a haze of smoke. "McGrath," he murmured.

"That's why we initiated the hospital program." Kinsman went on. "The old Air Force pioneered in flight medicine and it would be in keeping with Aerospace Force traditions and missions to build a hospital on the Moon. That would give us a presence on the Moon *plus* a role that has real meaning."

"And whose idea was it," Marcot asked, "to make the base a joint Soviet-American project? Durban's, wasn't it? Him and his internationalist pipe dreams!"

"That was done for funding purposes," Kinsman said. "It was easier to get the program started by showing that the Russians were going to share its costs."

"Well, the funding is about to run out," Marcot grumbled. "Our munificent Congress is backing out of the program now that the preliminary explorations are finished and it's time to commit major money for the permanent base."

"And we can't expect the SDI guys to divert funds from their program," General Sherwood said.

"Maybe we should forget about the Moon and concentrate on the antimissile defense. If we can prevent the Soviets from putting up their own version of Star Wars . . ." Marcot let his voice trail off.

"Leave the Moon to the Russians?" General Sherwood sounded almost alarmed.

"What good is the Moon?" Marcot asked. "It has no real military value."

Colt pointed out, "It will when it starts supplying fuels and expendables like oxygen for the SDI satellites. And for the factories the corporations claim they want to build."

"That's ten years away," Marcot said. "Twenty."

Kinsman said nothing, but thought to himself, So the Russians will win control of the Moon after all, in spite of everything we've done over all these years. He shrugged inwardly. Maybe they deserve it. Maybe men like Leonov will do better with it than we would.

"I still don't want Reds on the Moon alone," General Sherwood said. "Bad enough we have to share it with them. Ten, twenty, even fifty years from now—if and when the Moon has any military significance, then we must not allow the Soviets to have it totally to themselves. Especially by default!"

Marcot sank back in his chair, cowed temporarily by the General's fire. "Well, then," he said at last, sucking hard on his cigarette, "how do we get around this man McGrath —without compromising the spaceplane program?"

"We could brief him on the interceptor," Kinsman heard himself saying, "in exchange for a written oath of secrecy. I think a large part of his resistance to the Moonbase idea is that he feels out in the cold on the spaceplane."

Shaking his head, Marcot replied, "The White House has forbidden us to tell McGrath anything about it. He's a rabble-rouser—a secrecy oath won't mean a thing to him."

"I disagree, sir," Kinsman said. "I've known Neal since we were kids. He has a very strong sense of responsibility. If he signed a secrecy oath, he would keep his word."

But Marcot's head was still waggling negatively. "And he's nosing after the Minority Leader's job. From there he can aim for the White House. We can't give him anything that would help him along *that* route."

"But—"

"No," Marcot went on, tapping the ash from his cigarette, "I don't see any way around it. Either you convince McGrath that Moonbase is necessary or we have to forget about the Moon and concentrate all our resources on the spaceplane and strategic defense."

General Sherwood turned to Kinsman. "It's up to you, then, Major. Do you think you can handle it?"

"If he can't, sir, no one can," Colt said before Kinsman could open his mouth.

Colonel Murdock's expression could have turned sweet cream into paint remover, but he remained silent.

"The first thing I'll need," Kinsman heard himself say, "is a seat on that VIP flight Monday to Alpha. McGrath's going up for the dedication ceremonies. It might be a good chance to work on him."

"Or flush him out of an airlock," Marcot muttered.

Sherwood gestured to Colonel Murdock. "See to it, will you?"

"Yessir. But we'll have to bump—"

"Then bump," the General snapped. "Whoever."

Marcot blew a big, relieved cloud of smoke toward the ceiling. "That's it, then. We push ahead with the interceptor program and handle the Moonbase problem separately."

"And let McGrath determine whether we build Moonbase or not," General Sherwood muttered. He was not pleased.

"He's going to make that determination anyway," Marcot said. "We might as well face up to the obvious."

Kinsman said nothing.

Returning to his office, Kinsman slumped behind his desk and stared at the old photograph of a lunar landscape he had taped to the wall. The picture showed an astronaut —himself—kneeling in his lunar suit, working over a gadgety-looking piece of scientific gear. He had forgotten what the equipment was, what it was supposed to do. The photograph was faded, its edges browned and curling.

Getting old, he said to himself. And useless.

Beyond the machine and the man in the picture, the broad plain of a lunar *mare* stretched out to the abrupt horizon, where a rounded worn mountain showed its tired-looking peak. Above, riding in the black sky, was the half-sphere of Earth. Years earlier, when the photo had been new, the Earth had been a brilliant blue and white. Now it looked faded and gray, along with everything else in the office.

Suddenly Kinsman got up from his desk and went out into the corridor, heading for Colonel Murdock's office.

What are you going to tell him? he asked himself.

The answer was a mental shrug. Damned if I know. But I've got to tell him *something*.

You can quit, you know. Walk away from it. Murdock would be happy to see you go.

The voice in his head became sardonic. And do what? Wait till I'm Durban's age and have them carry me to the Moon on a stretcher?

There's more to life than getting to the Moon.

He answered immediately, No there's not. Not for me. That's where I've got to be, away from all this crap.

They're going to bring all this crap with them! You know that.

He shook his head doggedly. Not if I can help it.

The Colonel's outer office was empty again. Not even the secretary was there. Kinsman went straight to Murdock's door and rapped sharply on it.

"What? Who is it?"

Kinsman smiled at the thought of how the Colonel must have jumped at the unexpected knocking. He tried the door, but it was locked.

"It's Kinsman," he called. Then, thinking there might be

a superior officer locked inside with Murdock, he added, "Sir."

Footsteps. Muffled voices. Then the door opened. Murdock looked flustered.

"What is it?" the Colonel demanded, holding the door open just a few centimeters.

Kinsman heard the other door, the one that opened directly onto the corridor outside, snap shut softly. Whoever had been in the office with Murdock had left.

"I've got to talk to you," Kinsman said, "about this McGrath business."

Colonel Murdock was one of the few men Kinsman knew who could look furious and terrified at the same time. Now he also looked sheepish, with a little boy's caught-in-the-act expression on his chubby face.

He yanked the door open all the way. "All right, come on in."

"If I'm interrupting anything . . ."

Murdock glared at him. "Just a White House liaison man, a representative from the National Security Agency who briefs the President every morning. That's all!"

"I spooked him?" Kinsman punned.

Murdock ignored it. He went behind his desk and plopped into his swivel chair. "Make it fast, Kinsman. I've got a golf date that I can't afford to miss."

Taking the chair directly in front of the Colonel's desk, Kinsman realized he did not know quite where to begin.

"I . . . it's this McGrath thing," he said. "I've been put squarely on the spot. If I can't turn Neal around, Moonbase goes down the tubes."

Murdock nodded. "That's right."

"I don't like it."

"You don't like it? You don't like what?"

"The whole setup," Kinsman said. "Making the whole Moonbase program hinge on my ability to pressure McGrath."

"You can apply all the pressure to him that you can lay your hands on. We'll back you."

With a shake of his head, Kinsman replied, "That's what I don't like."

"So what?" Murdock snapped. "You still have to follow orders, just like the rest of us."

"But Neal's been a friend of mine since—"

"Which is why you got picked for this job. You ought to be able to find a few things in his background that could help to persuade him. Everybody's got bones in their closet."

"Yeah," Kinsman murmured. "Everybody."

"It's either a success with McGrath," the Colonel pointed out needlessly, "or the whole Moonbase program goes into mothballs."

"And the Russians get the Moon to themselves."

"And all of us—including you, Kinsman—get transferred to the Strategic Defense Initiative Office. Since you're grounded, you won't even get to play with the spaceplane. You'll sit at a desk here in the Pentagon for the rest of your life." Murdock smiled slyly.

"It's wrong."

"It's *decided*. You heard the Deputy Secretary. Your job is to convince McGrath. Otherwise, forget about Moonbase."

"We shouldn't be throwing the Moon away," Kinsman insisted.

"Then get McGrath to vote in favor of the base. Get him to swing the minority vote on the committee. Put Durban to work on him. Do whatever you like."

"Durban's in the hospital."

Murdock shrugged.

"Dammitall!" Kinsman exploded. "I don't want this! I don't want any part of it. I want to be flying, not crawling around these goddamned corridors like some roach!"

"Listen to me, hotshot," Murdock snapped back, his face reddening. "You're grounded. Understand? You'll never fly another Air Force plane or spacecraft again. Never! We should never have let you back on flying duty after you killed that Russian."

Kinsman could not answer. His voice choked in his throat.

"You want the Moon so goddamned much," Murdock was yelling now, "you better get your friend McGrath to vote the right way! Because the only way you're ever going to get off the ground, mister, is as a passenger!"

Kinsman's pulse was thundering in his ears the way it had

so long ago, when he had let his temper run away and lead him to murder.

But Murdock was smiling triumphantly at him now. "I know you, Kinsman. I know what makes you tick. You want to get to the Moon and leave us all behind you. Fine! I'm all for it. But you'd better make sure there's a base up there for you to go to; otherwise, you'll be flying a desk for the rest of your life."

"McGrath," Kinsman croaked, "will never go for it. Never."

"I've sweated blood over you," Murdock went on, ignoring Kinsman's words. "You always thought you were so goddamned superior. Hotshot flier. You and Colt, a couple of smartasses. Well, you just goddamned better do the job you're assigned to do or you'll be shuffling papers at a desk until you drop dead!"

For a moment Kinsman said nothing. It took every effort he could muster not to get up from the chair and punch the fat leering face gloating at him.

Finally he said, "I could resign my commission. I could quit the Aerospace Force."

"And do what?" Murdock asked smugly. "Get a job with NASA? Or one of the aerospace corporations?"

"You don't think I could?"

The Colonel's stubby-fingered hands were rubbing together as if by their own volition. "I don't know who would hire a man with a disturbed mental background like yours, Kinsman. After all, if they ask us for your background, we'd have to tell them how . . . unbalanced you can be."

Kinsman was on his feet and grabbing the Colonel's lapels before he realized what he was doing. Murdock was white-faced, half out of his chair, hanging by Kinsman's fists.

Closing his eyes, Kinsman released the Colonel.

"Okay," he said, forcing his breath back to normal. "You win. I'll work on McGrath."

Murdock dropped back into his chair. He smoothed his tunic and looked up at Kinsman furiously. But there was still fear in his eyes.

"You'd better work on McGrath," the Colonel said, his voice trembling. "And the next time—"

"No!" Kinsman leveled a pointed finger at him. "The

next time you try holding that over my head, the next time you say anything about it to me or anyone else, there'll be another murder."

"You . . . you just get to McGrath."

"Sure. I'll get to him." Kinsman headed for the door, thinking, I'll take him just like Lee took Washington.

He was staring at the ceiling, waiting for the sleep that was taking longer each night to reach him, when the buzzer sounded. In the darkness he groped for the switch over his sofabed. "Yes?"

"Chet, it's me. Diane."

Wordlessly he groped for the button that opened the lobby door of the apartment building. Only after he let go of it did he think to ask if she was alone.

He rolled out of the sofabed and turned on the battery-powered lamp on his end table. The main electrical service was shut down for the night, of course. Only battery-operated devices, like the building's security locks, could be used after twelve-thirty. Kinsman often wondered if his refrigerator was really insulated well enough to keep everything fresh overnight. He never kept enough food in it to worry over.

By the time Diane knocked on his thin apartment door he was wrapped in a shapeless gray robe and had lit a couple of candles. His wristwatch said 1:23 A.M.

He opened the door. Diane stood there alone, wearing a light sleeveless blouse and dark form-fitting slacks.

"I thought you were in New York," Kinsman said.

"I took the bus back after dinner," Diane replied, stepping into the room.

Even in candlelight the apartment looked shabby. The open sofabed was a tangled mess of sweaty sheets. The desk was littered with paperwork. The room's only chair looked stiff and uninviting.

"It's been an exhausting day," Diane said. "Those bastards in the Public Safety Office damned near canceled Friday's concert. Said my songs were too inflammatory. Thank God for Larry."

"Would you like a drink?" Kinsman asked as he locked the door. "I've got some scotch and there's a bottle of vodka around here someplace."

"Any beer?"

"Might not be very cold."

Diane unslung the heavy leather bag from her shoulder and let it clunk to the floor. She sat on the edge of the bed, kicked her boots off, and leaned back tiredly.

"Beer's fine . . . even warm beer."

"Why the hell did you come back tonight? And how'd you get from the bus terminal this time of night?"

"Phoned for a cab and waited at the terminal until they scared one up for me."

Kinsman took the four steps to his kitchenette and bent down to open the refrigerator. The beer bottles seemed fairly cold to his touch.

"That terminal's not a good place to hang around," he said, peering into the shadowy shelves above the sink for a clean glass. "Especially at night."

"There were a couple of cops. I talked with them while I waited. They recognized me from my videos. They even encouraged the taxi company to find a cab for me."

Handing her the bottle and a glass, Kinsman said, "It pays to be beautiful."

"And famous," she added immediately.

"But . . . why?" he asked, sitting on the floor beside the bed. "What was so important about getting back here?"

She took a swallow of beer from the bottle. "That was a pretty heavy message you laid on me this afternoon."

"Yeah, I guess it was. Have you had a chance to see Neal?"

"Not yet."

"When?"

"Tomorrow. I mean, later today—right after his committee hearings."

"Good."

"But I've got to know something, Chet. That's why I'm here."

"I can't go into the details, Diane. They're classified. But it's damned important that Neal realizes what's at stake."

"What the hell *is* at stake?" she asked.

"I can't tell you all of it . . ."

"Is this room bugged?"

He shook his head in the shadows. "No, I go over the

place pretty thoroughly every few days. And I've got a couple of friends in the Pentagon who keep track of who's listening to whom. My conversations with Neal are monitored, but I'm not important enough to have my apartment wired."

He could not see her face too well in the flickering candlelight, but Diane's voice was high with concern. "Is Neal always watched? Is his office wired, or . . ."

"His office must be. And his home was during the party. They spot-check his phones, I'm sure. That's pretty standard procedure for a senator. He knows about it; they all do. And they know how to protect themselves from it. But it means that I can't tell him everything that he needs to know."

"Just what is it he needs to know?"

Instead of answering, Kinsman got up and padded to the kitchenette for the scotch.

Almost an hour later, after two more beers for Diane and several long pulls of scotch for himself, he was saying, ". . . and that's the politics of it. I can't tell you what the other program is all about, but Marcot and the White House will clobber Neal if they get the chance. Unless, of course, he goes along with the Moonbase program."

Diane asked, "But what about you, Chet? Where do you stand in all this?"

"Right in the middle. I want Moonbase because I want to be there. I want to live on the Moon. I want to set up that new world I was telling you about."

"But if it's a military base . . ."

"Yeah, I know. Even if we start out as a hospital, even if we work jointly with the Russians, there's always the chance that the brass will start turning it into a supply center for a *real* military effort."

"They could do that?"

"Sure. Mine the lunar ores and build military satellites out of them, then place them in orbit around the Earth. Just like the corporations want to build their solar power satellites."

"But the Russians will be there too, won't they?"

Kinsman nodded. "And they'll do the same thing, once they see us do it."

"And you're caught in the middle of all this."

"Yeah, they've got me surrounded." He leaned his head

back against the wall and heard himself go on, "But that doesn't matter. It's where I've got to be if I'm ever going to make it back there."

"There?"

"To the Moon."

"It's like an obsession with you," Diane said.

He smiled at her. "Leonardo da Vinci."

"What?"

"He built gliders and tried them out himself. They never worked too well, but it was enough to make him write, 'Once you have tasted flight, you will walk the Earth with your eyes turned skyward. For there you have been, and there you long to return.'"

Diane smiled at him. "I see . . ."

"Do you?" Kinsman asked. "Do you know what it's like to have everybody around you call you a nut? You were nice about it, you called it an obsession. At the Pentagon they calls us *Luniks*."

"Us?"

"Yeah, there's a few of us, here and there. A couple in NASA, too. Guys like me. Guys willing to fight with everything we've got to get the hell off this lousy dungheap and out into the new world. Hell, I'll bet I could build a mountain just out of the paperwork in the Pentagon that'd reach the Moon. We could *walk* there!"

Diane laughed.

"Murdock and Sherwood and Marcot think we're crazy. Maybe we are. But they use us. They use us to get what they want."

"And you?"

"Sure, I'm using them to get what I want, too. But now the game's getting rough and I don't think we can all stay happy. The big boys are starting to use their muscle on us, and we *Luniks* don't have much muscle to fight back with."

"So what are you going to do now?"

"You know, once I said I'd sell my soul for the chance to get back to the Moon. Now I might have to make that choice."

"You need Neal's help, don't you?"

"He's got to vote for the Moonbase program. If he doesn't there'll be nobody left in space except the warbirds."

"Chet . . . do they know about us? Can they use our relationship to hurt Neal? To threaten him?"

Suddenly confused, Kinsman asked, "Us? What relationship?"

"Neal and me . . ."

Kinsman felt as if he were in free-fall, everything dropping away.

Diane pulled herself bolt upright on the bed. "You didn't know about us?"

"Mary-Ellen," Kinsman heard himself mutter.

"She knows," Diane said. "We've tried to keep it as quiet as possible, of course. Nobody in Washington would really care, but they would use it against Neal back in Pennsylvania. A divorce case and an affair with a pop singer—they'd crucify him back home."

"You and Neal," Kinsman said, still stunned by it. "And Mary-Ellen knows."

"We love each other, Chet. Neither of us wanted it to happen, but it has."

"Then when you stayed at their place after the party . . . Jesus Christ, I talked him into going out and finding you, way back in San Francisco!"

"Yes, that's when I first met him. But it wasn't until the Presidential campaign, when I was doing benefits for the New Youth Alliance . . ."

"And Mary-Ellen's just sitting back and letting the two of you have your fun. Or does she have a lover, too?"

"She's being awfully good about it. Says she doesn't want to hurt Neal's career. It makes me feel like hell."

But you sleep with him anyway, Kinsman growled silently. In her home. Aloud, he asked, "Are they going to get a divorce?"

Diane pushed her hair back away from her face with an automatic gesture. "I don't know. We'll see what happens after his re-election campaign next year."

Kinsman pictured Neal campaigning through the state, the solid family man with his wife and two children by his side and Diane waiting for him in motel rooms.

"I think I'm pregnant," she said in a small, almost frightened voice.

"Jesus Christ."

"I can't let anyone know it's Neal's baby. He doesn't know it himself yet."

"What'll you do?"

She shook her head. "I don't know. Have an abortion, I guess."

"And he invited you up to the space station. It wasn't just public relations." He put a slight emphasis on the word *public*. "It's a chance to be with you."

"Your people in the Pentagon don't know about this, do they?" Diane asked. "I mean, if they did they could use it to pressure Neal to vote their way . . ."

He looked up at her. "Diane—I'm one of those Pentagon people."

"But you're his friend. You wouldn't . . ."

"I'm Mary-Ellen's friend, too."

"She doesn't want him hurt."

"Yeah."

Diane swung off the bed and sat on her heels beside Kinsman, on the floor. "Chet . . . you're *my* friend, too. You wouldn't hurt the three of us, would you?"

"And what about me? What do I get?"

Diane reached out and put a hand on his shoulder.

He wanted to laugh. "When you came tapping at my chamber door, I had the crazy notion that you had come all the way down from New York to see me, to be with me."

"That was part of it," she said.

"I wanted you, Diane. I really did. I needed you."

"I'm here."

He brushed her hand away. "No. Not as a bribe. Not because Neal's home with his wife and you're lonely. Not to make me think there's a chance you might leave him for me."

"Chet . . . what can I do? What can I say?"

"Nothing. Not a damned thing."

She got to her feet. "I'd better go, then."

"Where to? There are no taxis this time of the morning. Bus service won't start again until six. You can't walk the streets after curfew."

"But there's no room here."

Kinsman stood up beside her. "Stretch out on the bed. Get some sleep. Just don't take your clothes off."

He padded around to the other side of the bed, blew out

the candles and lay down in the darkness. He could feel the warmth of her body next to his, hear her breathing slowly relax into sleep.

For a moment he thought of his interrogation by Tug Wynne. If he could see me now! Kinsman grinned at the irony of it. Sleeping next to a pregnant woman. He did not have to reach down to his crotch to know what was happening. I'm not impotent. Stupid, maybe. But not really impotent.

Several times his eyes closed and he drifted toward sleep. But each time he saw the cosmonaut drifting in silent space, her dead arms reaching out toward him.

McGrath took Mary-Ellen and their two children back to Pennsylvania, where they would stay while he flew to Florida and the new space shuttle that would take the VIPs to the dedication ceremonies aboard Space Station Alpha.

Kinsman spent the weekend doing Murdock's work for the Colonel. He pulled a fistful of Pentagon strings and became a VIP, much to the disappointment of a one-star general at Wright-Patterson Aerospace Force Base, who received a sudden phone call informing him that he had been bumped from the Alpha dedication junket.

Before flying down to Kennedy Space Center, Kinsman visited Walter Reed Hospital, where Fred Durban was. The old man was a permanent invalid now, in the cardiac ward. Kinsman sat beside his bed, the smell of antiseptics and quiet death everywhere; the clean, efficient, coldly impersonal feel of the hospital setting his nerves on edge. Durban's room was bright with flowers. The window looked out on leafy trees and a bright lovely blue sky. But the bed next to his held a retired admiral engulfed by life-support equipment that snaked wires and tubes into every part of his body. He was more machine than man.

It did not bother Durban, though. "I know it looks awful," he said cheerfully, "but that's just what I want them to do for me when I'm sinking below the red line. None of this 'death with dignity' for me! I intend to fight for every minute I can get."

He was painfully emaciated. His once-reddish hair was now nothing more than a wisp of white. His arms were bone-thin, his skin translucent. He belongs in a china shop, not a hospital, Kinsman thought. But those shaggy eyebrows were still formidable, and Durban's voice was doggedly optimistic.

"I'm just trying to hang on long enough so that you youngsters can build my lunar hospital. Up there I'll be a whole lot better. I've warned the staff here that they better keep me alive until they can transfer me to Moonbase."

Kinsman nodded and tried to smile for him. "We're working on it. Working hard."

"Damned right. Wish they had room to set up a hospital section aboard the new space station, though. I'd settle for that, right now."

"I'm going up there tomorrow."

"To Alpha? Good! Tell me about it when you get back."

"I will."

"But how's our Moonbase program working out?"

Kinsman shrugged. "The usual snags with Congress. Committees . . . you know."

Durban closed his eyes. "I've spent my entire damned life arguing with those shortsighted bastards. Anything farther downstream than the next election—forget it, as far as they're concerned."

"They don't have much foresight, that's true."

Durban lay quiet for a moment. The conversation stalled. Then he asked, "But the survey work . . . the site selection and the preliminary planning . . . that's all been done, hasn't it?"

"Yessir. I can bring you the reports, if you like. Once we get the appropriation for the coming fiscal year we can begin actual construction."

"Good." Durban smiled. "In a couple of years I'll be on the Moon, getting my second wind."

Kinsman said nothing.

Still smiling, the old man lifted a frail hand. "I know what you're thinking. In a couple of years I'll be six feet under."

"No . . ."

"Don't try to kid me, son. I can read your face like a blueprint. Von Braun never made it into space at all. Neither did Clarke or Sagan. At least I've been in orbit."

"We'll get you to the Moon, don't worry."

"I don't have a worry in the world. I know they'll never let me ride the shuttle in the shape I'm in now. If I can build my strength back up, then fine. If not, I'll die here . . . probably in this room."

Kinsman had nothing to say.

Durban went on, "But I'll *still* be with you on the Moon. I've left instructions in my will that I want to be buried there. At Moonbase. And I've got enough money stashed away to pay for it, too, by damn!"

"You're a stubborn *Lunik.*" Kinsman smiled.

"Damned right, sonny. One thing I learned early in this game. It takes more than talent, more than brains, more than connections, even. Takes stubbornness. Look at von Braun. Not the world's most brilliant engineer, but a hard-driving man who knew what he wanted and went after it, hell or high water. By God, World War Two was an *opportunity,* as far as he was concerned! The Cold War, the Space Race, he turned them all to his advantage. Other people sneered at him, called him a Nazi, an opportunist, an amoral monster. But he never wavered from his goal. He wanted the Moon and he went out and got it. We *all* got it, thanks to him."

Not all of us, Kinsman answered silently.

"You go get Moonbase started," Durban said. "Don't let them sidetrack you."

"We're trying."

"Going to the new space station, eh? Rubbing shoulders with the politicians and their sycophants. Good. But don't let them stop there. Keep driving for the Moon."

"Yessir."

Durban lifted his head slightly from the pillow. "I'll watch the ceremonies on TV. At least I can turn them off when they get too boring."

Kinsman laughed. The old man was still as feisty as ever.

"All right, son, you run along now. No fun watching an old man trying to stay alive." Durban winked at him. "Besides, I'm due for a bath . . . got a cute young nurse who thinks I'm too feeble to do her any harm."

Getting up from the bedside chair, Kinsman said, "I'll come back when I return from the ceremonies."

"Fine. I'll be waiting right here. I'm not going anyplace."

* * *

Even in the earliest morning the Florida sun was blindingly hot. Merritt Island was flat and scrubby, not at all like the hilly California coast at Vandenberg.

Kinsman had flown to Patrick Aerospace Force Base the previous night on a government charter jet filled with Congressional aides and their families. He had slept at the base's Bachelor Officers' Quarters. Now, just after dawn, he had driven a motor pool car to the space center to see the place before the newshounds and tourists cluttered it up.

In the old days of the Apollo moon shots and the original space shuttle launches, the roads and beaches would be covered with upward of half a million onlookers, as thick as ants on sugar. Official guests would have to arise at two in the morning to get to the VIP viewing stands before the roads became totally blocked with tourist cars and campers. But now, with government restrictions on travel and synfuels astronomically expensive, the roads leading to Kennedy Space Center were nearly empty. People watched launches on television, if they watched at all.

Most of the old buildings were still there, including the mammoth Vehicle Assembly Building, the largest enclosed structure on Earth, which was still used by the NASA people. The ancient launch towers, tall stately spiderworks of steel standing against the brazen sky, were strictly tourist attractions now. History had been made there, blasting out flames and mountainous billows of steam as the Saturns and Deltas and shuttles had launched men and automated probes into space. Now they stood empty and quiet, gawked at by a trickle of visitors from all around the world, lectured over by National Park Service guards surrounded by eager, curious youngsters and their sweating, sunburned, slightly bored parents.

The real action now was at the airstrip, where the new shuttles took off and landed. Unlike the older vehicles that Kinsman had flown in, the new designs were truly reusable spacecraft that took off and landed like airplanes.

The shuttle was a double-decker craft, two vehicles one atop the other, joined together like a pair of technological Siamese twins. The bottom one was the jet-powered Lifter. It was all fuel and engines, with a tiny cockpit perched high up on its massive blunt nose. It flew to the topmost reaches of the atmosphere, more than a hundred thousand feet above the ground, and then released its piggyback partner. The Orbiter, smaller of the two mates, carried the passengers and payload on into space on the thrust of its rocket engines. Both planes landed at the airstrip, separately, to be reunited for another flight.

Standing at the airstrip's edge, Kinsman stared at the ungainly-looking pair, one atop the other. *She'll never fly, Orville. Gimme a good old rocket booster and a lifting body re-entry vehicle like the Manta, the way God meant men to go into space.* But he knew that this new shuttle was making space operations practical. Military men could rocket into orbit atop bellowing boosters, but businessmen and their cargoes rode the new shuttle and saved money. It was cheaper, more efficient, and the gee loads on the passengers were negligible.

Fred Durban could ride into orbit on that bird, Kinsman knew, if he was healthy enough to get out of bed.

The shuttle would carry fifty passengers on this trip. NASA was making three flights with the same bird to the completed space station, all on this one day. The entire world would watch the station's official dedication ceremonies via satellite-relayed television.

"Hey, you! What the hell are you . . ."

Kinsman turned to see an Air Policeman yelling at him from a jeep parked a dozen meters away. The AP was in crisp uniform, with gleaming helmet and dead-black sidearm buckled to his hip. Kinsman was in his summer-weight blues. He walked slowly toward the jeep.

"Oh, sorry, Major. I couldn't see your rank with your back turned." The kid sprang out of the jeep and saluted. He dwarfed Kinsman.

"You expecting trouble, Sergeant?" Kinsman asked, returning the salute.

"Hard to say, sir. We were told some kook groups might try to stage an antigovernment demonstration. Or maybe something more violent by terrorists, like a bomb attempt."

"Well, I'm on your side. I just wanted to see the bird before everybody else got here."

"Sorry I hollered, sir."

"It's okay. Can you give me a lift back to the administration building parking area?"

"Yessir, sure." He waited for Kinsman to seat himself in the jeep, then sprinted around and slid under the steering wheel. As he switched on the nearly silent electric motor, the big sergeant asked incredulously, "You *walked* out here from the admin building, sir?"

Kinsman nodded as the salty breeze blew into his face. All the way back to the administration building he wondered at the insanity of anyone who would even think of bombing a beautiful piece of hardware like this shuttle.

The rest of the morning was a hateful blur to Kinsman. *Now I know what it's like to be invaded and conquered.* Crowds of strangers. Solicitous young Air Police—men and women—pointing you in the right direction. Smiling unctuous public relations people from NASA and the big corporations taking you by the elbow and telling you how proud and happy you should be that you're here to help make this day a success.

Not one of them knew Kinsman. No one recognized his name. No one commented on the astronaut's emblem on his tunic. He was a six-foot chunk of meat to them, a statistic. *I was working in orbit when you were in high school,* he fumed at them silently. But they just smiled and pointed and moved him along: an anonymous visitor, a VIP, a nonperson.

Kinsman was locked into a group of forty-nine strangers and walked through all the preflight ceremonies. A brief physical exam, little more than blood pressure, heartbeat, and breathing rate. The medic giving the blood-pressure tests muttered something about everybody being so excited about flying into orbit that all the pressures were reading high. Kinsman shook his head. *The equipment's miscalibrated,* he thought. *I'm not excited enough to raise my blood pressure.*

The safety lecture was designed to soothe the nerves of jittery civilians who had never gone into orbit before. Then came a five-minute video about how to handle the brief spell of weightlessness until the shuttle docked with the space station—mainly how to use the retch bag under zero-gee conditions. And every minute of the preflight rites took place under the staring eyes of the news cameras.

Kinsman resented it all: these newcomers, these strangers, these moneygrubbers who had fought against *any* programs in space until their boards of directors finally became convinced that there were profits to be made Up There.

His forty-nine "shipmates" included sixteen news reporters (eight female), three freelance writers (one a scenarist from Hollywood), eleven board members of thirteen interlocked corporations (none of them less than fifty years old), nine NASA executives who had never been out of downtown Washington before, and ten men and women (five each) who had been chosen by national lottery to represent "average taxpayers."

They all looked excited and chattered nervously as they were marched from the briefing room, past a double column of news cameras, and out into the muggy morning sunlight. A couple of the business executives seemed to be having some qualms about the thought of actually taking off in a vehicle that was built entirely by the lowest bidders, and several of the NASA desk jockeys looked a bit green. Maybe the space-sickness video got to them, Kinsman thought.

"I thought there were going to be entertainment stars," said one of the women taxpayers.

"They're on the other flight," someone answered.

The PR guide hovering nearest them said, "Two dozen stars from various fields of entertainment will be aboard the second flight, together with an equal number of senators and Congresspersons. There will also be religious leaders from all the major denominations coming up, as well."

Feeling thoroughly out of place and resentful, like an architect who is forced to serve as a clown, Kinsman climbed aboard the big glass-topped, air-conditioned bus that would take them out to the shuttle waiting on the airstrip. He took the seat that a young PR woman with a frozen smile directed him to.

"Have a pleasant flight, Colonel," she said.

"Thanks for the promotion," Kinsman replied to her departing back.

The bus chugged into motion and the speakers set into each chairback came alive with the news report of the momentous day:

"And there goes the first busload of visitors to Space Station Alpha. They're on their way!" gabbled a voice that had spent most of its life hawking consumer products. "This marks the beginning of a new era in space! Fifty ordinary people, just like you and me, will be riding to the space station just as easily and comfortably as we ride the daily bus to our homes and offices and shopping malls. Ordinary people, going into orbit, to a great man-made island in the sky . . ."

Ordinary people, thought Kinsman. Am I ordinary? Is anybody?

One of the "average taxpayers" was seated beside him, on the aisle. She stared at him for several minutes as the bus huffed slowly toward the airstrip and the radio voice prattled on.

"They didn't tell us there'd be any soldiers on this flight," she said at last.

Kinsman turned from the window to look at her. A youngish housewife: softly curled light brown hair, oval face. Dressed in a brand-new flowered pantsuit.

"I'm not a soldier," he answered, almost in a whisper. "I'm in the Aerospace Force."

"Well, why are they letting *you* up? This isn't a military satellite." She looked almost resentful.

An educated taxpayer. Glancing around and keeping his voice low, Kinsman replied, "Confidentially, I . . . well, I used to be an astronaut. They're letting me see what this new stuff is all about. Sort of like a homecoming for me."

Her minifrown softened. "Oh, I get it. Like inviting the old graduates to the school reunion."

Nodding, "More or less."

"I was wondering why you looked so cool and relaxed. You've been through all this before."

"Well, not exactly anything like this."

"Gosh . . . I've never met an astronaut before. I'm Jinny Woods. I'm from New Paltz, New York."

"Chet Kinsman." He shook her hand lightly. "And if you don't mind, I'd just as soon stay in the background here. I'm just a guest. You're the stars of today's show."

She wriggled with pleasure at his flattery. "You mean I shouldn't tell anybody you're an astronaut?"

"I'd rather you didn't. I don't want a fuss made about it."

"Okay . . . It'll be our secret."

Kinsman smiled at her while his mind recalled a line that

a friend of his had once uttered: Hell is, I'm booked into Grossinger's for a week and every girl's mother in the place knows I'm an unmarried medical student.

The bus ride was mercifully brief, but Kinsman wound up being placed beside the same woman inside the shuttle. The interior of the orbiter was much like the interior of a standard commercial jet airliner, except that the seats were plusher, the decor plainer, and there were no windows. Each seatback had a small TV screen built into it. The seats themselves were large, roomy, comfortable, and equipped with a double safety harness that crisscrossed over the shoulders and across the chest.

Jinny Woods fumbled with her harness until Kinsman leaned across and helped her with it. She told him about her two children and her husband back in New Paltz, who was a salesman. He nodded and admired the way she breathed.

And then they waited.

"What's wrong? Why aren't we moving?" Jinny whispered to Kinsman. She looked as if she were afraid of making a fuss, yet genuinely frightened at the same time.

"It'll take several minutes," Kinsman answered. In his mind he pictured what was going on in the cockpit of the orbiter, and in the massive lifter beneath them.

Range safety?

Clear.

Main engine fuel pressure?

Green.

Life support systems?

All green.

Full internal power.

On.

Shuttle One, you are cleared for taxi.

Roger, Tower. One taxiing.

One-quarter throttle. And steer clear of the bumps on the ramp. Let's not shake up the passengers.

The muffled whine of the lifter's hydrogen turbine engines vibrated through the cabin's thick acoustical insulation. Kinsman felt the shuttle surge forward. Sitting in the heavily padded seat with nothing to look at but the gray curving walls of the cabin or the dead eye of the TV screen in front of him, Kinsman imagined himself sitting in the Command Pilot's seat, nudging the throttles forward and handling the controls. The huge, cumbersome double-plane rolled out along the approach ramp and swung onto the five-kilometer-long runway: a broad black road that reached to the horizon and the sky beyond.

Shuttle One, hold for final clearance.

One holding.

Range tracking Go.

Range safety Go.

Meteorology Go.

Mission control Go.

All systems green.

Shuttle One, you are cleared for takeoff.

Roger.

Give 'em a nice easy ride, Jeff.

Only way to fly!

Full takeoff flaps. Full throttle.

Rolling.

Kinsman felt the acceleration pressing him back slightly in his seat. But it was gentle, gentle, nothing like a rocket boost. Hardly any vibration at all.

Two hundred.

Rotate.

The nose came up. Kinsman's hands clutched on his lap, thumb pressing an imaginary controller, and the giant rocket-plane lifted off the ground.

He turned to the woman beside him. "We're up."

She was staring at the TV screen in front of her, still looking scared. Kinsman glanced at his own screen. It showed a view from the camera in the nose of the orbiter as it rode piggyback on the lifter. He could see the bulbous nose and cockpit of the lifter below them, and scudding clouds that they had already climbed past.

"When did they turn the screens on?" he wondered.

"Just as we started down the runway. Didn't you notice?"

"No."

Within fifteen minutes they were high over the Atlantic, a cloud-flecked sheet of hammered gray metal far below them.

The intercom speakers hummed to life. "This is Captain

Burke speaking. I'm the Command Pilot of your orbiter aerospace craft. Our big brother down underneath us will be releasing us in approximately five minutes. They'll fly back to the Cape while we light our rocket engines and head onward into orbit and rendezvous with Space Station Alpha. You will hear some noise and feel a few bumps when we separate. Don't be alarmed."

The separation, when it came, was barely discernible. Kinsman felt a slight sinking sensation as the TV screen showed the lifter swing away and out of sight. Then a dull throbbing pulsed through the cabin, felt in the bones more than heard. The cabin vibrated slightly as the orbiter nosed up.

"Look!" Jinny Woods exclaimed. "I can see the curve of the Earth!"

I know. I've been there. But Kinsman felt the thrill of it all over again. Swiftly their weight diminished until they were in zero gravity, hanging loosely against their restraining harnesses.

Jinny swallowed hard several times but managed to keep herself together. Kinsman watched her closely.

"It feels like falling, at first," he said. "But once you get used to it, it's more like floating. Just don't make any sudden head motions."

She smiled weakly at him.

He relaxed and luxuriated in the freedom of zero gee. How many times has it been? Lost count. Someplace back there I stopped counting. He wondered what would happen if he unbuckled and got up from his seat and glided freely along the aisle separating the double rows of seats. Probably the PR guides would get hysterical. He pictured himself drifting up to the cockpit, going inside to join the crew and their smoothly functioning equipment. He laughed to himself at the thought of commandeering the spacecraft, bypassing the space station and heading on to the Moon. The first space hijack, he mused. Oh, for ten toes!

Soon enough the flight ended as the orbiter lined up with the loading dock at the center of Alpha's set of concentric rings. This was a piece of piloting that Kinsman had never done, and he watched the TV screen, fascinated, as the ship approached the space station like a dart seeking the bull's-eye. Alpha looked like a set of different-sized bicycle wheels nested within one another. Kinsman knew that the biggest one, the outermost wheel, was turning at a rate that would induce a full Earth gravity for the people who lived and worked inside it. The smaller wheels—most of them still under construction—had lighter gravity pulls. The loading dock at the center of the assembly was at zero gee, effectively.

The rendezvous and docking maneuvers were flawless, and soon Kinsman and the other passengers were shuffling, still weightless, along the narrow ladder that led through the orbiter's hatch into the station loading bay.

The loading bay was even more tightly organized than the groundside takeoff had been. There was a NASA or corporate representative for each of the fifty visitors to personally guide each of the individual visitors to the stairs that led "down" to the main living quarters in the outermost wheel.

Kinsman was relieved to be separated from Jinny Woods, although his guide—a sparkling bright young industrial engineer—treated him like a fragile grandfather.

"Just this way, sir. Now you don't actually need the stairs up here in the low-gravity area, but I'd recommend that you use them anyway."

"I've been in zero gee before," Kinsman said.

Ignoring him pleasantly, the young man went on, "We'll be going down—that is, outward toward Level One—where the gravity is at normal Earth value. Your weight will feel like it's increasing as we go down the stairs."

He led Kinsman to a circular hatch set into the "floor" of the loading bay. A metal stairway spiraled down to the other levels of the station.

"Easy does it now!" he said cheerfully, holding Kinsman by the elbow as they took the first steps down.

Kinsman wanted to break free of his grip and glide down the tube until the gravity built up enough for him to walk normally. Instead, grumbling inwardly, he patiently allowed the young engineer to guide him along.

"It's easy to get disoriented in low gee," the kid said.

Feeling like an invalid, Kinsman let himself be led down the stairs. The metal tube they were in was one of the "spokes" that connected the hub of the station with its various wheel-shaped levels. The tube was softly lit by patches of fluorescent paints glowing palely along the circular walls. No power drain, Kinsman realized.

Once safely down to Level One, the fifty first comers were organized into a guided tour. Kinsman endured it, together with the sullen weight of a full Earth gravity that tugged at him like a prisoner's chains.

The station's first level included some laboratory areas, individual living compartments that made submarines look roomy, a galley, and a mess hall. It all looked efficient and compact, although the decor was depressingly familiar to anyone who worked in a government office: bare pastel walls and spongy plastic floor tiles. But the floor curved upward no matter which direction you looked in, and the occasional windows showed stars turning over and over in lazy spirals against the blackness of infinity.

The tour started at one end of the mess hall and finished at the opposite end, where a bar had been set up. Kinsman took a plastic cup of punch from the automatic dispenser just as the second batch of arrivals appeared, exactly at the spot where his own tour had started.

Looking across the bolted-down tables and swiveling chairs along the sloping floor, Kinsman spotted Neal McGrath's tall, dour form among the newcomers. McGrath stared straight at Kinsman and scowled. Kinsman lifted his cup to the Senator, wondering, Is that his normal scowl or is he really sore at me?

Diane was in McGrath's group, surrounded by station personnel and public relations flaks. They all want to be in show biz, thought Kinsman. He did not recognize any of the other personalities.

Gradually the mess hall filled with visitors. Kinsman chatted quietly with several people and tried to avoid being pinned down by several others—including Jinny Woods, who had that "I've got a secret" gleam in her eye whenever she looked Kinsman's way.

Some of the station people hoisted Diane atop one of the bigger tables. As she began tuning her guitar the chattering voices of the crowd diminished into expectant silence.

"I've never been in orbit before," she said. "At least, not this way." They all laughed. "So I'd like to sing a song that's dedicated to the people who made all this possible, the farsighted people who pioneered the way here. It's called 'The Green Hills of Earth.'"

Kinsman ignored the words of her song and bathed in the magic of Diane's voice. Everyone was silent, turned toward her as flowers face the sun, listening and watching her sad, serious face as she sang.

He felt Neal McGrath's presence beside him. Kinsman turned slightly and McGrath said in a throaty whisper, "We've got to talk."

Kinsman nodded.

McGrath put a hand on his shoulder. "Come on."

"Shh. Wait a minute."

"Now!"

A surge of anger welled up in him and Kinsman brushed McGrath's hand off his shoulder. But then it ebbed away and he whispered back, "All right . . . where to?"

McGrath led him back through the corridor that ran the length of Level One, to the area where the living quarters were. He found an empty cubbyhole, no name on the door, and gestured Kinsman inside it.

The two of them filled the tiny compartment. There was nothing much in it: just a bunk built into the curving wall, a sliver of a desk with a bolted-down swivel chair in front of it, and some cabinets along the other wall. Kinsman tried the bunk. It was springy, comfortable, but narrow. He knew that if he stretched out on it, it would be barely long enough for him.

"You'd have a hard time sleeping on one of these," he said to McGrath.

"What's that supposed to mean?" McGrath growled. Neal had taken the chair. It looked pitifully small for him. Kinsman thought of an underfed burro bearing an overfed American tourist.

Shrugging, he replied, "Not a damned thing, Neal, except that these are pretty damned small bunks."

McGrath's scowl did not ease. "Diane told you about her and me."

"That's right."

"Who've you told about it?"

"Nobody."

"Nobody yet," McGrath said, emphasizing the second word.

"Yeah," Kinsman agreed. "Nobody yet."

"Mary-Ellen knows all about it."

"So Diane said."

Hunching forward in his chair, spreading his hands in a gesture that would have indicated helplessness in a smaller man, McGrath asked, "What are you going to do with the information, Chet?"

"I don't know."

He could see the pain on McGrath's face. It was not easy for the man to beg. "Most of the people around me know about it."

"But your constituents back on the farm don't."

"We . . . I was planning to get the divorce after I'm re-elected."

"After you become the Minority Leader."

McGrath nodded.

"Mary-Ellen's going to help you campaign, and you'll troop your kids all across the state, and after the voters send you back to Washington for another six years you'll get your divorce. Pretty sweet."

"What else can I do?" McGrath asked, real misery in his voice. "It's not the divorce so much as the timing. Should I throw away my chance for Minority Leader over a matter of a few months?"

"Those farmers and coal miners and churchgoers wouldn't like knowing that you're going around with a singer, an entertainment star, a left-wing ex-radical from show business. They'd think you're pretty lousy, cheating on your wife. Wouldn't they?"

"Yes," he admitted. "They would."

"They'd be right."

McGrath's eyes flashed. "Don't be too righteous about this, Chet. I never would have met her if it weren't for you."

"I know." Kinsman felt his own temper rising. "And she never would have gotten her chance for stardom if it weren't for me. And you wouldn't be in the Senate if it weren't for my family's money and connections."

McGrath took it like a body blow, the breath gushing out of him. But he dropped his chin only for a moment before plunging ahead. "I fell in love with her right off the bat, the first time I laid eyes on her. I just didn't do anything about it . . . until . . ."

"Will Diane marry you after the divorce?"

"I don't know. We've talked about it. The baby complicates things. I want to marry her, but she's not sure."

"She'd make a lousy senator's wife."

Exploding out of the flimsy chair, McGrath raised his hands wildly. They banged into the compartment's low plastic-sheeted ceiling. "Christ Almighty! I didn't want any of this! I didn't go out looking for it. I never intended to break up my marriage. It wasn't all that good anymore, between Mary-Ellen and me, but . . . Chet, when I'm with Diane I feel like a kid again! Just being in the same room with her! And then when she told me she felt the same way about me . . ."

Kinsman leaned back on the bunk and watched his old friend pace the tiny compartment. Middle-age change of life, he told himself. Neal always was precocious. He found himself envying the fact that McGrath could let go of himself so completely.

McGrath stopped in front of Kinsman. Looming over him he asked, "So what are you going to do about it?"

"I told you, Neal. I haven't decided what to do. Probably nothing."

"If you're thinking of using this to pressure me on the Moonbase deal, forget it! I won't knuckle under."

Kinsman looked up at him. Is Neal stubborn enough to throw his career into the flames?

"The trouble is," Kinsman said evenly, "if I've found out about it, it's only a matter of time until guys like Marcot and the rest find out . . ."

"They won't. Congress takes care of its own."

"Neal, some crap artist like Tug Wynne will nudge it out of somebody sooner or later."

"Wynne's bureau chief is a friend of mine. He'll keep it quiet or he'll lose a helluva good inside source. More than one. Other senators will clam up if he breaks silence. And their aides."

Shaking his head, Kinsman countered, "Look, Neal, I haven't been around Washington as long as you have, but I know this much: the White House is out to get you. Somebody in the Administration sees you as a threat. And they've got their own channels into the media, you know. You're playing in the big leagues now."

McGrath slowly sank down on the bunk beside Kinsman.

"Do you think for one second," Kinsman went on, "that Wynne or his bureau chief will sit on your story when it comes out of the Pentagon? Or the White House? For God's sake, somebody like Marcot could break it to the fucking *National Enquirer* or plant rumors in any of sixty daily columns. They could give it to the Hollywood gossip-mongers. Diane's a video personality, you know."

"I know."

"And when the Pentagon does find out about you," Kinsman said, "you're going to think I told them."

"What you're saying is that you might as well tell them yourself and collect the credit for it because they're going to find out about it sooner or later anyway."

Kinsman snapped, "No, that's *not* what I'm saying! Goddammitall, Neal, I'm warning you that you're going to have to face this pressure one way or the other."

"And if I vote for your Moonbase program the pressure will be off."

"That's right."

"For the time being. Until they want something else."

"I won't be involved in anything else," Kinsman said. "All I want is Moonbase."

"A military base on the Moon."

"It's not a military base, Neal. Not in the sense that it has anything to do with weapons."

For a long moment McGrath said nothing. Then, "This spaceplane thing . . . it's being built so we can knock out Soviet satellites, isn't it?"

"I'm not supposed to say anything about that."

"But you don't deny it?"

"No," Kinsman said. "I don't deny it."

"It's not a very well-kept secret. They've already spent nearly a billion on the design phase."

"So?"

"I'm still against your Moonbase," McGrath said quietly, but with the implacability of a glacier. "No matter what you say, Chet, they'll turn it into an armed military camp."

"No. They can't."

"Of course they can. They've already escalated the arms race into orbital space. First the antimissile satellites with their lasers and particle beam weapons. Now a manned interceptor to knock out the satellites. Next they'll start the interceptors shooting at each other. They're going to fight a war out there, and your Moonbase will become part of it whether you want it to or not."

Wearily, Kinsman pulled himself up from the bunk. "Maybe you're right. Maybe."

"But you want to go to the Moon anyway."

Turning back to face him, "I sure as hell do."

"At any cost."

"At *almost* any cost."

"So what should I do about it?" McGrath muttered, more to himself than to Kinsman.

"I wish I knew," Kinsman said, feeling trapped and helpless. "I sure as hell wish I knew."

When they got back to the bar at the galley Diane was nowhere in sight. McGrath went off to look for her. Kinsman took another cup of punch. It was weak stuff, but his mouth felt dry, his soul arid.

People were drifting through the mess hall, drinks in hand, conversing in small groups. Kinsman wandered over to one of the hall's small oval windows and stared out at the slowly revolving stars. Most of the PR flaks had disappeared, leaving the visitors to themselves for the time being.

"Well, Major, what do you think of it?"

Kinsman turned to see a cheerful-looking man of about fifty standing before him, two beer bottles clenched in each hand.

"Very efficient." Kinsman grinned at him.

"Oh, the beer! Beats going back to the bar every five minutes. But I was referring to the station." He tucked two bottles under his arm and extended his right hand. "I'm T. D. Dreyer. My outfit did the main structural work on this flying doughnut."

"Your outfit?"

"General Technologies, Inc."

"General Tech. You're *that* Dreyer!"

T. D. Dreyer grinned boyishly, happy to be recognized. He was slightly shorter than Kinsman, barrel-chested and burly of build. His blue-gray leisure suit had been carefully tailored to make him look as slim as possible, but his face betrayed him: a heavyset, happy ex-footballer who constantly battled overweight. It was a deeply tanned face. He either has a sunlamp at his desk, Kinsman concluded, or he spends most of his time in the field.

"And I know who you are," Dreyer said. "You're Major Chester Arthur Kinsman, former astronaut, now part of the Aerospace Force's team for Moonbase."

A faint chill of panic raced through Kinsman. "You've got a good intelligence network."

Dreyer's eyes lit up. "You bumped a Wright-Patterson general who's been giving one of my divisions a hard time over a contract we have with him. I was going to try a little friendly persuasion on him while we were both here and away from our desks. When I heard my pigeon had been bumped I made it my business to find out who had bumped him—and at the last minute, too. That takes some clout."

"Hell, if I had known . . ."

"Naah, don't worry about it. I'll catch up with him next week." Dreyer moved half a step closer to Kinsman and lowered his voice slightly. "Frankly, I have a feeling the guy's scared to fly. I was kinda looking forward to watching him shit his pants when I dragged him over to the observation window."

They laughed together.

"You've been up here before," said Kinsman.

"Sure. Big job like this, I come up and look as often as I can get away from that damned desk in Dallas. Gives my insurance people fits, but I like it up here. It's a relief to be away from all those damned numbers crunchers and ribbon clerks."

"I'll drink to that!" Kinsman lifted his cup.

After a long pull of beer, Dreyer said, "Y'know, the trouble with being chairman of the board is that you're supposed to be dignified and conservative. My board members don't believe me when I tell 'em we should be pouring every dollar we can into space operations."

"They think it's too risky?"

"It's not that so much as the fact that it's so easy to take government contracts instead. The profit is low but it's guaranteed. No risk at all, as long as you do a halfway decent job."

"What about the talk I hear about private companies building their own facilities up here? Factories and research labs and solar power satellites?"

Dreyer made a sour face. "Yeah, maybe. But not anybody who's got a board of directors to satisfy. Not as long as there are government contracts to be had."

"Dreyer! I thought that was you." A tall, lithe, hollow-cheeked man with a small pointed beard joined them. He seemed to Kinsman to be in his thirties. He wore a white one-piece jumpsuit. His face was lean and bony, ascetic; his reddish-brown hair was shaved so close to the scalp that he almost looked bald. His hands were empty.

"Well," the newcomer asked, gesturing out toward the view of space, "what do you think of it?"

"Very nice," Dreyer answered. "I think there's a future in it."

"You're being facetious."

"No, but I'm not being polite. Major Kinsman, allow me to introduce Professor Howard Alexander of Redlands University. Howard, this is Chet Kinsman."

Alexander's hands stayed at his sides. "I didn't know that any Air Force people were on the invitations list. You're on duty with NASA, I take it."

"No," Kinsman said.

"Chet's a former astronaut. Now he's on the Moonbase team."

"Oh, *that*." The temperature of the conversation dropped fifty degrees.

Dreyer seemed amused. "Professor Alexander is the apostle of the True Faith. He wants the military out of space so he can build colonies and make them into heavenly paradises."

"And you want to build them and make profit out of them," Alexander shot back testily.

"Sure, why not?"

"Because space should be free for all humankind, that's why. Because we shouldn't bring our selfish, petty greeds out

231

into this beautiful new world."

"Right on," said Kinsman.

Alexander turned to him. "Nor should we be trying to build weapons and fortifications in space. This is a domain for peaceful existence, not for war."

"I couldn't agree more."

The professor blinked at him.

Kinsman said, "I think it would be wonderful if we could leave all the greed and anger and suspicion of our fellow men back on Earth and come out here fresh and clean and newborn."

"I got news for you, fellas," Dreyer said, with a rueful grin. "It ain't gonna happen that way."

"I'm afraid not," Kinsman agreed.

Alexander shook his head, as if dismissing such unpleasant thoughts from his mind. "It *will* happen that way if we make it happen that way."

"How'm I gonna do that?" Dreyer asked, suddenly very serious. "You think my board of directors will risk the company's capital on dreams? They want profits and they want 'em *now.*"

"They'll get their profits, from the solar power satellites."

"Sure. Twenty years downstream. We could be in receivership by then. We can't tie up billions of dollars for twenty years at a time. Nobody can. So where are you going to get the capital to build those big-assed colonies of yours? Plus the lunar mining facilities, the processing plants, the factories . . ."

"It would only take five or six billion."

"Per year!"

"Surely the major corporations could invest that much in their own future," Alexander said. "And in the future of the human race."

Dreyer shook his head. "Like I said, we're not in the investment business. We work for profits. This year. Nobody in his right mind is going to risk the kind of money your space colonies require."

Alexander countered, "Think of the profits you'll eventually make from selling energy back to Earth once you've built a few solar power satellites."

"I know," Dreyer said, gesturing with a beer bottle in his hand. "But you don't need your supercolossal colonies to build solar power satellites. All you need is a tough crew of workmen on the Moon, where the raw materials are, and another crew in orbit, where the construction will take place."

"But there's more to it than just building the satellites," Alexander insisted. "The space colonies will also be involved in building more colonies, more self-sufficient islands in space."

"What for?" Kinsman asked.

"So that more people can leave the Earth and live in space!" Alexander's exasperated tone reminded Kinsman of a Sunday school teacher he and Neal had once suffered through.

But how do we know that God loves us?

Because the Scriptures tell us so!

But how do we know the Scriptures are right?

Because they were inspired by God!

But how do we know they were inspired by God?

Because it says so, right in the Scriptures!

Repressing a grim smile, Kinsman told himself, At least the Quakers never fell into that dogmatic tailspin. I'll bet Alexander was schooled by Jesuits.

"And who's gonna pay for these additional colonies?" Dreyer was asking.

"They'll be paid for out of the profits from the solar power satellites!" Alexander was getting edgy.

"Let's sit down," Kinsman suggested, pointing to an empty table. Most of the visitors were still clustered around the bar.

"Lemme get a refill," said Dreyer, hefting his emptied beer bottles.

The three of them pushed their way to the bar. Dreyer got another pair of beers, Kinsman another cup of the weak punch. Alexander abstained. Then they sat at one of the long mess tables, Dreyer at its head, Alexander and Kinsman flanking him on either side.

Kinsman took a sip of the punch. It felt cold and sticky-sweet.

"Now look," Dreyer said to the professor, "don't get me

wrong. I like the colony idea. I've liked it since O'Neill first proposed it, back in the Seventies. And I agree that solar power satellites could make a considerable profit—in time. *If* the government doesn't nationalize them, once they're built. But how do you raise the initial capital? You're talking about a hundred billion bucks or more."

"Over a ten-year period," Alexander said.

Dreyer shrugged. "That's still ten billion a year, minimum. That's a helluva lot of bread. With no payoff until way downstream, and maybe not even then. Who in hell is going to buy into this? My board of directors would toss me into the loony bin if I tried to put that past them."

"If the corporations would all work together and pool their resources . . ."

"They won't. They can't! The antitrust guys would be all over us in ten minutes."

Kinsman said, "I thought NASA was involved in this."

"Only on the transportation end of it," Dreyer said. "NASA's not going to build any colonies. Congress won't appropriate that kind of money."

"Not for solar power satellites?" Kinsman wondered.

Dreyer explained, "See, the power satellites and the colonies are two different things. The power satellites are gonna get built, probably by the government, at least the first one. But nobody's going to put up the money for a colony that'll house ten thousand university professors in a big suburbia in the sky."

Alexander frowned.

They talked around and around the subject, Alexander waxing poetic and pathetic by turns, Dreyer shaking his bulldog head and insisting on the economic facts of life. Kinsman looked over his shoulder at the star-filled window and saw their reflections in the glass: Alexander in profile, earnest and ascetic as a saint; Dreyer massive and solid as reality; his own face lean, dark, bored with their arguments that circled as repetitiously as the stars outside the window. But there was something nagging at Kinsman's mind, something that the two of them were overlooking. What?

Finally it hit Kinsman. He broke into their argument. "How are you going to defend this colony?"

"Huh?"

Alexander looked aghast. "Defend it? Against what? The Martians?"

"Against other Earthlings," said Kinsman. "Maybe the Soviets won't want a capitalist colony in space. Or terrorists. Your colony would be wide open to a small nuclear bomb. Look what they did in Cape Town."

"That's ridiculous," Alexander snapped. "Why would the Russians attack a space colony? And terrorists could never get up to a space colony. We wouldn't allow any weapons aboard it."

"You're not afraid of the Russians?" Dreyer asked.

"No. Why should I be? They're cooperating with us in our civilian space program, aren't they?"

"And competing with us to put their Star Wars system in orbit."

Alexander dismissed the idea with a wave of his hand. "The space colonies will be far beyond the militarists and their weapons."

"I hope you're right," said Kinsman.

Turning to Dreyer, Alexander asked, "I want to know how much your corporation is willing to invest in the space colony project."

"Nothing."

"Nothing?"

"Zero."

The professor's mouth went slack, but only for a moment. "Nothing at all? Are you serious?"

"Nothing at all," Dreyer said, with a good-natured grin. "Nothing for the colony. The lunar mining operation . . . now that's a different story. I think maybe we could go in on that. But not as part of your colony scheme. Find another pigeon for your flying Garden of Eden."

"That's *extremely* shortsighted!"

"Yeah, maybe. But if I was as visionary as you I would've gone bust years ago."

Abruptly Alexander pushed his chair back as far as it would go on the little track welded to the floor. Standing, he looked down on Kinsman and Dreyer.

"Someday we will have our space colonies and we will start a new era for the human race—without soldiers and without capitalists!"

"Good luck," Kinsman said. Dreyer grinned and took a pull of beer.

Alexander stalked off.

Dreyer watched him. "That's why he isn't afraid of the Russians. He's a goddamned socialist himself." He shook his head and laughed bitterly. "When he finds a place that doesn't have soldiers or capitalists he's going to be in heaven."

"Guess he'll snub Saint Michael," Kinsman said, "unless Mike puts away his armor and sword."

"Yeah. And there's a few capitalist saints he won't get along with, either."

Kinsman chuckled.

"He reminds me," Dreyer went on, "of what a kid in the office said about the head of the Office of Technology Assessment: 'He's no prophet; he's a loss.'"

They laughed together and got up and went to the bar for another drink. As they walked slowly back toward the window that looked out on the stars, Kinsman said:

"I've been thinking . . . let me ask you a hypothetical question."

"Shoot."

Kinsman put out his free hand and touched the plastiglass. It was cold. Space cold. Death cold. He could feel it drawing the heat out of him, pulling his soul into space.

He yanked his hand away and said to Dreyer, "Suppose the government was willing to sink a few billion dollars into building a mining facility on the Moon. Would your board of directors be interested in putting some of your own money into the operation?"

"Sure!" Dreyer answered immediately. "If Uncle Sugar is taking most of the risk, why the hell not?"

"That's what I thought," Kinsman said.

"You talking about a space colony now or something else?"

"Not a colony. Just the lunar mining facilities. And factories, either on the Moon or in orbit."

"To build solar power satellites?"

"No. Something else."

Dreyer said nothing for a long moment. Then, "Just what do you have in mind?"

Kinsman shook his head.

With a knowing grin, Dreyer said, "There used to be talk about building the Star Wars satellites in space, out of lunar raw materials."

Kinsman answered, "So I've heard."

Dreyer's grin spread. "We'd be happy to work on that kind of project. With the government providing the investment capital and the Aerospace Force behind it, it would be a project we could depend on. We'd be willing to sink a helluva lot of our own discretionary funds into it, too."

"Do you think the other industrial contractors would feel the same way?"

"Why the hell wouldn't they?" Dreyer said. Then he started laughing again. "I'd like to see the look on Alexander's face when he finds out that his precious idea for building colonies in space has been bumped by factories for turning out military hardware!"

Kinsman nodded and tried to smile back at the man, but he could not.

He sat once again next to Jinny Woods on the shuttle's return flight to Florida, but Kinsman's mind was a quarter-million miles away.

"I didn't see you hardly at all," the woman was saying, "once we got up there. You were always in *deep* dark conversations with somebody or other. Who were all those people anyway? Wasn't one of them Senator McGrath? I saw him on television, one of those late-night talk shows. He's so handsome!"

Kinsman made noncommittal noises at her while his mind raced:

Is this the way history gets made? Somebody wants to find a retreat, a place to hide, and we get a lunar base out of it? Somebody wants to make a buck, open a new trade route, get the tax collectors off his back. That's what makes the world go 'round?

". . . and the way she sang! I'll bet you didn't even hear her, did you? I looked for you but you weren't anywhere in sight. You missed the dancers, too. They took us down to the low-gravity section . . ."

I'll have to spring it on Murdock first. No, first I'll tell

Frank about it. If there are any flaws in the picture he'll spot them. Pick out the weak points and fix them. Then Murdock. Then we'll work up a presentation for General Sherwood. Probably for Marcot, too. It all ties together so neatly. Why haven't the others seen it?

"You haven't been listening to a word I've said," Jinny Woods complained.

"I'm sorry," Kinsman said. "I was thinking about some of the problems I've got ahead of me, back at the office."

"You sound just like my husband. I guess I talk too much. That's what he tells me."

"No . . . it's my fault."

She brushed a curl away from her eyes. "I'm just so excited by all this! It's all old stuff for you, I know. But nothing like this has ever happened to me before. It's all so new . . . so thrilling!"

She's kind of pretty, Kinsman noticed. Nice eyes. Happy as a kid.

"It's exciting for me, too," he told her. "Don't let this calm exterior fool you. No matter how many times you go into orbit, it's always a ball."

She seemed pleased. "Really? It's not just me? I guess I just never learned to control my feelings very well. I get awfully gushy, don't I? Do you think we'll ever get up there again?"

Do I think about anything else?

She went on, "They said they're going to bring us to Washington next week for a press conference. You live in Washington, don't you? I've never been there before and Ralph says he can't take any days off to come with me. I'll be alone in the city."

"Where will you be staying?"

"Some government hotel, I guess. They haven't told us where."

Kinsman nodded. "Well, I'll find out and phone you when you're in town."

"Oh, that'd be wonderful! Do you have a card or something, so I can call you? That'd be easier . . ."

"I'm afraid I can't give out my phone number," Kinsman said, taking on a man-of-mystery disguise.

She fell for it. "Really? Why?"

He put a finger to his lips. "I'll find out where you're going to be staying and give you a call when you get into town. Trust me."

She nodded slowly, her eyes filled with something approaching awe.

And that was the last time he thought about her.

As soon as he arrived back in his one-room apartment Kinsman phoned Fred Durban. But the old man had slipped into a coma and the hospital would allow no visitors except family.

Then he called Colt and invited himself to Frank's apartment for a drink.

Colt's pad was lush compared to Kinsman's spartan little cell: richly carpeted living room with a balcony that overlooked Arlington National Cemetery; big bedroom with a fake zebra hide thrown over the water bed.

Scotch in hand, Kinsman explained his idea to Colt. The black officer listened silently, stretched out on his synthetic leather recliner.

". . . and that's it," Kinsman finished. "We mine the ores on the Moon, process them there, ship them to orbital factories, where they're manufactured into the antimissile satellites. Instead of working against the SDI Office, we make Moonbase a partner of theirs."

For a long moment Colt said nothing. Then, "People talked about building the satellites in orbit when the SDI idea was first proposed."

"I know. But we can do it now. All the pieces are in place—almost."

"You got all the pieces tied together," Colt said. "One big program that's got something for everybody. Moonbase becomes an important mining center instead of a geriatrics hospital. The big corporations get Uncle Sam to finance factories in orbit for them. And the Star Wars guys get their ABM satellites deployed for half the cost of building them on Earth and launching 'em from the ground."

"Not really half the cost," Kinsman said. "It won't be that cheap, I don't think. They'll want to continue to build the first-generation satellites on the ground. The space-manufactured stuff is for the next generation, the satellites that'll be carrying the high-power lasers."

Colt kicked his recliner upright and bounced to his feet. "Shee-it, man, you've got it made! You've pulled the two projects together into one big beeyootiful program that makes sense! Nobody could vote against it! It'd be like spittin' on the motherlovin' flag!" Colt laughed and stuck his hand out to Kinsman, palm up. "Man, it's the best piece of strategical thinking since Moses led the Children of Israel out of Egypt!"

Kinsman slapped at his hand, then grabbed it. "You really think so?"

"Hell yes! The brass'll love it. And you get your goddamned Moonbase out of it. Shrewd, man. Shrewd."

A sigh of relief eased out of Kinsman. "Okay, great. Now the first thing we've got to do is tell Murdock about it."

"First thing tomorrow we'll corner him."

"Could you do me a favor, Frank?" Kinsman asked. "You tell him. Leave me out of it. As soon as I try to tell him anything he shuts me off. If I bounce this plan off him he'll find a million reasons to junk it without bucking it further up the chain of command. It'll die right there in his office."

Colt eyed his friend. "Yeah, maybe. But you're the guy who knows all the shit about this. I don't. I couldn't put it across to Murdock as well as you could."

Glancing at the purpling sky and the dark shadow of the Pentagon on the horizon, Kinsman said slowly, "Well . . . we've got all night to rehearse it. Unless you have something else to do."

Colt frowned. "Lemme make a phone call. This is gonna break the heart of the best-looking piece of ass the Secretary of Agriculture ever had working for him."

"Aw, hell, Frank, I didn't want . . ."

With a wink, Colt said, "Forget it, buddy. She'll keep. And you're right, I *do* impress Murdock with my keen military bearing."

Kinsman would have paced his office if it had been big enough. Instead he sat at his desk, the chair tilted back against the faded pastel wall, and had nothing to do but think.

You're selling out, you know that. You're giving them what they want: a military base on the Moon. Neal was right; you're spreading the arms race all the way to the Moon.

You're willing to start a war up there.

But another part of his mind answered, They're putting up the ABM satellites anyway. And the manned interceptor comes next. This way, at least we get a Moonbase out of it. At least I'll be there, away from all this madness.

And what are you going to do, he asked himself, when you're on the Moon and they order you into battle? What are you going to do when they start blowing up the cities of Earth?

He had no answer for that.

Colt burst into his cubbyhole office, his grin dazzling. "He bought it! He was on the horn to Sherwood before I even finished. Man, did he go for it! Whammo!" Colt smacked a fist into his open palm.

Suddenly Kinsman felt too weak to get to his feet. "And General Sherwood?"

"He wants to see us this afternoon."

"Us?"

"Yeah. I told him this was all your idea. After he finished talkin' to Sherwood. You shoulda seen his face! Like he crapped in his pants!" Colt roared with laughter.

General Sherwood tried to contain his enthusiasm, but as he sat behind his big, aerodynamically clean desk listening to Kinsman, he began nodding. At first his head moved only slightly, unconsciously, as Kinsman unfolded the logic of his plan. But by the time Kinsman was summing up, the General's head was bobbing vigorously and he was smiling broadly.

Colonel Murdock was sitting on the edge of his chair, alternately watching the General intently and eyeing Kinsman suspiciously, waiting for a misstep or an outright goof. Soon, though, his own bald head was going up and down in exact rhythm with the General's. Colt sat farther from the desk, back far enough so that Kinsman could not see him.

Standing in front of the General's desk, too wrapped up in presenting the ideas to feel nervous, Kinsman ignored Murdock, ignored Colt, ignored the self-doubts that gnawed at his innards. This is the only way, he kept telling himself. We'll never get to the Moon any other way. It's this or nothing.

Finally he finished. Kinsman stood in front of the General's desk, arms limp at his sides, sweat trickling down his ribs. My uniform must be soaked, he thought.

General Sherwood stopped nodding, but his smile remained. "Fascinating," he said, in a voice so low that he might have been talking to himself. "We can bring the Moonbase program up to full partnership with the Strategic Defense program, and bring the aerospace industry along with us."

Colonel Murdock objected slightly, "But the idea of building the satellites in orbit out of lunar materials—that's not really new."

"True enough," said the General. "But I think it's an idea whose time has arrived."

"Oh, well, of course . . ."

Sherwood turned back toward Kinsman. "Good work, Major. Very good work. Get the presentations staff and the numbers crunchers into this immediately. I want a detailed presentation of this plan before the end of the week."

All his exhaustion blew away. "Yes, *sir*," Kinsman responded crisply.

The rest of the week was a madhouse of meetings, rehearsals, discussions, arguments. Kinsman raced along the Pentagon corridors from cost-computing analysts to technical artists drawing the block diagrams, from long scrambled phone conversations with industrial leaders such as Dreyer to longer face-to-face meetings with their local marketing representatives and engineers. Days, nights blurred together. Meals were sandwiches gobbled at desks, crumbs spilling onto printout sheets of numbers, coffee staining artists' sketches of lunar installations. Sleep was something you grabbed in snatches, on couches, in a chair: once Kinsman dozed off in the shower of the officers' gym.

The full-scale presentation took two hours. Deputy Secretary Marcot chain-smoked through it. Kinsman stood at the head of the darkened conference room, squinting at the solitary light of the viewgraph projector, half-hypnotized by the clouds of blue smoke gliding through the light beam as he explained picture after picture, graph after graph, list after list. He could not see his audience but he could tell their interest from the rapt silence and, after the lights went on again, from their eager questions.

"What was the basis for the cost estimates on the lasers?"

"Latest industrial information, sir."

"And the comparison between the costs of lunar raw materials and raw materials on Earth?"

"The comparison, sir, is between finished products manufactured in space from lunar materials and finished products manufactured on the ground and boosted into low Earth orbit. The space-manufactured items average five to eight times cheaper, including the capital costs of the lunar facility."

"That's based on what, Major?"

Kinsman grinned. "Mainly, sir, on the fact that the Moon is an airless body of natural resources that has only one-sixth the gravitational pull of the Earth. It's twenty times cheaper to launch a pound of payload from the Moon to low Earth orbit than it is to boost a pound from the Earth's surface."

Marcot's sarcastic voice offered, "And those figures are based on Isaac Newton, not some industrial contractor who wants to buy into the program. You can trust Newton. He's dead."

Everyone around the table chuckled.

They questioned Kinsman for another hour after the final slide had been shown and the overhead lights turned on. Colt fielded some of the questions, as did some of the other men and women who had worked on the presentation. But Kinsman remained at the head of the room and took most of the questions himself.

Finally Marcot got to his feet. Waving his inevitable cigarette in Kinsman's general direction, he said, "Okay. Hone it down to half an hour and be prepared to show it to the Secretary first thing next week."

Back in his own office, Colt grabbed Kinsman by the shoulders. "We're on our way, man! The Secretary of Defense! The big brass boss his own self. Marcot bought it!"

Kinsman was too tired and numb to feel exultant.

"C'mon, I'm gonna buy you a drink."

"I just want some sleep, Frank. Thanks, anyway."

Colt shrugged. "Yeah. We got a weekend's worth of work figurin' out how to squeeze all this gorgeous stuff down to half an hour."

Kinsman said, "Let me lock up all this gorgeous stuff in the vault." The pile of viewgraph slides was scattered across Colt's desk, each stamped along its border in bold red letters: TOP SECRET.

It took both of them to carry the pile of slides over to Kinsman's cubbyhole. As he wearily tapped out the combination on the electronic lock to his file cabinet, Colt beamed happily at him.

"Man, you were a ball of fire in there. You coulda sold General Motors stock to the Kremlin. You've really changed, man. You've really come out of your shell."

Over his shoulder Kinsman said, "I want to go to the Moon, Frank. Even if I have to bring the whole goddamned Aerospace Force with me."

Colt grinned. "You figured it out, huh? You wear The Man's uniform, you gotta do The Man's work. That's the law of life, my friend. But it's good to see you thinking like an Aerospace Force officer. Always thought you had a good head on your shoulders. No more of this peaceful hospital crap."

Kinsman piled the slides into the file drawer, then shut it and clicked the lock. He took the card atop the cabinet and turned it from the white OPEN side to the red LOCKED side.

"Frank," he said, turning back to Colt, "don't get the wrong idea. The Moon is still legally restricted, as far as military weaponry goes. The mining operation, okay. What they do with the ores after they leave the Moon is somebody else's business. But Moonbase will never be used as a place for war. Understand that. Never."

Colt's grin faded. "And how are you gonna get the Russians to go along with that? They're gonna be up there with you, remember? You start mining operations, they'll start mining operations."

"We'll work it out some way."

"Without fighting."

"That's right."

"Damn! You're just as dumb as you always were."

Late Monday afternoon Kinsman stood at the head of the long polished mahogany table in the private conference room of the Secretary of Defense. No need to turn out the lights here; his slides were presented on a wall-sized rear projection screen. Kinsman spoke directly to the Secretary himself, despite the fact that the table was occupied by Marcot and two Under Secretaries of the Aerospace Force, four generals, including Sherwood, and a half-dozen civilian advisers to the Secretary. Colt was in the next room, feeding the slides into the projector.

Every man at the table watched Kinsman intently. The same thoughts were going through each of their heads, he knew: How does this affect my programs, my organization, my position in the Defense Department?

"To summarize," Kinsman said to the Secretary, "we can bring down the costs of strategic defense by a factor of five or more if we build the ABM satellites in orbital facilities, using raw materials mined from the Moon. The major industrial contractors are eager to begin space manufacturing operations, but have hesitated to risk the resources necessary for the task. This program will, therefore, have significant spinoff value in the civilian economy. More than significant: the eventual payoff to the civilian economy could more than pay for the investment made on this program. Thank you, gentlemen."

The men around the table stirred, glanced at one another, then all settled their gazes on the Secretary. He sat at the far end of the table, looking relaxed and thoughtful. He was the tweedy gray university type. An unlit pipe was clamped in his teeth.

"We are deploying the ABM satellites under any circumstances," General Sherwood said, filling the silence. "This plan allows us to build them more cheaply—and replace them more easily, in case of attrition."

The Defense Secretary nodded and started lighting his pipe.

"And by building the satellites in orbit," Kinsman added, still standing in front of the now-blank screen, "out of lunar materials, we not only get the SDI network, we get a powerful industrial capacity in space and a full-scale, permanent base on the Moon."

"A base," General Sherwood pointed out, "that will be under the administrative control of the Department of Defense."

The Secretary slowly took the pipe from his mouth. "You mean you blue-suiters get your Moonbase, eh, Jim?"

General Sherwood broke into a boyish smile. "Yes, sir, that is exactly what I mean."

Smiling back at him, the Secretary said, "Well, it seems to me that the important thing here is that America's industrial power is brought into space in a meaningful way. The President will like that. It's about time that industry really moved into space."

He's buying it! Kinsman's heart leaped. He's bought it!

"I think you're perfectly right about that," said Ellery Marcot. "Perfectly right."

"What I'd like to know," the Secretary said, with a nod toward one of his civilians, "is why our hired geniuses and university consultants never brought the whole ball of wax together the way the Major has, here."

The aide flushed. "Well, it's one thing to be sitting out in left field . . ."

"Relax, George," the Secretary said, making a patting motion with his free hand. "Relax. I was only tweaking you."

He got up from his leather-backed chair. "A very good presentation, Major. Good thinking. I'll speak to the President about it at tomorrow morning's briefing."

Kinsman could only say, "Thank you, sir." It was so weak that he wondered if the Secretary heard him.

Turning to General Sherwood, the Secretary asked, "Jim, see that my people get copies of those slides and all the backup material, will you?"

Sherwood rose, beaming. "Certainly, Mr. Secretary. Be glad to."

They all filed out of the conference room, leaving Kinsman standing there rooted to the spot. We did it, he told himself. Then he corrected, No, *you* did it. Don't blame anyone else.

He walked slowly out of the conference room. The others had already started back toward their own offices. All except Marcot, who was standing by the window talking with Murdock. The Colonel had been waiting in the anteroom all through Kinsman's presentation. He must've walked off the soles of his shoes, pacing up and down, thought Kinsman. Murdock looked rumpled, exhausted; hands clasped behind his back, the expression on his face halfway between eager anticipation and utter dread as he talked with Marcot.

Frank Colt jounced into the anteroom, the slim pile of slides clamped under one arm. He gave Kinsman a big grin and a thumbs-up sign.

Marcot came up to Kinsman, with Colonel Murdock trailing behind him. For once there was no cigarette in the Deputy Secretary's mouth.

"Major, you've done an impressive job. For the first time since I've been here I feel we have a logical, cost-effective program that not only meets the nation's defense needs, but will promote the civilian economy in a major way, as well."

"Thank you, sir."

"You pulled it all together into a coherent whole. That's exactly what we needed." Marcot jammed both his hands into his jacket pockets.

Feeling awkward and a bit foolish, Kinsman merely repeated, "Thank you, sir."

Marcot pulled out a fresh cigarette and lit it. "But we're not out of the woods yet." He blew a cloud of smoke toward the ceiling. "Not by a long shot."

"What do you mean?" Colt asked.

"There's still the Congress. They'll have to approve an even bigger Aerospace Force appropriation than we started with, to get this larger program going. We'll still have to face McGrath and his ilk."

It still boils down to that, Kinsman said to himself. He had almost allowed himself to forget Neal in the past hectic week.

Murdock patted Kinsman on the shoulder and said, "We're on top of that situation, aren't you, Chet? You're getting to McGrath."

"I've been trying . . ."

Colt said, "But with this new program, the way it all fits together and ties Moonbase into the rest of the Defense Department's space programs, not even McGrath and the peaceniks in Congress can vote against it."

"Can't they?" Marcot's long, hound-sad face had years of bitter experience written across it. "I can just see McGrath rising on the floor of the Senate and making a very eloquent speech about the Aerospace Force's paranoid schemes for extending the arms race to the Moon. I can see his cohorts telling their constituents back home about the hundreds of billions of dollars the Defense Department wants to throw away in space instead of spending down here on welfare and urban renewal."

"Bullcrap!" Colt snorted.

"But it works," Marcot answered. "It gets votes."

"Then we've got to stop McGrath," Colt said. "He's the leader of this faction. Get him to vote our way, pull his fangs, do *something* . . ."

Murdock bobbed his head. "It's up to you, Chet. It's your job."

Kinsman looked at the Colonel. Thanks. Thank you all. To Marcot he said, "Very well. I'll handle McGrath. But I want something in return."

Murdock looked shocked. Officers don't make deals; they carry out orders. But Marcot grinned wolfishly, the way a politician does when he's trading favors and expects to come out ahead.

"You want something?" he asked Kinsman.

"Yessir. The original motivation for this program was to make certain that we go ahead with Moonbase. That base will need a commanding officer. I want to be that man."

"But that'd be a colonel's slot!" Murdock blurted.

"Then I'll need a promotion to light colonel to go with it," Kinsman answered evenly.

Marcot glanced at Murdock, then said, "First we've got to get the Congress to approve the funds. Then, when we know there's going to be a Moonbase, naturally we'll want someone who's thoroughly familiar with the program and its implications to command the base."

Colt nodded. Murdock still looked bewildered.

Without a smile, without even daring to admit to himself that this was happening, that *he* was forcing it to happen, Kinsman said, "Thank you. I appreciate it."

Raising a tobacco-stained finger, Marcot emphasized, "But first we've got to get the Congress to vote the funds."

"I know," said Kinsman.

"Very well. We understand each other." Marcot glanced at his wristwatch. "I'm going to be late for a reception. Japanese embassy. Their military attaché has been pumping me about our ABM satellites."

They walked out into the corridor. Marcot headed off toward his domain; Colonel Murdock, Colt, and Kinsman took the stairs that led up to their lesser offices.

As they climbed the steps, Colt burst out, "You did it, man! You finally did it! Terrific!"

"We've all been working on this," Kinsman said.

"Naw, I don't mean that. You stood up to 'em and told 'em what you wanted. Commander of Moonbase. And he took it! Man, you got the power now."

They reached the landing and pushed through the scuffed gray metal doors into the corridor as Kinsman said, "I just want him to know that I want to be on the Moon, not down here."

"You talked yourself into a damned quick promotion," Murdock snapped.

"But, Colonel," Colt said quickly, "don't you see? If they move Chet up to light colonel they're gonna hafta give you a general's star."

Murdock blinked and almost smiled. "There's no guarantee . . ."

"You'll still be in command of the overall lunar program," Colt argued smoothly. "And the program's going to be a lot bigger than anybody had thought. You'll be running the whole operation from Vandenberg while we're up at Moonbase. They'll have to give you a star."

Breaking into a contented grin, Murdock said, "You know, you might be right. It's more responsibility, bigger budget, bigger staff. They couldn't pass me over again."

The two majors left the smiling Colonel at his office, then continued down the corridor to their own cubicles. The hallways were empty; the Pentagon had only a skeleton crew after 4:30 P.M. Their footsteps clicked against the worn floor tiles and echoed off the shabby walls.

"You finally came around," Colt said. "I never thought you'd make it."

"You make it sound like a religious conversion," Kinsman grumbled.

"Just the opposite, man. Just the opposite. You finally got it through your skull that if you want something you gotta give something. You want to be commander of Moonbase, you gotta let them have what they want. No other way."

"We're not going to put weapons on the Moon."

Colt looked at him. "Yeah, I know. But those mines and ore processors . . . long as we're using them to ship raw materials to orbital factories so they can build laser satellites, then they're part of a weapons system."

Kinsman did not break stride, but inside he stiffened.

"You're gonna be commander of a military base, *Colonel* Kinsman. Moonbase is gonna be the key to the biggest military operation the world's ever seen."

And that's the price for my soul, thought Kinsman. He left Colt and slipped into his own cramped office. The air-conditioning had been turned off at the official quitting time for the daytime staff. The paper-strewn cubicle was already muggy and stuffy.

It may be a military base, Kinsman told himself, and it may be there to supply raw materials for weapons systems, but there'll be no fighting on the Moon. Not while I'm there.

Then Marcot's cagey, cynical face appeared in his mind. "First get the Congress to vote the funds," he heard the Deputy Secretary saying.

"The Hungarian recipe for an omelet," Kinsman muttered. "First, steal some eggs."

With a sigh he sat at his desk and tapped out Neal McGrath's phone number. An answering service responded. Kinsman did not bother to leave his name on the tape. Then, out of pure routine, he tapped his own message key on the computer board. The display screen spelled out in green letters: PLS CALL MS WOODS: 291-7000 EXT 7949.

Kinsman stared at the message for a long moment. Persistent woman, he thought. As he punched the number she had left, he grinned at her use of the "Ms." Helps her forget she's married, I guess.

Jinny's face looked blander, plainer than he remembered it when she appeared on the tiny display screen.

"Oh . . . Major Kinsman! You got my call. I was in the shower. They've been touring us all around Washington all day . . ."

No makeup, he realized. That's what it is.

"You said you'd call me when we got into town," she was gushing, "but we were out all day and I never trust hotel switchboards to get messages straight and nobody down at the desk speaks English anyway so I called the Pentagon, I remembered you said you worked at the Pentagon, and asked them to look you up. All I remembered was that you were in the Air Force and you had been an astronaut. I even forgot your rank, but they found your number for me anyway!"

"I'm glad they did, Jinny," he said. The old oil. You do it automatically, don't you?

They met at a Japanese restaurant on Connecticut Avenue. Marcot's not the only one who'll nibble on sushi tonight. They had no trouble getting a tatami room for themselves, where they took off their shoes and sat on the floor. The restaurant was nearly empty. Even in the best parts of the city business disappeared once the sun went down.

"I'm sorry I wasn't able to call you earlier," Kinsman said as they sipped sake. "It's been a wild week for me."

"Me, too," Jinny said, looking at him over the rim of her tiny porcelain cup. Her hair was carefully done, her makeup properly in place. She wore a sleeveless frock with a neckline low enough to be inviting, yet still within the bounds of decorum.

Does she or doesn't she? Kinsman asked himself. As if it matters.

When they left the restaurant Jinny wound her arm around Kinsman's and said, "I'm so tired . . . they had us on the go all day long. Do you mind if we just go back to my hotel room and have a drink there?"

Like the cobra and mongoose. But which is which? Kinsman wondered.

Her hotel was a cut above standard government issue. The bed was a double, the furnishings fairly new and in reasonably good condition. The room was clean without smelling of disinfectant. Kinsman put money in the automatic liquor dispenser and bought a scotch for himself and a vodka tonic for Jinny. He poured the liquor and soda into plastic glasses, and found that the Styrofoam ice bucket was already filled with half-melted cubes.

"I've just got to get out of this dress," Jinny said, picking up her pink travel kit and heading for the bathroom. "I'll only be a minute."

Kinsman took the room's only chair and shook his head.

This game's pretty silly, you know. A voice inside him answered, Don't be scared; you're doing fine.

On an impulse he went to the phone and, sitting on the edge of the bed, tapped out the number for Walter Reed Hospital. The hospital's information display glowed on the phone screen:

MAY WE HELP YOU?

"Yes," Kinsman said. Speaking as clearly as he could for the computer, he asked, "The condition of Mr. Frederick Durban."

SPELLING OF LAST NAME?

"D-u-r-b-a-n. Frederick."

ARE YOU A FAMILY MEMBER?

"His son," he lied.

DURBAN, FREDERICK. DECEASED 1623 HRS TODAY. FUNERAL ARRANGEMENTS ARE BEING HANDLED BY . . .

Kinsman slammed a fist against the phone's OFF button. I know what the funeral arrangements are, he said to himself. Looking out the window at the darkening city, he thought, Four twenty-three this afternoon. Right in the middle of my goddamned presentation. Right in the fucking middle of it!

"What's the matter, Chet? You look awful!"

He turned to see Jinny standing a step inside the bathroom door, her hair loose and tumbling to her shoulders, an iridescent pink nightgown clinging to her.

"A friend of mine . . . died. I just called the hospital and found out."

She came to him and put both hands on his shoulders. "I'm so sorry."

"He was an old man. I expected it. But still . . ."

"I know. It's a shock." She sat beside him on the bed and slipped her arms around his neck and kissed him. He kissed back and felt her mouth open for him.

She disengaged and reclined languidly on the bed. Patting the covers, she said, "Come on, lay down beside me."

He remained sitting. "Jinny . . . I can't."

She gazed up at him, smiling. "If it's my husband you're worried about, never mind. We have an understanding about this kind . . ."

But he shook his head. The picture was forming in his mind again. He could see her floating helplessly, arms outstretched, reaching toward him, screaming silently, eyes wide and blank.

"No," he said, more to himself than to her.

She was staring at him now, looking uncertain, almost afraid.

"I've got to go." He got to his feet.

Jinny sat up on the bed. "Because of the man who died?"

"Yes."

"He was someone close to you? A relative?"

"You really don't want to know about it," he said, feeling clammy sweat on his palms. Almost pleadingly, "Please don't ask me anything more about it."

"Are you . . . a spy, or something?"

He focused on her for the first time since shutting off the phone. She was wide-eyed, lips parted, nipples erect with excitement.

"I can't tell you anything," he said, trying to make it tight-lipped. "I've got to go. I'm sorry."

"Will I ever see you again?"

"Maybe. But probably not. Where I'm going . . . probably not."

He went to the door. She rushed after him and gave him a final kiss, hard and desperate. He left her there clinging to the door, playing the role of the abandoned *femme fatale*.

Kinsman loped past a row of phones in the hotel lobby and grabbed the last remaining taxi standing at the curb. As it growled and rattled out into the sparse nighttime traffic he gave the black driver the McGraths' address in Georgetown.

Mary-Ellen let him into the apartment, a puzzled look on her face. "Chet, you look as if you're ready to take on the entire Sioux nation. What's the matter?"

"Where's Neal?"

She led him back to the parlor where the party had been. No one was there now except the two of them. The big room was filled with sofas and wingback chairs, the empty fireplace, mirrors, paintings, lamps, bookcases, end tables, the big circular Persian etched brass hanging between the French windows, a hundred pieces of bric-a-brac acquired over the years of their marriage.

"Neal's out," Mary-Ellen said. "He won't be back for a few days."

Kinsman looked at her. "The committee hearings are still running."

"He hasn't left town," she said, weariness in her voice. "He's just . . . not here."

"He's with Diane."

She nodded.

"And you're letting him do it?"

"Do you know any way I can stop him from doing it?"

"I'd think it would be pretty easy for you, if you wanted him to stop."

She dropped into the sofa nearest the dead, dark fireplace. "Chet, nothing is easy."

"Do you love him?" he asked, sitting down beside her.

"Do I breathe?"

"Hey, I'm the one who's supposed to give flip answers to hide his feelings."

Mary-Ellen's hands made a helpless flutter. "What do you expect me to say? Do I love him? What a question! We've been married nearly sixteen years. We have three children."

"Do you love him?"

"I did. I think maybe I still do . . . but it's not so easy to tell anymore."

"He said you agreed to a divorce after he's re-elected."

"Yes."

"But why?" Kinsman asked. "Why are you letting him do this to you? Why are you taking it like this?"

"What else can I do? Wreck his career? Would that bring him back to me? Threaten him? Force him to stay with me? Do you think I want that?"

"What the hell do you want?"

"I don't know!"

"You're lying," Kinsman said. "You're lying to yourself."

Tears were brimming in her eyes. "Chet, leave me alone. Just go away and leave me alone. I don't want . . ." She could not say anything more; she broke down.

Kinsman took her in his arms and held her gently. "That's better. That's better. I know what it's like to hold it all inside yourself. It's better to let it come out. Let it all out."

"I can't . . ." Her voice was muffled, but the pain came through. "I shouldn't be bothering you . . ."

"Nonsense. That's what shoulders are for. Hell, we've known each other a long, long time. It's okay. You can cry on my shoulder anytime. Maybe if I'd had the sense to cry on yours when I needed to . . ."

She pulled slightly away, but not so far that he could no longer hold her.

"We have known each other a long time, haven't we?"

"All the way back to Philadelphia," he said.

"I've known you as long as I've known Neal."

"I was jealous as hell of him," Kinsman remembered.

"He . . . he said I'm . . . he said that I couldn't give love. That I'm incapable of it."

Kinsman grimaced. "I haven't been able to give love to anyone for years."

A new look came into her eyes. "Is that what happened to you? All those rumors . . ."

He pulled her closer and kissed her. Gray-eyed Athena, goddess of wisdom and of war, I'll take you over treacherous Aphrodite every time. Their hands moved across each other's bodies, searching, opening, pulling clothes away.

Still half-dressed, he leaned her back on the couch and was on top of her, into her, before the picture of the dead cosmonaut could form in his mind. He heard her gasp and felt her clutching him, hard, furiously intense, alive, molten, burning all the old bad images out of his brain. Everything blurred together. He found himself sitting on the edge of the couch beside her, staring into those strong, wise gray eyes. Wordlessly she got to her feet and led him to the bedroom. She shut the door firmly. In silence they finished stripping and went to the bed. They made love and dozed, alternately, until the sun brightened the curtained windows.

"God," she murmured, and he could feel her breath on his cheek, "you're like a teenager."

"It's been a long time," he said. "I've got a lot of catching up to do."

He showered alone, and when he came back into the bedroom to dress she had gone. He found her in the kitchen, wrapped in a shapeless beige housecoat, munching a piece of dry toast as she sat at the counter that cut the room in half. An untouched glass of orange juice stood on the counter before her.

"Hungry?" she asked, wiping toast crumbs from her lips.

"I'll get something from the cafeteria in the Pentagon," he said.

"Have some juice, at least." She pushed the glass toward him.

"Thanks," he said.

"Thank you."

Suddenly they were both embarrassed. Kinsman felt like a sheepish kid. Mary-Ellen stared down at the toast on her plate.

He did not know what to say. "I . . . uh, guess I'd better be going now."

"It's awfully early. I don't think the buses are running this early."

He shrugged. "I'll walk for a while."

"Aren't you tired?"

And they both broke up. Kinsman lifted his head and roared. Mary-Ellen laughed with him.

"Tired? For God's sake, woman, I'm exhausted!"

"I should hope so," she said. "You had me scared for a minute, there."

She came around the counter and put an arm around his waist. He took her by the shoulders and together they walked through the parlor, toward the house's front door.

"I do thank you, Chet," Mary-Ellen said. "You've helped me to see myself—everything—in a new light."

"My pleasure."

"Not entirely yours."

"I . . . feel kind of funny about it, though," he admitted. "Christ, it's almost like incest!"

She smiled at him. "I know."

"It was a one-time thing. I mean, I don't think either one of us could . . . well, *plan* something like that."

They were at the door now. Gently she disengaged from him. "No, it was a surprise. A once-in-a-lifetime, wonderful surprise. If we tried to repeat it, it wouldn't work."

Nodding, "No, I guess it wouldn't."

"But it was good."

"Damned good. Thanks, Mary-Ellen. You've chased away a devil that's been haunting me for a long time."

"Then I'm glad."

They kissed, swiftly, almost shyly, and he left.

The door burst open as if it had been kicked and Neal McGrath's bulk filled the doorway.

Kinsman looked up from his apartment's desk. The clock at his elbow said 10 P.M. He had spent the day in the Pentagon, ignoring McGrath's committee hearings, working with the Secretary of Defense's staff on the briefings they were giving at the White House.

"You sonofabitch!" McGrath growled.

He slammed the door shut and took two strides into the shabby room. His tall, rangy body seemed to radiate fury.

"You bastard!" McGrath's fists were doubled, white-knuckled. "You screwed my wife."

"While you were screwing your girlfriend."

McGrath took another step toward him, raising his fists.

Kinsman stopped him with a pointed finger. "Hold on, Neal. You're bigger, but I've trained harder. All you're going to do is get yourself hurt."

"I'll kill you, you sonofabitch." But he stopped and let his hands fall to his sides.

"I don't blame you," Kinsman said softly. "What happened last night . . . it was completely unexpected. Hell, Neal, I came to your house looking for you. Neither of us planned it. It just happened. You ought to know about things like that."

"Don't hand me that!"

"I know, I know," Kinsman said, keeping his voice low. "Now we're talking about your wife, and that's different. Okay. But maybe now at least you know a little of what she's been going through."

McGrath said nothing. He stood in the middle of the small room panting like a bull in the arena that was confused by the noise and the light.

"It's not going to happen again," Kinsman added. "We both agreed on that."

"I thought you were my friend," McGrath said, his voice cracking with misery.

"Yeah, I thought so, too." Kinsman turned and pulled

the chair away from the desk. "Come on, sit down. I'll get you a beer. We've got a lot to talk about."

Numbly McGrath took the chair. Kinsman went to the refrigerator and pulled out two cold bottles of Bass ale. Fumbling in the drawer for a bottle opener, he wondered, Will the English ever come into the twentieth century and put screwtops on their beer? He found the opener, pried the tops off, then walked over and handed one bottle to McGrath.

"Hope you don't want a glass. They're both dirty."

McGrath gave a grunt that was almost a laugh. "What are we drinking to?" he asked, not looking up at Kinsman.

"To understanding," Kinsman said, stretching out on the open sofabed.

"Understanding what?"

The real world, man. The real world. "Understanding why I came over to your house last night, trying to find you. Understanding what's happening in the Pentagon and the White House, and what's going to hit the Congress in the next few days."

McGrath sat up straighter in his chair. "What the hell are you talking about?"

"I'm not authorized to tell you, Neal, but I'm going to anyway and if anybody's snooping on this conversation they can go rush their tapes to whoever they want to."

Inadvertently McGrath's eyes scanned the room, looking for microphones.

"The Aerospace Force has been working for some time," Kinsman said, "on the development of a manned interceptor spaceplane that will be used to destroy Soviet ABM satellites."

"I know that. Nobody in the Pentagon has seen fit to brief me about it, but I've got my own sources."

"Okay. You know, then, that this will mean we're going to actively pursue the objective of preventing the Soviets from deploying a Star Wars type of defensive shield in orbit."

"Yeah, and they're going to try to stop us from deploying our own," McGrath said. "That's what I've been fighting against since I came to the Senate."

"You're shoveling shit against the tide, Neal. It's going to happen whether either one of us likes it or not."

McGrath muttered something unintelligible.

"And we're going to start building our own ABM satellites," Kinsman went on, "in orbital factories, out of materials mined from the Moon."

"The hell you are."

"The hell we're not! The whole Department of Defense is behind this one, Neal. It's not just a little hospital of a Moonbase anymore. It's not just us *Luniks*. The entire military-industrial complex is in the act now. And so is the White House."

Understanding dawned in McGrath's eyes. "So that's why Dreyer's people have been huddling with the committee chairman. And the big aerospace primes are starting to give cocktail parties . . ."

"They're lining up their votes."

With a stubborn shake of his head McGrath said, "Once we start mining operations on the Moon the Russians will do exactly the same thing. Or worse: once they see that you're using lunar resources to build Star Wars hardware, they'll try to stop you. World War Three could start on the Moon and spread to Earth."

"No, it won't, Neal. There won't be any fighting on the Moon. I promise you that."

"How can you—"

"I'm going to be the commander of Moonbase."

"You want to spend a hundred billion dollars on top of everything we're already spending and bring the world to the brink of nuclear war, just so you can play soldier on the Moon."

"You know me better than that, Neal. We'll keep the Moon demilitarized. There won't be any armaments on the Moon. Just the mines. And the hospital." And a graveyard, he added silently.

McGrath shifted on the chair, making its wooden legs creak. "I'll do everything I can to stop this nonsense. I'm dead-set against it."

"The Pentagon will roll over you like a steamdriver, Neal. This isn't just a minor Aerospace Force program anymore, the kind you can nibble off the list and then go home and show the voters how much money you've saved them. This is the big time. Corporations like General Tech and the other big aerospace primes are coming in on this. It'll mean employment for those half-empty shops and factories all across Pennsylvania."

"It will mean inflation . . . and war."

"No, dammitall!" Kinsman raised his voice. "The ABM satellites will protect us against missile attack. The cheaper we make them, the easier it becomes to replace damaged or defective ones, the *safer* we'll be. Right now, this minute, somebody in Russia or China or seventeen other nations can push a button and inside half an hour this whole country will be just one big mushroom cloud. There's no way to stop a missile attack! Not until the ABM satellites are deployed."

"We're going to deploy them; you're getting your Star Wars system."

"Building them from lunar resources will make them cheaper and easier to deploy. We'll be able to protect more people, more parts of the world, sooner."

"Unless you provoke the Soviets into a preemptive strike because they're afraid we'll attack them once we have all our satellites in place."

"But they'll be putting up their own ABM satellites. You said so yourself."

"And you're building your goddamned interceptor to knock them down. What happens when the two of you start fighting in orbit? You could start a nuclear war here on the ground."

Kinsman took a swig of ale. "If that's going to happen, it'll happen whether we have a Moonbase or not. Neither one of us has any control over that."

"But I'm not going to vote to help you make it easier for them to start a war," McGrath insisted.

"But war isn't the only possibility, Neal. Look at the benefits we can get."

"Such as?"

"A solid industrial base in orbit. Shipping lunar ores to orbital factories can start the ball rolling on the solar power satellites and all the other peacetime industries in space that will help people on Earth. Opening the door to all the raw materials and energy in space. New jobs. New technologies. New industries. Space is our escape hatch, Neal. If we use it wisely we can put an end to the causes for wars on Earth. We can get out of this coffin we've built for ourselves down here."

"We've been through all that before. It'll take twenty, thirty years before space industries even begin to help the poor and disadvantaged here on Earth."

"Even so," Kinsman said, "what other program do you have that can help them? Everything else is taking from Peter to pay Paul. That's what causes wars, Neal: trying to steal a bigger slice of the pie. All those welfare programs you're pushing, all they do is prolong the misery. Space operations can open up new sources of wealth, make the pie bigger."

"For the rich. For the corporations."

"For everybody! If you do it right."

"I don't believe it, Chet. And I can't vote for it. It's impossible."

"Then you'd better kiss the Minority Leadership goodbye," Kinsman said. "And maybe your seat in the Senate, too."

He stared at Kinsman for a long, silent moment. "So it boils down to that, does it?"

"You knew it would."

"All this high-flown talk about the future and the benefits to the human race . . . it all comes down to the fact that you're willing to blackmail me just to get your ass up to the Moon."

"That's right."

"You *are* a sonofabitch. And a cold-blooded one, at that."

Kinsman grinned at the angry, smoldering Senator who had been his friend. "Neal, a fanatic who's willing to sacrifice his life for his cause is perfectly willing to sacrifice *your* life for his cause."

"So you can get to the Moon. You'd wreck my career, my life, you'd wreck the whole world just to get what you want."

"You'll live through it. And the world has a way of taking care of itself. Believe me, you'll both be far better off with me on the Moon. Me, and a few thousand other *Luniks*."

McGrath drained the last of his ale, then hefted the empty bottle in his big hand. "I can't vote for it. Even if I wanted to, I couldn't switch my position on this. My own party would crucify me."

"Yes you can. And I'll bet those big, bad industrialists in Pennsylvania will even contribute to your re-election campaign if you do."

"No," McGrath said firmly.

"It's suicide to vote against the national defense appropriation, Neal."

"I have always voted against wasteful spending."

"But this isn't wasteful! It'll create jobs, for Chrissake. Look on it as an employment program."

"That will lead us into war."

"That will lead you into the White House someday. Sure, some of your supporters will get disenchanted and turn against you—for a while. But you'll gain more supporters than you lose. You'll end up with a much wider base of support."

"By going against everything I believe in."

Suddenly exasperated, Kinsman burst out, "What the hell do you believe in, Neal? Your opinions about space are stupid! You're just as blindly ignorant about it as my father was. All those programs you back, for helping the poor and the needy—they've squandered more goddamned money on bureaucratic bullshit than anything that's ever gone through Congress. And they don't work! You've got *more* unemployed, more welfare cases right now in your own state than you did when you first came into the Congress. Look it up, I've checked the numbers."

"That's not the fault of the welfare programs."

"But those programs aren't helping! You want to be Minority Leader, you've got ambitions to head the party, but you're turning down an offer that's guaranteed to bring you more support than you've ever had because of a stubborn ideological bias that's just plain stupidly *wrong*. Just what the hell do you want?"

"I want to be able to live with myself."

"And with who else? Diane? Mary-Ellen? Both of them? Do you want to be able to live with those unemployed workers back home? To be an unemployed worker yourself? Take your pick."

McGrath got to his feet. For a moment Kinsman thought he was going to throw the empty bottle against the wall. But he let it drop from his fingers. It bounced once on the thin carpeting and rolled toward the sofabed.

Kinsman stood up, too.

"I've heard enough," McGrath said. "I'm leaving. If I ever see you near Mary-Ellen again . . ."

"You won't," Kinsman said. Then, grinning, he added, "Of course, one way to make sure of that is to send me a quarter-million miles away."

McGrath glared at him.

"You can have your Minority Leadership, Neal. All I want is the Moon."

The committee hearings were scheduled to go on for another week before the senators voted. Kinsman spent the time briefing White House staffers and key Congressional leaders, including Senator McGrath. The State Department reared its head and mewed about upsetting the delicate balance of offensive and defensive armaments that had been negotiated so painstakingly at Geneva over the past decade. But the Central Intelligence Agency cut State's legs off at the knees with evidence that the Soviets were developing a spaceplane that looked so exactly like the USAF interceptor they suspected the plans had been stolen.

Then came the critical vote on the defense budget by the Senate Appropriations Committee. The budget included a small supplemental item for Moonbase: the first year's funding, "a scant fifty million," as Marcot put it, "the nose of the camel." Everyone knew, thanks to Kinsman's briefings, that the full camel would cost twenty billion or more.

The first test came almost unnoticed, except by Kinsman and the other *Luniks*: no senator proposed an amendment to the budget that would eliminate the Moonbase program.

The second test was the roll-call vote of the committee. Kinsman sat in the rear of the ornate committee chamber, holding his breath as the roll call went down the long green-topped table. Only three senators voted nay. Two abstained. McGrath of Pennsylvania was one of the abstentions.

Moonbase passed. Kinsman leaned back in his chair and let out a year-long sigh.

You've got what you wanted, he said to himself. Now all you have to do is worry about whether it was the right thing to want.

Immediately he answered himself, No! All you have to do is to *make* it the right thing.

"So that's how Neal's going to handle it," Kinsman was telling Frank Colt that evening as they celebrated at a bar in Crystal City. "He's not going to vote in favor, but he's not going to stand in the way."

The bar was jammed. Half the Pentagon seemed to be there, clamoring for drinks. Music blared from omnispeakers set into the red plush-covered walls. The lights were glittering, splashing off the mirrored ceiling. Colt and Kinsman stood at the bar, wedged in by the frenetic crowd.

Colt hiked his eyebrows. "Politicians! They got more tricks to 'em than a forty-year-old hooker."

Grabbing his drink from the bar before the guy next to him elbowed it over, Kinsman shouted over the noise, "Who cares! We're going to the Moon, buddy!"

The guy next to him gave Kinsman a queer look.

Colt laughed, then turned to look over the crowded, throbbing room. Kinsman did the same, resting his elbows against the bar. All the tables were filled, people were milling around the dance floor, hollering in each other's ears, laughing, drinking, smoking. There was not a square foot of empty space.

Looking over the noisy crowd, Kinsman realized that he would be leaving this kind of scene far behind him. No great loss, he told himself. No real loss at all.

Then he noticed a stunning Asian woman sitting at one of the tiny tables with an almost equally good-looking blonde. The Oriental had the delicate features of a Vietnamese.

Colt spotted them, too. He nudged Kinsman in the ribs. "Now *that* looks like a scrutable Oriental."

"They do look lonely," Kinsman said.

Colt nodded. "And hungry. Probably waitin' for a couple of gentlemen to offer them a square meal."

"Or a crooked one."

They started pushing through the crowd, heading for the women's table.

"Seems to me," Colt yelled at Kinsman over the blaring music, "it's been a helluva long time since we tried this kinda maneuver together."

Kinsman nodded. "A helluva long time."

Colt's grin was pure happiness.

Washington lay sweltering in muggy late August heat. The air was thick and gray. The sun hung overhead like a sullen bloated enemy, sickly dull orange. Any other city in the world would be empty and quiet on a Saturday like this, Kinsman thought. But Washington was filled with tourists. Despite the heat and soaking humidity they were out in force, cameras dangling from sweaty necks, short-tempered, wet-shirted, dragging tired crying children along with them. Waiting in line to get inside the White House, swarming up the steps of the Lincoln Memorial, clumping together for guided tours of the Capitol, the Smithsonian museums, the Treasury Department's greenback printing plant.

Kinsman waited in the cool quiet of the National Art Gallery beside the soothing splashing of the fountain just inside the main entrance. Wing-footed Mercury pranced atop the fountain. Kinsman laughed at the statue's pose. Looks like he's giving us the finger.

Diane showed up a few minutes late, looking coolly beautiful in a flowered skirt and peasant blouse. Kinsman went to her and they kissed lightly, like old friends, like siblings.

"How'd you get my phone number?" she asked. "I'm only in town for a few days . . ."

"Neal's office."

"But he's back in Pennsylvania during the recess."

"Yes, but his office is still functioning."

He took her by the arm and began leading her back toward the museum's main doors.

"Where're we going?" Diane asked.

"I want to take you to dinner. This is my last day here. I'm moving out to Vandenberg tomorrow."

"I know. Neal told me."

They stepped outside into the glare and soupy heat. "He's up there in the cool Allegheny breezes mapping out his campaign for the Minority Leadership, playing family man for

Mary-Ellen and the kids and the voters down home."

"He's pretty sore at you," Diane said as they walked down the steps toward the jitney stop.

"Yeah. I guess he's got a right to be."

"He said he's going to fight against your defense programs once he's Minority Leader."

Kinsman looked at her. "That's his way of salving his conscience, Diane. Behind all the rhetoric, he's going to let us go ahead and do what needs to be done. He's got the White House on his mind now."

"You took advantage of him. And me."

"That's right. And of Mary-Ellen, and the Aerospace Force, the Pentagon, the White House—the whole human race."

She did not answer him.

Their talk through dinner was trivial at first, impersonal, almost like strangers who had nothing in common. Avoid arguments during mealtime, Chester, Kinsman could hear his mother telling him. If you can't say something pleasant, then say nothing at all.

But finally he had to ask, "How'd the tests come out?"

"The tests?" Diane seemed genuinely puzzled, then she realized what he meant. With a plaintive little smile she said, "Oh, I'm pregnant, all right. It's going to be a girl."

"You're going to have it?"

She nodded.

"And Neal?" Kinsman asked.

"I don't know." Diane's smile turned slightly sadder. "*He* doesn't know what he wants—now."

It was still hot and bright outside when they left the restaurant, but the downtown Washington streets were already emptying. The tourists were hurrying for their air-conditioned hotels and restaurants, exhausted and sweaty after a day of tramping around the city. They wanted to cool off and relax before the electrical power was shut down for the night.

"Hey, I've got an idea," Kinsman said. "Come on."

He flagged down a dilapidated taxi and helped Diane into it. She looked puzzled. "Washington Monument," he told the driver.

The line of tourists that usually circled the monument

266

was gone by the time they arrived there.

"Is it still open?" Diane asked.

"Sure. I've never been up the top. Have you?"

"No."

"Then now's the time!" Kinsman gripped Diane's hand tightly as he led her up the grassy slope to the immense obelisk that loomed before them. On either side of the path the silvery solar panels that provided electricity for the monument's night lighting looked like miniature fairy-tale castles, stretching all around the spire. As they approached the gigantic column, with the sunset sky flaming red and orange behind it, its marble flanks began to look gray and dingy.

"The world's biggest phallic symbol," Kinsman said. "Dedicated to the Father of our Country."

Diane grinned sourly. "You would look at it that way, wouldn't you?"

There were only half a dozen other people waiting inside, speaking German and another language that Kinsman could not identify. They milled around for a few minutes and then the elevator came down, opened its doors, and discharged about twenty bedraggled tourists.

As the elevator groaned and creaked its way up to the top of the monument, Diane whispered, "Is this thing safe?"

Kinsman shrugged. "I'd feel a lot better if it had wings on it."

Finally the elevator stopped and its doors wheezed open. They stepped out and went to a tiny barred window. The entire city lay sprawled below them, smothered in muggy, smoggy heat. The sun was touching the horizon now, and lights were beginning to twinkle in the buildings that stretched as far as the eye could see.

"If I have some good luck," Kinsman said, "this is the last time I'll see Washington."

Diane asked, "Why did you call me, Chet? What do you expect from me?"

Surprised, he answered quickly, "Nothing! Not a damned thing. I just wanted to . . . well, sort of apologize. To you, and to Neal. He won't even talk to me on the phone, so I sort of figured I'd tell you."

"Apologize?"

"For . . . using you both, as you put it. I think it would have happened anyway, sooner or later. Somebody else would have twisted Neal's arm the way I did. But I was his friend and now I've made him into an enemy."

"You certainly have," she said.

"And you?"

She looked out at the city, so far below. "His enemies are my enemies. Isn't that the way it's supposed to be?"

"So I've heard."

He stood beside her, gazing out at the buildings and the scurrying buses and cars, all those people down there, all the cities and nations and people of the entire planet. Suddenly, finally, the enormity of it hit him. Grasping the iron bars set into the stone window frame, Kinsman could feel himself falling, swirling out into emptiness. Good God, he thought. All those people! I've set myself up against all of them. I've forced them to do what I want, without a thought for their side of it. What if I'm wrong? What if it's not the right thing?

Almost wildly he searched for the Moon in the darkening sky but it was nowhere in sight.

"Neal says you're going to start a war in space," Diane said, her voice low but knife-edged. "He says your Moonbase is going to lead to World War Three. You're going to kill us all."

"No." The word was out of his mouth before he knew he had spoken it. "Neal and the rest of you, you just don't understand. The most important thing we'll ever do is to set up permanent habitats in space. It's time for the human race to expand its ecological niche, time we stopped restricting ourselves to just one planet. Our salvation lies out there, Diane, maybe the only chance for salvation we'll ever have."

She turned to him. "That's just a rationalization and you know it. You say it's important because it's what you want to do."

"Maybe. But that doesn't change a thing. Maybe history is the result of huge massive forces that push people around like pawns. Maybe it's the result of scared, lone individuals who're driven to pull the whole goddamned human race along with them. I don't know and I don't care. I'm going to the Moon. The rest of you will have to figure things out the best you can."

"And you're leaving all this behind?"

He looked out at the sprawling city. "What's to leave? This whole planet's turning into an overcrowded slum. If we do get into World War Three it won't be because of a few thousand people living in space. It'll be because six or seven billion people are stuck here on the ground."

"But those people are worth fighting for!" Diane said. "We have to struggle for social justice and freedom *here*, on this world. We can't run away!"

"I'm not running away, Diane. I'm helping you. I'm on your side, honest I am. I'll be sending you back all the energy and natural resources you need for your struggle. I'll be helping those poor people to become rich. And I'll send you back some new ideas about how to live in freedom, too."

She shook her head. "You're hopeless."

"I know. We both decided that a long time ago."

"You're really going to the Moon. In spite of everything."

"*Because* of everything. Want to come along?"

"Me?" She looked startled.

"Sure. Why not? You could be the first woman to give birth on another world."

"No, thanks! I'll stay right here."

"Then we'll never see each other again," Kinsman said. The sadness of it, the finality of it, left him feeling hollow, empty.

With a knowing look Diane said, "Oh, you'll be back, Chet. Don't get dramatic. You won't stay up there forever. Nobody could. You'll be back."

But his eyes were focused beyond her, on the window at her back. Through its narrow aperture he could see the full Moon topping the hazy horizon, smiling crookedly at him.

"Don't bet your life on it," he said.

BOOK 2

MILLENNIUM

It is not death that a man should fear,
but he should fear never beginning to
live.

—Marcus Aurelius

To Barbara, with all my love

Wednesday 1 December 1999: 0900 hrs UT

THE DIGITAL CLOCK on Kinsman's desk said nine. Not that the arbitrary time made any physical difference in the underground community. Up on the surface of the Moon it was sundown, the beginning of a night that would last three hundred thirty-six hours. But here, safely underground, a man-made day was just beginning in the community called Selene.

As the highest-ranking American on the Moon, Colonel Kinsman was entitled to a private office. It was small and functional. There was a desk tucked into one corner, but he rarely sat at it. He preferred slouching on the plastic foam couch that was set against one wall. It had been one of the first products of Selene's recycling facility. The plastic had originally come from packing crates hauled up from Earth. The foam was a fire-retardation spray that had outlived its useful life and had been replaced by a fresh unit. A Belgian chemist, a visitor to Selene several years earlier, had hit on the method of converting the foam to a comfortable padding for furniture.

There was no file cabinet in the office. No paper in sight. Not only was paper a rare and valuable commodity a quarter-million miles from the nearest forest, but Kinsman hated "paper shuffling." He preferred to talk out problems face to face. A computer terminal sat on his desk, linked to Selene's mainframe. Its display screen also served as a picture screen for the telephone. Another phone terminal was at Kinsman's elbow, on the stand beside the couch. Two slingchairs completed the office's furnishings. The floor was covered with hardy, close-cropped grass, more practical than esthetic: green plants provided vital oxygen in this underground outpost on an airless world.

Three of the office's rock walls were covered with large display screens. One showed Earth as it appeared from Selene's main dome, up on the surface. The other two were blank at the moment.

Kinsman was sprawled on the foam couch, one arm stretched lazily along its back cushions. He was no longer as lean as he had been on Earth; his middle was starting to fill out. His dark hair was touched with gray, and he still wore it rather longer than Aerospace Force regulations permitted. There was no insignia of rank on his blue coveralls; it was not necessary: everyone in the underground community knew him on sight—even the Russians.

His face was long, slightly horsey, with narrow-set gray-blue eyes, a nose that he had never liked, and a smile that he had learned to use many years earlier.

Facing him, sitting on the front four centimeters of a slingchair, was one of Selene's permanent residents, Ernie Waterman, a civilian engineer. Tall, angular, gloomy. He looks like Ichabod Crane, thought Kinsman. He smiled as he said, "Ernie, I don't like hounding you but Selene can't truly be self-sufficient until the water factory's brought up to full capacity."

Waterman's voice was edgy, ready for an argument. "So it's my fault? If we bring up more equipment from Earth . . ."

"Wish we could." Kinsman glanced at the blue crescent glowing on the wall screen behind the engineer. "Dear old General Murdock and his friends in Washington say no. Too heavy and too expensive. We're on our own. But there's no reason why we can't build our own equipment right here in the shops, is there?"

Waterman gave a guarded smile that was close to being a grimace. "An optimist, yet. Okay, look, so we've got some raw materials and some trained people. But where's the six million other things we need? We don't have tooling. We don't have supplies. It takes us four times longer to do anything because we always have to start from scratch. I can't pick up the phone and order the stainless steel I need. Or the wiring. Or the copper or tungsten. We've got to make do with what we can mine out of these rocks."

"I know," said Kinsman.

"So it takes time."

"But you've been at it two years now."

Waterman's voice went up a notch. "Now don't start blaming everything on me! I've only been up here a year and I've been on this job six months. I'm *supposed* to be retired . . ."

"Whoa, whoa, cool down," Kinsman soothed. "I didn't mean you personally. And you know you were going rock-happy in retirement, Ernie. You're not a man of leisure." Make him smile. No fights with the volunteer help.

The engineer's long face unfolded slightly into a small grin. "Yeah, well maybe it was getting to me. But what bothered me most was your blue-suit skyboys trying to make like engineers. Those idiotic solar ovens . . ."

"Okay, okay, you win." Kinsman threw up his hands in mock surrender. "You're on the right track, I know. I shouldn't push you. But the water factory's our key to survival. We need the extra capacity. If there's ever an accident and we lose what we have now—it's a long haul back to Earth. A long time to wait for a drink."

"You think I don't know? I'm pushing as hard as I can, Chet. It sure would be helpful to get more equipment from Earthside, though."

"That's out."

With an elaborate shrug, Waterman said, "All right, so we'll keep doing it the hard way." He hesitated, then added, "But I don't see what the big hassle is all about. The factory's already turning out more water than we use. You could even refill that precious swimming pool of yours with fresh water every month instead of recycling it."

Kinsman put on a grin. "That pool is Selene's one luxury. And the factory was deliberately overdesigned to make sure we could accommodate extra people up here —such as retired engineers."

"With gimpy legs. Yeah, I know." Waterman fell silent for a moment. Then, "But do they know Earthside about how you're expanding the factory?"

A jolt of electricity flashed through Kinsman. Mildly, though, he replied, "Oh, sure. Of course they know."

"I mean, about your trying to double its capacity?"

Kinsman remained silent for a moment, then answered

evenly, "Self-sufficiency has always been our goal, Ernie. Water is the key to survival. Without water we couldn't even keep the grass under our feet alive."

"Yeah, but . . ."

"But what?"

Waterman spread his hands. "You've already got a big-enough capacity to take care of more people than we have on the American side of Selene. Doubling it means we could provide water for the Russians, too."

"Is that so terrible?" Kinsman asked.

Waterman said nothing, but his face darkened.

"I didn't design this place," Kinsman said. "Selene got put together when the Russians were cooperating with us on the space program. We've got to live with them next door. All right, so far we've gotten along fine, much better than Earthside. But if the shoe starts to pinch, don't you think it'd be better if *we* have control of enough water to take care of both sides? Then, if something should happen to their water supply, they'd have to ask us pretty please, wouldn't they?"

The cloud over the engineer's face vanished. He laughed. "I get it. Okay, you want double the capacity for the factory, you'll get double. Only stop breathing down my neck every day, will ya?"

Relieved, Kinsman said, "How about every other day?"

They laughed together as the engineer leaned on his canes and pulled himself erect.

Kinsman stood up beside him. "You know, Ernie, when I found out that you were an engineer and interested in the water factory, I almost got religion. Waterman: just the omen we needed for the factory."

"Religion," the engineer said, his voice suddenly low and serious. "That's what you get when you find you can walk again, when you can get out of your wheelchair and do something useful and be a man again." He tapped the metal braces beneath his trouser legs with a cane.

"Low gravity is one of our greatest assets. A real tourist attraction," Kinsman said as he slowly ushered Waterman toward the door.

The engineer waved one of his canes. "It's not just the gravity. It's the whole attitude around here. The way people do things here. None of the red tape and horse manure like they have Earthside. No standing in lines or spending your days filling out forms. People have *faith* in each other up here."

And their faith has made them whole, Kinsman quoted to himself. He answered Waterman, "They're free, Ernie. We've got enough room up here to be free."

Waterman shrugged again. "Whatever it is, it's like a miracle."

"You don't miss Earth at all?" Kinsman asked, stopping at the door.

"The Bronx I should miss? Hell no! My two daughters, yes. Them I miss. But the rest of it—it's just a crummy slum, from sea to polluted sea. It's going to hell so fast there's no way to stop it."

Kinsman thought about his last days on Earth, more than five years earlier. His sudden yearning to see Diane one last time. The madhouse battling with the airlines to wrest a seat on a plane to San Francisco. The shock of seeing a city he had loved turned into a vast concrete jungle: the once-gleaming towers rotting with decay, their elevators useless without electricity; the bridges rusting with neglect; the Bay dotted with houseboats and black with scum. And Diane never showed up; her concert had been canceled.

"And what about you?" Waterman was asking. "Do you miss it? You've been here longer than almost anybody."

Kinsman avoided the question. "I can go back when I really want to. I'm not physically restricted."

"I thought you had a heart problem. I heard . . ."

Shaking his head, "Don't believe all the rumors you hear, Ernie. Selene's like any small town: ten parts gossip to every one part of fact. A little high blood pressure can turn into open-heart surgery on the rumor mill."

The phone buzzed.

"Duty calls," Kinsman said.

The engineer left the office and closed the door behind him as Kinsman went back to the couch. Leaning across it he touched the phone's ON button. One of the wall screens glowed, but no picture came up on it. Instead, the computer's honey-warm feminine voice said, "Colonel Kinsman, you asked to be reminded that the shuttle bringing new arrivals is scheduled to touch down at oh-nine-thirty hours. Traffic control confirms that the shuttle is on schedule."

"Right," he said, and punched the phone off.

He left the office and started down the corridor toward the power ladder. *Wonder what Ernie would do if I told him we'd share our water with the Russians in an emergency? Would he quit the job? Would he yell back to Washington?*

Officially, the American settlement on the Moon was called Moonbase. The Russians called theirs Lunagrad. Officially, the two bases were separate and independent of each other. Military planners in Washington and Moscow scowled whenever they thought of the brief rash of international amity that had led to building the two bases side by side.

Technically, Moonbase and Lunagrad were each self-sufficient, each capable of surviving without help from the other. Actually, the Americans and Russians who lived with each other as neighbors all called themselves Luniks and their community Selene.

Now Kinsman strode through the big cavern that linked the two halves of Selene. It was a vast underground chamber with a high chalky white ceiling and rough gray stone walls. The Russians and Americans had turned it into an open plaza with green lawns and tree-lined walkways. Tiny shops and refreshment centers, established by entrepreneurs from several Western nations, competed with government-owned exchanges that provided a meager flow of personal goods from Earth. The plaza was always busy with off-duty people: it reminded Kinsman of a New England village green, restrained and quiet in the soft, low-gravity, highly controlled lunar style.

Kinsman nodded and smiled hello to almost everyone as he went through the plaza. He knew all the permanent residents by name—there were only about a thousand of them.

But as he rode the power ladder up to the main surface dome his thoughts returned to Waterman. *How many of our people still think as if they're Earthbound?* he wondered. By the time he stepped off the ladder and onto the rock floor of the big dome he was scowling.

Follow the yellow brick road.

The dome was kept darkened; faintly luminescent arrows crisscrossed the fused rock floor, pointing the way to various destinations. Kinsman padded along the yellow arrows, heading for the main airlock.

The dome was as large as a modern cathedral, and just as empty. It was the biggest structure on the Moon's surface, a symbol of the eternal spirit of brotherhood and cooperation between the peoples of the United States and the Soviet Union. That spirit had died a little before the dome was finished, poisoned in a world choked by too much population and too few resources.

The sound of Kinsman's slippered feet scuffing along the fused rock floor was swallowed by the dark, sepulchral dome. He could feel the cold of the new lunar night seeping up through the rock, tingling the air. The dome's ceiling was also made from lunar stone, supported on a geodesic framework of aluminum scavenged from spent rocket stages. The main walls of the dome were transparent plastiglass, hauled up from Earthside kilogram by precious kilogram.

Rows of tractors and crawlers and other heavy equipment were lined up mute and unmoving in their assigned parking lanes. Facing the main airlock, the right side of the dome was for American equipment, the left side for Russian.

That's political nicety, Kinsman told himself.

Crossing the dome floor, Kinsman did not merely walk along, he prowled. His years on the Moon had led him to an unconscious compromise between his Earth-muscled legs and the low lunar gravity. The result was a gliding, almost floating slow-motion stride that resembled nothing so much as the silent purposeful advance of a stalking cat. In the shadows thrown by the dim, faraway overhead lights, his bony long-jawed face and dark-browed scowl added to the impression of a hunting feline.

He came to the heavy metal structure of the main airlock and detoured around its once-gleaming walls, to the observation area. Despite the low lighting, he could see a faint reflection of himself in the plastiglass wall. You're getting paunchy, he thought. Too much office work and too little exercise. The curse of the middle-aged executive. Looking past his own image, he gazed out at the desolate lunar plain.

The Sea of Clouds.

It was a weary, pockmarked rolling plain of naked rock, pounded for eons by a constant rain of meteors and more recently scoured—close to the dome—by the landing jets of spacecraft. It was a frozen sea of stone, bare and utterly lifeless, with boulders strewn carelessly across it like a half-finished construction job that the maker had abandoned, left to brood gray and ghostly in the light of the gleaming crescent Earth.

If it really were a sea, or even clouds, we wouldn't need the damned water factory. Kinsman's frown deepened as he thought of it. He hated to argue with people, despised the need to prod and pressure them. Maybe we won't need the extra water. But water is life and I don't want to have to refuse it to anyone, including the Russians. He glanced at the beckoning, beautiful blue and white crescent of Earth. Especially the Russians, he added silently.

Turning slightly, he looked across the silent dome's wide expanse to the transparent wall on the other side. The tired, rounded humps of mountains huddled there, guardians of the lunar ringwall Alphonsus, a crater wide enough to hold any city on Earth, including its suburbs. The thought of a teeming, fetid, decaying city here on the Moon disgusted him.

He turned back toward the Sea of Clouds and looked upward for some glimpse of the arriving shuttle. No flare of jets. No glint of Earthlight on smooth metal. He saw the horizon, close enough almost to touch. And beyond it, the blackness of infinity. No matter how many times he confronted it the sight still moved him. A few bright stars could be seen through the dome's thick plastic window. The eyes of God, Kinsman said to himself. Then he added, Superstitious idiot!

The pressurized tractors of the ground crew were starting to move out of the big vehicle airlock and arrange themselves around the landing area. Lights were winking on out there, so the shuttle must be coming down. Sure enough, Kinsman saw a puff of bright color, dissipated in an eyeblink. Then another, and the heavy squat shape of the shuttle took form, falling like a stone in a nightmare, slowly but inexorably, falling, falling—another puff of rocket thrust, then still another . . .

The bare rock of the landing area seethed into a miniature sandstorm where it had looked a moment earlier as if nothing as Earthlike as dust could exist. The shuttle landed like a fat old lady settling into a favorite chair: slowly, carefully, and then *plop!* The landing struts touched the ground and bowed under the spacecraft's weight. The engines shut off and the dust storm subsided.

The ground crew's tractors clustered around the still-hot rocket, faithful mechanical puppies greeting the return of their master. A flexible access tube snaked out from the personnel hatch of the airlock toward the main hatch of the ship.

Kinsman nodded to himself, satisfied with the landing. A new batch of ninety-dayers, almost all of them on their first tour of duty on the Moon. They would arrive calling this place Moonbase, the official designation given by Colonel Kinsman's superiors on Earth. Just as the new Russians called their base Lunagrad. But those who stayed on the Moon, those who made their homes in the underground community —no matter how reluctantly at first—would come to call this place Selene. Kinsman had hit upon the name several years earlier and it had stuck, even among the Russians. The ninety-dayers who could see the difference between Moonbase and Selene would return for more tours of lunar duty; Kinsman would see to that. The others would never come back; he would see to that, too.

Turning to face the airlock's inner personnel hatch, Kinsman watched the newcomers step in. They were women, eight of them, all talking at once. And four silent men. Boys, really. All but the one in the lead bounced clumsily as they tried to walk in the low lunar gravity, a sure sign of the newcomer. The women were wide-eyed, chattering, excited. Their first time.

Kinsman recognized the kid in the lead. He wore a captain's bars on his coverall collar. Perry: Christopher S., he recalled. The youngster spotted Kinsman and flicked a salute. Kinsman returned the salute lazily as Captain Perry led his file of newcomers toward the power ladder that went down to Selene's living and working areas.

The women ignored him, still chattering and ogling the grave lunar landscape. He was just an anonymous figure in plain coveralls standing in the shadowy expanse of the dome. You can hardly blame them, Kinsman said to himself. The landscape out there *is* a damned sight more interesting, especially the first time you see it.

The group walked past him and toward the ladder. One of them caught his eye as they pranced past.

Diane? He almost called out her name. But it couldn't be. Diane would not be among a group of government employees assigned to Moonbase for a ninety-day tour of duty. Couldn't be. But she certainly resembled Diane: tall, lithe, dark-haired. The distance and the shadowy lighting prevented a good look at her face. And her hair was shorter than Diane had always worn hers, barely shoulder length.

Kinsman shook his head. No, it could not be Diane Lawrence. You're seeing things that aren't there. Diane wouldn't come to the Moon, no matter how much you'd like her to.

More than six hours later, at precisely 11 A.M. Eastern Standard Time, the President walked slowly, almost reluctantly, into the Cabinet Room. The members of the National Security Committee, already in their places around the polished oval table, got to their feet.

"Sit . . . sit down." The President forced a smile and fluttered his hands at them. He took his seat at the head of the table as the others murmured a dozen versions of "good morning."

The Secretary of Defense was not smiling as he sat down. "Mr. President, I must bring up a matter that just came to my attention this morning and therefore is not on the agenda."

The President was black. Not very black. His complexion and bone structure both showed decided Caucasian influences, a fact that had cost him votes. His close-cropped hair was peppered with gray, his body had the slim-yet-soft look of a man who played tennis for exercise. He had a warm smile and a gift for making people feel he was on their side. Some said it was his only gift, but they were usually jailed as bigots—no matter what their color.

The Secretary of Defense was cold and spare, with a body as lean as a saber blade. His face was sharp-featured, with piercing gunmetal eyes. Behind his back he was called "the Hawk," which referred to his profile as much as his attitudes. The name secretly pleased him.

The President blinked at him. "Not on the agenda? Why not?"

"This information is barely a half-hour old. There wasn't time . . ."

Looking around the table at the others, the President tapped the single sheet of paper before him. "A half-hour ought to be enough time to revise the agenda. After all, that's what an agenda's for."

Nodding curtly, the Secretary of Defense said, "Yes, I realize that. But there wasn't time. The Soviets have disabled three of our ABM satellites today—that's since midnight, Universal Time, which means seven P.M. last night, Eastern Stan—"

"Don't get us all confused with time zones." The President raised his rich baritone voice. "What's the score over the past week?"

"Over the past seven days," the Defense Secretary said, shuffling through the papers in front of him, "the Reds have knocked out—yes, here it is . . . they've disabled seven of our ABM satellites and we've hit only four of theirs."

The President shrugged. "That's not so bad. Was anybody hurt?"

"No, there have been no deaths or injuries since that captain collided his spacecraft with one of their satellites. And that was purely accidental, apparently."

A four-star general in Aerospace Force blue nodded. "We've investigated very thoroughly. There was no possibility of enemy action in that case. Unless the satellite was booby-trapped in some new manner."

"I don't want anybody hurt," the President said.

The Defense Secretary frowned. "Mr. President, we are playing for stakes of the highest sort here. It will be necessary to take some risks."

"I don't want anybody hurt."

With a glance at the General and the others sitting around the table, the Defense Secretary said, "We have been trying to complete deployment of our strategic defense network for the past two years. The Soviets have been incapacitating our satellites to prevent us from finishing the system. If you'll look at these graphs"—he slid three sheets of paper toward the President—"you will see that they are now knocking out our satellites almost as fast as we launch them."

"And what about their satellites?" the President asked without looking at the graphs.

The General answered sternly, "We are restricted in the number of antisatellite missions we can fly. There are only so many trained astronauts available, and only a shoestring of funding to get the job done. Meanwhile, the enemy is increasing the frequency of his launches, putting up more and more ABM satellites. And his newest ones are decoyed and hardened—much tougher to find and eliminate."

The Secretary of State cleared his throat. "You keep calling them the enemy. We are not at war." He was balding, wore rimless glasses, spoke with a soft Virginia accent.

"That is not quite true," rasped the heavy-jawed, hulking man at the end of the table. His voice was a labored, tortured whisper; his face a perpetual red angry glare. "With all due respect, we *are* at war and have been for the past two years. Ever since we and the Soviets started launching ABM satellites, we have been attacking each other. Each side knows that whoever finishes its ABM network first will have a decisive advantage: the satellites can destroy the entire strategic striking force of the other side. The nuclear stalemate will be broken."

He paused for a moment and took a deep, labored breath. No one spoke. Leaning heavily on his forearms, eyes blazing with pain or anger or both, he resumed his harsh whisper. "When one side completes its ABM network it can dictate terms to the other side with impunity. We dare not allow the Soviets to finish ahead of us in this race. We dare not!"

The President fidgeted uncomfortably in his chair and looked away from the burly, angry-faced speaker.

The Defense Secretary said crisply, "Entirely correct. If the Soviets complete their ABM network before we do, they'll be able to knock down our missiles as soon as we launch them. We will no longer have a nuclear retaliatory force. We'll be at their mercy."

"It *is* war," General Hofstader affirmed. "Just because there's no shooting on the ground and no casualties so far, don't be fooled into thinking that this is just a game."

"And there will be casualties, sooner or later," said Defense.

"What? What do you mean?" For the first time the President looked startled.

"If you will look at the graphs I gave you," Defense said, with weary patience, "you will see that we can't keep going the way we have been for very much longer. We need a minimum of a hundred-fifty satellites in low orbit to cover the entire world adequately against Soviet and/or Chinese missile attack."

"The Chinese don't want to attack us," the President mumbled, his face down as he spread the graphs out side by side on the table.

"But they could attack the Russians, who might retaliate blindly at us," came the rasping whisper from the far end of the table. "They could start the pot boiling, and once it starts, who knows where it will end?"

Defense resumed, "We need a hundred-fifty satellites in orbit and functioning. We have been maintaining about eighty of them. Over the past few weeks the Soviets have been disabling them as fast as we can launch new ones."

"Why don't we repair the damaged ones?"

"Economics, sir," General Hofstader answered. "It's cheaper to launch a mass-produced unmanned satellite than to send a human repair crew to fix one that's damaged."

The President blinked, puzzled. "But I thought that those lasers were so expensive . . ."

The General produced a tight-lipped smile. "Yessir, they are. But maintaining men in orbit is even more so. It's costly enough just to keep our manned command-and-control centers in orbit, and they are housed in the space stations that were already in orbit when we began this program."

"I see." But the President shook his head as if he did not really understand or necessarily believe all that he was being told.

"Meanwhile," Defense went on inexorably, "the rate of Soviet launches is increasing. That's on the graph you have in the middle, there. Today they have thirty-nine satellites functional in orbit. Four weeks ago they had only thirty, even though we found and destroyed eleven of their satellites over that time span. Unless we do something about it, the Soviets will complete their network in another year—eighteen months, at most. And we'll still be far short of having completed ours."

"They'll have won," said General Hofstader.

"They will be in here dictating terms to you," whispered the burly man at the end of the table.

The President rubbed at the bridge of his nose. "Well, what do you recommend?"

Defense nearly smiled. Tensing slightly in his chair, leaning forward, he ticked off points on his fingers. "First, we must increase our own satellite launch rate by at least fifty percent. Doubling the present launch rate would be preferable.

"Second, we must increase our kill rate of Soviet satellites, otherwise they will pass us in a matter of months.

"Third, we must prepare for the possibility of striking their orbital command centers. One successful blow at a command center could incapacitate their entire network for weeks."

"Right!" snapped the General.

It took a moment for the President to realize what was being suggested. Then his mouth dropped open in sudden comprehension. "You mean attack their manned stations? That . . . that would kill people!"

"It would mean war!" the Secretary of State gasped.

"Not necessarily," Defense countered calmly. "Even if a few Russian technicians and cosmonauts were killed, they probably wouldn't go to war over it. Our computer forecasts show less than a forty-percent chance. Remember, neither side has publicly admitted that there are military operations going on in orbit. And they certainly won't attack when we have more functioning ABM satellites in orbit than they do."

"But that's precisely when they *would* attack," State insisted, his normally placid voice going shrill. "They'll attack when it becomes clear to them that we can complete our ABM network before they can complete theirs. They'll attack before we finish it and have them completely outgunned. That's what *we* would do. That's what you Pentagon people call a preemptive strike, isn't it?"

General Hofstader shook his head. The Defense Secretary frowned across the table at State.

The President said, "I don't want to run the risk of starting a nuclear war, and I don't want anyone hurt . . . unnecessarily."

"Sir, I am not making these recommendations lightly," Defense said. "The life of our nation is at stake, and—"

"I understand that," said the President. "But I still don't want any blood on my hands. You can increase your own satellite launches and shoot down more of theirs—your first two recommendations. But no attacks on people!"

"We may be forced to, sooner or later," muttered Defense.

The General asked, "What do we do when they attack our manned stations?"

The Secretary of State leaned back in his chair and stared at the ceiling.

His voice slightly shaky, the President repeated, "No attacks on people. Not for now, at least."

The Defense Secretary nodded. "Very well, Mr. President. Now, for the first item on the agenda, these food riots in Detroit and Cleveland . . ."

It was late afternoon in Selene. The clock on Kinsman's desk read 1650.

He had just come back into the office after spending most of the day prowling around the underground community, popping in on people as they worked, listening to problems and gripes before they became major complaints, making certain that everyone knew there was a direct pipeline to the commander and no need to go through official channels to get things done.

His phone was buzzing as he slid the door back and stepped into the office. Flopping onto the couch, he touched the ON button. One of the wall screens lit up to show the face of a young communications technician. One of the new girls. A cute young blonde.

"We are receiving a top-priority message from Vandenberg, sir," she said, impressed with the seriousness of her new job. "Captain Maddern thought you would want to see it as soon as the computer has finished decrypting it."

"Right," said Kinsman. "I'll be right there."

Top-priority messages were always hand-carried, by strict

regulation. With the Russians living on the doorstep it was virtually impossible to prevent interception of radio messages or taps of phone calls. It took about five minutes for Kinsman to walk to the communications center. The corridor was narrow, low-ceilinged, and not very straight, one of the earliest tunnels to be hewn out of the lunar rock. The rough walls were sprayed with plastic to make them airtight. Catacombs, Kinsman thought. Got to get these walls covered with something more attractive. The overhead lights were long tubes of fluorescents, dim in visible output but rich in infrared for the grass that lined the floor.

The comm center was a beehive of desks and electronics consoles and display screens that linked Selene with the three big manned space stations in orbit around the Earth. Through the space stations the lunar base could communicate with any place on Earth. The Russians had their own space stations in orbit, and a completely separate communications system of their own.

A broad balcony rimmed the busy working "pit" of the comm center. Kinsman went to the rail and glanced down at the humming, chattering jumble of people and machines below. He thought, Dante's Inferno . . . or maybe Marconi's.

The balcony was also jammed with desks and busy people, but not so many as below. Kinsman made his way around, one hand on the railing, nodding to the regulars whom he recognized. He reached the thin translucent partition that separated the cryptographic area from the rest of the center, opened the flimsy door, and went inside.

It was much quieter inside. There were four big desks grouped around a stand-alone minicomputer, a four-foot-high gray metal machine that was reserved entirely for cryptographic tasks. Only two of the desks were occupied. At one of them sat Diane Lawrence.

She looked up and recognized him just as the shock of seeing her hit the pit of his stomach.

"It *is* you!" he blurted.

Diane smiled at him, a smile that mixed sadness and anger and much, much more. "Yes, Chet, it's me. Surprised?"

He sagged down onto the empty chair at the next desk.

"Hell yes! What are you doing here? I never thought . . ."

She was just as lovely as he remembered her from five years before. Maybe even more beautiful. Her high cheekbones and dark eyes had always given her an ascetic, almost otherworldly appearance. But now there was strength in her face, an awareness that can only come from experience and pain. Instead of the black turtlenecks and tight jeans that had been her trademark since he had first seen her in a Berkeley coffeehouse twenty years earlier, she wore plain blue standard-issue coveralls with the insignia of a communications clerk on the shoulder.

"Your hair," he realized.

Diane shrugged. "It took too much time every day to keep it that long."

It had cascaded down to her waist, midnight black and lustrous. Now Diane's hair was barely shoulder-length and was pulled back off her face.

"I don't understand," Kinsman said. "Why didn't you tell me you were coming here? What happened?"

Her smile faded. "You need a license to be an entertainer, these days. The antisubversion laws, you know."

Kinsman shook his head. "I've been up here for five years . . ."

"Well, anyway, they revoked my license. Because of a concert I gave in Detroit, where they had the riots."

A thousand questions boiled through Kinsman's mind.

"I had to find something to do." Diane gave a nervous little laugh. "Would you believe that I was broke? By the time the IRS finished with me, there wasn't a damned thing left. So I went out and got a job. When I saw an opening for a tour of duty on the Moon, I applied for it. Extra pay, you know."

"You should have let me know . . ."

Her eyes shifted slightly away from him. "I didn't know if you'd want to have me here."

"Not have you . . . ?"

"I was wrong, Chet," Diane said quietly. "About a lot of things."

"So you came up here."

Brightening slightly, she echoed, "So I came up here. To see what your brave new world is all about. To see you, I guess."

"And Neal?" Kinsman asked. "He's still in the Senate, isn't he?"

"Oh, sure. He's back with Mary-Ellen. He and I broke up pretty soon after you left Washington. He might get tapped as the party's Vice Presidential candidate next year."

Kinsman muttered, "The sacrificial lamb."

"It's not good down there, Chet," Diane said, with a slight shudder. "I don't know what's going to happen to them, but you were right to get out and get away."

Suddenly he wanted to change the subject, move on to something more cheerful. Gesturing to the computer keyboard in front of Diane, he said, "They didn't waste any time putting you to work."

"No, they didn't. Your people are very efficient."

Kinsman mused, "The government revoked your entertainer's license, but here you are in the most sensitive section of the base."

"The guy in charge here is an old fan of mine."

"Harry Pierce?"

"He just asked me if I could run a mini and I said yes."

He wanted to laugh. "So much for checking the security records."

Her face grew serious again. "I really wasn't sure you were still up here, Chet. It's been so long . . ."

"I'm here. And I'm going to stay here."

"That's what you told me the last time we met."

"You can stay, too, Diane."

Her eyes shifted away again. "I don't know about that, Chet. It's . . . I just arrived, after all. Give me a chance to catch my breath."

"Okay. Sure." He glanced at the display screen on her desk. "Is that the message from Vandenberg for the base commander?"

"Yes. It's classified."

"I know."

"To be hand-carried to the base commander."

"That's me." Kinsman fished in the breast pocket of his coveralls and pulled out the worn, warped plastic card of his ID. "My holy picture."

Diane glanced at it. "Holy picture?"

"People look at it and say, 'Jesus Christ, is that you?'"

Diane laughed, and Kinsman felt good for a moment.

"Welcome to Selene, Diane," he said.

"Thanks."

"When are you off-duty?"

"This shift ends at six—eighteen hundred hours."

He grinned at her. "You're getting very military."

"I have to be."

He let that pass. "Listen. How'd you like to attend a surprise birthday party up in the rec dome?"

She did not hesitate. "Sounds wonderful."

"Good. I'll pick you up at twenty hundred. That's . . ."

"Eight o'clock. I know."

"Okay."

"Whose birthday is it?"

"Mine."

"You . . . yours? A surprise birthday party and you already know about it?"

"I'd be a lousy base commander if I didn't know, wouldn't I? Are you good at looking surprised?"

"I don't know!" she said, laughing.

"Well, we'll have to try to look surprised. Now, how about a copy of my message?"

"A paper copy? The first thing Harry told me was that we're not supposed to make paper copies unless it's specially authorized. Paper's very scarce up here."

"No kidding? I've planted four trees with my own hands, you know." Kinsman hesitated a moment, but when Diane did not reply he said, "There's reusable plastic in the bin next to the computer."

Diane muttered, "Oh, right," and leaned across her desk to pull a thin sheet of plastic from the computer tray. Puzzling momentarily, she flexed it, then slid it into the printer beside her display screen. Turning to her keyboard she touched a series of pressure pads, very carefully, one finger at a time. Her nails were all trimmed short, but not for the guitar anymore.

"I've got to be careful," she said. "Working the keyboard is funny in this gravity." She gave Kinsman a sidelong glance. "And I was never very good at typing anyway."

Abruptly the printer erupted into furious action, buzzing out line after line across the thin plastic sheet with inhuman speed. Then it stopped dead. Diane pulled the plastic out of the printer and handed it to Kinsman.

"You've got to sign for it," she said.

Kinsman nodded, scribbled his signature on the display screen with the electronic stylus she handed him, then got to his feet.

"Diane . . ." He found himself almost at a loss for words. "I can't tell you how great it is to have you here."

She said nothing, merely looked up at him with those dark, deep eyes.

"I'll pick you up at twenty hundred," he said.

"You don't know where my quarters are."

"I'll find you," he said. "You've come a quarter-million miles, I'll make it across the last few hundred meters."

He felt buoyant as he made his way through the din of the comm center and out into the shadowy silence of the tomblike corridor. Then, in the dim light of the overhead fluorescents, he read his decoded message:

TO: COL. C.A.KINSMAN/CDR, MNBS   I DEC 99
PRIORITY: ONE-ONE-ZERO   REF: RMM 99-2074
SECURITY CLASSIFICATION: TOP SECRET
INCREASED ORBITAL OPERATIONS REQUIRE LOGISTICS
AND MANPOWER SUPPORT FROM MOONBASE. URGENTLY
REQUIRE YOUR LATEST ASSESSMENT ON MOONBASE
CAPABILITY TO IMMEDIATELY SUPPLY LOGISTIC SUPPORT
FOR TEN (10) MANNED ORBITAL SEARCH AND DESTROY
MISSIONS PER DAY, PLUS MANPOWER SUPPORT FOR
MISSIONS AND/OR BACKUP PERSONNEL FOR STATIONS
ALPHA, BETA, GAMMA.
PRIORITY RATING FOR THIS REQUIREMENT IS ONE-ONE-
ZERO. CONSIDER POSSIBILITY OF YELLOW ALERT STATUS
IMMINENT: RED ALERT POSSIBLE. REQUIRE DETAILED
RESPONSE IN TWENTY-FOUR (24) HOURS.

B/G R.M.MURDOCK
COMMANDING OFFICER
USAF LUNAR OPERATIONS

Kinsman stood alone in the empty corridor, staring at the flimsy plastic sheet in his hand. Suddenly he was trembling, his entire body shaking while in his mind he saw it all again: the weightless, soundless, slow-motion fight; the cosmonaut's space-suited figure revolving slowly, slowly against the backdrop of solemn staring stars; the face inside the helmet frozen in the sudden terrified realization of death.

They're going to do it, Kinsman's mind screamed at him. They're going to make me kill again.

Wednesday 1 December 1999: 2120 hrs UT

ALL SPACE OPERATIONS worked by Universal Time. Not only those in the lunar community, but all space activities in orbit near the Earth, as well.

Colonel Frank Colt flicked a glance at the fuel gauge readout on the instrument panel in the cockpit of his small, sleek, one-man spaceplane.

"Alpha to Mark One," said a voice in his helmet earphones, gritty with static. "Repeat: We read your fuel reserves approaching redline."

Colt was strapped into the padded contour seat, sealed inside his pressurized suit. The spaceplane looked almost like a fighter aircraft, except that its wings were much too small and its tail surfaces nearly nonexistent. It was long and needle-slim, glittering silvery against the blackness of space.

Colt was a lieutenant colonel, the highest-ranking black man among the Aerospace Force's astronaut corps. He had spent the past several hours in orbit, chasing down "unidentified" satellites. Precisely two hundred and ninety-six kilometers to his left stretched the achingly beautiful blue and white Earth, dazzling clouds lacing the South Atlantic, the coast of Africa a thin gray haze on the horizon, approaching fast.

But Colt paid no attention to that. Inside his sealed suit

he itched and sweated, and after being weightless for more than an hour his legs were beginning to go to sleep again. They tingled annoyingly.

He wiggled his toes furiously, frowning at the radar display on his instrument panel. His radar had acquired four "unidentified" satellites so far on this sortie and they had all turned out to be decoys: nothing but metallized balloons. No markings, but everyone knew that if they were not made in the USA they came from Soviet Russia.

"C'mon, Frank, give it up," said the disembodied voice in his earphones. "You've got to start back now or else the mission controller will be required to ask Command for a standby rescue scramble."

"Stuff it," Colt snapped into his helmet mike. "Where they got decoys they're decoying something. What was the location of that other blip you had?" His tiny oval radar screen showed nothing now but random sparkles.

The communicator's voice in his earphones sighed. "Man, you're more trouble than the rest of this outfit put together."

"You're pickin' on me 'cause I'm black," Colt said, with a deliberate hint of Motown in his voice. "Where's that other blip?"

"It's out of your plane. You can't reach it."

"Gimme the coordinates."

He saw the data transmission light flickering madly on his computer panel, then the display screen showed a graph and a string of numbers. Colt tapped on the computer keyboard with a single gloved finger.

"You can't make that maneuver with the fuel reserve you've got!" the communicator said.

"Wanna put some money on that?" Colt laughed. "Watch this."

Colt closed his gloved left hand around the tiny sidestick controller and worked the thruster button with his thumb. The spaceplane dipped obediently down toward the Earth, while a background mutter of voices in his earphones told him that the communicator and mission controller back at Vandenberg were arguing over whether they should transmit a recall order or not. If they did, and Colt failed to heed it, whatever happened afterward was on Colt's record, not theirs.

The plane's nose was visibly heating, turning a dull red.

Colt thought he could hear air whistling past the cockpit, even through the insulation of his helmet, but he knew that it was his imagination.

"You are hereby ordered to discontinue your orbital plane-change maneuver," the controller's voice said, heavily, officially, "and position your vehicle for re-entry and return to base."

"Roger," said Colt. "Discontinue and attain re-entry heading."

But the plane plunged deeper into the atmosphere as Colt grinned happily to himself. With pressures on the controller as delicate as a lover's caress, he rolled the spaceplane and made it turn, feeling the weight of acceleration as the silvery aerospace craft bit into the thin air of the high atmosphere. He pulled the stick back ever so slightly and the plane's nose reared upward. Colt felt himself pushed back into his seat. His eyes flicked across the instrument panel. The computer screen showed a glowing white dot pulsing along a gracefully curved line.

"Right on the money," Colt muttered to himself.

The spaceplane was trading kinetic energy for altitude now. Colt took his hand off the control stick, felt his arms hang weightlessly.

"That's a helluva re-entry attitude, Colt!" the mission controller's voice snapped.

"Just savin' fuel, Mary," he replied, almost jovially.

The radar screen showed a fat blip gliding from one edge toward its center. Colt touched another button and the screen displayed a telescopic optical view of the satellite, with range data and a targeting reticle superimposed.

"There she is," Colt said calmly into his microphone. "Real one this time. Big mother, too."

In his earphones he heard a muffled, grudging, "The sonofabitch can fly, I'll give him that much."

The satellite was dead black, but studded with glassy protuberances that made Colt think it might be an x-ray laser. He glanced down at his data recorder and saw that it was taping everything his sensors picked up. X-ray lasers were powered by small nuclear weapons. Nuclear weapons in orbit were illegal, outlawed by the Space Treaty of 1967. The tapes ought to provide some ammunition for the diplomats wrangling in Geneva, Colt thought.

His fuel was too low for him to try an actual rendezvous with the Soviet satellite. He would have a chance for one shot at it, and that would be all.

Is there a nuke on board, and is it salvage-fused? Colt thought briefly about whether it would be better to be blown away by a nuclear fireball or fried by a blast of x-rays. He smiled grimly and toggled the ARMED switch of his missile control panel. Its tiny light glowed a baleful red.

As the course of his spaceplane carried it through the plane of the Soviet satellite's orbit, Colt touched the AUTOFIRE stud on the missile control panel. He felt a quiver shake the cockpit as the missile launched itself. On the display screen he saw a tiny flash on the side of the satellite. No explosion. No x-rays.

He blew out a breath that he had not realized he had been holding in. Punching an extreme closeup of the satellite he saw that several of the lenses were shattered and there was a ragged hole where the missile's solid head had hit it.

"Scratch one," he sang out.

"We copy satellite interception," said the communicator's voice, flat and professional.

"Okay," Colt said, "re-aligning attitude for re-entry. Please update navigational program."

The controller's voice responded, "Set channel frequency to 0415 for computer update on optimum transfer trajectory."

Colt tapped out the numbers on the keys to his right. "Freak 0415, check . . . Hey, what's today's score?"

"You got the only one so far—"

He grunted.

"—and they got three of ours."

Selene's recreation dome was much smaller than the main dome, where the shuttles landed. It was set on slightly higher ground, so that someone standing at the edge of the swimming pool could see the main dome, the undulating plain of the Sea of Clouds, and the slumped shoulders of the ringwall mountains of Alphonsus. The main viewing attraction, of course, was Earth, hanging blue and white and gleaming against the dead-black sky. The planet was a fat crescent, almost half full, its light strong enough to bathe the lunar night with far greater brightness than the full Moon lavished on Earth.

Kinsman and Diane stepped off the moving power ladder together. She was wearing red slacks and a gray sweater that clung to her. She carried a tiny plastic bag.

"Nobody told me you could swim up here," she was saying. "I had to borrow a suit from one of the women. I hope it's not too small for me."

Kinsman put on a leer. "There's no such thing as a too-small swimsuit."

She made a sour face at him. "Don't tell me you've reverted to male chauvinism out here on the frontier."

"Yeah, I guess maybe we have." On impulse, he reached for her hand. "Christ, I'm glad you came up here! It's the happiest surprise I've ever had."

Diane squeezed his hand. "I'm glad you're still here, Chet."

They stood grinning at each other for a foolish, happy moment. Then Kinsman said, "Now remember to look surprised."

"Okay, boss." They walked from the ladder through the humid, warm atmosphere toward the row of lockers that lined one side of the dome. The lockers had started service as temporary life-support modules when the first manned outposts were being set up on the Moon. Kinsman and the other lunar explorers had fondly referred to them as "telephone booths" when they had to live in them for two weeks at a time.

"Funny—I don't smell chlorine," Diane said.

"We don't use it," explained Kinsman. "There's plenty of oxygen available from the rocks, and plenty of solar energy, so we make ozone and keep the pool clean with that. Breaks down into oxygen. No more stinging eyes."

He led her to the lockers and helped her step up into one, then entered the one next to hers. Kinsman simply unzipped his coveralls. He was already wearing his trunks. He had not bothered to bring a towel. With electric heat lamps plentiful in Selene, he had almost gotten out of the habit of toweling himself.

Stepping out of the locker he scanned the pool area. A crowd was already there, filling the dome with noisy echoing laughter and splashing. A few families had their children with them. A teenage boy and girl executed simultaneous dives off the thirty-meter platform, pinwheeling slowly in exact synchronization. Impossible on Earth, but only marvelously difficult in one-sixth gravity.

The rec dome complex represented several years' worth of cajoling and arguing with General Murdock, who had stubbornly refused to see the need for such luxury at Moonbase. It was only after Kinsman had procured a year's supply of scotch for the base's three psychiatrists, and they began sending out reports on the vital need for recreational facilities at this distant outpost of human habitation, that the dome got built. Officially, Murdock still did not know that the Luniks had built a pool for themselves.

Pat Kelly spotted Kinsman and padded up from poolside toward him, trying desperately to look nonchalant.

"Uh, hi, Chet. About that order that came through this afternoon . . ." Kelly was a little guy, wiry, with a pleasant, open face marred by an oversized set of teeth and undersized squinting eyes which made him look something like a rabbit. His quick, nervous way of talking and moving added to the impression. Sandy hair, darting pale blue eyes. He was very bright, young, and coming on strong. He had already put in two tours of duty on the Moon and was now on his third. He had just made major, and Kinsman had picked him as his second-in-command.

"The order from Murdock?" Kinsman felt his insides go cold. "Any problems?"

"No, no. Just wondering what it's all about. Why do we have to get up a detailed report on our manpower and logistics by twelve hundred tomorrow?"

"Murdock wants to know how much help we can give the manned stations," Kinsman answered evenly.

"Yeah, that's obvious. But why? What's going on? What about this yellow alert?"

Shrugging. "Don't know, Pat. But you know Murdock. He's always been a wet-pantser."

Kelly still looked bothered. "Listen, Chet, is there really gonna be trouble? I've got a wife and kids down there. If there's gonna be real trouble, I want to be with them."

"I told you a long time ago to bring them up here. Even if

the shit hits the fan Earthside, we can ride it out up here."

"With half the place owned by the Russkies?" Pat's eyes widened in disbelief.

"If we have to fight here, at least it'll be with handguns, not nuclear missiles."

"You get just as dead."

Kinsman clutched the younger man's shoulder. "Pat, if I could order you to bring your family here, I'd do it."

"You feel that strong about it?"

"They'd be much better off."

His face seemed to twitch, rabbitlike. "They're not in such bad shape, you know. Good government housing. Got two whole rooms for themselves, off the base. Pretty good location—no break-ins, not even any electricity rationing, except in the summer."

"Bring them here," Kinsman repeated.

"You think I should?"

"I'll get the travel authorizations processed. Do it tomorrow."

Kelly still looked undecided. "Maybe you're right . . ."

Great way to start a party, Kinsman thought. Trying to decide if your wife and kids are going to get blown up this month or next.

Diane came up beside him. "The view here is incredible!"

Eyeing her green and yellow bikini, Kinsman agreed, "It certainly is."

She grinned at him. "I knew you'd say that!"

"You gave me the straight line."

"Just testing," she said airily. "Like Pavlov and his dogs."

Kinsman nodded once. "You have rung my chimes and I am salivating."

"Hopeless case of chauvinism," Diane murmured.

Kinsman was about to reply when Kelly cocked his head in the direction of the ladderway entrance. "Here comes Dr. Faraffa."

"Now you'll see what real male chauvinism is like," Kinsman whispered to Diane.

Dr. Faraffa was only slightly older than Kelly. He had a broad, bald, brown-skinned face with none of the acquiline features so often associated with Arabs. He walked directly to Kinsman, nodding briefly to Kelly and ignoring Diane altogether. He wore a rumpled tan pair of slacks and a light shirtjacket, the only person in the dome not in a swimsuit.

"Colonel Kinsman," he said in a voice as mellow and golden as Turkish tobacco, "I have been informed by my colleagues at Alpha that there is some talk of a new crisis."

The word spreads fast, Kinsman thought. "I believe that any rumors to that effect," he replied carefully, "are highly exaggerated."

Faraffa stepped close enough for Kinsman to feel his breath on his face. It carried an odor of something sweet, almost cloying.

"Highly exaggerated? Perhaps. Such as the occupation of the oil sheikhdoms by your Marines? That was once a highly exaggerated rumor."

Kinsman shrugged. "I'm not a diplomat. The Marines and the occupation are real. A new crisis is not."

"Not yet."

"Not yet," Kinsman repeated.

"If such a crisis does occur, I expect that all foreign nationals here on the Moon will be returned to their homes," Faraffa said stiffly.

Only if they're fools, Kinsman replied silently. He said aloud, "We always make every effort to accommodate our foreign visitors."

"Of course."

"Within reason," Kinsman added.

Faraffa's eyebrows arched upward. Then, with a slight smile, he added, "I understand that this gathering tonight is to celebrate your birthday. My felicitations, sir."

"Thank you." Kinsman could see from the expression on Diane's face what she thought of the Egyptian's attempt to spoil the surprise of the party.

"It is very interesting," Faraffa went on. "You are the most visible man here in Selene. Everyone knows you and admires you. Even the Russians."

With a small bow of acknowledgment, Kinsman said, "My life is an open book."

"Not quite." Faraffa's voice became almost a whisper,

but harder, sharper, a thin little dagger of sound. "I have attempted to learn more of your life. I am very interested in you, Colonel Kinsman. Yet, while the computer records are completely open, they extend back only a few years. Before that, your personnel file is a blank. A total blank. You are a man without a past, Colonel Kinsman."

Very evenly Kinsman replied, "The personnel records go back to the point where I first assumed command of Moonbase."

"But no further."

"No further."

"Why is that? All the other files extend back to the person's education, at least."

Keeping his voice low and steady, choosing his words very carefully, Kinsman said, "I received my degree from the Air Force Academy."

"Indeed."

"There's no need for more detail."

"A man without a past," Faraffa repeated. "It makes one wonder what you are hiding from us."

"Modesty," Kinsman said, making himself smile. "I have a highly developed sense of modesty."

"Or secrecy?"

"Call it privacy. If you really need to know something, ask me."

"No," Faraffa said. "I shall ask my government. Perhaps they can learn more than I can."

"Why all this interest in my early life?" Kinsman asked, trying to make it sound light.

Faraffa shrugged elaborately. "Ahh . . . call it curiosity, Colonel. I am a scientist, after all. Scientists are intensely curious. Especially when they find a mystery."

"There's no mystery," Kinsman lied, guessing at what was driving the Egyptian. "Ask me what you want to know and I'll tell you. Including the months I flew patrol out of Cyprus."

Faraffa's head rocked back. "So you *were* part of the so-called peacekeeping force."

"Yes, I was."

"I thought as much." The Egyptian nodded and smiled,

more to himself than to those around him.

"All you had to do was ask," Kinsman said, feeling a trickle of sweat down his ribs.

"Yes, of course." Faraffa made a stiff little bow, more with his head than his torso, and walked away without a further word.

Diane watched him go, then turned to Kinsman. "Do you have many foreign visitors here?"

"About forty or so—mostly Western Europeans and Japanese. A few Third Worlders. And Faraffa."

"No Israeli refugees?"

"Six. But they're here permanently, with their families."

More than fifty people were already by the pool, in swimsuits, with more pouring into the dome every minute. The prevailing skin tone was white, with a few browns and only two blacks. Several people were swimming, and the usual handful of muscular exhibitionists had pushed the teenagers off the high platform to make spectacular—if poorly coordinated—low-gravity dives. They sliced downward in dreamlike slow motion. The water splashed around them with equal languor. Most of the people around the pool ignored them, busy talking with drinks in their hands.

There were only a few Russians in the crowd, Kinsman noted. Leonov's not here. What orders did *he* get today?

"Ah, there you are!"

Kinsman turned to see Hugh Harriman knifing through the crowd, drinks in both hands, bearing down on him like a heat-seeking missile. Harriman was short, round, bald, bearded, popeyed, loud-mouthed, irreverent, dirty-minded, a self-professed coward, and probably the brightest human being within roughly 384,405 kilometers.

"Our esteemed leader!" Harriman bellowed. "Have a drink!"

Kinsman took the proffered plastic cup as people in the crowd turned to watch, and handed it to Diane.

"Oh, shit!" Harriman snapped. "Might've known you'd have a gorgeous woman with you. Should've brought an extra drink. I'd give you this one except I've already pissed in it."

"That doesn't matter." Kinsman took the cup from him. "The alcohol purifies everything."

"You sonofabitch!" Harriman yelped.

"Diane," said Kinsman, "this is Hugh Harriman. He's half Irish, half Jewish, half Spanish . . ."

"Portuguese, dammit! Watch your mouth, Kinsman."

"This is Diane Lawrence," Kinsman finished.

Harriman's bellicose expression suddenly melted into baby-blue innocence, all rolling eyes and a cupid's-bow smile. "Charmed, I'm sure." He reached for Diane's free hand and kissed it.

"I'm pleased to meet you," Diane responded.

A thoughtful expression crossed Harriman's face. "But aren't you the famous folksinger?"

"The ex–famous folksinger," Diane said sadly. "The government got tired of hearing me."

Everything went absolutely still. No one said a word or made a murmur. No one knew what should be said.

"Diane's starting a new life here on the Moon," Kinsman said firmly. Turning to face her, he added, "And I guarantee you that nobody here will get tired of hearing you."

A mutter of agreement went through the crowd. But it was only a mutter. Most of the people there intended to return to the States to spend the remainder of their lives.

"Tell me," Diane said to Harriman, "what do you do here at Moonbase?"

"Selene, my dear," he replied. "Selene. That's the name we have given to this haven of refuge." Harriman paused for a breath, glared for an instant at Kinsman as he sipped his drink, then smiled back at Diane. "I am a political exile, my dear. An unfortunate victim of diabolical forces. Would you care to hear the story of my life?"

"He's a secret agent," Kinsman said, "but we haven't been able to figure out which side he's working for—or against."

"Doesn't matter," Harriman said.

Kinsman asked, "Who set up the bar? What's going on around here tonight?"

Harriman went back to glaring. "Fuck off, Kinsman! You know damned well this is a surprise party for you. But you don't know what the *real* surprise is."

Kinsman was about to answer when a clamor erupted from the general direction of the ladderway, and a deep voice proclaimed: "Greetings and felicities from the peace-loving peoples of the Soviet Union of Socialist Republics to the money-grubbing imperialist lackeys of Wall Street!"

Suddenly Kinsman felt better. "Leonov." He grabbed Diane by the wrist and towed her through the crowd toward the ladderway. "It's Piotr Leonov, the commander of the Russian half of Selene."

Leonov was flanked by two smiling Russian women in zipsuits. Damned good figures, Kinsman noted automatically. The Russian was in full uniform, with colonel's insignia on his shoulders. He was slightly shorter than Kinsman, a bit heavier. His face was dominated by brilliant ice-blue eyes, very expressive, and a full-lipped mouth. His hair was already iron-gray, but it flopped boyishly over his forehead; he was constantly brushing it back with his hand.

"Chet! Bloated reactionary plutocrat! Happy birthday!"

He grabbed Kinsman around the ribs and lifted him off the ground.

"Hey, Pete, whoa!" Kinsman laughed.

With his bare feet on the grass again, Kinsman said, "I was afraid you wouldn't be coming."

"What? Miss the birthday celebration of my fellow Lunik? My friend?"

Nodding toward the two women, Kinsman said, "You seem to have a few friends of your own."

"Hah! Secret police. They have come to spy on you and keep an eye on me."

The women smiled and tried not to look uncomfortable.

I wonder how much truth there is to what Pete's saying? Kinsman asked himself. Is he trying to warn me about something?

Time was almost meaningless in Antarctica. It was daylight. It had been so since September and would continue to be so until March.

The coldest air on Earth settles atop the mile-high plateau that rims the South Pole. Dense, frigid, this high-pressure air spills down the plateau walls like an invisible waterfall. Invisible, but palpable, audible. It howls across the glaciers and snowfields with gale force, driving blizzards whenever there is moisture aloft.

This day the sky was clear, the air utterly dry. Still

Lieutenant Commander Richards shivered inside his electrically heated parka. The wind cut through the hooded suit with remorseless indifference.

Richards stood outside the big crawler, mentally counting the days until he would be relieved of duty and on his way back to civilization. Like most of the men who served under him—scientists and Navy alike—he had grown a shaggy beard during his months in Antarctica. Now it was flecked with ice, condensed and frozen from the moisture of his own labored breath.

One of the enlisted men slowly approached him, so heavily muffled in his parka and hood that Richards could not identify him until he was only a few paces away. Even then his goggles hid most of his face.

"Sir, the scientists say we're right on top of a big deposit. Scintillation signals are very strong and getting stronger as we head northwest."

Richards nodded. "Very good. Can we track the signals from the crawler, or do we have to stay on foot?"

"Looks like they wanna stay on foot, sir. They're picking up rocks and jabbering among themselves."

Inside his hood Richards scowled. "Damnation. I'm going inside to make a radio check."

Richards watched the sailor trudge back to the group of geologists clustered around a big rock outcrop, bending or kneeling like fur-wrapped pilgrims who had finally arrived at their shrine.

The valley was dead dry, one of those strange Antarctic deserts. No snow, no vegetation of any kind, not even soil. Nothing but rocks and gravel and more rocks. Some scientists had said the area was like the planet Mars, and suggested that astronauts bound for that distant planet could do their training here. White-topped mountains glistened all around them in the howling wind, poking their sparkling peaks into the painfully bright sky. But here in this bone-bare valley there was no water, not even frozen. No life of any kind. Except the duty-driven Americans, searching for coal deposits to feed the voracious cities back home.

Slowly, stiff with cold, Richards walked back to the crawler. His boots crunched on pebbles. The metal rung of the ladder felt burning cold even through his heavy gloves.

He clambered up and pushed through the hatch, into the rear compartment of the mammoth vehicle.

Warmth. Glorious soaking thawing warmth. He pulled off the gloves and pushed down his hood and reveled in its glow. It took half an hour and several cups of coffee before Richards began to feel human again. He sat alone in the driver's cab, parka off, boots planted directly in front of the heater outlet. He finished his radio check with McMurdo and settled back in the big padded driver's seat. He could watch the geologists from here.

Suddenly they all gathered together in a tight knot. Richards sat up straight and watched through the bulging bug-eyed windshield of the crawler. They were pointing at something and talking animatedly about it. Heatedly. Arms waving and gesticulating. One of them pointed to the crawler and then off to the sawtoothed horizon. He detached himself and sprinted for the crawler.

Puzzled, Richards pulled himself out of the seat and ducked through the hatch into the rear compartment, where the bunks and galley and worktables were. The outside hatch opened, letting in a slug of frigid air. The man was the same sailor who had spoken to Richards before. Pushing his goggles up to reveal bloodshot wide eyes, he said excitedly, "Sir, they've found a marker out there! Made of metal. Russian writing on it."

"Russian?"

"Yessir. Dr. Carlati says it looks like the Russians have been here already and staked a claim to this valley."

Richards frowned. "Stop talking like a Western movie, Bates. This is international territory. Nobody's allowed to claim any damned thing."

The sailor shrugged. Richards reached for his parka and hauled it on. Zippering it up he muttered, "Come on, let's see this. Do any of the scientists read Russian?"

"Dr. Carlati does, sir."

As he climbed down from the hatch and set foot on the rocky ground again, Richards heard the sailor call out from above him, "Hey, look there, sir! Another crawler coming up the valley."

Richards saw it. A dark speck edging along the gray

rocks. He looked up the ladder at the sailor, who was still standing at the hatch. "Get one of the carbines and load it. Bring it with you."

"Should I radio McMurdo, sir?"

Caught for a moment between two priorities, Richards shook his head. "No. Get the carbine. We'll fill in McMurdo after we've talked to the Reds."

By the time Richards and the sailor got to the group of scientists the Soviet crawler was close enough to make out its red star insignia.

"The richest deposit of coal I've ever seen," one of the geologists was saying. "This must be what the Montana beds were like before the Sixties."

"Yes," said another parka-muffled man. "But apparently *they* were here first."

"There's plenty here for everybody."

Naive fool, Richards thought.

The Soviet crawler was advancing on them, looming bigger and more menacing with every clank of its treads. Richards stood watching it, no longer aware of the cold or the wind. The scientists seemed tense, too.

One of them said, "Do you think Podgorny might be with them?"

"Is he here this year?"

"That's what I heard."

"I haven't seen him since the Vienna conference."

Richards broke into their conversation. "I think you civilians had better get back to the crawler. Ensign Jefferson, go get two more carbines."

Jefferson raced for the American vehicle, while Bates hefted his carbine and stepped closer to the Lieutenant Commander. The scientists fidgeted irresolutely.

Dr. Carlati said, "Richards, aren't you being melodramatic? What could cause trouble that would call for firearms?"

"I really think you should all get back to the crawler," Richards replied. "Since I'm responsible for your safety, I'm going to have to insist."

"But this is nonsense!"

"Please . . ."

Ensign Jefferson reappeared at the crawler hatch, two carbines in his arms, and started down the ladder. His foot slipped and one of the guns dropped from his grasp. It hit the stony ground and went off with a single sharp bang.

Immediately an answering *crack-crack-crack* came from the Soviet crawler. Chips of stone sprang up around the Americans. Richards saw a man sitting atop the Soviet vehicle, aiming an automatic rifle at them.

"Get down!" he screamed at the scientists. Pulling the carbine from the stunned Bates, still standing next to him, Richards turned to face the advancing crawler. It loomed huge and gray now, like an army tank. Richards cocked the carbine, hearing one more *crack* as he did so.

An incredible force slammed into his chest, knocking him over. He never felt hitting the ground, but suddenly he was staring at the sky. Hooded faces slid into his view. They were blurry. The pain! His body was in flames.

"My god, they shot him!" It was a distant voice, fading, fading.

"I think he's dead."

Kinsman had drifted away from the crowd around the pool. Nursing his third drink (Or is it my fourth?) he stood apart from the clustering crowd of partygoers, near the base of the transparent dome. He turned to look out at Alphonsus's weary ringwall, billion-year-old guardian of nothingness.

In the midst of the crowd Diane was singing:

"Oh, do you remember sweet Betsy from Pike,
  Who crossed the wide prairie with her lover
  Ike . . ."

She had been singing for nearly an hour. Inevitably, somebody had produced a guitar and asked her to perform. She was swept away from Kinsman by the crowd, as much a prisoner of her marvelous voice as he was of his haunting memories. Now, as he gazed out at the bleak beauty of the Sea of Clouds, her singing ended and Kinsman could hear snatches of whispered conversation among the partygoers:

". . . Takamara says there hasn't been a dolphin in the

North Pacific all year. They've gone the way of the whales, looks like."

". . . get back in time to do some Christmas shopping. The kids will be so excited . . ."

". . . just rounded up the whole department and marched them off to an internment camp. Claimed they were deliberately holding back on developing the new pacification gas."

"The whole damned department?"

"Eighteen men and women. Took their families, too. They're all in Nebraska someplace, working in an Army base. The ones who refused to go are getting re-educated with electroshock therapy and mindbenders."

"Without a trial? Or due process?"

"Hah!"

"They can't do that! It's against the Constitution!"

"Sure it is. But don't say it too loudly. You could get a paid vacation to Nebraska, too, you know."

Hugh Harriman came up beside Kinsman. But now the little round man was quiet and serious. With a lift of his eyebrows, Harriman asked, "What's this I hear about a yellow alert?"

"Christ," Kinsman muttered. "Aren't there *any* secrets in this town?"

"I know we civilians aren't supposed to know," Harriman said, "but how serious is it? Are you and Leonov going to arm-wrestle, or is this the real thing?"

"I wish I knew."

Harriman gulped at his drink. "That bad?"

"It won't be arm-wrestling."

"Damned fools."

A thought struck Kinsman, and he almost smiled. "Hey, if we're ordered to seal our half of the base from all foreign nationals, what the hell are we going to do with you? Brazil still hasn't come through with your papers, have they?"

"Of course not, the bastards. It's been almost two years now. I'm officially a stateless person. Another few months and I won't be able to stand up straight on Earth. They've got me by the balls—invite me up here with their sociology team and then revoke my citizenship."

"Cheer up. Socrates got hemlock."

"It's a rough world for us philosophers," Harriman said with a sigh.

"You mean gadflies."

"Whatever. You know who they put in my chair at São Paulo? A dimwitted colonel. A colonel in the fucking army is the chairman of the philosophy department in the largest university in Brazil! A colonel!"

"Something to look forward to when I retire."

"You should live so long."

"That's not funny, Hugh. Not tonight."

Harriman stared at him for an instant, mouth open and ready for his next reply. But when he realized what Kinsman meant he said, "Yeah. They're closing down all the schools. Luxuries, you know."

He walked away. Kinsman turned and looked outward again, feeling the numbing cold of infinity seeping into him despite the heated curtainwall, watching the tantalizing beauty of Earth hanging there, out of his reach. Seven billion people getting ready to destroy themselves.

A hand on his shoulder. Diane.

"You're supposed to be having fun, whether you like it or not."

"Oh, yes. I forgot."

"I think there's some kind of grand unveiling coming up." She gestured back toward the pool.

Kinsman saw a huge package at poolside, covered by a blue plastic tarpaulin. It had an odd shape. Kinsman could not make it out.

"They sent me here to bring you back," Diane said.

She had changed back into her slacks and sweater. Kinsman noticed her absently rubbing the fingertips of her left hand and realized that it had been a long time since she had played a guitar.

"I can think of better places for us to go," Kinsman said.

Diane smiled but said nothing. They walked together through the crowd that was clustering around the mysterious package. It was almost as tall as a man and much wider than his arms could stretch. The crowd's chatter and murmurs faded to an expectant hush as Kinsman and Diane approached.

Piotr Leonov was standing beside the veiled shape, grinning broadly. Everyone was silent now.

"Ah," said Leonov, "the guest of honor approaches. The magic hour has arrived."

Kinsman tried to look relaxed but he was really burning to know what was beneath the wrap.

"Before I unveil your birthday present," Leonov said, "I have a speech to give . . ."

Everyone groaned.

"Wait, wait!" Leonov held up a calming hand. "It is not a political speech. It is short. Only two sentences."

"We're counting!" came a voice from the crowd.

"Very well. One: We did a great deal of research into your background to select this present, Chet."

The face of the dead cosmonaut drifting helplessly. Kinsman drove the picture from his mind.

"And two: Every permanent resident of Selene gave up two months' worth of personal freight allowance to get this—thing—up here. Dr. Nakamura lent his personal assistance and used family connections to acquire the—ah —object. And the dedicated workers of Lunagrad provided the necessary technical assistance to make the thing work correctly."

"That's four sentences, Leonov!"

The Russian shrugged. "I am within a factor of two of my original estimate. That's quite good, compared to what some of you scientists have been doing."

Everyone laughed.

Turning back to Kinsman, Leonov went on, "Very well, then! From all of us Luniks, Chet—Lunagrad, Moonbase, Selene—happy birthday!"

He tugged at the plastic tarpaulin and nothing happened. Everyone roared. Suddenly red-faced, Leonov pulled again, harder, and it slipped to the floor. Revealing a gleaming ebony baby grand piano.

Kinsman felt his jaw drop. "Holy God in heaven."

For a long moment he simply stood there, too dumbfounded to do anything but gape. Then everyone was clapping hands. Somebody started singing "Happy Birthday." Diane stepped up to him, threw her arms around his neck, and kissed him soundly. More applause.

"You do know how to play it, I trust?" Leonov inquired.

Keeping one steadying arm around Diane's waist, Kinsman said, "Haven't touched a key in years. I used to be fairly good."

Pat Kelly came up beside them. "We found out you were a child prodigy."

"Bullshit," Kinsman snapped. "I had a recital when I was fifteen or so—my parents pushed me into it." And I always preferred flying planes to practicing piano.

"Play!" Leonov insisted. "I had to keep this thing in hiding in Lunagrad for weeks. I had to find someone to tune it, since there is no such talent in your den of capitalist Babbitts. Now, play something—Tchaikovsky, at least."

Shaking his head, Kinsman said, "You'll be lucky if I can remember 'Chopsticks.'"

He sat at the bench and stared at the keys. Black and white. Like morality. His hands were shaking. Why? Scared or excited or both?

He touched the keys, plucked a few experimental notes, ran through a few scales. The hands remember. Then he knew what the first piano music played on the Moon should be.

He actually closed his eyes. Involuntarily. He was surprised when he realized he had done it, and snapped them open again. By then his hands were well into the opening bars of the "Moonlight Sonata."

The crowd was absolutely silent. The soft, measured notes floated through the dome, nearly three hundred years and almost half a million kilometers from their place of birth.

Kinsman got about halfway through the first movement and then flubbed. He tapped out a few notes from a childhood exercise and then stood up. Everyone applauded.

Leonov came up to him. "Congratulations! But you must move the instrument from this dome. Too humid. It will never stay in tune here."

Kelly said, "We can put it in your quarters, Chet. We checked. There's enough room."

"No," Kinsman said. "Everybody ought to be able to use it. Put it in the assembly hall downstairs."

"They'll ruin it in a month. And the kids . . ."

"No, they won't. And we'll borrow Pete's tuner when we need him."

"Agreed," said Leonov. "On two conditions."

Kinsman cocked a brow at him.

"First, that you allow my frustrated musicians to use the instrument now and then."

"Of course."

"And second," Leonov raised two fingers, "that you *keep* it here on your side of Selene so that I don't have to listen to them!"

"Sure," Kinsman said. "And your secret police can plant their bugs in it, too."

"Wonderful. That will make them very happy."

Harriman was standing beside Diane. "Regular Renaissance man, aren't you, Kinsman? Musician, soldier, astronaut . . ."

"I used to be a swordsman, too. On the Academy's saber team."

"Humph. Goddamned Cyrano de Bergerac in our midst!"

"My nose isn't that bad," Kinsman said.

"I like your nose," said Diane.

Harriman tried to make his round face frown, and almost succeeded. "I'm consumed with jealousy," he groused. "You get to do everything, Kinsman. I can't play a note. I can't even get my stereo to work right."

With a laugh, Kinsman answered, "Playing a piano is like politics, Hugh. The secret is not letting your left hand know what your right hand is doing."

Several other people tried their hand at the piano. The dome rang with concussion rock, Chopin, soul, Strauss. One of the new ninety-day youngsters ran through some of the neo-Oriental style that was getting popular back in the States.

"Bah! Peasants and degenerates," Leonov grumbled at last, and plopped himself down on the piano bench. He pounded out some heavy-handed Mussorgsky, then broke into melancholy Russian folk tunes.

"Hey, I know that one," Diane said. She sat down beside Leonov and sang in Russian.

"What do the words mean?" she asked when they finished.

Leonov smiled at her. "What difference, beautiful one? Just to hear such a voice makes the words pale into insignificance."

With a reluctant sigh, Leonov hauled himself up from the piano and began saying goodbye to everyone. "I must return to the workers' paradise," he told Kinsman.

"Thanks for the surprise, Pete. Feel free to come over and use it anytime. It belongs to all the people of Selene: Moonbase and Lunagrad alike."

Leonov closed his eyes briefly. It was a gesture he used in place of a nod. "I understand." He hesitated and carefully refrained from glancing over his shoulder. Lowering his voice, he said, "My friend, we must get together for an inspection tour of the route for the buggy race. Just the two of us. Do you agree?"

"Away from the lip-readers?" Kinsman smiled grimly.

"Exactly."

"All right. Tomorrow?"

Leonov blinked slowly again. "I will call you."

"Good."

"Happy birthday, comrade. May you have many more of them."

"May we all."

"Indeed."

The party was breaking up. Leonov and his two female companions left, followed by a trail of admiring glances.

"They *are* intelligence agents," Harriman assured a young blonde with whom he was sharing a joint.

Finally Kinsman found himself walking slowly down a smooth-finished corridor with Diane, his arm around her slim waist, her head leaning sleepily on his shoulder.

"It was a great party," she said softly. "Nice of you to arrange for my first day."

He laughed. He had enough alcohol in him to feel relaxed, not enough to be uninhibited.

"They're a great bunch of people," Kinsman said. "Salt of the Earth."

"You mean the Moon."

"Right. They're good people. This is really just a small town, you know. A frontier town. Everybody knows everybody else. We all help each other. Got to. It's too damned dangerous up here otherwise."

"I never saw anybody look so surprised," Diane said, her voice light with laughter.

"They really got me with that piano," Kinsman admitted. "I never expected that."

They stopped in front of the door to her quarters. He pulled her to him and kissed her. Her breath caught and she clung to him for a moment. But then she pushed away slightly.

"Chet . . . I . . . ." Diane's eyes were filled with a fear he did not understand. "Let's take it slow, okay?"

"Sure," he said, releasing her.

"It's a lot to adjust to," she said. "I'm a long way from home."

"And Neal."

"That's all over," she said quickly. "It's been over for a long time."

"Okay. I'll see you tomorrow, I guess. Good night."

"Good night, Chet. And thanks."

He shrugged and made a crooked grin. But as he walked away down the corridor his mind filled with the old pictures of the dead cosmonaut, and the new memory of General Murdock's memo.

Kinsman strode past his own quarters, prowling the corridors, sleepless, angry with himself and not knowing why. Without conscious direction, he wound up back at the rec dome. It was empty now. The litter of the party cluttered the floor. The overhead lights were off, but the pool lights glimmered softly. Earth hung bright and motionless overhead.

Kinsman sat down at the piano and tinkered with it. He got all the way through the first two movements of the "Moonlight Sonata," decided against risking the third and botching it. He tried some Bach. It was miserable and so was he.

Then he felt her hand on his shoulder. He knew it was Diane without looking up. She sat on the bench beside him.

"I don't want to be alone," she said.

It was like the first time he had flown in orbit. The

breathtaking freedom of weightlessness. Free-fall. All the bounds of Earth slipped away. Nothing else in the universe except himself and this lovely warm woman. Kinsman even forgot the crowded, beckoning, troubled Earth and the star-eyes of God that watched him.

Thursday 2 December 1999: 1550 hrs UT

SPACE STATION ALPHA WAS a set of concentric rings connected by spokelike tunnels. At the central hub spacecraft docked. From a distance it looked rather like a set of bicycle wheels of different sizes nested within one another. Closer up, you could see that things were nowhere near that neat: antennas and equipment pods and odd-shaped structures poked out from the wheels every few meters. Like all human cities, Alpha was suffering from urban sprawl.

When it was first built, Alpha was intended to be a center for commercial industry, even tourism. But as the United States began developing its strategic defense satellites, armed with lasers capable of destroying ballistic missiles over ranges of several thousand kilometers, the military took over more and more of Alpha's facilities, and those of the other two major space stations, Beta and Gamma. Now Alpha was almost entirely manned by Aerospace Force personnel, a center for manufacturing the strategic defense satellites out of lunar raw materials, for deploying them in orbit around the Earth, and for command and control of the globe-spanning defensive network of laser-armed satellites.

Alpha had also become a base for the manned interceptor sorties against Soviet strategic defense satellites.

Frank Colt was supervising the overhaul of his spaceplane. The sleek one-man interceptor rested inside a tubular metal hangar, pressurized to normal Earth atmosphere so

316

that technicians could work without cumbersome space suits hampering them. Men, women, and equipment drifted easily in the nearly zero gravity, hovering around the stubby-winged spaceplane. Only a few weeks ago it had been gleaming, polished silver. Now it looked used, the metal finish pitted and dulled by hours of solar particle bombardment and fiery dives into the atmosphere, where the air turned incandescent from the shock of its hypersonic maneuvering.

Like the technicians, Colt was in stained, well-worn coveralls. He was hovering above the stump of the rocket-plane's tail, where the main rocket nozzles poked their black snouts out from their streamlined fairings. Pointing with an outstretched accusing finger to one of the smaller maneuvering thrusters set into the fairing, Colt muttered, "That's the one." He looked up at the technicians hanging upside-down above him and yelled over the clamor of the machinery that echoed through the hangar, "That's the mother that froze up on me."

The tech was white, young, with red hair and freckles. New to Alpha. He steadied himself by planting one hand on the spaceplane's skin and peered at the tiny jet nozzle. "Looks okay to me," he said, then added, "sir."

Colt pushed his face to within a centimeter of the tech's. "Listen, Sergeant, I don't give a shit how it looks to you. It froze on me. Get it out of there and find out what's wrong with it."

"Take out the whole thruster assembly?"

"Perform a hysterectomy if you got to. Find out what's wrong with it and fix it."

"But my shift is over in ten—"

"Sergeant, your shift is over when I'm satisfied that this thruster works right. Understand that? And the way I'm gonna find out is to bring you with me on a test flight. Now, you can either bust your ass in here or get fried out there. Take your pick."

The kid's face turned as red as his hair. But before he could say anything, the loudspeaker blared, "Colonel Colt, top-priority communication from Earthside. Acknowledge immediately."

Colt glared over his shoulder at the loudspeaker, set into

the nearby bulkhead. Then he turned back to the technician. "I'll be right back, Sergeant. Neither one of us sleeps until that thruster works as designed."

After Colt pushed away and went gliding toward the nearest hatch the technician muttered, "Black sonofabitch." But he began the laborious task of removing the thruster assembly.

Officers' quarters aboard Alpha were styled after the compartments of submarines. Compact. Functional. Barked shins and numbed elbows until you learned how to live gracefully inside a furnished telephone booth.

Colt plopped down on his bunk, automatically ducking to avoid the cabinets set above it. He touched the ON stud of the intercom panel on the bulkhead next to his pillow. The display screen glowed to life.

The screen showed one of the communications techs, a cute young blonde that Colt had occasionally dated when they had both been stationed at Vandenberg. It frosted enough people that Colt made a point of dating her. Now she maintained a conspicuous formality as she said, "We have a message for you, sir, from General Murdock. Personal and scrambled."

Colt scratched at his chin. "Okay, pipe it through. . . . And you can at least smile for me, sugar."

She smiled.

"That's better."

The screen went into a crazy flutter of colors as Colt leaned across the arm's-length span of his compartment and took his hand-sized decrypting computer from the writing desk. "Goddamn crap," he muttered as he plugged the unit into the intercom receptacle.

The picture stayed scrambled, but he heard a man's voice say, "Please identify yourself for voiceprint verification."

Scrambled Earthside, too? Colt was impressed. Even for Murdock this was elaborate. "Franklin D. R. Colt, 051779, Lieutenant Colonel, USAF."

There was the slightest instant's delay, then: "Thank you, Colonel Colt. Go ahead, please."

The picture cleared up and showed General Murdock sitting at his desk.

"There you are," the General said.

"Yessir."

Murdock was round, bald, and nervous. Colt had never seen the man look happy or pleased. The General had a new little gray mustache, still tentative, hyperthyroid eyes, and an apparently endless supply of the jitters. His hands were never still. "I'm having you reassigned to Moonbase, Colt. The paperwork is already on its way to Alpha. I want you to leave on the next available shuttle."

Colt immediately thought of the technician he had left working on the spaceplane's thruster. "May I ask why, sir?"

"It's . . ." Murdock seemed to glance around furtively, even though he was alone in his very secure office. "It's part of a new buildup we're putting into effect, to protect our network and prevent the Soviets from completing theirs."

"Then why'm I being sent to Moonbase? I oughtta be out flying double shifts, knocking off as many of their satellites as I can. You'll need every qualified astronaut to—"

"We've got a batch of replacements coming up. Leaves are being canceled, new people sent up ahead of schedule. There'll be plenty of manpower for the orbital missions."

With a shake of his head, Colt objected, "But, look, sir, it sounds blowhard to say it, but, hell, I've got the highest score of any of the rocket jocks here. If you want—"

"I don't want any arguments, dammit!" The General's normal tenor voice rose higher, and his face started to show splotches of purple. "You fly-boys turn every order into a debate. I want you on Moonbase."

"But I don't understand why, sir."

"You know why. I don't have to draw you any maps."

Colt rolled his eyes heavenward. "Sir, this may surprise you, but I can't read your mind."

"Dammit, Colt!" Murdock actually drummed his chubby fists on the desk, like a little boy having a tantrum. "Do I have to spell it out? You know Kinsman's commanding Moonbase. He refused rotation last year, claiming medical reasons, and those fools on staff let him get away with it."

Now it was becoming clear. Colt almost smiled. "You want me up there to look over Chet's shoulder during the buildup."

"That's right."

"Because you don't trust him."

Murdock glared. "I've had to deal with Kinsman for more than fifteen years. He's too emotional. Too unreliable."

It was unkind to tease the General, but Colt could not resist. "Then why don't you relieve him? Rotate him out of Moonbase. Nobody's supposed to serve on the Moon for more'n a year, anyway. How long's he been there now —three, four years?"

"More like five," Murdock answered, his bald head glistening with sweat. "But it's not that simple. Everybody up there's fanatically loyal to him. And it would be hard to find a qualified man of high-enough rank who'd be willing to stay on that rockpile for a year straight. Would you take the job? Willingly?"

"Hell no!"

"You see? And besides, Kinsman's got some medical problem in his record—a heart flutter or something like that. Probably faked, but if he's relieved of duty he could stay on the Moon as a medical case. Who'd want to take over as commander with *him* standing over his shoulder?"

Colt wanted to laugh, but instead he probed deeper. "Yeah, but Chet gets the job done, doesn't he? Moonbase is coming along fine, from what I hear: everything on schedule or ahead."

Murdock did not take the bait. Instead, he leaned forward confidentially and lowered his voice. "Listen, Frank. I know Kinsman. And I know a good deal more about him than you do. Things nobody else knows. I don't want him up there with a totally free hand if a crisis comes up. He's gotten very friendly with the Russians up there. He's just too soft all around. I want you up there so that you can take command, if and when the crunch comes."

Colt heard himself say, "Chet and I were buddies. We've been through a lot together."

"I know that. But he stepped right over you to grab the Moonbase assignment for himself. And a full colonel's eagles," Murdock said. "But I know that when the chips are down, you'll react like an American and an officer—not like a weak-kneed neurotic."

Neurotic? The word made Colt's stomach tighten.

"In an emergency situation," Murdock continued, grim-faced, perspiring, "I know that you'll put your orders and the nation's well-being above your personal feelings."

Colt's eyes widened as he realized what Murdock was saying. "You mean you think Chet would commit *treason*?"

"I'm not accusing anyone of anything," Murdock said, obviously doing just the opposite. "I'm just being careful."

As he packed his spartan travel kit Colt began to understand what Murdock was doing. The sonofabitch is *using* me! Because I'm a friend of Chet's and he trusts me. Gonna look great. Like Brutus sticking in his blade. He zipped the bag viciously and hefted it in one hand. And Murdock knows I'll do it, too. I've come too far and fought too many of those lily-white bastards to back down now. Never duck a tough job. Never turn down a chance for a promotion. Don't give 'em a chance to pass you over. And if I have to step across Chet's body to get the next step up—shit, if I don't do it somebody else will.

As he reached for the door of his compartment Colt remembered the technician working on his spaceplane. Fuck him. Let him work his white ass off. And he stepped into the corridor and strode off toward the Moonbound shuttle.

"When you said we were going for a walk I didn't realize you meant up here," Diane said.

She and Kinsman were in lunar suits, walking slowly and carefully across the inlet of the Mare Nubium that covered Selene and lapped up to the base of Alphonsus's ringwall.

Kinsman loathed the pressure suits. It was like being inside someone else's skin. Sluggish, difficult to move even in the gentle lunar gravity. They always smelled of plastic and machine oil and somebody else's sweat. He was annoyed with himself for not having the guts to order a special suit custom-made for him. The commander's entitled to it, especially if you're going to spend the rest of your life up here. But you're afraid of looking less than egalitarian. Kinsman the nice guy, that's the image you want them to have of you.

"Everybody ought to see the surface," he said to Diane. "Too many ninety-dayers come here and stay down below all through their tour. Might as well be in the Pentagon or the New York subway."

"What's that?" Diane pointed toward a rounded plastic dome, more than a kilometer away. He could not see her face behind the helmet's glare-proof visor. Her voice was an electronic approximation in his earphones.

"That's the original Lunagrad dome," Kinsman explained. "Leonov's people still land their shuttles over there." And why did Pete beg off meeting me today? What's going on with him?

Diane stepped closer to him, waddling ponderously. "How come the two bases were built right next to each other?"

"That was back when the watchword was cooperation. We were going to share most of the facilities: electric power, water factory, the farms . . . cheaper for both sides."

"It didn't last long, did it?"

"Earthside politics," Kinsman said. "The food shortages, the energy crunch—we started getting orders to make Moonbase self-sufficient. Not to depend on the Russians for anything. They got the same orders. But we'd already been living together for several years. It's hard to distrust people when you live with them."

Diane said nothing.

Spreading his arms, Kinsman turned slowly and asked, "Well . . . what do you think of the place?"

She may have tried to shrug inside the suit, it was impossible to tell. "It looks so barren . . . desolate. And it's so *empty*."

"We've got lots of space," Kinsman agreed. "And energy—free, almost, from the sun. What we don't have is water. Have to process it out of the rocks. Funny: energy's cheap here and water's expensive. On Earth it's just the other way around."

"Water isn't cheap on Earth anymore," Diane said. "Not drinkable water."

Kinsman shook his head even though Diane could not see the gesture. "You'd think that would be the last thing they'd mess up on a planet brimful of the stuff."

He took her gloved hand and guided her up the gentle slope of a small crater rim. The ground was pockmarked with craterlets a few centimeters across. The blower in Kinsman's suit hissed at high speed; still he felt hot inside it.

"The horizon's so close," Diane said.

"The edge of the world. Makes you half think you could fall off."

"I thought we'd be able to see the stars better."

"Your visor's pretty heavily filtered."

"It's just so *dreary*! I've never seen such desolation."

What did you expect? he said to himself. Aloud, he asked, "Diane, what made you come up here?"

She turned ponderously to face him. "I told you. It was a good job opportunity. Extra pay."

"And that's all?"

She hesitated. "I found out that you were right, Chet. All along, you were right and I was wrong. I tried it Neal's way, I tried working for the poor and the oppressed. All that happened was that they got poorer and the government got more oppressive. It took a lot of years, but I finally figured out that you were right. We *need* a frontier—even if it's a desolate emptiness way off in space someplace."

But there was something in her voice that hinted at deeper reasons, hidden motivations.

"Is it that bad, Earthside?" he asked.

"Yes," Diane said fervently. "The government doesn't release unemployment statistics anymore, that's how hard things are. And the super-morality fanatics make it even harder when you've got a fatherless child to support."

"You have a baby."

"She's almost five years old."

"Neal's baby."

"I decided against an abortion." For a long moment she was silent, then, "I guess I thought it would make him leave Mary-Ellen and marry me." She laughed bitterly.

"Where is the child?" Kinsman asked.

"With an aunt of mine, for the time being. In Arizona."

"While you're up here in the land of opportunity."

"Learning a new profession in a new world. For ninety days."

"You could stay longer. I could extend your tour."

"I've got a daughter to take care of."

Kinsman mused, "We could get her up here, too."

"You could do that?"

With a shrug he replied, "Rank hath its privileges."

They stood silently next to each other in the lonely vacuum of the roiled bare lunar plain for several long moments. In his earphones Kinsman could hear Diane's breathing.

"You'd let me stay permanently?"

"If you want to."

"With my daughter?"

Neal's daughter, he thought. "Yes, sure. Why not?"

"I . . ." Diane's voice almost broke. "Chet, that's really . . . I can't . . . I just don't know what to say."

"You don't have to say anything."

"But it's such a commitment. I don't know if—"

He cut in, "There's no strings, Diane. I can extend your tour indefinitely. You can have your daughter sent up. She'll be a helluva lot safer here than in Arizona, with all those airbases and hydroelectric dams. But nobody's going to force you to stay in Selene. If things don't work out the way you want, you can always go back Earthside." If there's an Earth to return to, he added silently.

"No strings," she repeated. Her voice sounded doubtful, wary.

"Come on, we ought to get back," he told her. To himself he said, No strings. No commitments. Not on either one of us. Not now. Maybe someday, but not now.

She paced alongside him as they headed across the uneven ground. After several minutes' silence, Diane said, "You're held in very high esteem around here, you know."

"Am I?"

"From what I hear, you're a very dashing and romantic figure."

"Sure I am."

"You are," Diane insisted. "Women talk. You can have your pick of the women here, and you often do."

"Well . . ."

"But no lasting relationships. Nothing permanent. Nothing even long-term."

"Dammitall, Diane, this is getting ridiculous."

"Is it?" Her voice sounded very serious. "I think it's important. I'm trying to understand you, Chet. And myself. I

324

never could figure you out, not from the first time we met, back in Berkeley."

He forced a laugh. "And I sure as hell have never been able to figure *you* out." Then he said very seriously, "But I've never been able to get you out of my mind, either. Not since that first time in Berkeley."

They walked in silence for a few more moments.

"So how about dinner tonight?" Kinsman asked.

She hesitated long enough to let him know that she considered it very carefully. "I'm afraid I've already made a date with Harry Pierce. He asked me this morning."

"Your section supervisor? You're going to have dinner with your boss?"

"Does that shock you?" she teased.

"Remember, kid, Selene is a very small town."

"Oh, but going to dinner with the base commander is a different thing, is it?"

Kinsman pulled himself to his full height, unnoticeable inside the bulky suit. "The base commander," he replied, "is a very dashing and romantic figure—so I'm told."

They laughed and clumped back to the main dome, hand in gloved hand.

"Chet," Diane said, "I don't want to make any commitments, either. I can't. Not yet."

"Sure," he said. "I understand. I shouldn't be dawdling over romantic dinners, anyway. I've got plenty of work to do." And I've got to find out why Leonov backed down.

Jill Meyers was just finishing her rounds in Selene's hospital. Like most of the underground community, the hospital was built in two interconnecting sections, one American and one Russian. Nearly all the facilities were duplicated.

Jill looked almost as youthful as when she had been an astronaut trainee, fifteen years earlier. Her bright-eyed, round, snub-nosed face, framed by short-clipped straight brown hair, would look young well into her golden years. But within her tiny frame was strength and skill and a quality that was rare in a physician: empathy.

The hospital was large and staffed out of all proportion to Selene's total size. It had been the original justification for a permanent lunar base, and now most of the permanent lunar residents—Russian and American—were on the Moon for medical reasons: bad hearts, bad lungs, muscular diseases. Jill herself had developed an intolerable set of allergies that had incapacitated her Earthside. Here in the controlled environment of the lunar community she was virtually perfect.

Jill looked tired now as she left the last of her patients and headed for the hospital's core of administrative offices and monitoring stations. She got as far as the first station, a horseshoe-shaped set of desks covered with display screens that monitored the sensors watching over a dozen patients' heart rates, respirations, alpha rhythms, and other parameters. The nurse sitting inside the horseshoe called to her, "Dr. Meyers, phone for you."

Jill stopped and accepted the handset from the young woman. Leaning wearily against the desk she watched the phone's picture screen crackle with momentary interference; then it cleared to show a bearded, dark-eyed man whom Jill immediately recognized as one of the Russian doctors. He looked very grave.

"Alexsei, what's wrong?" Jill blurted as her free hand unconsciously went up to smooth her brown hair.

"We have a difficult situation on our hands," he said, in smooth American English. "Cardiac infarction. Our emergency equipment is not available at the moment; one of the carts is in use and the other broke down yesterday. If you can't loan us an aortic pump system I'll have to decide who to help and who to let die. It's not a decision I want to make."

"Of course. Can you move the patient here?"

"Not without a pump in him."

"I'll be there in ten minutes," Jill said. "No, five."

"Good."

Turning to the monitoring nurse she said, "Put me through to the base commander, and while I'm talking to him get the emergency team across to Dr. Landau with a heart pump cart."

Pat Kelly's face showed up on the picture screen. "Kinsman's off someplace. Not to be disturbed except for cataclysms." He grinned toothily to show what he thought of the commander's absence.

Jill outlined the problem in two sentences. Then, "I'm taking an emergency unit to the Lunagrad section."

Kelly hiked his eyebrows. "Regs don't permit that, you know."

"Then either find Chet in the next three minutes or send an armed guard down here to stop me! There's a life at stake."

"Not one of ours."

"Oh, you're not a member of the human race? I'll remember that the next time you come in here. What you do with your regulations is your problem, but I can make a medical suggestion . . ."

"Okay, okay!" Kelly threw his hands up. "I'll write out the order and ask Chet to sign it when he gets back to his office."

"All right," Jill said. "Thanks."

"Don't thank me. I'm just doing what Kinsman would do if he was here. If it was up to me . . ."

But Jill had already dropped the handset and was racing down the corridor toward the Russian half of the hospital.

Four hours later she was slouched on a softly padded sofa, sipping a glass of scalding tea. Alexsei Landau sat next to her. He was tall, with broad shoulders and the strong, sure hands of a surgeon. Behind his beard he was smiling.

"There is an old Russian proverb that I just made up: If you have five cardiac emergency units available, you will get six cardiac emergencies."

Jill smiled back at him. "At least we got him in time."

"H'mm, yes. But he's going to need support for many days. Weeks, more likely."

"We can bring him back to our side. There's plenty of room."

Landau shook his head. "The rules forbid us to send our patients to your side of the hospital."

"Rules!" Jill snapped. "If we played by their rules your patient would be dead now."

The Russian nodded gravely.

"I'll have Kinsman talk to Leonov. They'll work it out."

"I doubt it. Leonov is due to leave shortly anyway. We don't know who will be taking his place."

"Chet Kinsman will figure out a way to do it," Jill said firmly, dismissing the problem. "Who is the patient? He looked vaguely familiar to me."

"He should. He is Nicholai Baliagorev."

"The ballet master?"

"Yes."

"I didn't know he was here!"

"He just arrived. They sent him here to rest his heart, but the rocket flight was almost too much for him."

"Oh, Alex, we've got to save him! We can't let a man like that die because of red tape."

Landau shook his head wearily. "Red tape has killed more people than bullets, dear girl. Far more."

Friday 3 December 1999:
1120 hrs UT

IT WAS STILL NIGHT on the Sea of Clouds, a night that would continue for another week. But the waxing crescent of the Earth, nearly half full now, cast a soft light on the lunar landscape.

Kinsman stood on a slight rise that overlooked the broad undulating plain, listening to the sound of his own breathing and the suit's airblower. A pair of dune buggies were inching their way across the plain, off in the distance. Not far from where Kinsman stood, a group of lunar-suited Americans and Russians were deep in earnest conversation.

Next to him stood Colonel Leonov, in a bright red pressure suit almost identical to Kinsman's own, except for slight differences in the helmet and backpack.

"It should be a good race," Leonov said. Kinsman heard the radio voice in his helmet earphones.

"Yes," he answered. "And this year we ought to win, for a change."

"Hah! Wait until you see the special buggy we have put together."

"Not another rocket job?"

"You'll see."

While they talked, Kinsman took a pad from his belt. Clumsily, with his gloved hands, he wrote, "Is your suit bugged?" He held the note up before Leonov's visor.

"I checked this suit personally before putting it on," Leonov answered. "It is perfectly safe."

"We ought to take a look at this crater," Kinsman said, clumping to the rim of a thirty-meter-wide depression. "It's close enough to the racecourse to be marked off, don't you think?"

"That depends on how steep the interior is." Leonov followed him.

They walked slowly down the interior slope, picking their way through rocks and loose rubble by the lights on their helmets, until they were out of sight of the race committee and the standing crawlers and buggies. Out of sight meant out of radio contact. Now they could talk to each other without being overheard.

"What happened yesterday?" Kinsman asked, lowering his voice unconsciously. "Your message wasn't very clear."

"Too much to do. I couldn't get away. It would not have looked right to drop important business because of the race committee."

Nodding, Kinsman changed the subject. "I got a call from one of our doctors. She wants to transfer a heart patient of yours to our side of the hospital."

"Yes, I know. Baliagorev, the former dancer."

"She says your regulations won't let you send him over to us."

Leonov answered, "Of course. And *your* regulations do not allow you to take him in without permission from your superiors Earthside."

"Hell, Pete, I'll just do it and get them to okay it after the fact. There's a human life at stake."

"Ah, but your superiors are much easier to handle than mine. Mine would absolutely forbid transferring a Soviet citizen to your side of the hospital. Absolutely."

"Then he's going to die?"

"No, he's on his way to your side of the hospital. I gave the order this morning before I came out here to join you."

Kinsman stopped dead on the gravelly slope, sending a few loose pebbles rattling noiselessly down toward the shadowed bottom of the crater. "You . . . Pete, sometimes you astound me."

"You think it's impossible for a good Communist to be flexible? To fly in the face of authority? You think only you Americans have feelings?"

"Oh hell."

Leonov put a hand on Kinsman's shoulder. "Old friend, I am being relieved of duty. I am being sent back to Mother Russia, to my wife and little ones. We will never see each other again."

"Shipped out? When?"

"In two weeks. Perhaps less. I'm not certain who my replacement will be, but the indications are that he will be a hard-liner. A good Marxist and a good soldier. Not a soft-hearted fellow like me. Not a collaborationist who attends capitalist parties and wastes the people's time and money on frivolities."

"You're in trouble?"

"I am always in trouble," Leonov said, trying to make it sound jovial. "That's why I was given the Lunagrad post in the first place. This is even better than Siberia—a banishment that appears to be a promotion. Most of the people in Lunagrad are exiles."

"If they're anything like the people in our half of Selene," Kinsman said, "they wouldn't want to go back to Earth. It's too crowded down there, Pete. Like rats, that's the way they're living."

"I know. But our superiors don't realize that. They are still living in the past. They still think of Lunagrad as a sort of exile for troublesome officers."

"They're calling you back, though."

"Yes. The game is becoming serious. They have finally realized that we supply most of the oxygen and foodstuffs and fuels for the space stations. Lunagrad—forgive me, Selene —is a vital logistics center for the orbiting platforms. And the men in those stations are in charge of the antimissile satellites. So we here on the Moon hold the key to all the military operations going on in orbit around the Earth. That is why I am being replaced. They want a reliable soldier up here."

Kinsman turned his head inside the helmet of his pressure suit. His nose wrinkled at the smell of sealant grease and fear. The rim of the crater blocked everything from view with a continuous wall of solid rock. He and Leonov could not see the other men and women, the crawlers and buggies, the lunar plain, or even the ever-watchful Earth. Nothing could be seen except the rock-strewn crater slope, the solemn unblinking stars directly overhead, and this other human being standing before him. Kinsman's eyes saw only the outside of a bulky, impersonal lunar suit; even the visor was a mirrored blank. But he could sense the man inside, the soul that animated the plastic and metal.

"Pete, I'm not supposed to tell you this," Kinsman said, "but something big is brewing. I don't mean just tinkering with the ABM satellites. That's been going on for a long time. I think they're getting ready to take the next step."

He could sense Leonov nodding slowly. "Yes. That is why they want to remove an unreliable officer from command of Lunagrad."

"They're sending up a 'good soldier' to be my second-in-command, too," Kinsman said. "Pat Kelly's being rotated back Earthside and Frank Colt's coming up to keep an eye on me."

"Colt? The black one. Yes . . . I remember him."

"Dammitall!" Kinsman balled his fists. "They're going to have their war. They're going to start killing people in orbit and they'll end up destroying everything."

"History is inexorable."

"Stop talking like a goddamned robot!" Kinsman snapped. "This isn't abstract. It's you and me, Pete! They're going to try to make us kill each other. Those shitheads won't be satisfied with tearing the Earth apart; they're going to send us orders to go to war up here."

"I won't be here," Leonov said quietly. "I'll be home in Kiev with my wife and children, waiting for your missiles to fall on us."

"And you're just going to let them do it to you? You're not going to try to do anything about it?"

"What *can* we do?" Leonov's voice deepened to a growl.

"We have talked about this many times, Chet. But what good is talk? When the actual moment comes—what can I do? What can you do?"

"I can refuse to fight," Kinsman heard himself say. "And so can you, for as long as you're in command up here. We can stop them from making war here on the Moon."

"Bravo. And what about the seven billions of human beings back on Earth?"

Kinsman stared at his friend. He had no answer.

It was almost fully dark in Washington. Streetlights and store windows were lit because the damage and danger of darkened streets was far worse, experience had proved, than the drain of energy from keeping the lights on. Commuters were scurrying for the police-protected buses that would speed them to the relative safety of their suburban enclaves, leaving the city to the poor, the black, the angry.

The President stood at his office window, staring across Lafayette Park to the National Christmas Tree. It soared nearly forty feet high, a triumph of plastic technology and chemical fluorescence. A Marine honor guard paced around it with bayoneted automatic rifles.

"Nobody comes to see the tree anymore," the President murmured. "When I was a kid we used to watch the tree being lit up on television every year. The first time I came to Washington we saw the Christmas tree. Now nobody comes at all. Nobody pays any attention to it . . ."

The Secretary of Defense coughed politely. "The orders for the contingency plan, sir—they require your signature."

Reluctantly, almost petulantly, the President turned away from the window. "We ought to do something. There must be millions of kids who'd like to see the tree."

"They do see it, on television," said the Defense Secretary. "It's difficult for them to get to the city." He was standing in front of the President's broad desk of genuine cherrywood, unconsciously tapping a thick sheaf of papers resting on the desktop.

"Um, well, I suppose they do." The President shook his head and then lowered his chunky body into the high-backed plush swivel chair behind the desk. He looked too small for the chair, for the broad desk itself.

"Now what am I supposed to be signing here?"

"These are the orders for the contingency plans, part of our follow-up on the ABM satellite problem."

"Oh." The President reached for his gold pen, then looked up at the Defense Secretary again. "And what's different about these that they need my signature?"

Defense's narrow, sharp-featured face clouded momentarily. "The contingency plans cover the possibility of a Soviet attack on our manned space stations. They provide for manpower and logistics backup to prevent such an attack from succeeding."

"Beefing up the stations' defenses?"

"Exactly."

"What's this going to cost? Are you sure we need it?"

"Sir, it's obvious the Russians are up to something big. The shooting incident in Antarctica—one of our naval officers was killed, you know."

"What?"

Defense raised a calming hand. "We've only gotten scrambled reports out of McMurdo Station. They're investigating the incident. Our monitors have also intercepted similar reports from the Russian base at Mirnyy. All we know for certain is that a team of Russians and a team of Americans fired on each other. One American officer is dead."

The President's hands were trembling. "They killed one of our men?"

"Apparently. We'll know more shortly."

"I want a full report as soon as the information becomes available."

"Of course."

"No matter what hour of the day or night. Do you hear me? A full report."

"Yes, sir. Certainly."

His voice still hollow with shock, the President went on, "Now, what's this got to do with the space stations?"

Defense said, "It's all part of a pattern. They're getting tough in Antarctica. They're building up their troop concentrations in Syria. Intelligence reports show that they intend to replace their present commander at Lunagrad, a coexistence type, with a hard-line full general straight out of the Kremlin. They're up to something big."

Wordlessly the President scribbled his signature on the top page of the sheaf of papers.

"Thank you, Mr. President." Defense snatched the sheaf of papers from his desk and strode quickly out of the office.

In the anteroom outside, the burly angry-faced man paced across the plush carpeting. He walked with a slight limp, as if his feet were not meant to be in the shoes he was forced to wear.

He glared up at the Defense Secretary. "He signed?"

The harsh tortured whisper made Defense want to shudder. "Yes," he replied. "Of course."

"He realizes that the plan includes preparations for an attack on the Soviet space stations?"

Defense shook his head. "That did not come up in our conversation."

The angry one almost smiled. "So be it. We can explain the value of a preemptive strike to him later. Gradually. If time permits."

The meeting of the State Security Committee had been long and bitter and sometimes loud. The Kremlin had often rung with the shouts of angry men, and many times such rancor had led to violence.

General Secretary Bereznik was determined to restore harmony.

"Comrades!" he called sharply, slapping a heavy palm on the table before him. They all jerked their attention to him, dropping their hot arguments for the moment.

"Comrades, we should be directing our energies to the solution of this problem. Wrangling will produce no positive results."

"Firing on our scientific expedition is an inexcusable provocation!" Marshal Prokoff shouted.

"But we killed one of their men," said the Foreign Minister, his puffy face florid with passion. "There was shooting on both sides."

"They are increasing their orbital missions," repeated the Intelligence Minister. "More satellites and more attacks on our satellites."

The General Secretary glared in helpless frustration.

Sometimes he wished he had Khrushchev's boldness: it was canny old Nikita who had often carried a pistol to these meetings.

"My father gave his life for the Soviet Union at Stalingrad," Prokoff was saying heatedly, "and I will not allow *any* foreign transgressor to destroy what he fought to preserve."

"But what of the Chinese?" someone asked, his voice quavering from the general din around the table. "What are they going to do?"

At the far end of the table the Nameless One got to his feet. All the arguing stopped dead. He was not truly nameless, of course, but he insisted on using his unpronounceable Tadzhik tribal name, so the Russians jokingly called him the Nameless One. What he thought of the joke, no one knew; he neither smiled nor complained.

Ah, thought the General Secretary, now a little clear thinking will enter the discussion. I was wondering how long he would remain silent. But he suppressed a shudder as he nodded acknowledgment at the Nameless One. The man was uncanny, frightening in the way that a snake frightens: inspiring a terror that goes far deeper than rational understanding. None of the men around the table was a stranger to force or violence. But for an Asian to reach the inner counsels of Mother Russia took a special sort of cold, ruthless ambition.

"It is clear," he said in his icy, quiet, slightly sibilant tone, "that we face a crisis of will." The Nameless One was neither tall nor imposing from the standpoint of physical size. His face was thin, with a slightly Oriental cast to the glittering, hypnotic eyes. His ears were slightly pointed, his hands long and thin and graceful.

"The peoples of the Soviet Union urgently need the coal that our scientists have discovered in Antarctica—especially if we are to continue selling natural gas to the West in return for hard currency. The Americans desire that coal, also, for their own needs and markets. Our strategic deterrent force is matched by their missiles. Our antimissile network of satellites is incomplete, and so is theirs. We are in a stalemate, unless . . ."

He let the word hang while the ministers and military

officers leaned forward on their chairs.

"Unless," he went on, "we are prepared to steel ourselves for the next step."

Marshal Prokoff nodded firmly. "Put the bombs in orbit."

"Exactly," agreed the Nameless One.

"But that would be a violation of a treaty that we solemnly . . ."

The General Secretary rapped his knuckles on the table-top. "That treaty was signed more than three decades ago. The world is very different today."

"Yes, but—"

"We have no choice," said the Nameless One, with infinite calm. "If we are not prepared to keep the Americans from attacking us, we will lose everything. The orbiting bombs will be a threat that the Americans—and the Chinese, as well—cannot ignore."

The discussion went on well into the night. But at least, the General Secretary thought gratefully, it is a discussion and not a brawl.

The Nameless One did most of the talking.

It was nearly midnight in Selene before Kinsman got to the hospital. He looked in on Baliagorev in the intensive-care unit. Jill Meyers was there and they wound up having coffee together in the hospital's tiny automated cafeteria.

The place was deserted. They took their steaming mugs from the dispenser and sat at the nearest table. It wobbled on uncertain legs.

"Damned place always smells of antiseptics," Kinsman grumbled. "And the light panels are too bright—glaring."

Jill laughed tiredly. "Yeah, boss, how about that? I'd look a lot better in candlelight."

"You look fine, kid. Tired but happy." It was true. There were dark fatigue circles under her eyes, but Jill was smiling.

She slumped back in her plastic chair. "It's been a long day, but a good one. I think Baliagorev will make it."

"And you've got Landau orbiting around you."

"Alex? Oh, he's an old friend. We met years ago . . ."

Sipping gingerly at the searing coffee, Kinsman said, "I was watching you two back at the ICU. Do you realize that you actually fluttered your eyelashes at him?"

Jill's face went deep red. "That's not true!"

"Oh no? He's asked to stay here overnight."

"He wants to be with his patient."

"And pigs have wings. He wants to be with you, kid."

She grinned, but her hands seemed to go out of control. They fidgeted around the coffee cup and then up to her face. "You're joking. You really think so?"

"Looks pretty obvious to me. I wouldn't be surprised if he ran the old man halfway around the Ocean of Storms just to get him to keel over."

"You're terrible!"

Kinsman smiled back at her. "Yeah, I guess I am. But I'm not the only one who's noticed the way you two have been looking at each other. Half the hospital staff is sighing with romantic rapture about you. The female half."

Jill tried to frown but her pixie face was not made for it. "What about you and this new girl in the comm section?"

Kinsman scratched at his stubbly chin. "Diane? I've known her for years. She was a pretty well known singer a few years back. Diane Lawrence."

"That's Diane Lawrence?" Jill seemed impressed.

Nodding, Kinsman said, "She ran into trouble with the government and that ended her singing career."

"But the First Amendment . . ."

"Is in trouble," Kinsman said. "Just like the rest of the country."

Jill rested her chin on a tiny fist. "She was *good*. I used to buy her tapes."

Brightening, Kinsman said, "There's no reason why she can't sing here. We could use a little entertainment around the old joint."

"That's right."

"She'd still have to work her regular shift, at least for the time being. But we could get her to moonlight after shift . . ."

"That's a terrible pun!"

Surprised, he asked, "What is?"

"Moonlighting."

"Oh—on the Moon. I see." Kinsman grinned. "It wasn't intentional."

"And there's nothing serious between you two?"

"Not really."

"You look awfully happy, all of a sudden."

He shrugged.

"It's about time you got serious about somebody, don't you think?" Jill asked, running a finger around the rim of her coffee cup. "You're getting a little elderly for the playboy lifestyle."

"Yeah. Maybe you're right. I'm too young to be a *roué*."

With a knowing smile Jill asked, "So what are you going to do about it?"

What can I do? he wanted to shout. Instead he merely muttered, "This is a lousy time to get my personal life tangled."

"Why?" Jill asked. "What's so bad about this particular time?"

He hesitated. "Things . . . are brewing. Trouble's coming. Big trouble." He reached across the table and grabbed Jill's wrist. "Listen, kid. You and your Russian friend better grab whatever fun you can get, and grab it quick. Because in the next week or two the lid could blow off. All hell's going to break loose. And soon." Then he heard himself add, "Unless we can stop it."

Saturday 4 December 1999: 1830 hrs UT

KINSMAN STOOD AT the airlock hatch in the main dome, waiting for it to open. Outside, the shuttle rocket sat squat and ungainly, connected to the hatch by an airtight access tube.

The hatch popped ajar with a sigh, then swung smoothly back. Kinsman felt a slight stir of air as the pressure in the dome equilibrated.

Frank Colt stepped through the hatch and into the dome.

He carried a single small travel kit and wore a regulation Aerospace Force blue uniform the way officers did Earthside, with a chestful of decorations, instead of the casual lunar coveralls.

Kinsman was always surprised at Colt's lack of physical size. The black astronaut had a giant's strong personality but physically he was slight. A black Alexander Hamilton, Kinsman thought. Tough, waspish. Then he remembered that Hamilton had been killed in a duel by a man later called a traitor to the United States.

At the sight of Kinsman, Colt snapped to bayonet-stiff attention and saluted crisply. Suppressing a grin, Kinsman returned a lazy salute, then reached for Colt's hand. "Frank, you old ass-kicker—good to see you! Welcome aboard."

Colt grinned widely. "How're you, pal? Letting your hair grow, huh?"

With a glance at Colt's close-cropped fuzz, Kinsman countered, "Jealous?"

"Shit, man, if I let mine go natural I'd never get a helmet over it."

Laughing, they made their way to the power ladder.

"You can drop your bag off at your quarters and have dinner with us," Kinsman said as they stepped aboard the moving rungs.

"Sure, sure. But shouldn't I be presenting my orders and officially checking in?"

"We can do that tomorrow. You must be hungry. And the food at Alpha hasn't improved any, I'll bet."

Colt laughed as he clung to the handgrip in front of him. "Hell, no."

They rode down four levels as the ladder's distant electric motor whined faintly. As they stepped off the ladder Colt said, "Maybe I can wait a couple more days and officially take my new post on Pearl Harbor Day. That'd have a nice historical touch to it."

"Pearl what?" Kinsman asked.

"Pearl Harbor. December seventh. World War Two. It was in all the papers."

Kinsman led him down the corridor. "You've got an odd sense of humor, Frank."

"History, man. History. It's my big subject."

Half an hour later they were in the cafeteria. It was a small place, with only a couple dozen tables. Most of them were filled, but the acoustical insulation kept the background noise down to a muted murmur.

Colt's face was grim as they sat down. "Aren't those Russians over there?" He cocked his head in the direction of the table where Jill Meyers was sitting with Landau and a pair of Russian medi-techs.

Kinsman nodded. "We've got one of their people in our intensive-care unit. Heart condition."

"Chet, this is *supposed* to be a military installation. It's bad enough to be sitting right next door to the enemy . . ."

"Hey, relax," Kinsman said. "These people aren't enemies of ours."

Colt shook his head warily.

Kinsman went on, "There's not enough military activity here to make it worth worrying over. You know that, Frank."

"Suppose you stopped supplying food and oxygen to the space stations. Then what?"

"Come on."

"No, I'm serious, man." Colt jabbed a fork into his pork cutlet, the first real meat he'd had in months. "Suppose they knocked out Moonbase or took it over. How'd our guys in the space stations get supplied?"

"From Earthside, of course."

"Yeah? You know how long it'd take to set that up? And what it'd cost? If they knock off Moonbase, they cripple our space stations and the whole system of ABM satellites. They win the battle, man. They own everything from a hundred klicks off the Earth's surface. Which means they own the Earth."

"It won't happen, Frank."

"It could." Colt attacked the cutlet with vigor. "That's why I've been assigned here. Murdock's worried about just that."

Kinsman suddenly was no longer hungry. "I guess I should've taken a look at your orders after all."

"Wouldn't do you any good. Ain't spelled out in black and white. But Murdock gave me a personal call, scrambled at both ends. He thinks you're a mushmelon and he wants me to make sure this place doesn't get bagged. That's why I'm here."

"Terrific," Kinsman said. He pushed his tray away from him. "And the next step will be to get prepared for taking over Lunagrad."

"Could be."

"That's stupid," Kinsman snapped.

"Is it?"

Hold it, Kinsman told himself. Don't let them start a fight between the two of us! With an effort he forced his temper down.

"Frank, do you remember Cy Calder?"

"Who?"

"Old Cy Calder. Way back in the early days, when we were training. Cy was a newsman . . ."

Recognition dawned on Colt's face. "Oh, yeah, the old dude. He was quite a guy."

"He told me a story once," Kinsman said, "about when he flew a bomber in World War One."

"Yeah, and the Mile High Club."

"No, this was a different story. He used to fly bombing runs in the early months of the war. Open cockpit, scarf-in-the-wind kind of stuff."

"No shit."

Kinsman grinned at the memory of Calder's story. "He flew a two-man bomber. Cranked her up to maximum altitude over the trenches—about five thousand feet. All the soldiers in the trenches shot at any airplane. Didn't matter whose plane it was. They all hated the fliers."

Colt laughed.

"Cy flew mostly night missions. Never saw another plane in the sky. Then one night, as they were coming back from a bombing raid on some farmhouse, they passed a big German Gotha bomber coming back from a raid on the Allied side of the lines."

"Yeah?"

"Cy waved at the German pilot and the guy waved back. They were both excited just to see somebody else up there."

"Those were the days," Colt muttered.

"Well, a couple of minutes after they passed each other,

Cy's gunner turned around to him and started yelling, so he could be heard over the engines, 'That was a *German!* What the hell were we waving at him for? Turn around, let's shoot the bastard down!' "

Colt nodded.

"Cy pushed the gunner back away from him and told him, 'You silly sonofabitch, it's dangerous enough up here without shooting at people!' "

Colt started to laugh, but it never became more than a half-hearted chuckle. "Okay, I dig it. It's dangerous enough up here on the Moon without shooting at people. But I've got my orders, Chet. And maybe the Russians never heard your story."

Kinsman replied slowly, "Anyone who's spent any time on the Moon knows that story. They've saved our guys a thousand times and we've saved theirs. Most of their people speak English and a lot of ours know Russian. We live together, Frank. In peace."

"Shee-it," Colt deliberately exaggerated the accent, "next thing you know you're gonna start singing gospel songs. You live in peace, huh? For how long, pal? How long? What happens when they get orders from Earthside to do it . . ." Colt slowly squeezed his thumb down on the tabletop as if he were squashing a bug. Or pressing a FIRE button.

Kinsman said nothing. Colt went on, "It's getting down to the big crunch, man. All this messing around with the satellites. And some Navy dude got himself shot down near the South Pole . . ."

"What?" Kinsman felt a lightning flash of startled fear in his guts.

Colt nodded. "Yeah. Couple days ago. Things are warming up."

"In Antarctica? They're shooting at each other in an international zone?"

"Why not? World's biggest coal beds down there. They're gonna fight over it—or something else. Maybe the Middle East again; there's still a lot of oil left there. It's coming, man. Lotta hungry people and not enough resources to keep 'em all going. They're gonna fight over it, sooner or later. Nothing we can do to stop it. We gotta be prepared to *win* it."

Kinsman started to reply, but there was nothing he could say. He sat there, defeated. Then he saw Pat Kelly coming up, holding a dinner tray.

"Mind if I join you?" Kelly asked. He did not wait for an answer, but put his tray down next to Colt's and pulled out the chair.

"Frank, you know Pat, don't you?" Kinsman asked.

Colt nodded as Kelly sat down. "Just made major, didn't you?"

"Yep," Kelly answered. "Pretty soon I'll outrank you, Flash." His usual rabbit's face looked different: tense, almost angry, flushed with expectation.

Colt flicked him a lazy glance. "I'm not planning on retiring that soon. And what's this 'Flash' crap?"

With a shrug, Kelly said, "You're the hotshot rocket jock, everybody knows that."

"I don't know," Colt said. "Tell me about it."

Kinsman sat there and watched it happen. He felt helpless and fascinated at the same time. Kelly was a good man, bright and dedicated. Frank Colt was just as bright, maybe more so. And whatever was burning inside Colt was far hotter than Kelly's flame, Kinsman knew from long experience. Yet there was something about Colt that called lightning down from the sky. Men either loved him like a brother or hated him. There was no neutral ground.

Kelly was tight-lipped. "Look at you, wearing that uniform like you're at an Academy parade. You know damned well we don't do that up here. But you've got to be the superhero. All-time champion hotshot."

"And you keep your uniform stowed in a closet so everybody'll think you're Mr. Nice Guy, huh? Ever been shot at?"

"That's got nothing to do with—"

"Hell it don't! Know why you're here, Mr. Nice Guy? D'you know why you can dance around on the Moon and collect rocks and advance in rank every three years?"

"Now, wait . . ."

Colt silenced him with a long forefinger jabbed toward his face. "You're here on the Moon, *Major* Kelly, because it's cheaper to supply our space stations and orbital factories from lunar resources than from Earth. That's it. I don't give a shit how many scientists you got up here or how many cripples you've saved. The only reason the taxpayers of the United States support this fairy palace is because it's cheaper than boosting supplies and raw materials into orbit from the Earth. Got that?"

Kelly was white-faced now. "That's about what I'd expect from you. Did you bring any bombs with you?"

Colt leaned back in his chair and laughed. "Shit, baby, you know nuclear weapons are outlawed in space. We signed a treaty with the Russians thirty years ago. No weapons of mass dee-struction. I bet if you swung a search-and-destroy patrol through Lunagrad right now you wouldn't find more'n three or four nukes."

Kinsman butted in. "Both you guys are supposed to be officers and gentlemen. How about acting that way? You're giving everybody a helluva floor show."

Kelly glanced over his shoulder. The people at most of the other tables were staring at them. Including the Russians. Colt just sat back and toyed with his fork.

Very quietly, Kelly said to Kinsman, "Chet, you had me just about convinced to bring my family up here. But I can see that it's useless. It only takes a few Neanderthals to ruin everything, whether it's Earthside or on the Moon."

He got to his feet and walked stiffly out of the cafeteria, leaving his untouched tray at the table.

Colt pursed his lips and looked at Kinsman. "He's too soft to be an officer."

"He's a good man, Frank."

"Yeah, but nice guys finish last. And in a two-man race, only the winner survives."

They finished their meal in silence with Kelly's food getting cold beside them, a mute reminder of their differences.

Kinsman took Colt back to his own quarters after dinner. "I've got a bottle of homebrew," he said as Colt plopped on the living-room couch. "See what you think of it."

Kinsman slid back the partition to the kitchenette and reached into a closet built in above the microwave cooker. He pulled out a bottle of colorless liquid. "It's sort of a cross between vodka and tequila. The guys in the chem lab made it."

Colt was relaxed happily on the couch. "Y'know," he said as he accepted a plastic cup from Kinsman, "I had forgotten what luxury you cats live in. A living room, a bedroom, a kitchen, all the electric power you want, all sorts of display screens and gadgets—fan*tas*tic!"

Kinsman pulled up one of the webbed chairs that had been scavenged from a wrecked dune buggy. "I guess it *is* pretty soft compared to the orbital stations."

"Compared to Earthside, man!" Colt said fervently. "Compared to Washington or Vandenberg or anyplace else. You'd have to be damned well off to have quarters this nice."

"Well," Kinsman filled Colt's cup and his own, "welcome to Selene, Frank."

He hoisted his cup and Colt returned the salute. Kinsman sipped at his drink, carefully letting the burning liquid slide over his tongue. Colt gulped.

"Aargghhh!" Colt squeezed his eyes shut and shook his head viciously. "Wow! That's some chem lab you got, man!"

"They do good work," Kinsman admitted, grinning.

"On their own time, of course. No taxpayers' money wasted on frivolities."

"On their own time," Kinsman said. "And under careful supervision from the management. I won't let any bootlegging operations get started around here."

Colt took another swallow. He held the cup up and admired it. "Real rocket fuel, all right." He downed the rest of it.

Kinsman put his cup down on the phone terminal next to the couch. Colt did the same.

"Frank, you really shouldn't clobber kids like Kelly the way you did."

"Hey, he jumped me!"

"I know. He's scared. He's got a wife and kids sitting next to a SAC base."

"So whattaya want me to do, turn the other cheek?"

Grinning, "That'll be the day."

Colt spread his hands. "Look, Chet, I'll try to go easy on these peaceniks you got up here. But I've got a job to do and I'm gonna get it done. If it takes splitting heads or bruising delicate egos, I can't help it. This base has gotta be prepared against an attack."

"I know," Kinsman admitted. "But just don't go out of your way to batter people. Most of them aren't in your league. It's unfair to sock 'em so hard."

"Yassuh," Colt joked. Or maybe it was only half joking. He got up from the couch and started shuffling, stooped over, toward the door. "Us colored folks know our place, massah. Don't want to make no trouble, no how."

"Go to hell," Kinsman said, laughing.

"See ya," Colt said at the door.

"Can you find your way back to your quarters okay?"

"Blindfolded."

"Good night, Frank."

As soon as Colt shut the door behind him, Kinsman leaned over and touched the ON button of the phone terminal. The screen lit up but showed no picture.

"Pat Kelly, please."

For a moment the phone hummed to itself, then the computer's synthesized voice said, "Not in quarters."

"Find him."

It took several minutes before Kelly's face appeared on the screen. He still looked tight-lipped, tense. Behind him, Kinsman saw a stenciled sign on the wall identifying his location as corridor C, area twenty.

"Taking a walk?" Kinsman asked.

Kelly replied, "I was trying to cool off and do some thinking."

"Listen to me, Pat. I want you to get something through your skull. Colt's going to be deputy commander of Moonbase. There's nothing I can do about that. But I can create a slot for an aide to the commander. I want you to take the job. You won't have to go Earthside. You can bring your family here."

Kelly's voice was dead flat. "Not while he's here. What's the use?"

"We can make it work out okay," Kinsman insisted. "I've known Frank since we were in astronaut training. There isn't a helluva lot we agree on, but we're friends. Brothers, almost. He saved my life once. I've helped him through some rough times."

Kelly said nothing.

"But as close as we are," Kinsman went on, "I'll never

know what it's like to be black. And neither will you. He's fought goddamned hard to get where he is now. He's had to jump over hurdles that we can't even imagine."

"Come on now, Chet," Kelly said. "That poor little underprivileged kid from the ghetto—I've been hearing that routine all my life. It's phony as hell."

"People still burn synagogues, Pat. And they still kick niggers. It's getting worse, not better. Frank's got the scars to prove it."

"And I'm supposed to—"

"You're supposed to act like an adult," Kinsman snapped. "You do the job that needs to be done and you bring your family up here where they'll be safe."

"Even with *him* around?"

"Even with him around," Kinsman said.

Kelly looked doubtful. But some of the anger had left his face.

"Start the paperwork tomorrow first thing," Kinsman said. "That's an order. You are now my aide. And your family comes up on the next available shuttle space."

"Well . . ."

"And while we're at it, dig into the personnel files and find out how many of the permanent residents here have immediate family Earthside."

"My God, are you going to start a rescue service?"

"Call it an immigration service," Kinsman replied. He snapped off the phone and Kelly's face faded from the screen.

Then he touched another button and turned to the big wall screen across from his chair. It showed the Earth.

"You know damned well you can't take them all," he whispered to himself. "I can't save them all. God, there's seven billion of them!"

Kinsman could not sleep that night. He got into his bed and turned off all the lights and display screens and stayed wide awake.

Seven billion of them.

And ye shall hear of wars and rumors of wars . . . For nation shall rise against nation, and kingdom against kingdom: and there shall be famines, and pestilences, and earthquakes . . . And woe unto them that are with child, and to them that give suck in those days!

But pray ye that your flight be not in the winter, neither on the sabbath day:

For then shall be great tribulation, such as was not since the beginning of the world to this time, no, nor shall ever be.

"Apocalypse," he whispered to himself.

Sitting up in the sweaty, wrinkled bed he fumbled with the keyboard on the nightstand and then stared at the display screen image of Earth floating in the darkness of his room.

". . . famines, and pestilences, and earthquakes . . . nation shall rise against nation . . ."

He squeezed his eyes shut and saw the dead cosmonaut again. Hanging in space. Oxygen lines ripped out.

"By my hand."

Kinsman held his hands out before him in the shadows of the darkened room. So you're going to survive while everybody else dies. You're guiltier than they are. You've killed. You didn't push any buttons; you did it the old-fashioned way. With your own hands.

"And if thy right hand offends thee, cut it off." The sound of his own voice in the darkness startled him. He knew it was not the correct quotation, but it fit. It fit.

Sunday meetings. The Sunday they found that a squirrel had gotten into the Meeting House and chewed up half the leather upholstery on the benches.

"Serves us right," his father had said. "Upholstered benches are an affectation."

This from the richest Quaker in Pennsylvania. A strange collection of contrasts he was. Wish I had known him better.

The school kids teasing him because he was a Quaker. Calling him William Penn. The tough ones, the big ones, ganging around him. "Let's see you quake, Quaker." How to get your nose broken. How to learn to talk your way out of a fight.

But there's no way to talk yourself out of this one.

Never to fly a plane again! If they wipe themselves out there will be no airplanes. No airfields.

"Who're you trying to kid?" he asked himself. "You couldn't handle one now. Not after years of living in low gee. You're soft as a sponge. Reflexes gone. Pushing forty."

Why do they have to have their war? In a half century of

Cold War, haven't they learned anything? Why must they blow up everything?

He knew why. For the same reason he had killed the cosmonaut. Exactly the same reason. It was not necessary. It wasn't. But you get the fury into you and you can't stop. Not until it's too late.

The alarm buzzer sounded. The bedroom lights slowly turned on to half-intensity. Time to get up.

To hell with everything and everybody, he told himself. This is the way it is and this is the way I've got to play it.

Things always look different in the light of day, he mused, even when the light is artificial. Not easier. Not better. But more rational. You can deal with things logically in day's light. In the dark, fearful shapes haunt the shadows.

Kinsman put in a phone call for Leonov, then dry-showered and dressed while he waited. Finally the phone buzzed and the computer told him that the Russian commander was on the line.

The screen went gray, but no picture took form. Leonov's voice came through strong and clear. "I didn't realize that capitalists got up so early in the morning."

Kinsman shot back, "That's how we stay ahead of you centralized bureaucrats."

"Hah! A slanderous provocation."

Getting serious, Kinsman asked, "You've heard about this Antarctica thing?"

"Yes."

He waited for Leonov to say something more. When nothing came, he asked, "Any further word on your replacement?"

"No, not yet."

Leonov's voice sounded strained. They're bugging his line, Kinsman realized. And probably mine, too.

"We've got to get together, Pete, and discuss things. The buggy race and all . . ."

"I can't," Leonov immediately replied. "Not today. Too many other problems to attend to. Possibly in a day or two."

Nodding to himself, Kinsman said, "Yeah. Okay. Call me."

He shut off the phone and stood there naked for a few

uncertain moments, then punched the keyboard once again.

"Get me a flitter," he said to the flickering gray screen. "Long-range flight. I'll fill out the flight plan in the operations office. Be there in half an hour."

Sunday 5 December 1999: 0945 hrs UT

KINSMAN RODE ALONE across the ghostly landscape. The flitter boosted into a high arc, gliding silently through the long lunar night. The ground below him was softly lit by Earthlight, a jumbled panorama of gray rocks and craters.

He was strapped into the pilot's seat of the tiny rocket-driven craft, coasting over the highlands east of Aristarchus. The Sea of Tranquility was a dark smear on the horizon ahead of him.

He flew alone. The craft was pressurized, so he could keep his visor up. The pressure suit was bulky and uncomfortable, but he willingly kept it on. If anything happened to the flitter, the suit could save his life. It had happened before.

The highlands slid by, far below, pocked and roiled mountains sandblasted and worn smooth by eons of meteoric infall. The only sounds inside the flitter's cockpit were the faint hum of the electrical power system and the even fainter hiss of the air circulators.

This is silly, Kinsman second-guessed himself. A damned stupid waste of time. But the craft was locked onto its course by the unyielding laws of ballistics. The pilgrimage, once begun, had to be carried through to its destination.

By twisting around in the pilot's seat and leaning as far forward as the harness would allow, he could see Earth beckoning. He leaned back again and checked the instruments on the panel before him. But this occupied only a fraction of his attention. He kept seeing Jill's face, and Diane's and Kelly's and Leonov's and those of the people he knew in Washington, California, back home in Pennsylvania. Worst of all he kept seeing children: playing, running, in school, at sleep, all burned away in the searing glare of a fireball.

Keep thinking with your tear glands, he raged at himself. That's a terrific way to solve a problem!

His helmet earphones buzzed. Flicking a switch on the control panel he said crisply, "Kinsman here."

"Comm center, sir. We're picking up a news broadcast from Earthside. Officer of the Day thought you would want to hear it."

"Okay, pipe it through."

There was a barely discernible click and a momentary hum. Then: ". . . of Lieutenant Commander Ernest Richards. White House spokesmen have emphasized that the shooting took place in international territory, although last year the Soviet Union and several Latin American and Asian nations served notice that they intended to exploit the mineral resources of Antarctica."

The smoothly professional broadcaster's voice continued, "The United Nations has debated the issue of exploitation since its opening session this fall, with the United States taking a sharply different position from that of the Soviet Union.

"Senator Russel Montguard of North Carolina has called the shooting of Navy officer Richards, quote, 'An act of international murder; yes, an act of war.' Unquote. Other reactions from around the world include . . ."

Kinsman snapped the radio off. Now it's an international incident. An act of war. Just the excuse they've been looking for.

The control panel's lights and instruments winked at him, amber. The computer display screen flashed numbers and a view of his landing site. The radar altimeter's digital readout began spiraling downward.

The rocket engine fired without Kinsman's aid, programmed by the computer. He felt inordinately heavy for a few moments. Then the thrust shut off and almost simultaneously he felt the springy thump of the craft's landing struts touching down on the Sea of Tranquility.

The guidance system checked the local landmarks and

peered at the arrangement of stars overhead through the flitter's stereo telescope. Then it proclaimed, with a loud beep and a bright green circle drawn on the computer display screen, that they had indeed touched down at precisely the destination point programmed. All the lights on the control panel burned a steady green.

"Proud of yourself, aren't you?" Kinsman asked the humming machinery.

He slid his helmet visor shut and sealed it, then unstrapped from the seat while the pumps sucked the air out of the cockpit with a diminuendo clatter and stored it in the tanks built into the craft below the cockpit. Kinsman opened the canopy hatch and clambered down the ladder to the sandy lunar soil. He started across the uneven ground, leaving footprints that would last for eons.

He topped a small rise and there it was: the seismometers, the laser reflector, the stiffly proud flag, the gold-wrapped lower half of the landing module. Just as they had left it thirty years ago. The only change was the clear plastic cover that had been lovingly sprayed over the ground to protect the original footprints of Armstrong and Aldrin.

"Tranquility Base," Kinsman murmured.

Picking his way through the assorted hardware left by the astronauts, Kinsman walked around the landing module until he found the plaque. The stainless steel was still polished and gleaming, even in the faint light from Earth:

HERE MEN FROM THE PLANET EARTH
FIRST SET FOOT UPON THE MOON
JULY 1969, A.D.
WE CAME IN PEACE FOR ALL MANKIND

Kinsman stared at it for a long time, especially the last line. Then he lifted his eyes toward the beautiful Earth and muttered, " 'Nation shall not lift up sword against nation; neither shall they make war any more.' . . . At least, not *here*."

A flicker of movement caught his eye. Stepping away from the Apollo module he looked upward as far as his helmet would allow his vision to rise. A flash of light—rocket thrusters. The tiny gleam of another lunar flier solidified into a full-sized craft, engines flaring silently, landing struts poking rigidly outward. A Russian flitter.

It touched down close enough for Kinsman to watch its noiseless landing. The bubble canopy opened and a red-suited figure rose out of the cockpit and climbed slowly down the ladder.

Kinsman walked toward the newcomer. "Pete?" he called into his helmet microphone.

"Yes," Leonov's deep voice answered.

Kinsman's spirits soared. "How the hell did you know I'd be here?"

Leonov trudged over to him and laid a heavily gloved hand on Kinsman's shoulder. "My spies watch you very closely," he said flatly. "And so does my radar. It was rather simple to fix your trajectory and puzzle out your destination. No?"

"And you came out after me."

"Officially, I am discussing the need for tighter security with our radio astronomers at the Farside Station. As far as my intelligence officers back at Lunagrad are concerned, I have made this stop to see what you are up to."

"I'm making a pilgrimage in the desert," Kinsman said. "When I saw your ship I was hoping you were doing the same."

"To a shrine dedicated to American success? Hardly."

"There are medals for Gagarin and Komarov in there." Kinsman hiked a thumb in the direction of the lunar module.

"Yes, I know." Leonov hesitated a moment, then, "What really brings you out here?"

Kinsman said, "I couldn't sleep."

"Neither could I."

"What are we going to do about it?"

"Chet, my comrade, let's not begin to torture ourselves again."

"There must be something we can do!"

"Hah! I'm going to be replaced in ten days and you have your black superpatriot snarling at your heels."

"So whatever we do, it's got to be done in the next ten days."

Leonov said nothing. Kinsman could sense his disapproval.

"Come on, Pete!" he snapped.

"Do you have a plan of action?" the Russian asked softly.

"I wish I did." Kinsman stamped his booted foot, stirring up a cloud of dust. His legs felt itchy and it was impossible to scratch them inside the cumbersome suit.

"So," said Leonov. "You talk and worry and stay awake nights—but you have no idea of what can be done."

"Do you?"

Leonov raised both hands above his helmet. "Spare me this endless self-flagellation!"

"Now, don't get excited," said Kinsman. "Before we can lay any plans we've got to agree on how far we're willing to go."

"In what direction?"

"Well . . ." Kinsman suddenly realized that he had known the first step all along. "To begin with, suppose you refused to return Earthside. Suppose you requested that you remain in Lunagrad. What then?"

The shoulders of Leonov's red suit moved vaguely, as if he were shrugging inside it. "I have several weeks' leave due to me. I could ask to spend it in Lunagrad rather than at home. But it would be a very suspicious move."

"Suppose you refused to relinquish command of Lunagrad?"

"Mmm . . ." The Russian's voice grew somber. "That would be a direct disobedience of orders. Treason against the state. Very serious."

"What about your wife and children?"

"I doubt that the security police would bother them. Nothing like that has been done in twenty years, despite the horror stories concocted by your Western press. But, frankly, I would worry about the children."

"And your wife?"

He almost laughed. "My darling wife would be quite happy to see me shot. It would free her completely."

"Oh, I didn't know . . ."

"It is not something one boasts about."

An embarrassed silence settled over them. Finally Leonov asked, "Well, you obviously have something in mind. What is it?"

Without letting himself stop to think, Kinsman answered, "Declare independence."

Leonov said nothing.

"Make Selene a nation, declare our independence from both the United States and the Soviet Union and apply for membership in the United Nations."

It took a long time for Leonov to reply. "I thought so. I was afraid that would be your brilliant idea."

"Look at it point by point," Kinsman urged, starting to feel some enthusiasm. "First, we won't have to fight here on the Moon. If we unite, we won't fight. The only way we can unite is for both of us to stop taking orders from Earthside. The only way we can stop taking orders is to declare ourselves independent . . ."

"We would starve to death in a matter of weeks."

"Not so!" Kinsman snapped. "Moonbase's water capacity can more than take care of all our needs. If we combine it with yours we can irrigate more farmlands and grow enough crops and livestock to be completely self-sufficient."

"If we have enough water."

"We will. We'll have enough in a few months for everything we want to do, plus an emergency backup, as well."

Before Leonov could say more, Kinsman went on, "The only way to make our independence stick is to have the UN recognize us. I think there are enough unaligned nations in the General Assembly that are fed up with both the West and the East to vote us in."

"That debating society!" Leonov stamped a few paces away from Kinsman. "Chet, my lunar brother, I expected better of you. This idea of independence is nonsense, idiocy. It cannot work. I myself have thought about it a thousand times. But it cannot succeed!"

"But if the UN would recognize an independent Selene . . ."

"Hah! So what? What good would it do? Long before the question of our glorious independence is even placed on the debating society's agenda, both Moonbase and Lunagrad would be buried alive under troops from Earthside. Our court-martials would be finished and our bodies fertilizing the pig farms before the UN bureaucrats could lift a finger."

"But—"

"Admit it!" Leonov nearly shouted. "We have no military strength. You could not even be sure that enough of your own Moonbase people would go along with your insane idea. All you would do would be to foment civil war inside your own community."

Kinsman shook his head. "No. That much I'm certain of. You forget, I've been selecting the permanent residents of Moonbase for the past five years. I know who they are and what they'll do. The ninety-dayers—yes, we'd have trouble with some of them. But nothing we couldn't handle."

Leonov snorted. "Well, I know what would happen in Lunagrad. Half the populace would shoot the other half, and I have no idea who would be left alive when the smoke cleared. Possibly no one."

Despite himself, Kinsman grinned. "I thought you said Lunagrad was filled with exiles."

"Yes—but they are *Soviet* exiles. Not citizens of some new nation called Selene."

"And they're not sufficiently intelligent to see that a free Selene is to the advantage of everyone, including Mother Russia?"

Leonov's voice went from scornful to curious. "What do you mean?"

"If we declared our independence it would startle both America and Russia. If we stopped supplying oxygen and water and supplies to the space stations, it would upset their orbital operations quite a bit . . ."

"For a month or two, possibly. No longer."

"All right." Kinsman glanced at the ungainly Apollo lander squatting nearby. He could not see the plaque from where he was standing. "But we'd cause enough of a fuss, enough of an upset to their plans, that they'd be forced to delay this war buildup. This Antarctica incident would be pushed from their minds. By turning their attention to us we could stop them from going to war against each other."

Leonov sighed heavily. "I wish it were that simple, my friend. But it is not. Nothing will stop them from fighting their war. They will bow only to superior force, and there is no force superior anywhere on Earth or the Moon. History is inexorable, just as Marx said."

"No, it doesn't have to . . ."

"Chet, you are being naive! Assume the best possible results. Assume that your most optimistic hopes come true: We become independent and the UN recognizes us. Your nation and mine do not interfere, and we are allowed to remain independent. Their war is averted. For how long? Six months? A year? Have we provided more food for anyone on Earth? More energy? Sooner or later we will be exactly where we are now: standing here helplessly and watching them build up for war. *There is no way to avoid it!* The Earth is too crowded, resources too scarce. Why do you think they are shooting at each other in Antarctica? Both of them *need* that coal!"

Kinsman agreed reluctantly. "With the oil running out, there's not enough for everybody."

"Even with the success of the fusion experiments," Leonov said, "they won't be able to produce enough energy to make any difference for another ten or twenty years."

"If we could hold off the war for that long . . ."

"We could not hold it off for ten months," Leonov said.

"You're right," Kinsman admitted.

"So, my idealistic friend, declaring independence for Selene will achieve nothing. It will change nothing."

Kinsman said, "It will guarantee that more than a thousand human beings will survive the war, without being killed off later by disease or starvation."

Leonov went silent. He turned and paced toward the landing module, then stopped as the American flag came into view from behind its spidery body.

"Do you seriously believe," he asked slowly, without turning back to face Kinsman, "that any of us could watch our homelands being destroyed without going mad? Do you honestly believe that their war will not destroy us, too?"

Forcing his voice to stay calm as he walked to stand beside his friend, Kinsman answered, "We could get through it without fighting. If we tried."

The Russian's voice was infinitely sad. "No, old friend. I

might trust you and you might trust me, but to expect a thousand Russians and Americans to trust each other while they watch their families being killed—never."

Kinsman wanted to scream. Instead he heard himself whisper, "But Pete, what can we *do?*"

"Nothing. The world will end. The millennium is rushing upon us. A thousand years ago most Christians believed that the world would end at the millennium. They were off by a factor of a thousand years. It will end now. And there is nothing we can do."

The flight back to Selene seemed longer and lonelier than the flight to Tranquility Base. Kinsman tried to blank everything out of his mind, think of nothing whatever. Impossible.

The world will end. There is nothing we can do.

Wrong! It had to be wrong. There must be *something* that can be done. Something!

As he gazed at the richly blue Earth hanging above the horizon the enormity of it struck him. He was ready to rebel against the United States of America, against the mightiest nation the world had ever known, against the three hundred million people he had sworn to defend and protect. Leonov's right, he thought. It's madness.

Kinsman's mind flooded with memories: Thanksgiving dinners, sitting in school watching filmstrips about the Declaration of Independence, the maddening bus ride each morning from Crystal City to the dingy old Pentagon, the first time he had ever seen the Grand Canyon, pledging allegiance to the flag as a solemn little kid and then the special flip of saluting the same flag at retreat that first day he wore his shining new gold lieutenant's bars, snap-rolling an F-16 under the Golden Gate Bridge, "Don't Give Up the Ship," "Send Us More Japs," "Give Me Liberty or Give Me Death," "Government of the People, by the People . . ."

We're the people! he told himself. They've got no right to make us fight their goddamned war.

All that history, all that training, three hundred million programmed people . . . How could Selene hold out against it? Each man, woman, and child in Moonbase trained and indoctrinated since birth. "My Country, 'Tis of Thee . . ."

And then he remembered a line from a physics class, a chalk-dusty little man of a teacher with a pinched face and the same gray suit every day of the semester saying, "Give me a lever long enough and a place to stand and I can move the Earth."

Is a quarter-million miles long enough? Kinsman wondered.

To anyone who took notice of such things, Jill Meyers and Alexsei Landau made an incongruous couple: the tall, grave, bearded Russian and the tiny, perky, moonfaced American woman.

At the moment no one was noticing. Jill and Landau stood in the midst of a knot of people watching a TV newscast from Earth. They were in Selene's central plaza, the wide high-domed arcade that had started as a natural cavern, been converted into a quartermaster's depot, and grown into a multitiered complex of privately owned shops that seemed to grow organically around the government-issue outlets.

There was little buying and selling right now. The crowd stood in tense silence in the middle of the arcade, watching the big TV screen set up in the archway at the far end. An Earthside newscaster was grimly narrating the day's events while the screen showed videotapes of the American base at McMurdo Sound, where Lieutenant Commander Richards's flag-draped coffin was being loaded aboard a jet transport plane.

The scene switched to Washington, the old Pentagon, gray and forbidding.

"While no word has yet been received from the White House," the newscaster was intoning, "informed Pentagon officials have hinted that American military units around the world have been alerted for possible action. Satellite monitors have identified a Russian task force steaming at top speed for Antarctica from Vladivostok, and East European troop maneuvers continue in Poland and Czechoslovakia, under the guise of winter exercises . . ."

Jill turned to Landau. She had to crane her neck to talk to him, but the inconvenience never entered her mind. "Alex, do you think they're going to do it this time?"

He shook his head. "Madmen, all of them. Insanity. It comes from heavy metal pollutants in the air—they cause brain damage."

"Be serious," Jill insisted. The people around them began to glare and shush them.

Landau took her by the arm and started pushing through the crowd. "I am being serious. It begins to look as if the end of the world is really at hand."

Jill felt a shudder go through her. She let Landau lead her out of the crowd, then toward the power ladder that went down to the living quarters. He slid his arms around her and pulled her close.

"If we have only a few days, little one, let us use them wisely."

By the time he got back to his office Kinsman realized that he could not face the evening alone. He called Diane and asked her to dinner.

In the phone's small picture screen, she seemed genuinely happy to hear from him. "Dinner will be fine. Why don't you come over to my place?"

He hesitated. "You're probably busy enough . . ."

With a smile, she said, "Don't be silly. I like to cook."

And she cooked quite well, Kinsman decided. Lunar food consisted almost entirely of home-grown vegetables, a precious smattering of chicken, pork, and rabbit, and an occasional luxury item such as fish or spices from Earth. Diane's dinner consisted almost entirely of soybeans in various disguises, plus a dessert of barbaric splendor: cherries jubilee.

Kinsman had brought one of his rare bottles of Burgundy, and they were savoring the last of it when Diane told him her news.

"Harry Pierce is going back home on the shuttle next week."

Kinsman felt his eyebrows rise. "He told you that?"

She nodded.

"He hasn't sent through a request yet."

"He will. He wants to get back to his family. All this talk of emergencies and war has him scared."

"He'd be smarter to bring his family up here."

"That's not the way he sees it," Diane said. "He wants to go home. And he's going to recommend me to take his place."

Kinsman felt shock. "You?"

"Me."

"But you've just come up here . . ."

She looked at him steadily. "He's going to recommend me. But the recommendation needs the base commander's approval. Will you turn it down?"

Trying to suppress a frown, Kinsman heard his own voice say, "Is that why you invited me over here? To cement the deal?"

Instead of getting angry, Diane broke into a grin. "You're still the total chauvinist, aren't you? You think I got Pierce's recommendation in bed."

"Did you?"

"That's none of your damned business," Diane replied, still looking smug. "But Harry was a fan of mine, you know, back Earthside. He collected my records."

"A patron of the arts."

"And it might further interest you to know," Diane continued haughtily, "that my aptitude scores and work records rate me higher than anyone else in the comm section —anyone who's staying here, that is," she finished more soberly.

He nodded. "A lot of them are going to want to go back home. Damned fools."

"You can't blame them, Chet."

"They'd be a lot safer here," he said.

Diane shook her head. "That's just logic. You're dealing with emotions."

"Panic."

"Very close to it," she agreed.

"What about you?" he asked. "What about your daughter?"

"I don't know what to do," Diane said. "Could I get a few days off to return to Arizona and bring my daughter here?"

"You could ask the base commander for an emergency leave," Kinsman said. Before she could speak he added, "But you won't get it. You're going to stay here, Diane. Have your daughter sent here; I'll okay that."

"But she's too young to travel by herself."

"I can get an Aerospace Force officer to bring her up here. But you're not going back Earthside," Kinsman said. "It's too dangerous. The balloon could go up any minute. You're staying here."

"Whether I want to or not?" Her eyes locked on his.

He nodded. "That's right. Whether you want to or not. Now that you're here I'm not going to let you go."

Monday 6 December 1999: 0345 hrs UT

KINSMAN PULLED HIMSELF up to a sitting position on the bed. He stared into the darkness of Diane's bedroom, running his tongue across his lower teeth. They felt gritty.

She turned beside him. "You're not sleeping?"

"No."

"What's the matter?" Her voice sounded hollow, as if she were stifling a yawn.

"Can't sleep," he said simply.

She sat up beside him. He could smell the musky odor from their lovemaking. "You're really worried about this war emergency?"

"Shouldn't I be?"

"They've had these crises before. It'll blow away."

"Not this time."

She put her hand on his back. "You don't think they're really crazy enough to start throwing nuclear bombs around, do you?"

"This time it's for real." He turned toward her, and could barely make out her face in the shadows. The only light in the room came from the digital clock built into the wall alongside the bed. "I'm going to try to talk Pierce out of leaving. I'll tell him to bring his family up here, instead."

"You really think it's that serious?"

"We're going to declare our independence from Earth. Leonov and I. I want as much of everybody's family as possible to be here when the shit hits the fan. Is there somebody back Earthside who can take your daughter to Cape Canaveral?"

"I don't know." Diane's voice was a frightened whisper.

"I'm hoping that our declaration of independence—and cutting off the supplies to the space stations—will throw a monkey wrench into their war preparations."

"Will the Russians go along . . . ?"

"Pete's saying no, but he means yes. We'll work it out."

"And if you don't?"

He shrugged. "At least we'll have brought as many families up here as we can. We'll survive here."

"Is that why you never went back to Earth once you got here? You've been worrying about this moment?"

Kinsman looked off into the darkness. "I never thought of it. Not consciously, anyway. Maybe you're right. Maybe I have been getting myself ready for this."

"Then your medical record is faked?"

He turned back toward her. "How do you know about my medical record?"

Her voice sounded faintly amused. "I have access to the personnel computer."

"H'mm."

"There's nothing secret about your file, is there?"

"No . . ." But he felt all the old fears welling up inside him.

"The file does go blank, just as Dr. Faraffa said. It makes you very mysterious."

He did not reply.

"And there's a medical notation about a heart condition."

"Officially," Kinsman explained slowly, "I'm supposed to have a heart condition that makes a full Earth gravity dangerous for me. It's only a little hypertension, but Jill Meyers wrote it into my file so that I can stay here in Selene indefinitely."

"Officially," Diane murmured.

"Unofficially," he went on, "it's because I don't want to give Murdock or any of the Earthside brass a chance to call me back and keep me down there. I decided a long time ago that this is where I want to be. This is my home."

He could sense Diane shaking her head. "So those are the official and unofficial reasons. Now what are the real reasons?"

The fear was still inside him, but it felt strangely muted, distant, fading.

"Chet," Diane said, tracing a finger along the length of his thigh, "you haven't told me anything you wouldn't tell Pat Kelly or one of your other buddies. We've known each other a long time. I don't care about your politics or your Air Force brass. I want to know what's going on inside your head."

"Why?"

"I've never been able to figure you out," she admitted. "And now I want to. I've got to. I need to know everything about you. Everything."

A picture of Samson and Delilah flashed through his mind. "You want to know why I haven't gone back Earthside for five years."

Her answer was so immediate it startled him. "I want to know what you're afraid of."

"It's too beautiful," he said. "And too ugly. It's too big and exciting, and too small and crowded. It's . . ."

"It's home," she said for him.

He nodded. "Right. Everybody up here knows that. All the permanent Luniks. We feel like exiles, no matter how much we tell each other that Selene is better than New York or Moscow or London or Tokyo. It *is* better up here! That's the hell of it. We have more freedom, more food and energy, even more living space per capita than most Earth cities. A better, more intelligent society . . ."

"But Earth is home."

"The elephants' graveyard," Kinsman said. "If I spent a few days on Earth—especially if I got out into whatever's left of the countryside, saw a blue sky with clouds, or a hill covered with grass, trees . . ."

"They're mostly covered with housing developments."

"No they're not. Not by a long shot. I can see them from here, through the 'scopes. Montana, the Canadian Rockies, the Mongolian grasslands—there are still herds of horses running wild out there! And the oceans! If I stood on a beach and watched the breakers coming in . . ."

He stopped. His voice had risen. He was losing control.

Calmer, he said, "You don't have to worry about Pierce staying. I know him. He'll take the shuttle and go back to his family, no matter what I tell him. He'll head for the elephants' graveyard to die, all right."

"And we'll stay here."

"Right."

"We'll survive."

"Yes."

Diane sighed. "We're the strong ones, aren't we?"

"I wish I knew," he said.

"Are we going to have a life together, Chet?"

He looked away from her and mumbled again, "I wish I knew."

"What's the secret, Chet?"

Don't act surprised; you knew she was going to dig that deep, he told himself. For a long moment he was silent, trying to identify the feelings swirling inside him: anger? fear? pain?

"Whatever it is," Diane said softly, "it won't hurt half so much after you've shared it."

How do you know you can trust her? he asked himself. You've known her almost all your life and yet you hardly know her at all.

But he heard himself saying, "It was on an orbital mission, years ago. Before we started cooperating with the Russians, before we came back to the Moon. I was inspecting one of their satellites . . ."

His mind detached from his body. He watched himself numbly reciting the ancient story, sitting there in bed beside this beautiful woman and opening himself to her as he had never opened himself to anyone in his life.

"It was a big mother, just launched. Our intelligence people were afraid it might be an orbital bomb. The cosmonaut came up in a separate capsule while I was in the midst of examining their satellite. We fought—like a couple of sea elephants barging into each other. We didn't have any real weapons. We just pawed at each other."

He was floating again. Weightless.

"I could have backed off and gotten back to my own spacecraft, but I stayed and fought. Very patriotic. Very full of righteous wrath. I fought. I wanted to fight. I pulled out her airhose. I killed her."

"Her?"

Nodding, seeing her face in the bulbous helmet behind the heavily tinted visor, screaming silently, going rigid.

"I didn't know it was girl." His voice was as dead as she was. "Not until I had already ripped out her air line. That's when I got close enough to see into her helmet."

He stopped.

"And you've been carrying around this load of guilt about it ever since." Diane took one of his hands in both of hers.

"I swore to myself that I'd never kill anyone again . . . I wouldn't let them make me kill anyone . . ."

"Chet, it wasn't your fault."

"Of course it was. *I* fought the cosmonaut. I *wanted* to kill! I wanted to rip the sonofabitch's airhose out of his helmet. I didn't have to. But I wanted to."

"And you didn't know it was a woman."

"No. How could I?"

Diane started to say something, but he went on, "Now I've got to convince Leonov that he can trust us, can trust *me*. With this thing sticking in my guts. And he probably knows about it; they have intelligence files on it. How can he trust me? How can he trust any one of us?"

"But you trust him, don't you?"

"He never killed any of us."

Diane asked, "Had you killed other people, before, when you were flying combat missions in fighter planes?"

"Never. I never even touched the firing button."

"And if it had been a male cosmonaut," she went on, "would you feel so guilty about it?"

He stared at her. "No, I guess not."

"Why not?"

"I don't know," he said vaguely. "Men expect to fight, I guess. It's different . . ."

366

"You've let this thing hang around your neck for how long now?"

He shrugged. "Ten years, just about."

"That's long enough," Diane said firmly. "It's over. It's done with. You can't bring her back. And it wasn't your fault, to begin wi—"

"I've had all the psychology lectures," he snapped. "It *was* my fault. Nobody else's."

"So you've got a built-in excuse for keeping a wall around yourself and not taking any chances on getting hurt again."

"*Me* get hurt?"

"Yes, you! You're not worried about some Russian woman you never knew. You're worried about Chester Arthur Kinsman, worried that people won't like you if they knew you killed somebody. Worried that Leonov won't be your buddy anymore. That's what's eating at you. Not her. She's been dead for ten years."

"Don't tell me what's churning my guts!"

"Chet," Diane said more softly, leaning her head against his bare chest, "you lost control, didn't you? For the first time in your life you let your emotions take over."

"And committed murder."

"So ever since then you've kept yourself all bottled up, kept your emotions under lock and key."

He nodded silently. Diane was right, he knew.

"That's why you're so afraid to let your emotions loose again, isn't it?"

Kinsman felt tears in his eyes. "I can't, Diane. Even when I try, even in bed—I can't let myself go."

"You're a very good lover," she said.

"I'm good at the mechanics, maybe, but the emotion isn't there," he whispered, admitting it to himself more than to her. "I'm just going through the motions, conscious of every move I make."

"You could have fooled me." Diane giggled.

He smiled in the darkness. "Yeah, but I can't fool *me*."

Diane reached up and kissed him lightly on the lips. "My poor Chet. Even when I first met you, you were the most self-contained guy I had ever seen. All these years I couldn't figure you out."

"So now you know."

"I'm beginning to understand you." Diane sounded pleased. "I'm beginning to think maybe I can get through the wall you've built around yourself. If you let me."

"And what happens then?" he heard himself ask.

"Maybe I can help you to be happy, Chet. Maybe you can help me to be, too."

"That would be good," he said. Then he realized, "Oh Christ!"

"What?" Diane sounded startled. "What is it?"

"Pete. I'll have to admit the whole thing to him, too."

"Pete?"

"Leonov."

"Leonov." Diane's voice went low and calm and measured, "Yes, you've got to tell Leonov about it."

He felt hollow inside. No longer angry. Not even fearful. Empty. Nothing was there but a dull, distant ache.

"I don't know if I can," he said.

"You can."

"It's not that easy. Admitting it to you—even admitting it to Pete—won't exorcise the demon."

Diane put her hand on his cheek. It felt cool and soft to him. "It will always be with you, Chet," she said. "You'll never get rid of it completely. But you can't let it stand in your way. You have important things to do, and you can't let this keep you from doing them."

He knew she was right. Still, it scared him.

Pierce's request for a transfer was on Kinsman's desk when he got to his office that morning. He called the communications chief and tried briefly, perfunctorily, to argue him out of it. Pierce was politely adamant. And he recommended Diane Lawrence to take over his position.

Tight-lipped, Kinsman agreed. Pierce smiled and thanked him.

Leaning back in his desk chair, Kinsman punched a button on his desktop keyboard and an Earthside newscast filled the main wall screen. The view was of the speaker's podium in the General Assembly chamber of the UN building in New York. The Soviet delegate was fulminating, glaring at the Americans sitting in the front row, his brows knit angrily, arms gesticulating. The interpretation was being spoken in a young woman's British voice as calm and flatly unemotional as Selene's computer:

". . . the capitalist imperialists were obviously guilty of invading territory that was clearly marked by representatives of the USSR, thereby deliberately provoking the incident. This aggression was rightfully repelled, as American aggression has been repelled by freedom-loving peoples all over the globe."

There was a commotion and the TV camera swung to the American desk, where the chief delegate was on his feet bellowing, "Mr. Chairman, how long must we listen to this pack of lies and distortions? There can be no meaningful resolution . . ."

The Russian speaker pounded the podium with his fists and shouted something unintelligible. The entire American delegation came to its feet, yelling.

Kinsman watched, stunned, while the cameras panned across the huge chamber. It looked as if a riot was about to break out. Shouting, screaming, arm-waving. The only person who remained in his seat was the Chairman, up at his desk above the podium. A slim, dark Latin American with big sad eyes, he merely sat there shaking his head.

The last, best hope of mankind, Kinsman thought. He snapped off the newscast and sat staring at the blank screen for a moment. Then he got up from his desk.

Better make the rounds, he told himself. He decided to start with the water factory.

He spent half the morning there, listening to Ernie Waterman complaining about how difficult everything was, over the noise of the construction crews. Yet they were making considerable progress, Kinsman saw. The dour-faced engineer was cautious to the point of being morose, but Kinsman knew that Selene would have plenty of water for all its needs, even if those needs suddenly doubled.

The water factory was actually half an ore-processing plant and half a water-purification facility. The rock crushers dwarfed human scale, taking in fresh loads of ore from the mining crawlers that came from as far north as the Straight Wall and as far south as Fra Mauro. Kinsman clambered over the big crushers, feeling the rumble of their heavy machinery in his bones. This was the most expensive equipment in

Selene, hauled up from Earthside over a three-year period. Selene's technicians could maintain and repair them but it would be years before they could even attempt to build such machines on their own.

Following the clattering conveyor belts that carried the pulverized rock, Kinsman came to the electric arcs humming steadily inside their stainless steel jackets. From here onward the factory was a maze of plumbing: pipes overhead, underfoot, lining kilometers of tunnels, sweating beads of precious ice-cold water no matter how much insulation the engineers put on them. Kinsman stepped over, ducked under, squeezed between the pipelines that carried Selene's lifeblood.

Waterman dogged behind him, leaning on his canes, unhappily cataloging his real and projected problems all the way through the factory. Finally, as they walked through the relatively quiet corridors of the factory's office and control area, Waterman said:

"I still don't see what all the rush is about. I wish you'd let me ease off; some of these guys have been working double shifts. They're getting tired enough to start causing accidents."

Kinsman stopped in front of the window that looked in on the computer control section. Watching the nearly unattended machine's lights flickering in some internally meaningful pattern, he answered, "Ernie, we've got a yellow alert slapped on us. We've got to be prepared for a real emergency. Earthside might suddenly need double, triple the rocket fuels we send them now."

"Then we ought to be beefing up the electrolysis facility, not the water production."

"First things first," Kinsman said. "Hydrogen and oxygen propellants come from water. If they want more rocket propellants we have to increase the basic water supply."

"Yeah, eventually, but in an emergency . . ."

"First things first," Kinsman repeated. The tautologist's handbook, he thought. When in doubt, fall back on slogans.

"But what about the interconnects with Lunagrad?" Waterman asked. "Why in hell do we have a full crew working to connect them with our increased supply lines when we're just going to have to cut them off when the fighting starts?"

"There isn't going to be any fighting," Kinsman said. "Not here."

Waterman's mouth hung open for a moment. Then he asked, "Whaddaya mean?"

"Just what I said, Ernie."

"I don't get it."

"You will," Kinsman said. "You will."

And he left Waterman standing in the corridor, scratching his head unhappily.

Kinsman worked his way through the underground farms, the workshops and laboratories, the central computer section, the communications center. He did this almost every day, but in no set pattern. Say hello, look for problems, listen to gripes or suggestions. Maintain a high profile, good visibility. Everyone knew him. More important, he got to know everyone in Moonbase, even the ninety-dayers.

The hospital section was always the quietest, most relaxed, and sanest part of his rounds. As soon as he stepped through the big double doors of the hospital lobby area Kinsman could feel himself calm down. Soft pastel walls, soft voices—even the intercoms and P.A. speakers were muted. Pleasant place to be, he thought, as long as you don't let them get their hands on you.

But today was different.

Two nurses scurried past him, pushing small wheeled consoles. They looked worried, and they went by so fast that Kinsman did not notice just what kind of equipment they were rolling. They disappeared down a corridor that led off from the lobby. A harried-looking young doctor hustled after them.

The P.A. system came to life. A man's voice, sharp and unusually loud, called urgently, "Dr. Meyers. Dr. Meyers. To the ICU immediately!"

The intensive care unit, thought Kinsman. My God, Baliagorev! He sprinted down the same corridor that the nurses and doctor had taken. That's all we need, for him to conk out on us. Talk about international incidents.

He flashed past the ICU monitoring station, where a male nurse spun around from his bank of display screens and yelled, "Hey, you can't . . ." Then, recognizing Kinsman, he said weakly, "Sir?"

Kinsman saw a huddle of white uniforms ahead of him. He skidded to a stop, then shouldered past the outermost ring of nurses.

"I will not talk to any of you enema-wielding vampires! I want Dr. Meyers!"

It was Baliagorev. A wisp of a man, feather-frail. But his voice was like iron. He was pale, face seamed with age. A dozen tubes and wires connected to various parts of his body. Someone had cranked his floater bed up to a sitting position.

One of the consoles that the nurses had wheeled in was a videocassette recorder, Kinsman saw. The Russian reached toward it.

"Don't! You'll pull your IV loose!"

"Then take it away!" Baliagorev roared. "When I want to be entertained by brainless videotapes, I will tell you. Where is Dr. Meyers? Where is she?"

Pushing his way through the remaining knot of nurses and the young doctor, Kinsman said, "She'll be here shortly, sir. I'm Chet Kinsman, the commander here. I'm glad to see that you're feeling so strong."

"Bah! I feel miserable," Baliagorev snapped, in impeccable English. "How would you feel, wired up like a marionette?"

"Well, I . . ."

The Russian shook his head. "I am a simple man. I can accept the fact that my countrymen regard me as a revisionist fool. I can accept the fact that my own heart has turned traitor on me. I can even accept the fact that I am surrounded by Yankees who have all the cultural sensitivities of a Latvian smuggler. All I want is to see Dr. Meyers. Why can't this one simple request . . ."

"Here I am, Maestro."

Kinsman turned and saw the others clear a path for Jill. Behind her strode the Russian doctor, Landau. Both of them had funny expressions on their faces: happy, but —embarrassed?

"Ahhh, Jilyushka, my ministering angel. Where have you been?" Baliagorev's tone changed completely. He went from truculence to grandfatherly sweetness in an eyeblink.

Jill grinned at him. "You know, Maestro, there *are* other patients in this hospital, and—"

"Nonsense! You were off in some corner kissing this bearded oaf."

Landau's face went beet-red. Jill giggled. Kinsman turned to the other nurses and said quietly, "I think the emergency is over."

They started filing out of the room, whispering among themselves.

"Don't you go," Baliagorev called to Kinsman. "I have a request to make of you."

Kinsman stopped at the open door and looked back at the Russian.

"I should like to stay here in the American sector, rather than return to Lunagrad. At least for a while."

Kinsman did not know whether to laugh or frown. "I thought we Yankees had the cultural sensitivities of Latvian smugglers."

Completely unflustered, Baliagorev answered, "When you have spent as much time as I have in the tyrannical grips of hospital orderlies and nurses, you learn that there is really only one way to treat them—with contempt. However," his tone softened, "I sincerely wish to remain here."

"Well . . ." There's something crafty about this old man, Kinsman realized. "May I ask why?"

Baliagorev shifted his gaze to Landau momentarily, then looked back at Kinsman. His eyes were ice-blue. "Put it down as the whim of an old man. The women here are much prettier. The nurses at Lunagrad are *awful*—huge beasts, ungainly, hopeless."

"That's not true," Landau murmured.

"Bah! Why should I hide it? I want political asylum. I was seeking asylum in France when my countrymen arrested me and carted me to a hospital in Siberia. A *psychiatric* hospital! That is where my heart broke."

Kee-rist! Just what we need. Kinsman kept his eyes off Landau as he replied, "This is a very touchy time to ask for political asylum, you know."

Baliagorev pursed his thin, bluish lips.

Jill cut in, "There will be no discussions of politics of any sort as long as my patient is in intensive care." Turning sternly to Baliagorev, she shook a stubby finger at him. "We haven't brought you back from clinical death just so you can kill yourself with excitement over politics!"

Landau broke into a laugh. "She's right, Nicholai Ivanovich. This is no time to discuss politics."

The old man raised his wispy eyebrows. "Very well. You have performed your miracle, and you don't want your Lazarus to suffer a relapse, eh? But will *you* be discussing politics with our countrymen, Alexsei Alexandrovich?"

The Russian doctor shook his head gravely. "No. I promise you."

"You can trust Alexsei," Jill said.

"I'm sure *you* can trust him," Baliagorev muttered. Then, with a crooked grin that threatened to turn into a leer, "Admit it, Jilyushka, you were necking with this bearded rascal, eh?"

"As a matter of fact, yes, I was," Jill admitted cheerfully. "And if you don't stop teasing, I'll put nothing but male nurses in here with you."

The Russian hesitated only for a moment. "H'mm . . . if they are young and tender . . ."

"You're impossible!"

Kinsman managed to say, "All right. Listen, Jill, Alexsei: your patient will have to stay here several more days, won't he?"

"At least a week," Landau answered.

"I could arrange to have a relapse," Baliagorev said.

Kinsman raised a hand. "Let's allow things to work themselves out for a week." Before they could argue or object, he ducked back out through the doorway and headed down the corridor.

But he heard the ballet master's voice saying gently, "Now then, Jilyushka, there is no reason why you could not become a first-rate dancer here on the Moon. With this low gravity, and me to teach you, we could work miracles."

Kinsman shook his head and wished that he felt good enough to smile.

The corridor lights had just turned down to their evening level as Kinsman padded from his office toward his quarters. Got to talk to Leonov again, he was telling himself. Maybe he can get his kids to visit him here before—

"Chet! Chet, wait up, will you?" It was Jill Meyers

scampering after him. She had a child's wide grin on her face.

He smiled back at her as she ran up and said breathlessly, "He's proposed to me!"

"That dirty old man?"

"No, not Baliagorev," Jill replied, beaming. "Alexsei! We're going to get married!"

Something inside Kinsman went cold.

"You're invited to the party," Jill was saying. "It's already started, over at my quarters."

"Married," he repeated.

"Yes! 'Here Comes the Bride' and all that stuff! Isn't it wild?"

"Why?"

Her grin froze. "Why what?"

"Why does he want to marry you?"

She planted her hands on her hips. "I *presume* it's because he can't live without me, and wants to spend the rest of his life with me. A lifetime commitment—but you wouldn't understand that, would you?" Her eyes were snapping at him.

"Dammitall, Jill, you know what I mean. You two can live together without having a legal contract drawn up. Why talk about marriage? What's behind it?"

"Argh! Chet Kinsman, you *stupid*, insensitive . . ."

He reached out and put two fingertips over her mouth. "Jill, you and I have known each other too long to pull punches. He loves you, okay. I can believe that. You love him. Fine. But where does marriage come into it? Does he plan to try to become an American citizen?"

Jill pushed away his hand, but her tone was quieter, less angry. "I . . . we haven't even discussed it. I thought I'd move into Lunagrad with him."

"Uh-huh. And suppose he figures out that he wants asylum, like Baliagorev . . . or that he's scared the Russian security people will nail him for the old man's defection?"

"Chet, that's a shitty thing to say!"

"I know. I'm a bastard. But I'd rather see me hurt your feelings than have him break you in half—him, or anybody else."

"I love him, Chet. I want to be with him wherever he goes."

A lifetime commitment, even if their lives only last

another week, Kinsman thought. "Jill, you can *be* with him. Hell, you've been living together for the past few days, haven't you?"

"Few days?" she echoed, wide-eyed. "We're talking about a pair of lifetimes."

"You two can live together for as long as you want to," Kinsman said. "But when he brings up the idea of marriage, that gets into legal and political problems."

"Chet, you're talking like a big brother. I'm old enough to take my own risks."

He shook his head. "Don't rush things, Jill. There could be—"

"You can't stop us," she snapped.

"Yes, I can. Or Leonov could. You know that."

Clenching her tiny fists, Jill said in a barely controlled whisper, "Chet, just because you can't work out your own head well enough to make a lasting commitment to anything or anybody doesn't mean that I'm as scared and screwed-up as you are. I love Alexsei and I'm going to marry him."

"On the strength of a few days' living with him."

"We've known each other for three years, off and on. Why do you think he came up to Lunagrad?"

Kinsman actually took a step backward at this news. Jill came after him, a furious little sparrow pursuing a confused cat. "You must think I'm some brainless child that you've got to protect and watch out for. Well, if either one of us needs a keeper, *Colonel* Kinsman, it's you! You haven't got the brains to realize when somebody loves you. But I do! And I'm going to enjoy his love as fully as I can. Understand *that*, big brother!"

Suddenly Kinsman found himself laughing. "Okay, okay," he said, putting up his hands as if to fend her off. "So I'm a suspicious bastard."

"You're an idiot."

"That too."

"And, and . . ."

"I'm trying to protect you," he offered.

"I'll protect myself, thank you. And if what you think is true, I'd rather face it than spend one minute less with Alexsei than I need to."

"Okay," Kinsman said. "Message received and understood."

"All right."

"Uh . . . am I still invited to the party?"

"You'll behave yourself?" She was starting to grin again.

"I'll be the model of decorum."

"No politics?"

"I'll just sit in a corner and won't even open my mouth—except to sip a little medicinal brandy."

"Then you can come."

"Thank you, ma'am." He bowed. "I'll just run to my quarters and change into my best coveralls."

She sniffed at him, then suddenly threw her arms around his neck and squeezed mightily. She had to stand on tiptoe to manage it.

"Oh, Chet, I'm so damned happy! Don't spoil it for me."

"I won't," he said. But he was already wondering. Will Pete Leonov be at the party?

He was not. A few Russian medics were there, crammed in among the crowd that bulged Jill's two-room quarters. But Leonov and all the other Soviet military and administrative personnel were conspicuously absent.

The place was impossibly jammed. The party was already overflowing out into the corridor by the time Kinsman got there. He had brought a bottle of Earthside scotch with him. Everyone brought their own bottles to these parties. When Kinsman had taken the scotch from his kitchenette cabinet he saw that it was the last one and he told himself, Got to get the guys to bring me reinforcements on the next grocery run. Then he realized that there might not be another replenishment mission; the shuttle flights from Earth might stop at any moment. No, he told himself, trying to calm the fear burning inside him. They'll take a few weeks to bring things to a boil. Ten days, at least.

Kinsman wormed his way through the crowd, holding his bottle over his head. He realized he could never spot tiny Jill in this mob, so he looked for Landau. He found him in the bedroom, standing to one side of a slightly smaller knot of people who were standing, sitting on the bed, slouching on other pieces of furniture, squatting cross-legged on the floor.

Jill was beside Landau, Kinsman saw as he made his way through the noisy conversations and laughter. Her back was to the doorway, so she could not see him approaching. He wrapped his free arm around her, pulled her to him, and kissed her mightily.

"Congratulations," he said at last. "I didn't get to say that before." Releasing her, he put his hand out to Landau. "And congratulations to you. You're getting the best girl there is."

"I know," the Russian said seriously. "Thank you."

Within minutes Kinsman was sitting on the floor, a plastic cup full of scotch in one hand, his back propped against somebody's knees, listening to a discussion that was getting steadily drunker and less coherent. Diane was nowhere in sight. He wondered if she had been invited to the party. Maybe she's on duty at the comm center?

Then Frank Colt pushed his way into the bedroom. For a moment he stood in the doorway, looking uncertain. At least he's wearing fatigues, Kinsman thought. Landau started to extend his hand. Jill reached up and put a hand on Colt's shoulder.

"Kiss me, I'm the bride-to-be."

Colt pecked at her, then shook hands with Landau. Before he could sit down, though, a swarthy lean-faced man sitting on the other side of the bed said loudly, "Here comes supermouth."

Kinsman started to say something, but Colt got there first. "Hey, it's a party—save the brain-damage stuff for later."

The guy was potted. Kinsman knew him slightly, a civilian engineer, one of Ernie Waterman's people. His name was . . . Kinsman searched his memory, then it clicked: Jerry Perotti.

"You been pretty mouthy all day long, Colt," Perotti said. "Why get shy with us here? Give us all the benefit of your keen military mouth."

"Stuff it," Colt snapped.

Everyone else in the room went silent. Kinsman's brain seemed to be working in slow motion. He panned across the room, looking at the faces of the people: surprised, amused, upset. Perotti looked sore. God knows what Frank did to him today. Colt himself looked tense but fully in control, almost smiling. The fastest gun in the West, facing yet another foolhardy challenger. I ought to stop this right here and now . . .

"No, I won't stuff it," Perotti was saying. "You and your goddamned gold braid. Who the hell do you think you are?"

Colt abruptly turned and took three strides into the bathroom. Before anyone had a chance to say or do anything he came out again and tossed a precious roll of toilet paper at Perotti, who automatically snatched it, one-handed, against his chest.

"Here, that's what assholes need," Colt said.

There was a split-second of shocked silence, then everyone broke up. They roared. Everyone but Perotti. He pushed himself to his feet in the midst of the laughing people, face darkening. He slammed the toilet-paper roll down on the bed and stomped out of the room. Colt stood back from the doorway and let him lurch past.

"Another notch on the ol' six-gun," Kinsman mumbled, suddenly realizing that the combination of lack of sleep, tension, and scotch had made him drunk already.

Colt spotted him and came over to squat on the floor beside him.

"What is there about you that makes people instantly want to give you a hard time?" Kinsman wondered aloud.

"Skin, man," said Colt.

"Oh, hell, Frank. There are dozens of blacks in Selene. We had a whole delegation from Chad last year. Nobody threw knives at them."

"Yassuh, but they's nice folks," Colt said in his Dixie yokel accent. "Me, I'm a sonofabitch. If you're white and a sonofabitch, nobody hardly notices. But if you're black, it all hangs out."

The party glided on. Kinsman drank slowly, steadily, maintaining a soft glow that blurred the edges of reality just enough to make everything pleasant.

In the apartment's main room the drifting currents of humanity had washed Pat Kelly and Ernie Waterman into the same corner. They made an incongruous pair: the tall, hound-sad engineer and the stubby, rabbit-faced major.

"Just how serious is this yellow alert?" Waterman was asking.

Kelly rubbed at his nose with a hand chilled from holding an iced drink. "About as serious as they come. I've been working all day on the logistics programming."

"I mean, shouldn't we be pretty damned careful about these Russians? They're right in our laps, for Chrissakes."

"I know," Kelly said. "I warned Chet about it. And now he's got 'em in our hospital and marrying into our people."

Waterman shook his head dismally. "You know what he said to me? He said we're not going to fight up here. Like he was guaranteeing it."

"Yeah? That's what he told you?"

"That's exactly what he said. Now, how can he keep from fighting here? If the orders come through he has to obey them, don't he?"

"He sure does," Kelly said, "or somebody else will. That's why they brought Colt up here. It'd only take a one-line message to relieve Chet of command and put Colt in."

"That might not be such a bad thing," Waterman mused. "I like Chet, but . . ."

"I wouldn't worry about it," said Kelly, looking worried. "Chet's an easygoing guy, great to work for, likes to have everything friendly and relaxed. But when the orders come, he'll follow them. Don't you think otherwise. When we get right down to the nut, Americans will act like Americans and Russians will act like Russians. Friendships end once the missiles are launched."

"You think so?"

"You don't?"

Waterman shrugged. "He seems so damned determined to get the water factory's output up to the point where the Russians can use it. You think maybe he's planning to let them walk in here and take over?"

"What?" Kelly looked startled.

"Well, he says there won't be any fighting up here. The only way he can guarantee that is to let the Reds take over without firing a shot. Right?"

"That's crazy!"

"Maybe so, but do you see him making any plans to take over Lunagrad?"

"We've got contingency plans . . ."

"When's the last time *he* took a look at 'em?" Waterman asked.

Kelly hesitated, then, "No! Chet wouldn't do that. He's easygoing, but he's not a traitor."

"Maybe he don't see it as treason." The engineer waved a hand at the chattering crowd all around them. "Maybe he thinks that any kind of fighting up here would kill everybody, so he won't fight, no matter what."

"Like the peaceniks back home, before they were all rounded up?"

"Uh-huh."

"Jesus Christ," Kelly muttered. "I sure as hell hope that's not what's on his mind."

Waterman looked as if he were about to cry. "It could be. He could be ready to sell us all down the river, just to avoid fighting."

"Hell! You know what that means, don't you?" Kelly looked genuinely distressed now.

"What?"

"I'm gonna have to go to Frank Colt and get *him* to review all our emergency contingency plans—behind Chet's back."

"If that's what's gotta be done . . ."

Kelly grimaced. "I hate to go around Chet. He's a nice guy and all that." His frown deepened. "And I hate like hell having to work with Colt."

"If you've got to, you've got to," Waterman said.

Kelly nodded unhappily. "I've got to."

More people jammed into the party. Others left. For a long time Kinsman could see neither Jill nor Landau in the roaring, jammed, body-heated apartment. He spotted Kelly and Waterman talking solemnly together off in a corner, looking grimmer with each word. Then Jill and the Russian appeared. The apartment started to get a little less crowded. People were drifting homeward.

Kinsman threaded his way carefully through the living

room and back into the bedroom, marveling at how well and steadily he could walk. Colt lay sprawled on the bed now with a bosomy redhead alongside him, propped on a pair of pillows. She was wearing a wine-red party dress, low in front and slit-skirted. One of the newcomers, Kinsman realized.

Jill and Landau came into the bedroom, the Russian standing protectively beside her.

Colt gave them a long look. "Ain't gonna be easy for you two, y'know," he said. His drink was perched precariously on his stomach, his hands were clasped behind his head. Only someone who knew him as well as Kinsman did would realize how drunk he was.

"I was married once to a girl who looked kinda light. She wasn't white, but try telling that to some drunk Florida rednecks." Colt's voice was absolutely flat, no emotion detectable. Like a pathologist reciting the details of an autopsy.

"We are intelligent people here," Landau said. "Jill and I can live in Lunagrad without difficulties."

"You mean your security people will let her in? Without worrying that she might be a spy? I just don't believe it."

Jill said, "We can live here."

"Then *I* have to try to find out if he's spying on *us*," Colt shot back.

"Come on, Frank," Kinsman said, knowing that his speech was slightly slurred. "Don't piss on the wedding cake."

Colt looked over at Kinsman. "Hey, man, you still up and around?"

"Well, it *is* a lot easier if I hold on to a wall or something."

Landau said, "Wait, this is serious. Suppose my government makes it impossible for Jill to live at Lunagrad? Could I take up residence here in Moonbase?"

" 'S'okay with me," Kinsman said, "but I don't think your own people would let you do it. Leonov had to break six hundred rules to let Baliagorev come over to have his goddamned life saved."

"But—"

"No buts," Colt said. "This is *very* serious. You guys

might have gotten along as friends up here so far, but things are changing very fast."

"Frank, old buddy," Kinsman said, holding himself as stiffly erect as he could manage, "I don't pull rank often, but I don't want this stupid crap to go any further." He turned to Landau. "Alex, husband-to-be of the woman who is virtually a sister to me, if you want to live here, you are welcome to. I am not going to permit this chickenshit from Earth to make a mess of things here. No way. Not now. Not ever. Not as long as I'm in command here."

Colt chuckled lazily. "That's a great way to make me commander of Moonbase, pal."

Kinsman found himself tottering down the corridor toward his own quarters with no idea of what time it was or how the well-built redhead got attached to his arm.

By concentrating so hard that it made his head hurt, he could remember the conversation with Colt and Jill and Landau. The tense silence that ended it. Going back to the bar in the living room and finding that all the scotch was gone. The girl popping up beside him . . .

With an effort, he focused his bleary eyes on her. Even in the unflattering overhead fluorescents of the chilly corridor she looked good. Young, soft, large of eye and full of lip. Big boobs. Her dress had slipped off one shoulder and her hair was disarrayed. She smelled of lost and forbidden memories: flower gardens and soft summer evenings.

She smiled up at him. "You got awfully quiet."

"I am old enough to be your father," he said, feeling stupid. "Just about."

"Oh, don't be silly," she said. "You're cute."

Cute? Holy shit. Cute! He scowled at her, but she only smiled all the more. *Diane doesn't show up at the party and I'm dragging teenagers home with me.*

"Cute," he muttered at her.

He knew why. He did not like it, but he knew. *Don't ever put yourself into a spot where your survival depends on one individual. Don't let yourself become so vulnerable to Diane or anyone else. Armor plate. Surround yourself with it. Otherwise it's too fucking easy to get shot down.*

"Cute," he grumbled at her again.

She laughed and slid her arm around his waist and snuggled closer as they walked.

What the hell, he thought. Maybe she's a good lay.

Tuesday 7 December 1999: 1025 hrs UT

"GOOD MORNING, CHEERFUL campers! And how's our peerless leader today?"

Through the haze of a throbbing headache Kinsman squinted up at Hugh Harriman. The little round man was smiling broadly and clasping something behind his back.

"Go away," Kinsman muttered.

"Now, now, don't be testy." Harriman was standing in the doorway of Kinsman's office. He walked all the way in and leaned over the couch slightly to peer into Kinsman's eyes.

"Nicely bloodshot," he pronounced. "Must have been a good party."

Kinsman leaned back on the couch and rested his aching skull against the cool stone wall. "It was quite a party, I'll grant you that." Then, remembering, "Why weren't you there? Where the hell were you last night?"

"I thought you'd never ask." Harriman plopped himself down on the couch beside Kinsman and revealed what he was holding: a thermos bottle. "But first," he said, unscrewing the cap, "try some of Old Doc Harriman's surefire hangover cure. Never fails."

Kinsman watched warily as Harriman poured a reddish liquid into the cup that had been the top of the thermos. He took the cup, but asked, "Aren't you having any?"

Harriman's eyes went round with innocence. "Suspicious this morning, aren't you? Well, if you insist." He hoisted the thermos in salute and put it to his lips.

Kinsman sipped from the cup. It had been a Bloody

Mary originally, that much he was sure of. But Harriman had added things to it. It tasted almost sweet, very smooth, very soothing.

"Not . . ."—his voice was a choked whisper—"not bad."

"Good! A little LSD never hurt anyone." Harriman seemed genuinely pleased. Wiping a bit of red foam from his mustache with the back of his hand, he went on, "Now, to answer your original question . . ."

"My question?"

"You *are* accelerating slowly this morning! You asked why I wasn't at the party last night."

"Oh, yeah." Kinsman could feel his whole nervous system vibrating like the strings of a harp that had been wedged into a supersonic wind tunnel.

"I was doing a bit of homework yesterday, and I got so engrossed in it that I stayed up all night. Haven't been to sleep yet."

Impressed, Kinsman said, "You look damned chipper for a guy who hasn't slept at all."

"That's because I've been stimulating my brain with creative thought, not soaking it in alcohol."

"Touché."

"Ah! A linguist. I had no idea. Well . . ." Harriman's face suddenly went completely serious. The smile vanished, the eyes became intense. "You realize, of course, that everybody in Selene knows you've been muttering about refusing to follow orders and declaring us independent of Earthside control."

"There are no secrets here," Kinsman admitted.

"Not the way you handle them! At any rate, I've been spending the past few days casually talking things over with lots of people—Americans, Russians, foreign visitors, permanent Luniks, ninety-dayers. I've also gone over the personnel records of most of the people here, their psychological profiles mainly . . ."

"How the hell did you get access . . . ?"

Harriman held up a pudgy hand. "You think you're the only one around here who has a way with women? After all, I'm considered a dashing and romantic figure by some of the weaker-minded broads. Besides, I told the kids in charge of the computer files that I wanted to search for people who might be interested in starting a university here. They fell for it."

Kinsman said only, "H'mm."

"It's your own fault, Chet. You run a very lax operation here. No wonder they sent Colt to tighten security."

"Don't tell me my troubles."

"All right. Near as I can compute it, about eighty percent of the permanent Luniks would support a move for independence. And the surprising thing is that the ninety-dayers are split about fifty-fifty. You can carry it off, friend, if you want to."

Kinsman shook his head, and immediately regretted it. The throbbing grew worse. "I've thought it over, Hugh. Declaring independence won't change things Earthside. They'll still start their war; all we'll be able to do is delay them."

Harriman blinked at him owlishly. "You mean you haven't figured it out? You're kidding! A brilliant military mind like yours? Not even Leonov has seen it?"

"Seen what?"

"How to make Selene independent and stop the friggin' war before it starts!"

Kinsman forgot his headache. He straightened up in the couch. "What the hell are you talking about?"

Harriman laughed. "My God! Are philosophers really the only people who can think?"

"Hugh . . ."

Running a hand over his bald pate, Harriman said, "I thought you had already worked it out for yourself."

"Worked *what* out?"

"Taking over the satellites."

"What?"

With a heavenward roll of his eyes, Harriman explained, "Look, neither the United States nor the Soviets has enough ABM satellites in orbit to provide a fully effective shield against the other side's missile attack. Right?"

"Not yet."

"How many satellites have to be on station for an orbital ABM network to be considered workable?"

"That's classified information, Hugh."

386

"So's my hairy ass! Anybody with a pencil and paper can figure it out, for Chrissakes! You want to be sure you've got several satellites over every possible launching area —including all the oceans—every minute of the day. If the satellites are in low orbit, which they are, to save on laser power, then you need between a hundred and a hundred-fifty to do the job. Right?"

With a grin, Kinsman said, "You're making the numbers, not me."

"All right, how many working satellites does the U.S. have in orbit right now?"

"Classified."

Harriman glared at him. "How many do the Russians have up?"

"Ask Leonov."

"How many are there between the two?"

Kinsman started to answer, then it struck him.

"Ah-hah!" Harriman crowed. "Dawn is breaking inside that murky skull. There are *already* more than a hundred satellites in orbit and in perfect working condition. Right? And if you and Leonov can grab *all* of them, Selene would have an ABM network that could prevent *anybody* from launching *anything*! Right?"

Kinsman heard himself say, "Including troop shuttles to take Selene away from us."

"Exactly!" Harriman said. "You get an *A*. Go to the head of the class."

Suddenly Kinsman was out of breath, winded as if he had sprinted through an obstacle course. He could feel his heart thumping inside his ribs. "Hugh, if we could do that . . ."

"It would guarantee Selene's independence, our freedom from attack, and it would prevent them from starting their war—at least, they wouldn't be able to launch missiles at each other."

"But . . ." Kinsman was still trying to catch his breath. "But to seize control of the ABM networks we'd have to take over the manned space stations."

"Right. Which is probably why you didn't think of the idea yourself."

"Why?"

"Simple psychology, friend," Harriman said. "Despite

your lofty military rank, you're not a violent man. You don't want to hurt anybody. You could see your way to declaring Selene independent because you don't think there'd be any fighting involved. But taking the space stations is another matter. Those guys in the station aren't Luniks. They'll fight you."

Kinsman nodded.

"It'll take bloodshed," Harriman said, very gravely. "There hasn't been a political movement in all of history that hasn't spilled blood. Dammit."

Pat Kelly had spent much of the morning searching for Frank Colt. After a fruitless couple of hours trying to get the computerized phone system to track him down or page him, Kelly finally left his cubbyhole office and the work he was supposed to be doing and set out himself to look for the black Lieutenant Colonel.

It was nearly noon when he found him, out at the catapult launching facility, at the extreme end of the longest tunnel in Selene. The facility was mainly underground, although the ten-kilometer-long catapult itself was up on the surface, its angled aluminum framework looking frail and spidery compared to the heavy construction of Earthside structures. Yet it still seemed strikingly bold and gleaming new against the tired ancient hills and worn pockmarked plain of the Sea of Clouds.

The control center was in a small surface dome. It looked rather like the control tower of a minor airport Earthside, mainly because it served much the same function. Instead of guiding aircraft into and out of an airport, however, this control center handled outgoing traffic only: the drone supply packages that were launched to the manned space stations in orbit near the Earth.

As Kelly stepped off the power ladder and onto the plastic-tiled floor of the dome, he saw Colt standing in the middle of the clustered desks and electronics consoles that lined the long curving windows across the way. The dome was dimly lit. In the shadows a dozen men and women were sitting tensed over their desktop control panels, watching the flickering computer readouts, listening to the commands and data updates through the pin-sized earphones they all wore.

Through the window Kelly could see a bulky wingless cylinder squatting at one end of the long catapult track. Colt stood at the opposite side of the dome, silent and unmoving, as the launch crew carried out the final stage of their operation in the cool, clipped tones of their profession.

"T minus thirty seconds and counting."

"Beta Station acknowledges."

"Sled power on."

"All track relays green."

"Fifteen seconds . . ."

Across the sweep of the control panels tiny lights were changing from amber to green, like a Christmas display. At the extreme right end of the curving row of consoles the ARM and FIRE lights of the launch controller still glared red. The controller herself sat with her back to Kelly, her eyes riveted to the panel lights.

"Internal power on."

"Terminal guidance and control green."

"Thrusters green."

"Ten seconds . . ."

The launch controller manually lifted the two switch covers with her right hand, and the two red lights went amber.

"Automatic sequencer on."

"Energize full track."

"Beta acknowledges time and recovery angle."

"All systems green."

"Three . . . two . . . one . . . launch!"

The squat cylinder became a blur and disappeared in less than an eyeblink. The entire crew glanced up at the now-empty track.

"Radar?" the launch controller asked, cool and professional.

From across the row of consoles came another woman's voice, "Through the keyhole."

The launch controller yanked the earpin out and stood up. "Okay, well done. But nobody moves until Beta Station picks her up and acknowledges the trajectory."

They leaned back in their chairs. A few pulled out cigarettes and lit up.

The spell broken, Kelly walked grimly toward Colt. "Frank, can I talk to . . ."

Colt spun around at the sound of his name. He looked surprised, then puzzled, then surprised again as Kelly came close enough to be recognized in the dim lighting. "Pat? What're you doing up here?"

"Looking for you."

"Yeah?" Colt's eyes narrowed with suspicion. "What for?"

Kelly felt the glacial chill of Colt's distrust. He wanted to turn and run, but knew that he could not. "I've got to talk to you. Someplace where it's quiet."

Colt gave him a long look. "I'm here checking on the defensibility of the launch center. Be easy for the Reds to knock this place off—all they'd need's a couple bazookas."

Kelly fought down a surge of anger. The black man was right, he knew that. "But they'd have to trek over the surface to get here," he pointed out. "The tunnel can be defended pretty easily."

"Hey man," Colt grinned, "you're making noises like a soldier!"

"And anybody moving on the surface is damned vulnerable," Kelly finished, ignoring the thrust.

"They're vulnerable if you know they're coming and you realize their intentions," Colt said.

"We could set up perimeter alarms—lasers, low-power ultraviolet, so they wouldn't be seen."

Colt raised his eyebrows. "Yeah, that'd work, wouldn't it?"

Damned right it would work, superhero, Kelly said to himself. Aloud, he repeated, "I've got to talk to you. Privately."

With a glance around at the chatting, relaxing launch crew, Colt said, "Okay, let's go back down the tunnel. I want to check on how secure the heat and power lines are, anyway."

As they stepped onto the power ladder they heard one of the launch crew sing out, "Beta's acquired our bird on their radar—on trajectory, time and angle on the double-oh."

Down in the long chilly tunnel, in the glare of the overhead fluorescents, Colt's skin looked bluish. Otherworldly. "Okay, what's this all about?" he asked Kelly again.

Pat suddenly wished he were somewhere else. Change

the subject. Forget the whole thing. But he heard himself saying, "It's Chet. He's been making some damned broad hints about refusing to fight, if and when the time comes."

Colt's expression turned sour. "Yeah, yeah. So what else is new?"

"Frank, I think he means it. He really will refuse to obey orders—maybe he'll turn us over to the Russians!"

Colt raised his hands as if to grab Kelly's coverall front. "Listen," he snapped. "Chet may be a do-gooder and an easygoing fool, but he's not a traitor. Understand that? He won't sell us out. He might need a little push when the time comes. That's why I'm here."

They walked for several moments in silence, listening to their shoes clicking against the rough stone flooring of the tunnel.

Finally Kelly said, "You and Kinsman have been friends for a long time. But I've been looking over his shoulder for the past couple of months. I know what he's been saying and what he's thinking. He's ready to do *anything* rather than fight. He's been palling around with Leonov and letting Russian nationals into our side of the hospital. He's closer to *them* than he is to our own people Earthside."

Colt said nothing.

"If he . . . fails to obey orders," Kelly went on, "he won't think of it as treason. He'll think he's doing the right thing. But he'll be crippling America's chances of winning the war."

"You're bringing your wife and kids up here, aren't you?" Colt asked suddenly.

Kelly stopped walking. "What's that got to do with it?"

Shrugging, Colt replied, "I'd think that you'd be on Chet's side of this. You anxious to have a shooting war up here, with your family on the way?"

"They'll be safer here than Earthside," Kelly said. "But I'd rather have them in the middle of a battle here than hand them over to the Soviets. We're Americans. We're ready to fight for freedom if we have to."

"Ready to die for it?"

Kelly nodded.

Colt laughed. "Ready to fight and die. . . . Ready to fight and die."

"What's funny?" Kelly could feel his face going red.

"My brother, man. You sound just like my brother." Colt's laughter echoed weirdly in the tunnel, ringing off the metal heat pipes and electrical power lines, bouncing off the cold stone that surrounded them.

"He beat the shit outta me when I joined the Air Force," Colt said. "Told me I was a traitor to my people. I told him I didn't want to die for my people, I just wanted to live good. Told him it was time we got enough of our own people into the chain of command to make it *our* Army and *our* Navy and *our* Air Force."

"I don't see . . ."

"Back then the fighting was going on inside the States. The black man didn't give a shit about the Communist menace. We didn't know the goddamned Russians were just sittin' back and waitin' for us to do their work for them, tear down the U.S. of A. from the inside. My brother tried. He worked hard at it. He fought for what he believed in: black power. Wound up in a shittin' hut in Dahomey, in Africa, hidin' out from the FBI and CIA and Lord knows who else. Know how he died? Some motherfuckin' Communist guerrillas sprayed the crappy little airport down there with machine guns and grenades. He happened to be there, waitin' for a plane. They killed him."

Kelly felt confused. Colt was not making sense.

"Listen," the black man said. "One thing I learned early and learned good. Don't fight city hall. Get inside city hall and take it over—but do it slow and easy, without any fuss. Too many guys call themselves revolutionaries, all they want is some quick publicity and easy pussy. The real revolutionaries carefully protect the system—'cause they want it for themselves."

"You're not . . ."

Colt grabbed him by the shoulder and shook him, schoolyard rough. "Listen, Irish Catholic God-fearing American. Black power don't mean shit if there's no America left, if it all goes up in a mushroom cloud. So I've gotta protect America, you dig? And at the same time, I wouldn't at all mind becoming commander of Moonbase. So give Chet enough rope to hang himself. Give him plenty of rope."

"You sonofabitch," Kelly said in a shocked whisper. "You say you're his friend . . ."

"I *am* his friend! But if he turns traitor then he's not my friend or anybody else's. And *you're* tellin' me he's gonna turn traitor."

Kelly fell silent.

"Well?" Colt demanded, his voice booming. "Ain't that what you're saying?"

It was hard to make his voice work. "Ye . . . yes," Kelly managed. "I guess that's what I'm saying."

"Yeah. You guess. And you're willing to have your wife and children in the middle of a shoot-out, to protect and defend America. Goddamned noble of you, whitey. Goddamned noble."

"Now listen, Colt . . ."

"I had a wife and family. I saw them die. Wonder how you'd feel."

Kelly wanted to run, to get as far away from this man as he could. Anywhere . . .

But Colt still held his shoulder with a grip of fury. "Listen to me, Kelly. I want to know everything Chet's doing, everything he's thinking, even what he dreams about at night. I want to know what he's going to do before he knows it himself. Because, if you're right, then I'm going to have to kill him."

"Kill!"

"That's right, baby. Kill. Chet might look easygoing, but underneath he's as stubborn as a Christian martyr. And damned popular around here. He's turned Moonbase into a freakhouse for all the eggheads who think they can live with the Russians. When the button gets pushed, Chet's going to be *very* hard to stop. *Very* hard. Talking won't do it."

"But . . . killing him . . ." Kelly was suddenly afraid.

"I know. It sucks. So's everything else. Maybe we can get away without it coming to that. But we gotta be ready to face it."

Kelly pushed at his thinning hair. "I don't know . . ."

"But I do. That's the difference between us, baby. And one other thing," Colt said, iron-hard. "Everything I've told you is based on the assumption that you're right, and Chet's going to hand this base over to the Russians. If I find out you're wrong, this whole planet won't be big enough to hide you. I will personally take you apart, little friend. Count on it."

Academician V. I. Mogilev was livid with rage. He flailed his arms angrily in the tight confines of the space station's compartment as he bellowed into the face of the station's commander.

"But this is insanity! It's preposterous! Bureaucratic interference with scientific research that has won the highest approval from the Supreme Soviet . . ."

The station commander listened with Oriental patience. The son of an Uzbek herdsman does not rise to the rank of captain in the Soviet Strategic Rocket Corps without learning patience. He had been screamed at by true experts; this little professor was a rank amateur.

After some time the academician wound down. "You can understand what idiocy this is, can't you?" His voice was almost pleading now. "We are in the middle of such delicate studies. All the instruments are at last aligned and working well. The quasar's peak of radiation intensity will be reached in another fourteen hours, if Chalinik's calculations are correct, and . . . and . . ."

"My dear professor," the Captain said as politely as he could, but still coldly enough to leave no doubt as to who was in command, "I appreciate the extreme importance of your work. But you must realize that orders from the Kremlin leave no room for argument. I cannot refuse to obey my orders. Do you want to have me shot?"

"No, no, of course not." There seemed to be some little doubt in the academician's tone, despite his words.

The Captain shrugged elaborately. "Then what can I do? I have my orders. You and your assistants must be prepared to leave within another . . ."—he glanced at his wristwatch—". . . another three hours."

"But our work . . . the instruments . . ."

"We will take care of the instruments," the Captain said. "No one will disturb them, I assure you."

The astrophysicist continued muttering as the Captain rose and squeezed out from behind his little desk and escorted the older man to the airtight hatch that opened onto the space station's main corridor.

"You will allow the instruments to keep recording the quasar's activities?"

"Of course. Certainly."

The scientist went slowly down the corridor, shaking his head and mumbling to himself. No sooner had the Captain seated himself at his desk again than a younger officer stepped through the open hatchway. He was stocky and blond, a true Russian.

He'll advance faster than I will, thought the Captain as he glowered at the younger man.

"Sir," the young officer said.

"Sit down, Lieutenant. Your craft is ready to take the scientists home?"

"Yessir, although they seem quite unhappy about it."

The Captain allowed a small smile to creep across his face. "They are civilians. You can't expect them to understand military matters."

The Lieutenant nodded.

"Of course, you understand such matters, don't you?" The Captain turned in his chair and reached for the small thermos resting on the shelf behind his desk.

"I believe I understand military matters, yes," the Lieutenant said to his back, then added, "sir."

"H'mm . . ." Taking two glasses from a desk drawer, the Captain asked, "Drink?"

"No, thank you, sir. I will be piloting the shuttle rocket."

"So? Tea upsets you?"

"Oh!" The Lieutenant was taken aback, a sight that pleased the Captain. "Well, yes, in that case. Thank you."

As he poured the steaming brew the Captain asked, "So you understand military matters, eh?"

"I think so. Sir."

"Then tell me"—he slammed the thermos on the desk hard enough to make the tea jump out of both glasses—"how do those Earthbound desk pilots expect me to defend a Soviet military installation that is defenseless? Heh?"

"I . . . sir . . ."

"Look at this place!" The Captain waved a hand. "It's made of straw. One of the Americans' laser beams could slice us apart like goat's cheese. How are we to defend ourselves against attack?"

"I didn't realize that an attack was imminent," the Lieutenant answered, keeping his hands carefully in his lap and not reaching for the tea.

"A commander must always assume that an attack is imminent! Learn that! Get it into your skull and into your blood! Never relax your guard!"

"Yessir."

The Captain glared at him for a moment, then pushed one of the glasses toward him. The Lieutenant quickly snatched at it.

"Why do you think they've ordered all the civilians off our little island in the sky? Heh? We are on alert status. At any moment the word may come that war has broken out. Do you have a family? Wife? Children?"

The Lieutenant blinked once. "My mother . . . in Moscow."

"Mmm. My children will be safe enough from the bombs," the Captain said. "But the fallout . . . the fallout, that's what will kill them. A lingering death."

"It may not happen," the Lieutenant said, very quietly.

The Captain eyed him. "Do you know what your cargo was? What you brought up here for me to sit with, in place of the scientists?"

"No sir. It was sealed, and my orders did not specify the container's contents."

"But something that big must have aroused your curiosity, heh? A single package, sealed and guarded. Heh?"

"Well . . ." The Lieutenant smiled, almost. "There were rumors at Tyuratam . . ."

"Rumors? Such as?"

"Well, that the package was part of a new weapon, a system that will defend the space station against American attack."

"Hah! I wish it were."

"Then it's not?"

"No, Lieutenant, it is not. It's a weapon, true enough. But it won't help to defend us. If anything it will make us an even more important target to the Americans."

"What is it, then?"

The Captain gave his best inscrutable smile. "Come now, Lieutenant. You must realize that I cannot tell you. The information is highly classified."

The Lieutenant drank his tea in stony silence and departed. Some time later the Captain got up from his desk and strode the length of his tiny station to the loading dock. He watched the shuttle, filled with the complaining scientists now, as its rockets puffed briefly and it arced away to be quickly lost against the glare of the looming Earth.

Then another spark caught his eye. The package that the shuttle had left hanging in orbit a few hundred meters from the station's main airlock.

The bomb. Tomorrow the shuttle would be back with another one. And the day after that, still another.

I must check with Lunagrad to be certain that they are giving the highest priority to sending us more lunar soil, the Captain told himself. Maybe we can get enough to protect the bombs, as well as the station.

Then he got an inspiration. Turning from the tiny porthole where he had been standing he told the nearest technician, "Dismantle all that scientific junk and plant it on the outside skin of the station. It might help to deflect laser beams if we're attacked."

Without a word of argument, the technician moved to obey.

Friday 10 December 1999: 1250 hrs UT

IT WAS A glum meeting.

The Farside Astronomical Observatory had briefly been a thriving center of exciting exploration. The vast array of steerable twenty-meter radio dish antennas seemed to fill the Sea of Moscow—at least, all that was visible from Farside's main dome. Up on the ringwall crest stood the spidery framework of the thousand-centimeter optical telescope and its clusters of electronic amplifiers and satellite telescopes. The UV and infrared, the x-ray and gamma ray detectors. The constant shuttle of eager young men and women, balanced by the older, more patient, but no less eager permanent staff. The computer links. The thrill of searching the universe for knowledge, for life, for intelligence.

Now Farside was like a ghost town.

Kinsman slouched back in a webchair, letting his mind drift from the droning voices of the men and women around the table. He stared through the conference room's window at the gleaming telescope framework outside. The largest optical telescope ever built, sitting in the airless open of the lunar plain, unattended and useless.

The sky out there looked dark and empty without the Earth to brighten it. The astronomers loved that; it made Farside a perfect site for their research. But it made Kinsman uneasy, frightened at the deepest level of his being. Earth was never in the sky, here on the far side of the Moon. What if it was gone when he returned to the near side?

"The only remaining item to be discussed," Dr. Mishima was saying, his soft voice slow and measured, trying hard not to reveal the bitterness he felt, "is the protective dome for the thousand-centimeter."

"I have examined the cost figures," said one of the Russian administrators. "The dome is too expensive for our current budget allocation."

Dr. Mishima drew in his breath. "If the observatory is to be shut down the equipment must either be transported to Selene or protected from meteoric erosion, so that it can be used again—when the times are more favorable and the gods of the budgets are more kindly disposed toward astronomy."

What the hell's the matter with Diane? Kinsman asked himself, staring out at the empty sky. Five days now and she hasn't answered my calls. Since she got Pierce's job. Is that all she wanted from me?

One of the Americans was saying, "It's not that we *want* to abandon Farside. They just haven't given us the money to keep it open."

"I understand that you regret this unfortunate turn of events more than words can express," Dr. Mishima said with elaborate politeness. "Still, it is imperative to think of the future. I cannot believe that astronomical research will cease entirely and forever . . ."

"Keep it open," Kinsman heard himself say.

They all jerked with surprise and turned toward him: Mishima, up at the head of the table, the Americans and Russians (sitting on opposite sides, Kinsman noted wryly), the three men and four women representing the other nations that had staff or equipment investments in Farside, and Piotr Leonov.

It was Leonov, sitting directly across the table from Kinsman, who asked, "What did you say?" The expression on his face was hard to read: almost a smile, eyes curious, as if he agreed with Kinsman but was not certain he had heard him correctly.

"I said we should keep Farside open. It would be a tragedy to close this place down."

"I agree," said Leonov. "But the funds have been cut off. It's the only thing our two governments have been able to agree on, all year."

Fuck them both, Kinsman said to himself. Aloud, "Dr. Mishima, just how much do you need to keep going here? You've got the big equipment and the computers and life-support and housekeeping stuff. What else do you need?"

The Japanese astronomer seemed stunned. "Er . . . our major costs over the past two years have been maintenance, housekeeping, basic supplies, things of that nature. And, of course, the largest cost has been that of bringing up tempo-rary people from Earth and transporting them back home again."

"Pete, why can't we keep Farside going? We don't need Earthside replacements every ninety days. There's enough of a staff among the permanent Luniks to keep the research going here."

Leonov finally did smile. Sadly. "I have orders to close the center."

"If your orders read like mine," Kinsman countered, "they merely inform you that no further Earthside funds will be allotted for Farside, and that you're to take the necessary actions. We still have our own resources."

Half the people around the table started talking at once,

and the silent ones either grinned hugely or glowered at Kinsman. The grinners were astronomers. The glowerers were administrators from Selene, mostly ninety-dayers.

Leonov got to his feet and called for silence. "Wait! Wait. This is something that Colonel Kinsman and I must discuss in private before we go any further."

"Right," agreed Kinsman. He got up and started around the table. "Why don't we break for lunch? Colonel Leonov and I can talk right here and see if we can come up with a meeting of the minds."

The others—some puzzled, some upset—left the room in a buzzing, chattering group. When the door clicked shut behind them Leonov turned to Kinsman and smiled sardonically.

"Very well. You've been trying to get me alone for the past three days. What is it?"

Kinsman walked toward the window. "I wondered why you didn't return my calls."

"I am being carefully watched. So are you."

Nodding, "Think this room's bugged?"

"I doubt it." Leonov came to the window and glanced out at the idle telescope. "Even if it is," he said, pulling a tiny flat dead-black plastic square from his pocket, "this will keep the bugs from biting us."

Kinsman felt his eyebrows go up a notch. "Scrambler?"

"No, a new type of transmitter that broadcasts at the frequencies of most listening devices. I have programmed it with decadent American hot-rock music; my security people will think you are carrying a jammer."

Kinsman laughed. "Wonder what *my* security people will think?"

"That is your problem, old friend."

Lowering his voice, Kinsman said, "I think I've got a solution to our other problem."

"Not your independence idea again!"

"Yes, but . . ."

Leonov closed his eyes. "I have received my orders. I will not be sent home, after all. I will be stationed at the Tyuratam launch complex for the duration of the emergency. All space-qualified officers have been placed on maximum alert basis. No leaves."

"Red alert?"

Leonov nodded. "Only for space-qualified personnel. All other military units are on standby alert."

"When do you leave?"

"My replacement arrives in five days."

"God damn!"

Leonov turned and stared out the window. "Well, my idealistic comrade, what do you do about that?"

"That's not the question," Kinsman said. "The real question is, what are *you* prepared to do, Pete?"

He turned back and gazed at Kinsman, his face somber, his eyes grave and weary. "Anything," he said in a near-whisper. "Anything that will save my children from being killed."

"They're really going to do it? Launch the missiles?"

"Of course they are!" the Russian exploded. "They can't come this close without pushing the final button. Oh, they will talk and argue and threaten each other for a few days more—a week or even two, perhaps. They will stretch everyone's nerves to the breaking point before they convince themselves that they must attack. But they'll do it, and when they do, it will seem almost like a relief. One of them will press the button—for the glory of the Motherland, or to save the world for democracy. Then the rest happens automatically."

"It's up to us to stop them."

Leonov laughed bitterly. "How? By declaring independence? By waving a piece of paper at them? I said I would do anything, but it must be something that will *work*! I will not sit up here safely and watch my nation . . . my people . . . my *children* . . ."

"Okay, okay." Kinsman put both hands on his shoulders. "Take it easy. Cool down."

"No, I will not cool down!" Leonov shouted. "I am not an automaton. I am not a creature of ice water, as you are. I have blood in my veins! Russian blood! The world is about to explode and you expect me to stand here calmly and discuss politics with you. How can you . . ."

"Stop it!" Kinsman snapped. "They won't need bugs to hear us."

Leonov's face was glistening with sweat. His chest heaved.

"I just want to know one thing," Kinsman said. "Are you willing to disobey orders and stay here?"

"Stay at Lunagrad instead of . . ." Leonov's voice trailed off for a moment. Then, clenching his fists with the effort of decision, "Yes. I will be doing the children no good by pushing buttons at Tyuratam."

"All right." Kinsman licked his lips. They tasted salty. Maybe I'm not ice water after all. "This is what we need to do: The ABM satellite networks are both unfinished, but *together* they can effectively cover the whole Earth and shoot down any missiles launched by either side. Or anybody else, for that matter."

"Together?" Leonov echoed.

"Right. We take over the space stations at the same time we declare Selene independent. If we can grab the command and control centers for the satellites, we can stop the war before it starts. And enforce our own independence."

"But they'll send troops."

Kinsman could feel the sweat trickling down his ribs. "They can try. But they'll have to send them in shuttle rockets. If the satellites can shoot down ballistic missiles they can shoot down troop-carriers, as well."

"You . . . could do that?"

"I'd warn them first. But they probably wouldn't listen."

"Your people would shoot down Americans?"

"We'd have to. Wouldn't want your people to do that; it might cause bad feelings among us."

Leonov seemed to sag against the window.

"It's the only way," Kinsman urged. "Neither side can stop a war, not the way they've been going. One of them would have to back down and neither of them is going to do that. Only an outside force can stop them. We've got to be that outside force."

"A handful of people . . . How many are we? A thousand?"

"But we're in a special position. We can pull their fangs. We can stop them from fighting."

"They'll call us traitors. They will kill us."

Kinsman nodded. "They'll try. Your government will probably take your kids."

"Yes."

"We could hold some of the officers from your space stations as counter-hostages."

"That might work." Leonov seemed dazed; his face was blank, his voice distant and toneless.

"Would they . . . kill the children?"

With a slow shake of his head, Leonov replied, "No. I doubt it. What good would that do them?"

"They'd be dead anyway, if the war . . ."

There were tears in the Russian's eyes. "So my choice is to have them bombed by the Americans or shot by the security police?"

"I . . ."

"No, no, it won't work. It could never work. It is madness even to think about it." Leonov paced away from the window.

Kinsman stood there and said nothing. He watched the Russian's back, the tension in the corded muscles of his neck. "It could work, Peter," he said. "We could make it work."

Leonov wheeled around to face him. "What would you have me do? Betray Russian and take away her only defense against American attack? Leave my homeland, my children, my whole life, to remain an exile forever here on this rock? Put my trust in a handful of strangers? Lunatics? Americans? How do I know I can trust your people? How do I know I can trust *you*?"

"You're afraid—"

"Of course I'm afraid!"

Kinsman felt the cold of that empty sky seeping into his guts. ". . . because I killed one of your cosmonauts."

Leonov rocked backward half a step. "Then it's true." His voice was hollow.

"It's true."

"I didn't believe the intelligence reports. Sometimes they contain exaggerations—outright lies, propaganda."

"I killed her," Kinsman said.

The Russian stepped close to Kinsman. Tears still glistened in his eyes. "I never meant to force you to confess to me."

Kinsman felt lightheaded, almost giddy. It was like coming out of anesthesia. "It was something I had to tell you; it had to be removed from between us."

Leonov closed his eyes.

"I can't kill anyone again," Kinsman said. "Not even if it's only by sitting back and letting others push the buttons. I have to try to stop them. *Have to*, Peter."

"And you cannot do it without Lunagrad's help."

"Without *your* help."

"Forgive me, old friend. I could never have trusted you if you had not told me. It's ridiculous, but I could not have trusted you."

They stood side by side, looking out the window at the bleak landscape and empty sky.

"Too many of us have died," Kinsman told him. "It's time to stop the killing."

Staring at the barren rocks, the ancient weary mountains, the stark framework of human artifacts, Leonov asked quietly, "Do you think there are enough people like us in Selene to carry it off? Can we make a success of it, or will we merely start the war here on the Moon? I have no desire for a glorious failure. Only the victors write the history books."

"Dammitall, Pete, if we don't try there won't *be* any history books."

"The world's savior," Leonov said. There was no sarcasm in it. He gestured toward the window and the unused telescope. "You want to make the blind see. You've already brought a dead man back to life. And now you want to save the world from hellfire." He sighed deeply. "They will crucify us, you know."

Kinsman shrugged.

Then, with a smile that was more sadness than anything else, Leonov slowly raised his hand and extended it toward Kinsman. Taking it in his, Kinsman gripped the Russian's hand firmly.

"Wasn't it one of your revolutionaries who said, 'We must all hang together, or we will surely all hang separately?'"

Kinsman laughed. "Franklin."

"We must act swiftly," Leonov said. "And we must start *now*."

Now, Kinsman repeated to himself as he sank into the foam couch of the ballistic rocket. Takeoff from Farside was felt rather than heard. A pressure squeezing you into your couch. A distant rumbling that was more a vibration in your bones than an audible sound.

The engine thrust cut off and Kinsman felt the pressure ease to zero. Free-fall. Floating. His hands drifted off the couch's armrests. He still leaned back in the couch, unable to see the dozen other passengers cocooned in their own couches, their own thoughts.

Swinging the couch up to its sitting position, Kinsman touched the communications keys on the right armrest. The screen on the seatback in front of him flickered to life and within a few moments he was looking at Pat Kelly's worried, lip-nibbling face.

"What do you hear from your wife and family, Pat?" Kinsman asked.

Kelly looked puzzled that the boss would call from the Farside ferry rocket with a personal question. "They were at Kennedy yesterday. I haven't checked with Alpha yet, but they ought to be transshipping to the lunar shuttle this afternoon. That's the schedule."

"Good. Listen, Pat. Get Alpha on the horn and find out exactly when that shuttle took off and who's on it. I want the crew and passenger list on my desk when I land back at Selene."

"Okay. Sir."

"There's more," Kinsman said. He pulled the pin mike from the armrest and lowered his voice as he spoke into it. "I want you to set up a red-alert condition . . ."

Kelly's mouth dropped open.

"No, it's not really a red alert. But I want you to get the whole base buttoned up as if it were. The best people we have at all the critical centers: communications, power, water factory, launch center. Only permanent Luniks, no ninety-dayers. The program's all set up in the command computer, all you have to do is run off the orders."

Kelly scratched at his thinning hair. "Well, are we on red alert or aren't we? What do I tell—"

"Just do what I told you and do it now! I want the base buttoned up tight before midnight."

With a perplexed shrug, Kelly said, "People are going to ask a lot of questions."

"Keep it as quiet as you can. No fuss, no alarms ringing in the corridors. Don't scare the civilians. Just get the right people to the right places. Now!"

Kelly looked distinctly unhappy when Kinsman breezed into his office, more than an hour later.

"What's the word?" Kinsman asked, going straight to his desk.

Kelly had a thick sheaf of plastic reports in his hand. "We're scrambling hell out of everybody's work shifts, but the base is getting buttoned up. Lots of questions being asked, lots of grumbling."

Sitting in the desk chair, Kinsman said, "I told you to do things quietly."

"You can't shove half the population of the base around quietly!" Kelly complained.

Kinsman looked up at him. "Okay, Pat. Okay. Sit down." He pointed to the couch. "Give me a rundown."

By the time Kelly was finished, Kinsman was satisfied that everything was going as smoothly as could be expected.

"What about the shuttle?" he asked.

"Left Alpha on schedule."

"The passenger list?"

"In the computer."

Leaning back in his chair, "Okay, good. Put in a call to the shuttle. Tell them to increase boost and get here on a maximum-energy trajectory. Clear the launch center for them. Talk to your wife while you've got the channel open."

Kelly shook his head as if to clear it. "Maximum-energy trajectory? Chet, what the hell are you doing?"

Kinsman grinned at him. "Your wife and kids are aboard. Aren't you anxious to see them?"

"Yeah, but . . ."

"How many kids do you have?"

"Uh . . . six."

"You don't sound too sure."

It was Kelly's turn to grin. "Well, I haven't seen her for a couple months. She might know something I don't."

"Goddamned sex maniac."

"Me?"

"Get moving. I want to know exactly when that shuttle

can touch down. And I'll be inspecting the base at midnight. God help all of you if I'm not satisfied with the security status."

Mumbling incoherently, Kelly got up and left.

Kinsman immediately turned to the computer display screen and started going through the files of all the military personnel in Moonbase, especially the ninety-dayers. He knew most of them, had selected them from previous tours of duty. *Wonder how many I've rejected over the years? The unthinking martinets. The clumsy ones who would kill themselves up here. The stupid ones who'd kill others with their mistakes. The idiots who can't live in close contact with people of other races, other nationalities. The soft ones who'd never have the guts to . . . to . . .*

"To commit treason," he said aloud. "Face it. Treason. Like Washington and Jefferson. Like Benedict Arnold. It depends on who wins; that's the difference between treason and patriotism."

Out of the one hundred twenty-two military personnel among the ninety-dayers Kinsman identified forty whom he knew would be reliable. Forty men and women who would be willing to follow him, who would see a free Selene not as a threat to America but as the only way out of a deadly negative-sum game.

The highest-ranking officer on the list, next to Pat Kelly, was a captain. "Christopher Perry," Kinsman muttered, looking over the Captain's personnel file. The picture in it showed a clear-eyed, square-faced blond youth. Pleasant expression; almost innocent. Kinsman remembered a long conversation with him during his previous tour of lunar duty: how he was fed up with flying helicopters on riot control over Washington. "Yeah. He's one of us."

The door buzzer sounded. Looking up from the display screen, Kinsman called, "Come in."

The door slid back and Frank Colt stepped into the office.

"I was just thinking about you, Frank."

The black man kept his face expressionless. "What's going on around here?"

"Sit down, buddy. Relax."

Colt ignored the couch and pulled a chair from the wall.

"Kelly says you've got a mock alert going. You suddenly getting security conscious?"

"Yep. That's what it is. I'm security conscious."

Colt did not look convinced at all. "Why you keeping the ninety-dayers out of it?"

"Because Murdock wants us to have enough people available to help out with the manned stations," Kinsman answered smoothly. "Can't send the permanent Luniks, can I?"

"You could in a pinch. Only one section of the stations are at Earth gee."

"Yeah, but the ninety-dayers would be better for orbital duty. Not us soft, decrepit medical cases."

Colt frowned.

"What's wrong, Frank? I thought you'd be delighted that I'm taking Murdock's hysterics so seriously."

"How come I wasn't notified? I'm the deputy commander and I—"

"The emergency procedures program hasn't been updated since you arrived, I guess. You found out anyway, didn't you?"

"Because I bumped into Pat Kelly in the fuckin' corridor and he looked scared as shit!"

"So you didn't find out through official channels," Kinsman said. "But you did get the word."

"What are you pulling, Chet?"

"When I pull something," Kinsman responded, "you'll be the first to know. I'll even go through regular channels."

Colt jumped to his feet. Still unaccustomed to lunar gravity, he knocked the chair over backward. "Goddammit, Chet, you're gonna get your ass killed! I know you're up to something crazy, and I know it's not Murdock's orders. Now take some advice from a friend, man, and—"

"Frank!" Kinsman cut in. "I don't want advice. I know what I have to do."

"Don't do it, Chet! I'm asking you. Don't do it, whatever crazy scheme you're cookin'. You're gonna force me to kill you."

"There won't be any killing, Frank."

"I don't know what the hell's going through your head," Colt's voice was trembling, almost breaking, "but don't put me on the spot. I don't want to have to choose between your life and mine."

"You won't have to choose," Kinsman said, trying to keep his voice calm despite the tightness gripping his chest.

"If you try to hand this base over to the Russians . . ."

"Don't be silly!"

"Or do anything against the United States . . . Chet, I'll have to stop you. I'll have to!"

"You'll have to try, I guess. If and when the time comes."

"Chet! Dammit!"

Rising slowly from his chair, Kinsman said, "Frank, if and when the time comes, we'll all have to do what we think is best. If you've got to kill me . . . Well, everybody dies sooner or later."

"Jesus H. Christ on the motherfuckin' cross!" Colt threw his hands up and stamped out of the office.

Kinsman stood there for a long time, leaning on the desk, waiting for the tension to ease away from his chest.

Saturday 11 December 1999:
0112 hrs UT

IT WAS EVENING in Washington, dark and raining.

General Murdock shivered as he humped his overweight body against the limousine's jumpseat. It was not the rain or the cold that sent the shudders down his spine, although God knew the rotten weather made the bedraggled tinsel and gaudy decorations of the downtown stores look even cheaper and drearier than usual. No one—absolutely no one—was walking on the streets. A mud-brown Army combat patrol car stood at every street intersection, glistening in the wan streetlights and steady downpour of rain, turrets buttoned up and guns aimed along the sidewalks.

Even General Hofstader looked gloomy. His uniform

was crisp, his ribbons shone in the darkness of the limousine. But his face was gray, creased, shrinking into premature old age from the tensions that he was forced to endure.

It was the other man's voice that made Murdock shiver. That harsh, labored whisper, like a demon clawing its way up from hell.

"Enemies within as well as without," he rasped, pointing a heavy hand toward the empty streets. "With the Soviets about to attack us, every fool pacifist and Communist sympathizer in the land is preparing to stab us in the back."

"I didn't realize . . ." Murdock began, then immediately wished he had not. General Hofstader froze him with a glare.

"Didn't realize," the other man said, his rage-filled face twisting even more. "How many Americans do realize the seriousness of this crisis. Few. Very few. Precious few."

He lapsed into silence for a moment. Neither general dared to speak. The limousine sped through the rain, its turbine whining shrilly. There was no traffic to hinder them. The only other sound was the *thwack, thwack* of the windshield wiper on the back window. The front of the limo was acoustically sealed off from the rear.

"We precious few." The man wheezed. It was as close as he ever came to laughter. "We will live through the holocaust and then begin a new world—begin afresh, the right way, the way that made this nation great."

General Hofstader cleared his throat. "I should be at Cheyenne Mountain if an attack is imminent . . ."

"It is important to have the Joint Chiefs together for this meeting. In person. Top security." He turned his burning eyes on Murdock. "And you. I want to hear the latest intelligence from your mavericks on the Moon."

Murdock swallowed hard. "They seem to be taking the crisis much more seriously now. Apparently they've gone into a maximum-security status . . ."

" 'Apparently'?"

"From . . . from . . . the latest report. This afternoon."

"And the Soviets?"

"I don't know." Murdock felt helpless. "I don't have access to that information."

"I suppose you also do not know that the Soviets are deploying nuclear weapons in orbit."

"Ohmygod."

"Indeed. Now, tell me, what is your personal assessment of the commander of Moonbase?"

Murdock blurted, "Kinsman?"

"That is his name, isn't it? I understand he is a dubious factor."

"Well, he's . . ."

"Yes?"

His eyes were boring into Murdock. Hofstader was staring at him, too. Miserably, Murdock answered, "He's been a good administrator but I'm not certain that he's the best man for the job in an emergency situation."

"Then get rid of him."

Murdock turned to Hofstader.

"Remove him," the Four-Star General said. "Do you have a reliable second-in-command up there?"

"Oh, yessir. Very reliable!"

"Put him in command. Send whatever-his-name-is back down here."

"He can't. Medical disability."

The other man leaned forward and put a heavy hand on Murdock's knee. "Get him out of there. If you have to arrest him and put him in a life-support capsule for the rest of his life—get him out of there!"

"Yessir. Right away, sir," Murdock squeaked.

It was close to 0200 hours when Kinsman finished his inspection rounds of Moonbase.

Everything's buttoned up tight. Shuttle's down and won't move until I say so. The base is as secure as it can be. Reliable people on duty. No screams for help from Leonov.

Kinsman was pacing down a corridor in the residential section of the base. Most of the people were sleeping, as if this night were the same as any other. He turned at an intersection and started toward Diane's quarters.

"She can't be working all the time," he muttered to himself.

He put all doubts behind him as he hurried down the corridor, passing under the eerie bluish light of one set of fluorescents into the shadows between lamps and then back into the light again. It was warm down at this level, but

Kinsman still felt a clammy cold sweat that made his coveralls stick to his chest and arms and back.

He knocked at Diane's door. No answer. He knocked again, louder, then put his ear to the thin plastic of the door. A scuffling sound inside. Muttering. The door opened a crack.

"Oh, hello." Diane's voice was thick, her hair tousled, eyes puffy.

"Can I come in for a minute?"

She opened the door wide enough for Kinsman to step through. Diane was wearing an ankle-length shift. It had been pink once, but had faded considerably. No frills on it. High Chinese collar.

"Is something wrong?" she muttered. "I was relieved of duty in the middle of my shift . . ."

He stood on the grass-covered floor and surveyed the room. The door to the bedroom was closed.

"Something's wrong," he said.

"What?"

"You haven't returned my calls. You've been avoiding me."

"Not now, Chet. I can't . . ."

"Now," he said. "I've got to know why."

She rubbed at her eyes.

"Why?" Kinsman took her by the wrist. "Why have you been avoiding me?"

"Because you scare me," Diane said.

"Scare you?"

Her voice shaky, her eyes avoiding his, she said, "I didn't realize . . . you mean it! You're really going to try it!"

"Of course I am. I told you."

She pulled her hand away from him. "I don't want any part of it. It's crazy! All you're going to accomplish is getting yourself killed. You're committing suicide over some woman who died ten years ago."

"That's ridiculous."

"It *is* ridiculous. And frightening." Diane backed a step away from him. "And then you say you're not going to let me go back to Earth. I don't want to stay here, Chet! I don't want to be here when they kill you!"

"Nobody's going to kill me."

"Yes, they will. You're going to keep pushing at them until they have no choice but to kill you."

"Everybody dies," he muttered.

Diane pushed a lock of hair back away from her face. "Sure. Be a hero. Save the world. I can't stop you. I won't even try. But I've got a daughter to think of, to protect. I don't want to die and I don't want her to be killed. I don't want *you* to die!"

"So what do you want to do?" he asked.

"I want to find someplace safe."

"Where?" He almost laughed. "There aren't any safe places. There's going to be killing here, Diane. Maybe a lot of it. Frank Colt won't let me take Moonbase away from America without a fight. Leonov will have to shoot his way to independence. Then we'll have to take the space stations —more killing. It's inescapable. We've got to kill to prevent killing. It's a cosmic joke."

"There's nothing funny about it."

"I know."

"I can't go with you on this, Chet. You'll have to do it without me."

"I know." He had known it all along.

Pat Kelly looked scared. There's no other word for it, Kinsman decided. Pat is scared.

The two officers had spent most of the morning going over all the contingency plans for repelling attack and keeping Moonbase secure. He and Kelly had checked, using the picture phones, every vital area of the base. They had then called in, one by one, every key person, military and civilian: the personnel chief, the head of maintenance, the director of the hospital, the Officer of the Day—every man and woman in charge of a department or an important group of people or a vital piece of equipment.

To each of them, Kinsman gave the same speech: "We are in a maximum-security status. War is imminent. I intend to declare our independence from Earthside and try to prevent the war from starting. We will act together with the people of Lunagrad. Selene will become an independent nation. Both the United States and Soviet Russia will try to stop us, and there might be bloodshed. We'll try to avoid it, but we've got to be ready to face that possibility."

The night fears were gone from his mind, or at least buried deep enough so that he could ignore them. Kinsman felt strangely calm, at peace with himself for the first time in a decade.

The people he spoke to were shocked, surprised. Some smiled with sudden relief. Some were angry and showed it. Of those who agreed with his purpose, Kinsman asked only that they explain the situation to the people under them. To those who became tight-lipped and clench-fisted, he offered a shuttle flight back to Earth. And then called in their second-in-command.

As the long day wore on, the entire absurd idea began to seem almost natural, inevitable. We're thumbing our noses at the two most powerful nations in the world. Why? Oh, because I killed a Russian girl once. And, incidentally, we're trying to save the world. So what's new with you? Kinsman began to feel lightheaded.

Diane was the last one to come into his office.

"You know what's going down," Kinsman said to her as Kelly watched nervously from the couch. "Can we depend on your cooperation, or should we relieve you of duty at the comm center?"

Diane smiled, despite herself. "I just got the job; I'd hate to give it up so soon."

Kinsman felt his hopes soar. "Then you'll work with us?"

"I guess I'll have to."

"I thought you didn't want any part of this," Kinsman said, remembering their conversation earlier that morning.

Without an instant's hesitation Diane replied, "I don't. At least, I didn't. I was scared. Middle-of-the-night scared. But it's daytime now. You're going ahead with it, even though it's crazy."

Kinsman nodded.

"Okay," Diane went on. "If you're going to do it, then I've got to go along with you."

"Even though . . ."

"Even though it scares hell out of me, yes," Diane said. "I can't sit on the sidelines. I've got to be a part of this, whether I like it or not. I've been trying to warn people about this government for a long time, you know. Some of us saw where they were leading us way back when. Some of us saw this war coming years ago. Why do you think they stopped me from singing? Why do you think they exiled me up here?"

"You're on our side, then."

"What you're doing is right, Chet," she said. "I don't think it's going to work. I think we're all going to get ourselves killed. But you're right; we've got to try."

"We'll make it work," he said grimly. "We'll *make* it work."

"You'll want the comm center shut up tight." Diane seemed to draw herself up to her full height. Her decision made, she became businesslike, professional. "All Earthside messages routed straight to you?"

"Right. And no traffic beamed Earthside without my specific okay."

"No traffic at all?" Diane asked. "Won't that make them suspicious?"

He shrugged. "Can't take the chance on somebody sneaking a message out."

"I can monitor the outgoing messages for you."

He stared hard at her. "Do you want to?"

"Yes."

"You'll accept that responsibility? I didn't think you wanted to be involved . . ."

"We can keep the routine messages flowing," Diane said, ignoring his question. "And the computer data exchanges, of course. I can monitor all the personal messages and make certain they don't contain anything damaging. I could even run them through the cryptographic computer, just to be certain no one's sending coded messages."

For a moment Kinsman wondered if he could truly trust her. But he said, "Okay. Good. And thanks."

Diane left the office. Kinsman turned to the worried Kelly. "Who's left?"

"That's everybody." Kelly's voice was shaky.

"What about Ernie Waterman?"

Kelly flinched as if slapped. "Ernie's not a department head."

"I know. But he's a key man. I want his reaction. Didn't I ask you to call him earlier?"

Kelly started to shake his head.

"And Frank Colt. Where's he? Get somebody to track him down."

"Okay."

Kinsman watched Kelly working with the phone. The guy's scared half to death!

"Pat."

Kelly jerked away from the phone keyboard. "Yeah? What?"

"Calm down," Kinsman said softly. "It's going to be all right. Everything's going better than I had hoped it would. There's not going to be any shooting."

Biting his lip, "Yeah. Maybe."

"I'm going to try to get Leonov on the phone. Meantime, you call Chris Perry in here."

"Perry? What for?"

Kinsman was already punching Leonov's number on his desktop phone. "Chris is going to lead one of our missions to the space stations. His group will take Beta. I'm going to Alpha. And we've got to find a reliable guy to . . ."

Kelly's face looked stricken. He went white, his mouth hung open, his hands froze on the phone.

"Pat! You okay?"

With an effort Kelly croaked out, "I didn't know you were going to attack the stations. You never told me . . ."

"We're not going to attack them. We're going to take them over. Quick and neat and with no fuss. And Leonov's going to do the same on his side."

"You're going to leave the United States defenseless."

"No," Kinsman answered. "We're going to take over all the defenses ourselves. Then we'll make sure that nobody can attack anybody else."

Kelly got up slowly from the couch. He was visibly trembling. "Chet, I . . . You've got to let me out of this. I never thought . . ."

"Hold on, Pat. Nobody's going to get hurt if we can help it."

"You can't . . ." Kelly's eyes were darting, looking for a

way out. "You never told me you were going to take over the ABM network. I'm not . . . I can't . . ."

Kinsman stared at him. "Okay, Pat," he said at last. "I don't want you to do anything you don't want to do." But in his mind, Kinsman was startled. *Pat's not on our side! I was so certain of him. But he can't make the crossover. How many others am I wrong about?*

Kelly hurried out of the office. Kinsman watched the door slide shut behind him. For long moments he did nothing.

Finally he returned his attention to the phone and tapped out Leonov's number. The screen stayed blank and a man's voice said, "Sir, all communications with Lunagrad are down."

"The lines are cut?"

"Nosir. No physical damage. They've just closed down their comm center. No traffic in or out. Our monitors show no Earthside traffic, either."

They're fighting, Kinsman realized. *It must be a real civil war over there. And there's not a damned thing we can do to help Pete. That's all he'd need—a bunch of armed Americans marching into Lunagrad.*

But he could not stay in his office any longer. Kinsman punched out the number for the comm center and told the answering technician, "Page Captain Perry and have him meet me at the access hatch to the main Lunagrad tunnel."

There were a dozen points where Lunagrad and Moonbase touched each other: the main plaza, the hospital, the recreation dome. The main tunnel was the oldest and most strategic point of contact. It was here that the two separate bases had originally been united. And in a show of everlasting trust and friendship, much of the life support plumbing and electrical power cabling had been routed through this tunnel.

Kinsman never got there.

As he hurried down the corridor that led to the main tunnel the P.A. loudspeakers set into the rough stone ceiling suddenly blared:

"KINSMAN . . . CHET KINSMAN!"

He skidded to a stop under one of the speakers. As he stared at it, set overhead between the fluorescents and some piping, he recognized Frank Colt's voice.

"Chet, listen to me. We've taken the water factory. Ernie Waterman's here, and so is Pat Kelly and a lot of other loyal officers. We're going to shut down the water supply for Moonbase in exactly one hour unless you surrender yourself to us. If you try to take us here we'll blow the whole fucking water factory sky-high."

Saturday 11 December 1999: 1520 hrs UT

THE HOUR WAS nearly over.

Kinsman stood at the railing of the balcony that rimmed the communications center. *Everything looks so damned normal,* he thought.

Down below, on the main floor of the center, the technicians were bending over the consoles and display screens. All of Moonbase seemed serene and secure. All except the water factory. And there had been no contact with Lunagrad for more than six hours.

Chris Perry came up beside Kinsman. He was taller and broader in the shoulders than Kinsman, with a wide-boned, open Norseman's face: eyes the color of a summer sky. "We've triple-checked every person in the base," he said, in a youthful tenor voice. "Only thirty-two people are missing, mostly Aerospace Force ninety-dayers. They must be the ones at the water factory."

"Thirty-two? Kinsman echoed. "So the hard-core dissidents are that few." *But more than enough to stop us.*

Diane was sitting at a desk not far from where he stood. She, too, had been working steadily. But now she got up and walked slowly to Kinsman, a plastic message sheet in her hand.

"Priority message from General Murdock," she said, looking straight into his eyes. "We just finished decoding it.

418

You've been relieved of command. Frank Colt is the new commander of Moonbase. You're ordered to report to Washington immediately."

Kinsman reached out and took the plastic sheet from her fingers. It had been used so many times that the electrostatically formed letters looked blurred and smudged. Or is my eyesight going bad on me? The back of Kinsman's neck was knotted painfully. His chest ached.

"This just came in out of the blue?" he asked Diane.

She nodded. "They don't know that anything unusual's going on here. Not yet. The change of command has nothing to do with your revolution."

Turning to Perry, Kinsman said, "The Great White Father has relieved me of command. What do you think the Indians will say?"

The young Captain shrugged his husky shoulders. "We're not taking orders from Washington anymore. We take our orders from you."

Kinsman stared hard at the blond youth. "You're sure that you realize what you're saying? You can avoid a lot of grief. If we fail . . ."

"We won't fail," Perry said with a quick smile.

We'd better not! Aloud, Kinsman said, "Okay, Chris . . . here's what I want you to do . . ."

It was five minutes before Colt's deadline when Kinsman arrived at the water factory entrance.

As he stepped off the power ladder he saw that the entrance—an open space that had once been a natural cave—was now guarded by two unarmed men. Guns were carefully locked away in Selene. Only a few were available at any time, and Kinsman had control of most of them.

He recognized one of the men: a middle-aged accountant who worked in the procurement group. He was an asthmatic, and this excitement was not helping his heaving chest. The other was younger, a newcomer, one of the ninety-day shavetails. Kinsman had seen him before, but could not recall his name. He wore ordinary gray fatigues without insignia or color code.

Wordlessly they walked him through the rough-hewn

chamber. The overhead fluorescents glowed, the rock walls felt cold. Forcing himself to smile, Kinsman murmured to them, "Relax. Nobody's going to get hurt."

They did not answer. At the end of the chamber, the redhead from Jill's party was standing tensely in front of the doors that opened onto the factory's office area. She looked angry.

"I didn't expect to see you here," Kinsman said.

She was not wearing a party dress now; just a pair of green fatigues that marked her as a member of the life-support group. But they could not conceal the ripeness of her figure.

"Follow me," she said.

She pushed open the door and led him down the curving corridor, in silence. Kinsman could not help noticing the way her butt moved inside the fatigues. They passed the computer area and he stared hard through the long windows as they walked by. The computer's lights were flashing away as usual even though no one was sitting at the desk stations. They haven't shut anything down, Kinsman realized. Then he added, Yet.

"I never did get your name straight at the party," he said to the redhead.

"Doesn't matter."

He pulled alongside her. "Come on now. Politics is one thing, but you don't have to be inhuman about it."

In coldly clipped tones she said, "What happened at the party was strictly business."

"Business?" Even as he said it, Kinsman realized, Kee-rist! Internal Security Agency! No wonder she's sore. She took all the trouble of going to bed with me and didn't learn a thing. Probably looks bad on her file.

Soon they were out of the corridor and into the factory area itself. She led Kinsman through a maze of piping, up onto catwalks that threaded through the electric arcs and main pumps. He could feel the machinery throbbing like a giant mechanical heart, making the metal grillwork of the catwalk vibrate. Off in the distance the muted thunder of the rock crushers went on without slack.

Pat Kelly was standing on a platform on the next level

above the catwalk. Under the harsh lights, Kinsman could see that Kelly was fidgeting nervously, his rabbit's face a picture of anxiety. He wore a gun in a holster buckled to his hip.

The redhead stopped at the base of the ladder that led up to the platform. "Major Kelly will take over from here," she said.

"Tell me one thing," said Kinsman.

She looked at him warily.

"Still think I'm cute?"

She flushed angrily and spun away from him so fast that her shoulder-length hair swung over her face momentarily. Kinsman watched her stamp back down the catwalk for a few seconds, admiringly, then reluctantly turned to the ladder and started climbing.

Kelly was genuinely frightened. He could not look straight at Kinsman.

"Come on," he said, gesturing down another spidery catwalk. "We don't have much time."

"I didn't expect you to be with them," Kinsman said, falling in step beside the younger officer.

"I didn't expect you to be handing Moonbase over to the Russians," Kelly answered, keeping his eyes straight ahead. "Or to hand them our defense satellites."

"You're wrong about that, Pat. We're creating a new nation here."

Kelly shook his head.

"You know, if you blow up the water factory you'll be killing everyone up here."

"They can send us water from Earthside."

"How soon? Two, three days? A week? A month? And how much? Enough for a thousand people, every day? Don't be stupid, Pat. And don't think they'll do *anything* —especially if the shooting starts."

Kelly did not reply.

"It's your wife and kids, Pat. You'll be killing them, too."

"You're the guy who made me bring them here! Was that your idea, to use them as hostages?"

"I'm trying to save their lives."

For the first time Kelly turned to face Kinsman. "By

handing them over to the Russians? So *they* can shoot them?" He banged a fist against the catwalk railing, making it reverberate hollowly. "If we go to war they're as good as dead anyway. I'm not going to let you help the Russians beat America."

"Then why don't you help me to prevent the war from happening?" Kinsman's voice rose enough to echo off the huge metal machinery below them.

"You can't talk your way out of this," Kelly said, starting to walk along the catwalk again. "You can't avoid the war by giving the enemy everything he wants."

"Leonov and his people aren't the enemy."

"They're Russians! That's the enemy! I took an oath to protect and defend the United States of America!" Kelly shouted, his voice cracking. "So did you. It might not have meant anything to you, but it's the most important thing in my life."

"It won't work, Pat."

"I know what my duty is!"

"And your family?"

"I know what my duty is!" Kelly was nearly screaming.

Very quietly, ignoring the growing sullen pain in his chest, Kinsman said, "Joseph Goebbels."

Kelly blinked at him. "Who?"

"Goebbels. Propaganda minister for the Nazis, under Hitler. During the final days of World War Two, when the Russians were pounding Berlin to rubble, he gave cyanide to his wife and kids. Six or seven of them, I think. Then he took some himself."

With a disgusted snort, Kelly sped up his stride along the catwalk. He was almost running.

"I could never understand how a man could do that," Kinsman went on, easily keeping pace with the shorter man. "Not since I first read about it, in high school. Now I know."

Kelly flushed deep red.

"Hold it right there!" It was Frank Colt's voice, coming from somewhere below them. Kinsman peered over the catwalk railing. There he was, down on the floor of the water factory, three levels below. The black Lieutenant Colonel was wearing his regulation fatigues, Aerospace Force blue, with his silver oak leaves pinned to the collar and a heavy automatic pistol strapped around his middle.

"Search him," Colt ordered.

Kinsman took a palm-sized transistor radio from the chest pocket of his coveralls. "This is all I'm carrying." Plus the homing beacon inside my left shoe.

Kelly searched him anyway and missed the flea-sized signaling device as he patted down Kinsman's arms, torso, and legs. They clambered down the long ladder to Colt. Kinsman went slowly; he found that he was panting, short-breathed. Kelly followed him down.

Stepping out onto the stone floor of the factory, Kinsman said to Colt, "Congratulations, Frank. Murdock's made you commander of Moonbase."

Colt's eyebrows shot up. "Yeah? That's good. Makes everything legal and official."

"Except for the fact that Moonbase no longer exists," Kinsman said, forcing a grin. "Murdock doesn't know that yet, but he's always been behind the curve." More seriously, "This is now the nation of Selene, Frank. Washington's orders have no authority here anymore. Neither do Moscow's." I hope! he added silently.

Colt glanced at his wristwatch. "In another minute and a half there won't be any water factory, buddy. Unless you call this shit off."

"Frank, we've been friends for a long time."

"This isn't friendship anymore, Chet. It's treason."

Looking up at the hulking metal shapes throbbing around them, Kinsman asked, "Where's Waterman?"

"Busy." Colt gestured vaguely.

"Planting explosives."

"That's right."

"Frank, if you do this you're not only going to kill everyone in Selene. You'll be killing everyone on Earth, too."

"Stuff it. Nobody's gonna die if you tell your people to forget this independence shit. I'll even see to it that the whole thing's hushed up. Nobody arrested, no hassles. You can go back Earthside . . ."

"And get nuked."

Colt's jaw muscles clenched. He looked at his wrist again. "The explosives are set to go off in less than a minute. You better make your move."

Despite the roaring in his ears, despite the pain flaring in his chest, Kinsman forced himself to say calmly, "When your explosives go off, Frank, you'll be killing the entire human race."

"You goddamned fool!" Colt's voice was molten steel. "Leonov's pigeon. They've set you up, man! Can't you *see* that? They've set you up! Peace and love and friendship—and you turn the whole ABM system over to them. Fuck that!"

"You're wrong, Frank. We can trust Leonov. He's one of us."

Turning to Kelly, Colt snapped, "Gimme that radio he brought." He took the palm-sized plastic box and thrust it at Kinsman. "Call it off, Chet. Tell 'em to stop. You got fifteen seconds to go."

Kinsman stood unmoving, hands by his sides.

"For Christ's sake!" Kelly screamed. "Do it! Don't make us—"

The lights went off. The rumble of machinery died. Before anyone could say anything the tiny emergency lamps came up, scattering pools of grayish light sparsely amid the dark looming machinery.

Kinsman spoke first. Calmly. Coolly. "Your explosives are electrically fused?"

"Sonofabitch!" Even in the dim lighting Kinsman could see Colt's hand nervously rubbing the holster at his hip.

"There'll be troops coming through here soon," Kinsman told them. "They'll be armed with sniperscopes and gas grenades. Remember, Frank? The stuff you insisted we stock, on your last tour here, so we could fight the Russians without shooting up valuable equipment."

"You haven't won, Chet." Colt yanked the gun from its holster. "Not yet."

He gestured with the gun, ordering Kinsman and Kelly along the walkway that led between the big steel domes of machinery. It was tricky going in the semidarkness, but within a few minutes they met Ernie Waterman.

"They shut off the fucking power!" Waterman cried.

"How the hell am I supposed to . . ." Then he recognized Kinsman and shut up.

Colt waved the gun. "Jury-rig something. You can use batteries, can't you?"

"Yeah, yeah. That's what I was on my way for —batteries."

"Well, get 'em!" Colt's voice was urgent.

Kinsman asked, "Ernie, could you actually blow this up, after you worked so hard to build it?"

A dull, muffled boom made the floor shake. "There's your answer," the engineer replied. "One of the other teams has found some batteries. It's only machinery, *Colonel*. It can be rebuilt. Machines do what they're designed to do. Not like people. People can turn on you."

"And people can behave like machines," Kinsman snapped back, "following programming that's obsolete."

"Patriotism isn't obsolete."

"It is when it leads to the destruction of the nation you're being loyal to."

"Cut the crap," Colt said, "and go find some goddamned batteries."

Waterman hurried down the walkway, his canes clicking on the stone floor. Kinsman wondered, What did they blow? How much damage did they do? He felt as if his chest were being rubbed raw, from the inside.

Another explosion. Closer. They all winced. Kelly put his hands to his ears.

"They're all finding batteries." Colt smiled grimly.

They walked to a row of electric arcs, a line of stainless steel jackets that looked like cannon shells the size of a man, standing on heavily insulated supports. Conveyor belts carried pulverized rock slurry into one end of each jacket; a maze of piping at the base carried away water and minerals. Standing there neatly in a row the arcs reminded Kinsman of missiles waiting for the final push of the red button.

The conveyor belts were still now. The arcs silent and powerless. Somewhere in the darkness Kinsman could hear the *drip, drip* of slurry leaking through a seam in the belting. Like the drip of blood from a wound. Then his eyes caught an ugly cluster of red packages wedged under one of the arcs:

explosives, electrical detonator, coils of wire.

Colt holstered his gun and leaned against one of the stainless steel jackets. Kinsman stood before him.

"You're killing everybody here," he said simply.

"No," Colt replied. "*You* are."

"And everybody on Earth." Where's Perry and the cavalry? If they blow the arcs we're finished. We'd never be able to rebuild them without help from Earthside.

Wearily, Colt said, "Chet, you can afford to be a high flier. You take your own chances, it's only your own white ass if you get caught. But what happens to every black man in uniform if I turn traitor? What'll their lives be worth if Washington thinks I'm helping you?"

What's he trying to tell me? Kinsman asked slowly, stalling, "What are their lives worth now, Frank? What happens to them when the missiles are launched? Most of the blacks in the States are living in urban areas, aren't they? Right in the prime targets."

"But *you're* the one who's gonna let the Russians launch their missiles!"

"No, Frank."

"Yes! Dammit, man, open your eyes! If you let the Russians grab the ABM satellites they can nuke the hell out of America and stop any counterstrike we launch."

"Nobody's going to use those satellites except us," Kinsman said, his voice rising. "The people of Selene. And we'll use them against any and all missiles—Russian or American. Or Chinese or French or South African!"

"Bullshit!" Colt snapped. "You've been conned, man! Once the Russians get their hands on our satellites, you know they ain't gonna cooperate with you. They been sweet-talkin' you and you fell for it."

"We can trust Leonov."

"Like hell! Can't trust Reds. Not any of 'em."

Kinsman felt as if he'd run a thousand meters—no, a thousand kilometers. "Frank, you're scared of trusting anyone. You're scared of taking the risk. And I'm telling you that unless we trust Leonov and his people, unless we start trusting one another, the world's going to go up in flames."

Colt stubbornly shook his head.

"You're chicken, Frank. Scared of trying something new.

So you fall back on the regulations. When in doubt, follow the rules. Right?"

"Right!"

"Play it Murdock's way. Obey all orders blindly. Do what they tell you. Tote dat barge, lift dat bale . . ."

Colt punched him. A short savage right that came from the hip and clipped Kinsman squarely on the jaw. Kinsman actually felt himself lifting off his feet, flailing ridiculously in the low lunar gravity, and collapsing in a heap—ass, spine, shoulder, head—on the stone floor. His feet were the last to touch down.

Pat Kelly stared at him, frozen with surprise.

For a moment Kinsman lay there, tasting blood in his mouth. "That's the way, Frank. Kill and be killed."

A tangled skein of expressions worked across Colt's face. He said nothing.

"Frank," Kinsman said, still on his back, propping himself up on one elbow, "the black people of America, of Africa, of *everywhere*, are going to die. Before the month is out. Maybe before another week is out. Is that what you want?"

"And you're gonna save 'em by turning 'em over to the Reds?"

"I'm going to save them by making them free."

"Ahhh . . ." Colt's face went sour. "You sound like a fucking dumb revolutionary. I been that route. It sucks."

"Why isn't Ernie back?" Kelly worried out loud. He peered nervously down the dim walkway.

Maybe Perry's men intercepted him, Kinsman hoped. Another explosion boomed faintly. Far off. Gas grenade? More likely another chunk of the factory being destroyed.

Kinsman got slowly to his feet. "Frank, Pat—have either of you thought about what it is that you're defending? The United States of America. Is it really the nation you want it to be? Does it work the way you want it to?"

"Don't start that," Kelly muttered.

"Think about it," Kinsman said. "Look at what's happening down there. Fuel shortages. Food shortages. Riots. More people in jail than on the streets. Army patrols in every city. Curfews. Surveillance. What the hell kind of a nation is that?"

"So you want to let the Russians blow it up?"

"No! I want it changed. But they're not heading toward change. They're heading toward war."

"The United States will never start a war," Kelly said.

"What difference does it make who starts it?" Kinsman snapped. "Who's going to *prevent* it? We're the only ones who can."

"The United States . . ."

"Pat, stop spouting schoolbook lessons! There are people down there who *want* the war! They think they'll live through it while the rabble get fried."

"That's Communist propaganda!"

Kinsman shook his head. "The two of you—open your eyes. That wonderful land of the free and home of the brave—it's gone." With a chill in his heart, Kinsman realized it was something he had known for years, but ignored, buried, hid away from his conscious thoughts. "That beautiful nation died in 1963, while we were still kids. Maybe someday it'll be beautiful and free again, but not the way it's going now. Not if it's subjected to a nuclear attack."

For a long moment the three men stood facing one another, an unresolved triangle of silence.

Suddenly a rumbling noise startled them. Turning, they saw Waterman limping along the walkway, painfully towing a handcart laden with bulky, heavy-looking shapes.

Where is Perry? Kinsman screamed to himself.

"Got batteries, connectors, firing actuators—everything we need," Waterman said tiredly. "Had to come the long way around, though. Soldier-boys all over the place, swarming on the catwalks, everywhere. They're ripping out the explosives wherever they find them."

It's only a matter of time, Kinsman told himself. Maybe the factory isn't too badly damaged. Maybe we can still make it happen.

Wordlessly he watched Waterman and Colt work at fever pitch to connect the batteries to the explosives. But if they blow the arcs here, we're finished, Kinsman knew.

"A matter of time," he said aloud.

Waterman glanced up from his work at Kinsman.

"C'mon," Colt urged the engineer. "We gotta get it off

before the troops show up." He looked over toward Pat Kelly. "Go down the walkway there as far as the end of this row of arcs. Lemme know when they're in sight."

As Kelly started down the dimly lit walkway Kinsman took two quick steps, brushed past the kneeling Colt, and grabbed Waterman by the back of his collar. He yanked the engineer away from the explosives and sent him staggering backward. Colt sprang to his feet and pulled the pistol from its holster as Waterman landed on the seat of his pants with a painful *thwack*.

For an instant no one moved. Kelly stood a few paces up the walkway. Waterman sat sprawled on the floor. Colt pointed his gun at hip level toward Kinsman.

"You're not going to do it," Kinsman said. "Even if I'm dead wrong, this is the only chance we have to get out without a war." He stooped down and grabbed a fistful of wires.

Colt's voice was gunmetal cold. "You're not just gonna be dead wrong, Chet. You're gonna be dead."

"Goddammit to hell," Waterman moaned. "You bent my goddamned brace. Hey, leave those wires alone! If you touch that red one to the battery terminal . . ."

Kinsman's fingers tightened around the wires.

"Chet!" Colt raised his gun, arm fully extended. The muzzle was ten centimeters from Kinsman's face, a yawning black tunnel to eternity.

"That's the only way you'll stop me, Frank." Kinsman heard his own voice as if it were coming from a long way off: strangely flat and calm, as if he were reading lines that had been rehearsed eons ago.

"Chet, I'll kill you!"

"Then do it. If you have your way, everybody's going to die anyway."

Kelly found his voice. "Shoot him! What are you waiting for?"

"Chet," Colt said again, "take your hands off the wires and step away. If you don't, I'll have to shoot."

"No way, Frank."

Colt pulled the gun back slowly, then with his left hand slid the action back, cocking it with a loud metallic *click, clack*.

"I mean it, Chet."

"I know. It all boils down to the two of us, doesn't it? It's you and me, Frank. Life or death."

"If you're wrong," Colt said, his face shining with sweat. "If you're wrong . . ."

"Leonov is with us. He's doing the same thing in Lunagrad that we're doing here."

"That's what he wants you to think."

"That's the truth."

"No . . ."

"Yes! The only way to prevent the end of the world is by trusting him. And if you can't trust him, Frank, then trust *me*. This is the only way, Frank. *The only way*."

The gun wavered just the slightest fraction of a centimeter.

"Don't listen to him!" Kelly screamed. "Shoot him! Shoot!"

Colt let his arm drop. He turned to Kelly. "You shoot him, hero. You get the job done."

Kelly blinked a half-dozen times. "Me?"

"Chickenshit," Colt said. "It's all right for the black boy to do your dirty work, but you haven't got the guts to do it for yourself."

Waterman, still sprawled on the floor, said, "You've gone crazy. All three of you—you're nuts!"

"Nobody's going to shoot anyone," Kinsman said. He yanked at the wires and pulled them away from the explosives. Then he stood up as Colt holstered his gun.

In the distance Kinsman could hear the clatter of men running. Faint voices. Lights flashing around the silent machines, casting eerie flickering shadows along their looming bulk.

Waterman broke into sobs. "You're gonna let them nuke the United States. You're gonna let them kill my girls, you stupid sonofabitch."

"No," Kinsman said firmly. "We're going to stop them from destroying themselves. If there's enough of this factory left to keep us alive."

"You hope," said Colt.

"It's the only hope we have," Kinsman answered.

"You'd better be right," Waterman said, his voice trembling. "You'd just better be right. If they kill my girls, I'll kill you. I swear it on my wife's grave. With my bare hands I'll kill you, Kinsman."

Silently Kinsman replied, Get in line, Ernie. There are plenty of others ahead of you.

His office was jammed with people.

It surprised Kinsman. He was bone-weary, soaked with fear, sweat, and exhaustion as he trudged the final length of corridor to his office door. He felt totally alone, wrapped in apprehension. What's happening at Lunagrad? Why hasn't Pete called?

Then he slid the office door open and saw more than a dozen people packed into the small room. All the display screens were blaring. Diane sat behind his desk, the phone's handset clamped to one ear and her hand pressed against the other so she could hear over the noise of the crowd. Nearly every light on the phone keyboard was lit. Hugh Harriman was working the other phone, at the couch, yelling and waving his arms.

Kinsman went straight to the desk. Diane looked up at him. Simultaneously they asked, "Are you all right? How bad's the damage to the factory?"

The ghost of a smile flitted across Diane's face. She brushed a hand across her forehead. "You don't look so good."

"I could use a drink. What's the word on the damage? How bad is it? I didn't stay to see it all."

"Hugh's getting reports from the maintenance team."

Chris Perry pushed his way to Kinsman's side. "We've done it, sir! Everything's secure. The whole base is ours. The only real resistance was at the water factory, and they're all rounded up."

"Fine. What about the damage reports?"

People were clustering around Kinsman, grinning, flushed with victory. But Harriman was still gabbling a steady stream of rapid-fire talk into the phone at the couch.

Kinsman made his way toward the couch; people cleared a path for him. "Hugh, how bad is it?"

Harriman flailed a pudgy hand at him. "I'm trying to find out, dammit! Give me a minute or two!"

Perry asked, "Sir, what about the, uh, prisoners from the water factory?"

"Return them to their quarters. Put an armed guard at the end of each corridor. Just see that they don't get into any more mischief." Kinsman's head was buzzing. "Any word from Leonov?"

Diane answered, "We received a call from Lunagrad about half an hour ago. Not from Colonel Leonov, but from one of the scientists. It was a personal call for Dr. Landau."

"Landau? No other communications from them?"

"No."

Puzzled, Kinsman turned toward the desk. On the wall display screens he could see that the sections of Selene currently being shown looked quiet and secure, completely normal, except that the main plaza was crowded with people in a holiday mood. They were milling about, looking happy, excited. But then one screen changed to show an area of the water factory: an explosion had ripped open half a dozen pipes and precious, sacred water was gushing out, flooding the area knee-deep as a team of repair technicians sloshed in it, trying to stem the flow. Kinsman felt as if one of his own arteries had burst: that was his life's blood being wasted.

He sank into the chair next to the desk and reached for the phone's extra handset. Diane handed it to him, without taking the receiver she was using from her ear. Briefly their eyes met; neither of them smiled.

Kinsman took the handset and punched an open line on the keyboard. "Lunagrad," he said into the phone. "Colonel Leonov."

A communications tech's voice answered, "Sorry, sir, but the links with Lunagrad have been very spotty. We're getting no response at present."

Jesus Christ, what's going on over there? Kinsman struggled to keep his voice calm. "Use the laser comm system. Swing it from the lock on the space station to lock onto one of Lunagrad's receiving mirrors."

"Sir, I'll need authorization for—"

"This is Kinsman. I'm going to put Captain Perry on the

line, and by the time he gets here that laser had better be pointing at a Lunagrad mirror. I want a link established and I want it *now*!"

"Yessir."

Kinsman waved Perry to the desk and explained what he wanted done. He went back to the couch where Harriman was still deep in agitated, animated conversation.

What are all these people doing here? he asked himself. Scanning the crowded room, he saw the chief of the engineering section, two of the top scientists, a couple of young Aerospace Force noncoms who normally worked the catapult facility, several others from various administrative sections, and a few he could not place. And Diane. She got up from the desk and came to him.

"How's it going?" she asked.

He shook his head. "Don't know yet. The water factory's damaged. And there's been no word from Leonov."

"Are you all right?"

"Yeah. Fine. How about you?"

"I want to help. What can I do?"

Shrugging, "Sit and sweat it out with the rest of us." And then he understood why the others were here. Why the people were gathering in the main plaza. Waiting. Waiting to see if it was going to work. Waiting to learn if they would live or die. On my responsibility, Kinsman thought.

Harriman snorted and slapped his free hand on his thigh. "All right, all right!" he yelled into the phone. "Keep feeding all the details into the computer so we can update the assessment."

Kinsman was standing in front of him as he slammed the receiver down on its cradle.

"Well?" Kinsman demanded.

Harriman rolled his eyes and made a fluttering motion with one hand. "Not too good, not too bad. I got all the damage-control teams to put their preliminary assessments into the computer and then let the stupid machine mull it over for a few minutes."

"And?"

"Preliminary analysis: water production down roughly forty percent. Minerals and ores down a little less, maybe twenty-five, thirty percent. They blew a lot of plumbing, but the big hardware—the rock crushers—they just didn't have enough explosives to really damage those monsters."

"Forty percent," Kinsman muttered. "For how long?"

Harriman said, "Two weeks. But that's too damned preliminary to count. Say a month, at least."

Kinsman did a quick mental calculation. "We can live with that. Water'll be scarce for a month or so, but we can do it."

Harriman lurched to his feet. "So we'll drink our booze straight, eh?"

And suddenly they were all laughing, almost cheering, with relief. Perry's strong tenor voice cut through the noise. "I've got Lunagrad! They're bringing Leonov to the phone!"

The office went absolutely silent. It all hangs on Pete, Kinsman knew.

He went to the desk. Perry got up from the chair and handed the receiver to Kinsman. He felt suddenly weak and dwarfed beside the younger man. Sitting, he glanced at Diane, who swiveled the phone screen around for him to see it.

The screen was a blur of rainbow static. Then it abruptly cleared and Piotr Leonov's face took form. He looked serious, his iron-gray hair disheveled.

"My apologies, old friend," Leonov said. His voice sounded slightly hoarse.

Kinsman's heart seemed to stop beating.

"I should have thought of the laser link earlier," the Russian went on. "The hard-liners tried to seize the main communications and power centers."

"Tried to?"

"Yes. There was some shooting. I'm afraid we had to kill a few of them. But it's over now. We are in firm control."

A collective gasp of relief from everyone in the office.

"Fine, Pete, fine," Kinsman said soberly. "We've got this end of Selene under control, too."

For the first time Leonov smiled. "Congratulations, then. We must toast the birth of Selene, the newest nation of humankind!"

"Not yet," Kinsman said. "Not until we take command

434

of the space stations. Without them, what we've done so far is meaningless."

Leonov shook his head slowly. "That cannot be done overnight, you understand. But I am already picking reliable men for the task. And the stations themselves are manned by a great variety of peoples—Ukrainians, Uzbeks, even a few Poles and Czechs."

"Really?" Kinsman could feel the tension among the people around him fading. "How did that happen?"

His smile returning, Leonov answered, "A few years ago I served a tour of duty as personnel director for orbital operations. I managed to place emphasis on training, education, and technical skill, rather than Party affiliation and nationality. Enthusiasm and Leninist ideals—although basically correct, you understand!—are no substitute for technical capabilities when you are in a space station."

"Agreed." Kinsman felt himself relaxing a little, too.

"One unhappy thing." Leonov's face grew somber again. "Those two girls I brought to your birthday party. They *were* security agents! One of them shot me."

"Holy hell. Where? Is it serious?"

The Russian scowled. "In the back . . . lower back. I think she was trying to humiliate me. At any rate, the doctors tell me I will live and enjoy life—but I won't be sitting comfortably for a few days."

They all roared. But even while Kinsman was laughing his mind was warning him, The space stations. We've got to take them quickly. Or fail.

Tuesday 14 December 1999: 1200 hrs UT

LIEUTENANT COLONEL STAHL STOOD before the main screens of Space Station Alpha's cramped communications center. "Holiday traffic's starting to build up, I see."

Major Cahill smiled weakly at his boss's joke.

The comm center was a shoebox of metal and plastic with six monitor desks nested so tightly that if one of the technicians tried to stretch an arm it would knock the headset off the person next to her. When they spoke to the spacecraft that were approaching or leaving the station, it was in the low, whispering, economical jargon of flight controllers everywhere.

Major Cahill sat at a cramped desk of his own, built into the metal bulkhead off to one side of the compartment. The entire forward bulkhead was a checkerboard of radar and video display screens, a kaleidoscope that showed all the traffic around Station Alpha.

Stahl always felt claustrophobic in here. His armpits went clammy. The room was too small, too densely packed with humming electrical gear and muttering human beings. It always smelled sweaty, tense. He pointed to one of the screens that showed a nearly empty field of view. Only one speck was discernible against the background of stars.

"Is that the shuttle from Moonbase?" Cahill nodded and touched a stud on his desktop. Alphanumerical symbols sprouted on the screen alongside the lunar shuttle, telling its position, estimated time of arrival, cargo, and crew.

Major Cahill was lanky and lantern-jawed. During his tour of duty aboard Alpha he had allowed a sandy mustache to grow; it was now thick enough to curl at the ends. He intended to shave it off before returning home for the holidays. If the world lasted that long. Cahill's job included keeping track of both the American and Russian unmanned ABM satellites. He knew that the lasers aboard those satellites could slice Alpha into very small pieces. And there was nothing he or anyone else could do about it, except threaten to treat the Soviet space stations to the same kind of surgery.

Lieutenant Colonel Stahl—chunky, solid, squared-off face seamed by age and weather, nose bent from a fracture incurred at a long-forgotten Academy football game—was commander of the station. If he worried about their vulnerability, he gave no sign of it.

"We have another bird approaching," Cahill told his commander. "The emergency troopship coming up from Vandenberg, to beef up our crew. Its ETA is going to conflict with the lunar shuttle."

"The troopship has priority," Stahl said crisply.

Cahill agreed with a nod, but said, "You know, boss, we haven't had a supply shipment from Moonbase for two days. Their catapult's on the fritz."

"Yes, I know."

"Right. Well, if you take a look at the cargo the shuttle's carrying . . ."

Stahl leaned forward slightly and squinted at the symbols on the screen showing the lunar shuttle.

"The LXY FDSTF means 'luxury foodstuffs,' Harry. Chicken, fresh vegetables, maybe even some fruit. It might be a good idea to get them packed away safely *before* those green troopers come stomping aboard."

Stahl pursed his lips. "H'mm. Green troopers, you say."

"None of 'em been on orbital duty before. There's going to be a lot of upchucking, a lot of wasted food. And if they see the good stuff being offloaded, we won't be able to keep it just for us senior types. Their officers will want their fair share."

"Who's in command of the detachment?"

"Some major straight from Murdock's staff. He'll have a pipeline right back to the General."

Stahl tugged at an earlobe, then grinned. "All right. Vector the troopship into a parking orbit while we offload the goodies and stash them safely away. Then we can let Murdock's snoops come on board."

Cahill grinned broadly. "Right you are, boss."

* * *

Strapped into the contour seat, Kinsman felt the slight bump when the shuttle hard-docked with Alpha's landing collar. He forced himself to stay relaxed, remain in the seat, as tinier bumps and vibrations told him that the station crewmen were attaching the access tunnel to the shuttle's main hatch.

Kinsman was in the front seat of the shuttle's passenger compartment. The spacecraft carried no cargo, despite the information radioed ahead to Alpha. There were twenty-six men aboard, the maximum the shuttle could carry. The cargo hold was empty. The men were armed.

It had been a long thirty-six hours in free-fall, between Selene and Station Alpha. Kinsman had always loved the feeling of weightlessness, the sense of freedom that it brought. But this time he felt confined, pinned down, trapped. He kept in constant contact with Selene by tight-beam laser link, impossible for the space stations or Earthside to intercept. Everything was under control. Apparently. Earthside suspected nothing. Apparently.

You could be stepping into the midst of a nasty reception committee, he told himself. They might have seen through your story about the catapult being inoperative. Even if they haven't, you've only got twenty-six men to seize control of Alpha. Kinsman knew there were several hundred people aboard the space station. But most of them were technicians, scientists, civilians working for the Aerospace Force. Only about forty of them were real troops capable of organized resistance. No more than forty. If we can surprise them, move fast enough . . .

And is everything really under control at Selene? Kinsman wondered about his decision to trust Frank Colt. And Diane.

It had happened on Sunday, after a night of cautious celebration during which the Americans and Russians had mingled freely—all except the dead and the prisoners. That morning, as Kinsman went over the list of available personnel and tried to puzzle out in his mind how many men he would need to seize all three space stations *and* maintain a strong hand in Selene, he realized that there were not enough people to go around. He called Colt and Diane and Hugh Harriman to his office.

Harriman looked tired but happy. He had spent the hours of drinking and quiet celebration the previous night telling everyone that at last he could become the citizen of a nation once more and stop being a stateless person.

Diane was calm and cool. Too cool, Kinsman thought. As if she had to maintain a certain distance away from him. Projection, Kinsman told himself. You're blaming her for feeling about you the way you feel about her. But you *can't* get too close to her, he knew. Not yet. Not now.

Colt looked wary and . . . something else. Kinsman could not put his finger on it. Uncertain. Undecided.

They sat. Colt on a slingchair, looking as relaxed as a mountain lion surrounded by hunters. Harriman slumped on the couch, muttering about homebrew vodka and pain thresholds. Diane sat beside him, quietly, her eyes searching Kinsman's.

Kinsman stayed behind his desk. El Presidente, he said to himself. The successful revolutionary who now has to worry about counter-revolutions.

"How's everything in the comm center?" he asked Diane.

"Fine," she replied. "No hint of suspicion from Earthside. All traffic perfectly normal."

Kinsman licked his lips. "Good. Now, the next step is to take the space stations. If Diane's right they don't have an inkling of what happened here yesterday."

"Yet," Colt murmured.

"And they won't," Kinsman countered, "as long as we've got a loyal crew at the comm center." He looked at Diane as he said it. She gazed back at him. "With the exception of keeping the comm center and the launch facilities guarded," he went on, "I don't see any reason why everything can't go on normally here at Selene."

"The barriers between Moonbase and Lunagrad are down," Harriman agreed.

"They were only paper barriers. We're all part of the same nation, the same people. We have been, for years. There aren't any walls between us."

Colt made a grunting sound that might have been a half-stifled derisive laugh.

"I'm going to need every military man available to take the space stations, plus a few to keep the comm center and launch facility secure. The catapult is shut down."

"And the Russians?" asked Colt.

"Leonov is going through the same exercise. He's already got his shuttles heading for their stations. No other flights in or out of Lunagrad."

Harriman said, "It's one of those lovely ironies that the Yanks and the Rooskies don't trust each other, so they don't tell each other what's happening at their bases. But it's only a matter of time before they figure out that nothing's leaving *either* Moonbase or Lunagrad. They'll get suspicious then."

"That's why we've got to move fast." Kinsman got up and stepped around the desk. "Hugh, I was thinking of asking you to act as chief honcho around here while I'm gone."

"Lord no!"

Kinsman raised a hand to calm him. "I know, I know. You're not the right man for the job. Philosophers aren't leaders of men."

"Shit! You've got a nice way of deballing people."

Turning to Colt, "But military officers are, by training and attitude, leaders of men."

The black man looked startled. "What're you saying?"

"I'm asking, Frank. Asking if I can trust you to run our half of Selene until I get back from the space stations."

Colt laughed bitterly. "You're crazy, man."

"I need you, Frank. I need the job done, and done well. You can do it."

"I'm not on your side! Haven't you caught up with that fact yet?"

Kinsman leaned back on the edge of the desk. "Frank, you could have stopped me there at the water factory. But I asked you to trust me and you did. I think you can see that Leonov's keeping his word . . ."

"They can still pull the rug out from under you anytime, buddy. Anytime at all."

"Maybe. Maybe Leonov's bluffing, although I don't think he'd get himself shot in the ass just to . . ."

"Shot where?"

Harriman bubbled, "You should've seen him last night! Had his goddamned ass in a sling! For real!"

Colt shook his head, bewildered.

"Frank." Kinsman was serious. "I'm asking you if you will run Selene for a few days—our half of it, at least. Get the repairs started on the water factory. Make sure everything runs smoothly. What you'll be doing will have nothing to do with which side you're on. You'll be taking care of several hundred men, women, and children, making sure that this place runs smoothly. Whether I win or lose is something else entirely."

Colt started shaking his head.

"All I ask is that you promise not to try to contact the space stations or Earthside. Just take care of the job that needs doing here. Can I trust you?"

"Let Pat Kelly do it," Colt said.

Kinsman could feel his jaw muscles clench. "I can't trust Pat. Besides, he's in no emotional condition to do anything. If we get through this alive and the war is stopped, we'll ship him and his family home."

Colt repeated, "I'm not on your side."

"I don't care which side you're on," Kinsman said. "Can you run our half of Selene for a few days—as a temporary neutral?"

"That'd be *helping* you, man!"

"I'll do it," Diane said.

Kinsman blinked at her. Harriman mumbled something undecipherable.

Diane smiled at them. "Don't look so shocked. I can be a leader of men, as you so neatly put it, Chet."

Harriman's brows rose and he shot Kinsman a quizzical glance.

"Don't think that running road tours all those years didn't take leadership skills," Diane said. "I've dealt with drugged-out musicians and union bosses looking for payoffs. The people you have here are all pussycats, by comparison. I can manage the base for a few days."

It took several seconds for Kinsman to say, "You'd want to . . . to take that responsibility?"

With a nod, Diane answered, "Somebody's got to. And I really am on your side, you know. I can run the base."

Kinsman admitted, "I never thought of you as base commander."

But Diane had already turned toward Colt. "I'd expect you not to make any trouble while Chet's back is turned."

Kinsman returned his attention to the black Major. "How about it, Frank? A temporary truce. Will you promise not to try to grab the comm center or the launchpad?"

Colt frowned and blinked and struggled visibly with himself. Finally, "Aw, shit. Okay. I won't make any waves. But I want to be on the first damned shuttle that goes Earthside! I want no part of your crazy revolution."

Harriman looked dubious, but for once he kept his silence. Kinsman felt uneasy and must have looked it.

"What's the matter, Chet?" Diane asked, with a knowing little smile. "Afraid to let a woman run the show? Even for a few days?"

He shrugged and grinned and surrendered gracefully. After all, he told himself, what choice do I have?

A green light was flashing, breaking Kinsman's troubled reverie.

"Okay for egress," the shuttle pilot's voice came over the intercom.

Kinsman unstrapped his safety harness and got out of the seat—floated up, weightless. It had seemed a long thirty-six-hour journey to Alpha. Now it was too short, too soon finished. They had gone over their "battle plan" fifty times. Now he wished for fifty more.

"All right, men." Boys. "Just follow the assignments we've mapped out and they'll never know what hit them. Move fast. Don't shoot unless you have to. Good luck."

Their young, serious, scared faces looked back at him. A few nodded. A couple of others checked their weapons. They all carried pistols, nothing bigger. Dartguns, designed to stop a man with a combination of impact shock and sedative. Not strong enough to puncture the thin metal skin of a spacecraft or space station. Or to knock down a charging opponent.

Kinsman floated past them all to the airlock hatch. He felt and heard the thumps of the station crewmen on the other side, undogging the hatch. Hefting his pistol in his hand, Kinsman pressed the button on the bulkhead alongside the hatch that unlocked it from the ship's interior.

The hatch swung open, revealing a hefty tech sergeant and two airmen in work fatigues. "What . . . ? We were expectin' . . ." Then the Sergeant saw Kinsman's gun.

"Just stand back and don't give us any trouble," Kinsman said.

"What the hell is this?"

They backed the three men out of the cramped metal chamber of the airlock, into the larger area of the unloading bay. From this zero-gravity hub of the many-wheeled station the lunar troops fanned out along three main tubes, the "spokes" that led from the hub through each wheel and out to the farthermost ring. Their objectives were the communications center, the electrical power station, and the officers' quarters. Five men were left in charge of the loading bay. Three teams of seven men each rushed to take their three objectives.

Kinsman remembered the first time he had come to Alpha, the day of its official dedication. Diane had sung for the assembled VIPs. Neal McGrath had been among them, not yet an enemy. The station was going to be a center for private industry, for scientific research and exploration of the heavens. How quickly it had become a purely military base, a control center for the network of antimissile satellites and their powerful laser weapons.

Still, most of the men and women aboard Alpha were civilian employees. Ignore them, Kinsman knew. Take the high ground and the rest comes free. Control their electrical power and you control the station. Cut off their communication with Earthside. Round up the officers before they can organize an effective defense.

Kinsman led the group heading for officer country. They clambered down the long, nearly endless spiral ladder that wound around the tube's inner wall, dropping in free-fall at first, then grabbing at the ladder's handrail and half walking, half leaping as the first gentle pull of gravity returned. Officers' quarters are at Level Four, which spins at a lunar grav, Kinsman knew, thankful that he would not have to face a full Earth gravity—not yet, at least.

They pushed past two startled civilians who were making their way up the tube. Neither of them said a word as the armed men hustled past them. Let 'em go. By the time they figure out what we're up to we'll be in command of the station. They clattered on, footsteps echoing metallically now through the narrow, dimly lit tube.

At last they burst out on Level Four and rushed down the central corridor toward the officers' area. His heart pounding against his ribs, Kinsman searched the nameplates on the doors they passed. There he is! L/C H. J. STAHL. He pushed the door open. Empty. Bed, desk, photos of wife and children, tape cassettes, but the man himself was not there.

Two other station officers were being pulled out of their compartments by Kinsman's grim-faced aides. One of them was Art Douglas; they had gone through astronaut training together. He was as bald and round-faced as Kinsman remembered him from the last time they had met, but he had added a "station tour" mustache to his upper lip. "Chet! What're you doing here? What the hell's going on?" Flanked by the armed youngsters, Douglas and his buddy both looked surprised and more than a little annoyed.

"We're taking over the station, Art. Where's Harry Stahl?"

"Taking over? What do you mean?"

"Just what I said," Kinsman answered, walking down the corridor toward them. "Where's Stahl? This is no time for playing games."

Douglas was looking angry now. His buddy was staring at the guns that the young officers were holding. "This may come as a surprise to you, Chet, but the Colonel doesn't always take me into his confidence about every move he makes. Maybe he's in the head. How the hell should I know?"

Kinsman grimaced. "All right. Move—down into the mess hall." To his half-dozen men he said, "Clean out every compartment along the corridor. Herd them all down to the mess hall."

Douglas and the other officer walked ahead of Kinsman. They did not raise their hands over their heads, and Kinsman tucked his pistol into its holster. But they all knew what was happening.

"This is crazy, Chet. You can't get away with it."

"Just keep walking, Art."

The corridor sloped upward in both directions; it looked

as if you were always walking uphill, although it felt perfectly flat and there was no sensation of climbing at all.

The mess hall was nothing more than a widened section of the corridor with bulging blisters on both sides to make alcoves where people could sit and look outside. It had enough tables to accommodate fifty people at a time. Both ends of the mess hall were open to the corridor, which ran through Level Four like the inner tube of an old-fashioned bicycle tire. At the far end of the mess hall the corridor passed through the galley and a series of storage bays. Kinsman seated the two officers at one of the tables, then walked to the galley and waved a wide-eyed cook and his helpers to seats near Douglas and his smoldering friend.

The Earth slid past the window beside their table as the young lunar troops began bringing other station officers and men and women into the mess hall. They looked shocked, angry, bewildered. A few of them had obviously been awakened from sleep. Although a number of the enlisted personnel were women, only three of the officers were female; the highest-ranking was a captain. Lieutenant Colonel Stahl was not among the prisoners.

"Colonel Kinsman," the overhead speaker blared. A young man's voice. "Colonel Kinsman, please call the comm center."

Kinsman went to the wall phone in the galley, keeping his eye on the rapidly filling tables. Men and women were coming from both sides now, urged by gun-wielding youngsters.

"Kinsman here," he said into the phone. "Put me through to the comm center."

The station's computer buzzed briefly, then a young man's voice said, "Communications."

"This is Kinsman."

"Yessir. Lieutenant Reilly here, sir. We have Colonel Stahl. He was in the comm center when we got here."

Involuntarily Kinsman let out a sigh of relief. "Very good. Bring him up to the officers' mess. You've secured the center?"

"Oh, yessir. No trouble at all."

"Good. Call me when the power station team calls in."

"Will do."

The mess hall was filling with grumbling, frightened-looking men and women when Lieutenant Colonel Stahl was led in by one of Kinsman's youngsters.

"Kinsman! Just what the hell do you think you're doing here?"

"Declaring independence."

"What?" Stahl stood defiantly in the center of the mess hall, legs slightly spread, fists clenched. He looked as if he wanted to spring at Kinsman.

"We're taking over all three of your stations," Kinsman said slowly, walking up to within two feet of him, "as part of creating the independent nation of Selene. It's a funny name, I guess, but the best one we've got. The Russians are doing the same with their space stations."

Stahl's face went white. "You . . . you and the . . . the Russians?" He seemed dazed.

"Moonbase and Lunagrad together, that's right."

"You can't—"

"We have."

The two men stood facing each other, neither one moving, neither one speaking. The loudspeaker broke their stalemate: "Colonel Kinsman, please call the power station."

The kids at the power station were jubilant. No casualties on either side, everything under control. Kinsman congratulated them and told them to stand by for further orders.

He scanned his own men, then nodded to the oldest-looking one. "You men escort these officers back to their quarters, then seal the emergency hatches on both ends of officers' country and station a guard at each end." That'll keep them in their own cabins, where they can't make waves, Kinsman thought. "I'm going down to the comm center."

The communications center was down in the next wheel, Level Three, spinning fast enough to produce nearly half an Earth gee. For the first time in nearly five years Kinsman felt a pull stronger than the Moon's gentle gravity. It was like wading through hip-deep surf.

He sank gratefully into the chair Major Cahill had recently occupied and looked over the display screens that were now showing mostly the various interior sections of the big space station. His chest felt heavy; he was puffing like an overweight jogger.

The mop-up operations took several hours. There were

almost a hundred civilians aboard the station, almost all of them in the outermost wheel, Level One, at a full Earth gravity. Kinsman left them alone for the time being. He concentrated his meager forces on the military areas, hoping he had enough men to do the job. And it began to look as if his gamble had worked. There were only a few other officers who were not in their quarters or at the comm center, loading dock, or power station. There were many more noncoms and technicians spread around the station, but Kinsman's gun-brandishing Luniks rounded them up quickly and efficiently.

Kinsman watched it all from the communications center, slumped heavily in his seat, perspiring with the effort of lifting his chest to breathe. Reports came in from Stations Beta and Gamma: all secure. Those stations were much smaller, with only a squad or two in each. Some of the crewmen on Gamma had recovered from their initial surprise and tried to rush the Luniks with their bare hands. They were all gunned down after a brief scuffle.

"I can't believe it's going so well," said one of the young officers after Captain Perry reported success at Beta. "Weren't these stations on yellow alert, same as Moonbase?"

Kinsman nodded. Even that was an effort. Slowly he said, "Yes, but yellow alert here means stand by to shoot down unfriendly boosters—not repel boarders. Good old S.O.P. Screws you every time."

The kid laughed.

Civilians were starting to phone the comm center, aware that something strange was happening elsewhere on the station. Some of them tried to climb up from their wheel to the inner levels, but they were turned back by Kinsman's guards, stationed at the connecting tubes.

"They're getting kind of panicky," said one of the men at a communications console. "They don't know what's happening, and it's getting to them."

Kinsman said, "Pipe me through the P.A. system."

The kid studied the rows of buttons on the console before him, puckered his face into a frown, then carefully touched two of them in sequence. Turning back to Kinsman, he said, "You're on, sir—I think."

Watching the display screens that showed the central corridor of Level One, Kinsman said calmly, "Attention, please. May I have your attention, please."

In the display screens he saw conversations stop, people walking down the corridor come to an abrupt halt, heads turning up toward the overhead loudspeakers.

"My name is Chester Kinsman." Suddenly he did not know what to say. "Umm . . . today, a group of us from Selene—Moonbase, as you call it—have taken over command of this space station, as well as Stations Beta and Gamma. Our Russian neighbors from Lunagrad have taken similar actions with their space stations. We have formed a new nation, which we call Selene, independent of the United States and Soviet Russia. Independent of all the nations of Earth."

He watched their faces. Shock, incredulity, apathy, anger.

"We've taken the space stations as a matter of self-protection. We intend to transport anyone who wishes to return Earthside, just as soon as possible. In the meantime, please carry on your work as usual. Nobody's going to hurt you or bother you. But for the time being we'll have to ask you to remain in your own sector of the station. Please stay on Levels One and Two, and don't try to get any higher than that until we announce that it's all right. And, oh, yes—there will be no communications Earthside for a while, so don't try to get any messages through the comm center. Thank you."

He studied their faces in the display screens. They looked stunned, for the most part. Most of them looked frightened and angry. A few looked surprised, but not particularly uptight. Europeans, Kinsman surmised. Or Americans who can see past the ends of their noses. One or two faces even smiled. But only one or two. Within half a minute there were knots of babbling, arm-waving conversations filling each display screen.

Kinsman set up temporary headquarters in the rec area, up in Level Six, where the effective gravity was even less than lunar. The walls, floor, and ceiling of the big gymnasium were all padded. Appropriate, he thought. Amidst the rowing machines, oversized barbells, and a magnetic pool table, Kinsman and a few of his men pushed together some benches and a Ping-Pong table next to the only wall phone in the area.

Men scurried in and out constantly, bringing reports and problems to Kinsman. The phone buzzed incessantly, papers piled up on the table. They just grow, Kinsman thought of the papers, like mushrooms.

The captain of the waiting troopship was told to abort his docking with the station and retrofire for return Earthside. He sputtered indignantly about dropsick troops until told that there were several cases of an unidentified viral infection aboard the station. Then he blasted away gladly. Kinsman had the comm center call Earthside with a request for an immediate medical evacuation mission to take more than a hundred uninfected people off the station.

That brought up a bee swarm of calls from Earthside, including one from General Murdock. Kinsman's officers handled them all from the comm center, sticking to their story, claiming that they were on skeleton-crew status because of the infection.

By 1800 hours Kinsman could relax enough to have a brief dinner brought up from the galley. He was just finishing a not-quite-thawed piece of soyloaf when the phone on the wall, just behind his ear, buzzed. "Kinsman here," he said into the speaker.

"Sir," the voice sounded worried, "one of the civilian scientists down in Level One is putting up a terrific squawk. Claims he has a crucial experiment on weather modification going on and he's got to get to the observatory section by 1900 hours or several years' worth of work will be wasted."

"The observatory's in the zero-gee area, next to the loading and docking facilities," Kinsman thought aloud. "What nationality is this man?"

"American, sir. But he claims he's working for the United Nations—UNESCO, if you can believe it."

"The Weather Watch." Kinsman thought it over for a swift moment. "Send him up here. I want to talk with him."

"Yessir."

Kinsman finished his small meal, wondering how Leonov was doing. Too early to expect any word from him. Shouldn't expect everything to go as smoothly for him as it has for us.

Within a few minutes a Lunik officer and a civilian entered the recreation area and crossed the padded floor to Kinsman's makeshift command post. The civilian did not look like a scientist. He was well over six feet tall, with broad shoulders, an athletic body. He glided smoothly across the padded floor; low gee did not bother him. His face was hard, hawk-nosed, set in a looking-for-trouble scowl. The stump of an unlit cigar was clamped in his teeth. He was completely bald, except for the thinnest white fuzz across his skull. He reminded Kinsman more of a Turkish wrestler than anything else—and an angry one, at that.

Kinsman stood up behind the Ping-Pong table as the trio of young officers working beside him made room for the newcomer.

"Ted Marrett," the civilian said, keeping his beefy hands at his sides. He loomed over them all.

"Chet Kinsman."

"Now listen. I don't have time to be polite or repeat what I say, so listen good. I've got a rainfall augmentation experiment project going—been working on it for six fuckin' years. Moving rainfall patterns along the upper Niger valley, trying to hold back the Sahara from creeping farther southward. If I'm not directing the catalysis experiment that starts at 1900, six years' work will fall through, a few million people will starve, and people down on Earth will know that something wonky is happening at this space station."

Kinsman let himself sink back onto the bench. "You're directing the experiment from here?"

"Where the hell else?" Marrett boomed, still standing. "I can see what's happening from here. Key to the whole motherin' setup is the wind and current patterns between the African coast and the Canary Islands. What do you think . . ."

"Whoa, slow down." Kinsman put his hands up, almost defensively. Grinning, he asked, "Do you understand what's happened here today?"

Marrett gave him an even sourer look. "Some of you Lunatics took over the station. Your glorious leader wants to proclaim the independence of the Moon. Big shit. I've got *work* to do, buddy."

"I see," said Kinsman. He looked into Marrett's steel-gray eyes. "I'm the glorious leader."

Now it was Marrett's turn to grin. "Should have guessed. My mouth always has been bigger'n my brains. But, c'mon, time's wasting. I've got to be in touch with my people back on Earth. It's important."

Kinsman realized it would help to allay any suspicions Earthside if the experiment went through on schedule. "You won't mention anything about what we're doing here?"

"Hell, I'm no politician. As long as I can get my work done."

"I'll let you go ahead and do it," Kinsman said slowly, thinking it out as he spoke, "but I'm going to ask the lieutenant here to stay with you and make certain you talk *only* about your work."

"Fine by me," Marrett replied easily. "Only, this job might take ten, twelve hours."

"We'll send a relief if we have to."

Shrugging his big shoulders, Marrett turned to the young officer. "C'mon, sonny," he said.

It was not until they had left that Kinsman asked himself, How in hell would any of us know if he's sticking to his work or sending some sort of nonsense gobbledygook that'll stir up suspicions Earthside? It's one thing to trust Frank Colt; Frank's with us whether he realizes it or not. But this Marrett character is a complete stranger. The one I'm really trusting is that kid lieutenant, and I can't even recall his name.

The phone buzzed again. From the speaker on the wall a scared, shaky voice said tinnily, "Sir, several of the station crew have broken out of confinement down here on Level Four. They shot two of our men, sir. One of them's dead. The other—he's hurt bad, sir."

Tuesday 14 December 1999:
1810 hours UT

KINSMAN SAGGED BACK on the bench, felt his shoulders slump against the padded walls of the gym. The young officers around him froze in their tasks: one was holding a sheaf of papers; another, sitting across from Kinsman, had been reaching for the coffee mug; the third simply stood staring at the phone on the wall, slack-jawed.

Strangely, Kinsman felt no surprise, no shock. You knew all along that it wouldn't go without fighting. They'd never give up so easily. There had to be blood.

His voice as bleak as his soul, he said into the phone grille, "Seal all the hatches leading into Level Four. Nobody in or out."

"But sir," the kid on the other end of the phone objected, "a couple of our men are still in there."

"Seal off Level Four," Kinsman repeated, with more iron in his voice. "Airtight. Get a couple of men EVA at once and dog down all the outside hatches, too. I don't want a molecule getting out of that level. Understood?"

The barest of pauses. "Understood, sir."

He punched the phone off. Turning to the officer with the papers in his hand, "How many men does Stahl have down there?"

The youngster pawed through the sheets. "Duty roster, personnel assignments . . . here we are!" He pulled a flimsy sheet from the stack. "According to this checkoff list there are thirty-five men down there—no, make it thirty-three. Two are in sick bay."

"How many of 'em are women?" asked the kid with the coffee cup.

"Looks like ten."

"They won't fight," the kid said smugly.

"The hell they won't!" snapped Kinsman. "Give them guns and they'll shoot you just as dead as any man." They fight, Kinsman knew. They die, too.

The officer who was standing seemed to pull himself together. "The small arms supply is down on Level Four. They'll have submachine guns."

They were starting to look scared. The seriousness of the situation was sinking in.

"If Stahl has Level Four, then we're cut off from the comm center, and . . ."

"And they're cut off from us and the loading bay."

Kinsman nodded. "Which means that half our force can't get through to our escape route back to Selene."

"Jesus!"

Half turning on the bench, Kinsman touched the phone button. "Comm center," he called.

Swiftly he outlined the situation to the men at the communications center.

"Yessir, we can see them on the monitor screens here," answered the officer in charge. "They've got guns, all right. And they're starting to break out some of the emergency pressure suits."

"That's what I thought," Kinsman said. "Turn off their air."

"Sir?"

"Tell our guys at the power station to pump the air out of Level Four. In fifteen minutes they'll all be unconscious down there."

"Not if they're in pressure suits."

Kinsman said, "There's only a handful of suits down there. Not enough for all thirty-three of them."

"But they've got three of our guys in there, too. One of them seems to be hurt pretty bad. We've got to try to get him to sick bay."

Kinsman hesitated. "Put me on the P.A. system for Level Four only. Patch in their answers to this phone."

"Yessir."

The hatch at the far side of the gym swung open and a young officer burst through. His coveralls were stained with sweat as he lurched crazily toward Kinsman, trying to run in the low gravity. "Sir . . . I got up here . . . fast's I could."

Kinsman recognized the voice; the fear also showed in his eyes. "All right, all right. Take it easy. Calm down. Just what happened on Level Four?"

"I . . . Hard to say. Everything happened so fast. We were standing guard outside the hatch between the mess hall and officers' country. They just broke through the hatch. Popped the explosive bolts. Knocked us flat on our asses. Never had a chance. . . . Shot Polanski while he was lying there—right through his chest!"

"How'd you get away?"

One of the young officers handed the kid a cup of steaming coffee. Another was searching through the medical kit that he had opened on the table.

"The blast from the hatch knocked me behind a table." He took the cup in both hands; still the coffee sloshed from his trembling. "They didn't see me the first couple seconds. I got up and emptied my dartgun at them. Jumbled 'em up enough. They sort of fell over each other and ducked down. I ran out of the galley and then went up the ladder to Level Five. I sealed the hatch behind me."

"Okay, fine. You did the right thing," Kinsman said soothingly.

The kid gulped at the coffee. "I saw Polanski die. They just shot him . . . never gave him a chance." His face was flushed. The officer with the medical kit took out a hypospray syringe.

"It's all right. Everything's under control," Kinsman lied. To the officer sitting next to him he ordered, "Find another phone, fast. Get our men standing by the hatches to disarm all the explosive bolts."

"Yessir!" The youngster was on his way before Kinsman had finished speaking.

The kid finished draining the coffee cup as the other officer pressed the hypospray against his sleeve. "Tranquilizer," he said. "Settle your nerves."

"Shot him," the kid was muttering. "Colonel Stahl himself. Just pointed the gun at Polanski and shot him while he was still on the floor."

Warrior of the week, Kinsman fumed silently. Stahl will get a medal for heroism, shooting kids. Then he thought, And if we win, Polanski will be our first martyred hero. We'll probably put up a statue to him. Big consolation.

The phone buzzed. "Sir, the air pumps to Level Four also supply parts of Level Three, including the comm center, where we are."

Shit! "Better get into pressure suits damned fast," Kinsman said.

The voice sounded distinctly unhappy. "Yessir."

"And what about that P.A. hookup to Level Four?"

"All set, sir, whenever you want it."

"Are they pumping the air out?"

A brief hubbub of background noise. "Yessir, they've just started now."

"All right," said Kinsman. "Plug me into the P.A."

"You're on . . . now."

Kinsman hesitated a moment. Then, "Stahl, this is Kinsman. You'd better stop now, before anybody else gets hurt."

For a moment nothing but a sizzling hum came out of the phone grille. Then Stahl's voice crackled clearly, "Kinsman, the game's over! You've got five minutes to give yourself up, or we'll recapture the station, level by level. I've got the men and the weapons to do it!"

He sounds happy, Kinsman realized. Elated. The sonofabitch is *enjoying* this. He's high on it!

"Stahl, listen to me. You can't get out of Level Four. All the hatches are sealed."

"That's your story."

"We've disarmed the explosive bolts."

"We've got primacord and thermite from the engineering section. We'll get through the hatches. Come on, Kinsman, you're beaten. Give up."

It always comes down to this, Kinsman told himself. You knew it would. There's no such thing as a bloodless coup. Now you make your choice: let them win or be ready to kill them. No idle threats. You can't talk your way out of this one. You've got to be ready to kill them. All of them. That's all they understand.

"Come on, Kinsman!" Stahl snapped impatiently. "We've got three of your own men here. One of them's bleeding to death. You'd better give up quick so we can get him to sick bay in time to save his life."

Rage suddenly boiled past Kinsman's self-control. "You damned hypocritical bastard. You shot the kid, and now you're using him as a hostage!"

"Damned right! I only wish it was you—*traitor!*"

And just as suddenly, with that word, Kinsman's rage turned glacier cold. It was not gone. The fear and anger were still there, greater than ever. But instead of bubbling hot within his guts, now they were frozen into an iron-hard purpose. Beyond all trembling. Beyond all self-doubt. Stahl was no longer a threat, a man to be feared. He was an obstacle that had to be hurdled, a barred gate that must be broken through. Kinsman almost smiled. Idly he glanced at the faces of the men around him: apprehensive, questioning, frightened.

I am sitting in a padded room with a gaggle of kids, rebelling against the United States of America. In the name of humanity. In the name of peace I am going to kill thirty-some men and women. For openers. And God only knows how many more. In the name of peace.

"If this is treason," he said slowly into the phone, "then make the most of it. We started pumping the air out of your level ten minutes ago." A lie; it was more like three, four minutes at the most. "You've got about five minutes before your men start passing out."

"You're bluffing!"

"So you want to be a hero, Stahl? Fine. You've already killed one man, and you're letting another bleed to death. How many pressure suits down there? Twelve? So figure out who among you is going to live and who's going to die. That's a perfect task for a hero, Stahl: pick out the people you're going to murder."

Kinsman punched the phone's off button. Immediately, he called the comm center again. "What's going on down on Level Four? How many suits do they have?"

"We're checking the screens, sir. And we're getting into suits ourselves. It's not easy—takes time."

"What's Stahl doing?" Kinsman demanded, his voice rising.

"Colonel Stahl is waving his arms and yelling for everybody to be quiet. They're all shouting, arguing. They've got

about ten suits out, but nobody's anywhere near sealed up in 'em."

"All right. Get our men on the other sides of those hatches leading to Level Four into suits. I'm going to suit up also and come down there."

"Uh, sir, if we keep the air off long enough it'll kill them, or cause brain damage. And our own men—"

"Just do what I told you," Kinsman snapped. Then he added, "There isn't anything else we can do, son. Not a goddamned thing."

By the time Kinsman had suited up and clumped down to the hatch that opened onto Level Four, the comm center reported that most of Stahl's people had collapsed. Only five had successfully sealed themselves into pressure suits, the Colonel among them. Kinsman ordered them to stop evacuating the air from Level Four; bringing the area down to hard vacuum would accomplish nothing more.

Kinsman had his men pop the hatches all at once, and they moved into Level Four—ten space-suited men holding dartguns in their gloved hands. Kinsman clambered down a ladder that led to the galley hatch. A younger man, unidentifiable in his bulky pressure suit, pushed through ahead of him. No one in sight. The only sounds in Kinsman's ears were his own breathing and the whisper of his suit's air pump.

Pushing through the galley, into the mess hall, they found bodies. Sprawled, blue-faced, but still alive. "Get the emergency oxygen masks on these people," Kinsman ordered.

Six bodies. Two women. He clumped past them and into the corridor that ran through officers' country.

"Got two guys here!" his earphones crackled. "They're surrendering."

"Two men in pressure suits?" Kinsman asked.

"Yessir. No fight. They gave up."

That left three more. He met two of his own men coming down the corridor toward him and almost fired at them. But he quickly recognized that their pressure suits were orange and red—colors that could be easily spotted on the desolate lunar surface—rather than the white of the orbital station's crew.

Together they poked into each compartment along the

corridor. Empty. Reports were pouring in over the suit radio. Men and women found asphyxiated in other parts of Level Four. Most were still alive. Eight were dead, including the wounded man from Kinsman's group.

Kinsman pushed open a compartment door and his nerves flashed red inside him. A space-suited figure sat on the bunk, a submachine gun in its lap. The dartgun in Kinsman's hand was cocked and pointed as his brain screamed, Is it a man or a woman? Is she threatening you?

"Put the gun down on the floor!" Kinsman shouted.

The figure on the bunk took up the gun by its muzzle with two gloved fingers and laid it gently on the floor.

"Stand up."

"Please don't shoot me." Through his earphones, Kinsman heard a man's voice, high-pitched, frightened. "I'm just an adjutant with the Judge Advocate Group. I'm not here to fight!"

A lawyer. Kinsman almost laughed with relief. A mother-humping lawyer! How did he get into a suit while others suffocated?

There was one more suited man to find. And Colonel Stahl.

Stahl's quarters are down this way, Kinsman told himself as he and the other two Luniks behind him plodded down the corridor. Be just like him to start a shoot-out. The thought of their dartguns against a submachine gun did not please Kinsman, especially in the narrow confines of the corridor and the tiny compartments.

Shots! A muffled string of shots coming from up ahead. Kinsman broke into a galumphing sprint, leaving the other two pressure-suited youngsters behind him. Sure enough, there was Stahl's door. Shut. Probably locked. And the shooting? Kinsman kicked at the door. It swung open. Stahl was sitting at his tiny desk, his back to Kinsman. He was in his pressure suit. The submachine gun was on the floor, still smoking.

With the inevitability of a Greek drama, Kinsman knew what he would find. He did not even bother to call to the Colonel. He saw the entire event in his mind's eye: Stahl sitting there at his desk, defeated. Maybe starting to write a

note to his wife or commanding officer. Realizing that he had lost the station to people he considered traitors. Unable to write with the suit's clumsy gloves. Knowing that it was just a matter of time before he would be taken prisoner. Thinking about all that tradition, centuries of military history piling up inside his head, all the gallantry and honor and bravery that had failed.

He believed all that crap, Kinsman thought as he crossed the three-paces-wide compartment.

Stahl facing defeat, disgraced in his own eyes. Staring down at the gun. Holding his breath and lifting up the visor and resting the gun's muzzle against the lip of his neck ring and setting it on semiautomatic and squeezing . . . His last thought: *Don't let me die in vain. Remember Space Station Alpha.* Kinsman knew it as if Stahl had implanted the words telepathically in his brain.

He put his hand on the shoulder of Stahl's space suit and turned the Colonel toward him. The chair swiveled easily. There was not a speck of blood anywhere, except inside the helmet. For the first time in his life Kinsman retched in his pressure suit.

VAFB/SCM TO SACHQ/SJL
COMMUNICATIONS WITH STATIONS ALPHA, BETA, GAMMA INOPERATIVE. PLS ADVISE.

SACHQ/SJL TO VAFB/SCM
BACKUP SYSTEM USE AUTHORIZED. EMPLOY LASER LINK IF NECESSARY.

VAFB/SCM TO SACHQ/SJL
NO RESPONSE ON ANY FREQUENCY, INCLUDING LASER LINK.

SACHQ/SJL TO VAFB/SCM
HOW LONG HAVE ORBITAL STATIONS BEEN OUT OF CONTACT?

VAFB/SCM TO SACHQ/SJL
LAST ROUTINE AUTOMATIC CHECK-IN AT 1700 HRS UT.

NO RESPONSE TO PERSONAL CALLS, ROUTINE TRAFFIC, ETC SINCE 1745 HRS UT.

SACHQ/SJL TO VAFB/SCM
HAVE YOU CHECKED SOLAR ACTIVITY? JAMMING? OTHER POSSIBLE INTERFERENCE?

VAFB/SCM TO SACHQ/SJL
FULL TEAMS OF COMM SPECIALISTS CHECKING FOR PAST THREE HRS. NO INTERFERENCE. THEY ARE JUST NOT ANSWERING. LAST MESSAGE WAS CALL FOR MEDIVAC. CLAIMED INFECTION SPREADING THROUGH ALPHA. POSSIBLE COMM CENTER PERSONNEL INFECTED AND UNABLE TO PERFORM DUTIES?

SACHQ/SJL TO VAFB/SCM
UNLIKELY TO CAUSE BLACKOUT AT BETA AND GAMMA. WILL QUERY TOPSIDE. STAND BY FOR POSSIBLE RED ALERT.

VAFB/SCM TO SACHQ/SJL
WHAT ABOUT MEDIVAC MISSION? IT HAS ALREADY LIFTED FOR ALPHA.

SACHQ/SJL TO VAFB/SCM
CONTINUE MEDIVAC MISSION. IS COMM LINK WITH THEM OK?

VAFB/SCM TO SACHQ/SJL
READ THEM LOUD AND CLEAR. WILL CONTINUE MISSION AND STAND BY FOR RED ALERT.

SACHQ/SJL TO AFHQ/SJL, ADC/SCM
COMMUNICATIONS WITH ORBITAL STATIONS ALPHA, BETA, GAMMA CUT OFF. HAVE INITIATED STANDBY FOR RED ALERT. AWAIT FURTHER ORDERS.

JSC/SJL TO ALL COMMANDS
RED ALERT. REPEAT, RED ALERT. ARM ALL MISSILES PREPARATORY TO STRIKE ORDER. FULL SECURITY ALL BASES AND SUBMARINES. ALL LEAVES CANCELED. THIS

IS NOT A DRILL. REPEAT, THIS IS NOT A DRILL. ACTIVATE
SUBROUTINE 98-00622.

QUERY. QUERY. QUERY. NETWORK REQUIRES AUTHORI-
ZATION FOR ACTIVATION OF SUBROUTINE 98-00622.

AUTHORIZATION SUBCODE JCS/AAA 11813175441514.

AUTHORIZATION SUBCODE ACCEPTED. SUBROUTINE
98-00622 ACTIVATED.

ACK.

SUBROUTINE 98-00622 BEGINS:

CHIEF OF STAFF TO ALL BASE AND FBMS COMMANDERS:

MEN, WE ARE ON THE BRINK OF THE NATION'S SUPREME
TEST. THE WORLD DEPENDS ON US TO FACE DOWN THE
AGGRESSORS WHO THREATEN CIVILIZATION. I KNOW
THAT EACH OF YOU WILL DO HIS DUTY, AND FUTURE
GENERATIONS OF AMERICANS WILL BE PROUD OF YOUR
HEROISM AND DEDICATION. GOOD LUCK. GOD BLESS
AMERICA.

By 2000 hours Alpha was securely in the hands of the
Luniks. All of Stahl's men were back in their quarters, cowed
and disarmed. Several were in sick bay, oxygen masks and IV
tubes feeding into them while medical teams grimly tried to
keep their oxygen-starvation injuries to a minimum. The dead
were being prepared for shipment Earthside.

Kinsman split his tiny command into three groups and set
up a sleeping routine. He put a lieutenant in charge as Officer
of the Day, then made his way down to Level Three and the
comm center. The extra weight there was still painful. He
braced himself in the doorway as he received reports. Extra
men and women were on their way from Selene. The troopship had re-entered Earth's atmosphere and made an emergency landing at Patrick Aerospace Force Base, in Florida.
The medivac mission would rendezvous with the station in
less than an hour.

"There's all sorts of queries and messages from Earthside," the youngster running the comm center told him. "Should we continue radio silence?"

Kinsman nodded slowly, and it made his head feel like a cement mooring block. "Got to. We can't let them know what's happening until we've got enough of our own people here to run the whole ABM system."

The young officer shrugged. The heavier-than-lunar gravity did not bother him in any discernible way.

Kinsman quickly returned to his makeshift headquarters in the rec area, grateful for the diminishing weight as he made his way up the metal ladder that wound through the tubular spoke connecting the station's various levels.

They'll go on red alert, he knew. But then they'll find out that the Russians are cut off from their stations, too. They'll wait to puzzle it out. They'll wait. They won't launch the missiles. Both sides will wait. But the burning in his chest contradicted the logical certainty his mind was trying to establish.

Four civilians were waiting to see him, sitting along the bench at his table as Kinsman padded across the gym floor. He spent the better part of an hour with them, assuring them patiently that they could stay at the station or leave for Earthside as soon as transport could be arranged. One of them was a wispy little Japanese astronomer, fragile and aged.

"We are scientists, not politicians," he said in a quiet, calm voice. "We do not wish to abandon our work here. Several of us are caught in the midst of experiments or observations that must not be interrupted. We have no desire, however, to be caught in a cross fire between armed troops."

"Nothing could be further from my own desires," Kinsman answered, unconsciously picking up some of the formal cadence of the Japanese manner of speech. "I sincerely believe that you can all be assured that no one will interfere with your work. It would please me if you would continue your investigations as if nothing has happened."

"Well, I'm not a scientist," said one of the other men, hotly. He was younger than the others, built on the chunky side and starting to flesh out too much. Youthful muscle turning into the premature flab of middle age.

"I'm a civilian contractor from Denver, a U.S. citizen," he went on. "Came up here on government contract to work on the computer system they put in here. Now just what . . ."

Kinsman silenced him with a pointed finger. "You'll be going back home within an hour. Better get your gear packed."

"What? But I'm not . . . you can't . . ."

Kinsman said, "There's no time for arguing. Get packing!" He turned to the other three. "That goes for all of you. Anyone who wishes to return Earthside may do so. The shuttle will be here in less than an hour."

The contractor lurched to his feet. "You're letting foreigners stay, but a taxpaying American has to clear out?"

"The scientists can stay if they want to," Kinsman replied calmly. "The rest will be better off going home. This station is no longer American territory. It is now part of the independent nation of Selene."

The contractor blinked, uncomprehending. The Japanese astronomer sighed knowingly.

"I don't get it," the contractor said.

"You will, once you're Earthside," Kinsman told him. "Now, hurry; you don't have much time to spare."

One of the younger scientists claimed Kinsman's attention. "We're being held incommunicado. Your men won't allow us to call our colleagues or families at home."

"Only for a short time more."

"And what have you done with Dr. Marrett? He disappeared with one of your officers after putting up a row, and he hasn't been seen since."

"He's in the observation section, carrying out his experiment."

"You mean that he's allowed to have radio contact with Earth?"

Nodding, Kinsman replied, "Only with his own special outposts, and only for the experiment he's working on. We have an officer up there with him to make sure he doesn't . . . do anything political."

"This is insane," the young scientist argued. His accent was definitely British. "You're going to have half the troops in the United States pouring in here as soon as they realize what's happened. We'll all be clay pigeons in a shooting gallery."

"Maybe," Kinsman said evenly.

"Of more serious consequence," said the Japanese astronomer, "is the possibility that America might unleash its nuclear missiles, for fear that this situation has been caused by the Soviet Union."

When they realized what the older man had said, the others turned toward Kinsman. But he had no answer for them.

Captain Ryan closed his codebook with an audible snap. The other officers in the wardroom were staring at him. Not a smile on the eight of them. The Captain's personal codebook was used only for the very highest priority messages, the kind that were marked FOR YOUR EYES ONLY. All lesser priority messages were decoded by the submarine's computer.

"It's the red balloon, all right," Ryan said. The tension in their faces actually eased a bit. The known fear was always easier to face than the unknown. "And a personal message from the Chief of the Joint Staffs. He expects us all to do our duty and make our kids proud of us."

Garcia's kids are living in the open housing development south of San Diego, Captain Ryan knew. They won't be around ten minutes after the button's pushed. He scanned the faces of his fellow officers. Same for Mattingly and Rizzo. Same for my own—and my new grandson!

"Well," he said, leaning his elbows heavily on the green felt tabletop, "it looks as if the shit has really hit the fan. And we've got a job to do."

They showed no enthusiasm at all.

"Listen to me," he said evenly. "When those missiles go, there's gonna be a helluva lot of Americans killed. Our job is to seek and destroy enemy subs. There are two of 'em in our area, according to this morning's sweep, and they wouldn't be patrolling around here if they weren't missile-launching bastards."

They glanced at one another, still showing no sign of fire. It was the captain's responsibility to instill a high morale among his crew, especially his officers. The officers must set an example for the men, and the captain must set an example for his officers.

"Now, one of those subs has at least one missile that's got San Diego for a target," he went on. That moved them. They stirred. They sat up straighter.

"We've got to stop that missile from being launched."

"Sir," Garcia said, "I don't see how we can do that. I mean, a red alert doesn't mean that war's been declared."

"There won't be a declaration of war, Mike," argued Mattingly, with his damned nasal Princeton accent. "The button is pushed and the missiles are launched. No paperwork. No diplomatic niceties."

"Then how do we stop them from launching it?"

Captain Ryan said, "We go for those subs *now*. Not after they've launched their missiles. Not after we get the codeword from Fleet HQ. *Now!*"

"But—"

"You want to wait until they've blown San Diego off the map?"

"No, but we can't move without orders."

"A red alert gives the captain of a warship discretion to act on his own initiative in case of communications failure."

"But we don't have a communications failure," Rizzo said, his voice a bit hollow.

"We do now," Captain Ryan answered.

No one argued against him.

The rec room looked more like a real command post now. Men going in and out constantly. Several small tables and chairs had been moved in. A computer terminal hummed at one table, a communications console with four small display screens lapped over the sides of another.

Kinsman was wolfing down a hasty sandwich. It was well past 2100 hours now. The medivac shuttle had taken most of the civilians off the station. Word of what had happened was screaming up the chain of command to Washington.

"Sir, we have Colonel Leonov on screen four," said one of the technicians, a woman who had volunteered to stay aboard the station with the Luniks.

Washing down a mouthful of unidentifiable soybean

product with a gulp of synthetic coffee, Kinsman made his way to the comm console.

Leonov looked triumphant on the tiny screen. "All three of our orbital stations are completely in our hands!" he reported. "There was amazingly little shooting. Surprise and a good deal of agreement with our aims carried almost everyone. I was *very* eloquent." He arched his brows, daring Kinsman to dispute him.

"Good work, Peter," was all that Kinsman could think to say. "We had a few bad moments here, but everything's under control now. Beta and Gamma are secure, and our people are checking out the ABM control systems on all three stations."

"They are bypassing the controls in the Earth-based stations?"

"Right. I presume your people are doing the same."

"It is already done. Our network of satellites can now be controlled only from the space stations. The Earthside control links have been removed from the circuits."

"Good work," said Kinsman.

"You have sent the prisoners back to the States?" Leonov asked.

"Most of them. There wasn't room in the one medivac ship for all of them, so we still have a few here. And there are more coming from Beta and Gamma. We'll hold them here until they send another ship up from Earthside."

"If I were you, Comrade, I would hold on to the remaining prisoners. They might be valuable as hostages. That is what we are doing here."

Kinsman nodded. "You might be right."

"Now then," Leonov broke into a smile, "what about announcing our actions to the former owners of these space stations, eh?"

"The evacuees must be yelling their guts out into the radio aboard the medivac ship right now," Kinsman said. "Washington should be sorting out the story very shortly."

"Yes, but do you realize they are on full alert down there? They could send off their missiles before we are ready to stop them. We must make some sort of announcement jointly so they won't bombard each other."

"I know, Pete, but I'm afraid if we make the announcement before we can really control the ABM satellites, they'll either shoot at us or send troops up. I'd rather wait until the reinforcements get here from Selene and we have enough people to man the ABM control centers properly."

Leonov slowly blinked his eyes. "I understand. But it is much faster to launch a missile or troopship from Earthside than to get extra technicians down here from Selene. Even with our ships accelerating at maximum energy . . ."

He stopped. Someone off-screen had caught his attention. Leonov snapped a few words in Russian, and an excited voice babbled breathlessly at him. Leonov's face went white.

"Chet, it's too late! One of our . . . a Russian submarine has been torpedoed and sunk off the coast of California. The war has started!"

Tuesday 14 December 1999: 2148 hrs UT

"THEY'VE LAUNCHED THE missiles?" Kinsman's voice was a shocked, high-pitched little boy's squeal of fear. His guts were frozen, a block of lunar ice. But his mind was racing.

Got to tell them right away that we've taken over. Got to! Got to scan the missile farms—Idaho, Montana, Texas, Siberia, China. Jesus Christ! The oceans. The subs. We'll need every sensor on every satellite. Got to be in touch with Perry and the others, make sure we can fire the lasers, get the radars tracking, all the sensors—get 'em ready to shoot at anything that moves. Fast!

"No," Leonov was answering. "Nothing has been launched yet. But the standby orders have gone out. It's only a matter of hours now. Perhaps minutes."

Can't do it from here, Kinsman realized as he watched the Russian's dismal face in the tiny display screen. Got to go down to the comm center.

A clattering noise made him jerk his attention away from

the screen. One of the young officers had let a plastic food tray slip from his hands. He was visibly shaking as he knelt to pick up the mess. The others were fixed on Kinsman: standing, sitting—one of them leaning his fists on the computer terminal, his face a tense death mask, white, taut, unblinking—all of them staring at Kinsman, waiting for him to act, to tell them what to do.

"Pete, get on all the broadcast frequencies you can manage and tell your people Earthside what we've done. I'm going down to our comm center and do the same thing. We can stop 'em if we yell loud enough." You think! "But we've got to tell 'em now!"

"Yes, yes, of course. But do you think—"

"Tell 'em we're prepared to shoot down any missile launched from anywhere on Earth. Make 'em believe it!"

"But can we really do it?"

"You tell me!"

Leonov rubbed a hand over his forehead. "I don't know! We have teams of technicians working, but how can we be certain that all those satellites will respond correctly?"

Forcing a grin, Kinsman answered, "The machines don't care what your politics are, Pete. If the lights come on green, then everything's working."

"Sheer materialism."

"Yep. And you thought I was a romantic. Get moving. There's no time to spare."

"*Da* . . . Good luck, *tovarich*."

"Godspeed, friend." Kinsman pushed up from the chair and started across the padded gym floor for the hatch that led to the downward-spiraling ladder. "Get the comm center on the horn," he commanded the youngsters around him. "Make sure they understand what's happening. Tell them I'm on my way down there and the techs had better be able to use every fucking laser on every fucking satellite we've got!"

"Yes, *sir*!" yelped one of the officers as Kinsman yanked the hatch open.

Level Three was like slogging through knee-deep mud. One-half normal Earth gravity, and Kinsman was quickly out of breath. By the time the comm center crew made a chair available for him, his legs ached and his heart was thumping heavily. Even the air felt soupy, humid and thick, hard to breathe.

The comm center reminded Kinsman of a string sextet flying through a Mozart allegro: wildly ordered activity, measured frenetic action. The comm techs were buzzing commands into their pin mikes; the giant insect-eye of display screens—bank on bank of them—showed strangely incongruous scenes.

The bright, soul-thrilling beauty of the broad Pacific, a globe-spanning expanse of blue water decorated with intricate patterns of dazzling white clouds, swirls of giant storms, files of cumulus puffs marching dutifully in response to sunlight and earthspin. How many submarines hidden in that beauty? How many missiles with hydrogen bombs tucked inside their nose caps?

The tense, sweat-streaked face of a technician urgently yammering into the earphone of a comm tech who sat nodding in front of that particular screen.

Captain Perry, standing in front of the elaborate fire control panel aboard Space Station Beta, talking to someone in what seemed to be an easy, professional, competent tone. Kinsman could not hear what he was saying, of course, unless the audio from that individual circuit was piped into the earphones that rested in his lap. The fire control panel's idiot lights were almost all green, Kinsman saw. The ABM satellites were in operational condition.

Display screens showed lovely rural Earthside scenery, where ICBM silos dotted the countryside. Half a dozen major cities. A Russian comm tech frowning as he talked with his American counterpart. No, Kinsman corrected himself. Not Russians or Americans anymore. Luniks. Selenites.

Kinsman took all this in with a single glance as he slumped heavily in the seat near the comm center's hatch.

"Reports look good," said the officer sitting next to him. "And we've got a dozen or so volunteers from the station's crew helping us. They decided to stay with us."

Kinsman nodded, and even that was an effort. For the first time it registered in his mind that three of the six techs working the consoles were women.

"I need to be patched in to the top-priority network right

away," he said wearily. "White House, Pentagon, SAC headquarters, commanders of the Atlantic and Pacific strike forces—the works."

"The gold-braid circuit. Yessir, can do," the youngster nodded easily, grinning. He started flicking fingers across the master keyboard.

He'd make a good piano player. Kinsman realized that he himself would not be able to play well in this gravity. Or at all, in a full Earth gee. He pushed everything to the back of his mind. Closing his eyes, he leaned his head back, annoyed momentarily that the chair they had given him had no headrest.

So far no missiles had been launched. So far the reports from all the space stations and the unmanned ABM satellites looked good. Now he had to make Washington aware of the new situation. Convince them that we can and will shoot down anything they launch.

He rubbed at the back of his neck, corded with tension and aching sullenly. It's not fair, dammitall! Jefferson had weeks to write his Declaration. I've only got minutes.

The display screens that filled the main bulkhead of the center's crowded compartment were beginning to show Earthside military men. Communications technicians at first, but quickly each one was supplanted by an officer: colonels and generals and a pair of admirals scowled or glared or licked their lips nervously, waiting for the message from Space Station Alpha. They were not accustomed to waiting.

"What about the White House?" Kinsman asked.

The youngster looked up from his keyboard, one hand on his earplug. "They're working their way up through a gaggle of flunkies. They say General Hofstader will speak with you. Is that okay?"

Kinsman nodded painfully. "He'll do."

"They have to find him and patch him into the circuit. It's still sleep-time down there."

"Tough. I doubt that any of them are asleep."

The central screen shifted from a female colonel to show the handsome, silver-maned image of General Hofstader. The paneling of the office wall behind him looked more like the Pentagon, to Kinsman, than the White House. A furled flag stood behind him, and he seemed to be glancing at other people who were in the office, off-camera.

"General . . ."

"What is this, Colonel?" Hofstader's voice was crisp, deep, the very model of a commander's decisive tone. "Why have the space stations been off the air and out of contact? Are you under attack?"

"Nosir. We've taken control of the stations, and the ABM network."

" 'Control'? 'We'? What are you talking about?"

All the faces on the smaller screens around the General looked alarmed, surprised, concerned, angry. Kinsman almost laughed. It was like watching a living Rorschach test.

"The people of the Moon," Kinsman said slowly and carefully, "have decided to form the independent nation of Selene. We have taken control of all the space stations, both American and Russian."

For a moment he thought the words had not gotten through. They all just sat there, with no reaction. Then came the eruption. Fury, shock, rage. They all tried to talk at once. General Hofstader's eyes went absolutely round, his mouth fell open, he seemed to slump inside his well-pressed uniform. For several moments Kinsman let them babble. Finally Hofstader broke through the confusion.

"That's impossible," he snapped. "You can't . . ."

"We have. And we intend to enforce an absolute ban on all rocket launches. Anything, launched by any nation, from any spot on Earth, will be immediately destroyed."

"This is treason!"

A civilian pushed into view, crowding the General and forcing him to lean back in his plush leather chair. Kinsman recognized the hawklike features of the Secretary of Defense. "Do you realize that the Soviets are counting down for a full-scale nuclear strike?" he bellowed into the camera. "Are you insane, man? You're destroying your nation, your homeland!"

"No missiles have been launched," Kinsman replied evenly. "And if they are, we'll shoot them down long before they near their targets."

General Hofstader edged around the Defense Secretary's elbow to roar, "I'll give you five minutes to surrender and turn yourself in! Otherwise you'll see the full striking power of—"

"Bullshit, General!"

Hofstader sagged. The Defense Secretary grabbed at his arm, as if to keep him from falling off his chair.

"Now listen, all of you," Kinsman said to the many faces in the screens. "This is no joke and no idle threat. We will stop any rocket launching. No matter where in the world it's launched from. We will not allow the destruction of Americans, or Russians, or anyone else. There will be no war. Is that clear? No war!"

Kinsman could feel his heart banging wildly, making his ears roar. He took a deep, painful breath and went on, "There is no way that we can hurt you. Our armaments were specifically designed to defend against missile launches. The nation of Selene is no threat to any nation on Earth. But we will not allow missiles to be launched! And if you try to send troops to these space stations to take them away from us, we'll be forced to destroy your troop-carrying rockets. Check with your technical staffs, gentlemen. We can do it. And we will. Now, good night. It's been a long and difficult day up here."

He turned and nodded once to the officer beside him. All the display screens went blank.

"Stay in touch with them," he commanded. "Answer their questions. Tell them that we make only one demand: that they refrain from launching any rockets. Tell them we'll shoot anything that moves above the atmosphere."

"Yessir."

Slowly, Kinsman pulled himself to his feet. Like a ninety-year-old, he thought as he made his way back toward the rec area, toward the blessed ease of low gravity.

It was well past midnight by the time he got to bed. His men set him up in the VIP quarters on Level Five. It was jokingly referred to as the honeymoon suite. The low gravity, even less than lunar gee, was considered to be better than a water bed. Kinsman smiled as they showed him the tiny two-compartment suite. He recalled the old Zero Gee Club of bygone days, so many years ago that it seemed like another century. Damned near is another century, he realized as he stretched out gratefully on the bunk. The millennium is almost here.

He knew he should call Selene. He knew he should check on Diane and Colt, and talk with Harriman. He knew he should tell them that he was all right and everything had worked out better than they had any right to expect. But he was too tired. Too tired to talk, to think, even to sleep. I'll never sleep, he told himself, tossing in the bunk. Too keyed up . . .

He awoke with a pang of fear burning in his gut. The phone was buzzing. The only lights in the compartment were the yellow 0351 of the digital clock and the pulsing red eye of the phone. He reached over, instantly wide awake, and punched the phone on.

"Yeah?"

A woman tech said, "Station Gamma reports a rocket launch from the Chinese mainland."

He sat up in bed, forgetting his nakedness and the fact that the room's darkness hid it. "When?"

The woman glanced at something off-camera. "T plus one hundred fourteen seconds."

"Lemme see."

The phone's tiny display screen flickered, then showed a telescope view. The brown, cloud-streaked mountain country of western China. A single luminous thread of a rocket exhaust.

A male voice came on. "Trajectory extrapolation gives an impact in the mid-Pacific. Doesn't look heavy enough for an ICBM. Exhaust profile matches a scientific high-altitude sounding rocket more than anything else."

"Burn it," Kinsman snapped.

"We're already tracking it and have programmed a kill as soon as it clears the coastline," the man's voice answered, almost casually. "Got three different satellites lined up on it. If the first one misses . . ."

"Good work," said Kinsman. Very practical people, the Chinese. The only ones with sense enough to use a cheap scientific rocket to see if we mean business.

The rocket was too small to be seen visually, even in the best telescopic magnification. Instead, the various satellite sensors were being overlapped to give an optical view of the

Earth background and a combined radar-infrared image of the rocket—which looked on the display screen like a reddish blob, slightly longer than it was wide. Suddenly it blossomed into a white glare. *Got it!* The fireball was much too small for a nuclear explosion but bright enough to see optically. It quickly dissipated.

"Well done," Kinsman grunted. "Now let me get some sleep. Call me only if something critical happens."

The comm tech reappeared on the screen. "Sir," she asked worriedly, "who's to decide what's critical?"

"The Officer of the Day, honey. He's the man on the spot."

But Kinsman could not sleep anymore. He tossed in the bunk for what seemed like a week, got up and padded around the darkened compartment, bumping into the dresser that was built into the bulkhead beside the bunk. Finally, when the glowing digits of the clock said 0700 he put in a call to Diane. The phone screen stayed blank as Selene's computer tracked her down. She was not in her quarters or at the communications center. Finally her face appeared on the small screen. Kinsman recognized the background instantly; she was in his own office.

"You're up early," he said.

"You too. Is everything all right?"

"I was going to ask you that."

Completely serious, she said, "Everything's running smoothly here. No trouble from Colt or any of the other dissidents."

"Good."

Diane frowned slightly as she said, "We got the word that everything went well, at first. But then there were reports about fighting. Nobody seemed to know what was happening for a while. Finally word came through that you had taken control of all three stations, and that Leonov had taken the Russians' stations. There was quite a celebration, the Russians and us."

"Sorry I missed it."

"When will you be back?"

"I'm hoping I can leave today. Be back, um, Thursday sometime. We'll work out an exact ETA later."

"All right."

Christ! he thought, we might as well be talking about the weather! How can she just . . .

"We saw the Chinese rocket intercept," Diane said. "It happened in the middle of the party. Everybody was in the main plaza. And when the Orca missiles were fired . . ."

"Orca?"

She brushed a strand of dark hair back from her eyes. Kinsman began to realize that she probably had not slept all night. "Yes. We watched the whole thing on the big screens in the plaza. Everybody cheered when they were shot down."

"Yeah, I'll bet," he said weakly.

She peered into the camera. "Are you all right?"

"I just need a little rest."

"The worst is over now," Diane said. Then she added, "Isn't it?"

"Yes. The worst is over," he answered, wishing he could believe it was true.

As soon as Diane signed off Kinsman punched the code for the comm center and asked for the Officer of the Day.

"Why wasn't I informed about the Orca missiles?" he demanded.

The youngster wore a lieutenant's bars and a wispy light brown mustache. "Sir, you gave orders that you were not to be disturbed unless something critical happened. The submarine launched six missiles in salvo from the mid-Pacific. We assume it was an American sub, since the projected trajectory of the missiles was toward targets in Siberia. Our fire control crew aboard Gamma tracked the missiles while the ABM system engaged them in automatic mode and shot them all down within four minutes of launch. No sweat. Sir."

Kinsman sagged back on the bunk and grinned. "I see."

"We have videotapes, sir, if you wish to review the action." The Lieutenant was very sure of himself, as only a young officer can be when he has the rules working on his side and he knows it.

"No. I'll take a look at it later. Any messages from Washington?"

"Oh, yessir. A whole tankful of them!"

It was two hours later that Kinsman realized he was hungry. He went down to Level Four, where the mess hall

475

was. He got a tray of hot food from the galley and sat at a long table that was crowded with young officers and crewmen, and a few civilians. The more elaborate automated restaurant down on Level One had been shut down by its departing crew, so the remaining civilians were forced to eat up in officers' country.

Most of the civilians seemed relaxed enough, even friendly. But one pair—Americans, by their clothes and accent—got up from the table when Kinsman sat down and moved to a smaller table on the far side of the mess hall. A few of the Europeans seemed ill at ease, tense. The Orientals were polite and professionally inscrutable.

Nobody knows where this is going to end, Kinsman realized, watching them work at their food and their conversations. But they all want to avoid the pariah.

Ted Marrett walked in. Fatigue lines were etched around his eyes. He moved his big frame stiffly, as if he had been cramped in one position for much too long. Kinsman followed the broad-shouldered meteorologist with his eyes as Marrett punched out two cups of steaming black coffee from the dispenser in the galley and carried them wearily into the mess hall. One of the scientists at Kinsman's table, a slim, sharp-featured Moroccan, called to him. "Ted, here. Come join us."

Marrett shuffled over to them and sat next to the Moroccan, two seats down from Kinsman.

"How did the trial go?"

"Pretty good." Marrett took a huge gulp of scalding coffee, winced, then took another. "Missed two of the correlation factors we're looking for, but it looks like all the major factors checked out. We'll know more in a month, and still more when the winter season's over."

"If you can stem the encroachment of the Sahara . . ." the Moroccan mused.

Marrett grimaced. "Could do better'n that if we had the authority to operate in the Mediterranean. That's where the crux of the motherlovin' problem is. But they won't give us permission. 'Fraid we'll screw up their humpin' weather."

The Moroccan shrugged. "We mustn't hope for more than can be accomplished. As I told you earlier, if even a ten percent increase—"

"Ten percent! Hell, we could stop the goddamned Sahara cold if they'd just let us work things right!" He drained the plastic cup, slammed it on the table, and grabbed the second cup. Then he recognized Kinsman. Raising his cup in greeting, Marrett asked, "How's your revolution going?"

Kinsman arched his brows in a "here's hoping" expression. "So far, so good. Had some trouble last night but everything seems cool now."

"Yeah, I heard. Got some interesting queries from my confreres Earthside. Even a few priority calls from Washington and Paris."

"Paris?"

Marrett reached into his shirt pocket. "Damn! No more cigars. Yeah. Paris. They were fronting for NATO headquarters in Brussels, I think. And UNESCO's interested in what you're doing, too."

"H'mm." Kinsman thought a moment. "Leonov and I ought to make a worldwide broadcast."

"Might help to settle people's stomachs."

Kinsman nodded abstractedly, then turned his attention to his cooling breakfast. Marrett kept talking nonstop to the Moroccan and a couple of younger men who joined them. Before long, Kinsman realized that they had stopped talking meteorology and were talking about flying: ultralight planes, jets, soarplanes, even rocket gliders. Kinsman joined their conversation by saying, "I never got the chance to try rocket gliders; they came in after I became a permanent Lunik."

One of the younger men broke into an animated, "Jeez, there's nothing like them!" Using his hands to illustrate, "You stovepipe up to fifty thou, straight up, then drop the boosters, and . . ."

And they were brothers. Fliers, all of them. Without nationality, or race or any creed except the excitement of flying.

"You can keep the rocket stuff," Marrett said, with a wave of a meaty hand. "I'll take soarplanes; that's where the real fun is. I want to make love to those fat humpy cumuli. I want to get into those thermals. I want to *feel* that goddamned cloud. Feel it."

Kinsman decided he liked the man. Trusted him. On the strength of his enjoyment of flying? Yes, Kinsman realized.

On nothing more than that. It's enough. Reluctantly, though, he got up and started out of the mess hall. There's more to do than shoot the shit—dammitall.

As he headed down the corridor for the tube that led up to his command center, he heard Marrett's voice behind him.

"Got a minute, Colonel?"

He turned. "Better call me Chet. I think my commission in the Aerospace Force might not be worth much this morning."

Marrett laughed: a strong, healthy, joyful sound. He was too big for this narrow corridor; he needed a much wider setting to accommodate him. "Okay, Chet. Look, I've got a question. Maybe it's dumb, but I figure there's no such thing as stupid questions, only stupid answers."

Kinsman grinned back at him. "What's your question?"

"Just what in the seven tiers of heaven are you trying to accomplish with this revolution of yours?"

"You want the answer in twenty-five words or less?"

"Less."

They stood facing each other, the big meteorologist with his heavy hands planted on his hips, Kinsman looking up at him, the rest of the corridor empty and sterile-looking, a row of plastic doors set into aluminum-framed curtainwalls.

"Well, Dr. Marrett . . ."

"Ted."

"All right, Ted. What we're trying to accomplish is peace. No war. No missile strikes. No fighting between Russians and Americans on Earth, at least no nuclear fighting. So there'll be no need to fight on the Moon."

"That's about what I thought." Marrett gestured toward the tube hatch. "Goin' upstairs?"

"Yes. To Level Three."

"Good. I'm headin' back to the observation bay." He started walking toward the hatch. Kinsman followed. As they padded up the metal steps, circling the thin metal wall that held the cold vacuum of space at bay, Marrett said, "Got another question for you."

In the dim lighting of the tube Kinsman could not see Marrett's face too well. But his voice was low, serious, as it echoed along the metal cylinder.

"What is it?" Kinsman asked.

"Your new nation gonna apply for membership in the UN?"

"I suppose so. Why?"

"Listen. I've been working for the UN for more than ten years now, watching the best weather-modification work in the world get pissed down the drain because one nation or another blocks it."

"You don't look that old."

Marrett cast a baleful eye on him. "How do you think I got bald? X-ray treatments?"

"Okay," Kinsman said as they continued climbing the metal steps. "So your work has been stymied by individual nations."

"And blocs. Western Europe, Pan-Arab—you name it. They all think of themselves as the one and only outfit on the planet. Nobody else counts. And UNESCO, the whole diddling UN, is helpless as long as one nation refuses to go along with our ideas."

"So?"

Marrett stopped. Two steps above Kinsman, he loomed in the shadowy lighting like a menace from an old Gothic tale. "So here you are," he said quietly, rationally, "pulling off your revolution. You stop the United States and Russia from using their missiles on each other, but they've still got other ways to fight. Germ warfare or nerve gas or some old manned bombers to drop nukes."

"We can stop them," Kinsman said. "And cruise missiles, too, if we have to."

"Can you stop tanks? Artillery? Genetically engineered disease viruses smuggled into a country in somebody's luggage?"

"No," Kinsman admitted.

"Okay! In the meantime you want to be recognized as an independent nation—what the hell you gonna call yourself, anyway?"

"Selene."

"Ugh. Okay, Selene, if that's what you want. You think the U.S. and Russia are gonna recognize an independent Selene?"

"Not at first."

"Damned right they won't! And what makes you think

479

any of the other nations are gonna run the risk of alienating the big boys, just to make you feel good?" Marrett leaned down over Kinsman and jabbed a forefinger against his chest. "They won't. Not unless there's something in it for them."

"We can act as an international policeman," Kinsman said, "as long as we control the ABM satellites."

Before Marrett could reply, he added, "And we can knock out any orbiting satellites we want to. We could cripple communications satellites, for example. Military *and* civilian communications would be screwed up all around the world. The economic threat alone—"

"Negative advantages," Marrett snapped.

"Huh?"

"Those are negative advantages. So you prevent a nuclear war and all the fallout and crap. That doesn't put any rice on the table in Burma. Neither will shooting out commsats."

"I don't follow you." Kinsman got the feeling that Marrett was being deliberately non sequitur.

With a sigh, Marrett hunkered down and sat on a stair. His long legs straddled four steps. Kinsman leaned back against the tube's curving bulkhead. The metal felt chill.

"Look," Marrett said, with great patience. "Suppose you could go to the smaller nations of the world, especially some of the Southern Hemisphere nations—although the Europeans would be interested in it, too, come to think of it—well, anyway, suppose you went to 'em and promised not only a policeman in orbit, but weather control."

"Weather *control*?"

"Right. Not modification. Control. We can control the goddamned weather all across this planet. Optimize crop yields, improve health, make fortunes for resort areas, divert storms, improve fish populations, maybe even save the dolphins before they go the way of the whales—the whole big ball of wax. But we need two things: these space stations as bases of operations, and the political muscle to override the objections of individual nations and the big power blocs."

"They're against weather control?"

Marrett frowned. "It's a long and bloody story. Big-power politics. Basically, the big nations are against letting the UN have any real power. The only way weather control can possibly work is on a worldwide basis. You can't slice off a chunk of the atmosphere and separate it from the rest of the world. No single nation can achieve weather control all by itself. And the big powers won't let the UN have a shot at it, either."

"Orbital police and weather control." Kinsman's mind was churning.

"It'd give the UN some godawful power," Marrett said. "If a nation doesn't behave, we'll just turn off their water."

"You could do that?"

"More or less."

"But that would mean a tremendous upheaval in the UN itself. They're not set up for anything like that. You'd have to revamp the whole structure."

"Damned right." Marrett was grinning hugely now.

In those gloomy shadows, with the twisting metal steps snaking off into darkness above and below them, Kinsman felt suspended between—what? Success and failure? Life and death? Heaven and hell?

"Are there people in the UN who'd be willing to consider this?"

"I know one," Marrett said.

"Who?"

"Emanuel De Paolo."

"The Secretary General?"

"The very same."

Wednesday 15 December 1999: 1700 hrs UT

IT WAS PRECISELY noon in Washington, although from the curtained windows of the Oval Office nothing could be seen but the swirling wind-driven snow of the season's first blizzard.

"Big wet flakes," the President said, idly gazing out the windows as he leaned back in his desk chair. His eyes were puffy from lack of sleep, his hair tousled. "The kind that's heavy to shovel. I remember, back in Roxbury, when I was a kid, we would . . ."

The Defense Secretary looked pale, drawn. "Mr. President, there's no time for childhood reminiscences."

"Oh, no?" the President asked, his mouth tightening. "What else can we do? This, eh, colonel—what's his name?"

"Kinsman," General Hofstader spat.

"Yes. Kinsman. He's got us stopped, doesn't he? We can't lift a missile off the ground. We can't attack, and we can't be attacked. So there's nothing to do except what we used to do in blizzards when I was a kid: sit back and enjoy it."

"What makes you certain that we can't be attacked," came the burly man's tortured whisper.

The President blinked in puzzlement and the reflex response of fear. "Why? Do you think . . . ?"

It was eight o'clock in the evening in Moscow, but the same questions were being asked.

"Are we so certain," the Nameless One was asking in his stiletto-thin voice, "that this is not a clever American trick? What guarantee do we have that these lunar rebels will stop an American attack on us?"

The General Secretary shifted his bulk uneasily in his

chair. The long table was almost empty. Only Marshal Prokoff, the Minister of State Security, and the Nameless One were present.

"Didn't they shoot down half a dozen American missiles?" the General Secretary demanded.

"What are a half-dozen missiles?" the Nameless One countered. "A ruse, a decoy, aimed at lulling us into relaxing our guard. Tomorrow, or next week or next month they could strike while our defenses are in a state of sleepy lassitude."

"That's right," General Hofstader was saying. "This could all be a goddamned trick to catch us with our pants down."

"And keep us from instant readiness to launch a counterstrike," the Defense Secretary added.

"Or a preemptive strike," Hofstader said.

The burly man whispered harshly. "More than that. While our attention is focused on the drama in space, we still face a very real crisis here on Earth. The Antarctic coal fields, the battles between our fishing fleets last summer . . ."

". . . and they sank one of our submarines," Marshal Prokoff insisted, waggling one stubby finger in the air. "Do not let this trickery with the satellites blind us to the realities of Earth!"

Wearily, the General Secretary objected, "But this new situation has greatly altered the correlation of forces. What do you recommend as a new course of action? Clearly we cannot launch a missile strike against the West—for which ill fortune, I think, we should perhaps be grateful."

"Perhaps," the Nameless One said. Then with a thin smile he added, "But it will be necessary to send troops to recapture the orbital stations."

"Can it be done?"

"We will find a way."

"Remember, they have the orbital bombs with them at the space stations," Marshal Prokoff said. "We cannot allow them to hold these weapons over our heads."

The General Secretary glared at him. "The bombs that *you* insisted we place in orbit."

The Security Minister cleared his throat. "We should

arrest the family of Colonel Leonov and anyone else who is part of this lunar rebellion."

"What good would that do?" the General Secretary grumbled.

"They might become useful hostages."

"Idiot! Think of the hostages *they* have at their mercy!"

"Hostages?"

Rapping the table with his knuckles on each word, the General Secretary counted, "Moscow, Leningrad, Smolensk, Volgagrad, Kiev . . ."

"Then we're agreed," the Defense Secretary said, "that recapturing the space stations is our first order of business."

"Yes," whispered the burly man.

General Hofstader nodded.

"I'm not so sure," the President said. "How can we get troops up there if they're going to shoot down all our rockets?"

"We'll have to work out a plan," said Hofstader.

"There are a *lot* of things we'll have to work out," the Defense Secretary agreed.

"Yes," came the angry whisper. "A lot of things."

It was nearing midnight when General Murdock read the TWX for the last time. He was still in his office, at his desk. The lights of Vandenberg Aerospace Force Base were still blacked out; the red alert had not yet been lifted.

His wife had phoned three times, and each time he had told her he would be home in an hour. He had not mentioned the TWX to her. He stared at the flimsy sheet of paper. "Right out in the open," he muttered. "Not even a private communication. Everybody on the base must know about it. They knew about it before I did."

He was past crying. He had blubbered for an hour when the TWX had first arrived. His secretary had tried coffee, bourbon, womanly comforting that went from a motherly caress to an offer to bed down for the night. The base chaplain had come in to talk to him briefly. "It's an investigation—that's all that a court-martial means. They can't find you guilty of treason or dereliction of duty." Shaking, Murdock had ordered him out of his office.

A psychologist, a golf-playing friend of the General, had dropped by long after the dinner hour. "But why do you think they're going to blame you, Bob? You had nothing to do with it."

Murdock moaned. "I'm the one they can reach. I'm the commanding officer of the men who rebelled. It's my responsibility. Haven't you studied military history? Don't you know what happened to General Short, after Pearl Harbor? What do you think they're going to do to *me*?" He had screamed the last words.

Prayer did not help. Neither did tranquilizers. Murdock knew what they were going to do to him. Knew it quite clearly. "You're killing me, Kinsman," he murmured as he sat at his desk, head in his hands, his uniform dark with sweat despite the gusting air-conditioning that riffled the papers on his desk. But not the TWX. It was magnetically pinned to the deskpad. Nothing could blow it away.

Court-martial. Inquiry. Trial.

Brigadier General Robert G. Murdock rose from his desk and walked unsteadily to the bathroom off one side of his handsome office. Idly, he thought how much easier it would be if he had a gun. But he had not fired one in years and had never used one in anger.

"I've never tried to hurt anyone," he said to himself. His voice sounded little short of whining. "Not even Kinsman. All these years he's laughed at me, made a fool of me. And now he's killed me."

He turned on the hot-water tap, then reached for the medicine chest above the sink for a razor blade.

Thursday 16 December 1999:
2250 hrs UT

"RETROFIRE IN FIVE minutes. Please prepare for landing."

The pilot's voice coming through the tiny speaker in the seatback in front of him woke Kinsman. For an instant he did not know where he was; disoriented, he felt a flash of panic surge through him. Then everything settled into place: the lunar shuttle, the young officers around him, the safety harness crossing his chest and thighs, the windowless metal tube of the spacecraft's passenger section.

"I must have dozed off," he muttered.

The kid sitting beside him grinned. "About four hours ago, sir."

Kinsman grunted and rubbed his eyes. It had been a long flight, a minimum-energy boost, but a busy one. He had spent more than twenty hours straight in urgent communications with Selene, the space stations—where he had left Chris Perry in charge—and with Ted Marrett, going into deeper and deeper detail on the politics of global weather control.

There had been a flood of messages from Earthside: urgent, angry, inquisitive, apprehensive. Kinsman had Perry or Harriman answer most of them. He refused to speak to anyone lower than the President of the United States or the General Secretary of the USSR's Communist Party. With an inward grin, he admitted to himself that such haughtiness guaranteed he would not have to take any calls. The heads of state would not speak with him, that would be too big an admission for them to make. It simply was not done in the protocol-conscious world of international diplomacy.

He spoke briefly with Diane at Selene, using the compact display screen before him. All was quiet. Apparently both sides were still on red alert, but there had been no further warlike incidents, no further rocket launches, no further threats or blusterings from Washington or Moscow.

They're playing wait-and-see, Kinsman knew. They're digesting the new situation, running it through their computers and think tanks, trying to figure out what to do next. The calm before the storm.

"Retrofire in thirty seconds."

We've got to get Marrett back down to New York, Kinsman realized. He's got to talk to De Paolo. We're going to need weather control, even if it's just a threat or a promise, to give us some leverage on the big powers. Of course, we could knock out their commsats and other satellites if we had to. And we've got the Russians' orbital bombs . . .

He shook his head. Dismantle the bombs. Take them apart so that nobody can use them. We got into this business to prevent a nuclear war, not to start one.

The braking thrusters fired and Kinsman felt a firm but gentle hand push him down in the foam cushion seat. There was no noise from the retrorockets, only a faint shudder of vibration.

Over the intercom, the pilot sang out, "Last stop: the free and independent nation of Selene. Population, one thousand and umpty-two. Everybody off the bus!"

Kinsman grinned. Home sweet home. He realized that he was indeed *home*. Diane was here, and Harriman and Frank Colt and all the other people and things that made this corner of the universe his home.

He had been sitting up at the front end of the passenger compartment. Most of the other men and women aboard were between him and the egress hatch, but they stepped aside wordlessly, automatically opening the aisle for him to go to the hatch first.

Kinsman looked at them for a moment. They were all watching him. "What is this, a parade?" he joked. "Go ahead, go on out. I don't have to be the first in line."

He followed them through the access tube that connected the shuttle hatch with the airlock of Selene's main dome. It felt like a long walk. Behind him was the excitement, the terror, the passion of action: the swift, fearful climax of so many years of self-doubt, so many weeks of indecision and mounting tension. Now it was done and men had died because of it. *Because of me*, Kinsman knew. But strangely he felt no guilt. Only weariness, and the beginnings of dread.

Kinsman realized that this revolution, if it really was one, had barely begun. The fighting may be over but the real struggle had only started. *Now we have to make it stick. Make a nation of little more than a thousand people stay independent of the seven billions on Earth. We've got a long lever and a place to stand—but is it enough?*

The inner airlock hatch was closed when Kinsman stepped into the metal chamber. "Something wrong?" he asked the youngster ahead of him.

The officer shrugged. "Dunno. It was open and people were going through, then somebody outside yelled 'Stand by,' and they shut the damned thing in my face."

Before Kinsman could go to the wall phone the hatch swung open again. The young officer stepped through and Kinsman followed him out onto the floor of the main dome.

It was thronged with people. Off to his right, a motley collection of musicians struck up a barely recognizable version of "Hail to the Chief," playing a battered slide trombone, a dozen or more recorders and kazoos, a few homemade instruments, at least one violin, a few drums made from oil cans, and a dulcimer. Everyone was shouting and cheering. Kinsman was so surprised he did not have the strength even to stagger. He stood frozen to the spot. The trombonist was *smiling* as he played!

The crowd was still yelling as the band ground to a ragged stop. The dome reverberated with their cheers. Hugh Harriman somehow appeared beside Kinsman, pounding him on the back. Leonov was there, too, grinning and kissing everyone in sight, man or woman.

"Congratulations, Chet!" Harriman was yelling in his ear. "We ran an election this afternoon and you lost! You're the Chief Administrator of this crazy nation."

"And I am Deputy Chief," Leonov beamed. "In charge of immigration. I get to interview all the girls who want to come live here."

It was a dizzy, crazy whirl. Diane came out of the crowd and took Kinsman's arm as the whole population descended upon him, laughing, cheering, grabbing for his hand, telling him and each other that they were ready to defend their new nation and follow his leadership.

Kinsman lost all track of time. Diane climbed up on the fender of a tractor, guitar in hand, tears in her eyes, her voice nearly choking as she reached the words she had not been allowed to sing for so many years:

"It's the hammer of justice,
 It's the bell of freedom,
 It's the song 'bout the love between my brothers
   and my sisters,
 All over this world."

Food appeared as if by magic, and drink: all sorts of drink, from precious bottles of champagne to locally distilled rocket juice that seemed to be still fermenting. After what seemed like hours of ear-numbing noise and crowds and music and folk dancing that snaked all across the dome and down the corridors below ground, a small group of them ended up in Diane's quarters: Harriman, Leonov, Jill and Alexsei Landau, Diane herself.

"Immigration?" Kinsman was asking. His head was still spinning, and there was a tall drink in his hand. Diane was perched on the arm of the couch beside him.

Leonov nodded vigorously. He had a vodka bottle in one hand and a tiny shot glass in the other. He was standing, his boots were planted solidly on the grassy floor, but his body weaved slowly from side to side, like a fern in a fishtank. Kinsman could not decide if it was his own eyesight or the Russian's stabilization system that was going kaput.

Leonov boomed jovially, "Do you realize how many requests for immigration visas we have received in the past twenty-four hours? Thousands! From almost every nation in the world."

"We've already been officially recognized by several nations," Diane said. "Starting with Sri Lanka."

"And the government of Israel in exile, surprise, surprise," said Harriman, buffing his fingernails against the chest of his coveralls. "I'm not without influence among certain of the more civilized people of the Earth, I'll have you know. Besides," he added, "Selene is the only nation that the Jews haven't been thrown out of."

"Maybe we could offer them a promised land up here,"

Diane said. "They're desert people; the Moon's certainly bleak enough for them."

"Too much," Kinsman muttered. "It's all too much."

"You're entirely right," Jill Meyers said, fixing Kinsman with a professional medical gaze. "You look like you've been through several wringers. I want you in my office at oh-nine-hundred hours tomorrow morning."

"You mean *this* morning," Alexsei said softly. "It's already past three."

"To bed, all of you," Jill commanded. "Can't have our Chief Administrator collapsing from exhaustion his first day on the job."

Harriman pursed his lips. "There are several lewd remarks I could make, but considering your exalted position, Mr. Chief Administrator, I will maintain a kindly and courteous silence."

"You're just sucking up for a good political job," Kinsman said.

"How right you are! How about making me Minister of Education?"

"No. I want you to be our Foreign Minister."

Harriman was aghast. "Me? A diplomat? One of those mincing faggots?"

"You'd start a new trend in foreign affairs, Hugh. You've already influenced one government, by your own admission."

"I won't wear striped pants!"

"Hugh, you don't have to wear any pants at all, if you don't want to. What I need is—"

"Tomorrow!" Jill said firmly. She got up from her chair and Alexsei rose with her, towering above her tiny form. Diane got up, too, and they all drifted toward the door. But Kinsman lingered as the others left.

Harriman's voice was still echoing down the corridor as Kinsman said to Diane, "Well, I made it. They didn't kill me."

"They tried," she said.

He reached out to push the door shut but she did not let go of it.

"You did a fine job, taking care of everything while I was gone."

"Thanks."

He did not want to make polite conversation. He did not want to talk about anything, or even to think. Not about politics or war or death.

"Diane—let's make love."

"Instead of war?" She smiled faintly as she pushed the door shut.

Kinsman slid his arm around her shoulders as they headed toward the bedroom.

Jill Meyers took up the first couple of hours of the new day, running Kinsman through an extensive physical, clucking and frowning and shaking her head as the readouts came from the medical sensors and integrating computer.

"You think this heart murmur of yours is just a dodge to fool the brass Earthside," she scolded. "Well, take a look at this EKG." She handed him a ribbon of plastic tape across her bare little desk.

Kinsman examined the jagged line. "Bad?"

"It's got the shakes. Have you been feeling any chest pains? Sharp twinges along your left arm or side?"

With the innate distrust of medics that all fliers feel, Kinsman answered merely, "Some discomfort when I was down in the high-gee section of the space station, that's all."

"That's all." She glowered at him, spoke a prescription for pills into the computer input mike, and then waved him out of her office cubicle. He got as far as the door, a single step.

"You're not immortal," Jill said sharply. "We're all depending on you, Chet. You'll be no good to any of us dead. Slow down."

"Sure." He made himself grin at her. "The worst is over. It's all going to be downhill from here on in."

It was not until he was halfway down the corridor that led into the water factory that he realized how many different connotations "downhill" could have.

Ernie Waterman was embarrassed to see him. The dour-faced engineer actually blushed when Kinsman arrived at the rock crushers, where an explosion had wrecked two of the six conveyor belts that carried pulverized rock from the giant machines to the electric arcs.

"I . . . I figured as long as I'm here . . ." Waterman stammered over the clamor of technicians yelling to each other and the spark and hiss of welding lasers. The four working crushers pounded out a basso accompaniment to the higher-pitched noises. "Well . . . I figured I might as well help out. It's better than sitting around doing nothing, ain't it?"

"That's fine, Ernie," said Kinsman over the din of the construction crew. "I appreciate your help."

"How soon do I have to leave?"

"Leave?"

An air compressor screamed to life and Waterman raised his shrill voice even louder and leaned on his canes toward Kinsman's ear. Their hard hats actually clicked. "When are you going to be shipping me back Earthside?"

"Nobody's going Earthside!" Kinsman yelled back. "And nothing from Earthside is coming up here—not until we get some of the politics straightened out. And whether you leave Selene or not is your decision, Ernie. I can't send you back to a wheelchair. If you can stomach what we're doing here—or even better, come over to our way of thinking —you're welcome to stay as long as you like."

Waterman's mouth moved but Kinsman could not hear what he said.

"I mean it, Ernie," he shouted. "As long as you don't work against us you're welcome to live here."

"You'd . . . trust me?"

"Why not? Aren't you an honest man?"

Waterman merely shook his head in wonderment.

Much of the afternoon Kinsman spent going over personnel lists and combining the American files with Leonov's. The two of them worked in the Russian personnel office, alone except for the Lunagrad computer terminal that sat on a table in the middle of a large room. The Moonbase computer had not yet been fully linked with the Russian machine.

Leonov had to translate the Cyrillic symbols. Kinsman had the American files transferred electronically into the Russian data bank. He frowned as Pat Kelly's file appeared on the display screen. Kelly was still confined to quarters, under a psychiatrist's care. He had requested immediate transfer for himself and his family Earthside.

I failed with him, Kinsman told himself. He worked so close to me, saw everything I saw, everything I did. And yet he couldn't make the jump, couldn't change his thinking enough to grasp what had to be done. He'd rather see America destroyed than changed.

When he returned to his own quarters, just before dinnertime, he found Frank Colt sitting tensely on his living room couch. Alone.

"I was wondering when you'd show up," Kinsman said as he slid the front door shut.

"Yeah. I steered away from the partying last night. Figured you had earned a celebration without me screwing it up for you."

"I looked for you in the crowd. I wanted to thank you for staying out of mischief while I was away." Kinsman crossed the room and sat on the slingchair next to Colt.

"Took some guts for you to trust me," Colt said, eyeing Kinsman carefully.

"Took some guts for you to accept the responsibility, feeling the way you do."

Colt broke into a grin. "Listen, buddy. That lady of yours would've shot me down like a dog in a microsecond if I had stepped half a millimeter out of line. She's pretty and sweet—and tough."

Kinsman felt his brows knit slightly. He had never thought of Diane as being tough, yet the evidence had been obvious all along. No one built a successful singing career without inner strength and a steel-hard determination. And even after the government slapped her down, she bounced back and made it to the Moon.

"Do you still feel the same way?" he asked Colt. "That what we're doing is wrong?"

Colt did not answer right away. But when he did it was with a silent nod of his head.

"Even though you can see that the Lunagrad people are with us, and that we're both acting together to save the United States and Russia?"

Hunching forward in the couch, fists on knees, Colt answered, "Okay, okay, you're a bunch of do-gooders and you've got the best interests of mankind at heart. I still can't buy it. I'm sorry, Chet, that's just the way it is. I want out. I want to go back Earthside."

"But Frank, can't you see—"

"I can see the whole fucking thing! And I know which side I'm on. It ain't yours. I'm sorry, man. Maybe I'm wrong and you're right. But that's where it's at."

Kinsman searched his friend's face. It was a thinly masked mixture of pain and stubbornness. "There's nothing we can do?"

"Not a damned thing. Just send me back Earthside as soon as you can."

"There might be trouble for you down there. They might not believe that you were against us."

"I'll take my chances."

With a shake of his head, Kinsman said, "Frank, I just hate like hell—"

"Do it!" Colt snapped. "Stop thinking you can win everybody over with logic and a sweet smile. I am what I am, and you can't change that."

"And you *won't* change it."

For an instant Colt looked as if he would lash out at Kinsman. But the fire in his eyes dimmed and he answered only, "That's right. I won't change."

Something from the back of Kinsman's mind surfaced and he heard himself say, "Okay, Frank. You can be on the next shuttle to Alpha. I'll set up a special flight to Earthside from there. There are a few civilian scientists who want to get back, too. You can go with them."

One of those scientists would be Marrett, Kinsman knew.

"Fine," said Colt.

Kinsman sat back in his slingchair, thinking. You're using your oldest friend, letting him be the excuse for getting Marrett to the UN people.

"Is there anything else, Frank?"

Colt gritted his teeth before answering. "Yeah, one more thing." He sounded disgusted, ashamed.

"What is it?"

"Murdock . . ."

"Oh, shit. What's old wetpants want now?"

Colt's eyes evaded Kinsman's. "Diane asked me to tell you. She didn't know how to break it. Murdock's dead. Committed suicide two days ago."

"Suicide?"

"Sliced his wrists."

Murdock? That pudgy little kettledrum of a man? The guy we used to tease until he'd throw a tantrum? Clowns don't slice their wrists. It can't be for real!

"But why?" Kinsman asked.

Colt's voice was barely audible. "I guess they were looking for a scapegoat. They were going to investigate, court-martial him."

"Oh for God's sake!" The bastards. Kicking the weakest one. I should have known. I should have known. "Did he leave a note or anything?"

"A taped message. It was addressed to you. The communications people just got to it this afternoon—they been swamped and this had no priority at all."

"Addressed to me?" Kinsman felt his insides going hollow.

"I burned it," Colt said. "You don't want to hear it."

"What did it say?"

"It was shitty."

What did it say?"

Colt took a breath. "He said, 'Thanks for everything, Kinsman. This is the reward I get for covering up your murder of that Russian girl. I should have crucified you when I had the chance.'"

Thursday 23 December 1999:
1400 hrs UT

IT WAS 9 A.M. in New York. Ted Marrett paced impatiently past the floor-to-ceiling windows of the plushly carpeted office, high in the UN's Secretariat Building. A sleety rain pelted the windows; across the turgid, oily East River, Brooklyn and Queens were only a gray smear.

"You're going to wear out your boots," said Beleg Jamsuren. He was sitting placidly in a leather easy chair, his round, flat Mongol face a picture of stoic calm. He was a young man who carried his formidable name easily, as confidently as if he were an ancient warrior atop a shaggy Gobi pony wearing padded armor and a steel helmet with a short bow strung over his shoulder. Instead he was a bright young scientist, and he wore a plain brown business suit.

"Better than wearing out the seat of my pants," Marrett growled. He was in denims and a tweed sports jacket, puffing hard on the stump of a cigar clamped between his teeth.

Jamsuren silently thanked the gods for the ventilation system that sucked up the fetid cigar smoke. "He said he would see you shortly after nine."

"That's what it is now." Marrett tapped his wristwatch. "Shortly after nine. Where is he?"

"He does have a few other responsibilities."

"Nothing as important as this! Holy hell, we've been trying to see him for four solid days."

"The Secretary General doesn't often make time to see a couple of lowly UNESCO scientists. His schedule is arranged . . ."

Marrett wheeled toward the Mongol. "Don't give me that humble Oriental crap! I know you better. You're just as worked up about this as I am."

Jamsuren allowed himself a smile. "Perhaps I did use my

consanguinity with the Mongolian ambassador to further our cause."

"You betcha."

"But it won't do us any good if you're an incoherent wreck when . . ."

The door opened. Marrett turned, taking the cigar from his mouth. Jamsuren stood up.

Emanuel De Paolo was a slight, frail-looking man. His skin was dark, his hair as gray as volcanic ash. His eyes were utterly black, but alive, youthful and alert in an aging man's face. His suit was very conservatively cut, with cuffed trousers and a double-breasted jacket over his soft turtleneck sweater. But the suit was the blue of the skies over the Andes; the sweater Incan gold.

"Gentlemen," he said in a soft, almost musical voice. "Please do not be formal. Sit, sit."

Marrett eased his big frame slowly into the chair that Jamsuren had been using, without taking his eyes off the Secretary General. The Mongol scientist wordlessly moved aside and took another chair. De Paolo relaxed in a webchair of Scandinavian wood and rope.

"May I please ask you to be brief," the Secretary General said pleasantly. "There is a meeting of the Security Council this afternoon to discuss the recent events on the Moon, and I have several appointments on my calendar before the session begins."

Marrett glanced at his friend. Jamsuren said, "I am not sure of how much the Mongolian Ambassador told you, sir."

"Very little," said the Secretary General. "I must confess that he seemed to enjoy making this as mysterious as possible."

"It's not mysterious," Marrett said, stubbing out his cigar in the ashtray by his chair. "No more mysterious that the rain falling out there."

An hour later an aide knocked discreetly on the door of the room to remind the Secretary General of his ten-fifteen appointment. De Paolo told him to cancel it. The phone rang once, and De Paolo spoke harshly into it in Portuguese. They were not interrupted again, except for when the Secretary General suggested that they have some lunch brought in.

The Security Council meeting began without him. By

mid-afternoon De Paolo was asking, "Can all this really be done?"

Marrett was chewing the soggy end of his last cigar. It had gone dead hours earlier. "If you mean technically, the answer is yes. Sure, it'll be some time before we can tailor-make local weather on a small scale, but we know enough right now to ruin a nation's crops anytime we want to. And we've been able to steer major storm systems for years —when we're allowed to do it."

"Within limits," Jamsuren added.

The Secretary General had taken off his jacket. He dabbed at his forehead nervously. "But this is fantastic. Do you realize what power you are speaking of? Do you have any conception of what you are offering?"

"It *is* awesome," Jamsuren agreed quietly.

De Paolo pulled himself out of his chair and walked to the window. It was no longer raining but the sky was still gray. "I wish I had not agreed to listen to you," he said, staring out at the decaying city. "I wish I had never heard this. The temptation . . ."

Marrett tapped his watch. "In exactly five minutes you'll see some blue sky. The sun will break through."

The Secretary General glanced over his shoulder at the big man. "You are certain?"

Nodding, Marrett replied, "Just as certain as I am that the UN—or *somebody*—has got to grab this power. We can't keep it a secret much longer. There are plenty of meteorologists and fluid dynamicists who are aware of the potential. Once they work up the guts to admit to themselves that the weather can be controlled all around the world, it'll be the next big international crisis."

"And this Kinsman," De Paolo asked. "He is an honorable man? He can be trusted?"

"I think so. He wants to have his new nation admitted to the UN, and recognized as an independent country. He offers a way to enforce world peace."

The Secretary General shook his head. "It's frightening. Too tempting."

"You mean the potential power?" Jamsuren asked.

"That," the old man answered, "and the responsibility. We have all wrung our hands about the United Nations' political impotence for years, decades. But this changes everything. Everything!"

"It's using technological power to attain political power," said Marrett.

"I am not certain it's the right thing to do. I am not at all sure that we're ready for this. It's the use of force—a different kind of force, perhaps—but still . . ."

"Force is the only way to move an object," Marrett said.

"Newtonian physics," replied the Secretary General. He smiled wanly. "You see? I am not entirely ignorant of science."

He turned back to the window. A lance of sunlight broke through the gray clouds. A slice of blue appeared in the sky. "Your prediction was too conservative," De Paolo said to Marrett. "Five minutes have not elapsed yet."

Marrett shrugged. "I'm always on the conservative side."

"Are you?" The Secretary General squared his shoulders, like a man who had finally decided to accept a burden, no matter how heavy. "Very well. I suppose I must meet with this Kinsman. Do you think he would be willing to come to New York?"

The California sunshine was strong and brilliant, coming out of a sky so blue that it needed occasional puffs of white cumulus clouds for contrast.

Frank Colt squinted, even behind his polarized glasses. The glare coming up from the concrete runways and taxi aprons was powerful. But I can handle it, Colt told himself. That, and anything else they care to send my way.

The two Air Policemen walking in stride a few paces behind him were both over six feet tall, with football physiques and big automatic pistols holstered on their hips. They followed Colt wherever he went. Technically he was under house arrest and confined to this desert base until the masterminds in Washington decided whether he could be blamed for any responsibility in the lunar rebellion.

Colt grinned sardonically. Not every dude has his own bodyguards following him around. Status symbol.

Overhead a silvery speck started to materialize into an executive jetcopter, and Colt could hear the *wush-wush-wush* of its huge rotor blades even over the shrill scream of its turbine engines. Colt and his two guards came to a parade rest, quite unconsciously, at the edge of the painted yellow circle marking the helicopter landing area. A service truck was racing across the concrete off in the distance, coming up to plug in electricity for the copter's communications, lights, and air-conditioning.

The jetcopter settled down on the concrete landing apron in a scream of gale-blown grit and pebbles. As it squatted on its springy landing gear and the rotors slowed, Colt looked up and saw that it bore no insignia except for a standard USAF star and the identification number H003. The "three" in the number struck Colt at once. Number one's for the President, and two's for the Vice President, he knew. He was impressed with the man inside, the man who had come to see him.

The copter's main hatch swung upward and a lieutenant in spotless uniform stood in the hatchway as metal stairs trundled out and touched down on the concrete. He looked at Colt and saluted, sallow-faced, pinch-eyed, but very crisp and professional in bearing. Colt returned the salute and went up the stairs and into the helicopter. His two guards remained outside in the glaring sun. In the week that they had been escorting Colt everywhere, they had yet to say a word to him.

Get a good tan, fellas, Colt silently wished them.

Inside, the copter was frigid. The Lieutenant was tall enough to have to duck his head as they stepped through a smaller hatch set into a gray-painted partition. Colt stepped into a sort of conference room—a compartment, really; spacious for a helicopter, perhaps, but crowded already by the three people seated at its narrow table.

Colt snapped to attention and saluted. The weary-looking Two-Star General seated across the table flicked a salute back to him. He was flanked by a puffy-faced colonel and a civilian, a man in a dark suit who sat hunched over, his burly shoulders bulging strangely inside the suit jacket, his face seemingly stamped with the red heat of constant pain.

There was one lightweight plastic chair unoccupied. The General gestured to it; Colt sat down. The Lieutenant stayed at the hatchway, behind Colt's back. He had noticed that the Lieutenant wore an Air Police armband but carried no gun. Standing behind him, though, it would be possible for him to kill Colt with his hands if he were told to.

"I am Major General Cianelli," said the General. "This is my aide, Colonel Sullivan."

Colt nodded. But two-star generals don't get chopper number three, he knew. This bird must belong to the civilian. He turned expectantly to the red-faced man, who was sitting on his left.

"My name is not important," he whispered, harsh and labored.

For a moment there was silence in the compartment. Colt could hear the distant muffled drone of the service truck's diesel generator, nothing else.

General Cianelli looked pained. "We are here to review your case; that is, the statements you made to the investigating board earlier this week."

"Yessir," Colt said, going into his professional act. "I'd be happy to clear up any questions you have."

"You said that you led a group of counterinsurgents," Colonel Sullivan said, in a surprisingly high tenor voice, "and attempted to destroy Moonbase's water production facility."

"Yessir. We were only partially successful, though. We were overwhelmed by sheer numbers before we could do more than superficial damage."

"Only superficial damage?" came the tortured whisper from his left.

"I heard, while I was under arrest afterward, that our action cut down Moonbase's water production by about one third . . ."

"Ah?"

". . . but the damage could be repaired in a few weeks."

"Without needing any parts or supplies from Earth?" General Cianelli asked.

"That's right, sir. They have everything they need for the repairs there at the base."

"A few weeks," Sullivan mused. "That means the rebels are short on drinking water?"

"Not likely, sir," Colt responded. "The water facility can produce enough drinking, housekeeping, and irrigation water for both Moonbase and Lunagrad. They may be short on rocket propellant, though, since the hydrogen and oxygen are electrolyzed from the water that the facility produces."

General Cianelli frowned. "What sort of a man is this Colonel Kinsman?"

Careful, man! Colt warned himself. They know all about both of you. "He was a close friend of mine, sir. I've always regarded him as well-meaning, very likable, but politically soft."

They went on for hours. Colt carefully maneuvered around the fact that he could have shot Kinsman or could have attempted a counter-coup while the rebels were seizing the space stations. He gambled that no one else who had returned from Selene knew exactly what had happened and what role he had played. Only Pat Kelly might contradict him, but to do that Kelly would have to put himself on the spot. Gradually it became clear to Colt that they were no longer probing his loyalty or questioning his actions during the rebellion. They were pushing for information about the rebels themselves, Kinsman especially, and the defenses that the space stations and the lunar settlement possessed.

"Sir," he asked the General, "am I going to face a court-martial?"

General Cianelli glanced at the angry-faced civilian. "That's a matter to be decided . . ."

The burly man silenced him with the slightest movement of one hand. To Colt he said, "There will be no need for a court-martial. Quite the opposite. We are seeking a knowledgeable officer to assume the late General Murdock's command. A man who knows the space stations well enough to show us how to recapture them."

Colt closed his eyes momentarily and saw a general's stars. "Recapture the space stations," he echoed, looking straight into the civilian's pain-shot eyes. "I can show you how."

Cianelli looked surprised. Sullivan smiled. But it was the angry man who answered him. "How? The rebels have command of all the laser-armed satellites. They will destroy any rocket boosting up from Earth."

Colt faced him. "You've got to get them to agree to allow one flight to come up to Alpha. That's all you need: just one flight."

The man stared at Colt, his face red and scowling. Neither of the two Aerospace Force officers dared to speak.

Finally the burly man said, "Show me."

Colt asked, "Do you have a computer link aboard?"

The civilian looked up at the Lieutenant, still on his feet behind Colt. "Bring it."

It took some fiddling around with the terminal, a compact desktop unit, before Colt could link it with the files at Vandenberg. Finally the display screen showed views of Space Station Alpha, together with the records of the military crew needed to staff it.

"Even if we assume that Kinsman's put extra people in Alpha to protect the station," Colt said, "he couldn't have more than a hundred military men aboard."

"A shuttle carries only fifty passengers, max," General Cianelli objected.

"That's fifty civilians," Colt shot back. "We could pack more troops in, especially if you use the cargo space in the bottom deck."

The General sat up straighter. "We'd have to modify the shuttle, pipe life-support capability into the cargo deck—but that can be done."

"Certainly," Colonel Sullivan agreed.

Colt went on to show how the station could be overrun quickly and efficiently by a hundred well-armed, well-trained troops.

"They'd have to be well-led, too," Colt added.

"And you will be their leader?" the burly man asked.

"No," said Colt. "Not me. I'm not an infantryman."

Ignoring that, Cianelli asked, "So we recapture Alpha. What good does that do?"

Smiling to himself, Colt realized that he had them hooked. "Okay. Watch." He touched the computer keyboard again. The view showed an animated drawing of Earth with hundreds of satellites revolving around it. With a touch of his finger, Colt wiped out all the satellites except the three American space stations. "Now, look at the area each station 'sees' as it orbits around the Earth."

The display screen showed pale-colored ovals slipping across the Earth's surface: the area visible from each of the space stations.

"There are windows," Colt explained, "when Alpha and only Alpha is available to survey the Vandenberg area. Or

Cape Canaveral, for that matter. Once we seize Alpha, we can launch more troopships during those periods. And we time the seizure of Alpha so that we can follow it up within a couple of hours by launches that will take Beta, Gamma, and the Russian stations, too."

He clicked off the display screen and looked up at their faces. "If we can move fast enough and we do everything exactly right, we can take over the whole ABM network—the Russians' as well as ours."

"We'll have the Reds staring into our gun barrels!" Sullivan exulted.

"And we can march in on Moonbase anytime we want to," said Cianelli. "They'll be defenseless. They'll fall like a ripe plum."

"Lunagrad too," Colt said.

The other man said nothing. They all turned to him. He breathed a deep, labored exhalation. Then, "Consider yourself an acting full colonel, Mr. Colt. The General here will process your orders immediately. You will implement the plan you have just outlined. If it succeeds you will be raised in rank to brigadier general."

Cianelli's mouth tightened into a bloodless line. Sullivan's eyes were evasive.

Colt said, "One more thing."

The man's angry face seemed to swell and get even redder.

"I want," said Colt, "to meet the President of the United States. It's purely a personal thing. I want to meet the top man, even if it's just for a minute. I want to shake his hand."

The anger subsided, slightly. He almost smiled. "Of course. That can be arranged."

"When can we strike?" Cianelli asked suddenly. "This entire strategy depends on the rebels' allowing us to send a shuttle to Alpha."

The angry man mused, "Intelligence reports that many nations have forwarded requests for emigration to the lunar rebels. There have even been some Americans asking for exit permission."

"Americans?" Sullivan looked shocked.

"We have always had fools and traitors in our midst," the burly man said. "This will be a good way to get them to identify themselves to us. Then they can be re-educated."

"Christmas Eve," Colt said.

"What?"

"Or Christmas Day. Get Kinsman to accept the first flight of immigrants to the Moon on Christmas Day."

"Impossible!" Cianelli shook his head. "We can't pick shock troops and train them for this mission and modify a shuttle by tomorrow or the next day."

Colt frowned. "Kinsman's a sentimentalist, a romantic. He would buy the Christmas thing."

"What about New Year's?" Sullivan asked.

The three of them looked at Colt, waiting for his reaction. "New Year's *Eve*," he said. "That way they can start the first day of the new century, the new millennium, aboard the space station in their new nation."

"Didn't I read somewhere that the new millennium doesn't really start until the next year—2001? Is that right?" Sullivan wondered.

"Doesn't matter," Colt countered. "Kinsman will buy the New Year's Eve bit. And everybody counts the change from 1999 to 2000 as the millennium. Nobody gives a crap about the purists." Colt used the slight profanity very deliberately. No one reacted to it at all. You got 'em, baby! he told himself.

"New Year's Eve it will be, then," said the burly man.

Before the sun set that day Colt's guards disappeared. He was ushered into plush quarters and a big office where he found a pair of silver colonel's eagles on his gleaming new desk, together with the paperwork for the promotion.

"They work fast," he muttered to himself. Fingering the eagles, "Only two pieces of silver. Judas got thirty."

He looked out the window of his new office, and he could see the pale outline of the Moon rising over the low hills in the still-bright sky.

"I ain't gonna hang myself, though." His voice sounded bitter, even to himself.

Saturday 25 December 1999:
1612 hrs UT

"IT'S BEEN A busy day," Kinsman said.

"Haven't they all?" replied Diane.

They were sitting in the living room of his quarters, watching the start of the buggy race on the big wall screen across from the sofa.

"I guess they have, at that," Kinsman admitted. He had not seen Diane since the night of his return from Alpha, except for brief business talks in his office. He had appointed her Deputy Director of Personnel for Selene, under a former Russian psychologist.

Selene's first Christmas of independence had been celebrated by a huge dinner in the central plaza, with everyone bringing their own food plus something extra for the communal buffet. More than a thousand people sat on the grass and ate picnic style, celebrating the holiday together regardless of nationality, religion, or politics. After three hours of feasting, the buggy race had begun. Kinsman and Leonov officiated at the countdown, up in the main dome. Then Kinsman had invited Diane to have a drink with him.

Now they watched the ungainly lunar buggies lumbering across the uneven ground at speeds of up to thirty kilometers per hour, heading for the crater Opelt. It would take them more than a whole day to complete the nine-hundred-kilometer round trip.

The racing buggies had all started life as standard lunar surface rovers, but now they were barely recognizable as such. They all had bubble-shaped canopies up front where the crew sat: bulging cockpits that looked like insects' eyes and gave the term "buggy" a double meaning. There the similarities ended and individual inventiveness took over. Some of the buggies were wheeled, others tracked. One walked stiffly on sharply angled praying mantis legs that ended in spongy-looking hooves. Several had weird multicolored wings sprouting from them: solar panels designed to intercept different wavelengths of sunlight and convert them into the electricity that ran the motors. Some had boxy collections of fuel cells running their lengths, and one buggy had a steam generator and a solar mirror atop it just behind the cockpit. Their colors were all garish, and not for esthetic reasons alone. Each crew wanted to be easy to spot by searchers if their buggy broke down on the desolate lunar plain.

Kinsman sat on the sofa with a drink in his hand and Diane beside him, watching the slow-motion race. The buggies scrabbled toward the nearby horizon, climbing laboriously over the rises in the undulating ground and wallowing in the shallow spots like turtles seeking the sea. His mind flashed a memory of roaring balls-out in an F-18 thirty meters above the Mojave floor, throttle to the firewall, afterburners screeching, scrub and rocks and sand blurring into one continuous barely seen swatch of gray-brown as he focused his eyes on the hills rising in front of him. Then barely a nudge of the stick and she stood on her tail and hurtled skyward while the safety suit hissed and squeezed at him and he flipped her into a tight barrel roll just for the sheer hell of it.

Nevermore. He shook his head.

"Chet?" Diane broke into his reverie.

"Huh? What is it?"

"I just realized . . . You didn't get me anything for Christmas, did you?"

He thought swiftly, Should I tell her? Then he heard himself answering, "Well . . . not really."

"I didn't think to get anything for you," Diane said, her face quite serious.

"That's okay. What I'm trying to get for you won't be here for a while, anyway."

Diane sat up straighter. "You're trying to get something for me?"

"Not some*thing*," Kinsman replied. "Some*one*. Your daughter."

She gasped with surprise.

"I asked Hugh to see if he could arrange to have her sent here to you."

Diane threw her arms around Kinsman's neck and kissed him.

He held her tightly and the kiss grew warm with passion. Then the phone buzzed. They separated slightly as Kinsman sighed and punched the ON button. Hugh Harriman's face took form on the display screen. He was wearing his pixie expression.

"Am I interrupting anything?" he leered.

"Yes. We're planting a mistletoe tree. What do you want, Hugh?"

"While you two have been playing all day at your infantile games," Harriman answered, "I have been engaged in many hours of earnest and fruitful discussion with my fellow diplomats Earthside."

Kinsman sat up a little straighter. "On Christmas Day?"

"You sound like Bob Cratchit, for God's sake! Yes, on Christmas Day. It hasn't been easy to put all the pieces together, since nobody wants to go on the record with this. They'd rather talk from their homes on the holiday than from their offices during business hours. All under the table, highly unofficial and all that."

"For Chrissakes, Hugh, you're sounding more like a Foggy Bottom bureaucrat every day! What the hell are you talking about?"

"Well!" Harriman put on his injured look, but let it melt away immediately. "Okay, here's the story. One: Marrett called early this morning and told me that you could expect a personal invitation from the Secretary General of the United Nations to address the General Assembly in a special session. As a private person, mind you, not as a head of state. But he will invite you officially only if he knows beforehand that you'll accept. Can't afford to lose face and all that shit."

Kinsman felt his breath coming faster. "When?"

"Before the week is out."

Diane moved closer to Kinsman. "Will the American government allow someone from Selene to land there?"

"My dear child, what do you think I've been trying to arrange all day long? Do you think I'd miss the feasting and the girl-goosing of this festive occasion for sheer lack of team spirit?"

"Cut the crap, Hugh. What did you accomplish?"

"Plenty, if I say so myself." He hesitated only a moment. "I explained to Marrett that our position with the Yankee *Federales* is rather delicate. He understood and said the UN had already requested a safe-conduct guarantee for you and all your party."

"So?"

"So while I was wondering whether I should try to get a call through to the American State Department—knowing that nobody who could exert any authority would be available on Christmas Day—I received a call from an old chum of yours: *Colonel* Franklin Delano Roosevelt Colt."

"Full colonel?"

"Seems Frank's landed on his feet, Earthside. He was wearing a bird colonel's eagles."

"He's at Vandenberg?"

"Right. Apparently they've let him take over your General Murdock's command."

"Sonofabitch!"

"And," Harriman went on, "this request from the UN for handling a party of visitors from Selene has already reached his level. Approved by no less than the President of the United States his own self."

"You mean it's all set?"

Harriman scratched at his goatee. "Not only have they moved faster than anyone in Washington has since the riots of ninety-two, but they seem to be going out of their way to be nice to us."

"What do you mean?"

"They're asking permission to send up a shipment of people from all over the world who've asked to emigrate from their native lands to Selene. Leonov's kids might be among them. I might even be able to get your daughter included, Diane."

She said nothing, but Kinsman felt her fingers tighten on his arm.

He leaned back against the sofa's foam padding, wondering aloud, "I don't get it. Why are they being so accommodating, all of a sudden?"

"I asked myself the same question," Harriman replied. "There are several possible answers."

"Such as?"

"Well, for one thing, Colt's probably having some influence. He must be telling them that we really mean the United States no harm, and that an independent Selene friendly to the U.S. is better than a Selene that's hostile."

Kinsman nodded.

"Then, too, the think-tank people must have figured out by now that we could easily become allies of the Soviet Union, which would be disastrous for the U.S. Another reason for them to treat us carefully."

"Go on."

Harriman shrugged. "There's also world opinion: the big, bad U.S. picking on a helpless little new nation. That doesn't count for much, I think, but it might explain the request to send up a token bunch of immigrants."

Trojan horse? The thought flicked through Kinsman's mind. "I want to know exactly who these immigrants are. Complete data on each of them."

"Right."

"You've had a busy day, Hugh."

Harriman grinned toothily. "Yes, but it's been very rewarding. I even spoke briefly with the Russian ambassador to the United Nations. Marrett told me where to find him; he'd canceled a holiday trip home. It looks as if the Russians won't be averse to recognizing our independence—as long as they can inspect the space stations and the ABM satellites and satisfy themselves that we really are independent."

"Check with Leonov about that. And find out about whether or not his kids are in that shuttle-load of immigrants."

"Right."

"Do you think you really can get my daughter?" Diane asked.

"I'm going to try. Strike while the iron's hot, and all that."

"It all sounds terrific, Hugh. Almost too good to be true."

"Yes, it looks as if they're bending over backwards to be sweet to us. Maybe it's the Christmas spirit."

"I hope it's something deeper and more permanent."

"Amen."

"Anything else?" Kinsman asked.

"Two things. About the invitation to address the General Assembly. The hitch is that they want you 'at your earliest convenience.' But no later than this coming Thursday."

"Thursday?" Diane echoed. "That's so soon!"

"We can't let any dust gather on this," Harriman said, completely serious. "Things are rolling our way, we've got to take advantage of this favorable tide before something happens to change their minds."

"All right," Kinsman said. "Thursday. What was the other thing?"

"The other? Oh!" Harriman's eyes twinkled. "I spent an hour's time—my lunch hour, the way I figure it—tracking down the jackal who calls himself the Maximum Leader of my native land. Finally got him on the screen."

"To tell him that you're coming Earthside under a UN safe-conduct?"

"No." Harriman smiled with beatific delight. "I just wanted to see his pockmarked face once more and watch the expression on it as I gave him my personal Christmas greeting."

"You called to wish him a Merry Christmas?" Diane asked.

"Not quite. I told him to go fuck himself."

Sunday 26 December 1999:
1015 hrs UT

"THERE IS NO WAY," Jill Meyers said firmly, "that you are going Earthside, Thursday or any other day. It's medically out of the question!"

They were in Kinsman's office: Jill, Leonov, Harriman, Diane, and Kinsman himself.

"Come on, Jill," Kinsman said. "This is no time for lectures."

She was on her feet, frowning intensely at Kinsman.

"Chet, I'm not lecturing. I'm telling you the simple facts. You can't survive on Earth."

"Just for a couple of days . . ."

"Watch my lips," Jill snapped. Then she said with deliberate care, hesitating between each word, "You can not live on Earth."

Diane looked surprised. "Not ever?"

"Maybe with six months of special training and exercise," Jill replied, "but even then his heart . . ."

"Jill, let's not start swallowing our own propaganda," Kinsman interrupted. "You know damned well we cooked up that heart murmur to get around the duty regs about rotation."

Jill stood squarely in front of him, a tiny snub-nosed Raggedy Ann doll with a will of chrome steel. "Your heart problem is real," she said slowly, making every word diamond hard. "It was a slight problem five years ago, and with the proper balance of rest and exercise it could have been corrected. It can still be corrected, given time. But for the past five years you have been living in one-sixth the gravity of Earth. Your heart has become accustomed to doing one-sixth the work it would face Earthside. The muscle tone, the workload capacity, is gone. You simply can't survive Earthside gravity! You'll kill yourself!"

For a long moment the office was absolutely still. None of them moved or spoke. Kinsman found himself staring into the wall screen opposite his couch: Earth was hanging there, close and lovely, the jewel of the cosmos. Near enough to reach, in a day or two.

"Jill," he said at last, "I'm not asking you to tell us what we can't do. You've got to help us to accomplish what needs to be done. I've *got* to go Earthside. Do you understand that?"

Leonov cleared his throat. "Let me go instead. I am in good physical condition, thanks to Russian pride in manly strength, as opposed to decadent Western self-indulgence."

"I appreciate the offer, Pete," Kinsman said, adding silently, *and the attempt to make us laugh.* "But the simple fact is that the deal was set up for me. The Americans would get very twitchy if you showed up in my place. Even the Russians would start to wonder what's going on."

"Does it have to be a personal visit?" Diane asked. "Can't it be handled by phone? I mean, we could pipe it through the biggest wall screens and all."

Harriman shook his head. "No, dear lovely lady. The crux of this whole meeting is the chance for Chet and Marrett to get face to face with the key national leaders down there. In private, with no bugs or eavesdroppers. The speech and the public meetings are nothing more than window dressing. The important thing, the *vital* thing, is for Chet and Marrett to offer the smaller nations their double-barreled deal of ABM protection and weather control."

"And to subtly threaten the major powers' existing communications satellites and other space assets," Leonov added.

"Subtly," Harriman agreed.

"What about your health, Hugh?" Kinsman asked him. "Will you be able to make the trip?"

Harriman put a fist to his forehead and flexed his biceps. No motion was discernible inside his coverall sleeve. "I've been exercising at least six hours every week in the centrifuge ever since I came here. I always expected to go right back home again, remember?"

"I've checked his latest physical exams," said Jill. "He's in good-enough shape."

"You bet your sweet ass I am!" Harriman concurred.

"All right," Kinsman said. "So it's my frail heart that's the problem. I'll only be Earthside for a few days . . ."

Jill gave him a tight-lipped scowl. "How did you feel when you were aboard the space station the week before last?"

"Huh? Fine! No problems." As long as I stayed in the low-gee sections, he remembered. But that wasn't my heart. I just felt tired, heavy, and some trouble breathing . . .

"Your chest didn't feel heavy?" Jill probed. "You didn't feel any aches or sharp pains anywhere?"

"Nothing much."

"How much time did you spend on Level One, where there's full Earth gravity?"

"Um, well, I didn't get down there at all. But I was on Level Three a lot—it's about half an Earth gee, a lot more than we have here."

"And how did you feel?"

"Kind of tired—achy. But my heart was okay."

Jill shook her head. "When you got back here your EKG looked like a Richter point-eight seismograph reading. Do you have any idea of how much your heart function had deteriorated from Earth normal? And your entire body's muscle tone? You wouldn't be able to stand up under normal Earth gravity for more than a few minutes! You'd—"

"Shut up!" Kinsman snapped.

Jill looked shocked. But she fell silent.

"Now listen to me," he said more softly. "We live in an age of medical miracles and high technology. There's no reason why I can't wear a powered suit down there. The exoskeleton will hold me up and the servomotors will help my flabby muscles move my arms and legs."

"But your heart—"

"Do something about it! You've got pressure cuffs and booster pumps and God knows what the hell else. Pump me full of adrenalin or whatever it takes."

Harriman shook his head furiously. "No drugs, dammit! We can't have you high or dopey during these meetings, for Chrissakes."

Already Kinsman was feeling weary. He ran a hand across his eyes. "Yeah, you're right." Turning back to Jill, "Okay, you're going to have to prop me up with whatever mechanical aids you can produce. I guess I'll need a doctor with me, then."

"But I can't go back," Jill said, almost apologetically.

And that's why you're resisting the idea of *me* going back, Kinsman realized. He looked at Jill with new understanding, and the residue of angry frustration inside him melted away. Reaching out to touch her arm, he said, "I know that, Jill. I don't expect you to . . ." To risk your life, he thought, the way I'm risking mine. But aloud, he finished, ". . . to go back with me. Nobody expects that of you."

"Alex will go with you," Jill said. "There's no medical reason for his being confined here."

"But he's driving one of the buggies in the race," said Kinsman.

"Then call him back."

"But . . ."

Leonov raised a solemn hand. "She is right. The race is not as important as your medical safety."

"It would be good politics to have a Russian in our little delegation," Harriman pointed out.

"All right," Kinsman said. "Then it'll be Alex, you"—nodding to Harriman—"and me. A Russian, an Irish-Brazilian Jew, and an American. We'll outnumber 'em."

Kinsman and Diane walked back toward the living quarters together, silent as they paced down the long, rough, curving corridor. It was late afternoon; nearly the whole day had been spent planning the Earthside trip.

"Would you like to have dinner at my place?" he asked.

She would not look at him. "I don't think so, Chet."

A family walked by them, parents and two children, one barely big enough to toddle by herself. After they passed, Kinsman asked, "What's wrong, Diane?"

She stopped and turned toward him. "You know what's wrong. You're going to keep going at this thing until it kills you."

"Oh . . ." He hunched his shoulders. "I've got to. There's no way around it."

"I know," she said. "That's the trouble. I know that what you're doing is right, and good, and there's no one else in the human race who can do it."

"I'll be okay."

She shook her head. "They're going to kill you."

"Don't be so melodramatic."

Diane turned and started walking down the grass-floored corridor again. Kinsman caught up with her and grabbed her arm. "Diane, listen to me. It's just this trip Earthside. After that, things will settle down." He grinned weakly. "We'll bring your daughter up here. We might even be able to lead a halfway normal life."

She smiled back. "I wish it were true."

"It will be true," he insisted. "When I come back from this trip Earthside, everything ought to be pretty well settled."

"You don't believe that, Chet, and neither do I."

"It could happen."

"When?"

"Once this Earthside business is finished. I'll be back in time for New Year's Eve, I bet. We'll celebrate the new century together."

Diane's smile warmed. "The new millennium."

"And I'll make a New Year's resolution," he joked, "never to leave the Moon again. How's that?"

"It would be wonderful," Diane said. "Especially if you could keep it."

Frank Colt wore dress blues as he leaned back in the plush reclining chair of the jetcopter's passenger compartment. The seats were arranged two by two, facing each other. Sitting beside Colt was a Major, ten years his senior, now serving as his aide. Facing them was a pair of civilians, one from the State Department and the other from the Internal Security Agency.

"We have cleared visas for all of the foreign visitors and American citizens who want to emigrate to Moonbase," the State Department man was saying. He was a professional bureaucrat, businesslike and knowledgeable. "They will begin arriving in New York on Thursday morning. The lunar delegation can meet most of them at the reception being given that evening."

The ISA agent was small, paunchy, balding. He nodded, poker-faced. "That should allay any suspicions the Luniks might have. Then we'll stash the foreigners at Kennedy Spaceport, tell them there are technical difficulties, and keep them incommunicado."

"While the troops take off in their place and seize the space station," the Major finished. "All very neat."

"Timing's critical," Colt said. "No room for screw-ups."

"Everything is worked out to the second," the Major replied smugly.

"Then work it out to the millisecond," Colt snapped. "I'm meeting the President tonight, and I want to be able to assure him that those stations will be in our hands when the new year begins."

The Major nodded, his lips pressed together and his cheeks going a blotchy red.

The State Department man traced a well-groomed fingernail down the crease of his trousers as far as the knee. "There is one additional item."

"What is it?" Colt asked.

"Our situation analysts have run this entire plan through the computer one additional time, to see if there are any loopholes to be plugged."

"And?"

"And they have come up with an elegant suggestion. They think that you, Colonel, should be in New York with this Kinsman character when the troop shuttle takes off."

Colt controlled his surprise with a reflex clamp-down on his emotions. He kept his voice noncommittal. "Why?"

"If Kinsman has any slight shred of doubt about a Trojan horse situation, your presence in New York should ease his fears."

"Or put him on his guard."

"No." The State Department man smiled. "We have analyzed Kinsman's personality profile quite thoroughly. He tends to trust people rather easily, especially people he has known for a time. You were friendly with him for many years. He undoubtedly still feels deep ties of friendship toward you. He will see your presence at the UN as a gesture of amity, and that should put him off his guard quite nicely."

He does trust people too easy, Colt admitted to himself.

The ISA agent smirked. "Beautiful. You two can watch the takeoff on TV together."

"The final few hours of countdown will be more-or-less automatic," the Major chipped in. "There's no real need for you to be physically present at the Kennedy launch center, or even at Patrick."

Colt said, "I don't like it. I'd rather be where the action is, at the launch complex."

"But the computers," said the State Department man, "show that the plan's chances for success increase from eighty-five percent to ninety-three if you are in New York with Kinsman."

You want me to kiss him on the cheek, too? Colt fumed silently. But he hid his anger, hid his fear, and looked into the three white faces, each in turn.

"Okay," he said at last. "I'll do it."

Wednesday 29 December 1999: 0525 hrs UT

KINSMAN SNAPPED awake.

For a moment he could not remember where he was. Then it came to him. The VIP suite in the low-gravity section of Space Station Alpha.

He got up slowly. There was a plastic tube in his thigh, carefully wrapped in protective bandaging. He glanced at the digital clock set into the bulkhead. In another hour and a half that tube would be connected to a pacemaker and electric motor. Inside his leg, the tube wormed through his femoral artery and up his torso into the aorta, where the plastic balloon pump rested. It was quiescent now. Once the pacemaker and power unit were connected the balloon would act as an auxiliary heart, helping with the blood-pumping work that his natural heart would be too weak to do on Earth.

Jill had frowned through the entire surgical procedure. "The pump can't take more than fifty percent of the workload off your heart," she had said. "You're still going to be in trouble when you reach Earth."

Kinsman padded into the sanitary stall and dry-bathed, letting the sonic vibrations cleanse and massage his skin. Silly, he told himself, knowing that he could have luxuriated in a water shower. But the habit prevails. And I shouldn't get the bandage wet, I guess. He did not want to admit that a water shower would smack too much of a last-chance-of-my-life ritual.

He shaved carefully, then started to dress. Briefly he thought of putting in a call to Diane, back in Selene. But he shook his head against the idea. Better to leave it this way. If I get back—*when* I get back—maybe we can start putting our lives together. But not now.

He pulled on a T-shirt, shorts, and slipper socks. Nothing else. The bandage showed beneath the brief shorts and bulged against the inside of his thigh. It felt like an extra pair of balls.

Kinsman hesitated at the door to his compartment. He took a deep, calming breath, then slid the door open and headed out to meet with Jill and her medical team.

Two hours later he was sitting in a special foam cushion chair aboard a rocketplane as it bit into Earth's atmosphere. Kinsman was encased in a mechanical exoskeleton: a framework of metal tubing that ran along his legs, torso, arms, and neck. The silvery metal tubes were jointed in all the places where the human body was jointed, although the broad metal plates running along Kinsman's back could never be as supple as a human spine. Tiny electrical servomotors moved the suit in response to Kinsman's own muscular actions.

The rocketplane glided deeper into Earth's atmosphere, shuddering and groaning as the shock-heated air made its external skin glowing hot. Kinsman felt the gee forces building up and decided to begin testing his new skeleton. He raised his right arm off the seat's armrest. A barely audible hum of electric motors and the arm lifted smoothly, easily. Yet when Kinsman tried to flex his fingers, which had no auxiliary help, it felt as if he were trying to squeeze a sponge-rubber ball rather than empty air.

The exoskeleton would allow a normal man working in Earth's gravity to lift half-ton loads with one hand. Kinsman hoped the suit would allow him to stand and walk properly. The back of the suit included a rigid framework, much like a hiker's pack frame, to which would be attached the electrical power supply for the suit and the heart pump, the pacemaker controls and motor, and a small green tank containing an hour's supply of oxygen. Resting on the seat beside Kinsman was a clip-on oxygen mask. Jill had insisted on its being part of the equipment he carried.

It was difficult for him to turn his head because the neck supports of the exoskeleton were quite stiff. So, like a man with a sore neck, Kinsman carefully edged his whole body slightly sideways, restrained by the safety harness cutting across his shoulders and lap.

He looked at Landau and Harriman, sitting in the double

seats across from him. They were unfettered except for their safety belts, and deep in animated conversation. The rest of the rocketplane was empty except for the flight crew up in the cockpit and a trio of stewardesses who had all shown professional nurse's or paramedic's certifications to Jill before she agreed to let them serve on this brief flight.

Kinsman leaned back in his seat, to the accompaniment of a miniature chorus of electric hums. He closed his eyes. He knew perfectly well what was happening in the cockpit now—or, at least, what used to happen when he flew such craft, decades ago. Now they were controlled from the ground; everything was automatic, the airport computer giving commands to the ship's computer. The flight crew was there only in case of emergency.

But in his mind he felt the bucking control column in his hands as the ship buffeted through maximum aerodynamic drag. He saw the firetrail of re-entry as the ship blazed through the atmosphere like a falling meteor, torturing the air around it into incandescence. He remembered one flight he and Frank Colt had . . .

"Touchdown in three minutes," announced the little speaker grille. Even the voice sounded mechanical, automatic. No emotion at all.

Despite himself, Kinsman grinned. Only an old fart reminisces about the good old days.

There were no windows on the rocketplane, but the tiny display screen set into the chairback in front of him showed a pilot's-eye view of the craft's approach to JFK Aerospaceport. Sunlight glittered off steel-gray water, uncountable structures took form on the screen: rows of houses, factories, warehouses, parking garages, towers, churches, shopping malls, bridges, roads, streets—all out in the open, under the strangely pale and diluted sun.

Peering intently at the little screen, Kinsman still could not see any people, or even any individual autos on the streets. Just an occasional gray bus or olive-colored truck that looked more like an Army vehicle than a civilian. The long dark corridor of the runway rushed up at them. A jarring bounce, then another, and then the muffled roar of braking jets told Kinsman they were down. He smiled to himself. We could land 'em a lot smoother than that, he thought. The computer doesn't take any pride in its touchdowns.

And then he realized they were on the ground. On Earth. He did not move until the craft rolled to a stop at the terminal building. One of the stewardesses helped him undo the buckles of his safety harness. Then she stood back, an odd expression on her face, as he tried to stand up.

Must look pretty weird, Kinsman thought as the suit unfolded itself—unfolded him—and he got to his feet.

Landau moved behind him and started up the heart pump. Kinsman had expected to feel it throbbing in his chest, but he felt only a slightly warm sensation that quickly passed. For several minutes the Russian tinkered with the equipment on Kinsman's backpack as Harriman watched in moody silence.

"How does it feel?" he asked at last, his voice deep and grave and somehow irritating.

"Fine," Kinsman snapped. "Same as it did on Level One at Alpha when we tested it. I'll challenge you to a basketball game before we go home."

Harriman snorted, "Bragging already! Come on. If you're so good, move your ass off this tin can and let the people admire us."

But there were no people.

At least, no crowds. Kinsman and his two followers walked from the ship into an access tunnel that led into the terminal building. A small knot of officials and medical people were there, including a representative from the American State Department and several UN functionaries. One of them, Kinsman noted immediately, was a tall, striking blonde. Swedish, I'll bet.

No news reporters. No television cameras. No curious onlookers. All the other gates in this wing of the terminal building had been shut tight. The entire area had been cleared of people. As far down the corridor as Kinsman could see there was no one except a row of uniformed security guards spaced every twenty meters or so, wearing hard hats, with gas masks on their belts next to their riot guns and grenade pouches. Even the newsstands and gift shops were closed.

Then the tall, cigar-chewing figure of Ted Marrett pushed through the little knot of officials. "Welcome to Fun City!" he boomed, and all the others seemed to pale and melt back.

Kinsman extended a metal-braced arm and Marrett grasped his hand warmly. "I'm here as the unofficial greeter and personal representative of the Secretary General. We've got a squad of cars waiting outside to take you to UN headquarters. The three of you will be guests of the Secretary General."

But it was not that easy. The officials immediately formed themselves into a reception line and the three lunar visitors had to be introduced to each one of them. Kinsman wondered idly how they had arranged their pecking order, since they seemed to come from a dozen different nations and two dozen different types of government agencies, ranging from the United States' National Institutes of Health to the Ministry for Development of Natural Resources of Tanzania. A trio of photographers cruised around at a distance, discreetly snapping away without flashbulbs. Kinsman noticed tiny apertures in the walls and ceilings where other cameras might be recording their arrival, as well.

Kinsman shook hands with each of the officials, including the blonde, who turned out to be from Kansas City, representing the American Urban Council. A good front for an intelligence agent, Kinsman guessed. Glancing at her clinging sweater, he decided she had a good front for anything.

Finally they were ready to head down the corridor toward the main terminal building. One of the American medics offered, "We can get a wheelchair for you, Mr. Kinsman."

"No thanks. I can walk."

Landau came up beside him. "It would be better to conserve your strength."

"I feel fine."

"You are high on your natural adrenalin at the moment," Landau advised. "A wheelchair is advisable."

So they wheeled Kinsman, fuming inwardly, through the emptied terminal building. Security's tighter than a Mafia summit conference, Kinsman realized as he saw that the entire terminal of one of the world's busiest aerospaceports had been completely shut down. All the ticket counters were empty. All the TV monitors showing arriving and departing flights were dark. The fast-food counters and restaurants and bars were shuttered. Grim-faced, heavily-armed security guards were posted everywhere. The only sign of life outside of the funeral cortege flowing through the deserted building was the trio of photographers skipping back and forth with the agility of Oz's scarecrow, clicking away with their tiny cameras.

Kinsman and Landau were ushered into a sleek limousine, together with Marrett and the American State Department representative: a square-jawed young man with a deep tan and the kind of wrinkles around his eyes that come from being outdoors, not behind a desk.

If he isn't ISA I'll eat the upholstery, Kinsman told himself as he settled into the limousine's back seat. The braces of the exoskeleton poked into him uncomfortably. Landau sat beside him while Marrett and the State Department man took the jumpseats facing them.

"You okay?" Marrett asked. He had to hunker down on the jumpseat to keep his bald head from bumping against the plush-lined roof.

"As well as can be expected," Kinsman replied. He caught a glimpse of Harriman entering the car ahead of theirs, with the blonde from Kansas City at his side.

"How's that one-man jail cell feel?" Marrett asked as the chauffeur started up the car and pulled away from the terminal building.

"Not all that bad. It's a lot better than trying to get along without it, I guess."

The State Department man, whose name Kinsman had not caught, asked, "How does it feel to be back home again?"

Kinsman threw him a sharp look. "My home's almost half a million kilometers from here."

"Oh. Yes, I see . . . I meant . . ."

But Kinsman turned to stare out the window at the acres of totally empty parking lots surrounding JFK. "They've really shut down the whole damned airport? For us? What were you afraid of?"

"Nowadays anything can touch off a riot," answered the State Department man. "And you're not terribly popular with the plebeians, you must realize."

"Also," Marrett added quickly, "it's easier to control the news about you if the government's the only source of info. Right, Nickerson?"

Nickerson seemed to go darker, beneath his tan. "The news media can be very irresponsible, sensational."

Marrett laughed, a full-throated chuckle that filled the limousine's plush interior. "Sure. No sense letting them get sensational about a man who's led a successful revolt against the government and has come down from the Moon to visit as a guest of the United Nations."

Nickerson did not smile back. "Mr. Marrett," he said coldly, "you are an American citizen, even though you seem more loyal to the UN than to your own nation. I advise you to be more careful with your statements."

"Stuff it, sonny!" Marrett pulled a fresh cigar from his shirt pocket. Despite the winter chill outside, the big meteorologist wore only a leather jacket over his shirt and slacks.

Landau raised a protesting hand. "Please. No smoking."

"Huh? Oh." Marrett looked at Kinsman, then slipped the cigar back into his pocket.

The entire expressway leading into Manhattan was clear of all other vehicles except for an occasional police cruiser or Army armored car. Even the overpasses were empty of traffic and people. As the little parade of limousines and their escorts neared Manhattan an eerie sensation began crawling up Kinsman's spine. He had been here before. It all looked familiar, yet somehow different. Empty. They've pulled all the people away. No one on the streets, no cars or buses. Yet there was something more. Something was missing from the bare canyons of concrete and brick. Defoliated! Kinsman realized. Not a tree in sight. They've taken down all the trees. For fuel?

They swung up onto the Queensboro Bridge and Kinsman saw the skyline of tall gray towers that he remembered, half lost in a cold brown haze of smog. Uptown of the bridge a few private cars shared the East River Drive with phalanxes of steam-powered buses. But downtown of the bridge, where the drive led to the UN complex of buildings, the roadway was completely empty except for police and Army vehicles.

The river below looked oily and turgid, flowing sluggishly. And then it hit Kinsman. *Water!* Miles and miles of water, waves lapping gently, water that falls from the sky and makes noisy little streams like that time in Colorado flowing down the mountain slopes to form rivers that sweep out into the oceans. Rivers. Lakes. Oceans. A whole planet brimful of water.

He stared into the gray river. All that water, and look what they've done to it. Fouled their own nest.

He pulled his eyes away from the filthy river. "I just don't understand why you felt it necessary to clear out our whole path," he said.

Nickerson glanced at Marrett, sitting beside him on the other jumpseat. "Mr. Kinsman," he said, "it may come as a shock to you, but the majority of the American people regard you as a traitor. We thought it would be better for your own safety to provide a maximum of security for you."

"And a minimum of opportunity for me to tell Selene's story directly to the people."

Nickerson's nostrils flared, but it was the only betrayal of his feelings. He said evenly, "We do not want to run the risk of starting a riot and possibly having you or the others of your party injured or killed."

Marrett looked disgusted but said nothing.

Kinsman turned back to stare at the river. So much water! For free! This world is so rich—and they've fucked it up so thoroughly.

As they pulled off the East River Drive and down the short stretch of rampway that led directly to the UN garage, suddenly there were people. Thousands of them. Tens of thousands. Thronging the pedestrian mall and spilling over to block the bottom of Forty-eighth Street. A cordon of mounted policemen—They still use horses! Kinsman marveled—kept the crowd from surging onto the rampway and blocking the limousines' access to the underground garage.

Kinsman remembered the UN Plaza as a neatly manicured park, green with trees and flowering shrubs. The glimpse he got of it as the limousines slowed down showed it to be bare and treeless. And packed with people who clutched tiny American flags in their fists and angrily waved placards:

DON'T DEAL WITH TRAITORS!
THE MOON BELONGS TO U.S.

And others that were worse. Most of them were professionally printed, and many copies of them had been made available by somebody. The government? The hand-lettered ones were obscene.

Through the bulletproof windows of the limousine Kinsman could hear the seething roar of the crowd, booing and shouting at them. A woman's high-pitched screech: "Kinsman, you Quaker bastard, I hope they kill you like a dog!"

Nickerson smiled coldly. "See what I mean?"

"Good job of stage managing," Marrett muttered.

The cars slid past the mouth of Forty-eighth Street and beneath the overhang of the pedestrian mall, to a wild cacophony of screams and curses.

With great effort, Kinsman turned around to look out the rear window. Suddenly the crowd broke through the police line and surged onto the rampway. More police appeared almost magically and halfheartedly tried to hold them back from the entrance to the garage. In the background, Kinsman could see the mounted cops pulling gas masks over their faces while others slid gas masks over the muzzles of their horses.

"Stop the car," Kinsman ordered.

His voice was strong enough to penetrate the partition separating the back of the limousine from the driver's seat.

"Stop it!" he shouted.

The driver lurched to a stop.

"What are you . . ." Nickerson reached for Kinsman's metal-sheathed arm.

But he had already opened the limousine door and was climbing out, servomotors whining as he ducked through the door frame and stood erect.

A riot was beginning up at the entrance to the garage. The police were shoving at the crowd and the crowd was pushing back. Police clubs and electric prods were already in hand. The roar of anger was echoing down the concrete tunnel.

The air was foul. It stank of smells that Kinsman had completely forgotten: gasoline and rubber and burning garbage and urine. His eyes burned. But instead of going for his oxygen mask, he trudged up the ramp toward the maddened, flag-waving, struggling crowd.

Dimly he was aware that Landau was running up behind him. And Marrett. And Nickerson, who probably had a gun on him. The ramp's slope was unnoticeable to them. But to Kinsman it felt like climbing Annapurna. Step by plodding step: *click, whine, hum, thump*; *click, whine, hum, thump*. Frankenstein's monster invades Manhattan.

And suddenly the battling and shouting up ahead of him died away. Not all at once, but within the space of a half-minute it went from riot to silence, a shock wave passing through the crowd, numbing it to inertness. One gruff voice hollered, "Hey, what the hell is *that*?" Then utter silence from more than ten thousand people.

Except for the noises of Kinsman's exoskeleton. Slowly, laboriously, he worked his way up the ramp. Breathing was an exercise in concentration. His chest felt raw inside, too heavy to lift.

One of the policemen edged toward him, face shield down, gas grenade clutched in one hand, bullhorn in the other.

"The . . . bullhorn," Kinsman puffed. Christ Almighty! Twenty paces and you're half dead.

The policeman hesitated, then held out the bullhorn. Kinsman took it, with a click and whir of servos. He put the bullhorn to his lips.

"I . . ." His voice cracked, his throat burned.

Landau reached out to support him. Marrett and Nickerson came up on the other side.

"I am Chet Kinsman," he said, and heard his magnified voice boom hollowly off the tunnel walls.

The crowd seemed to flow backward a pace or two, buzzing. Like a rattler trying to make up its mind about striking, Kinsman thought.

"I'm the man who's being accused of treason." Kinsman took a deep, rasping breath. "I can only tell you . . . that we declared independence . . . for the Moon . . . in the same spirit that our forefathers . . . declared independence . . . for the United States."

Can't get air into my lungs!

"The people of Selene . . . would like to live in peace

. . . with all humankind. . . . There's no more reason for you to fear . . . an independent Selene . . . than there has been for England to fear . . . an independent United States."

The crowd was murmuring, wavering. Kinsman let his arm drop. Someone took the bullhorn from his fingers. There's more to tell them, he knew. But I can't. I can't. Too bloody tired.

Thursday 30 December 1999: 1332 hrs UT

FLOATING. HE WAS floating in free-fall, connected to reality only by the lifegiving umbilical snaking back to the spacecraft. Kinsman glorified in the freedom of it. Turning slowly in space he saluted each of the stars in turn: Rigel, Betelgeuse, Sirius, Procyon, the Twins, the Crab, the Scorpion with Antares glowering redly in its middle. Antares, the rival of Mars. Enemy of Mars. Enemy of war.

And then she drifted into his view. Dead. Arms still outstretched in terrified supplication, oxygen lines ripped away by his hands. She was turning slowly, ever so slowly, showing her back to him at first but slowly, slowly revolving so that now he could see the bulge of her helmet where the right earphone was built in and now the hinge of her dark-tinted visor and the first red initial of CCCP across the top of her helmet.

No! I want to wake up!

But she drifted closer to him, still turning toward him, her arms extended now in a cold embrace of death. He wanted to tear his eyes away, but instead looked deeply into that visor through the darkness and saw her face.

Diane's face. Dead.

"Noooo!" he screamed.

Kinsman was trying to sit up, eyes wide open, room still echoing with his nightmare shout. The lights snapped on harshly, painfully. Dr. Landau and two nurses burst into the room.

He saw that he was lying on a water bed, felt it sloshing wildly beneath his struggles. A light plastic web harness was fastened over him, making it impossible for him to get free. In his ears he heard the peculiar double beat of his natural and artificial hearts, thumping hard in syncopation.

"Chet, Chet! Don't try to get up!" First time Alex has ever called me by my first name, Kinsman realized with a detached part of his mind.

"I'm all right," he said, relaxing, sinking back into the water bed's warm caress. "Just a dream . . . a bad dream."

One of the nurses, a tall leggy African, had a syringe in her hand. Landau waved her away.

As they unfastened the web harness Kinsman lay back and let the buoyancy of the water carry him. The room was big, huge by lunar standards, and plushly furnished. The ceiling was richly paneled in wood, the floor thickly carpeted; deep comfortable chairs and couches were scattered in a smooth luxurious arrangement.

The other nurse touched a button on the wall and the drapes slid back, letting sunlight filter through the ceiling-high windows. There was a spacious desk by the windows, with various electronic gadgetry neatly arranged on its top and a special contour chair behind it.

For the freak, Kinsman realized as he saw his exoskeleton stacked beside the chair, like some smothering insect waiting to envelop him.

Most of the electronics was medical checkout equipment. Landau used it to test Kinsman's vital systems, shaking his head and frowning unhappily through the brief procedure. As the nurses helped Kinsman into his clothes and then into the braces, he asked the Russian doctor, "Well, Alex, how'm I doing?"

Landau, sitting on a regular chair next to the desk, bit his lower lip as he scanned the readout on the desktop display screen.

"Terribly, if you must know the truth," he answered. "The heart pump cannot sustain you through any physical exertion at all."

The black nurse lifted Kinsman's right leg and clamped

the foot brace on while the other—she looked Armenian to Kinsman, maybe Greek—did the same for his left.

"So I won't exert myself," he said lightly. "Who needs to, with such expert help at hand?" He would have patted their heads but his arms felt too heavy and he feared he could not coordinate them properly.

"This is no joking matter," Landau replied grimly.

Kinsman could not even shrug comfortably. "All right, Alex. So I'll sit still and do nothing more strenuous than talk."

"Your heart reacts to emotional stress also, you know."

The nurses bent him forward to hook up the back brace.

"Ummph. But, Alex, I feel a helluva lot better now than I did yesterday. What happened? Did I pass out or what?"

"You collapsed," Landau said. Bitterly, he went on, "And for a reason that I should have foreseen, but was too stupid to. The air you were breathing. It was heavily contaminated, polluted with carbon monoxide and soot and other filth. Your lungs were strained, which put an additional workload on your heart. You were faced with a serious cardiac insufficiency and you collapsed. The exoskeleton would not permit you to fall, so you hung inside, quite unconscious."

"I had a heart attack?"

Landau shook his head. "No, not what a layman would call a heart attack. Merely an insufficiency of oxygen-carrying blood getting to your brain."

"Like a blackout in a high-gee maneuver."

Landau frowned in concentration for a moment. "I suppose so."

"But I feel okay now."

"You have been sedated and resting in the most comfortable environment the United Nations could provide. The air in this room is mixed from bottled gases; you are not breathing city air at all, not even filtered city air."

Kinsman laughed as the nurses lifted his arms and clamped the braces on them. "I remember when New Yorkers used to boast that they didn't trust air they couldn't see."

Landau found it totally unfunny.

With the exoskeleton fully hooked up to him, Kinsman got to his feet and tried a few experimental steps across the

530

wide carpeted room. Just like the Tin Woodman. Hope somebody remembered to bring the oilcan.

Landau waved the nurses from the room. Within a few moments a pair of liveried waiters wheeled in breakfast. And right behind them came Hugh Harriman.

"Well!" he snapped with mock indignation. "Sleeping Beauty's finally up and on the job, eh?"

"I think I can make it through until naptime," Kinsman said.

"Good." Harriman waited until the waiters had set up the breakfast table and taken the food from the hot and cold sections beneath the white-clothed rolling table. Finally the table was neatly arranged with a variety of dishes and they left as silently as they had come.

Harriman pulled up a chair. "Bagels and lox! That's a really low blow. They've loaded this table with foods we can't get in Selene."

Kinsman found that his contour chair had a series of toggle switches set into its right arm. The first one he tried adjusted the back. The second rolled the chair forward. Like an airplane's joystick, he thought. He deftly maneuvered the chair up to the table.

Landau pulled his chair to the table, looked everything over, and murmured, "Caviar."

"Don't worry," Kinsman said. "We'll be getting this kind of stuff in trade goods within a few months."

"And what'll we trade them back?" Harriman groused. "Oxygen?"

Kinsman nodded unconsciously, and the whir of electric servomotors startled him. "Oxygen's already an important export item for the factories in near-Earth orbit, Hugh. If things go our way, those factories will start manufacturing peacetime goods. They'll need lunar aluminum, silicon, other raw materials from us. We also have tourist accommodations and research facilities. We've got lots of things for trade."

"I still think it's damned shitty of them to lay all these goodies in front of us," Harriman muttered.

Landau reached for the tea. "They are probably trying to be very polite to us."

"Or the fucking American and Russian security people are bribing the UN to make us homesick."

"All right," Kinsman said. "Let's get down to work. What did I miss yesterday?"

"Nothing much," Harriman replied. "A bunch of reporters and photographers crashed through the police cordon at the garage, but they were hustled off before we could say much to them. Then we met a lot of UN staff people in the afternoon. In the evening they trotted a dozen of the immigrants past us. They all wanted to meet you, of course, but they had to settle for my charming self."

"The people who are coming to live in Selene?" Landau asked.

Harriman nodded as he munched a mouthful of bagel, cream cheese, Nova Scotia salmon, and onion. "Uh-hmm." He swallowed mightily. "Fascinating group of people, all of them rather stupefied that their governments are allowing them to leave. They fly out of Kennedy tomorrow; they're on their way down there now."

"On their way down to where?" Kinsman asked.

"Kennedy Space Center."

"In Florida? Not the JFK Aerospaceport here?"

Harriman blinked. "No, they told me the American government was taking them to Florida."

"Why wouldn't they take off from here?" Kinsman wondered.

"Damned if I know. Probably some bureaucratic red tape somewhere along the line. Anyway, that's not the important thing. The Secretary General is scheduled to meet you at ten this morning—less than an hour from now. Are you up to it?"

Kinsman started to nod, thought better of it. I'm getting to hate the sound of electric motors, he thought. "I'm fine. Where will the meeting be?"

"Right here. Mohammed's coming to the mountain."

Kinsman raised his eyebrows. At least I can still do that for myself.

A few minutes before ten Ted Marrett barged into the room unannounced, with Beleg Jamsuren trailing behind him. "Best meteorologist Mongolia's ever produced," he said by way of introduction.

"For your information," Jamsuren said softly as he shook

hands with the seated Kinsman, "Mongolia produces comparatively few meteorologists. And actually, my training was in fluid dynamics."

"Well, the best in Asia," Marrett amended. "You seen the morning news? Your performance at the garage yesterday really's getting the big splash."

Without asking he crossed the room in a few long strides and touched a small inset wall panel. A holographic Chagall reproduction instantly disappeared from the wall, replaced by a three-dimensional image of a woman being wheeled through a hospital corridor. "Goddamned soaps," Marrett grumbled as he touched the panel again.

Kinsman sat back in his special chair and suddenly saw a holographic picture of himself striding painfully toward the crowd at the UN garage. The camera was somewhere in the crowd, heads and placards constantly getting in the way as his weird skeletal figure clambered up the garage ramp.

The newscaster's voice-over was saying things about "unearthly appearance . . . terrific physical strain of ordinary gravity . . . message of peace and friendship . . ."

Good Christ! Kinsman said to himself as he watched. I actually did raise my hands like an old-time Indian scout.

Marrett abruptly shut off the picture. "The government's gone apeshit," he said, grinning broadly. "They thought they had everything all buttoned up and orchestrated. No newsmen at the airport, nobody allowed to get near you guys."

"But there were cameramen in the crowd."

"Sure! Half of 'em were government goons, there to record the riot."

"There was *supposed* to be a riot?" Harriman asked.

"It is an old tactic," Landau said. "The government plants agitators in the crowd; natural leaders seize the opportunity to vent their passions; the riot begins, the natural leaders have identified themselves. They can be taken by the police during the riot or, if that is inconvenient, at least their pictures are recorded. They can be picked up later."

"And at the same time," Marrett added, "they have video footage to show the American public that the people are dead-set against you. It's called 'forming a climate of opinion.' Happens all the time."

"An old trick," Jamsuren agreed.

"Wonder who they learned it from?" Harriman murmured.

The Secretary General arrived precisely at ten. He came alone, without flunkies or fanfare. He merely knocked on the door once and opened it. As he entered the room, all five men present got to their feet. Kinsman ignored the whine of his servos.

"Please—sit down," said the Secretary General. "I insist."

As they did so, he added, "And since this is an informal meeting, please let us dispense with titles. My name is Emanuel De Paolo. I know your names: Mr. Kinsman, Mr. Harriman, Dr. Landau. So let us relax and speak freely. I can assure you that this room has been carefully inspected as recently as an hour ago to ensure that it is not wired by anyone."

Kinsman found himself immediately liking this slim, tan-faced man with the dark sad eyes. De Paolo took a chair for himself and brought it close to Kinsman's. Marrett pushed the breakfast table out of the way. The morning sunlight struggled through the murky haze of the city to make the room seem warm and bright.

"Now then, Mr. Kinsman," De Paolo said, "you have shown considerable courage and wit. You are an instant hero with the American public this morning. How long such popularity can last is questionable, however. Many Americans, perhaps most of them, honestly consider you to be a traitor."

"I'm sure most Englishmen considered George Washington a traitor," Kinsman replied.

De Paolo shrugged. "Yes, of course. . . . Eh, you have come here to seek recognition for your new nation, is that correct?"

"Yes. We want to create a political environment in which Selene can be free from the threat of attack by the United States or the Soviet Union. In return for this, we can offer to all the nations of the world a safeguard against missile attack—against nuclear war."

Dr. Paolo pursed his lips. "You offer us much more than that."

Glancing at Marrett, Kinsman said, "You mean the weather control."

"I mean much more than that. Much, *much* more."

Kinsman leaned forward in his chair. The seat back moved with him. "I don't understand."

With a smile that looked more sad than pleased, De Paolo said, "Let me try to explain." He paused. Then, "What causes war? You may say, political differences, conflict over territory, or even, the competition for natural resources. None of these is completely true. Wars are caused by nations. National governments decide that they can obtain by force something that they cannot obtain any other way. Once they have decided to use force, there is no way to prevent them from fighting."

"Go on," said Kinsman.

"Our world—this Earth—is faced with a myriad of staggering problems. War is only one of them. There is vast hunger, in my native land, in most of the Southern Hemisphere, even in parts of the wealthier nations. There is a struggle for natural resources. There is overpopulation and energy shortages, and pollution on a global scale. These are worldwide problems."

Harriman's face lit up. "Ahhh . . ."

"You begin to understand." De Paolo smiled at him. "The nations of the world cannot—or will not—solve these global problems. This is because the most fundamental problem of all is the problem of nationalism."

His voice was suddenly iron-hard. "Each nations considers itself sovereign, a law unto itself, with no higher authority to hinder its actions. All nations, even the youngest of Africa and Asia, demand complete authority to do as they wish within their own borders. What they accomplish is stupidity! Population crises, famines, racial massacres. And eventually, inevitably—there is war."

"We're a new nation, too," Kinsman said. "And we want our sovereignty, too."

"Yes, of course. But why have you come here? It is, I think, because you realize that no nation is completely sovereign, de facto. There are always restraints on action, political realities that cannot be ignored, the need to cooperate when you cannot coerce. The irony of it all is that you—living on the Moon!—you realize that you must cooperate with the other nations of Earth if you wish to survive. Would that the nations of Earth were that clear-sighted!"

Kinsman nodded, and the servomotors' buzz made his forehead twinge with the beginnings of a headache.

"Your own Alexander Hamilton knew the problem. He wrote, 'Do not expect nations to take the initiative in developing restraints upon themselves.' No. The nations of the world will not solve the problem of nationalism. They cannot," De Paolo said, very firmly. "For more than two centuries they have been trying to cure the sickness of nationalism, and every year it gets worse, more virulent, closer to the point of lethality."

The old man rose to his feet. "Every year . . ." he muttered, walking toward the windows. Kinsman felt confusion in his mind. De Paolo looked frail and yet strong; old and yet vital.

De Paolo turned and faced Kinsman, framed by the windows. "For twenty-two years I have watched them play their stupid games. The proud nations! Each so utterly convinced of its divine right to be as smug and stupid and brutal as it chooses. For twenty-two years I have watched people starve, villages bombed, whole nations looted, while diplomats politely stood here in this very building and made a mockery of ideas such as law and justice and peace. They are no better than the barbarian warlords they replaced centuries ago!"

He was staring beyond Kinsman and the others in the room, plainly disgusted by what his mind could see. "I know the games they play. I have given the best years of my manhood to make the United Nations a force for order and sanity in a world of madmen. But they refuse order and sanity. They have turned our political efforts into travesties. They loudly proclaim the need for international law, but then they use the power of money and weapons to take what they want, like the bandits and cowards that they are."

He gazed straight into Kinsman's eyes. "For more than two decades I have tried to use the UN's nonpolitical arms —UNESCO, the World Health Organization, the International Food Distribution Committee, yes, and even the Committee on the Peaceful Uses of Outer Space—but even there the proud nations have thwarted us. Their refusal to allow weather modification work is merely the most recent example of their nonsense."

"So you're proposing . . ."

The slim old man paced stiffly back to his chair. "I am proposing that we take the skill and courage that we possess and work toward an effective world government. With the antimissile satellites that you control we can offer the smaller nations of the world safety from nuclear holocaust."

"And threaten the larger nations' communications satellites," Harriman blurted. "If they don't play ball with us we can close down their damned telephone systems! That'll cripple their economies overnight. To say nothing of shutting off their television!"

"We're not here to make threats," Kinsman said.

Harriman beetled his brows. "Okay, *mon capitaine*, speak softly if you want to. But it won't hurt to let them know you carry a sizable stick."

"We have a much larger stick," De Paolo said. "Dr. Marrett's ability to manipulate the weather. With that, we can maximize food production and avert disastrous storms—and at the same time threaten any nation on Earth with unacceptable calamity if it refuses to cooperate with us."

Marrett nodded grimly.

For a long moment Kinsman did not know what to say. "That . . . that's quite an undertaking."

"Of course," said De Paolo. "And we cannot hope even to begin working toward this goal unless you join us. Your satellites are the key to everything."

"But . . ."

"I know," the old man said. "You fear that I am a megalomaniac, intent on world domination."

"Well . . ."

"But I am!" He smiled again, and this time the sadness was lessened. "I want to see a world dominated by *law*. By justice. By cooperation among peoples. Not by force and terror, as it is now."

De Paolo spread his hands expressively. "We know how to build an effective world government, a government in which each nation would participate and no nation would be held as a pawn or a slave. We can substitute the rule of sanity and law for the present rule of power and armaments."

"The nations of the world can't solve the problem of nationalism," Kinsman mused. "They need an outside force . . ."

"And together we can be that outside force," De Paolo answered. "I know that it sounds dangerous. I know how tempting it would be to strike for a world dictatorship and *force* the recalcitrant nations to do as we wish. It would have been easy for your George Washington to have himself proclaimed king, also."

"But he didn't."

"And neither will we."

Kinsman closed his eyes. "That's a lot to swallow in one sitting."

"I understand. But I intend to give you even more to chew on. This afternoon you are scheduled to address the General Assembly. However, the American delegation has requested that your address be put off until Monday—after the weekend and the holiday."

"I can't!" Kinsman snapped. "I can't stay here that long."

De Paolo nodded. "Yes, of course. This is a move by the Americans to prevent you from getting your message across to the peoples of the world. Unfortunately, the Russians are in agreement with the Americans on this, and between them and their blocs in the General Assembly they have enough votes to force a postponement of our special session. Actually, most of the delegates are away at home for this week, and a postponement suits them very agreeably."

"But . . ."

"Fear not," De Paolo said, with an upraised hand. "You can address the General Assembly next week from the Moon or one of your satellite stations. Your public address was not the real reason I wanted you here. There are a few dozen key people that you must meet, and we will take every advantage of your time here to bring them to you. They are officials from many different nation-states. Most of them are from very small and weak nations, but a few might surprise you."

"If they think you're okay," Marrett broke in, "then they'll get their governments to go along with us—to revamp the UN and move toward a real world government."

"Wait a minute," said Kinsman. "I'm not sure that *I* want to go that far!"

De Paolo smiled, and once again there were generations of human suffering on his face. "Your discussions with these men and women will help you to make up your mind, in that case. Obviously, none of us can move in any direction until we are all agreed."

"Fair enough," Kinsman said.

De Paolo got to his feet. "I must get back to my other duties. You may hear thumping along the walls and ceiling from time to time. Do not be alarmed; it is merely our security team sniffing for electronic bugs."

He walked to the door, alone. Stopping there, he looked back at Kinsman. "You believed you were acting to save your world—your Selene—from being destroyed by decisions made here on Earth. Then you found that perhaps you could save the people of Earth from destroying themselves. Now we offer you something much grander, and much more difficult to achieve: a chance to rid the Earth of the curse of nationalism. A chance to move human society to its next evolutionary phase. A world government is the only chance we have to avoid global catastrophe."

Through the long day they came, and well into the evening. One by one, very rarely two together, and only once did three visit Kinsman at the same time. Diplomats, representatives of many nations. Some of them had enough technical background to converse freely about missile trajectories and the logistics of orbital operations. A few of them had been on the Moon for brief periods, although Kinsman remembered only one of them: a striking olive-skinned, black-haired Italian geologist. She was now part of the UNESCO team studying global natural resources, and apparently reported directly to the Italian minister of finance.

"A father in high office," she murmured, with the trace of an accent laid over her British-style English. She smiled as if she thought her father's position was being aided by her work, rather than vice versa.

Marrett stayed with Kinsman and Harriman until the last visitor had departed. He spoke to the visitors of weather control, of optimizing their climate, of allowing them to plan their harvests years in advance and then see the predictions come true. Kinsman spoke about international stability, about peace based on the protection of the orbital ABM network, about substantial disarmament and the chance for the smaller nations to depend on world law rather than spending half their gross national product on armies that often turned on their own governments and ousted them in bloody coups.

The visitors to the plush, quiet room with the special air supply came from Africa, from Asia, from the scattered islands of the Pacific, from the overpopulated nations of Latin America. Kinsman was surprised to receive a three-man delegation from Japan, all smiles and polite bows and sincere wishes for good fortune, who knew a disturbing amount about the ABM satellite lasers and were quite familiar with Marrett's work in weather modification.

Beleg Jamsuren brought his uncle, the Mongol ambassador to the United Nations. The Italian woman was not the only European: the Scandinavian nations, Hungary, Czechoslovakia, Yugoslavia, Holland, and Denmark all sent representatives.

All very unofficial. Completely social. No agreements were made or even hinted at. No commitments. But they got the information they had come for and they left with new light in their eyes.

By 10 P.M. Kinsman was exhausted. He had the back of his contour chair cranked all the way down as Landau ran through the medical checks. Marrett and Harriman were wolfing hot sandwiches and beer.

"That water bed looks awfully good," Kinsman said tiredly as Landau disconnected the last sensor probe from the medical computer.

"It should," the Russian said. "Your blood pressure is very low." The miniaturized analyzer on the desk gave a gentle *ting* with its little bell, and automatically displayed its analysis of Kinsman's blood sample on the computer's screen.

"Ahh-hmm," Landau muttered, studying the readout graph's snaking lines. "Blood sugar is also low, as I suspected. You need food and rest."

Kinsman closed his eyes. "I'm too tired to eat. God, we

must have told the same story three dozen times."

"Sixteen times," Harriman corrected from the wheeled dining table. "Another dozen coming tomorrow."

Landau scratched at his beard. "Very well. Let's get you bedded down, and then we can feed you with the IV."

"No you don't." Kinsman's aversion to having holes poked through his skin overcame his fatigue. "I'll eat some real food." He cranked the seat back up and rolled to the dining table. "If there's anything left after these two chowhounds," he added, looking over the nearly empty table.

"Sixteen times," Harriman repeated thoughtfully, clutching a steak sandwich with both hands. "After listening to your *spiel* all day and night I could give your song-and-dance routine in my sleep."

"I'll do it sixteen thousand times," Kinsman said, "if it'll do any good."

"It did good," Marrett said firmly. He had a bottle of beer in one big hand; he disdained a glass. "Every one of the people who came in here today is connected right back to the power centers in their governments. No flunkies or dodos in the bunch of 'em. They might not all have had much rank, but hell, most big-shot diplomats are nothing but assholes anyway."

"Hey, watch that!" Harriman snapped, frowning.

Marrett raised his beer bottle in salute. "Present company excepted."

Harriman kept his stern visage. "There's a lot of nasty comments I could make about engineers."

"I'm a meteorologist."

Harriman glanced heavenward. "The Lord has delivered him unto my hands!"

Landau pulled up a chair and reached for one of the few remaining sandwiches.

"You think we got our message across to them?" Kinsman asked Marrett.

"Yep. They knew the story before they came in here. De Paolo's seen to that. They just had to meet you, size you up, and play their estimation of you against their estimates of what they stand to gain or lose by going along with De Paolo's scheme."

Kinsman shook his head once and got a fresh lance of pain from the servomotors whining just behind his ears. "I wonder about De Paolo's plan," he said. "He claims that he's not aiming at a world dictatorship . . ."

"You want to know if you can trust him?" Marrett asked. "He's honest. He means what he says."

"But what about the people around him?" Kinsman wondered. "And the people *after* him?"

Marrett started to shrug, but Harriman said, "What the hell did you expect, Chet?"

"What do you mean?"

With a shake of his head, Harriman explained, "Don't you see that De Paolo's plans are the logical extension of your own? Follows as the night the day. All he's doing is building a permanent structure where you've been improvising lean-tos and pup tents. De Paolo sees further than you do, my boy. What he wants is a solid edifice."

"You mean a jail?"

Harriman made a sour face. "Don't be such a muddlebrain! The only way you can prevent nuclear war is by producing a force that's stronger than nations. Selene by itself can't be that strong. But De Paolo's moving toward a *real* world government—with muscle. It's what we need. Hell, Woodrow Wilson recognized that! But up until now no international organization has had the muscle to *make* the nations toe the line. Well, now we do. Or we will."

"Damned right," Marrett agreed. "We're gonna build a whole new thing out of all this. A real world government. The age of nationalism is over, finished. Has been, ever since Sputnik. We're just trying to build something effective in its place to hold the world together."

Marrett took a long, thoughtful pull on his beer. Putting the bottle down, he said, "Listen. A world government isn't gonna solve all the world's problems overnight. And there's always the danger of a dictatorship on a global scale. But compared to what we've got today, a world government looks damned good to me."

Harriman added, "Chet, it's a question of quid pro quo. If we want these nations to recognize Selene, if we want to be admitted to the United Nations, to get the United States and the Soviet Union off our backs, then we've got to play along with De Paolo. There's no choice. It's a question of political reality. Help De Paolo get what he wants and he'll help us to get what we want. Quid pro quo."

"While the whole fucking human race hangs in the balance," Marrett added.

Kinsman asked, "These people we talked with today —they're going back to their respective governments?"

"They're on airplanes right now," Marrett said. "De Paolo will carry the ball from here on. All we need from you is your agreement to keep up your end of the bargain."

"And that will get us recognized by a large enough bloc of nations to have us voted into UN membership?"

"If none of the Security Council members vetoes our application," Harriman said.

"That means Russia and the States."

"Right."

"Why would they be nice to us?" Kinsman asked.

"Because," replied Marrett, "De Paolo's gonna let them know that weather control's on the way. They can't afford to be left out in the cold, and storm, and drought, and flood."

Kinsman stared at him. "You can really do that?"

"Sooner or later. A lot sooner than they think." Marrett let his big fists rest on the heavy white tablecloth. "Been doing it on a small scale for years. It's been used in war, mostly to increase rainfall and cause floods. Or wipe out crops. It's actually *easier* to do it on a big scale—you've got a lot more reinforcement factors working for you."

Harriman broke in, "And on the near term, we have the power to knock off all their commsats and other space assets. Let's see them try to get groceries from California to Connecticut without telephones or navigation satellites!"

Kinsman felt his face pull into a frown.

"But it's working, Chet!" Harriman insisted. "They know what they're up against. Why do you think the U.S. and Russia are trying to be nice to us and letting those immigrants go—including Leonov's kids and Diane's daughter?"

"Yes, maybe . . ." Kinsman wanted to nod, but instead found himself blinking, the way Pete did. "But they asked for a postponement of my speech to the General Assembly."

"I am in agreement with them on that point," Landau said. "You must avoid additional strain and return to Selene as quickly as possible."

Ignoring him, "But why did they push for a postponement?" Kinsman repeated.

Marrett shrugged. "Who the hell cares? They're just giving De Paolo a few more days to line up everybody. Time's on our side."

"Is it?" Kinsman wondered. "Is it really?"

Friday 31 December 1999: 1700 hrs UT

IN THE PACIFIC *and through much of Asia it was already the New Year. Holiday crowds celebrated in the summertime streets of Melbourne and Sydney. In Tokyo, where Western-style observances were frowned upon, the streets were silent. A waning crescent Moon looked down across China, the vast Himalayan wastes of high rock and ice, and the steaming subcontinent of India. If the new millennium was being celebrated there, it was quietly, in private homes or government palaces. Or in shrines.*

In Florida it was high noon. Fifty men, women, and children who had traveled from all over the world to the Kennedy Space Center were being led away from the sleek silvery space shuttle that they had expected to board.

They looked tired and more than a little bewildered as they marched in a ragged line under the high Florida sun, across the cement shimmering with heat haze, under the mirrored sunglasses of uniformed guards. They were better dressed than most refugee groups but they still gave an impression of bedraggled despair to the technicians and security guards watching them.

In a dozen different tongues they asked each other, "Why? What has caused this delay? When will we be allowed to take off for the Moon and our new lives?"

In a Southwestern twang, a crew-cut Army major, dressed in civilian clothes, told them, "We are experiencing some technical difficulties with the shuttle that was going to take you to Space Station Alpha. We'll let you know more as soon as we have further information."

The refugees were led into very comfortable quarters, complete with air-conditioning, separate bedrooms, color television, and an open cafeteria.

"You are the guests of the government of the United States of America," the Major told them cheerfully.

The one hundred U.S. Army Rangers who were checking their automatic pistols and gas grenades and electric stunners were housed only half a kilometer away, in a gray cement building that had no amenities except a Coke machine that took silver dollars and an immaculate white-tiled latrine.

The Sun raced across the other side of the world and the line of midnight swept westward, carrying the new year and the new millennium with it.

In New York City by 5 P.M. it was already dark. A cold wind had swept the city all day long and now as Kinsman stood by the high-ceilinged windows of his room in the UN Secretariat Building he could see a single star hanging high in the inky sky. Jupiter? Saturn? Or could it be Space Station Alpha?

"You should sit." Alexsei Landau's heavy voice came to him from across the room.

Kinsman turned slowly, to a grating symphony of servo noises. "Alex, I've got to move around. I can't stay in that damned chair all the time." But it's hard to stand, he admitted to himself. My back aches, head hurts. I'm falling apart like a geriatrics case.

"That was the last of the visitors," Harriman said glumly from the desk.

He's tired, too, Kinsman realized. And feeling the strain of being cooped up in this room. "Ted," he called, "how about taking us on a guided tour of the building."

"Huh?" The meteorologist looked startled.

"Absolutely impossible," Landau said. "I forbid it."

"Alex, we're going crazy in here!"

Landau shook his head. "The air out there is full of viruses and bacteria, dust, dirt, pollutants. No, it's impossible."

Frowning, Kinsman said, "I'll wear my oxygen mask, for Chrissakes!"

"And he can stay in the chair," Harriman added.

Marrett agreed. "We can take him down to the basement level and cross over into the General Assembly chamber. It's an impressive place. Nobody'll be there."

Landau scowled but capitulated. "Give me a few minutes to pack my kit. If anything happens, I must be prepared."

"Great!" Kinsman clapped his hands. Or tried to. The servos were out of sync just enough to make his palms hit slightly off-center, producing a dull thump instead of a sharp smack.

He got into his chair and said, "And while we're thinking about it, check on our shuttle. Is it still set to take us up at ten?"

Harriman said, "I called JFK fifteen minutes ago. They'll be ready for us at ten."

"You'll miss the New Year's Eve celebration," Marrett said.

"In here? Watching the celebration on TV isn't my idea of fun, even if it's a three-dimensional screen," Kinsman replied. "I'd rather be on my way home."

"We'll get to Alpha an hour or so behind the immigrants," Harriman said. "There'll be plenty of celebrating."

They made a strange foursome: Marrett leading the way, tall, an aging athlete's flat-stomached, hard-eyed figure, chomping on an unlit cigar; Harriman walking alongside Kinsman's powered chair, pudgy and round, a middle-aged cherub; Kinsman himself in his otherworldly skeleton of metal and machinery, his face hidden behind a green oxygen mask; and Landau, tall and taciturn, a dour bearded figure pacing solemnly behind the chair waiting for a tragedy.

There had not been a traffic jam in Manhattan for years. Most of the commuters were carried in and out of the island on government-operated buses and trains; private autos had disappeared almost entirely. But on this particular evening people poured into Manhattan. They jammed the buses, choked the trains. They drove petroleum-extravagant cars. They pedaled

*bikes and rode in taxis and limousines and horse-drawn cabs.
They clogged the bridges and tunnels where the toll gates had
been left open and the exorbitant fees went uncollected by a
strangely munificent government. They were filling the city,
which was normally empty and quiet after sundown. Times
Square was already packed with people, and for the first time
in a decade the Manhattan traffic computer system broke
down. The wind died away and clouds drifted across the face
of the Moon. It would be cold this night, but few of the New
Year's Eve fun-seekers would notice.*

The General Assembly meeting chamber was empty, as
Marrett had predicted. Almost. A little knot of schoolchil-
dren stood clustered by the speaker's rostrum, goggle-eyed at
the splendor of real wood and plush upholstery and paintings
and sculpture commissioned over the years by the United
Nations. The work of the world's best artists decorated the
chamber profusely.

To no avail, thought Kinsman as he sat at the far end of
the chamber, near the last row of visitors' seats. He tasted
oxygen in his mouth, felt the slight chill of the gas and the flat
tang of metal, as he looked out across the splendid and futile
chamber. *So much of the world's hope has been brought
here—and laid to rest. Buried under talk.* He noticed a
broad, sweeping mural of an underwater scene, very abstract,
but very recognizable. *The big fish eat the little fish.*

The schoolkids were trudging up the aisle, on their way
out. Their teacher somehow got into a conversation with
Marrett. She was a gray-haired dumpy woman with a bright
smile and expressive hands.

Marrett walked back a few steps and bent over Kinsman.
"Chet, these kids are children of UN employees. Mostly local
people. Parents work as clerks, janitors, and such. Some of
the kids'd like to talk to you."

From inside his oxygen mask Kinsman could not conduct
a conversation. He raised a hand, servos humming, and
pointed skyward.

"Upstairs," Marrett translated. "You'll talk to them up
in your room?"

Kinsman made a circle of thumb and forefinger. *At least
I can do that without servos,* he told himself.

Landau said, "They can visit only for a few minutes."

"Okay," Marrett said. "You take him back up and I'll keep the kids busy with a quick tour through the weather center. Be with you in fifteen, twenty minutes. Right?"

Kinsman nodded and Landau agreed.

The new millennium had already come to Moscow, Tehran, Tel Aviv, Berlin, and Vienna. All the other cities of Europe were preparing for it. News headlines proclaimed WAR THREAT EASES *in forty different languages. Happy, expectant crowds streamed through London. In New York the clubs and restaurants that normally closed at sundown were filling. The streets were crushed with people. Pickpockets and prostitutes had more business than they could possibly handle.*

In Florida at 5:30 P.M., Eastern Standard Time, the Rangers began boarding the shuttle. The entire Kennedy Space Center had been cleared of prying eyes. The news people were locked in the same plush prison as the refugees.

In Washington, the burly, red-eyed man shifted painfully in his chair as he watched the troop boarding on closed-circuit television.

"They take off at six?" he asked for the hundredth time.

"Barring delays," answered an Air Force colonel. "They should have Alpha secured by shortly after midnight, according to the schedule. Kinsman and his group will arrive no sooner than one A.M."

The man nodded.

"May I ask, sir," the Colonel added, "why we're allowing Kinsman to depart at all? Why not keep him here, under our thumb?"

"A dead martyr is a worse enemy than a live traitor."

"Oh. I see. Uh, Colonel Colt should be in New York by now, incidentally."

The man came as close as he could to smiling. "Yes, I know."

Colt was there when Kinsman returned to his room.

Harriman held the door open as Kinsman wheeled in, with Landau right behind him. Colt was standing by the windows, looking out at the night and the unaccustomed brilliance of the city's lights.

As he rolled his chair across the room and yanked off his oxygen mask, Kinsman said, "Frank! This is a pleasant surprise. What brings you here? I thought you were at Vandenberg."

Shrugging, Colt replied, "Couldn't let you get this close without hopping over to wish you a Happy New Year."

Harriman muttered, "Good old sentimental Frank."

"Yeah," Colt said, glancing at him. "Sentimental. That's me, all right."

"I'm glad to see you," Kinsman said. "Bird colonel, eh?"

Colt said nothing. Kinsman gestured him to a chair and wheeled up close to the windows. "Can't see the Moon. Too overcast."

Landau began to set up his instruments on the desktop.

"I thought you'd be busy with the final countdown at Kennedy," Kinsman said to Colt.

"It's going along fine. They don't need me breathing down their necks. If there's any problem they can reach me here."

Kinsman grinned at him. "That doesn't sound like the old perch-on-the-bastard's-ass Frank Colt that I used to know and love."

Colt turned slightly away from him. "I'm a big-ass bird colonel now. Got to show some dignity. Besides, I'd rather be up here with you."

"How come our first shipload of immigrants is being launched from Florida?" Harriman wanted to know. "Why not right here, from the commercial port?"

Colt did not answer. He licked the lower edge of his teeth with his tongue and frowned.

God, he's uptight! Kinsman realized.

"Listen," Colt said at last. "I . . ."

The door buzzer startled all of them. Kinsman turned his chair around as Harriman bustled to the door and opened it. Four very solemn-faced youngsters came in, three boys and a girl. The oldest must have been no more than ten. The girl and one of the boys were Latin-dark. Puerto Rican, Kinsman guessed. One of the other boys was black; the fourth a redheaded, freckled, street-wary Huckleberry Finn.

And their teacher. "Oh, it's *so* kind of you to let us visit you! I understand how busy you must be." She prattled on as she urged her youngsters into the room like a hen pushing its chicks.

The kids were silent, staring, but the teacher never stopped talking. Kinsman immediately realized that she was speaking to Harriman only to allay her own nervousness, using exactly the same tone and expressions that she used on her classroom kids.

"Oh, and you must be Mr. Kinsman—Chester Arthur Kinsman. Were you named after President Arthur? And you live on the Moon! Isn't that interesting, children? Would you like to live on the Moon someday?"

The girl reached a shy hand out toward Kinsman's exoskeleton. "Why you wearin' that?"

Kinsman smiled at her. The old lunar charm. "I need it to help me move around. See?" He raised one arm, and all four of the children hopped back a step at the sound of the servomotors. "My muscles are accustomed to the gravity of the Moon, which is six times less than the gravity here. I'm too weak to move by myself here. You're a lot stronger than I am."

That emboldened them. "My dad says you're a traitor. You're bein' bad to the United States," the black ten-year-old said.

"I'm sorry he feels that way," Kinsman answered. "The people on the Moon want to be free. We don't want to hurt the United States or anyone else. We just want to be free."

"When I grow up," the Puerto Rican boy asked, "can I go to the Moon?"

"Sure. You can live there, if you want to, or just come up for a visit."

"Would I have to wear one of those things?" He pointed at the braces.

"No." Kinsman laughed. "That's only for weak old men like me. And on the Moon, even I don't need it."

They asked a few more questions and then their teacher started to shoo them toward the door.

"Can girls go to the Moon, too?" the girl asked.

"Yes, sure."

"Come now, children. Mr. Kinsman is very tired. It's very difficult for a man from the Moon to stay here on Earth.

Smell the air in here? Even the air is different!"

"I don't smell anything."

"That's what I mean!"

By now they were outside in the hall and the door was swinging shut when one of the kids yelled, "Fuckin' traitor! We'll get ya!"

"George!" the teacher clucked. "Such language! And shouting in the hallway!"

Shout it from the rooftops, kid, Kinsman thought. Be a real patriot.

Harriman kicked the door shut. "George must be running for mayor."

Landau got up from his chair and went back to the desk. "I must run a medical check."

"More blood? Hugh, order up some dinner, will you? Frank, you'll stay and eat with us."

"I oughtta get going," Colt muttered.

"Come on," Kinsman urged. "We'll let you loose early. We've got to be at JFK for a ten o'clock takeoff. You can watch the immigrants take off on TV."

Hesitantly, Colt got up and went to the TV controls on the wall. With equal reluctance, Kinsman turned his chair toward the syringe-wielding Landau.

All traffic was being routed around Times Square. Policemen on horseback, in armored cars, in helicopters, all wore riot gear: hard helmets, plastic visors, gas masks, the armament of combat infantrymen. Thousands of people were pouring into the square and more throngs were congregating elsewhere in Manhattan. In strategically located armories around the island the Army assembled companies of men and armored personnel carriers and balloon-wheeled light tanks. Washington Square, Columbus Circle, the entire length of the Amsterdam Avenue Mall—crowds were thickening everywhere. Bottles and butts and pills were passed freely in spite of the fact that police patrolled the fringes of the throngs and flitted overhead with glaring searchlights probing down from their helicopters. But the people were happy, laughing, celebrating. Huge TV screens had been set up in the streets to show the launch from Kennedy Space Center.

Frank Colt puffed nervously on a cigarette as he sat on the couch and watched the final moment of the countdown.

The shuttle sat at the end of the runway bathed in the glare of a dozen huge spotlights. All the service vehicles had been cleared away from it. Only a thin wisp of vapor from the liquid oxygen boil-off indicated that the craft was occupied and ready for launch.

The TV announcer was gabbling, "In one of the most generous acts of international goodwill seen in this decade, the United States is allowing fifty people from foreign nations to engage in this historic journey to the Moon—despite the fact that the lunar settlement is still legally American territory."

Landau frowned as he packed away his medical equipment. Harriman was on the phone, checking again on the readiness of their own shuttle at JFK.

Kinsman sat tiredly in his special chair. The medical exams not only depressed him, but made him feel even weaker than normal. Somewhere far in the back of his mind a nagging tendril of unease flickered warningly. He turned his gaze from the TV screen to Colt, taking a hard drag on his cigarette. Frank never smoked, Kinsman told himself. Can the pressures of command be so heavy on him that he's started smoking?

The door buzzer sounded. Dinner arrived.

"Not again!"

General Maksutov listened for a solid four minutes, by the digital clock on his metal desk, his face growing more incredulous and grimmer at the same time. Finally he put the phone down, but not before saying into it, "Yessir. Immediately!"

"Dimitri," he said to his aide, who was sitting across the desk holding a glass of champagne in his hand, "that was Moscow. We must prepare for three manned launches immediately."

Dimitri dropped his champagne glass onto the thick Oriental carpet.

"Intelligence claims that the Americans are on their way to recapturing their space stations," the General explained. "If we don't take our own back from the counterrevolutionaries the Americans will get them. In a matter of hours!"

"But *three* manned launches? *Now?*"

General Maksutov nodded bitterly. "Rouse the men —full crews and full backups. I'll call Andrei and give him the joyful news. The ground crews must be alerted. See to it."

The aide nodded dumbly and pushed himself up from his chair. Absently, he noticed that the glass had not broken. He picked it up and placed it on the desk with a slightly shaking hand.

"Get the infirmary to issue wake-up pills. You'd better take some yourself."

"Yessir."

"Happy New Year, comrade," the General said bitterly. "And happy new millennium."

Dimitri shook his head. "This is too much like the old millennium."

"Yes, isn't it? Except that back in the twentieth century we didn't have the duty of killing our own countrymen, you and I."

The launch was shown on the mammoth TV screens set up in Times Square and other places where the crowds had gathered. The people watched, a sea of murmuring humanity, as the final few seconds of countdown ticked off and the shuttle sat bathed in the spotlights against the balmy Florida night, waiting, waiting . . .

"Three . . . two . . . one . . . Ignition!"

For an instant, nothing happened. Then the shuttle started to roll down the runway, a thundering roar propelling it faster and faster as it swept past the camera and hurtled into the dark sky, furnace-hot blossoms of orange glowing from the engine nozzles at its tail.

The crowds ooohed.

The shuttle climbed steeply and banked gracefully leftward, the glow of its engines reflecting off the low-lying mists from the nearby sea. The camera followed it until it became a distant speck indistinguishable from the stars scattered across the night sky.

And the TV announcer never missed a beat. "The liftoff is fine, fine . . . she's climbing precisely on course now, carrying the first load of interplanetary immigrants in the history of the human race . . ."

Dinner had been quiet, tense. Kinsman and the three other men had eaten quickly, sitting around the portable dining table without much conversation, watching the TV screen. It alternated between shots of the shuttle countdown and launch, views of the New Year's Eve crowds in Manhattan, and long dreary segments of "entertainment."

"Well, Frank," Kinsman said as the big wall screen showed a telescopic view of the shuttle in flight, "you can relax now. They got the bird off without you."

"Yeah," said Colt.

He's stretched so tight he's going to snap, Kinsman thought. What on Earth is eating at him? Something was terribly wrong, Kinsman knew, but his body ached too much for him to think. I know how Atlas must've felt, holding up the world.

"Chet," Landau said, "we must prepare for the ride to the airport. You will have to wear the oxygen mask."

Kinsman wanted to nod but he did not even try.

"De Paolo's got two cars coming for us," said Harriman. "Plus the escort. No local or federal cops. We sneak out quietly."

Suddenly Kinsman wheeled his chair to face Colt. "Frank," he blurted, "come with us!"

"To the airport?"

"No, to Selene! Come on. You know you don't belong down here anymore. You know what we're trying to do. Join us!"

Colt pushed his chair away from the white-clothed dining table. "Me? You're serious? You want me . . . ?"

"Why not?"

"After what I've done?"

"That's in the past. We're building for the future. You can help us! You'll be a helluva lot happier in Selene than putting up with all the chickenshit they throw at you down here."

Colt lurched to his feet. "You're crazy! I can't—"

"Sure you can," Kinsman urged.

Throwing his napkin down on the table, Colt shouted, "You damned fool! By the time you get back to the space station there won't *be* any Selene!"

"I don't get—" But the tortured look on Colt's face stopped Kinsman. "What do you mean, Frank?"

"Shit, man! Did you really think they were gonna let you get away with it? Did you really think that?"

Kinsman could feel fire flashing along his nerves. "Frank, what are you saying?"

Colt's face was a landscape of pain. "Chet, you soft-headed bastard—that plane's not filled with your goddamned refugees. It's loaded with a hundred armed troops! In another two hours we'll have Alpha. In twenty-four hours we'll have *all* the manned space stations, the Russian ones, too. Then we take Selene."

Kinsman closed his eyes.

"You sonofabitch!" Harriman raged. "That's how you got those eagles!"

"Yeah." Colt's voice sounded weak, miserable.

Landau muttered one word. "Jill . . ."

Kinsman looked at the three of them. Harriman and Landau were still sitting at the dinner table, food and wine unfinished. Colt stood, legs spread slightly, up on the balls of his feet as if waiting for them to physically attack him.

"Phone," Kinsman said, more to himself than the others. Wheeling toward the desk, "Phone link . . . JFK's got a link with Alpha."

Colt shook his head. "They won't put you through. Air Force took over communications at JFK an hour before I came up here."

Kinsman slid the chair to a halt at the desk. Turning it back to face Colt he said, "Then you've got to tell them to establish contact."

"*I've* got to?"

"You're the only one who can, Frank."

Colt was wide-eyed now. "You're crazy, man. That's insane."

The scene on the wall screen showed Times Square and the still-growing crowd there. Harriman went over to the controls and turned the volume down.

"Frank," Kinsman said, "you're on our side. You've always been on our side. You're the only one who hasn't recognized it."

Walking stiffly, shakily, toward him, Colt answered, "I'm on *my* side, Chet. That's the only side there is. Numero uno."

"Bullshit. You can't live with that and we both know it. So they make you a general. It's still a dying world out there, Frank. It's *dying*! Unless we do something to change it."

"By selling out the United States."

"By rising above it!" Kinsman shouted, and his chest flared with pain.

Colt was standing in front of his chair now, looming over him. "We know what you and De Paolo are doing—all those visitors you've had in the past couple days. It won't work, Chet. They're not gonna let it work."

Kinsman took a long shuddering breath and forced the pain down. "I don't care about that. I don't care about anything except Selene's independence. Because without our independence you'll be part of a nuclear strike that will kill all the people of the United States. There's no way around it, Frank. Either we control those satellites or there's going to be nuclear war. Which do you want?"

"I don't want either, dammit!"

His voice as hard as the braces he wore, Kinsman snapped, "It's got to be one or the other, Frank. And *you* have to decide which. The choice is yours. Choose."

Colt glared at him.

"Choose!"

Colt hesitated a moment, then turned to the desk and punched savagely at the phone keyboard. "JFK central switchboard," he said into the speaker grille.

The tiny phone screen glowed pearl gray but no picture came on. A man's voice said, "JFK Aerospaceport," in a bored, flat voice.

"This is Colonel Colt. Put me through to Major Stodt, in communications."

The voice suddenly became more alert. "Sir? Would you please repeat the order so that our audio verification equipment can check your voiceprint?"

Colt did it, and with a single flicker of the screen a pinch-faced man with a high domed forehead appeared. His blue tunic bore the gold oak leaves of an Air Force major.

"Stodt here."

Colt gave Kinsman a sidelong glance. Then, "I want a tight laser link with Alpha. Full scramble and no tapes. At once. Pipe it into this phone line."

The Major's narrow face seemed to tighten even more. "Sir, that is not in our operational plan."

"Did I ask if it was?" Colt snapped. "Do it!"

"But . . . but, sir, there's no way for us to monitor a laser link unless we have time to—"

"Stodt, you've got ten minutes to get that fucking link set up. In the eleventh minute you can start writing me a report explaining why an asshole of a communications tech has been promoted beyond his talents. Now move, *Captain*. Or do you want to try for lieutenant?"

The Major visibly trembled. "Right away, sir," he muttered. The screen went blank.

Colt turned back to Kinsman. "I don't know how long it'll take 'em to catch on to what you're doing and cut the link. Better talk fast—if you get the chance to talk at all."

The pain was a dull, sullen throb, like a cinder: charred black on the outside but red and glowering deep within. Kinsman said merely, "Thanks, Frank."

Colt shook his head but said nothing. He walked back to the couch near the silent wall screen and plopped down. The screen was showing the Guy Lombardo simulacrum smiling and waving its baton in perfect three-four time in front of an orchestra of robots. Real people were dancing on the floor of the Starlight Roof.

"We should be leaving for JFK ourselves," Landau said.

Harriman gruffed, "Those bastards won't let us go. They've got us by the balls here."

"No," Colt said. "I told them that it'd be okay for you to return to Alpha and then to Selene. We were gonna have Alpha under our control by the time your shuttle got there. That was our plan."

Kinsman listened with only half his mind. The rest was racing through the possibilities. Can't let them dock at Alpha. But they'll probably try to force a docking. Or maybe they've got enough pressure suits to jump across and grab the emergency hatches. God, if there's much fighting up there they could destroy the whole station. Diane . . .

The phone screen flashed into a sparkle of colors. A voice—not Major Stodt's—said, "Direct link with Alpha is coming on, sir."

The screen cleared and a female communications technician, looking faintly surprised, said, "Go ahead, JFK."

"This is Kinsman," he said, squaring the chair in front of the phone. "Who's in charge there?"

The girl blinked once. "Mr. Perry."

"Where's Leonov?"

"He returned to Selene yesterday, sir. I can patch you

through to him if—"

"No. Get Perry. Immediately."

"Right."

It took a few minutes. The other three men gathered tensely around Kinsman's chair. Finally Chris Perry's strong, youthful face appeared on the screen. The typical square-jawed adventure hero, Kinsman thought. I hope he's up to it. Perry was smiling broadly, but there were other people and a general hubbub in the background.

"We thought you'd be on your way here by now," he said happily. "Had a helluva party at midnight—our time, that is. But everybody's staying up to welcome the immigrants, and Diane Lawrence wants—"

"No time!" Kinsman snapped. "The flight from Florida is filled with soldiers, not immigrants."

"What?"

"It's a trick. A Trojan horse. We're still here at UN headquarters. That shuttle must not be allowed to dock. Understand? Under no circumstances."

"Yessir." Perry was completely sober. The laughing and chattering in the background had turned into absolute silence.

"Establish radio contact with them," Kinsman said. "Order them to retrofire and return Earthside immediately."

"Right. But what if they don't comply? They could try to force a docking. If there's any kind of heavy weapon play here—"

"I know." Kinsman's hands were clenched hard on the metal braces of his thighs. "That's why it's necessary to get them to turn around. If they don't comply—" He hesitated, squeezed his eyes shut for a moment, then commanded, "If they don't comply, use the ABM satellites. Warn them first, but use the lasers if they won't turn around."

Perry nodded, tight-lipped.

"Don't let them get close enough to the station to damage it," Kinsman said. "They may be carrying missiles, and they might try to use them if they can't board you."

"They will," Colt said from behind Kinsman's shoulder.

Perry looked grim. "Yessir. I'd better get on the horn to them right away."

He turned from the screen momentarily.

"Will he do it?" Landau whispered.

Kinsman turned and looked up at the Russian. The

braces made it a painful operation. "You mean will he kill Americans? We'll find out pretty damned soon." *You started this as a move to end war,* he raged at himself, *and it's turning into a civil war.*

"He'd better do it," said Colt.

Perry came back to the screen. "I've got to get down to the comm center. They've got the shuttle on the standard frequency, but I can't run all the parts of the show from here."

"Right. Keep this line open," Kinsman said.

But the screen erupted into flickering colors. The only sound from the speaker was a scratchy angry hiss.

"They tumbled to it," Colt said. "Cut the link."

Kinsman turned the chair around. "Hugh, find a phone someplace and tell our shuttle to hold. No telling when we'll be there—if ever. Then see who you can find in the UN chain of command . . ."

"Christ! On New Year's Eve?"

"Can't be helped! We've got to get some muscle around that shuttle. It's our link home, and . . ." A sudden surge of pain made him gasp.

"Chet!"

Landau reached for him. Kinsman pushed the Russian away. "No . . . I'm all right." He tried to catch his breath. "Hugh, for God's sake—we need De Paolo. Find him. Find some foreign diplomats. Marrett, news reporters, anybody. We've got to get the word out about this. Don't . . ." The pain hit again, searing flame across his ribs and down both arms. "Don't let them keep this a secret."

Harriman bit his lower lip. But he nodded and rushed toward the door.

Landau forced Kinsman's chair down to a reclining position. The ceiling seemed to be spinning. Kinsman heard the phone making funny noises, then a voice calling tinnily, "Colonel Colt! Colonel Franklin Colt!"

Landau's face was hovering over him. It was blurred, but very serious. Intent. So damned somber. *Wonder if he's that way in bed with Jill. He must smile sometime.*

"This is Colt."

"One moment, Colonel. Priority call from Washington."

"Great. Just what I need."

By turning his head slightly Kinsman could see the wall

screen. The dance floor was jammed with happy people. Old people, mostly. The scene shifted. Amsterdam Mall was crowded with dancing people, too. But these were young, black, Puerto Rican, other Latins. And their dancing was not stately or measured. Their music was not provided by a painstakingly detailed simulacrum of a long-dead orchestra. Kinsman could see steel drums and guitars and enough amplifiers to make him wonder sleepily, Where'd they get the electricity?

He forced himself awake. "Stop sticking needles in me, goddammitall!"

Landau laid a heavy hand on his shoulder. "Be still. Quiet."

"Colonel Colt." Kinsman could not see the desk, but the voice came through the phone speaker clearly. It was an angry burning whisper.

"Right here." Colt's voice was calm. He's made his decision, Kinsman knew.

"Congratulations, Colonel. You have earned yourself a firing squad."

"Guess again, baby. I'm on UN territory and I've asked for asylum in Selene."

"You are a traitor," the harsh voice whispered. "A turncoat. Worse even than Kinsman himself. You *knew* what we were doing. You helped to plan it for us. And then you changed sides. There will be no mercy for you, black man. No place to hide. You are a dead man."

"Everybody dies," Colt said, in his toughest ghetto snarl. "Including you."

"That is true. But you will die sooner than most. Our troops will not be thwarted. They will seize Station Alpha or destroy it."

"Better change their orders. They'll get their asses fried if they don't turn back."

"They will not turn back. And if your newfound friends kill American troops, not even the UN building will be safe for you."

"If I were you," Kinsman heard Colt saying quite distinctly, "I'd be heading for a bomb shelter instead of making threatening phone calls." Then he heard the faint snap of the phone switch.

"Alex," Kinsman said. "Don't put me under. I've got to stay awake . . . got to . . ."

"Your EKG is frightening," Landau said. "You will stay down and you will rest."

"He will not," Colt said firmly.

Kinsman fumbled for the controls on the arm of his chair and swung it around to a point where he could see Colt. Don't try sitting up, he warned himself. Don't get that brave. The pain was dulled now, but he knew that was from whatever Landau had injected into him. The drug had merely turned the volume down temporarily.

"Keep him awake and alert," Colt said, walking over to face Landau. "We're gonna need him. He's the one they'll listen to—the people up there and the people down here. If he's out of it, they're not gonna listen to you or me."

"There is Harriman," Landau said through barely opened lips.

"Keep him awake," Colt repeated.

"You'll kill him."

Before Colt could reply, Kinsman said, "Everybody dies." The two former astronauts grinned at each other.

"Frank," said Kinsman, "see if you can re-establish contact with Alpha. Perry's no fool. He's probably trying to make direct contact with this building's microwave receivers right now."

"Yeah, right." Colt went back to the phone.

Breathing very carefully so that he would not disturb the beast that was drowsing inside him, Kinsman told Landau, "Do whatever you have to, Alex, but don't put me under. Frank's right. I've got to be awake through this. I'm the only one they'll listen to. Maybe when Hugh comes back . . ." If he gets back, Kinsman thought. If he had to go outside the building they might have grabbed him.

"I could try electrical blockage for the pain," Landau muttered, and went back to his medical equipment.

Colt was grumbling and swearing into the phone. "Don't any of those fuckers on the switchboard speak English? Holy shit!"

Kinsman smiled to himself. Frank's made his choice. He came through.

The wall screen showed a huge clock built into the facade of one of the Times Square towers. It said 9:48. The crowd was like a single mass of people now, swaying, chanting, self-hypnotized.

"Yeah . . . whozzat? Perry! This is Colt."

Kinsman swung his head. Too fast. The pain lanced through him. Christ, I can't even move!

Colt dashed over to him. "Perry's on the horn. No visual, just voice."

He wheeled Kinsman to the desk.

"Chris, this is Kinsman." Can he hear me? My voice sounds so damned weak.

"Yessir. We've been trying to reach you."

"What . . . happened?"

"The shuttle refused to turn back. They even fired a missile at us."

Missile! "Where? How much damage?"

"No damage. We intercepted the missile with a laser beam and then got the shuttle itself with another laser."

"Got the shuttle?"

A long delay. "Yessir. Radar confirmed the kill. She split apart. Nothing but debris now. No survivors."

A hundred men. Nothing but debris. In orbit . . . floating like she did.

"Sir?"

"Yes, I'm here." His voice was weak. A groan.

"There was nothing else we could do. They refused to back off."

"I understand. You did the right thing. It's my responsibility. I gave the orders."

"Yessir." The phone went dead.

"Now you *must* sleep," Landau said. "There is no . . ."

But Colt said, "Look at this." He turned up the volume on the wall TV screen.

A grave, shocked-looking announcer's face filled the big screen. He was saying, ". . . destroyed by the rebels. The government has made no announcement of why the troops were aboard the space shuttle, or of what happened to the group of international émigrés who were scheduled to reach the space station at about ten P.M. Eastern Time."

The announcer glanced off-camera briefly, then resumed, "I repeat: The White House announced a few minutes ago that a space shuttle carrying one hundred American soldiers was destroyed as it approached Space Station Alpha tonight. All one hundred Americans—plus the shuttle's crew, who were also Americans—were killed. The shuttle was deliberately destroyed by the rebels who are in temporary command of the space station. More information will be released shortly, White House sources say."

The TV screen cut back to the view of the crowd at Times Square. They were frozen in place, stunned, immobilized. The big TV screens all around the square had shown the same announcement. Now one of them—the public educational channel—began showing an animated simulation of the shuttle approaching the space station. It disappeared in a blinding flash of light.

"They worked that up fast, the bastards," muttered Colt.

"They must have had it ready as part of a contingency backup plan," Kinsman said, his voice barely a whisper.

The scene changed to a closeup of a TV announcer down on the street, warmly bundled in an electrically heated suit, three heavily armed private policemen standing beside him.

"The crowd here at Times Square seems stunned, shocked, utterly unable to believe this sudden and tragic news," he said into his lip mike.

From behind him came a surging crowd of shouting bodies. The camera view cut back to an overhead shot from atop one of the towers around the square. But the announcer rattled on:

"The crowd is coming to life. I don't know if you can make out what they're shouting. It's rather profane, a lot of it, but the general gist of it is—the lunar dissidents have killed a hundred Americans. There's anger here, real rage."

Kinsman heard a woman's piercing shriek quite clearly, "The bastards are in the UN building!"

The announcer was speaking rapidly, as if covering a sports event. "The crowd's milling around, like a huge uncertain beast trying to make up its mind about which direction to go in."

"They'll be here," Kinsman said.

Colt nodded. "They're already starting to push out of the square. And the cops are letting them go."

The police were doing nothing as the crowd began streaming out of Times Square. The TV picture changed to show similar scenes elsewhere in Manhattan.

Kinsman tried to sit up. "Frank, we've got to get to our shuttle. Now." The pain bloomed inside him. It was like railroad tracks of red-molten steel clamping down across his chest, his arms, and then everywhere. No! he screamed to himself. Not now! But he could see nothing. It all went black.

Distantly he heard Landau's shocked voice. "It's too much . . . too much . . ."

Friday 31 December 1999: 2358 hrs UT

SOMETHING WAS SHAKING him. A loud whining roar rattled Kinsman's very bones. He could not move. His body felt glued down.

A voice. Marrett's? Shouting over the engine roar. "I told him we'd give 'em the goddamnedest drought this continent's ever seen. And we can do it, too. De Paolo's on the phone with the President right now."

Kinsman forced his eyes open. It took a massive effort of will. His head was turned to a small window. It all came together slowly in his foggy brain. Helicopter. They took us off the roof in a copter.

"So they tracked me down," Marrett was saying. "Hugh burst in on the party with a whole squad of UN security police. Half the people at the party thought it was a drug bust!"

Kinsman tried to focus on the scene outside. It was still night. There were city lights sliding past below them. In the distance was the river, the skyline of Manhattan . . . *Oh, God!*

Fire. Flames licking upward, doubly reflected in the river and the glass wall of the Secretariat Building. They're burning it. They're burning the UN buildings.

"Fire's getting worse," somebody said.

Marrett's voice answered. "Sure. Goddamn fire trucks can't get to it because of the mob."

"'What fools these mortals be.'" Harriman's voice, sounding very tired, very down.

"Hey, it's midnight."

"Terrific."

"Happy fucking New Year."

The voices buzzed on but Kinsman paid no attention. He watched the UN buildings being swallowed in flames.

The pain came and went and returned again. He could feel it snaking through his body. Tendrils of hot iron worming down through his arteries and veins, branching, exploring, searching. Down through the fine nets of the capillaries the pain spread. He felt it, he knew it was there, even though his brain kept insisting that the drugs were keeping the pain suppressed. Yes, but I can feel it moving through me like a conquering army, taking possession of the territory it's won.

Harriman's voice came out of total darkness. "It's De Paolo. They're going to meet tomorrow. The President's coming up to New York to look at the damage. De Paolo says to tell Chet that buildings can be rebuilt. And so can institutions. Stronger than they were before."

But we'll have to be so careful, Kinsman replied silently. It'll be so easy to turn it into a dictatorship. We've got to preserve human freedom—it won't work any other way.

They were moving him. He felt himself being lifted, placed. Carefully. Tenderly. Like a fragile treasure. He thought, Like a fossil.

Pressure and the muted thunder of rocket engines. The pain flared everywhere now, waking him.

Frank Colt was sitting beside his litter, brooding. Kinsman grabbed at his arm.

"There's so much to do, Frank." His voice sounded like a dying old man's.

"Hey, Chet. Take it easy, man." But Frank's voice sounded strange, too.

"Got to . . . listen, Frank. We've got to do everything we can. We've got to keep the doors open for the human race."

"Yeah, sure, baby. Don't get yourself excited."

Others were surrounding him now. Shadows.

"Frank, we can develop the raw materials from the Moon. And go on to the asteroids. We can develop it . . . there's a whole solar system of natural resources . . . nobody has to be hungry or poor. We can do it! We can make it all work out!"

"Yeah, okay."

"You understand, Frank? You know what I mean? I can leave it with you, can't I?"

Colt nodded gently as someone else pulled Kinsman's hand away.

"I know," Colt said. "Been thinking about it myself. I'll see that it gets done. Don't worry about it. You just rest yourself."

"Good," Kinsman said. "Good. You'll know how to get it done. Mine the Moon. A world of resources. And the asteroids. Plenty of power . . . everything we need . . . for everybody . . ."

Someone—Landau, he thought—pressed a needle into his arm.

Floating. He was floating. Voices flickered around him. They were moving him again, but now it was like floating out in the sea.

Don't go too far, Chester. There's a tide.

Yes, Momma. There sure as hell is.

"It's all right now, Chet. You're safe. You're back home."

Diane's voice. Her scent.

He tried to open his eyes. He tried to speak. With all the power of his being he tried to raise a hand to touch her.

Nothing.

He felt her hair brushing his face. "You're going to be all right, Chet. You're not going to die. Please. You can't die."

He moistened his lips. He got the feeling that his eyes were open but he just could not see anything. Maybe a blur, a faint gray against the enveloping darkness. Cold. Cold and dark as space itself.

"Chet, it's me, Diane. Please don't die. There's so much for us to live for. I love you, Chet. I've loved you all my life . . ."

And I could have loved you. I could have. I could. He wondered if she could hear him saying it.

But then the gray blur of the gathering darkness took shape and he saw her waiting for him, floating weightlessly, her arms outstretched to embrace him at last. Kinsman's final thought sighed out of him like a breath of relief. The debt is paid, the only way it could be paid. He joined her, completely and finally.